INFERNO PUBLISHING COMPANY, Houston, Texas.

For more information about this book, visit Giacomo's website.

Cover design by Natasha Brown

Book design by Giacomo Giammatteo

This edition was prepared by Giacomo Giammatteo gg@giacomog.com

Print ISBN 978-1-949074-12-3

Electronic ISBN 978-1-949074-11-6

❀ Created with Vellum

CONSUMMATE VENGEANCE

Rules of Vengeance, Book III

GIACOMO GIAMMATTEO

Inferno Publishing Company

INTRODUCTION

For he shall wear the crown of Arangar.
Whose head hath deepest scars, whose breast most wounds.
He holds fire in his hands, lightning in his eyes.
And in the furrows of his frowning brows,
Harbors revenge, war, death, and cruelty.
Let all men kneel before him,
And if one should stand, let him be brave,
For if he means to place himself before the Prince,
He must be armed and ready to wade up to the chin in blood.

PROLOGUE

She stared out at the world through eyes that were not eyes, held captive by walls that were not walls.

Things were proceeding as predicted, as she knew they would. Soon her prison would be gone, the aeons spent here just a memory. As for the mortals who had dared to forget her, they too would be gone. Relinquished to the worst of fates.

Most important of all, the gods of old would be gone, forever trapped in their own prison. An eternity of anguish as they watched her reign over their fawning worshipers of long ago.

Not much remained to do. Everything was set in motion. Soon their champion would die. Her freedom was heartbeats away. Heartbeats! When she had already waited for aeons. A sigh went unnoticed. No one to hear.

One dilemma did remain though. Should she kill her champion? Or simply turn him into a pawn?

Anger erupted inside her. There was one she knew she should kill— knew she would kill. Then a thought came from memory—no, not one, but many. Yes, she thought, many. Time grows short. I should prepare my list now.

3

LOST POEM OF SETHIA

I wander through this barren land, a paradise long gone.
Searching for an ancient grave amidst death and fury spawned.
The trees are gone, the rivers dry, yet something hides it still.
I seek the secret earthy base. It gives my heart a chill.
Sing to me oh rancid flesh, oh lost and weary womb.
Call to me, and point me to your long-forgotten tomb.

4

RETURN TO VALLAH

The air in the corridor rippled, coalesced, as the rift formed. The sound of silk caressing satin floated in the air, and the slightest hint of cinnamon came and went in an instant. Too quick to taste.

Ghruehne stepped through, careful to check for traps. He turned, then nodded to Sendra as she emerged, her boots silent as she moved across the marble corridor.

Sendra put her finger to her lips, then whispered, "I will do a Sensing."

She focused, scanning the whole of Vallah, then her eyes went wide. She stopped, focused more. "Aentarra and Mikkellana aren't here, but some of them are. It's just …"

"What?"

"I don't know. I sense them, but something is strange. They appear to be in Council." She looked at Ghruehne, a question written on her face. "But what would they be doing in Council without Mikkellana and Aentarra?"

Ghruehne's head darted from side to side, checking the corridor. "Suppose they are here. Remember, Aentarra has Stealth. This could be a trap."

Sendra had to lean in close to hear his whisper. She thought, shook her head. "Something is wrong with the Sensing. I think we'll have to examine this ourselves. Be careful. And stay close." She started off down the dark corridor, hugging the side to her left.

Ghruehne owned a lecherous smile, made worse by the scar Antar had put on his cheek. "I didn't know you felt that way, Sendra."

Her head whipped around, the glare silencing him.

They moved down the corridor at a measured pace, taking each step as if a trap awaited—chances were good that one did. "This way," she said and turned right.

At the end of the hall, a pair of massive doors led to the Council Chamber where they had once held meetings to determine the fate of this world. Sendra felt the pain of the familiar surroundings, the agony of memories from long ago. There had been many good years in Vallah, years of laughter and love; but those were followed by bitter arguments that led to battle.

Why couldn't we get along? Sendra pondered the thought as she moved down the corridor. In ages past the marble floors echoed with the sound of servants' footsteps as they carried carafes of khaffe and trays of food. Days when they had all lounged in luxurious beds, whiling away the mornings without a care in the world. She cringed. Never again would she have the time to enjoy the comforts of a sunny morning or lie in bed listening to the patter of rain on the roof.

"Sendra! Are you with me?"

She shook her head, clearing old memories. "Sorry, Ghruehne. Just thinking of times long gone."

A grunt from Ghruehne expressed his disapproval. "Keep worrying about the past, and we could be long gone. Aentarra could be lurking anywhere."

The realization of Ghruehne's words brought her alert. "I'm all right now." She moved ahead with a newfound sense of awareness. "I have missed this though," Sendra said. "We had good times here."

"The Sethian Palace is nicer."

"Perhaps." She still whispered, although her voice had gotten a little louder. "But Sethia isn't as nice."

Ghruehne frowned. Despite his admonishment of Sendra, he found himself drifting to ancient times. An image of the Council Chamber came to mind, of a time when he had occupied one of the chairs surrounding that giant blackthorn table. This was a world they could have split amongst them. Why had Lukaan wasted it all? He felt Sendra's hand on his arm, turned to her.

"Focus," she whispered.

Ghruehne shook the memories away, looked about. The statues lining the hall seemed to watch them as they moved closer. He gave the ancient figures a second look, ensured it was not Illusion at work, then continued the advance. Five more paces brought them almost to the door.

"They better not have touched my room," Sendra said.

"Your room?" Ghruehne had to stifle a laugh. "Why would you think of that now? It has been a thousand years."

"I don't care how long it's been."

"Focus on this for now," Ghruehne said, and stepped in front of her. With his hand gripping the door, he turned to look at Sendra. At her signal they burst in, Fire and Lightning ready to strike.

The large blackthorn table was still there, as it had been for so long, and the blackthorn chairs, massive pieces in their own right, stood rigid—sentinels guarding the perimeter. In each of the chairs—twelve of them—sat one of the immortals, as rigid as the chairs themselves. Ghruehne stared, at a loss for words.

Sendra walked closer. "What is wrong with them?"

"Are they dead?" Ghruehne asked.

She lay her hand over Mesan's heart, shock registering on her face. She pulled out the chair, needing two hands to accomplish the task, then placed her ear to his chest, listening. "I can't hear anything. But, no, they're not dead … I don't know. Feel them; they're still warm. This is why the Sensing was strange." When she moved, she stumbled, almost fell, then she quickly wiped a tear from her cheek.

Ghruehne kicked at Xanthes' chair, nearly toppling him, then he walked to where Kiris' head lie on the floor, beside her body. "I've never seen anything like this."

The glow of a Slicer caught Sendra's eye, one barely protruding from Mesan's head. She reached for it, then screamed as the jolt hit her. Her hand retracted like a viper returning to a coil. Smoke drifted from her fingers, and the smell of burnt flesh permeated the room.

"Slicers!" Ghruehne said.

"Aentarra!" Sendra added.

Ghruehne turned. "Your mind is protected?"

"Of course. Ever since we found Iazzo's body."

"You think Aentarra did this?"

She nodded her head. "Despite your harsh feelings about Melissara, she has an acute sense for that sort of thing. She can analyze a week-old carcass and determine what killed it." Sendra let it sink in. "Besides, Melissara would never let Mikkellana escape the blame if it had been her—not after what she did to Tarman and Canno on the old world."

Another set of memories flooded Ghruehne's mind. "I wish we were back on our world."

"As do I," she said. "For now though, we better search the room."

They turned, searching every corner of the room, peering behind curtains and double-checking each alcove, then they looked at each other.

"Why?" Ghruehne asked.

Sendra nursed her finger while she thought, and she continued walking around the table, inspecting every one of them. "There's a Slicer in every one. Only Aentarra and Mikkellana are missing."

Ghruehne bent down to get a closer look at Kiris. He avoided kneeling. Even though the blood was old, it didn't seem right to kneel in it. "No Slicer here. She removed it."

"She had no need of it since Kiris was dead." Sendra shook her head as she joined Ghruehne, staring at Kiris' head lying on the floor. "What could she have done to warrant that, after being in this condition?"

Ghruehne straightened, adjusting his shirt. "You can never tell with Aentarra. Remember what Lukaan said. Perhaps he was more right than I gave him credit for. But this makes it a lot easier for us."

Sendra stood quietly. Thinking. Her eyes continued to dart around the room. "Don't be too sure. I don't understand what happened here, but Aentarra did this for a reason." She slammed her fist on the table. "Damn her and those Slicers!"

Ghruehne finished his inspection of the bodies, careful to avoid the little crystal shards. "We'll have to be more careful."

"Yes, we will."

"Perhaps we should kill them."

"No!" Sendra remained in control of herself even though panic tainted her objection.

"Why not? If they were alive, we would."

Sendra stared at them—twelve helpless souls. "I don't know. It doesn't feel right."

"I have no idea why Aentarra did this, but we can be certain it was to benefit her in some way."

Sendra glared at him. "Leave them as they are, Ghruehne. I am going to my room then we can leave for Sykor."

"Let's go to Sykor now," Ghruehne said.

"Not yet. I want to see my room."

Ghruehne sighed but followed her. "We still need to be careful. It wouldn't surprise me to find Aentarra lurking in the corner somewhere."

"After seeing what she did here, nothing would surprise me." Sendra walked the long corridor, cautious at first, but soon she became oblivious to her surroundings an focused on the journey.

Anxious about her room. Ghruehne's banter followed her as she quickened her pace, and she returned an occasional response, though if asked about the content of her conversation she couldn't have attested to any of it.

She pictured the room as she had left it, so long ago. So very very long. What had brought them to that point? Why couldn't they have just gotten along? At the last turn, Sendra's pace moved from walk to run, but she stopped at the door, afraid to enter.

"I'll wait here," Ghruehne said.

Sendra nodded, then opened the door. A smile lit her face. The bureau was there, the one he had helped her make, shaping the wood with his own hands, cutting dowels, sanding it. The two chairs sat around a small table, the janga board still there, its pieces likely in the same position as the last game they had played. She could always beat him at janga, and though Tirzinitzia was the best, Sendra came close to equaling her.

She picked up a general, dusting off the cobwebs, and shooing a mother spider away. She fought the tears, recalling the times they shared in here. Alone. In secret.

Her books lay on the shelves as she had left them; she had a particular order, not alphabetically by title, but by the primary battle that had taken place in the book. The few that weren't about war sat on the bottom shelf, as lonely as old soldiers. She turned to the corner, almost afraid to look, but there it was—her bed—fresh as ever, with lavender sheets and that surprise quilt. She still didn't know where he had gotten that. Probably from a merchant in Khatara.

Sendra walked slowly to the bed, sat. She brushed off the ages, then lay her head on the pillow, closing her eyes as she did. Memories raced across time to long ago, to blissful nights spent playing games. And to passionate nights spent making love. Oh, how those nights pleased her, tempted her still with the ecstasy.

A smile turned to tears of what could never be again. A moment or two of weeping was a long time, a lifetime to those not accustomed to it. Soon, that emotion found other means to express itself. Vengeance! "I'm going to kill Aentarra. I'll kill her, then rip her limbs apart."

~

*G*hruehne paced the hall, recalling the good times here when they had all shared the palace. Shared the world. The thoughts kept taking him back to the Council Chamber and the twelve bodies that sat in a catatonic state. He went to knock on Sendra's door then changed his mind and headed back to Council.

As he entered, he again checked to ensure no trap awaited, then stepped over to the table. The dagger of House D'Norta lay there, begging to be used. Ghruehne picked it up, slid the blade along his arm, drawing a trickle of blood, then he smiled.

"I don't know if you can hear me, but blame Aentarra for your fate, not me." With that, he slit Xanthes' throat. It took a while for the blood to come, but when it did, it bubbled out like the eternal spring at Gorshan Cave. Satisfied, Ghruehne moved to D'Norta, then Solenna, cutting each one with precision, meticulous about his method. He didn't stop until he reached Mesan, the last of them. He thought of wiping the blood from the dagger, then opted for tossing it onto the table.

The blood had soaked into their clothes, run onto the floor and pooled under the table, spreading out to form a pond of red. Ghruehne smiled again. Whatever Aentarra had planned for them had been foiled.

~

Sendra rose, walked to the bureau, opened the drawer. Gasped! A letter lay there with her name on it. Unopened. Still sealed with his mark. She clutched it to her heart, fought a futile fight against more tears, then forced herself to do the inevitable. She knew she should burn it, not just tear it up but burn it. But she couldn't. It must be read.

The paper was his, fine-quality lightly tinted green, with that magnificent symbol of his family crest at the top.

~

My dearest love:

How can I even begin when there is so much to say? So many places I could start. By now, you are trapped in Sethia, that monstrous place where no one should live—especially you, who loves the rain. Remember when we shifted to Genoa just so we could enjoy the afternoon thunderstorms? When we walked through the streets, hand clutching hand, lips touching lips? Even now, I grow excited thinking about it—the things we did on the beach. Things hidden by the sound of the waves and the roar of the thunder.

There was thunder in my heart that night, the kind I can never forget. One of my deepest regrets is that you won't be able to enjoy the rain much, not in Sethia. I know I'll never be able to enjoy it until I can once again look at the lightning through your eyes, hear the thunder with your ears, and feel the rain tapping us as we hold one another.

*H*ow many times have I come to the Sethian Shield and stood there, trying to find the courage to walk through it? I yearn to see you one more time. I believe I would have gone through the shield if it weren't for you, knowing it would hurt you to see Lukaan kill me.

*A*t least I like to think I was that brave. I'm not sure. Not sure about much anymore. Since this happened, I seem to have lost everything. My courage. My spirit. My life. How can I get it back? I wish you could tell me. You were always the brave one, the smart one—look at our janga games. I hope I never face you in battle. My strategy would be a lost cause at best.

Sendra brought the letter to her heart again, bawling uncontrollably. The ink had been smeared at this point as if tears had fallen on it while he wrote. She composed herself, then continued.

*...W*ere the strong one. I pray you find the strength to live a good life in Sethia if that's possible. And I truly hope that someday you will be reading this letter while I watch you from the bed. Just lying there staring at your perfect figure, one that even my dreams could never duplicate, though I have tried every night for all of these years.

I'm going to stop now. My emotions have run away with me, and I need to keep a grip on what sanity I still have. Every prayer I have is for you, my love. If nothing else, I will be waiting at the Gates of the Sun.

Forever in love,

Mesan

Sendra cried more, then more still. Afterward, she ripped the letter to shreds, ripped it until she could do no more. She picked up every single piece, the smallest fragment, let them lay in her hands, then burned them. Her tears put the fire out, eventually.

A knock on the door startled her, though she was amazed it had not come much sooner.

"What?"

"It has been almost half a day, Sendra. When are you coming?"

She wiped tears, dried eyes, straightened her clothes, and made a vow of vengeance against Aentarra. "I'm ready now."

5

THE BOUNTY MAN'S TRAIL

Two days had passed without water, two blistering days with nothing to drink. Thirst scratched Gregor's throat and peeled the skin from scabbed lips. The hunger meant nothing; he had gone without food for five days once, but the thirst proved unbearable.

He had hidden in a crevice tucked into a side crack in the canyon walls. It was a two-span climb to the surface, and he feared he may be too weak to make it, even if a swift-flowing creek beckoned him.

The bigger fear was the Banished Ones. They had come after the attack. The attack! He recalled the night it happened, how could he not. Wolfen had seized him and Wehr and dragged them from the camp only to be hunted by Takar and Darstan.

By the grace of the gods! Darstan! He had used Fire on them—Fire! The sky lit with fire, and the wails of the Gnakas must have been heard for leagues as they burned. Gregor had barely escaped, but fortune had not smiled so bright on Wehr.

The biggest shock came afterward. He had been able to dispatch two Wolfen who had been guarding him when he heard noise from above.

Perhaps Darstan and Wisp have come to get me, he thought. He climbed up to investigate, and that was when he saw the Banished Ones, and, gods forbid, the Evil One himself. Gregor felt certain it was him, there was a blinding light surrounding an image of a man wrapped in a dark aura. It was not something he could make out definitively, but it exuded evil.

He crept back into the crevice and trembled, too terrified to move. He sighed. Something had to be done. If he didn't get water soon, he would surely die.

Gregor climbed, slowly, carefully, each hand securing a firm hold before any move was made—he would risk no loose rocks falling. As he peeked over the rim, he scanned the desert. With the first breath, he gagged, almost losing the battle to control his body's reaction to the stench. He had smelled it for a while, but being so close to the bodies seemed to make it worse.

Straining, he pulled himself the rest of the way, coming onto the ground, first with one knee then the other. He crawled a short distance away from the cliff, then stood, searching for any signs of trouble, though he felt certain that nothing could be out there.

With one final look behind him, he started out on shaky legs. As soon as they firmed, he increased the pace to a fast walk, then a feeble run. Soon he'd be out. He could see the spot where they entered a few nights ago. The bounty-man traveled fast, but quietly, being adept at moving with little or no noise.

Wild thoughts came to him as he ran. This was the Sethian Shield, something he thought to be a legend only days past, but now he had to concede its existence even if it remained invisible to him. He knew he was close though, close to where Darstan had spewed fire. Gregor saw the scorched ground scattered with bits of charred flesh and bones, lots of bones. It's not far now. Not far at all.

"Leaving us so soon?"

Gregor stumbled. Fear whipped his head around like a wolf's howl does a lamb. He lay on his back, propped up on wobbly hands, feet digging into the ground to push himself away. A woman stood above him, smiling. "Blood of Gods!" he swore. "You ... you're one of them!"

Her smile should have been warm, from any other woman this beautiful it would have been, but on her, it was colder than a steel blade. Her hair was honey-colored, with long tresses that tumbled off her shoulders, and her body was lithe as a mountain cat's, but he felt her to be more dangerous, much more dangerous.

"I am leaving ... My Lady!" His voice a plea. "I only came to be here by mistake."

Her eyes never left him, hawk's eyes—no, owl's eyes; not just deadly, but wise as well. He would not hide things from this one.

"A mistake? I'm sure. I feel quite certain that you didn't come here purposefully, yet fortune delivers us gifts at times, great and wondrous gifts."

Gregor felt something stir in his head, and without knowing how she was doing it, he knew she was somehow in this head. Understanding the process, or even what she did was beyond him, but he felt her in there, inside his head, crawling around like a serpent hunting prey. Fear consumed him, then pity, then hopelessness until tears streaked his cheeks.

"Stand, bounty-man. And find your courage!" A look of disdain crossed her face. "I have no respect for a man who sheds tears."

Gregor found the strength to speak. "What will you do with me?" That cold smile returned, perhaps it had never left.

"First, you will tell me everything I want to know. Then you will do anything I want you to do." She chuckled, then a harsh, sadistic taunt. "Then, I will give you to Tirzinitzia. I feel certain she will want to know more than I, much more." With that, she grasped his hand, and they disappeared.

REVENGE

Refugio led the army through the pass, stepping over the hacked and charred bodies of Chun and Cergalan soldiers. There was a certain euphoria that rode with the army now. The recent victory had raised them to hero status, but still ... the battle had taken its toll. Cergalans were accustomed to fighting, especially fighting the Chun of Arangar, but what had happened in the pass tainted them. To kill with swords and spears was one thing, but Black-Wolf's raging fire had destroyed the Chun in a few disastrous moments —many Cergalans too—and the men were afraid.

"Faster, men. We fight for Cergala today." Refugio went through the motions, after all, he was the commander, but in his heart, he didn't feel committed. They had won already. The Cergalans controlled the pass for the first time in five hundred years ... so why were they marching into Arangar? When you hunted deer, you didn't kill the whole herd.

Refugio found it difficult to breathe, trying his best to only do it through his mouth. At times, though, he would forget and inhale, the horrific stench providing a sharp rebuke.

He wiped his nose with his sleeve, spat on the ground—careful not to hit any bodies—and once again began breathing through the mouth. At the top of the pass lay a heap of bodies that only now were being moved to a clearing. BlackWolf would soon reduce them to ashes as he had so many others. Refugio shook his head yet again. This was no way to conduct a war.

Occasionally they would see a Chun soldier still alive, struggling to get up or crawl to safety. Refugio tried to warn a few of them to sit still, pretend to be dead, but they didn't listen or didn't understand. When BlackWolf saw them, he ordered them killed, or worse, he did it himself. One of Refugio's men tried helping an enemy soldier, Black-Wolf put his sword in the man's heart.

"Don't leave any of the Chun alive," BlackWolf said. "We didn't come here to heal them."

Five thousand Cergalans followed him through the pass, with supplies to last months. He kept the rest of the Cergalans to guard the pass and as reserves. Darstan chased the Chun through the mountains, tracking them and slaughtering them, sparing no one except women and children, and only them if they didn't resist. He razed the villages and destroyed the land around them, burning everything to the ground.

For days, several raiding parties harassed their flanks, then fled. Darstan chased them into a narrow valley, but when they got there, the Chun had disappeared.

Rocky paths overlooked steep slopes dotted with pines and a few hardwoods. Snow filled pockets in the hillside and the shaded spots behind trees and large rocks. Refugio's scouts warned against a trap, suggesting a small force be sent into the mountains on each side first to check them for Chun. Darstan would hear nothing of it. Vengeance and patience did not mix well.

"I'll lead the way, Refugio. It's me they're after."

Orders rang out from the senior officer. "Flank BlackWolf. Stay alert."

They marched into the valley in loose fashion, no columns or rows, no visible sign of discipline, yet they all had their places, and they knew what to do in the event of an attack. Two full patrols flanked Darstan on either side, some slightly ahead, others just to the rear. What appeared to be a few stragglers rode in front of him.

Two short coughs from one of Tesla's men indicated the Chun had been spotted. That he turned right and to the rear when he coughed gave them a direction. Afterward, another scout stopped to light his pipe. The fact that he held it in his left hand and lifted his head high when he puffed on it told Refugio the enemy was ahead on the left.

Refugio rode up beside Darstan. "We appear to be surrounded, BlackWolf."

Darstan stopped, studied the slopes; they were steep, but the few trees weren't enough to cause real damage if he set them on fire. He might kill a few, inconvenience them, even panic them, but not enough for it to be decisive. The cliffs above them appeared to be sheer rock, and there wasn't enough snow to create avalanches. Maybe he should have listened to Refugio. He could get through, and he would eventually kill them, but a lot of Cergalans would die.

"What would you do, Refugio?"

Refugio thought for a moment, called two of the scouts and conferred with them. "The road to the south leads around these mountains, a long way, but a safe one. We can take that and be confident of getting around the other side, but we would still have these forces to deal with, and they would be behind us."

Darstan nodded. "Go on."

"The only way for them to get down is to descend to this valley then come out this way, or go through the pass to the south." Refugio leaned in close to Darstan. "If we leave a force of fifteen hundred men camped on the hillside, they'll have the Chun trapped. They can wait them out."

"How many did the scouts say they had?"

"No more than three or four hundred, armed with bows and spears."

"So if we left fifteen hundred, it would be a massacre, and it would still leave us with a formidable force."

"And once our men finish with the Chun, then they can come through the pass to join us. They'll probably get there at the same time if not before we do."

"Pick the men, Refugio. We'll camp here tonight and leave in the morning."

~

The morning was crisp, the way Darstan liked it. It reminded him of Kamnor, back when life was good. He took his time having khaffe, ignoring breakfast altogether.

"It's a long ride, BlackWolf. You should eat."

"I'll eat when I'm hungry." He threw out the last sip of his khaffe and set the mug down. As he walked about the camp, the men all jumped, pounding out their formal, three-fisted salute as they addressed him.

"Good morning, BlackWolf." Or simply: "BlackWolf."

He nodded at each one. He didn't know their names, save a few. It didn't matter. They only saluted him out of fear. They had either seen what he had done in the pass or heard about it from others, and those tales were probably worse than what had happened.

Halfway through someone offered him more khaffe, a young soldier. He hadn't bothered to salute, and he didn't look afraid. Darstan stopped, accepted the mug. He was a boy, no older than Darstan, but he looked as if he'd seen a lot more. "What's your name, soldier?"

"Benson."

Darstan stared at him while he sipped the khaffe. It was hot. Good. "Benson? Doesn't sound like a Cergalan name?"

That comment, coming from BlackWolf, would have buckled some men's knees. Veterans at that. "Neither is Darstan, BlackWolf." Benson gave a slight nod. Kind of a half salute, but he didn't buckle.

Darstan stared at him. Sipped more khaffe, stepped closer. "You don't like me, do you?"

Benson didn't look away. "No, sir."

"Why?"

A long silence ensued. "You're just a boy. No older than me."

"And?"

"And you got no business leading us to war. Way I figure it, every time somebody dies now it's because of you. There's no need for us to be here except for your vengeance." He bowed his head. "Guess I said too much. Kill me if you want."

Darstan clenched his teeth. Paced. Stared at the boy. He felt the fire churning in his gut. How dare he question him. Vengeance! After what they did to Mirana.

Darstan felt the fire trying to get out of his arm. He fought it, struggled, then he reached out and handed Benson the mug. "Good khaffe, boy." Darstan smiled. "Let's make a pact. You keep making good khaffe, and I'll try not to get us all killed."

Benson breathed a huge sigh, smiled, then pounded out a formal three-fisted salute. "Yes, sir, BlackWolf. You come by anytime for khaffe. I'll have it ready."

Darstan patted him on the shoulder. "And keep telling me what's on your mind, soldier. Now pack up, we're getting ready to leave." Darstan walked off, making the final turn through the camp before coming full circle to where Refugio stood waiting.

"Let's go, General," he said, and climbed atop his mount, wishing it were Grayson. It wasn't the first time he'd wished he had Grayson with him and wondered again how the horse was doing—if he was even still alive. He turned around, gave one last look at the men they were leaving behind.

Darstan had wanted Refugio to stay with the men in the pass, but the general insisted that Tesla was as good, if not better than him. Darstan had seen Tesla in action at the pass. He was good. "He won't take chances?" Darstan asked.

Refugio shook his head. "He knows how to preserve men. And he knows how to kill the enemy."

Darstan smiled. "A combination I admire. Let's move out then."

They rode for four days through rugged terrain, continually fighting biting winds and bitter cold nights. The roads were bumpy, many with big holes in them, but they were well traveled and for the most part cleared of debris or any other obstacle. In all that time they never met a single Chun to fight, hadn't seen more than a few dozen. On the fifth day, a rider approached from the rear, riding hard. Darstan halted when the man approached.

"Message from Commander Tesla."

The rider was panting like a worn out dog. "Said to tell you we cleared the pass. Killed all the Chun."

The smile lit Darstan's face. "How many did we lose?"

"Twenty-seven dead. Sixteen wounded bad enough to send back. Tesla sent ... I mean, Commander Tesla sent one hundred men along to guard the wounded."

"Get food and drink and fall in, soldier. That's good news." Darstan turned to Refugio. "How long before we get to the other side of the pass?"

"Tomorrow. Maybe the next day. Tesla will already be there."

"The scouts said there are villages on the other side of these mountains."

"You expect trouble?"

"There are a lot of villages," Refugio said. "This is where most of the Chun live."

"You think they'll take a stand?

Refugio sat up straight in the saddle as if it might provide an answer. He looked around, staring into the woods, mountains, open fields. "They'll fight us here. I can feel it."

"Good," Darstan said, and spurred his mount to a faster pace. Then this is where they will die.

~

They passed by three villages the next day, all abandoned. Darstan burnt them to the ground, sparing nothing, not even the stables.

"They'll need a place to live," Refugio said.

"Dead people don't need houses," Darstan said and moved on.

Late in the afternoon on the following day, they reached the pass. Tesla and his men were already camped, with scouts posted a quarter of a league out for advanced warning.

"I got the report, Tesla. Excellent!"

Tesla nodded. "You must be tired. Sit and eat."

"Have you scouted the area?"

"It's not good. They seem to have left their towns and gathered together for a massive strike. There must be ten columns, not two leagues from here."

The news shocked Refugio. "Twenty thousand men!"

"My scouts are seldom wrong, Commander. I even sent Tiko to double check."

Refugio nodded. Tiko could count the leaves on a tree with one glance. If he said there were ten columns, Refugio would take his word for it.

"What are we going to do, BlackWolf? We should at least try to get you out of here."

"Relax. Have dinner."

"We can't fight ten columns. And if they have that many now, they're probably waiting for more." Refugio paced. "We need to do something. Now!"

"Eat," Darstan said. "I have a plan."

"My dinner would taste much better if I knew what this plan was."

Darstan looked at Refugio. "I don't even know how to tell you. Trust me. Somehow I know it will work."

Refugio looked to the mountain pass, noting how Tesla had the men deployed, then he turned, staring at the road leading in from the south —open ground. Difficult to defend. "They'll attack in the morning, BlackWolf. They'll come with the sun. If not tomorrow, the next day for sure."

"Perhaps not, my friend." Darstan stared at Ranal, hugging the mountain peaks, while Ranalla sat high on her throne in the sky. "Refugio, could you please have someone get me khaffe? I intend to be up late tonight."

As he started to leave, Darstan halted him. "And have the men play some music, sing perhaps."

Refugio looked at him as if he were crazy, but he simply nodded. "Yes, of course."

Tesla sent out a dozen more scouts with orders to stay in pairs and to report any movement from the Chun. "I'm going to position the men, BlackWolf. They might as well know tonight where we want them in the morning."

At BlackWolf's nod, he continued. "I'll put the archers up high. We can take a lot of them out before they hit our lines. And since we have the narrow pass, we'll be able to hold out for a while." He paused, fearing what he had to tell BlackWolf. "Also, I already sent four messengers to request reinforcements."

Another simple nod, then. "Good, Tesla. Now let me think."

Refugio returned to join them, and while Darstan sipped his khaffe, they talked about tomorrow. "We should put a small guard, perhaps five hundred, at our rear, just in case they have flanked us. The rest need to focus on the road. We can't afford to let them get to those groves—"

Then, news of a messenger rang through the camp. Tesla jumped up, rushing to greet him. His heart sank when he saw who it was—Marco—one of the four he had sent for reinforcements.

Marco saluted, then stood rigid.

"Report, soldier."

"Trapped, sir. They got the others. Barely got out myself."

"How many?"

"Four, maybe five columns. The pass is blocked. We're not going back the way we came, that's for sure."

Refugio nodded. "Forget all I said. Guess they've decided to take a stand. They want you, BlackWolf."

"What do you mean?"

"They know you have Fire, saw it at the pass. But they must be guessing you can't last forever with it. That's why they brought so many men. Plan on a lot of them dying."

Darstan stood. "Then I won't disappoint them."

7

QUEST FOR BLOOD

esla made his rounds, inspecting the guards and the encampment. "Fill your guts tonight. The Chun could attack at any time, and you don't want to go to battle on an empty stomach."

"Think they'll come early?" one soldier asked.

Tesla glanced but didn't recognize him. Could have been a recruit. "Get your rest, boy. No matter what time they come, you won't sleep through it."

"Sure is quiet tonight," the lad next to him said.

Tesla started off, but then stopped. He went back and sat next to them. These boys weren't much older than his son, and they were scared. He smiled as he took a seat. "I always liked a quiet night before a battle. Made me sleep better."

They nodded but didn't say anything.

"When it starts, whether it's tomorrow or not, find me and stay under my command. I'll watch out for you."

The smaller of the two smiled, but the other still looked worried. "What about our patrol leader? He—"

"I'll go tell him now," Tesla said and got up. He patted them both on the back just before he left. "And don't worry. I won't tell him why. He'll think you have a special assignment."

Smiles lit both of their faces. They said good night with newfound confidence.

"Get some sleep," Tesla said.

As he made his way to the rear guard, he worried. They had too many men like those two in the army. Boys who had tasted battle just a few months ago, hardened boys, for sure, but still just boys. And fear always found a place in a young man's heart. "Report!" Tesla called as he approached.

"They're showing us their strength, Commander. Got more fires lit than they'd need in mid-winter. Figure on worrying us, I guess."

"Is it working?"

"Yep. They're doing a very good job."

Tesla laughed. The soldiers who joked about being afraid, the ones who admitted it, those he didn't worry over. "What's your name, soldier?"

"Anju."

"Been with us long?"

"Been with Refugio since before he was weaned."

Tesla laughed again. "Then I'd wager you've taught him a lot." He patted Anju on the back. "Take care tomorrow. We need men like you."

Anju nodded. "You take care of BlackWolf. He's the one we need tomorrow."

He checked the rest of the guards, then went to get some sleep. He knew he would need it come tomorrow. As he lay down, he saw Black-

Wolf leaving camp by himself. Tesla wondered what he was up to. BlackWolf said he had a plan.

~

*D*arstan stepped lightly as he left the camp, not wanting to disturb the men. The forward guards saluted when they saw him, stunned by his appearance.

"BlackWolf, you surprised me. I didn't expect—"

"That's all right. I'm here to try a few things." He looked about, saw only two guards. "Get a few more men. We'll be taking a walk."

Puzzled, all the soldier could do was nod, then he found his voice. "Yes, sir," he said and hurried off.

He returned within moments, four veteran soldiers at his side. After another salute, he stood at attention, waiting for a command.

"What's your name, soldier?"

"Yago."

"All right, Yago. Bring the others and come with me. Leave one man on guard duty here."

Yago posted the most senior man on duty, then fell in line behind BlackWolf. "Where are we going?"

"To see the enemy up close."

They crept through the woods as silent as a snake on the hunt. The Chun were sure to have sentries posted, and though it didn't worry Darstan, he didn't want to have them alerted if he didn't have to.

When they got within a hundred paces of the camp, well inside of their outward sentries, Darstan ordered them to stop. They were on a small rise, nestled in a copse of trees that offered good protection. The moons were shining bright, like a Hunter's Moon, and much like that, it would prove to be a good night for hunting.

"Keep watch," he said. "Don't bother me unless they come." Darstan sat on the ground, arms folded. He let his fingertips touch the spot on his left arm, where his hand used to be, ever so lightly, then closed his eyes and focused. Soon he felt the beat of his heart, slow, pulsing. He listened to it for a while, felt its rhythm, let his breathing fall in step.

When he got like this, it sometimes felt as if he still had both of his hands. Before long the pulsing stopped, replaced by a vibration that traveled up his arms and into his chest. It circled in his stomach, then moved down his legs and up into his head. His whole world seemed gone, lost.

He was now one with this strange world. A world where he ruled, where everything was pure and simple. He didn't even know what it was he wanted, but he knew it was in there. He had seen it in his dreams, and he would recognize it when he saw it.

His mind separated into something that resembled rooms in a palace. He had heard about memory palaces, but this wasn't that. This was more like a palace of power. He saw a room where the BlackFire resided, and a room that held Lightning, though he had never used it.

Another room was in a constant state of flux, shifting and moving about—he'd have to explore that later—and he saw the room that held the Voice he had used on the way to Vennala. Several rooms had open doors, but he knew he had not been there before. He wondered what secrets they held, but he didn't have time for that now.

The palace was huge and held a lot of corridors and many stairs. He climbed to the next level, then several more beyond that. On the floor just before the top, he found what he wanted—ColdFire. The door was a whitish blue, like blue ice. He shivered when he saw it. That door was open; he had used it in Sethia when his hand had been cut off, but not since. Something always warned him about using it, something instinctive.

Next to the ColdFire, lay several more doors, one was pulsing in rhythm with his own beating heart. Just as he was about to enter, he noticed another set of stairs, spiraling to the top floor. He walked up, but there was only one corridor, long and dark, and at the end lay a door with a lock on it, an illuminated door. It too, pulsed, but to a different beat, an ominous throbbing that seemed alien to him. That same instinct that he had learned to listen to told him to go back down. He did, though he longed to find out more.

When he returned to his destination, he opened the door and walked in. The room was cold, very cold, and a mist filled the room from floor to ceiling, a thick fog that swirled and moved as if it had a life of its own.

This is it. This is what I need.

He opened his mind—opened his soul—and let the fog in. It seeped in through the pores of his skin, chasing goosebumps away with fear. Somehow it got into his veins, raced through him as if it were his blood. Filled him. Flooded him.

The palace disappeared, and Darstan opened his eyes. The soldiers stared at him as if he had changed as if he were something to fear.

"Are you all right, BlackWolf?" Yago asked.

"Fine." He rose, walked to the outer rim of the bushes. "I am going to be busy now, so listen closely. Don't disturb me unless we are in grave danger. And no matter what happens, don't touch or go near the fog you will see."

They nodded, backing up as Darstan turned toward the enemy camp. He focused, then reached inside himself, drawing on the newfound talent he had just discovered. He had learned its name when he opened the door—FearMist it was called, and it was a power of ColdFire.

The fog came from his stump, slowly, in a cylindrical column that moved down the hill, hugging the ground. Then, his fingertips glowed, and more mist came from there, tendrils of thick smoke that twisted and turned and danced its way toward the Chun. It curved around rocks, crept through branches and slinked along the creek bed, mingling with the water as it did.

The camp was quiet, save for the occasional chatter around the many fires. Guards were posted a short distance from the perimeter, and men had been posted to tend the fires as well. As it neared the camp, the column of mist split into many columns, all as large and as thick as the original one.

One of the guards saw it coming toward him, an oozing mass that moved with stealth. An eerie feeling ran through him, but he stepped aside as it approached. When he moved, though, the mist moved with him, following him, advancing. He stepped back a few more paces, and with a little more haste. The mist continued, not any faster, but with deliberate intent. Reason suddenly settled on him, and he held his ground. This was just fog, after all.

When the mist reached him, it curled over his boots, wrapped around his legs, went up under his pants. It climbed his legs, writhing, reaching all the time. Panic forced his hand. He brushed at it as if it were a cloud of bees, trying to get it off him but it wouldn't move. He screamed, running toward his camp, but the mist clung to him. Fear had a firm grip on the soldier, and it wouldn't let go.

The guard's shouts alerted the other Chun, but it was too late, the FearMist entered from all sides, slinking under tents, slipping into clothing, and wrapping around everything it touched. Soon the entire camp was full of shouting, screaming soldiers. Some cowered in their tents, or in dark pockets of the woods. Others ran in circles, more than a few catching fire as they stumbled or raced through the flames. Some even used their weapons on themselves, death providing relief from the insatiable fear.

The men with Darstan huddled together, a different kind of fear gripping them. They had seen the FearMist, wondered about it, now they heard the screaming, and they saw Chun running about on fire or chasing each other with swords.

After a while, Darstan turned to them, a smile on his face. "We shouldn't be troubled with them in the morning," he said. "Now let's get the others."

By the time he had finished with the Chun in the pass, and the last of the FearMist left his body, exhaustion was setting in. He felt as if it the Fear-Mist was taking part of him with it. He fought, struggled, but it tugged at him. When he could fight no more, he collapsed. Yago was slow to react, and BlackWolf cracked his head on a rock, blood oozing out.

"Help me," Yago called to the other men. "BlackWolf is hurt."

They picked him up, carrying him to the camp while praying he didn't blame them. The camp was in turmoil, men gathered in groups wondering what kind of madman they traveled with, and what this new power of his did.

It struck fear into their hearts, and more than just a few talked about going home. Tesla and Refugio made quick rounds, trying to encourage the men and console them, but it was difficult when they felt the same way.

Refugio tended to him for the rest of the night, desperately trying to wake him. He called camp healers, but they did nothing.

"All we can do is wait," Tesla said. "I'm going out with the men before they all go crazy with fear."

Soon afterward Darstan awoke. He came out of the tent just before dawn. "Time to go."

"Where?" Refugio asked.

"To finish the job." Darstan seemed stunned that he asked. "They're afraid, but they're not dead. Not yet."

"But, BlackWolf. You're sick. You—" He paused. "What did you do to them?"

"I told you before, Refugio. You wouldn't understand." Darstan looked out over the men, saw their fear. "Listen well, soldiers of Cergala. We came here to do a job. We're going to finish it. Tesla, take half the men and go into the pass. Refugio and I will take care of the others."

Tesla turned to go, with not even a salute.

"Tesla!"

"Yes, BlackWolf."

"I'm coming back through the pass. Don't let me find anyone alive."

He sighed. "Yes, BlackWolf."

~

*D*arstan led the march into the Chun camp, killing some stragglers along the way, men who wandered about as if they were lost. Most ran when they saw the Cergalans, but ran as if they were creatures from the Evil One himself, not mere men. The camp was filled with more of the same.

Refugio came upon a Chun cowering near a tent, sitting on the ground, head buried in drawn-up knees with hands wrapped around them. He was rocking back and forth mumbling something incoherent.

Darstan came up behind him. "What's the matter, Refugio?"

Refugio turned and stared at BlackWolf. "Look at him! This was a Chun warrior. By all the gods, BlackWolf, what did you do?"

Fire danced in Darstan's eyes as he stared at Refugio. There were twenty or thirty Chun all around them, cowering, lying on the ground, or hiding. He raised his left arm, focused, then shot columns of Black-Fire at the Chun. Their whimpering turned to screams of death. Cowering bodies now writhed in pain. The flames burned through them, turning flesh to ash.

"BlackWolf, no! This isn't right."

Darstan turned his head very slowly to Refugio. "I told you when we set out I planned on killing them all. Nothing has changed."

Refugio looked at the charred bodies. "But this... this is—"

"This is death, Refugio. If you can't do it, go back. Send me someone who can."

Refugio stood in silence under the scrutiny of Darstan's glare. At last, he nodded.

"Good," Darstan said. "Now get the men to help me. I want every soldier dead before we leave."

It took all day to do the killing, the men physically and mentally exhausted from the horrible task. More than half had taken turns throwing up; some even tried to desert, sneaking out when they thought BlackWolf wasn't watching. He had caught a few of them, giving them the same treatment as the Chun. Once the men saw that, the desertions stopped, but the sickness persisted.

"We'll camp, then start out in the morning."

"I'm not camping here," Refugio said. "I don't care what you do or what you want; I'm starting back now. I don't know how far I have to go to get away from this stench, but I'll know when I get there."

Darstan stared, but then agreed. "Fair enough. We'll march. But send runners to the other villages. I'm sure they've heard what happened by now. Some would have gotten away. Have them tell the villagers I'm coming. Tell them to take their women and children and go to Chingua. Tell them I'm coming for them. Soon!"

"There are a half a million people in Chingua," Refugio said.

Darstan nodded. "And I intend to kill them all."

8

ANOTHER BEGINNING

Kyra sat by the fire, tufts of mottled fur bristling in dawn's light. One of her claws had broken, and a wound in her side oozed blood every time she moved. *Perhaps I am too old to do battle,* she thought and attributed her failure to escape the dorgan's swipe to her aging body. Though many young had fallen too, and they had more agility and speed than she could muster.

It made her think of her son, Pharr, and she mourned his loss. Even the loss of Arton weighed heavily on her. Though he had slaughtered countless Krengs, he had become a friend, a blood protector, and it was Arton who had saved Phay. Aside from Pharr and Arton, many other members of her pack had gone on to the Eternal Hunt, taken there by dorgans. And now she was trapped in a strange world with strange people. *I should have stayed with Pharr.*

One of Phay's sharp claws stroked her back, while she pondered. "I miss him," Phay said.

"We will soon hunt together once again," Kyra said, her paw caressing his.

Mulka, one of the ancient race of Mordi, rose from his seat by a log and sat next to Kyra. "They will get you back to your lands, and I will soon be going to mine."

The Kreng nodded, eyeing Mulka and Garnock. "You do not belong. No more than the Kreng."

"No, we don't."

Kyra walked to where Sama sat, weeping on Kavi's shoulder. "When they take me home you can join my pack," she said to Kavi.

Kavi forced a smile. He had hunted with her in the Paaren where she had earned his highest respect. "We have our pack, Kyra, and though we lost our leader, another will take his place."

Kyra put her paws together and bowed. "A wise pack lasts forever. May your hunts be fruitful."

Kavi bowed in return, then continued to console his mother.

The Kreng wandered through the camp, but careful to keep a respectful distance from the blackthorns. Rhaven had told them all about the deadly poison. Kyra stood staring at the trees, rising halfway to the sky, and she wondered how they grew so tall, how they stayed aright in the winds. Rhaven moved up beside her.

"Remember I told you about the darts I make."

When she acknowledged, he continued.

"I thought that I could make some arrows, show you how to coat them. They might be strong weapons against the dorgans."

She stared at him for a long time. "I have no bow, and I don't know how to use one."

"I can give you a bow. And learning to shoot something as big as a dorgan should be easy enough. Then, with practice, you will get much better."

A quizzical look came over the Kreng. "You think it will work on a dorgan?"

"It's worth trying," Rhaven said. "Come with me."

They walked to one of the huge blackthorns, where Rhaven cut into the bark just below a large thorn, drawing a thick syrupy substance that oozed from the tree into a container. He took some white powder from a pouch and mixed it with the sap. "This powder keeps it potent for almost two years." After he got enough, he sat on the ground, and using a thin brush, he applied the mixture to the arrows, starting at the bottom and working his way up, but stopping short of the tips.

"Don't ever coat the tips," he told Kyra. "That way, if you happen to nick yourself there is no poison. And whatever you shoot, the arrow will go in enough for the poison on the sides to get to the blood."

"Dorgan skin is thick, but I think at the neck it would work."

Rahg had come over to watch, remembering when he had seen Rhaven do this so long ago. It seemed long ago, yet it was only last year. "You can have my bow and arrows, Kyra. I won't be needing them."

Rhaven looked as if he might admonish Rahg, but he smiled instead. "Rahg could teach you to shoot too."

Kyra's claws retracted, and she patted Rahg on the back like she had seen the furless ones do so often. "My pack is grateful."

～

*A*entarra put down her cup of khaffe. "I need to check on the Shield. See if I can tell who got out."

"Are you strong enough to risk it?"

"Do you truly care, sister?" With that, Aentarra shifted.

Rahg stood next to Mikkellana shaking his head. "You almost let her die in Sethia. Your sister!"

"She would do no different."

"She saved us all. Risked her own life. She—"

"Nonsense. She only saved her skin. Aentarra does nothing without—"

"No!" Rahg shouted. "She could have left on her own. And you let her bleed half to death." He stopped, shocked at the memory. "Just like she said you let your brother die."

"I told you before to keep your nose out of that, boy. Now—"

The air rippled, allowing Aentarra to slip through the thin rift into their camp in the Blackthorn Forest.

Mikkellana was sitting next to Rhaven, sipping khaffe. "What did you discover, sister?"

"He's still trapped, but Sendra and Ghruehne escaped. At least, if my Sensing is still accurate, they did."

"Who are they?" Rahg asked. "I mean, what are they like?"

Aentarra laughed. "They're Banished Ones, boy. They'll kill you the first time they see you. Kill anyone you're with too."

"Tobias, may I have more khaffe?" Mikkellana walked over to him, holding out her cup. "I'm afraid Aentarra is right about this, Rahg. Ghruehne is worse than Iazzo. He's a bitter man who loves nothing more than to cause pain." She sipped on the khaffe. "Ages ago my father gave him a scar on his face, and he has been repaying that to others for a thousand years."

Despite the fear coursing his veins, Rahg was excited. He had never heard either one of them mention their father. "Why did your father—"

"There was a war," Aentarra interrupted. "A great war. It was called the Wars of Light, though it should have been called the War of the Lights. There were seven worlds at war, and we—"

"You mean seven lands? Seven countries?"

"I mean what I say. Seven worlds. Just as your lands make up your world, we had seven in Nelstar."

"But how did you—"

"We shifted between worlds, at least those who were powerful enough did. My father was so strong he once shifted to Runella with ten thousand men, and that was three worlds away."

"If he was so strong how did he die?"

A long sigh followed. "I'm afraid I've already said too much. If I say much more, you'll be frightened to death."

Mikkellana stood. "Odd that we seem to be agreeing of late, sister." She stared at Rahg. "The only two people you need to know about now are Ghruehne and Sendra. I told you about him, but don't be fooled into thinking she is any less dangerous. Sendra may not kill for pleasure, but she will kill you as quickly, and she is ruthless and efficient. She once tracked fourteen assassins in three days. Killed them all."

Rahg trembled, though he tried not to let it show. "If you wanted to scare me, it worked. Now tell me what I'm supposed to do. I can't fight them alone."

"You're not alone," Rhaven said. "We're all with you. I don't think Mikkellana and Aentarra are leaving you to face them by yourself."

"He's right about that, Rahg, but we still have problems. Ghruehne and Sendra won't attack without full advantage. That means if they see us with you, they'll stay hidden until they can catch you alone. Sooner or later, they *will* get you alone."

"Why can't we go to Entiria? They can't find us there."

"How do you think Iazzo got there?" Mikkellana said. "He would have sent the Shift points to Lukaan as soon as he had them."

Aentarra grabbed a biscuit and khaffe from Tobias, but as she started toward her seat, she collapsed, biscuit dropping to the ground and her khaffe spilling all over her.

Tobias jumped to her side, knelt and held her head up in his lap.

"Is she all right?" Rahg asked, now standing at Tobias's side.

"Don't know, lad. She's breathin', but she seems unconscious."

"Move!" Mikkellana made her way over, pushing Camissa and Mulka out of her way. "Let me look at her." She knelt opposite Tobias and examined her, running her hands over her chest and then her head.

Soon, Aentarra became alert. "What's the matter?" Mikkellana asked.

Aentarra stared at her. "I think I know, but I have to check something first." She tried to stand, making it with Tobias's help. "I'll be back soon," she said, and shifted.

"Wait!" Mikkellana said, but Aentarra had already gone. "Fool, shouldn't be shifting in that condition."

"What happened?" Camissa asked.

"As of yet, I have no idea."

They soon returned to the discussion of where to go, Rahg pressing for Entiria despite the warnings.

Mikkellana sat still, saying little until the end. "Whatever we do, it had better be—"

Then a rift appeared, Aentarra stepping through. "I pray that you were going to say that whatever we do it had better be soon."

Mikkellana stared at her, still upset with her actions. "Why?"

"Unless I'm mistaken that wondrous shield of yours won't be holding Lukaan much longer."

Mikkellana's face wrinkled into a question. "Why? What happened?"

"Our allies in Vallah are dead."

Shock replaced the questioning look. "All of them?"

"Throats slit."

Mikkellana lashed out with a shield, battering Aentarra to the ground. As she stood above her preparing another attack, a Slicer emerged from Aentarra's pouch, stopping a hair's breadth away from Mikkellana's head.

A thin, sardonic smile appeared on Aentarra's face. "I don't think you want to do that, sister, but it is good to see you have a temper. I thought you might have lost it after keeping it under control all of those years."

Aentarra propped herself up on an elbow, rolled to her side, then stood, dusting off her pants as she glared at Mikkellana. "Don't ever try that again."

"Look what you've done!" Mikkellana shook her head as she walked away. "Fool!"

Rahg stood on the side, close to the fire. He had backed up, along with everyone else, when this had started. "What's wrong? Whose throats are slit? And what does she mean that Lukaan might get out?"

"None of your business." Mikkellana snapped.

Tobias stepped up beside Rahg, ready to defend him, but Rahg held him back. "It is my business all right. If you and Aentarra think I have something to do with this nonsense then what happened is my business." He glared at Mikkellana, then Aentarra. "I'm tired of being pushed around by you two."

Mikkellana stepped toward him. "Boy, I could ..."

"Yes, I know the things you could do to me, so do what you want; I don't care anymore." Rahg stared a moment longer, then went and sat by the fire.

Camissa sat next to him, a ferocious glare of her own directed at Mikkellana.

Mikkellana focused a scathing gaze at Rahg before shifting it to Aentarra, then she closed her eyes. Before long she seemed to be back in control. "Enough of our bickering. We need to be together now more than ever. Aentarra, have you any bright ideas?"

"I don't like Entiria, but he would be safe in Arangar, for now … unless Darstan is still there."

"Darstan won't hurt me."

Mikkellana's frown revealed too much. "Don't be so sure of what he'll do. Besides, it doesn't matter. We can't stay in Arangar forever."

"We have to use him as bait," Aentarra said. "We'll dangle him out there and wait for them to strike."

"Not me!" Rahg jumped up, spilling what was left of his khaffe. "I'm not going to be bait for anybody."

Mikkellana shot him a look to kill. "You'll do what we say, even if I have to put the hook in your mouth myself."

Rahg couldn't believe what he was hearing. Here the two of them were, talking about using him for bait with the Banished Ones and not caring one bit if he lived or died. "I want to go to Entiria."

"There's nothing for you there," Mikkellana said.

"I need to ask the shera some things."

"What?"

"Things that you don't know about, Mikkellana. There are …"

Aentarra nodded her head. "It's the mountain in the Paaren, isn't it?"

"What?"

"You heard me, boy. It's that mountain you went up to and stayed for so long." She held him fast with her glare. "What was up there? What did you see?"

Rahg sat silent for a long time. "I can't say. It's just—"

"The gods," Camissa said, and her knees buckled. "He met the gods there."

Rahg's head spun around to Camissa. "I can't believe you did that! Can't believe you told them." His breathing grew rapid, then faltered.

He struggled, finally calming himself. *By the gods, the dragon was right. I can't trust anyone!*

Mikkellana grabbed him by the shirt. "What about the gods?"

"I'm not saying anything. Kill me if you want. Probably will anyway."

"Let's go to Entiria," Aentarra said. "We can deal with Ghruehne and Sendra later."

9

ENTIRIA AGAIN

Aentarra's rift opened inside the Shulan's palace, in the corridor outside the rooms that they had used before. "Mikkellana, take them to the temple. I'll find that priest so we don't waste time."

"Mulka, tell Kyra and Garnock to stay close. The Entirians are peaceful, but you never know what people will do." Mikkellana turned to the others. "Rahg, you and Camissa lead us to the temple. Rhaven, guard Mulka and his companion."

"You mean guard the Entirians, don't you?"

"Either way."

Rahg led them down familiar corridors. They held no fond memories for him, but he remembered each hall and where it led. Perhaps it was the dread of the first visit here that had implanted them in his mind. That was when he had learned about his mission, learned he had powers, then found out he had to fight Iazzo, a Banished One. A lot of people died that day, good people.

He didn't look forward to his visits with the priests, but there were things he needed to know, things that these priests might have answers to. Since he was tied up in this mess, he had better find a way to survive.

~

Camissa walked alongside Rahg, her memories of Entiria mixed: some good, some frightening. She had almost died here when they had fought Iazzo and she had entered the Planes of the Mind. If it hadn't been for Aenaila, she probably would have died in there.

Camissa had not entered since that time, despite the fact that Rahg had begged her to teach him. She felt certain, that was not a good idea. Rahg didn't seem stable enough to handle the powers he had now, let alone setting him loose in that place. Her powers had greatly increased since that time, and though she doubted that the experience had anything to do with it, she sometimes wondered.

Camissa focused her thoughts on confidence and boldness, then sent it to Rahg as Suggestion, hoping to provide him with enough strength to make it through this ordeal. She knew how nervous he was.

~

As they turned down yet another corridor, Jarrell continued walking straight. "This way, Jarrell," Rahg said.

Jarrell looked to Rahg, then joined them in the procession, falling in like the last duck in a line. His thoughts had been wandering since returning home, jumping from excitement to despair then back again. He was the only Entirian to survive, he and the ones they left with the ship, though they would have long since returned home, assuming them dead by now. And nearly right they were.

Katsu, Torsla, the others, all gone. *They were the lucky ones*, Rahg thought, but then wondered if the ones who died weren't the lucky ones, considering the fate they all might face. *If the Evil One gets out like they say, I think I'd have rather been with Katsu.*

~

*R*haven watched as Tomkins gawked and stared.

"I'm guessing you haven't seen the likes of this," Rhaven said.

Tomkins shook his head. "Traveling with you people opened my eyes to a lot of things, but this palace is something new."

As they emerged from the building to a large courtyard, Rhaven stared upward as he walked, not paying much attention to where he was going.

"What's the matter?" Tobias asked.

"That building, the temple," Rhaven said. "There's no damage to it, yet when we fought Iazzo, his lightning hit it several times. I remember."

Tobias rubbed his whiskers as he tilted his head to stare. "I do believe you're right about that. I remember thinking what a shame it was that the temple would be ruined." He thought a moment more then started walking again, following Rahg. "Guess they fixed it. Looks good now."

"They couldn't have fixed it this soon."

"Someone did," Tobias said. "C'mon, let's go before the lad gets talkin' with the priests. I don't want them fillin' his head with nonsense that we don't know about."

~

*T*hey ran, catching up to Rahg as he crossed the courtyard. After a short walk, they made their way to the temple steps. Soon, Rahg's feet were pounding the blue-tinted stone slabs used as steps, and once again he counted them aloud as he climbed, though he didn't need to. There would still be twenty-one of them.

Across a promenade were the same bronze doors with the intricate carvings of odd symbols. And, once again, the doors seemed to open on their own as he approached, though now he knew it was due to a device the Entirians had rigged to the back of the doors. The guards stepped aside to let them enter.

Rahg stepped inside and stared. "It looks larger than before."

Hundreds of candles lit the room, casting an eerie glow to the walls, and the echoes made by Rahg's boots pounding the marble floors reverberated loudly.

Rahg made his way toward the center of the room where three priests stood, just where they had before, in the middle of three circular designs that were part of the floor. The shera stood in the middle.

The shera bowed his head, the others following suit. "It is good to see you again, Rahg. The gods must have smiled on you."

"They didn't smile on Katsu, or Jorn, or any of your other men, except Jarrell. And they didn't smile on the Krengs or Korg. But those names don't mean anything to you, do they? They're just more dead people to add to your prophecy."

Rahg stared them down. "They're all dead. Everybody you sent with us, except Jarrell and the ones we left with the ship. Them plus many more. And for what? We didn't do anything. Didn't get anything accomplished except get a lot more people killed."

"Sometimes the true meaning of what we do is hidden," the shera said.

Rahg reached for his sword, having to grit his teeth to restrain himself. "Don't start with your riddles. I've got questions that I wish you to answer, and I want no nonsense."

"Wishing and wanting are two different things," one of the priests said.

Rahg sighed and gritted his teeth. "Rhaven, if you don't kill him, I will."

Aentarra laughed. "That boy has less patience than I do." She walked to the shera and turned him to face her. "But he wouldn't kill you, Shera."

She glared at him. "I would though. Now answer his questions and do it truthfully. I'll know if you don't. And the first lie will earn you a slit throat."

The shera gulped, then bowed low to Aentarra and again to Rahg. "Please, go on."

Rahg took a deep breath. "What do you know of this place I went to, the place the amulet led me to?"

The shera cast a quick glance to Aentarra, then focused on Rahg. "Our prophecies foretold your coming thousands of years ago, about a warrior who could stop the Awakening. Along with those prophecies was a legend of the amulet that would lead you to the gods."

Mikkellana stared at the shera. "How could the prophecies tell about the Awakening that long ago? Lukaan wasn't here then?"

"What do you mean lead me to the gods?" Rahg asked.

The shera cast another stolen glance to Aentarra, then, "The ancient gods of our people. There were three of them: Zukaar, Shinaka, and Daurien. They have not been heard from in thousands of years, and it is said they now live in the lands you call the Paaren."

"On that mountain?" Rahg asked.

"In that mountain."

Rahg nodded. "I saw one of them. Zukaar."

The shera and his two priests fell to their knees, heads planted on the floor, lips forming the words of their chant.

"Quiet!" Aentarra shouted, then grabbed hold of Rahg. "You saw one of them!"

She scared Rahg, but he held himself straight. "More than that. I talked to him, and ..."

"And what, boy?"

"He gave me some power."

Aentarra stared, while Mikkellana moved to the front. "What do you mean, gave you power?"

"He said he ... infused me with Shield, so I wouldn't—"

Aentarra grabbed a dagger from her waist and stabbed him in the side.

Rahg screamed, jumped aside and reached for his wound but there was none. He looked at his hand, expecting to see blood, then his side, but nothing. No blood and no pain. "It worked! It really worked."

After he got over the surprise of his shield working, the realization of what Aentarra had done hit him. "You stabbed me! I could have been killed. Suppose it hadn't worked."

"Then you would have learned a valuable lesson about lying to me."

Everyone stared at him, but no one seemed more excited than Aentarra. "What else is in that forsaken place? And if the gods are hiding there, what, or who, are they hiding from?" She paused. *Of course.*

Aentarra reached over and grabbed the shera's robe, yanking him up from the floor. "What else do you know, Holy Man? Tell me everything."

He shook his head rapidly. "You must believe me. I know nothing else. I didn't ... I had no idea they lived there."

"You didn't believe?" She taunted. "Shame on you. Say extra prayers tonight, my friend, and every night from now on, because I plan on telling your gods how you've abandoned them."

The shera reached for her, then stopped, head bowed. "My apologies. And you are right. We had abandoned them ... but no more. I will spread the word, and we will begin anew. Perhaps with prayer, they will return."

It will take a lot more than prayer, my good shera. A lot more. Aentarra stared at Mikkellana. "You know where we have to go now, sister."

"It's the last place I want to go, but it looks as if we must." She turned to Mulka. "We're going to need you again. Garnock, too, if he'll come."

Mulka nodded, then turned to Kyra. "We are taking you home to rejoin your packs."

A guttural growl rumbled from her throat. Home.

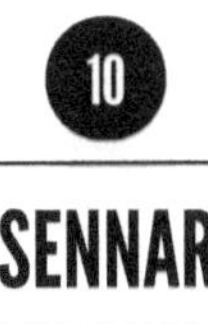

SENNAR

Mikkellana and the rest of them had just exited the temple when she heard a familiar voice.

"My Lady, ya' didn't think to sneak out of Entiria without seein' me, did ya'? Might have to stand in line, though, all the women want me now that this pretty face is fixed up."

Mikkellana laughed. The old salt had certainly changed his attitude since she had first met him. "I would have found you despite the lines, Sennar, though I might have nudged my way to the front."

Sennar hugged her, then Camissa, and shook hands with Tobias, Rhaven, and Rahg. He stared at Kyra and Garnock, then Mulka. "See you got some new friends too. Look a little saucy if ya' ask me."

"No hugs for me?"

Sennar heard the voice, so sensual it could melt a man's heart, make him do things he'd not ordinarily do, but he knew who it belonged to. He turned, stared at Aentarra. "I'm plum out of hugs today, My Lady. Please forgive me."

Her laughter put them all at ease. It was ever a guessing game as to how she might react to any comment. If she was in the wrong mood and took a comment as an insult ... Today must have been a good day, for all she did was laugh and move on, leaving the rest of them to talk with Sennar.

"What were ya' gonna' see me about?"

"I might need your help. Remember, I said—"

"No need to go further. I told ya' I'd do anything, and I'm a man who keeps his word. All that's left is the tellin'.'"

"The tellin'?"

"Tell me what you need me to do."

A smile crossed her face. Sennar's language was more colorful than Tobias's. She suggested they have some khaffe and food while they talked, and once they got there, she related the tales of what had happened since they left him in Entiria.

She told him of the Banished Ones who had escaped and how they now were sure that Lukaan would start troubles in all the countries. "War is inevitable, and we're going to need all the help we can get, Captain Sennar."

"What can I do?"

"Build a navy. Gather as many sea captains as you can. Genda has more ships than all the other countries, and it is imperative that we seize control of them before Lukaan strikes. Control of the sea will be important."

Sennar nodded while she talked, his mind racing. "I don't know how much the people of Genda will listen to an old tar like me, but I know one they would listen to, and he happens to be the best seaman in the world."

"Who?" Mikkellana asked though she felt certain she knew.

"Malakai. The Sword of the Sea." Sennar smiled. "They'll listen to Malakai 'cause they're scared of him, and 'cause they know he can command a fleet of ships better'n any man alive."

"How can we convince him to help us?"

"He'll listen to me." The voice came from nowhere, then Aentarra appeared, her famous smirk firmly planted on her face.

Sennar jumped up from his chair. "I don't want no harm comin' to the man. He—"

"Don't worry. I don't need to kill a man to get him to do what I want. Give me more credit than that."

Mikkellana worried about what she might do, but she nodded her head. "My sister can be persuasive. I suggest we let her try."

Sennar stared at her from the corner of his eye, a wary look on his face. "I'll get my men ready to sail. About time we got home anyway."

When Sennar had gone, Aentarra sat at the table where he had sat. "So, sister, how do we get to this place where the pirate is?"

"I've never been. My guess is you'll have to sail with Sennar."

Aentarra's glare looked as if she wanted to kill. "You knew all along. Knew I'd have to go with him. Fine, but I just might kill a few of his men for spite."

"Don't you dare!" Mikkellana's face turned rigid.

"Have you no humor, sister? I don't intend on sailing with that old man. I'll get a Shift point on the ship and join him when it's time."

Mikkellana nodded. "I should have thought of that." She paused. "You intend to use a Slicer?"

"It would be the easiest way."

"All right, then if we have nothing else here, let's get ready to go."

Aentarra asked Sennar about how long it would take him. Sennar had to consult with the Entirians. They had told him there'd be another way back, a roundabout way, but a safe one. He found Aentarra later that day. "More'n likely be two weeks before I can get there."

"Show me your ship then, so I can get a point to shift to." Before she left, she told Sennar to wait for her there, no matter how long it took. "And make sure that nothing is moved on this ship. I need that space right there, the same as it is now."

Sennar nodded, then watched her disappear.

THE CHOSEN KARN

Jen Pal stepped into the building, silent as ever. Always silent.

Shatir, busy fending off strikes from two opponents, stepped quickly back then spun toward him, smiling when she saw who it was. A raised hand stopped the others, and that brought the news to everyone. She had been practicing with a staff today, eager to learn the uniqueness of Suk Won's bedmate. "I presume we have news, Jen Pal."

Cherry-black eyes scanned the small group. "Ghruehne, the small god, has escaped."

If Ligarns gasped, they likely would have, but Ligarns seldom showed emotion, forbidden in their culture.

"But before he left he gave me the selection of the karn."

This was the news everyone had awaited, even those who had not participated were eager to hear. It was an honor for them. A line formed, and when they were all there, Jen Pal continued, wasting no time with pleasantries or unnecessary chatter.

"Shatir, Suk Won, and Triala will join me." They stepped forward and bowed. Jen Pal returned the gesture. "We leave in the morning." With that, he left.

Shatir woke early, long before the sun, but just lay in bed, hands folded under her pillow. She slept with one sheet and one thin pillow. On the coldest desert nights, a second sheet might be dragged from the closet, but never more than that.

Her husband, Bhaka, slept with nothing, not even clothes. She stared at him, still asleep, and traced a line down his chest with her finger, tickling him awake.

He smiled, leaned over and kissed her. "Today?"

"Yes."

"Have you told the children?"

"After our meal."

He rolled to his left, wrapped an arm around her and kissed her softly. "Should we wait?"

"When I return," she said, then got out of bed and began to dress.

Long, muscular legs as brown as a sentry tree's bark, flowed up to a perfect backside. Perfect, like two half moons, and as taut as a new bowstring. A thin layer of silk, disguised as skin, covered her ribs and the muscles in her arms remained hidden until needed. She put on pants, then her top and her belt, complete with sheaths. As she lifted each leg, a soft moccasin slipped on, becoming one with her feet.

Her clothes seemed to slide onto her, then hugged her as if they were a man longing to see her. Shatir's eyes were cherry-black—all Ligarn's were—and her hair made her skin appear pale.

Two knives lay on the table next to her, her bedmates. They were shorter than the Wolfen long-knife but long enough to run through a person's gut and out their back. Shatir had chosen the knife as her bedmate, though by all reports she should have chosen the bow. None could equal her with the bow, few with the knife.

The blade seemed simple enough, but the process of folding the steel and mastering the crafting of it was a mystery hidden by generations of Ligarns.

She caressed each knife as she slipped it into the sheath, recalling her Day of Naming. Her father went with her that day, offering comfort but no advice. A Ligarn must choose for themselves, as they wed for life, unlike a real partner. The primary weapon is the one they were expected to become an expert in—beyond the sense of reason. The weapon must become a part of them, and they must learn the weapon's needs as well.

For the bow that meant when to oil and stretch it, and what to do when the sun baked it dry. What string is best, and how tight to draw the bow. Which wood to choose, and how to carve and shape the wood. Shatir had done this, and more. She spent as much time with her bow as she did her husband, and with the exception of romantic nights, she enjoyed it more too.

She pressed the cold steel of the knife against her cheek, letting it slide slowly over her jaw. The metal for the knife was forged and folded meticulously, and as it cooled, with every few folds, the Ligarn touched it, rubbed it, caressed it—as if it were a partner on the night of mating. Before the final fold, a drop of the Ligarn's blood was mixed with the steel, binding them forever.

As important as the blade was, the handle was even more so. It had to be carved from a special wood dried in the Sethian sun, wood that seemed to exist for this purpose only.

The trees grew at the northeastern fringes of the desert, in the foothills of the Khataran Mountains. They lined the edges of the desert like a farmer's fencing and boasted lush foliage with sweet tasting nuts. The wood was unexplainably porous, yet hard, and legend claimed it was the roots of these trees that stole the life from once-green Sethia. If molded properly and cured to perfection, the handle of the blade would never slip because it absorbed its master's sweat.

Shatir slid a blade into each sheath, then repeated her mantra. She moved to the children's room, kneeling next to their bed. Two priceless boys, both of them eager to grow into men. She planted a soft kiss on each forehead, then an even softer one on each hand before leaving.

Her husband held her, kissed her lips. "Stay a while."

"Jen Pal will be waiting."

He nodded. "May the gods smile on your journey."

"If not, I will be waiting at the Gates of the Sun," Shatir responded, and walked out the door.

~

Triala mustered her energy, then darted off into the desert. Nothing felt as good as running through the sands before the sun rose. The desert night left it cool, inviting, and occasionally she would come across a yanta plant or two, upturned leaves offering their sacrifice of water for the day to needy animals.

She did this every morning, regardless of the weather. A warrior cannot worry about the weather. Bare feet pounded rocks and the occasional piece of thorny bush, but that never slowed Triala. She was accustomed to bloody feet, inured to pain.

A scorpion scurried across the ground, perhaps twenty paces ahead. Triala stopped, removed her bow, nocked an arrow—and with one fluid motion drew back the string and shot. The arrow flew true, as always, and the scorpion was knocked back four to five paces, the arrow still in it. Triala smiled. Shatir will have competition at the next contest.

She walked to retrieve the arrow, cleaned it off and put it back in the quiver. Arrows were never to be wasted. Whoever chose the bow also made the arrow from the same tree as the bow, so a Ligarn was expected to make as many arrows as they would need in a lifetime. As frugal as they were, that was far less than one might expect. Ligarns believed that an arrow cut from a different tree than the bow never flew as true.

As with all weapons, the Ligarns followed an age-old process. The crafting of arrows required that each arrow be anointed with a tear from their eye so that the arrow would go wherever their eye saw, never miss its mark. They used the fruit of the jatocha plant, the one that grew underground, to make their tears. These tears were allowed since they were not tears of emotion, but the "Blood of the Hunter's Eye."

Triala walked all the way home, breathing deeply and filling her lungs with fresh morning air. She entered the house, went to her bedroom, changed into fitting clothes, then prepared to leave. She slipped one knife into a sheath behind her, and she slung the bow over her shoulder, opposite a quiver of arrows.

As she exited the house, the sun peeked over the mountains to the east. She set off at a fast pace. Jen Pal would be waiting.

～

A desert fly made its third pass over Suk Won's bed. He lay still, eyes closed. He waited for the sound, then, as it drew near, his hand darted out and snatched the fly out of the air. He brought his closed fist close to his ear, heard the buzzing inside. Smiled.

Suk Won rose from the bed, walked to the stone patio outside his home, then set the fly free.

Enjoy the wind.

He always felt it good fortune to do a kindness before setting out on a karn, and what better kindness than to spare a life. No light graced his courtyard yet, but he made his way to the center, sat with legs folded, upturned hands resting on his knees. A ritual chant seemed to emanate from him, almost as if he were not singing it. It vibrated throughout the yard. Suk Won closed his eyes, focused, fell into rhythm with himself. Soon he was lost in another world, another time. In moments he returned, refreshed as if he had slept for days.

It was time to go, he knew, and stood, walked in to dress. His shirt and pants seemed to fall in place, then he slipped on calf-high boots, leather so supple it could be skin. He tucked a knife into a sheath in his boot, then grabbed his spear. As he was walking out the door he grabbed his staff; his hands seemed empty without it.

Like all Ligarn weapons, the staff required patience and diligence. The wood was chosen with meticulous care, usually from a chunta tree, or if one was available a jakallella. The tree must be old, at least seventy-five years, and the branch cut had to be twice as thick as the staff would be and half again as long. More than any other weapon, the staff must be perfect. Balanced to perfection. Hardened to ward off strikes from swords, yet flexible enough to be a whip in a master's hands.

The staff was one of the weapons of life. Ligarns categorized weapons as death or life-and-death. The weapons of death were used exclusively for killing: the bow, spear, flail, sling, garrote, whip, and axe. Weapons of life-and-death were used for both defense and offense: sword, staff, knife, and sai.

Suk Won flicked his wrist, twirling the staff as he walked. It sang for him, a tune like a morning dove. He smiled. This would be a good journey, but he must hurry, as Jen Pal would be waiting.

~

Jen Pal fixed his morning khaffe, while he made preparations to leave. There was little to do at home, the house was small and sparsely decorated: a table with a small chair in the kitchen, and a pot for brewing khaffe; a few pans with silverware for cooking; a bed with a thin sheet in the bedroom; and a cushion on the floor in the gathering room. The walls were empty save one lone painting of a woman, dark-skinned, young and beautiful.

When he had finished drinking the khaffe, he cleaned the mug then put it away. He picked up his knives, tucked them into sheaths in his belt, then grabbed his sai and headed for the door. On his way, he stopped at the picture, bowed, then kissed the woman goodbye. "I will clear your shame. I vow it."

As he left the house, Jen Pal fingered the blade on his sai, the feel of cold steel bringing a shiver to his body. He recalled the day of naming, when he had chosen his bedmate, and the rituals that accompanied his choice.

"The hilt must be chosen first," his mother had said, and she took him to the eastern border where a grove of sentry trees grew. It was a sacred grove, with many of the trees being grandfathers, claiming a life of hundreds of years. Thick, gnarly roots reached out of the ground, converging into a smooth, impenetrable trunk. The trees were squat, with far-reaching branches that hung low to the ground. They seldom drank water, and what little they did was preserved inside the impervious bark.

Jen Pal's mother waited patiently while he selected the tree, then nodded when he pointed to the one he had chosen—an ancient black wood with a first branch that dipped to the ground.

He took his pouch of water, carried all the way from home, and fed the tree, pouring it into a notch by the base where the bark was thin and porous. Once the tree absorbed the water, he cut a piece of branch slightly larger than what he would need. From a pouch at his side, he withdrew a special sap to seal the wound he had made, then bowed and said the prayers of thanks.

Eyes beaming now, he turned to his mother and smiled.

It took two days to walk home, then another two weeks for him to carve and shape the wood into the perfect hilt. The wood went through numerous treatments: rubbing with oils; heating; drying; then more oils until finally, it was ready. Two years after his naming day he went to the metal smith, the hilt for his sai already made. Measurements were taken, distance from tip of fingers to the bottom of the palm, and from wrist to elbow. The sai were not only offensive weapons but defense as well. A flick of the wrist converted the sai from a stabbing weapon to a shield for the arm.

As the metalsmith folded the steel, Jen Pal provided drops of blood. Every ten folds required a drop of blood from the one to wield the weapon, enough to ensure a strong bond, ensure that the sai sang for them when they needed and stayed silent when they didn't. Once they were finished, the practice began, years of training with masters at the sword and sai both. A master of sai must learn how to kill with them, but also how to disarm a swordsman.

Jen Pal ran the steel across his gut, slowly, gently, just enough to draw blood with each tip. He let the sai taste his blood, a fine way to start the day, imperative when beginning a mission. "Drink well, my friends. I will let you sate your thirst soon."

He rubbed his stomach with the juice from a yanta plant to seal the wound, then cleaned his sai before sheathing them. One final bow to the picture on the wall, then Jen Pal left the house, breaking into a run when he stepped outside.

OBELISK

The Gnaka leader cracked his whip over the back of a single laggard. Most of his men worked feverishly, knowing too well the repercussions of a less-than-fruitful day, but this one had decided to let others pull his weight, attempting to hide where the candlelight couldn't find him. Fool!

The whip snapped two more times, drawing blood on the last one. "A double shift for you," the leader said, then moved down the line. All four sides of the obelisk were being worked simultaneously in a zealous effort to please Lady Melissara—the alternative too frightful to conceive. "Dig with your backs!"

The Gnaka leader was about to turn a corner when a worker called him.

"Bottom, sir. We've hit bottom!"

Heart racing, he ran to see for himself. The worst he could do would be send Melissara false information. He jumped into the pit, grabbed a pick and swung it several times, hitting a solid surface with each blow. "Get shovels over here. Dig! I want this uncovered."

The leader lowered a candle close to the floor as he knelt to feel the surface. He stepped up out of the pit, excitement building. She would be pleased to hear the news. "Send me a messenger. Our fastest runner."

He waited until they uncovered an area large enough to verify the discovery, then once again inspected the find. "It's true," he said, "We've finally done it."

"Do we continue?" one of the workers asked.

"Uncover it on all sides and clear it back far enough to give her room for inspection." He turned to his messenger. "Go to the priest now, tell him to inform her that—"

"But, sir. It is the middle of the night."

"If we wait until morning and she finds out, we will all be buried with this obelisk. Now, hurry."

~

The messenger rapped persistently on the priest's door, praying for a response. Inside, Shera Jurre woke from a deep slumber. It was the middle of the night, and someone was pounding at his door. *Who could it be?* He slid off the bed, threw on a robe and walked to the door. "What is it?" he asked.

"The dig, Holy One, we have hit bottom. We are supposed to tell the Lady Melissara right away."

A smile came to Shera Jurre's face, the first in a long time. "Go, my son, I will relay the message."

As the door closed, he thought of the ancient times and what Sethia must have been back then.

Sethia had once been a paradise; now rotted wood lay where great forests had grown and prospered, providing lumber to build cities and the great temples of worship. Tawny brown sand had replaced the moist black soil that nourished and fed the crops that had fed half the world, and dry and cracked earth–like a web from a gigantic spider— covered massive depressions where lakes of pure water sparkled in the sweet rays of a kind afternoon sun.

The shera walked into his room, lit two candles then opened a chest he kept under the bed. A white sash lay on top of a purple robe with white trim. It had been made of the finest silk, back when the silk worms were only one of Sethia's many blessings. Under that were jade slippers, the soles a little worn from ages of wear, when other sheras had done their duty, honoring Her. Shera Jurre laid it all out on the bed, went and bathed, taking care to cleanse himself, then rubbed the blessed oils on his skin. Naked, he walked back outside, letting the dry night air caress him.

He went back and dressed. He had been meticulous, making sure he missed nothing. It might have taken a little time, but he would be in front of Her soon, nothing else would do.

As he made his way to Melissara's home, he saw a dry creek bed, reminding him of the massive ravines filled with pointed rocks, the only testament to the mighty rivers that used to run through Sethia. This river—or former river—had been fed by water from the Great White Mountains to the north and the Khataran range to the east.

He prayed that this would be the time he had read about in his scrolls, parchment so old that the slightest mishap would rip them asunder. He had made copies, painstakingly writing each letter of each word. It was not an easy task, for the words were written in the old language of Sethia, and only he and a few others knew how to translate it. But he had made out enough to know what lay under that desert, and he had learned enough to know about the obelisk. *Fools. Do they think to chal- lenge Her?* He only prayed that he would be there when the final day came. The Awakening.

He still recalled the day he had found the secret. He had kept it to himself all of these years, and now it had come to pass. No one else suspected, not even the other priests. They might have had suspicions —if he had given them that one critical piece of parchment, the one that completed the message.

Shera Jurre sighed, his pace increasing as he drew nearer to Melissara's home. Without that piece of parchment they would struggle and struggle, and all to no avail. But he knew what was there, and when the Awakening came, he would be prepared.

~

Tirzinitzia opened the door even before the shera knocked, startling him into obeisance. He fell to his knees, head bowed. "A message for Lady Melissara."

She almost laughed, but it reminded her too much of her supplication to Lukaan. "Get on your feet, Shera Jurre, and give me the message."

Despite the anxiety, he couldn't contain his excitement. He stood, all smiles and brightness. "They have reached the bottom, My Lady."

Her hand went to her chest, a deep sigh occurring with it. "They are certain?"

The shera bowed. "Otherwise, I would not be here."

Of course. They wouldn't dare disturb her at this time of night if not. "Stay here while I get Melissara. I'm sure she will want you there."

His hands joined in supplication, and he bowed his head low. *Soon my work will be finished.*

Tirzinitzia's long strides carried her down the corridor leading to Melissara's chambers. She shivered, though she couldn't tell if it was from the cold tiles on her bare feet or the excitement of the news. A light rap on the door elicited a quick response.

Melissara popped her head off the pillow, eyes still full of sleep. "What is it?"

"It's me. A message from the dig. Are you dressed?"

"Don't worry. Just get in here. What news?" She jumped out of bed and went to the dresser; goosebumps traced her sides as she slipped on undergarments.

"They have hit bottom."

"Finally!" Melissara said, and put on her pants and shoes. A top completed the dressing.

"Do you want khaffe or te?"

"No time for that. Let's go."

"Wait," Tirzinitzia said. "I need to dress. I will only be a moment. And besides, Shera Jurre is in the entry. He brought the message."

~

Melissara walked out the door and turned right, heading for the entry. Tirzinitzia went the other way, toward her room. "Meet me there," Melissara said, and quickened her pace. She was still talking to Shera Jurre when Tirzinitzia arrived. Immediately, Melissara grabbed her hand and shifted, reappearing in the cavern by the obelisk.

Melissara walked about it, while Tirzinitzia stared, Shera Jurre hurried to stand beside it. "What do you think?" Melissara asked.

"No door," Tirzinitzia said.

"There has to be," Melissara said. "Something is in there." She touched it, rubbed her hands over the stone, caressed it. It called to her, drawing her. "Something strong is in there."

Tirzinitzia kept her distance, staring. "Step back, Melissara. I want to try something."

Melissara stood beside her, motioning for the shera to do the same. "What?"

Tirzinitzia hurled a bolt of Lightning at the obelisk, a small force, but one that would crack stone.

"No!" the shera screamed and ran to prostrate himself before it. The obelisk absorbed the Lightning, then a Forcebolt struck at Tirzinitzia, knocking her off her feet and back several paces. At this, the shera stood again, trying desperately to hide his smile.

Melissara raced over. "Are you all right?"

Tirzinitzia lay on the ground gasping for breath. "I'm all right, but… What was that?"

"It ricocheted."

Tirzinitzia shook her head. "No. That wasn't my Lightning. That was something else." She sat up with Melissara's help but remained seated on the floor. "At least it answers my question. I thought we might force it open."

Melissara's brow furrowed. "We tried before. You and I both have hit it with Fire and Lightning and never experienced anything like this."

"It wasn't uncovered then." She shrugged her shoulders. "Who knows. Perhaps that made a difference somehow."

"But how?"

"That, I don't know," Tirzinitzia said, then reached her hand out. "Help me up."

Tirzinitzia brushed dirt from her pants, took a deep breath. "What do we do now?"

Melissara walked back to the obelisk. She glared at Shera Jurre. "What did you think you were doing?"

He tried to think of a suitable response. "I suspected there might be problems and did not want Lady Tirzinitzia to be hurt."

Melissara's eyes narrowed, stayed focused on him for a moment. "I don't believe one word of it, Shera, but for now I'll let you tell that lie."

She turned about, looking for the Gnakas. They had all moved away when the Forcebolt struck Tirzinitzia. She pointed to the one closest to them. "Take a hammer and strike it.

He looked at her as if she were crazy, but a glare convinced him to obey. The Gnaka walked over and swung the hammer into the obelisk. He immediately flew back. The rest of the Gnakas moved farther away while Tirzinitzia went to the Gnaka, lying on the ground. She knelt beside him, put her fingers to his neck. "He's dead."

Melissara acknowledged with a simple nod of her head. "Whatever this is, or isn't. It doesn't want us to get inside."

"It would seem so."

"And yet, we must get inside. There is power in there that we must have."

A smile came to Tirzinitzia's face. "Remember when they tried to dam the Paggo River?"

"What does that have to do with anything?"

"Too much power. You find a way to get whatever is in there, and it might do to you what the Paggo did to that dam."

Melissara chewed on her fingernail, a lifelong habit. "Something to consider," she said, "but for now, what do we do with it?"

Tirzinitzia ran her hands up one corner of the obelisk, feeling the smooth surface. "We can dismiss the Gnakas, for one. Now that it is uncovered they are no longer needed."

"Dismiss them then."

As Tirzinitzia headed off, Melissara called her back. "Remember to tell them they are under penalty of death if they so much as breathe a word."

Tirzinitzia nodded. "I'll make certain."

Melissara leaned in close to the obelisk, rested her head against it, then pressed her body firmly to it. She could feel the pulsing inside, feel a power that emanated from deep within. It sang to her. She smiled. Nothing was going to stop her from getting inside of there. Nothing.

13

DARSTAN'S WAR

They picked up Tesla and his men on the way back, Darstan taking time to inspect, make sure the Chun were all dead. He cast a suspicious glare at Tesla. "Any get away?"

"Some. Not many." Tesla lowered his head. "I have to say, BlackWolf, I don't like this. The men don't either. We didn't come to Arangar to slaughter innocent people."

"Innocent!"

Tesla drew himself up tall, his once-proud black-and-green uniform covered in Chun blood. "That's right, innocent. I'll fight soldiers all day. And the Chun were some of the best I've ever seen, but whatever you did to them, it turned them into something else. Something I don't even want to think about."

Darstan turned and walked away. "Let's go. We're moving out now."

Two days later they arrived at the Cergalan Pass to shouts of joy and victory. Men traded stories and renewed old friendships, all happy to be together again.

"Tell the men not to get too comfortable, Refugio. We'll camp here tonight and tomorrow, then move out."

"We should give them a rest. At least select different troops."

"We're taking everybody."

"All of them? And leaving the pass unguarded?"

Darstan paused. "Leave ten thousand here. The rest come with us. We're going to Chingua, and I expect we'll need them."

Refugio shook his head. "We can't be ready in two days. It'll take five days just to get supplies ready, and even then—"

"Five days then," Darstan snapped. "No longer. The rest of the supplies can catch up to us." He started down the pass, toward their former campsite. "Five days, Refugio!"

The general's salute was less than enthusiastic, a perfunctory three taps to the chest. "Yes, sir, BlackWolf."

Darstan made his way down the pass, the continuous mass of flesh quickly moving out of his way, pounding out salutes as if he were a god.

"To victory, BlackWolf" and "Death to the Chun!"

He heard these and an assortment of other greetings, but none registered. He was tired. Rest seemed to have eluded him since ... since ... he couldn't even think her name, let alone say it. How could he? How could he ever say her name again?

He caught a tear before it started. It wouldn't be good to show the men. When he neared the bottom, Mattu came to greet him.

His salute was formal, though somehow lacked respect. "I have heard the reports, BlackWolf. An undeniable victory."

"It's not over yet. Not until Chingua falls." Darstan kept walking, forcing Mattu to turn and follow.

"Chingua has half a million people! We have barely—"

"Everyone keeps telling me how many people Chingua has, but no one offers solutions on what to do about it." Darstan stopped, turned and stared at Mattu. "If you want to help, General, devise me a plan. I leave in five days."

His pace increased as he drew closer to Aenaila's tent. Word of his arrival must have preceded him. Aenaila and Wisp were outside waiting.

Aenaila rushed to greet him, offering a warm embrace. "Darstan, it's so good to see you. You had me worried."

He pulled back from her, smiled, for perhaps the first time in days.

Wisp grabbed his hand, shook it while he patted his back. "Come inside. Have you eaten? You must be starved."

Darstan's smile grew. "I am. The food I've been eating isn't the best. Conversation hasn't been much either."

As Aenaila held the flap of the tent open for Darstan and Wisp, she called her aide. "Flavia, would you please bring us some food?"

She followed them in and sat in one of the chairs next to Darstan, reaching out and touching his arm. "How have you been?"

He started to give a typical "fine" response but stopped himself. "I don't want to talk about her, Aenaila. I can't."

She folded her arms, face more serious. "Then let's talk about Arangar. This is not what I had in mind."

Darstan stood. "I knew it was a mistake coming here." He turned to Wisp. "I'm leaving in five days if you want to join me. If not ... stay with her." He stormed out of the tent, amidst protests from both of them.

*R*efugio led the army. It was immense, well-fed, and with a supply train to keep them fed for half a year. Three days into the march to Chingua they realized the Chun had changed tactics.

All of the villages were abandoned, and they hadn't seen a single Chun since they left the pass. Darstan razed each town they came to, but at least no one else was dying.

As they drew near the capital city, they ran across a band of warriors that fought with them despite the odds. The slaughter was quick, but not merciful.

At night they camped far from the bodies, but not far enough. The stench of burnt flesh had the Cergalans retching throughout the night, many of them questioning what they were doing there. The war had been won. What they did now was sacrilege.

The army spread across several hillsides, tents dotting the slopes like pine saplings in the fall. The night air was cool, cool enough for a fire, and most of the soldiers sat close, telling stories, though not all of them were good. Those who had traveled with Black Wolf whispered tales of horror.

Wisp and Darstan sat in a tent on the hillside. "How much is enough, Darstan?"

"Nothing is enough. I'm going to destroy Arangar. All of it."

"You can't bring her back. She's gone. No matter how many you kill."

A huge silence followed.

"I'm going back, Darstan. This isn't for me."

"I thought you'd stay the course. Stay with your friend."

"I have no friend now. I'm leaving a madman. A man I don't know anymore." Wisp stood, extending his hand. "For the friendship we had."

Darstan glared at him. "Go on. Go back to Aenaila. It's easy for you. You have her to go back to." Darstan stood and walked to the back of the tent. "Who do I have? I've got no wife. No son. No brother. And now, no friend."

Wisp opened the flap of the tent to leave, but stopped and turned back. "You won't know how much you still have until you lose it all. And at the rate you're going, BlackWolf, that won't take long. Good luck."

Fire danced on Darstan's fingers. Pressure built in his head. He would show Wisp. He'd show them all.

⁓

Wisp saddled his horse, packed what little he had brought, then rode out of camp. He glanced to the rear to see if Darstan was in sight. It felt wrong to leave him, but something had to be done. Besides, if anyone could stop him, it would be Aenaila. He'd go to her and bring her back.

Wisp stopped to stare at an odd rock formation, a good point to use for Shifting, then continued, spurring his horse to a gallop.

⁓

Darstan paced the tent, anger boiling inside of him. He almost smiled when the tent flap opened, thinking it was Wisp coming back—but when he saw the servant, his misery returned. "What is it?"

"I thought you might want some food, BlackWolf. You haven't eaten all day."

Darstan shook his head. "Bring me some wine, then leave me alone."

As the servant started to leave, Darstan called to him. "And post a guard at my tent. I want no one bothering me."

As the wine took effect, haunting memories returned—Magmar, killed by Victas at Twin Forks. Gregor and Wehr killed by Darstan's hand in Sethia. Then Rahg betraying him. Killing Mirana. Killing his son!

The wine glass broke under his grip, drawing blood, then fire spewed from his stump, searing the wound shut. He let the fire grow until it enveloped him then engulfed the tent.

Shouts of alarm rose from all quarters in the camp, soldiers rushing toward BlackWolf. Pails of water soon doused the flames, enough so that men could rush inside.

Refugio entered first—then stopped dead.

Darstan stood in the center of the room, his whole body aflame—and him, laughing aloud. Refugio threw a bucket of water on him, not knowing what else to do.

The laughter stopped, but a smile remained, perhaps more a smirk. "Don't worry, Refugio. I'm all right. It takes more than fire to kill BlackWolf."

Darstan's eyes narrowed and his steely gaze fixed Refugio. "You can tell the rest of them to remember that in case anyone thinks we should be going home."

Refugio bowed low. "Yes, BlackWolf. I'll tell the men we continue the march into Arangar."

Darstan nodded. "Yes, do that. We move at once."

Refugio straightened, panic showing on his face. "But ... the men have not yet slept. They will—"

"They'll find a way." Darstan put together a change of clothes, the second time he'd had to do that of late, and he vowed to keep his Fire controlled.

Refugio exited the tent, turmoil filling his gut. They had all wanted revenge on Arangar; all Cergalans wanted to conquer their enemy, but not like this. Never like this. What had their prophecies wrought?

A full day's march brought them to another abandoned village. "Camp here. Post a guard."

Long after nightfall, a small group of soldiers sat around a tent near the outskirts of town. "We're leaving tonight," one soldier said. "Not staying here to do any more of his killing."

"Isn't that why we waited for him all these years, to be led to victory over Arangar?"

"Not like this. I never wanted any parts of this."

The second soldier agreed. "Killing in battle is one thing. Slaughtering men while they're on the ground praying is another." He paused. "What by the holy gods did he do to them? Those were Chun warriors back there."

A third soldier sidled up close. "I once saw a Chun fight with a sword in his belly, fought like it wasn't even there."

"I'm going with you," the second soldier said.

"Me too," the third added.

"Wait till the second watch, then we'll leave."

Four of them crept out of camp, keeping low, staying silent. They made it through the small brush, and as they were about to enter the woods, a voice called to them from the side. "Probably not good to be seen leaving camp at night. Somebody might think you were deserting us."

Tesla seemed to tower above them, and his eyes, even in the dark, pierced their souls.

"Just stretching our legs, Commander."

"Don't make it worse with lies, Bando. Already costing me sleep I can't afford to lose." Tesla knelt beside them, whispering. "I'm gonna' go back to sleep now. If I find you missing when I wake up, I'm going straight to BlackWolf, and I'm going to tell him you deserted. But if you're there when I wake up, no one will know a thing."

"You know it's not right," Bando said. "This is—"

Tesla grabbed him by the collar and pulled him closer. "The only thing I know is if I tell BlackWolf you deserted, he'll hunt you himself. And trust me, he'll find you." Tesla shook his head. "Right or not, I wouldn't want to be you when he finds you. You've seen what he'll do."

Tesla stood, started walking toward camp. "Good night, men. Good luck."

Morning came too soon, but Tesla rose quickly, walking through camp in a roundabout way to get his khaffe. "Good morning, Bando. Glad to see you."

Bando saluted, fist pounding chest. "And you, Commander Tesla. It seems to be a fine day for killing."

Tesla bit his lower lip, scowling. "I hope you keep your sword as sharp as your tongue, Soldier. You'll stay alive a little longer that way."

"Yes, sir," Bando shouted, and saluted again.

Tesla smiled as he made his way for the khaffe. He hadn't wanted to lose those men.

While downing his second cup, Refugio approached. "A fine day, Tesla."

"I was speaking with Bando about that."

"I'm glad to see Bando is still with us, Commander."

Tesla nearly dropped his khaffe, eyes raised, face shocked. "Was he going somewhere, sir?"

"I'm not certain. Just had a feeling."

Tesla stood rigidly, but Refugio's smile relaxed him. "We should reach Chingua tomorrow, Tesla. Try and prepare the men."

"Prepare them for what? Do we know?"

"Only Black Wolf knows."

"God help us then," Tesla said.

Refugio lowered his voice to a whisper. "Commander, I'm constantly learning new things he can do, like whatever it was he did to the Chun at the pass. For all we know he might be able to hear things we can't. I would keep that in mind if I were you."

Tesla saluted. "Thank you, sir. I'll prepare the men as best I can."

"Good. We'll me marching soon."

*C*hingua came into view just before dusk on the third day, moonlight shining on tens of thousands of houses and shops. "Make the campfires bright, Refugio. I want them to know how insolent we are."

"It's not wise, BlackWolf."

"A lot of things I do aren't wise. I act with my heart, and it is telling me to build fires." Darstan turned to stare at him. "I like fires, Refugio."

The commander saluted. "As you will, BlackWolf."

AENAILA'S PLEA

Wisp stood outside Aenaila's tent, waiting for her. "Hurry up, Aenaila. I didn't come here to be ignored." Patience had never been a virtue he embraced.

A moment later the tent flap opened. "It wouldn't do to have the men see you come in here with me not dressed."

"I didn't know you weren't dressed, or I *would* have come in sooner."

Aenaila walked to the table, grabbing a piece of fruit from one of many baskets. "Have you eaten? These are fresh."

He held up his hand, and she tossed him one. He took a bite, nodded, then continued. "We've got to stop Darstan. He's killing them all. Even Refugio and Tesla want to quit."

"Have we lost many men?"

"Few of our own, according to Refugio, but he said Darstan's killed more than fifty thousand Chun. There won't be any Chun left if we let him go." Wisp shook his head. "This is no way to wage war, Aenaila. Victory is one thing. Slaughter another."

She nodded. "Tell Flavia we're leaving. I assume you have a Shift Point."

"I do. Get ready. I'll be right back." He told Flavia they'd be gone for a while then returned to Aenaila's tent, grabbing her hand.

She found the image in his mind then shifted, stepping through a rift near the boulders he had recalled. The camp, however, was gone, they were already on the move. "I can't believe he's marching them at night."

"I told you, he's not the same man we came here with."

"We'll follow on foot," Aenaila said. "Besides, I have a plan. The problem is this plan might kill me if it doesn't work. If he's as bad as you say."

"I thought you could control him. Back in Khatara—"

"That was before he knew how strong he was, when he was more afraid of his powers than others were. Now ... now is a different story. I believe he's as strong as a Banished One."

"Don't try it then. He's lost all control."

"We'll see. But let's not waste time. Move on."

Aenaila and Wisp followed the path of destruction, sickened by what they saw: bodies hacked to pieces and entire towns razed, some with charred bodies still smoldering. The stench was unbearable. "We've got to stop him, Wisp. He's not only destroying Arangar but himself as well."

They followed the trail for half a day, then it turned south. "I hope I'm wrong, but I don't think so. He's heading for Chingua."

Aenaila looked at Wisp, tears in her eyes. "There could be more than a million people there if the cities surrounding it sought refuge." She thought for a moment. "We need to move faster. I'm going to shift by sight. That will get us there quicker, then all we need to do is get into the city."

"I can help with that," Wisp said.

They waited until dark then sneaked past Darstan's sentries, making their way to the city. The gates were open to all, a necessary event since so many refugees were arriving from all over the country. "What now?" Wisp asked.

"We need an audience with their king."

"I don't think we can just walk in."

"If I tell him who I am we can," Aenaila said.

"He might kill you."

"I've thought of that too. But I think we'll be all right."

They walked through deserted streets, and where they did run into people, it was mostly panic: people afraid, talking about Black Wolf and how he had killed so many. Talking about the Cergalans and what barbarians they were. Aenaila listened and shook her head while stopping tears. "I could be walking through the streets of Cartena. This is exactly what our people say about them."

~

"It's always like that," Wisp said. "People don't know the other side of the story unless they've lived it. It's like being a thief; there are good thieves and bad ones. People who decide to make war should live with the enemy for a while before they decide to attack."

Wisp smiled after he said that. "I knew a thief once who used to go to work for a merchant that he was thinking of robbing. If, after thirty days or so, he found the man to be unscrupulous, he would continue with his plan and rob him, but if he found that the merchant had character and treated people fairly, he would abandon his plans."

"What ever happened to him?"

"He liked one of them so much that he kept working for him and learned a trade. He's now a respected merchant."

Aenaila smiled for the first time. "So there is hope for you."

"Not me."

Aenaila tugged on Wisp's sleeve. "There's a patrol of guards. Perhaps we can convince them to take us to the king."

"Don't be foolish. Follow me. I'll get us in."

When they reached the palace, Wisp used his Cloaking to get them inside; then, when no one was around, they started down the corridors toward the king's chambers.

The palace was exactly what he would have expected a king's palace to be: extravagant with unnecessary things everywhere. He thought of Aenaila's father's house in Cartena, and how humble it was in comparison. Perhaps there was hope for him after all.

Sometime near midnight, the king returned to his chambers, alone. He walked in, closed the door and made his way to the bed. Wisp chose that moment to appear, but behind the king, so he didn't notice.

"Your Majesty, please don't be alarmed. We mean no harm."

The king spun around, fear on his face. "How ... how did you get in here?"

He stared at them as if they were assassins, not knowing whether to call the guards or not. "Who are you?"

Aenaila stepped forward, bowed low. "Please, Your Majesty, relax. We mean no harm, but it was imperative we speak with you."

He continued to stare but seemed to lose some of the anxiety. "Go on."

"My name is Aenaila. I am the daughter of King Marro."

A cynical laugh erupted from the king. "And I'm to believe you mean me no harm. After you have slaughtered my people."

"We never intended for this to happen. Our general is out of control."

"Why should I trust you?"

Aenaila shook her head. "He has killed half your countryside. I've seen the carnage myself. Thousands dead, every village destroyed, and now he sits outside of Chingua wanting to destroy it."

The king started to interrupt, but Aenaila forestalled him. "Forgive me, Majesty, for speaking so bluntly, but this is not an ordinary war. This is no ordinary man. My people call him BlackWolf." She approached the king, staring into his eyes. "And please, believe me, he could destroy this city before the next sun rises."

Despair replaced fear on the king's face. "Then the stories are true?"

"I haven't heard the stories, but if they tell of a man who wields fire and death, then they are true. He could put this city aflame with just one thought."

"This BlackWolf has given us an ultimatum. Surrender the city by first light, or he will raze it."

"Trust his word. He'll do it unless we stop him."

"How can you stop him?"

"For that, I'll need the help of some of your women and children." Aenaila's face grew stern. "Volunteers only! They might die for this effort. But for what it's worth, I will be with them and could die just as well."

～

As Darstan's deadline approached, the front gates to the city opened and out walked a dozen women, a few carrying small children, others trailed by young boys and girls. They walked toward the camp on the hill, heads held high.

Darstan scowled. "They think sending women will satisfy me! I'll show them what I think of their women."

"No! BlackWolf, wait." Refugio grabbed his arm. "Look! Look at the one in the center. It's Mirana!"

All of the Chinguans were light skinned and blonde, all except the one in the middle. Darstan froze. He stared until tears formed in his eyes.

"It's her! By the Blood! She's alive." He walked toward her, unaware of anything else. Refugio and a dozen others followed, swords drawn, eyes alert. As Darstan neared, he ran. "Mirana!"

When he got right up to her, within paces, he realized it was not her, even though the resemblance was uncanny. Even more so as she was pregnant.

"We beseech you to spare our city, Great One," the Mirana look-alike said. "If you require a sacrifice, we offer ourselves and our children, but please, spare our city. Enough have died this year. Enough for many years."

Darstan kept staring. He placed his hand on her stomach, rubbed it gently, then he raised his hand and stroked her cheek. Tears flowed. "I had a wife ... a love who looked like you. She ... are you carrying a son?"

She nodded. "The Farseers say so."

Darstan smiled. "I had a son too. For a short while."

He stood still for several moments, staring, and caressing her, then his face hardened. He wiped the tears and straightened, staring into her deep brown eyes. "No one will die here today. No one need die anymore. Tell your king to see me. We will negotiate peace. A lasting peace."

The lady smiled, tears forming in her own eyes. She stepped forward to kiss him, but he jerked away, holding her at bay. "No! You're not mine. You look like her, but you belong to someone else. Please, go to him. Tell him how fortunate he is. Tell him his wife has saved Arangar."

Refugio fought to restrain his joy. He placed his arm around Darstan's shoulder. "You did well, BlackWolf. It is time for peace."

15

THE LONG ROAD HOME

The Nyauran countryside seemed strange to Gregor. He had been there before, after they had rescued Darstan from prison, but he had been traveling with a group, and they had their own provisions. In the city, few could equal his survival skills and adaptability, but he felt helpless in the country.

Being armed with a staff left him at a great disadvantage in the wild. It might be easy to take down a thief, even a guardsman or two, but game was different.

It had been almost a full day since he had water, two days for food. Lips parched, body weak, he struggled on, hoping to find a village or even a lone traveler. He shielded his eyes with cupped hands, staring west at the setting sun. It seemed so close, but he knew better now. The plains seemed to go on forever.

Already he had been walking for ten days, and it seemed as if he had made no progress, as if the sun and the mountains were no closer than when he started. He looked south, then west again. At least he still headed in the right direction.

As the orange sun made its final plunge, Gregor's limp grew worse.

Relying on his staff for support, he continued pressing; he yet had time before the cold forced him to stop. Another half a league, and he had to stop again. He looked at the staff, raised it up and laid it across both hands, felt its balance.

Where had this staff come from? He owned a blackthorn staff! Trying to picture it in his mind proved difficult, but he knew he was right. No one would forget owning such a staff. Dizziness set in. *Water. Must get water at least.* He pushed harder despite the pain.

Soon he found a small copse of trees, enough shelter to keep him warm and safe for the night even if there was no water. The wind drove him deep into a pocket between two of the trees, his cloak wrapped around his head and neck. As he grew more comfortable sleep tempted him, his head slipping to rest on his chest as he nodded off.

The sound of a horse's nicker awakened him. He grabbed his staff and jumped up. "Who goes there?" The words came out awkwardly, sputtering out of a dry throat.

"Tencha. Iron Hooves Clan."

Gregor made his way to him, hobbling along on a very stiff leg. "I'm Gregor. Trying to get home to Sykor." The words were flowing easier now. "Haven't had water all day."

The Nyauran let go of his horse's reins and moved to support Gregor. "Easy. These plains will dry you out in a hurry. Sit while I get you something to drink." He helped Gregor back to the tree where he had been, his horse following him all the way. Once Gregor was situated, the Nyauran grabbed his water, allowing him measured sips, though Gregor tried gulping it down.

Tencha laughed. "If you are that dry, your belly must be empty." He went to his saddlebags and got some dried meat and a hunk of cheese. "Chew it well. Eat slow. Drink slower."

Gregor tore off a hunk of meat with his teeth, chewing with firm, determined bites. "I am in your debt ..."

"Tencha."

"Sorry. I forgot." Gregor smiled. "I was only thinking about eating and water."

"I have been in your place before, my friend. I vowed never to be there again."

The bounty-man- finished the meat and cheese, drank more water, then sat up straight. "Everything feels better now. Still weak, but better."

"With a night's rest, you'll be fine." Tencha covered him with a blanket, then took out his bedroll. "Tomorrow I will take you to a village nearby. They can get you a horse and supplies and take you to the Caravan Route. Once you are there, you can find your way."

"I have no money. I—"

Tencha shook his head. "A stranger's money is no good on the plains. No one would take it if you had any."

"But—"

The Nyauran held up his hand, shaking his head at the same time. "Someday you will return the favor. Perhaps not to me, but to someone, somewhere." He stared at Gregor. "Once you know the Great God, this is your way of life."

The bounty-man nodded. "I will indeed return this favor, many times over."

In the morning Tencha took him to the village where the elders gave him a horse and food and water. An escort took him to the Caravan Route where Gregor said his thanks, then headed west toward Sykor. *It won't be long now.*

The gates of the city seemed strange after being out on the plains so long. So restrictive. So confining. Despite that, his heart beat faster. Sykor was home.

Two guards controlled passageway through the gate, with two additional ones logging in all data, including the names of who entered. He made it through the process, mechanically answering the questions as he stared at the moat and the tall walls erected long ago. Fifty paces brought him through those gates and into the city. A smile came to his face when his feet met the cobblestone street. It was all familiar to him now, returning to memory in a rush.

His limp seemed better. Everything did. Echoes from his boots clomping on the stones refreshed his smile, as did seeing Volger's jewelry store and Farlo's fruit stand. He passed the Trader's Inn in a hurry, resisting the urge to go in. Images of nights spent sipping on ale, mingling with other bounty-men—even with thieves. It didn't seem to matter; he was at least talking to someone besides himself.

Gregor stopped and turned, staring. The urge was strong, pulling him. He made half a step toward the inn, then found will power and reversed his course, heading home.

Six more blocks brought him to even more familiar territory, the streets he had trod every day. As he turned the corner toward his house, his chest tightened, and his breathing grew irregular. He stopped again, hand placed against the wall for support. Fear had him. He was afraid to see how he lived. How he had wasted his whole life.

A few deep breaths found courage, and he continued down the street. It seemed lonely, empty. As he turned the key in his lock, he listened for laughter but heard none. Laughter might crack the walls on this street.

He opened the door, lit a candle he always kept there, then began the climb. The steps to his house were even lonelier than the street, and his limp seemed to make it worse, draw out the long climb. Cobwebs clung to the corners of his doorway. He brushed them away gently. At least someone had made it home.

A rusty hinge squeaked, warning him away perhaps, and he reluctantly entered the most familiar territory of all. He lit another candle, hoping it would appear different than it was in memory, but when the door closed hope went with it. Nothing had changed. *Had it gotten worse?*

He hobbled to the kitchen, rubbed his leg when he sat in the chair—his favorite one, facing the window. Two empty chairs stared back at him. Laughing. Empty walls and an empty room joined the chorus. His heart sank into a pool of sorrow and self-pity.

He recalled the night he and Rhaven had caught Wisp and brought him here. That was the best night of his life. His home was full of people: Rhaven, Wisp, Darstan, Rahg, Camissa, Tobias, even the Black Rose.

Gregor stared at the empty chairs again. They had been filled that night, as had his sofa. People even sat on the floor. What a night that was!

He lay his head on the table, fighting emotions, but soon a tear rolled down his cheek soaking into the thirsty wood of the table.

16

TORTURE

Force Commander Ludar dismissed the guards when he finished with the day's business. He had been waiting all day for this, and he would find out what he needed to know. He removed the sword, took off the sheath, then walked toward the fountain in his quarters.

A secret door lay hidden behind the fountain. It opened when he pressed a particular tile at the bottom of the wall, swinging out on well-oiled hinges. Ludar went through, down two flights of stairs then east for several blocks through underground tunnels as old as the palace itself.

A few more turns placed him in a room designed for interrogation, a special kind of interrogation. Within a few moments footsteps sounded from the other direction. The door opened, and the guards ushered the prisoner into the room.

Sergeant Takar's face was swollen from continual beatings, and one of his eyes was closed. A broken nose prevented proper breathing, making a whistling sound with each inhalation. And when he smiled— which he must have done for spite upon seeing Ludar, gaps showed where three teeth previously occupied space. "Gettin' tired, Ludar?"

The Force Commander shook his head as he paced the room. "You will talk tonight," Ludar said while he examined some instruments on a table in the corner. He selected two vise-like clamps then walked to the center of the room and fastened them to hooks on the end of ropes attached to a pulley system. "Bring him here."

The guards grabbed Takar by the arms, dragging him toward the rope, but he fought them despite being handcuffed. He butted one guard in the head with his own, then lashed out at the other with his feet.

Ludar smashed a wooden mallet on Takar's head, rendering him unconscious. "Pick him up and bring him here."

The clamps had flat ends about the size of a big man's thumbs, and each one had a handle at the top to tighten it. Ludar lowered the ropes then attached a clamp to each of Takar's middle fingers. "Tighten them until I tell you to stop."

One guard turned the screw while the other stared at Ludar. "Force Commander, this will break his fingers. Surely we can—"

Fire burned in Ludar's eyes, not real fire, but it was there sure enough. He took a knife from his belt and placed it on the guard's neck. "Guardsman Callo isn't it?"

Fear showed in the man's expression, though he managed a nod.

Ludar's gaze burned into him. "If you do not do as I say, exactly as I say, when I say it, I will use this blade on you. It will not be pretty, Callo."

"Yes, sir," he shouted, and joined the other guard in tightening the screws.

Before they had reached five twists, Takar shot awake with a scream of agony. "Rats blood!"

He jumped to his feet, looked at each of his hands, then to Ludar. "No matter what you do the answer will be the same. I don't know where he is." Takar gritted his teeth, clenched his jaw. "Don't do this."

Ludar stared at the guards. "Why did you stop?" he shouted, and they immediately went to work again, eliciting another cry of anguish from Takar.

"Hurts doesn't it, Sergeant?"

"I'll kill you for this. I swear."

Mock laughter greeted him. "Yes, I'm sure you will."

After four more turns, his bones broke, the crunch drowned out by his wails. Two more turns brought tears to his eyes.

"Lift him up with the pulley."

Callo almost objected but caught himself. He grabbed the rope and tugged on it, raising the sergeant's arms, stretching them taut. Takar screamed when his body started to lift off the ground, supported completely by the two fingers the clamps held. The other guard worked with Callo, pulling hard, raising him. Soon the screaming stopped, and his head collapsed onto his chest.

Ludar walked over, and with his knife, poked Takar a few times, just enough to draw blood and make sure he wasn't faking. "That's enough for tonight."

As the guards got him down and unscrewed the clamps, Callo gasped. "Force Commander, look at his fingers. They're ..."

Takar's two fingers dangled from the sockets and were crushed to almost nothing at the ends.

"Useless," Ludar said. "Cut them off." He started to turn but stopped. "No, don't. We'll wait until tomorrow night when he's awake. No sense wasting the pleasure." Ludar walked to the door. "I want you two back here tomorrow. No one else."

"Yes, sir," Callo said, and the other guard followed.

They had to wait for Takar to wake up before they could move him back to the cell. He was far too heavy to carry. As he came to, Callo offered him water.

Takar took a sip, stared at his hands, bandaged at the top and tied to the others with a splint. "You do this?"

Callo nodded. "We both did."

"I ..." Pain choked him as he tried to talk. He placed his palms on his thighs and pushed, trying to stand, but the pressure shot pain throughout his hands. He collapsed again, though still conscious. Takar stared up at Callo and the other guard. "I know you lads don't I?"

They both shook their heads feverishly as if afraid it would be true, but Takar kept nodding his head, denying them the chance.

"You probably don't want me to know you, but I do." He nodded toward the second guard. "Your father served under me, boy. You've got his eyes. Ballard, isn't it?" Before he could respond Takar looked at Callo. "I don't recall your name, but you must have had an older brother. He was with me a few years back."

Tears came to Callo's eyes. "Callo's the name, sir. Was my brother Geoffrey who served with you."

"Ballard's right for me, Sergeant," the other one said, then he cried. "I'm sorry about this, sir. We didn't know. We—"

"Sh! Don't worry." Takar stared at them. "I know what he's like, and I don't blame you. I'm going to ask a favor though, a big one."

They both stared at him with teary eyes.

"Kill me."

"What!" Callo shouted.

"I said I want you to kill me. Just—"

No, sir!. We can't."

Takar managed to get up on one knee, then the other, though shots of pain accompanied each bit of progress. He stared at them with eyes stolen from a demon. "Take your sword and kill me. That's an order, lads. If you can't do that you're not soldiers."

Ballard looked to Callo, who stared back at him. Finally, Callo shook his head. "No, sir. We're not going to kill you, but we are getting you out of here."

"Don't try," Takar said.

Ballard grabbed his arm while Callo undid the cuffs. "We're leaving, sir. I hope you've got some friends who will hide us."

"I do."

"Hope they're good friends, sir, 'cause Ludar is going to tear this city apart to find you.

APPLE PIE AND BARDS

It took half the night, but Callo and Ballard managed to sneak Takar out of the dungeons and into the Dongrel section of the city. Not even guards patrolled the Dongrel at night.

"Where to, Sergeant? I don't mind risking my neck getting you out of the dungeons, but traipsing through the Dongrel is something else."

Takar gasped with each step. He suspected his left leg was fractured from an earlier session with Ludar, and he had more bruises and cuts than he could count. "There's a small house near the end of the next street. Next to the last house in the row. Right side."

Callo supported him while Ballard kept the guard up. "Almost there," Ballard said.

"You're going to have to knock," Takar said. "My hands are useless."

Callo knocked, and soon the door cracked open. A round face appeared about chest high on Takar and a loud voice, even at a whisper, greeted him.

"Sergeant Takar! What would you be doin' down here? Come to visit old Mollie did ya'?"

"He's hurt," Ballard said, and it was then she looked at his hands.

"By the hand of the Lady!" she cried. "Get him in here."

Callo looked both ways, then hurried Takar inside. Mollie was talking full speed and waving her hands almost as fast as she spoke. Finally, Takar interrupted her.

"Before you agree to anything, Mollie, I need to tell you. Ludar is after me. He'll kill you if he finds out you're hiding me."

She placed her hands on a set of spacious hips and stared up at Takar. "Listen to me, you big oaf. There'll be no one tellin' Mollie who she can, and can't, help."

She turned her glare toward the two guards. "Get him on that sofa."

As they moved him over there, she went to the kitchen and grabbed a few pieces of torn cloth. "You lads need a place to sleep?"

"No, we're going to go home."

Takar laughed. "Idiots! You can't go home. Not tonight or ever. You've got to leave the city, and you've got to do it before he knows I'm gone. After that, your life won't be worth a half a copper."

Ballard shook. "You think we can't go home. Not even to say goodbye."

Takar shook his head, same time as Mollie, but it was her that spoke. "Not if you crossed Ludar. He'll come to kill ya' before the morning. Better leave now." She turned and headed toward the kitchen. "I'll pack you up some food, got a few pies you can take too."

Mollie put some bread and cheese into a sack, wrapped her pies then handed it all to the guards. "Don't eat it all at once. I know you'll be tempted to eat those pies at the first meal, but you better save 'em." She leaned over and kissed each one of them on the cheek. "That's for bringing the big man to me. Everyone needs a friend at some time."

Callo fought tears, as did Ballard, then they said farewell to Mollie and Takar. "Better find someplace else to hide, sir. Ludar will be searching everywhere."

Takar nodded. "Get out of the city tonight. I'll take care of myself." As they turned to leave, Takar called them back. He pulled them both toward him and hugged them. "You saved my life. I won't forget that."

"Sir, I—"

"Get out of here," Takar said. "And hurry. Both of you."

After they left, Mollie moved into a higher gear, moving fast and thinking even faster. "Can't keep you here. If anything they were right about that. That blackhearted son of a cur will be lookin' in the Dongrel first. River's Edge next." She bit on the end of one of her fingernails. "What do ya' think about sendin' for Perl?"

Takar laughed. "Don't know the man well, Mollie. He did help me once before though when I got Darstan out of prison. Can't imagine that he'd be willing to go so far as to risk anything for me."

Mollie grabbed a candle from a shelf on the side wall, took a few strikers, then lit them and set them on the table next to Takar. "You let me worry about that. He'll do it if I ask him." She wiped sweat from Takar's head with a soft cloth, peeled back his eyelids to stare into his eyes, then checked his fingers, carefully removing the bandages between exclamations of pain. "Ludar did all this to you?"

Silence greeted her.

"If you're not saying he didn't do it, it's the same as saying he did. Why'd he do it?"

Takar stared at her. "You've heard tales about the one-handed man with Fire?" At her nod, he continued. "Ludar thinks I know where he's hiding."

Mollie finished taking the last of the bandages off of his fingers. "Done a good job of things, our Force Commander has. Looks like he didn't want you wielding a sword anymore."

Takar laughed. "He didn't want me wielding so much as a fork, Mollie. He planned to kill me tomorrow. If it hadn't been for those boys ..."

She cleaned his wounds, wrapped them again then got him some food. "Stay put. I'm goin' to find Perl. If he won't help, he'll know who to send me to."

~

*P*erl got the word from a serving girl at the City's Edge Tavern. "Mollie needs you." She seldom sent for him, and never unless it was urgent. He looked about, ensured that no one was watching, then paid his bill and left. A block from the inn he ducked quickly behind a wall, waited, checked to see he wasn't followed. When no one came, he continued, this time at a fast pace, one to mimic a good man in a hurry to get home. It wouldn't do for the guards to stop him for questioning.

The rap on Mollie's door came in code, and she answered quickly.

"'Bout time," she said as she opened the door.

"Hope this is important."

She nodded toward the sofa. "Takar's hurt. Escaped from the dungeons where Ludar's been wantin' to kill him. Now he'll want to kill anyone who's helpin' him too."

Perl threw his pipe on the floor, nearly breaking it. He stomped his foot while shaking his head. "Got no business messin' in the affairs of the guards, especially Ludar."

Mollie slowly advanced on him. "Got no business! After the things this man's done for us?" She snatched the pipe he had retrieved from the floor out of his hand and tossed it aside. Stared him in the eyes. "Perl, I'm ashamed of you. If your mother, bless her soul, was still alive ..."

Perl pulled her to him and hugged her. "All right. All right, Mollie. You win. Let me think about this for a while. I'll have to set some things up."

Mollie patted him on the back as she ushered him to the door. "Come see me tomorrow."

"Where's your husband?" Takar asked.

She laughed. "That no good left me years ago. People still think he's here, but I ain't seen him in almost two years."

"Sorry, Mollie. I didn't know." She brushed it away, then sat beside him to talk. They stayed up late, both of them lamenting what had become of the city they loved. Finally, when Takar had grown used to the pain, he was able to fall asleep. She soon followed him.

~

Takar awoke to the smell of pies baking in ovens. It was still dark outside, yet she was up and at it as if it were mid-day. "Getting a start on the day, Mollie?"

"Got to beat the sun every morning or you won't make enough money to feed yourself."

"Can I do anything for you while you're gone?"

"Stay out of sight until tonight. After that, it'll be all over."

Somewhere around mid-morning, Perl arrived at Mollie's stand. There were two customers standing close by. "I'll have a piece of that apple pie," he said.

She dished it out, took his money and chatted. "Another nice day. Hope it stays like this for a while."

Two guards strolled up, one an older man, perhaps Mollie's age, and the other a young recruit. They got some pie then stayed to talk with Mollie as they ate it. The older guard munched on his blueberry, licking his fingers clean when he finished. "Told my wife about your pies, Mollie. I think she got jealous that I talk about them so much."

A short cackle burst from her chubby frame. "Rightly so. At your age, a man's more concerned with his stomach than he is other things."

The recruit laughed, covering his mouth to keep from spitting out food, and the older man joined in. "If you weren't married already I might think about it. As it is I'm not getting the pies or the other things. Gotta' pay for both of them."

Mollie helped another customer, then turned back to the guard. "At least my price is fair. Stays with you longer too."

Perl, still standing with them, decided to get it over with. The guards would never suspect anything. "Mollie, you look like you could use a night out. You ought to take that worthless husband of yours to the Sentry's Watch Inn. Baldomere Testa will be there tonight, and they say he loves apple pie."

She shook her head. "Don't know if I can bring any pie, but I just might go see him."

Perl nodded, finished his pie, then left, heading in the direction of the Inn. He met with Testa, setting the final plans for the exchange of Takar so that he could be hidden or sneaked out of the city.

Perl looked around to ensure no one listened, then began. "Mollie will be there tonight. She'll offer you an apple pie, which means the original plan is on. We'll take him to the River's Edge and try to get him out the back gate during the night. Might be dangerous, might even come to blows with the guards, but I think we can do it."

Testa listened, never saying anything.

Perl checked the area around their table again. "If we change anything, I'll get word to you, and you can ask for a different kind of pie.

There are only two other possibilities. One is to keep him at Mollie's, which we don't want to do. It's only a matter of time before Ludar searches all the houses.

The other plan would be to take him to the Trader's Inn. Brock Larnigin will help us." Perl got up to leave. "Remember, there will likely be guards everywhere, and you can trust no one."

~

Mollie continued selling her pies all day, as she did every day, then returned home with a few extra ones. She cleaned up, prepared a few things for Takar and her to eat then headed out to take care of her part in the plan. "If you see that rotten husband of mine, kill him. He deserves it."

Takar looked at her as if she were crazy. "I thought you said he left two years ago."

"He did, but he might be back some day. More stupid than I thought if he doesn't come back."

The sergeant looked at her with warm eyes. "He is a blasted fool, Mollie. You'd be a good woman to come home to." She didn't say anything, which was just as well. As he picked at a pie she had given him, he asked. "Is Ludar looking for me?"

She chuckled. "His men came past my place ten, maybe twelve times today. He's got the entire guard searching for you, and he's not gonna' stop. Started searching homes earlier today in River's Edge. Near caused a riot."

"He will cause a riot if he keeps that up. You still think our plan will work?"

"We'll see about that," she said, and left through the front door.

~

The Sentry's Watch was a fine establishment situated just outside of the Dongrel, far enough outside to avoid the smell, but close enough to the merchant's district to draw the valuable trade from the rich traders and the visitors who came from other cities.

They typically served a good meal for patrons, and soon after it opened the reputation of the good food began to draw customers on its own. Seeing a business opportunity, the owners employed entertainment for the busiest nights. Tonight it would be Baldomere Testa—bard extraordinary.

Mollie walked through the front door to a raucous crowd. She looked about the inn, judging the mood of the crowd. Everyone seemed on edge, likely due to Ludar's orders for the patrols to stay on duty all day and night until Takar was found. There were at least a dozen guards in the inn tonight, and they weren't there to enjoy the show. She sat at a table next to two friends, ordered some bread and a mug of ale. Couldn't afford no real food.

"Loud tonight," one of 'em said.

Mollie nodded. "It'll quiet down once Testa gets goin'. He can quiet a room like a good killin'."

Perl walked by, but she ignored him, not even a glance, though she did greet a few customers who stopped by to say hello. Soon, Baldomere Testa entered the stage, and as Mollie had predicted, the crowd fell quiet.

Perl watched the crowd more than he did Testa, and while scanning the patrons, he noticed someone he knew at a table in the corner. Gregor!

At the first opportunity, he walked over to him. "Seat seems to be begging for someone to sit in it."

Gregor nodded between sips of ale, then kicked the chair out with his foot. "Must have been waiting for you." He narrowed his eyes until recognition hit him. "Perl, isn't it?" He used a whisper to ask.

Perl pulled the chair out, plopped himself in it then ordered an ale from the serving girl. "And you're Gregor, the bounty-man. I remember you well." Perl looked around the inn, checking all corners, then leaned toward Gregor. "Is our friend with you?"

Gregor set the mug down and wiped his lips. "I've been looking for him myself. So if you see him, tell him I'll be staying at the Trader's

Inn." The bounty-man raised his eyebrows. "You know it. It's where we met when—"

"Sh. I know it all right." Perl sipped some more ale, pulled his chair in even closer. He wrapped both hands around the mug and hunched over the table, whispering. "Gregor, we might need your help."

"What kind of help?"

Perl again looked about, though he tried to remain inconspicuous. "You heard about Takar escaping?"

Excitement seemed to take hold in the bounty-man. "That's why I'm trying to find Kender Darnell. We can hide Takar at my house, though I wouldn't suggest that; it's only a matter of time before Ludar searches all the houses." Gregor looked about. "But we could use the Trader's Inn. I know Brock would help, and he has a place in his cellar that is so good they would never find him."

Perl nodded his head. "I didn't know about that." He took a large swig of ale then set the mug down along with two coppers and his tobacco pouch. "I'll get back to you on this, Gregor. We might need you."

As he left, he weaved through the growing crowd, slowing as he passed by the door backstage where Baldomere Testa had just taken a short break. He stopped, pulled out his pipe and a striker, feigning an attempt to light it. "Don't take the apple pie," he said out of the side of his mouth. "I'd go for the cherry."

Testa nodded.

Perl lit his pipe, then returned to the table where Gregor sat. He reached over the chair to pick up his tobacco pouch. "Didn't know I left it until I went to light the pipe. Good thing I remembered, or I'd have had to go all the way to the Trader's Inn to get it. Don't know if I could have gotten there much before noon."

Gregor nodded. "I would have waited."

Perl nodded, then walked off into the crowd, enjoying Testa's show.

Testa gave a stellar performance, as he always did, a mixture of poems, stories, and wild imaginary tales of other worlds. After he was done, he made his trip around the room talking to customers and collecting his tips, the lifeblood of his earnings. When he approached Mollie's table, she threw a copper at him. He caught it with his hat, then bowed graciously.

"I applaud your generosity, famed lady of pies, but if I am forced to accept a gift from you, I would prefer it be a pie, not a copper coin."

Mollie blushed, her smile stretching from ear to ear over wrinkled skin. "That bein' the case, I'll fetch you an apple pie in the morning."

Testa made a big deal of tilting his head back and sniffing the air as if the pie lay right in front of him. "Ah, the sweet smell of cinnamon on apple. Now there is an aroma not unkind to the senses, my dear, but oh how I long for a cherry tart, one with just a hint of sourness to it."

Mollie laughed, pulled Testa close and kissed him on the cheek. "You're a long-winded man; I'll grant ya' that. If you spent that much time in bed with your wives, they might have stayed a little longer." She stood up to him. "But never you mind, I'll bring you that tart tomorrow. Before noon it'll be."

Baldomere Testa removed his hat and performed a sweeping bow, letting the feathers of his hat dust the floor. "A man can argue with many things, my friend, but it is difficult to argue with the truth. And as beauty has lost its grip on you, brevity has long since abandoned me. But my gratitude and eager anticipation await our next meeting. And as you say—may it be short."

The crowd cheered as he continued making his rounds. When he came arrived at the inn, he had not known who would be his contact, but Mollie worked perfectly. No one would ever suspect. And by tomorrow at noon, Takar would be safely delivered. Just one more stop after that, and he'd be home free.

SPECIAL DELIVERY

Mollie got up every morning before the sun. She did her normal routine, baking a few pies while it was still dark and sipping on strong khaffe to start her day. "You ready for this, Takar?"

He laughed. "Feels like old times, doesn't it, Mollie?"

She stirred something in a pot, but her head was shaking more than her stirring spoon. "Never get those times back. Shame about that."

Takar finished his khaffe and announced he was ready to go.

"You've got it right. No sense delaying anything." Mollie walked to the door, peeked out and turned back to him. "You stay here until I bring the wagon up. As I'm loading it, you can pretend to help me then climb into the back under the covers."

"And you don't think they'll look in there?"

"Not if I get them to help me," she said.

Takar hid under covers in the back of the wagon. Mollie covered him up with supplies, tablecloths, and other miscellaneous items. She moved slowly through the streets, greeting people and guards alike, as she always did.

At one corner, where four guards were inspecting wagons, Mollie called to them from halfway down the street. "Think you brutes could take enough time to stop lookin' for one man and help an old woman and her cart?" She had gotten out and acted as if it were a struggle to get up the street, tugging on the horse's reins.

Two of the guards laughed, brushing their hands at her, but one walked her way. When he reached her, he grabbed the reins. "Get in, Mollie. This horse is plenty strong enough. He's just old and stubborn like you."

She climbed into the cart and waited while the guard took hold and led the horse up the street.

"Where are you going this morning, Mollie?"

"First to the Sentry's Watch. Got to deliver a tart to that bard."

The guard patted the horse's neck. "Ought to be easier going from here to there. Not as many hills." At the top of the street, he handed the reins back to Mollie. "Have a good day, Mollie."

As she passed by, she tapped him on the shoulder. "You come by and get a pie from me. I'll show my thanks for a good man's help. Not you others though," she said, wagging a finger at them.

In the back of the wagon, Takar breathed a sigh of relief. It looked as if the plan would work after all. This had been the most difficult part, getting him to the inn. Two more streets brought them to the Sentry's Watch where Baldomere Testa came out to greet her.

She handed him the cherry tart, and while he nibbled on it, she waited for her clue—either confirmation of the plan to take him to the Trader's Inn, or some other place if a change had been made.

"This is a good tart, fair lady, though I dare say not as tasty as what I found at the Trader's Inn."

Ah, there it is. The Trader's Inn. "Go eat there from now on," she growled. "I didn't much care for your rhymin' anyway." She climbed back aboard her cart and headed toward the inn with a smile. Brock Larnigin would be takin' Takar off her hands soon.

Mollie took two turns left, went up a short hill, then turned right at the top. She pulled the cart into the stables, and as she climbed down, two full patrols of guards surrounded her.

"Move away," the patrol leader ordered. "Search the back."

Within a moment they pulled Takar from the wagon, locking him in chains. "Force Commander Ludar will be pleased to see you, Sergeant."

Takar spat on him, then tried to kick him.

Mollie stared at him with pleading eyes. "Wasn't me."

He smiled. "I know, Mollie."

One of the guards grabbed Mollie by the arm. "What about her?"

"Let her go. Ludar only wanted him." The guards formed a line, swords drawn.

As they marched down the street, they kept alert for danger, knowing the citizens of Sykor could, and would, attack a guardsman if they felt strongly enough about it and many of them still loved Takar.

A curtain moved slightly to the side from the window on the third floor of the Trader's Inn. Gregor peered out the crack staring at the Sykoran Guards as they hauled Takar away.

19

PRINCE OF ARANGAR

Darstan waited only a short while, then the gates opened and a small band of men emerged, the king leading them. No one was armed.

As he approached, he bowed to Darstan. "Is it you they call BlackWolf?"

"It's just a name," Darstan said.

The king stared at Darstan for a moment. "But ... you are just a boy."

"If only that were true," Darstan said, a sigh accompanying his words.

The king knelt, as did his followers. "Much more than a name, I believe. Even our legends have foretold of your coming, though you are called by a different name."

"Too many names," Darstan said. "Too much blood." He shook his head for a long time. "Please, get up. Together we'll arrange peace."

The king rose, a smile of hope lit his face.

"Careful, you might not like the terms," Darstan said.

"Go on."

"Cergala promises to keep the peace as long as Arangar remains true. No more incursions into our lands. No deaths, no matter the cause."

The king nodded at each statement, but Darstan knew that the last would be tough for him to swallow. "And Arangar will cede the Cergalan Pass and the surrounding mountain to Cergala."

The king paused. "If Cergala holds true to the agreement, it won't matter who controls the pass." He nodded. "Agreed."

"There's more," Darstan said. "Reparations must be made."

"We are a poor, starving people. There is nothing to give."

"I said reparations. Here are my terms. Each year, ten thousand of your young men will go to Cergala. They will work the fields, rebuild the city of Vennala. Clear the woods, learn the land."

The king frowned for the first time during the discussions. "Ten thousand slaves is a heavy price to pay. Too heavy. We need to rebuild our lands, now more than ever. And with this drought—"

Darstan growled. "I abhor slavery." He stared at the king. "I had not finished what I was saying."

When the king nodded, Darstan continued. "In exchange for your men, ten thousand Cergalans will come to Arangar. They'll rebuild the land I destroyed. They'll plant crops. And they'll bring food to feed the hungry." Darstan held the king's hand and stared into his eyes. "If our people are to learn peace, they must learn about each other. This is the only way."

Tears welled in the king's eyes, and in those of some of his men. He reached for Darstan's hand and grasped it. Then he knelt again and kissed it. The prophecies are true. You are the Prince of Arangar."

Darstan's mouth fell open. "What nonsense is this?"

"The prophecy said that we would be conquered, nearly destroyed, then the one who destroyed us would become our savior. This, they said, would be the true Prince of Arangar.

It was prophesied that he would come bearing fruit when our trees were barren. Wheat when our fields were dry. Meat when our cows were gone." The king removed his ring and gave it to Darstan. "Take this, Prince of Arangar, as a sign of my fealty. Wear it long and with pride."

Darstan nodded, and for the first time in a while, felt proud. "Send messengers to all parts of your land. Tell them what happened. I want no more blood."

"I will, My Prince." The king started to turn away when Darstan called to him. "Who was the girl?"

"Which one?"

"The brown-eyed one. Black hair, pregnant."

The king walked back to Darstan. "Black Wolf, I don't know what you saw. Perhaps the gods arranged it, but there were no dark-haired women at the gate. All of them had blonde hair."

Darstan nodded. *Which gods, I wonder?*

He looked about, checking for a face in the crowds. He wanted to be angry, but somehow that emotion didn't surface. Perhaps he had worn it out. *Gods arranged it? ... I'd wager it was an emerald-eyed god who did this, and a rat was her companion.*

20

PEACE AT LAST

Darstan rode into camp with a small contingent of soldiers. Wisp stood by a campfire drinking khaffe. "The war is over, Wisp, though you already knew that."

Wisp appeared shocked, started to speak.

"Don't bother denying it. I know it was her."

Aenaila emerged from the tent. "Welcome back, Darstan." She looked around. "Where are the rest of the men?"

"Refugio stayed behind to clean things up. He'll be along soon." Aenaila began to speak, but Darstan interrupted. "I want to go home, Aenaila."

She smiled. "We'll leave for Cartena at first light."

"Not Cartena. Home. I want to go back to my lands. Sykor. Kamnor."

"There's nothing for you there. In Sykor you are a wanted man. In Khatara you are hunted. And nothing is waiting in Twin Forks but old memories. Here, you are a hero."

"At least Twin Forks holds good memories. Besides, I swore to help Takar. If he's still alive, I need to get him out. He saved me once."

Wisp nodded. "I'll help. I owe him too."

Aenaila stared at Wisp. "I can't go with you now. I'll take you there, but I'll have to return later."

Wisp embraced her. "I know. I'll be back. As soon as we finish with this."

"Finish?" Aenaila shook her head. "You have no idea what you're going back for, do you?" He looked at her while she pointed a wagging finger at Darstan.

"He says he's going to save Takar, but that isn't the real reason. He's going after Rahg. Don't you see? He's going back to kill Rahg. That's why he wants to go to Kamnor. To find a trace. Find something to lead him to Rahg."

Wisp wanted to argue, but somehow he knew she was right. When he looked at Darstan, it left no doubt. "It doesn't matter, Aenaila. We're in this together. He needs me."

"Stay with her and Adju. I don't need anybody."

Anger flared in Aenaila. "And if you find Rahg? If you manage to kill him. What about Rhaven, and Camissa, and Tobias? Will you kill them as well? What of the prophecies, do you think—"

Darstan's hand shot for her throat, but Wisp grabbed his arm, yanking it away. Darstan screamed at her. "Curse your prophecies! Curse all the damned prophecies. They've brought me nothing but misery. An arm cut off. Powers. A dead wife ... a lost son ..." Tears streamed down his cheeks as his head lowered. "Curse your prophecies," he whispered.

Aenaila wrapped her arms around him. "I'm sorry, Darstan. Truly I am." She held him for a moment longer. "Tell me when you're ready, and we'll leave."

"I'm ready."

"Take hold then. You too, Kender."

Aenaila shifted to her father's home, the private meeting room. As soon as they arrived, she went to greet her parents, Darstan and Wisp following.

Marro's face lit up as she came through the door. "Daughter! What news do you bring?" As Darstan and Wisp came into the room, worry covered his face. "Have we lost?"

Aenaila smiled, hugging him. "No, Father. Not all news is good, but we have won the war, and we now control the pass. Even more importantly, BlackWolf has established peace with Arangar that has a good chance of lasting."

Marro dropped his arms, sat in his chair, silent. "Five hundred years," he whispered. "Five hundred years."

Aenaila's mother, Genea, embraced her. "You said not all news was good, child."

Aenaila gulped, staring at Darstan. "Mirana is dead."

Her mother hugged her, and Marro got up to offer comfort as well, but she shook it off. "She was carrying BlackWolf's baby."

At that, tears came to the queen's eyes, and she moved to hug Darstan. "I am sorry for your loss, BlackWolf."

Darstan nodded. "I'm going home."

Marro grasped his arm with both hands. "You are a legend already in our lands. I am sorry you had to lose so much to become one."

"He is more than a legend here," Aenaila said. "They have named him the Prince of Arangar."

Marro stepped back, almost as if he were afraid. "Who named him this?"

"Their king," Aenaila said. "He knelt and paid homage, then named him Prince of Arangar, relinquishing his own rule."

Marro nodded. "Then it's true," he whispered, almost to himself.

"What's true?" Aenaila asked.

"Nothing. I just meant that it was true—official."

Aenaila looked at him, head cocked. "I just said it was, father. But enough of this. I don't mean to rush you, but Darstan wants to go home. I will take him to get Adju then we will leave. I'll need a ship, of course."

Marro nodded. "It will take a few weeks for you to get to the island. Tell your brother to take care of it."

Wisp and Darstan reached out to grab her hands. "Another thing, Father, Mother. I'm going to stay with them for a while. They need my help."

"No!" Marro screamed.

"There's no need," Darstan said.

Aenaila seemed shocked by her father's vehemence. She hugged her mother, then Marro. "It's done, father. They came to help us. It's my turn." With that, she grabbed their hands and shifted.

Once they had gone, Genea came to Marro's side. "What troubles you, husband? I've never seen you like that."

Marro walked in circles, mumbling.

> Darkness looms behind the light.
>
> Waiting for the Prince of Night.
>
> From Arangar he comes with scorn.
>
> And when he comes, the world will mourn.

"I've never heard that before, Marro."

Marro hugged his wife. "That is the prophecy of the prince, and if it rings true, Black Wolf will be the death of us all."

Shock covered Genea's face. "But the other prophecies ... the ones that said BlackWolf would save us, would—"

"The other ones say he will destroy the Prince of Arangar, but now he is the Prince of Arangar. How this happened, I don't know, but it doesn't bode well."

"May the gods protect our daughter," Genea said.

"May they protect us all," Marro repeated.

● 21

RETURN TO ARANGAR

Rahg and his party stayed the night in Entiria, resting for the next phase of the journey. Rahg didn't want to go back to Arangar for many reasons, not the least of which was that Darstan was there. *How did things get so bad?* He thought, then lay down to sleep.

Morning came too early, and after a full breakfast, they prepared to shift. Mikkellana led them, taking them to the outskirts of the village where they had first met Tomkins. As they stepped through the rift into a clearing, Tomkins breathed a sigh of relief. He stooped to the ground and patted it then stood, smiling.

"Can't say as I was ever so glad to be home, Tobias. When I left here I planned on dying; now I couldn't be happier to be alive and to be back here, a place I swore I had no use for."

Tobias nodded, a smile on his face too. "I'm not home, Tomkins, but at least I recognize this place. Not the fondest of memories, but better than some we've had these past days." He pulled the pipe from his pocket, tamped it with his finger, then grabbed a striker to light it. "You know you're welcome to join us, Tomkins. Be good company if you did, but can't say if I were you that I wouldn't grab myself a lonely barmaid and bring her home. Plant myself right there."

Tomkins walked over and extended his hand. "I'll miss you, but I'm staying. My heart won't take much more of this."

Tobias nodded, and as they shook hands, Rhaven and Rahg walked over to say their farewell. Rhaven gave him enough food and water to last a few days, until he got back to town, then they sat to rest.

"When will we shift again?" Rhaven asked.

"Right now," Mikkellana said. "I don't need to rest." She turned toward Sama and Kavi. "We'll take you home first, then go to the Paaren. Everyone grab hold."

The rift opened in the square of Korg's village. As they stepped out, Camissa gagged, then fell to her knees, puking.

Sama screamed. "No! No! Not my baby." She fell to the ground, weeping. Kavi rushed to her side.

Rahg looked around, doing everything he could to stop himself from throwing up. All through the square lay bodies—mangled, charred, hacked to pieces, and torn apart by scavengers. The stench overpowered him. He shoved his face and nose into his shirt sleeve, but even that didn't help much. The shirt seemed to have taken on the odor.

"Darstan!" Rhaven said.

"He'd never do this," Rahg said.

Aentarra bent, examining the ground next to some charred soldiers. Mikkellana did likewise. "It was him all right. BlackFire did this."

Rahg stared at the houses burnt to the ground, people dead all over, not a single building standing in the entire town. Some of the people were burnt to ash. There were even women and children. *Darstan couldn't have done this. He couldn't.*

Rhaven patted Kavi on the back. "Help your mother. We'll stay a while."

Sama's tears began anew. She walked to the spot where her house had stood, knelt and ran her fingers through ash. Kavi hugged her when she returned, but she pushed him away. "Your father waits for me on the Chugarran Path."

"No! Mother, you can't."

"There is nothing left. He—"

"He has Reyna to share laughter and memories."

"What memories can she share—harsh and hungry winters; dry, hot summers." Sama shook her head, took out her knife. "I must go, son." With that, she grabbed the knife with both hands and plunged it into her stomach, gasping as she doubled over.

Kavi caught her as she fell, lowered her to the ground. "Mother! What have you done?" He rested a cheek next to hers, tears falling, then he cushioned her head with his coat and held her against him, rubbing her hand. "Tell father I miss him. And Reyna too."

She tried to speak, but no words came out. She nodded, her eyes holding him fixed.

"I love you, mother. May your walk be a short one."

Mikkellana stood behind him. "I could heal her."

Kavi held up his hand, shaking his head. "She would only do it again. No need for her to suffer twice."

Rhaven went to Kavi. "What will you do now?"

"Try to find my people. See if any are left."

"Take what food you need. Water, too." He turned to Mikkellana. "We need to find Argus. I left him here; Marchall, too."

"I doubt that Darstan, even in his maddened state, would have killed the animals. He—"

Rhaven's face turned red, anger taking hold. "He killed children! Nothing is worse than that."

"We'll find him," Mikkellana said. "For now, let's eat. We all need nourishment."

"I'm not eating here," Rahg said.

"We'll walk a ways, then rest," Tobias said, and headed north.

They soon found a clearing. Everyone ate, nibbled mostly, and all in silence. Kavi stood when he was done, walked over to Rahg and extended his hand. "Time for me to go. I wish you good fortune."

Rahg stood. "You, too, Kavi. I hope you find your people." As Kavi started to leave, Rahg called him back. "I"m sorry. Sorry about your family. It's my fault." There were tears in Rahg's eyes.

"It's no one's fault. The gods take us when they're ready."

Rahg nodded, said goodbye, but inside he wondered if the gods knew anything about what they were doing. If they were good gods, they couldn't let so many innocent people die.

Aentarra scanned the bodies, walked among them, careful to avoid staining her clothes with blood.

"Notice anything odd, sister?" Mikkellana asked.

"You mean the lack of Cergalan bodies? Or the fear etched on the faces of the ones not burned."

"Both," Mikkellana said. "What happened here?"

"I don't know, but I intend to find out."

Tobias approached from the side. "Where do we go from here?"

Mikkellana rubbed her eyes. "We might as well camp here for the night."

Rahg lay in his bedroll, not far from Camissa. She was already asleep; most everybody was except Rhaven. *He and Wisp never sleep,* Rahg thought, and recalled a few times in Sykor when Rhaven was coming in as Rahg woke, and a time in Pomanda when Wisp did the same. *Don't know how they do it.*

It was a quiet night if any night in the woods can be called quiet. An owl hooted now and then, and crickets held their scheduled chorus. A light breeze ruffled some trees and occasionally spurred the fire to crackle, but other than that, not much.

Rahg stared at the fire for a while, almost hypnotized by the dance it did, flames stretching and reaching out then curling around a small log, caressing it. Fires seemed enchanting at night, meant for the dark. He pulled his cloak around him to keep out the chill, and it was then he felt it—a pulsing, rhythmic throbbing. He pulled the cloak tighter and continued staring at the fire, not wanting to look anywhere else, certainly not inside his cloak.

The movement of the fire now seemed awkward, out of sync with the world. The only thing that felt right was the rhythm inside his cloak. The rhythm of the Slicer. He peeled the cloak back a bit, peeked inside. He thought he saw a faint glow and tugged it closed. *I should have given it back to Aentarra.* He had no business having this thing. The pulsing increased to match his heartbeat. Soon, he couldn't tell one from the other. Fear took hold.

His hand moved toward the Slicer, involuntarily. He tried to stop, but it was as if it had a mind of its own, slowly reaching for that thing in his cloak. "Ah!" he sighed when he touched it, felt the warmth rush into him. Flood his body. "No!"

"You all right, Rahg?"

Rahg jumped, his hand letting go of the Slicer as he sat up. "He looked about, saw Rhaven standing there. "Oh, yeah. I'm okay. Just a dream I guess."

Rhaven left, and Rahg lay back down, eyes wide open, staring at the stars. It was a long time before he went to sleep that night.

22

BACK TO THE PASS

Tobias got up first, sniffing the air. "Still stinks around here. I say we get out of here and eat somewhere else."

"No sense wasting time," Aentarra said. "We can shift right to the portal."

"What about Argus?"

"Even if we find the horse, he can't come with us," Aentarra said.

"That's true, sister, but we could at least try to find him, and if we do, then we can keep him safe until we return."

Aentarra brushed crumbs from her pants. "Do what you will. If it keeps Rhaven focused, it will be worth the trouble."

Rhaven jumped up, pacing, all nerves and anxiety. "Where will we look?"

"The pass," Mikkellana said. "Cergala will have men stationed there, and they'll know where any captured horses went."

"Darstan might be there!"

Aentarra smiled, recalling the shock Darstan had given her when he attacked with his BlackFire. "If he is, I'll teach that boy a lesson."

"Everyone take hold," Mikkellana said, then shifted.

The rift opened at the top of the pass on Arangar's side. Mikkellana and the rest of them stepped through, facing a group of armed soldiers. A quick glance and she surmised several hundred if not a thousand held camp, and from the looks of the plains below the pass, there were many thousands more. "I'm looking for Darstan. If he's not here —Aenaila."

Refugio stepped forward, his sword lowered, but drawn. Fear gripped him, but he controlled it enough to maintain a steady voice, and hand. "BlackWolf is gone. Went back to Cartena with Queen Aenaila."

"Queen Aenaila?" Rahg moved to Mikkellana's side. "Aenaila's a queen? And who is BlackWolf?"

Refugio bowed slightly to Mikkellana. "I saw how you came here, so I know you have powers. Are you the ones who fought us at the pass?"

Mikkellana stared at him, but never let her eyes drift from the rest of them. "Perhaps you should answer Rahg's questions first. Is Aenaila your queen? And, I too, want to know about BlackWolf."

Several patrols of soldiers had joined Refugio, all armed and anxious. "Keep weapons sheathed, men," Refugio ordered, and slowly slid his sword back into its sheath. "Keep your guard. Nothing has changed." He turned back to Mikkellana.

"Aenaila's father is our king, and soon she will be our queen. We do the honor of calling her that now."

A slight nod of Mikkellana's head. "And BlackWolf?"

Refugio paused. "The one you know as Darstan, the one with one hand. He is BlackWolf, the one foretold in our prophecy. BlackWolf led us to victory."

"The Cergalan Sword!" Rhaven muttered. "That sword he got in Sykor. It was called a Cergalan sword."

"It too was foretold in our prophecies."

"And the killing? The villages burned? Darstan did this?" Rahg asked.

Refugio nodded yet again. "Sometimes sacrifices must be made before peace is attained. People must die so others might live."

"He killed children!"

"And he isn't proud of that. But they killed ours, even worse, they killed the wife and son of BlackWolf. That's what started it."

"Speaking of killing, tell me what happened at the Chun village."

"Which one?" Refugio asked.

"The Chun home, their main city."

Refugio looked as if tears would fall. He struggled in the telling of it, but he told them about what Darstan had done, and what they had done.

FearMist! Aentarra shot a look at Mikkellana and knew she too, had recognized the description, though neither one of them had ever seen it. No one had ever seen it. It was a legendary power associated with ColdFire, but no one had ever been able to master it. Not even her father.

Refugio rushed to his defense. "He's changed. A different man than the one who did that."

"Never be peace now," Tobias said.

Refugio's forehead wrinkled, and his eyebrows rose. "There already is peace. The King of Arangar signed a treaty and swore allegiance to BlackWolf—the true Prince of Arangar."

"By all that's holy! Prince of Arangar! That's who Zukaar told me I must face. This can't be. It can't!"

Rhaven touched Refugio's arm lightly. "We left several horses in one of the Chun villages. One of them—"

The welcome sound of Refugio's laughter broke some of the tension. "I know the horse. BlackWolf saw him when we were fighting. He said if anyone hurt that horse, he would kill them himself."

Rhaven's face seemed to crack. "Then he's alive!"

"Alive and well, my friend. You must be Rhaven." He held out his hand. "I'm called Refugio, and your horse has been under my care." He looked to Rahg. "Your's too. BlackWolf made us care for both of them."

"Take me to him."

"We can't bring him with us," Aentarra reminded him.

"I want to see him, then I'll be ready to go."

"Follow me," Refugio said to Rhaven, then turned to one of his guards. "Nino, bring two others and walk with us."

Rhaven looked about. "You don't trust your men?"

"We just fought a terrible war. Many died and emotions were high. There is peace now, but ... sometimes men do not think before they act."

"I've seen it too. Many times." Too many times.

The glares of soldiers followed them through the camp, and though some seemed ready to draw weapons and fight, no one made a move. "Your men respect you, Refugio."

A hint of a smile crossed the Cergalan's face. "They fear me ... not me actually, BlackWolf. He left strict orders about keeping the peace."

They walked in silence for a while, Rhaven listening to the banter of the soldiers. It was the same everywhere. No matter what land you were in. "Is Darstan all right?"

"Are you his friend?"

"I saved his life a few times. Trained him in weapons. Watched him grow some. Aside from that, yes, I'm his friend too."

Refugio stopped, turned, and stared into Rhaven's eyes. "He suffers. I don't think I've ever seen a man suffer like him. Underneath it all, he's a good man. But he needs help." Refugio turned and started walking again. "If you ever get with him again, try to help him; be his friend."

A loud neigh sent chills down Rhaven's back. "Argus!" He ran the rest of the way to the pens where the horses were kept, Argus off to the side in one by himself. Rhaven leapt the fence and hugged him. "Good to see you, boy. It's been a long time."

He spent a long time with Argus, brushing him, checking his hooves, his teeth. Finally, Refugio came up behind him. "Time we got going. Your friends seemed to be in a hurry."

Rhaven patted Argus a few more times, gave him some hay, then joined Refugio for the walk back. Idle chatter kept them busy until they reached the top of the pass again. Rhaven looked at Refugio. "I'm afraid I'll have to ask you to watch him for a while longer. We have something that must be done."

Refugio clasped hands with Rhaven. "Don't worry. I promised Black-Wolf to watch him until either you or he came back. He'll be safe."

"Thank you."

"Ready?" Aentarra asked.

"I'm ready," Rhaven said, and he locked hands with Camissa.

Aentarra closed her eyes, focused on the Shift point at the top of the Forbidden Path, then shifted.

23

INSINUATION

S hatir let a shadow usher her way into camp, a secluded area tucked in amongst the hickory, spruce, and great oaks. "Sykor will present no problem. Six guards are posted at the gate with two more every two spans on the parapet, but they are lazy and see nothing. We can slip through easily."

J en Pal noted the smile on Shatir's face. Only his mother had a more beautiful smile. "Yes, Shatir, after so many silent moons, we will be written in the Books again." Jen Pal allowed himself the crack of a smile. "How many karns have had such blessings? None. Not even the great karns of old were honored so."

"Has any karn ever killed a king?" Suk Won asked.

"Long ago, Suk Won. Long before the Master came here. Jen Pal let excitement get hold of him. "But no karn has ever had three such missions: to kill a king; to kill the village boy, who the Master deems so important ..." Jen Pal's smile grew as wide as his face. "And to kill Black Death."

~

*S*hatir knew Jen Pal better than anyone, better even than his mother had, but there was something odd about his obsession with Black Death. It was an honor, to be sure, but Jen Pal had elevated this to a holy level. *What could it be?*

Jen Pal stirred the embers of their smokeless fire. "Suk Won, scout the side walls. See if there is a better way in."

While they waited for Suk Won, they talked of old times, of the legends of karns in ages past when they had missions every month.

"Will those times ever come again?" Triala asked.

Jen Pal looked at Triala. "No. I believe we are the last of the great karns. We need to make the most of it."

Suk Won returned from scouting the Sykoran wall. "There are only two sentries at this point. Can you hit them from this side of the moat?"

A smile came to Shatir's face for the first time in days. "You should know better, Suk Won. You've seen me shoot the beak off a crow in flight."

"I am only concerned with two Sykoran Guards, and whether they will sound an alarm."

"They will not have time to gasp, let alone cry out." Shatir withdrew two arrows, checked her feathers and, with bow in hand, she crept toward the moat under cover of the trees. She nocked one arrow, the other resting in a groove carved in her bow, specially designed to hold additional arrows to allow rapid firing.

The guards walked as most "frail ones" did; first toward each other, then they turned and headed back. She waited until they met in the middle and, just as they were executing the turn, she fired. The first arrow struck the guard in the throat, dropping him instantly. Before he even hit the ground, her second shot took the other guard in the nape of the neck—another mortal wound.

~

*J*en Pal heard the call, like the sound of an owl, and prepared the others. "Grab the rope, Triala; Shatir has finished. Suk Won, help me with this log."

They crept a few paces forward, then positioned a large log, the remnant of a downed tree, and rolled it toward the moat. Once in place, they used it to cross the moat.

Triala took only three attempts to fasten a hook over the wall, and within moments, the Ligarns were standing atop the parapet.

Suk Won watched as Shatir retrieved her arrows, cleaning them on a burlap cloth she carried at her side. "Perhaps Shatir *can* shoot the beak from a crow in flight." His laughter carried to her ears only. She smiled in return. Suk Won dropped one of the bodies over the wall into the moat.

"They will see the blood in the morning," Triala said, as she slipped the second guard over the wall. "Once they see the blood it will not take long to find the bodies."

"Nothing to be done about that. This will give us time enough to hide."

Soon the Ligarns were walking down side streets in Sykor, heads lowered with hoods drawn up on their cloaks to disguise their height. At night no one would notice them, but in the day their darker skin and stature would likely draw attention.

"This was too easy," Suk Won said.

Jen Pal's cherry-black eyes seared Suk Won. "We have completed nothing. All we did was enter a city that the rats have long found an open gate to. Are you proud of that? Or has it been so long since you have been on a mission that anything pleases you?" Jen Pal did not relent. "We do not know what awaits us. Black Death could even be here."

Shatir nodded her head while Suk Won kept his bowed low. "Of course you are right. My mind will not slip again."

"Nor your tongue."

They soon made their way to a room pre-arranged for them and sneaked in through the window. Sleep occupied the remainder of the night, but when the sun greeted them at dawn, all were awake. "Do you think he will be here?" Triala asked.

"Who?"

"Black Death."

Jen Pal stared at a blank wall, red brick with slicked joints. "I hope so, Triala."

She paced, staring. The floor was wooden planks, old, tongue and groove design. Long ago it might have been called gorgeous; now it was simply a floor. "What is so important about him. He is only a frail one."

Jen Pal's head shot around like an owl's at the squeal of a vole. Triala had braced herself for liberation, but Jen Pal simply stopped, once again staring at the brick wall.

Triala waited, but when he said nothing, curiosity compelled her to continue. "Do you know him?"

Shatir sat in the corner, arms wrapped around tucked-up knees. She shook her head at Triala. The message was clear—ask no more. This was a mystery she would have to uncover later.

"When will we strike?" Triala asked.

"We must first go see the pawn of the small gods, the one they call Ludar." Jen Pal raised the hood to his cloak. "Come, it is time we go. Triala, lead the way."

*L*udar instructed the young girl where to go, the side alley entrance that led to his quarters, though it would require two other guards to lead her through the maze to get to him. He did this often, brought young ones to his chamber—mostly girls, but there had been an occasional boy or two.

He longed for this one tonight; fresh, she was, and innocent, and longing to have Ludar's favors bestowed on her.

He dismissed the guards in his chambers, and from the inner rooms as well, only maintaining a watch on the exterior doors. When the rapping finally came to his secret entrance, he struggled to stifle his pulsing heart.

Just before he reached the door, a whisper from behind a pillar caught his ear. He whirled, sword drawn to the ready, stupefied that someone could have penetrated his chambers. "Guar ..." he almost called them in, when the realization struck him that it must be a messenger from the Master. Or the other one, he thought, recalling Aentarra's visit not so many moons past. It chilled him to form the image.

Jen Pal stepped from behind the pillar so lightly he could have been floating. No weapons touched his hand, but then none needed to. "Send the child away," Jen Pal said, his disgust evident.

Ligarns! Ludar had been warned they would come. Sweat loosened the grip on his sword.

Ludar spoke through the door. "Send her home, guard, then post a watch on the street," he said to his guard.

"Are you certain, sir?"

"Send her away!"

Ludar waited to hear the shuffle of footsteps, then focused once again on Jen Pal. "Ghruehne told me to expect you, but he said there would be four." Ludar glanced about. "Where are the others? I cannot afford for you to be seen in the city."

Jen Pal raised his hand, and the others slid into view. "We are here," Shatir said as she emerged from an alcove too small to hide a shadow. "And here," Triala said, appearing behind a chair as if she had stood there all the time. "And here," Suk Won's whisper carried from behind the waterfalls of the fountain.

Ludar's calmness was shaken. *How did they get in?*

"We were told to seek your help," Jen Pal said, "but we do not want it. Tell us everything you know, and who else knows about us."

Ludar gathered enough courage to challenge them. "Ghruehne said—"

Jen Pal's cherry-black eyes bored a hole in Ludar's gut. "Ghruehne is not here. I am charged with this mission. It is our honor that will be stained if something goes wrong." Jen Pal smiled. "All you can lose is your life."

Ludar talked through an entire bottle of wine. The Ligarns had none. He told them of Ghruehne's plans and why the king must die. "It is imperative that the people believe he was assassinated by the Pomandans. No one must suspect it was you or that the guard had any part in the conspiracy."

"No one will see us," Jen Pal said. "And since you are the only one in Sykor that knows, the secret is yours to conceal."

24

A VISIT WITH THE GODS

"**B**e careful when stepping out of the rift," Aentarra warned. "Remember, this is a narrow trail, and the drop is deadly."

Mikkellana and Rahg followed Aentarra out, careful to plant a firm foot onto the path. "I didn't remember it being so narrow," Rahg said.

"We were in a hurry last time. Your brother was shooting fire at us." Mikkellana laughed. "I do recall Kella had a difficult time."

Rahg looked at her as if she were crazy. "You talk about Kella like she was someone else."

"She is."

Kyra and Phay came out next, then Rhaven, Mulka, Garnock, Camissa, and Tobias all moved onto the trail, smoke from Tobias's pipe following him through the rift. "Can't say I'm eager to go back in there, lad. One of the few places you've led me that I'd just as soon forget."

"Me too, Tobias. But he told me I had to come back, and now's as good a time as any. I want to get this over with."

Mikkellana was the first one out on the ledge, and soon she went through the portal. The others followed, stepping into bright sunshine.

Mulka sniffed the air, eyes darting about. "This is not where we entered before."

Aentarra too, cast suspicious glances all around. "It's not. There were hills and a creek," she said, looking out across a dry, flat plain.

Mikkellana nodded. "It has ever been a strange place, sister. Remember the times when we would wake up and be somewhere different than when we went to sleep?"

"You were here before?" Rahg asked.

"I thought you already knew. Yes, we were trapped for hundreds of years."

Rhaven shook his head. "An unkind fate."

The wind blew out two of Tobias's strikers before he finally got his pipe lit again. "I say we get movin' before any of those creatures show up. Longer we stay in one place the more nervous I get." He puffed furiously to stoke the pipe then turned to Mulka. "Which way?"

Mulka pointed west and started off in that direction, but Rahg stopped him.

"That's not right. The amulet is pulling me the other way."

Rhaven looked to Rahg, then to Mikkellana. "I thought that Mulka—"

"They can. Give me time to think about this."

"No need to think," Aentarra said. "The Mordi is following a path that will take us back to where we originally entered, the first time. But as we all know, that isn't where we are now. His way will get us to the mountain, but it will be a roundabout way. The amulet will take us there directly."

"She's right," Mikkellana said and smiled. "You always did have father's logic."

"Among other things," she said, with a smirk.

Mikkellana laughed. "All right, we follow Rahg."

Kyra's guttural growl formed words easy enough to understand. She had learned the language well enough from Arton and others. "I go to join my packs now." She bowed low. "It has been an honor to hunt and fight with you. May your claws stay sharp for the Eternal Hunt." She then pulled out four long pieces of fur from her side, tied them into three small loops and handed them to Rhaven. "You may now count the Kreng as friend. If you meet any of my kind, show them this. Tell them that Kyra of the Three Trees Pack is your ally."

Rhaven bowed low. "It has been an honor to fight with you, Kyra, and I thank you for your gift. I have nothing to offer that could equal it. Only my friendship."

One of her claws scratched Rhaven's arm, drawing blood. She brought a drop to her lips, tasted it. "I am now bound to you as I was with the Nameless One, called Arton. May your journey be safe," she said, and headed off at a fast pace.

They followed Rahg for two more days, through terrain that all seemed new. Before they had a desert to contend with, now they had nothing but long stretches of plains. It proved to be an easy journey in comparison. There were ample supplies of water and game was abundant. Fruit and nut trees provided additional, unexpected food that they stocked up on in the event things changed.

Along with that was the constant fear of the dorgans. The beasts seemed to be on everyone's mind, at all times.

"How did you stay in here so long?" Rahg asked. "Always wondering about the dorgans."

"It wasn't easy," Aentarra said, "but imagine what Arton went through. He was in here for more than a thousand years, and by himself for the most part."

"How did you get trapped in here to begin with? Who was with you?"

"Aentarra's demeanor switched from pleasant to vicious, as she spun to face Rahg. "You don't need to know, boy. Stop asking so many questions."

They walked until dusk, then stopped for supper and to make camp. "Gonna' be cold tonight," Tobias said. "Be nice to have a fire."

"No fires." Rhaven moved alongside Tobias and Rahg. "As open as these plains are, a fire could be seen from too far off. No sense giving those creatures an advantage."

Tobias spat, then put out his pipe, stuffing it into his pocket. "Should've stopped earlier. Then we could have cooked something."

"We've got fruit. That will do for tonight."

"Might do for Mulka, but I need some meat. Couple of hot biscuits wouldn't hurt either."

Rhaven laughed. "Now I see where Rahg gets it from. He must have spent too much time around you in his youth."

"I'm going to sit with Camissa," Rahg said.

~

*A*entarra sat off from the rest of them, back planted against the trunk of one of the few trees they had seen, and her arms wrapped around drawn-up knees. She stared up at starry skies, searching for familiar patterns that she knew weren't there.

"Want some company?"

"My sister is always welcome," Aentarra said with a smile.

They both sat in silence for a long while. "You've been pleasant to be with of late, Aentarra. It has been a long time since we've shared so much."

Aentarra put her hands behind her head, rested against the tree. "Getting sentimental on me?"

"No. It's just that ... sometimes I miss home. These past few months have made me miss it more. Especially when I saw Melissara; it brought back memories of father and better times at the manor."

A scowl formed on Aentarra's face. "Nothing can ever bring it back. But we can get justice."

"You mean vengeance don't you?"

"Call it what you will. I'm going to kill every one of them, starting with Lukaan."

Mikkellana shook her head. "Even if you can kill Lukaan, how do you think you can get back to Nelstar? And how in the gods' name do you think you can kill the Lights?"

"I've got my ways."

"What? Your Slicers? What you did with Xanthes and the others?" Mikkellana stood, angry. "I know all about it. I don't fully understand it, but I know you've gotten stronger as a result." She stopped, staring Aentarra in the eyes. "Remember what the Lights did to father? It would take millions of the Slicers to get you enough power."

A small smirk flitted across Aentarra's face. *Yes, it would, wouldn't it?*

"You're smiling? Do you pretend to be crazy, or did you inherit more from father than his hair and eyes?"

Aentarra jumped up, fire dancing on her fingertips. She pointed a finger at Mikkellana. "Don't ever talk about him like that. If he went crazy, it was you and Melissara who did it to him. He loved me." Tears formed in her eyes. "He loved me!"

Mikkellana was stunned into silence. "I wasn't talking about love, Aentarra. I know he loved you, but—"

"Enough!" She screamed, then darted off into the darkness.

Mikkellana watched her disappear into the night, a thousand thoughts racing through her mind, but the one that rang the loudest wouldn't stop. *She is crazy. May the gods help us all.*

25

HOME OF THE GODS

The next day, Tobias called out from the lead position. "Think I see the mountain. Sure looks like it."

Anguish fought with relief inside of Rahg. He was relieved that the dorgans hadn't gotten them, and he was relieved that they were finally nearing the destination, but he was terrified to go back into the cave. The pain from the last visit still haunted him.

Several days of walking brought more nights with little sleep, dorgans dancing in dreams. Rhaven practiced his forms every morning before anyone awoke, and Tobias complained about not having fires to cook with. Aentarra used her Fire to let him make khaffe every morning, but that was only because she wanted it too. She cared less about dinner.

During long walks, Aentarra would intermittently throw fire at Rahg, a test to see how alert he stayed. Several times he got burnt. Mikkellana healed him, though she made him wait until night to do it.

"A painful lesson lasts longer," she told him.

On the third day, the terrain changed, the flat plains giving way to rolling hills peppered with short, squat trees. They were in the foothills of the mountains, the cold wind forcing heavy cloaks, even hats to come out. The next day, they reached the bottom of the mountain.

Rahg stared up at it, his gut twisting, throat parched. "Cook me a good meal tonight, Tobias. I'll get started early."

"You know the orders, lad. No fires."

"We have enough protection here. I think we can allow a fire," Rhaven said. "Besides, Rahg needs a full stomach. Last time he was gone for six or seven days."

"I'm going with you," Aentarra said. "If there's a god up there, I want to see him."

"I don't think you should, My Lady. He—"

Her eyes narrowed to slits. "Don't ever tell me what to do."

"Yes, My Lady."

Mikkellana studied her sister. "Do what you will. You always have. But I would heed the warning if I were you."

"I'll let fate steer my course."

Rahg awoke early, after a tumultuous night of sleep. He felt more tired than he had in days. *Might as well get this over with,* he thought, and began packing for his journey up the mountain.

"Want khaffe, lad?" Tobias stood next to Rhaven, sipping on khaffe. Camissa sat beside him.

It didn't surprise Rahg that Tobias and Rhaven were up, but seeing Camissa and Aentarra did surprise him. "I didn't think everyone would be up this early."

"Not everyone is," Aentarra said.

Tobias came over offering Rahg a cup.

"I don't want any, but thanks." He hugged Camissa, then shook hands with Tobias and Rhaven. "I'll see you when I get back."

"Good luck, lad. I'll have an extra biscuit for you when you return."

Rahg started up the mountain along a steep, tortuous trail. Aentarra followed him closely. The collar of fog that hovered near the peak started its descent the moment he began his climb, just as it did last time. By the time he reached the halfway mark, the fog had met him, enveloping him until he could see no more than an arm's length away.

Rahg shivered but kept walking. The trail would stop soon and then he'd have to scale the mountain by hand.

～

*A*entarra could no longer see the path ahead of her, couldn't even see her feet or where to place them. "Rahg!" There was no answer. She stopped, listening, but heard nothing. *How is he seeing in this?*

She crept along, slowly placing one foot, then the other until a misstep nearly sent her reeling off the mountain. She recovered, then looked ahead. The path was completely covered, yet behind her, she could see clearly. It was a definite sign, subtle but clear. She turned and went back down the mountain.

Rahg continued, finally reaching the top, then the cave. When he entered the dragon greeted him.

Back so soon, young one?

"It seems I have no choice."

Do any of us? The dragon said, then moved aside, allowing Rahg to pass.

Rahg wondered about the dragon's newfound beneficence, but he wasn't about to argue. He hugged the walls as he passed, keeping a wary eye on the dragon at all times.

Two paths waited ahead. Last time there had been three. He wasted no time pondering over a choice, simply chose one of them and moved forward. It was dark, pitch dark, and he had to use his sword, as he did before, to feel his way. Soon he came to the end, and when he turned around, a light greeted him, exploding from a cavernous room that he felt sure had not been there moments ago when he passed. Rahg squinted, held his head low, then entered the room, expecting the worst.

I am Shinaka, the god said, his voice filling the room. You have done well on your journey.

Rahg knelt, not daring to look up. "I need help."

We are aware.

"I don't know what you want me to do, and I'm afraid that ..." Rahg fumbled for the right words, but he knew a lie wouldn't do. "I guess I'm afraid."

You must conquer fear. There are more than a few lives resting on your shoulders.

Rahg shook his head. "So many have died already. I'm not strong enough for this. I can't fight Lukaan."

The light vanished. Rahg knelt in total darkness. The ground under him rumbled. He felt a vibration in his knees, then it ran up his bones, jarring him. He tried to stand, but couldn't.

You were told before you do not have to fight him. You were told not to go to Sethia, but you did. You put all at risk.

The rumbling stopped, and along with it, the pain.

"I didn't plan on going there. I almost died myself."

I care nothing about your life. The voice rang so loud in his head, he felt it might explode.

Rahg gulped, as if he were swallowing rocks. "Tell me what you want."

It was you who came to see me.

He paused, thinking. "Can you give me more powers? Make me stronger?"

The room brightened again, as if a thousand candles were lit at once. He was kneeling on a circular design in the floor, perfectly inside of it. The floor underneath him began a slow rhythmic motion, not like before; this was more entrancing than painful. Then a light shone from above, straight through him—actually through him.

Rahg tried to move, but he couldn't even blink. Couldn't close his eyes. The light hurt. His eyes watered, tears running down his cheeks, then things inside of him began moving.

Cold fear gripped him. He retched. How many times he couldn't tell, but it didn't stop until nothing remained. The heat built inside of him, coursing his veins. The temperature rose, growing hotter and hotter until he could take no more. His skin bubbled, and then, just as he felt sure he would die, flames shot out from his hands—two cylinders of fire that struck the cavern walls.

"I've got Fire!" he screamed.

You have always had it. I simply helped you find it.

Rahg beamed, proud of his new power. "I want to see the other one. Daurien."

The cavern walls rumbled. ***You are not ready for Daurien. You must go back and rest. Grow stronger.***

Rahg shook his head. "I don't have time for this, and neither do you. You told me I had to fight the Prince of Arangar. If I do, I better be a lot stronger than this."

Very well. Go see him.

The light disappeared, so too, did Shinaka. Rahg turned to see a doorway open in the cavern walls. He rose, walked over to it and into the dark corridor. The blackness enveloped him, and he had to once again use his sword as a walking stick. Soon, he hit the end and turned. As he made his way back, a doorway opened on the right side. Rahg entered.

The light was blinding, but he saw the form of a god against the far wall. Daurien seemed no different than the other two—ominous, threatening, omnipotent. "I needed to see you now," Rahg said. "There might not be time to wait."

What you need is of no importance.

Rahg was riding a confident wave. "Apparently it is. You seem to need me, too. And I don't have time to wait for you."

You don't have time not to wait? A long pause followed. ***We are giving you powers you would not get for a long time. To accelerate any faster might kill you.***

"Do it anyway."

No. Leave now. You will know when it is time to return.

"I'm not leaving. You can—"

The mountain rumbled, jarring Rahg to alertness. Lightning dashed across the room, striking the outside wall, splintering it. The crack opened wider, a gap large enough for a man to squeeze out.

Go! Or I will throw you out.

Rahg moved slowly to the exit, peered out, then made his way down. It was a moonless night, and it proved to be a slow descent, with the trail steep and riddled with pitfalls. By morning, he had made it within sight of the camp. Nothing ever looked so good.

Aentarra was the first to greet him, sniffing the air, using Sense. "There's a difference in you. You have more powers." She paused. "Fire! How did you get it?"

"He said it was always there. He just released it."

She looked up at the mountain, nodding. "I'll need to teach you how to use it. It takes practice, just like the shield."

They made their way into camp, where everyone chatted for a while, peppering Rahg with questions about his experience. "Time enough for that later," Tobias said. "We better get outta' here before any of those beasts come. Been pushin' our luck as it is."

They packed quickly and left, following Mulka's lead back to the portal. On the fourth day, they spotted a large group of dorgans in the distance. "They haven't seen us yet," Aentarra said. "I can use Illusion to trick them." They picked up the pace, and Aentarra used her Illusion to show a chasm between where the dorgans were and the path they had taken.

"Faster," Rhaven said. "That might not hold them for long."

The dorgans soon came to a stop at the chasm and began following it south, away from the path Aentarra and the others had taken.

"It's working," Tobias said.

"Only for a while," Aentarra said. "They'll soon come to a point where the Illusion stops, then they'll cross, and if they get our scent, they'll stay on it."

They ran as fast as they could, though Tobias was having a difficult time keeping up. He looked to the rear and saw them charging. "Here they come!"

"Run for those rocks!" Mikkellana yelled.

"We'll never make it," Aentarra said. "Our only hope is stealth. Everyone grab hold, and don't dare let go."

As soon as the Cloak took hold, the dorgans lost their scent, stopping, puzzled. They stared in all directions, then got on the ground sniffing, picking up dirt, examining everything. They spread out in a search pattern, groups of them moving in all directions, very methodically.

"I can't last very long with all of us," Aentarra said. "And the way those dorgans are searching, they're bound to find us sooner or later. We've got to keep running and not stop." She looked to them. "When I say so, be ready to move, and don't forget, you can't let go." She looked one more time, nodding.

"Okay, let's go." They ran for a long time, Tobias and Camissa gasping for breath, and showing signs of wearing out. "Keep moving," Aentarra ordered.

Before long, a town appeared in the distance; a small town tucked into a neat little valley. "That wasn't here before," Rahg said. "Mulka, I told you we had to go back the same way."

"This is the same way. Something is wrong with this place."

"Stop arguing!" Mikkellana said. "I don't care how the town got here, or where we are. We have to find shelter."

"Keep moving," Aentarra repeated. "We'll make it there before them. I hope there's someplace safe to hide."

They ran for the town, still Cloaked. As they got nearer, Rahg stopped, nearly causing them to break the connection. "It's Twin Forks! By all that's holy, that's Twin Forks."

"Keep moving, boy. I don't care what it is. Those dorgans are heading this way."

"They're following us," Camissa said.

"They can't be following us, girl, but they've gotten lucky and picked the right way to go."

"There's my house!" Rahg said, pulling to go that way.

Mikkellana yanked hard on him, moving toward the center square and what appeared to be an inn. "We'll take refuge inside there. We have to let Aentarra rest."

Aentarra collapsed as soon as they entered. "I couldn't have lasted any longer."

Mikkellana rushed to the window. "Watch for them. Tobias, take the other side. We can't let them know we're here or they will tear the place apart."

Rahg seemed dumbfounded and just stared out the window at the familiar buildings. Rhaven looked too. "I know that some things are difficult to explain, Mikkellana, but how is this possible?"

"The beasts are wandering," Mikkellana said, "searching everywhere. I hope they can't smell us in here." She looked to Rhaven. "As to your question, it isn't possible ... and yet, here we are.

Aentarra sat on the floor, leaning against a wall. "Remember that time we thought we saw the Manor?"

Mikkellana thought, then nodded. "I do. At the time I was certain it was the Manor. Later, I convinced myself it was an Illusion created by one of the others to torture us." She paused. "Not this time though. This is no Illusion."

"One comin' this way," Tobias said.

Mikkellana shot a look to Aentarra.

"Too soon. We'll have to hide and risk it until I recover."

"In the kitchen," Mikkellana said. "Everyone but Rhaven and Tobias." When those two turned to look at her, she explained. "Each of you take a watch. Let us know when they're almost here, but don't wait so long as to risk being seen." With that said, she moved into the kitchen with Aentarra, Camissa, Rahg, Mulka, and Garnock.

A huge, brown dorgan passed close to Havril's Inn but never stopped. Before long, all of them had moved through the town and had disappeared into the hills beyond. "Safe for now," Tobias said, as he came back from scouting the area.

"We should be going," Rahg said.

"Not until I'm ready. If we meet them in the open, I want to be able to Cloak."

Rahg nodded. "I'm going to see my old house. You want to come, Camissa?"

"I'd love to," she said, and followed him out the door.

They walked the short distance to his house in silence, then Rahg stood there, staring at the front porch. "This is it, Camissa. Where we grew up."

Images of Magmar sitting on the porch and of Darstan, chopping wood and mending fences, flashed in his mind. He closed his eyes and could almost smell a stew cooking on the stove, could almost hear his father calling him for supper.

"I don't know how this is possible, Rahg. I've never heard of anything like this."

"Strange things seem to happen to me. To us, I guess. Look at how many of us have powers. Something's wrong with that."

Camissa looked around her, nervous. "We better be getting back. I don't think we should venture far under the circumstances."

"The dorgans are gone."

"I'm not talking about them. I'm talking about this town. It wasn't here when we passed by just days ago. Suppose it disappears the same way it came while we're in it?"

Rahg thought for a moment, then grabbed her hand. "You're right. We need to tell the others in case they haven't thought about it." He ran toward Havril's Inn, Camissa trailing close behind.

She explained her concern to Aentarra and Mikkellana as soon as they entered.

Aentarra jumped up from the floor. "The girl's right, Mikkellana. I don't know why I hadn't thought of it." She headed for the door. "Let's get out of here before something happens."

After three days of walking, they approached a spot that Mulka recognized. "We've passed here before, just after we entered. Two more days and we should be out of here."

"Don't ever count on being out of here until we are out," Aentarra said.

They walked until dusk, everyone tired from the pace they had set for days. They came upon a small enclave of rocks, good for shelter, and Rhaven called for camp, but just as they were setting up Garnock alerted them.

Tobias looked to the side and saw them coming. "Dorgans!"

Six of them charged, the ground rumbling under the heavy footsteps. They were too close to use Illusion, and they were in an enclave of rocks that could be searched too easily for her to Cloak them. Aentarra jumped to the front. "Shield us, Mikkellana. I'll take the one on the left." Lightning struck in a constant barrage at the dorgan, while the others hammered on the shield. After a few more strikes, the first one fell. Aentarra used BlackFire on the next, all the while keeping a wary eye on the shield. "Keep it up, sister. Don't let them in."

"I've got a little time left. Not much."

"Let me at them," Rhaven said, holding the sword Mikkellana had given him in one hand and a sai in the other.

"Stay where you are," Mikkellana instructed.

Rahg, outside the shield, struck from the right, wielding Fire for the first time. He managed a small column of Fire that struck the dorgan's torso. The creature screeched, but smothered the flames with its hands and came at Rahg.

He erected a shield just as it reached him, but the pounding soon had his knees buckling. "Gods they're strong. Can't hold this."

Then, two arrows struck the neck of the dorgan, followed by a third. The dorgan screamed, reaching for the arrows and yanking them out, but it was too late. In less than a moment, it lay writhing on the ground, convulsing— then, it lay dead. Three more arrows struck almost simultaneously in the next dorgan in line, sending it to a similar fate. Kyra and Phay, leading ten other Kreng, charged into battle, all with bows and poisoned arrows.

Rahg dropped his shield and called on his Fire again, attacking one of the two remaining beasts. Aentarra had killed two, and Kyra and her pack two. Soon, the blackthorn tipped arrows took out the last two dorgans.

Rhaven bowed to Kyra as Mikkellana lowered the shield. "It seems they do work on dorgans."

A guttural growl that Rhaven had come to recognize as laughter emerged from Phay and Kyra. "It takes three of them, sometimes four, but they work. And we have to hit the neck or head."

"As long as we get out of here alive, I'll get you more poison. A lot more." He thought for a moment. "I'll tie the flasks to a rope and dangle it from a rock on the other side of the portal. That way, even if the terrain changes in here, the flasks will still be there." He looked to Mikkellana. "Assuming Mikkellana will take me to get it and bring me back."

"We owe Kyra that much."

All the Krengs growled. "Then we can hunt freely. I will look for your gift." She bowed and ran off.

"I'm not much for stayin' here now," Tobias said. "Might as well keep movin'."

They all agreed and continued the journey.

True to Mulka's estimate they reached the portal inside of two days and exited without a problem. Rahg stepped onto the ledge first, careful with his footing. He made his way slowly until he got to the trail. "It's fine," he hollered.

"Glad to be out of there," Tobias said, igniting his pipe.

"How long before we can go home?" Rahg asked.

"We need to get Argus and Marchall first."

"I can be ready at any time," Aentarra said. "It's up to Mikkellana."

Mikkellana looked at her sister. "I'll get the horses, then take Mulka and Garnock home. You get the others."

"Meet you in Vallah," Aentarra said, "then I've got to stop by and see that pirate."

"I had forgotten about that. And remember, be careful in Vallah. Ghruehne and Sendra might be there."

Aentarra smirked. "They wouldn't dare." She grabbed hold of Rhaven and the others, then shifted.

A rift opened in Aentarra's chambers, inside the palace at Vallah, and Aentarra stepped through, alert for trouble. She sniffed, then focused a Sensing. "They've been here," she said, "but they're gone now."

"This is beautiful!" Camissa said, marveling at her room. "I've never seen anything so nice."

Aentarra smiled. "It took me fifty years to get it the way I wanted. Even then, there were things that bothered me."

Camissa ran her hands over the sheets. "They're so smooth!"

"Lie down," Aentarra said. "Try it."

Camissa removed her shoes, then lay on the silk, wrapping it around her as she rolled from side to side. "Come here, Rahg. Try this out."

Begrudgingly, he lay on the bed, and while he didn't sound exuberant, Camissa could tell he enjoyed it. She frolicked about with him for a moment, then seemed to realize that Aentarra was there, watching. She lost some of her playfulness, sat up, and straightened the pillows. "That is a wonderful bed. I don't know how you sleep in any other after that."

Aentarra smiled. "I'll show you to your room. It's almost as nice, and the sheets are just as good." As they walked out the door and down the corridor, Aentarra turned to her. "Did I mention that Rahg's room will be right next to yours?" She didn't wait for a response, just kept walking down the hall.

Camissa caught the image that formed in Rahg's mind. It was a brief thought, but it was there. *Tonight. I'll get some time with him.*

26

SENNAR COMES HOME

A rift opened on the deck of the Sea Skate, the air rippling in a soft breeze. Aentarra stepped through, saw the guards surrounding her, called her Fire. At the last moment, she realized they were unarmed and bowing to her, not attacking.

"Good thing I was observant or you would all be dead. What fool posted you here?" Her legs were exposed past the thigh, almost to her buttocks, and her top left little to the imagination. Aentarra enjoyed dressing this way, especially when she knew she would be around men who could barely control themselves.

The first mate looked as if he tried not to gawk but found it impossible. The only decision he likely faced which part of her to look at first. "Captain Sennar told us." An ecstatic look remained etched on his face.

Aentarra's cunning smile appeared in a flash. She walked around him as if she were appraising a horse for purchase. "Get a good look, did you?" Her tone was taunting, but the words flowed like honey from her mouth, almost promising.

A panicked look came to his face. He'd seen her on the ship when they came to Entiria. Knew what she could do. "I'm sorry, My Lady. I—"

Aentarra laughed, patted him on the shoulder, letting her hand linger a little too long as she pulled it away and brushed his skin with a delicate touch.

He shivered, most likely a shiver of ecstasy, like an orgasm gone wild. Her touch was more than a night in bed with any other woman.

Aentarra leaned in close, whispered in his ear. "You would not survive the night," she said, and flashed that smile of hers, the one that could turn a man's gut. "But it would be worth it."

His face went white, and he bowed to her. "Yes, My Lady."

"Tell Sennar I'm here. And someone get that pirate, too."

"They're comin' even now, My Lady," a shipmate said.

When Sennar and Malakai came on board, they bowed to her. "My Lady," they said in unison.

"Are you blessed with a gift I don't know about or is our pirate friend that efficient?"

Malakai nodded his head in appreciation of the compliment. "A simple messenger system that alerted me when you arrived."

Aentarra studied him: a large man with flaming red hair but soft blue eyes. Many years ago some women might have clamored for him—those who favored the reds—but he was older now, perhaps more tame. Aentarra liked dark hair, the darker the better. And a chest like the mane of a wolf. "I didn't see anyone leave their post."

Malakai looked above and to his left, where banners flapped in the breeze. "Change the color or number or the arrangement, and it sends a message. It all means different things. An old trick from the sea. You can send a lot of messages with just a few simple banners."

"Interesting," she said, and immediately thought of uses for that in battle. "Did Captain Sennar tell you what we had in mind?"

Malakai stared at her with a firm gaze. "Said you needed help controlling the sea. That there was going to be a war."

She paced the deck, and each time she turned, the men's heads turned with her. Sennar signaled them to stop, but they weren't paying attention.

Aentarra snickered. "You can look all you want. It will make you worth something to your wives when you get home. Close your eyes and pretend it's me." Her laughter rolled across the deck.

As she came to a stop in front of Malakai and Sennar again, she grew serious. "I believe the best way to say it is with no frills. Lukaan is going to get out. I know that. And when he does, it will be a war like you've never seen. In the meantime, he will do everything he can to start wars between countries, so it is imperative that we control the sea. And to do that, our good friend Sennar believes we need you."

Malakai smiled. "I always said my old teacher had wisdom."

"I suggest you leave soon. Lukaan will not be idle for long."

"You haven't even asked me if I'm going," Malakai said. "We're risking a lot to leave here and go chasing a war that's none of our business."

Aentarra stepped up close to him, so close their bodies almost touched. "You're going, pirate. You'll go if I have to strap you to the mast."

She reached over and pulled Sennar to them. With her finger under his chin, she swiveled his head to the side. "You see his face, how pretty it is now?" Malakai nodded. "My sister did that. Healed him for his help in getting them to Entiria." Aentarra's lips and eyes both narrowed and her brow wrinkled. "But if you two fail me I'll make both of you look like he used to."

"I already told ya' I'd be goin'. Got no cause to be makin' threats. As for Malakai, he made up his mind days ago. For all the man's faults—and they're many—he's not one to shirk a duty."

"Good. I like that." She stepped back, then turned to leave. As she walked toward the center of the deck, Malakai called to her.

"Suppose I had said no."

Aentarra turned slowly, smiling. "I almost wish you had."

"Why?"

"Because then I would have killed you."

Malakai was shocked by her coldness. "And leave my wife with no husband. My child with no father?"

Aentarra's face lost all expression. She walked back to him, stared up into his soft blue eyes. "You misunderstand, my pirate friend. I would have killed all of you. Your wife, child, all of your men and their families too." She ground her teeth tight. "No one refuses me."

After she departed, long after the rift had disappeared, Malakai looked to Sennar. "Was she serious?"

"More than you'd ever know, my friend."

"Gods help us if she's the good one."

"Gods help us all," Sennar said.

27

PLOTS REVEALED

Favian paced the room, afraid. Always afraid. "How do you know this information is reliable? Where did it come from?"

Ludar stood, still as one of the columns in the room. "We have spent much time and money planting our spies, My King. The agents we have in Pomanda and Khatara are among our oldest and most-trusted. If it were simply one report from one agent that would be different, but two agents in Khatara have heard the same news, and one of the agents in Pomanda has confirmed it."

The king walked without questions until he had circled the room three times. "Do we know who the target is yet?"

"No, My King. But the news comes out of the merchant and guild districts. The action appears to stem from some trade disputes. I would guess that they will attempt to assassinate one or two of our biggest merchants or the leader of a guild."

"Insanity!" the king snapped. "What would they gain from that? Why even bother?"

"They could gain much. If several of the big merchant houses fell, the caravan route would be all but shut down. And who better to fill that need than some Khataran merchants?"

Favian's hand rubbed his beard in thought. "Hmm. And if we refused to do business with them?

Ludar smiled. "We are not in a position to refuse goods from Khatara. If I may remind you, My King, a large percentage of what we bring from the caravan route is resold to other cities, including, I might add, Pomanda."

Favian's eyes lit up. "Pomanda, yes. And they would stand to gain by cutting us out as the middle man."

"Indeed, My King, which is why I believe the plot is much deeper than just Khatara. I believe they act in alliance with Pomanda, perhaps others."

Favian sat while he pondered. "Is it the merchants who are targets? Have we agreed on that?"

The Force Commander shook his head. "Not necessarily. They are the most likely targets, but as I said, the guild ..."

"What would they accomplish by killing guild leaders? I understand what the guilds do, but they would simply elect new leaders."

"Not so, My King. The guilds function in a controlled fashion. Quality is mandatory, adherence to all guild laws is strictly enforced, and as long as the guilds' key members are in control any individual leader can be replaced; however, if suddenly chaos is thrown into the mix by several key assassinations, the rules will be tossed aside. If that happens, it again leaves us vulnerable to the competition from the other cities."

Ludar paused. "And remember, 'When unrest rules the city, the king rules unrest.' "

"I should address the people, Ludar. Tell them to hold fast in these difficult times, embrace our problems together."

Ludar shuffled nervously for the first time since the audience began. "My King, there is something else … I have given this much thought, and while I do not believe it likely, there is always the possibility that these assassins will try to kill you."

Favian's eyes went wide. "Nonsense! Not even the Khatarans would dare do that, and Pomanda would never ally themselves with someone planning a royal assassination."

Favian smiled and pointed a finger at Ludar. "Royal assassinations were banned centuries ago after all the lands nearly lost their rulers. The other rulers know that if they can kill me, they can also be killed; and a royal assassination requires a royal sanction. No, it will not be me. Fear not." The king smiled. "Besides, they would not risk war with us; not with you as my Force Commander."

Ludar nodded. "Just the same, My King, have you ever acknowledged publicly that Cynamar would be your heir? It would be a good time to let them know, show your people that you have no fear of naming your only daughter to the post should something unfortunate happen."

Favian scoffed. "A man's death is an unpleasant discussion, but I'll think about it. The promise of a male heir is certainly gone."

"Very well, My King. If there is nothing else, I will take my leave. There are patrols to inspect. The soldiers are getting younger and need more training."

Favian dismissed him with a friendly nod. "Yes, go. Go, Ludar. Put special attention on your guards that are watching the guilds and merchants."

Ludar began to speak, but the king cut him off. "And don't worry about me. You will best serve me by protecting my people."

"As you will, My King." Ludar's fist struck his chest three times, then he bowed, spun on his heels, and marched into the corridor. He made it look so simple, so fluidic—a soldier's soldier. Barely had the door closed when the smile came to his face. *Soon*, he thought. *So soon.*

28

FAVIAN'S SPEECH

After Favian announced his planned speech, Ludar returned to see the king.

He paced the room like a mother with a lost child. Paintings from the most gifted artisans decorated the walls and sculptures from the ancient masters adorned alcoves strategically placed throughout the room. "I don't like you doing this, My King. Something could go wrong."

"Nonsense! No one is going to try to kill me. Besides, the people have heard the rumors. If I don't show, they will assume I fear the worst."

"If you insist on going through with this then we should take more precautions. I will post guards along every street, and we will keep four full patrols around you at all times. And I want you to wear a suit of heavy mail."

Favian sighed. "Fine. Dress me in whatever you wish, but let us be on with it." The king flopped into a chair, resting himself.

Ludar had the king's mail brought for him, and while he waited, he gave his men orders. "Take extra patrols and disperse them into the crowds. Have them mingle, listen. Keep guards on every street along the procession and side streets too. Inspect stables, alleys, everything!"

The sergeant's fist pounded his chest three times. "Yes, Force Commander. Your will."

Ludar turned to Favian, still seated. "With your permission, Your Majesty, I'll go and inspect the preparations."

Favian brushed him away. "Go, please. I'll be ready shortly."

Cynamar sat on the bed while the valets dressed the king. "Father, I don't want you to go. If Force Commander Ludar is worried, there must be a reason."

Favian reached for a drink while they fussed over his wardrobe. "Nonsense, my dear. A king cannot be afraid to address his people."

She jumped off the bed, face flushed with anger. "If someone wants to kill you, you should be afraid."

"Ludar said he is concerned, yes, but I believe he is overreacting. I'm sure it's nothing more than talk and idle chatter. I intend to speak to my people, assure them that everything will be all right." Favian paced, shaking his head. "All of this talk about people with powers. It's got half the city frightened to death."

"And the other half fuel that fire, father. I know. Still, you should be more cautious."

Favian walked over, hugged his daughter and kissed her cheek. "I'll be well guarded, my dear. Now, get dressed. When the people see how beautiful you are they won't even listen to my speech."

"Is that your plan? For me to distract them so they don't know how bad it is?"

The king laughed. "And a good plan it is. Now, hurry. We don't want to be late."

"I'm never late, father. You know that."

Favian exited the palace surrounded by four patrols of guards with swords drawn. Four other patrols scouted the streets ahead of them and on the sides to ensure no traps awaited. Ludar walked at Favian's side. Cynamar would arrive a few moments later, escorted by a different set of guards. Ludar had insisted that they go separately in the unlikely event an attack did happen.

They arrived at the center square without incident and, after checking the surrounding buildings and the crowd, Ludar led the king toward the podium. Sykoran Guards stood in protective lines about the square, keeping a good distance between the king and the people.

Excitement grew when Cynamar arrived—always a favorite among the common folks—and once she got to her father's side he stepped up to the dais. People screamed for Cynamar. Young girls sat high atop their fathers' shoulders, craning their necks to get a glimpse of the princess. Some of the braver, or more eager ones, stood, balancing themselves precariously while they shouted and waved, hoping to draw Cynamar's attention.

Young men too, were not immune to the charms and beauty of the princess as they jostled and squeezed their way toward the front of the crowd. It wasn't every day that a common person could get a look at the princess. It took a few moments for the crowd to calm, then Favian began.

"Good people of Sykor, I wanted to speak with you today to allay any fears you might have regarding recent events in our city. There has been talk of people with powers, of unrest in the guard, even treason among some of our noble houses." Favian shook his head.

"These rumors have even reached the palace, where chambermaids and palace guards whisper stories in darkened corridors. I have heard them. Some gave me pause." Favian stood tall and leaned forward. "But I have faith in our Force Commander, and he has investigated the accusations. There was nothing of substance."

The king paused then let a smile light his face. "The men with powers were little more than bards capable of secreting a striker, thus giving the appearance of being able to produce fire at will. There were a few disgruntled guards, no more than at any other time, but we have 'suggested' they choose new occupations. Unfortunately, there was a treasonous noble family, one whose history in Sykor was as long as my own family's. They sought to undermine authority and were not an insignificant part in sparking many of these rumors. That family is no longer with us. We all know the penalty for treason."

Heads nodded throughout the crowd. No one liked a traitor. Favian waited, sipping on a drink provided to him by Ludar. When he deemed the time right, he proceeded. "But let's not dwell on what has happened before. We should look ahead to new days and better times. I have signed a new treaty with Genda, increasing our sea trade with them significantly. This will allow our merchants to ship goods directly from Khatara or our ports at the River's Edge."

The crowd cheered, but Favian held up his hands to quiet them. "This might be far off, but I have also negotiated with the Krovs, and they have agreed to let us build a road through the swamps just below the Pomandan border. This will let us reach Genda by land as well as sea."

Again the king had to stifle the crowd. "I have not forgotten our friends, the Pomandans. I have granted them passage through our lands so that they might trade with the Nyaurans or the Khatarans and not have to worry over road and trade taxes."

Favian noted the questioning looks on many of the faces. "Think of this, my people. If we let the Pomandans have free pass to trade, even though we won't collect taxes, we will benefit. They will stay at our inns, buy our food, enjoy our entertainment, and have their horses shoed by our blacksmiths. All of this and more will bring new business to you."

Before the crowd could begin the applause again, he continued. "Furthermore, I want to officially name my daughter, Cynamar, as heir to the throne."

The crowd reacted fervently, adoring Cynamar and not thinking about what kind of queen she'd make.

~

*M*ost in the crowd applauded and listened with selective ears, but not Talanvar. He watched the crowd, and he watched the merchants, and he watched the guards, especially Ludar.

Ludar looked not the least bit worried, strange that—when the city just had one assassination and now their king was giving a speech in public. Yet Ludar's eyes never searched the crowd, never checked with the other guards stationed throughout the courtyard.

Ludar wiped sweat from his brow and looked up to a building outside the courtyard. Talanvar glanced back but saw nothing. Then, he suddenly worried. Ludar wiped sweat from his brow!

For all that Talanvar despised the man, he was the consummate soldier. He would never break his stance during a ceremony to wipe sweat away! Not even if he stood in the flames of Chugarra?

Talanvar scanned the crowd again then the other guards and the building where Ludar had cast his gaze, but he saw nothing.

~

*F*rom atop a building across the square, the Ligarns watched the speech. "Remember to use a Pomandan arrow," Suk Won said.

Shatir shook her head. "All of this subterfuge. Why? If it were me, I would have walked up to him, held his eyes, and told him that in two days I would kill him. Then, I would have disappeared into the crowd, leaving him to worry about his death."

Suk Won laughed. "Perhaps that is why they put Jen Pal in charge of the karn and not you."

"Almost a shame to kill him," Triala said. "He seems different."

Bitterness dripped from Jen Pal's words. "He is a frail one."

"Besides," Shatir said, "the small gods want it done." She reached for the arrows that Jen Pal held, nocking one and laying the other next to her. She drew the string back slowly, sighting as she did. Then with one fluid motion, she reached the tension point and released. As soon as the string snapped, she nocked the second arrow and fired it.

The crowd was still cheering when the first arrow struck Favian in the throat, blood spewing all over Cynamar, Ludar too.

"Father!" She screamed, grabbing him just as the second arrow hit his chest. "No! By god, no!"

"Guards!" Ludar shouted, and a dozen men surrounded them.

"I've sent for a healer," one of them said.

Ludar cast a quick glance at Cynamar, then to the guard, shaking his head. "Close the city gates. Search everywhere. I want whoever did this found."

Guards raced through the city, rousing people, searching buildings, emptying merchants' carts. Some people wept, while others joined in the hunt.

"It was a Pomandan arrow," someone shouted. "They did this."

"Kill their king. That's what we should do."

Ludar knelt alongside his king, a consoling hand on Cynamar's shoulder. *Yes, good people, that is exactly what we should do.*

~

Talanvar was about to send some of his men to scout things when he heard the scream. "The king's been shot! Someone shot the king!"

Talanvar raced toward the rear of the crowd. He could do nothing to help the king—physicians and healers would do that, but he could try to find out who was responsible for this. Three of his men saw him rushing toward the gate, and they hurried outside to see if he needed them. "I think the shots came from that building," Talanvar yelled. "Search everything, all of you!" He started to turn, then called back. "Are you armed?"

"Are you dressed, My Lord?" Niel said.

Talanvar laughed despite the circumstances. "I'm putting out the word. Seal the city with eyes. We need to know who did this."

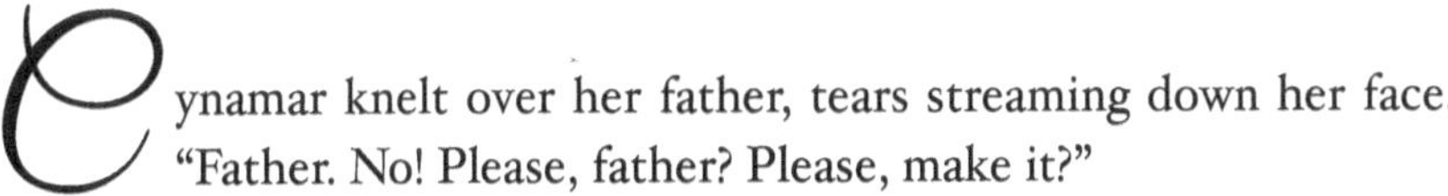

Cynamar knelt over her father, tears streaming down her face. "Father. No! Please, father? Please, make it?"

A healer pushed her aside, though gently, so he could work. "We haven't much time, Princess. There will be ample time for tears later, or for joy."

Ludar stood high on the balcony overlooking the courtyard, shouting orders to guards who appeared to be scurrying about like rats. "Search everywhere!" he shouted. "Anyone with a bow. Anyone from Pomanda. Anyone you do not know personally. I want to question them all." He knelt briefly to look at the king but saw the physician shake his head. Ludar nodded and stood.

"Hardik, take a full patrol and escort the Princess to her chambers. We cannot let any harm come to her."

At first, Cynamar was flattered by such attention at a time like this, but it suddenly struck her what Ludar was doing. *The king is dead! He is protecting his queen!*

More tears rolled down her cheeks, tears she could no longer control. *Father, dead! Me a queen!* "By all the merciful gods, where is that rat lover when I need him?"

Hardik turned at the sound of her voice. "Pardon, My Lady... I mean, Your Highness. Did you call?"

The address irked her. *How dare he!* she thought. Cynamar gave him a silent glare and a grim lip until he turned from her. Once inside the palace, they quickly reached her quarters. "I can manage from here, Patrol Leader. Tell Ludar I wish to speak with him later."

"At once, Your Highness." He snapped a three-fisted salute and began to hurry off, leaving four guards at the door.

Cynamar sat on the bed, then lay down. *How could this have happened? How could he be dead?* She kicked off her shoes, letting them slip to the floor as her head found the pillows. *How will I manage without father? How will Sykor manage without him?*

~

*T*he Ligarns climbed over the wall, lowered themselves, then made it across the moat the same way they had come in. Jen Pal turned west. "The small gods will soon control Sykor. Now we go to Pomanda."

"That was too easy,' Suk Won said.

Jen Pal nodded. "But after Pomanda our mission is to get the boy, and they say he is a small god himself. Besides, Black Death will be there," he said, and a glow came to his eyes.

29

PLANS TO RULE

Cynamar sat in the chair, but her fingers tapped nervously on the te cart. The people were already clamoring for war. Somehow it had been leaked that the Pomandans were to blame and now the populace demanded revenge. Cynamar, at first, experienced the same emotions—raise the army and destroy Pomanda! But caution was needed, and wisdom. She could ill afford to lead her people into a war with the Pomandans. *That may be just what they want.*

Why else murder the king? Surely not for trading routes! She stopped drumming her fingers long enough to form a thought. *Or would they?*

She shook her head to clear it. She needed help on decisions such as this. Ludar was all too ready to leap into war, and besides, she had not yet come to respect his counsel. His obeisance seemed to lay on a thin layer of silk, a very thin layer; and it caused her to wonder where his loyalties lay, if not with her.

"More te, Your Highness?" Hanna held the teapot ready to pour.

"Stop that nonsense, Hanna. If you call me that one more time I'll have you whipped." Cynamar rose from the chair and came to get her te, bare feet reflecting her pensive mood. She never could think with shoes on.

"Just like the royalty to do such a thing, whip one's loyal servant."

Cynamar laughed. It was a short laugh, but it was the first time since her father had died.

"You must be thinking, child. I see your shoes off a lot these days." Hanna rubbed her shoulders as Cynamar sipped her te. It was what she had done for her since she was a little girl.

"There is so much to think about, Hanna. So much that I know nothing of." Cynamar turned and embraced her. As Hanna hugged her the tears flowed again.

"Oh, Hanna! What am I to do? You're the only one I can trust. And we cannot run Sykor by ourselves."

Hanna let her cry out the tears. "Go on, child. It's not good to keep a tear inside you. Tears let out the poison, take away the hurt. You can't feel better till the last tear's gone."

Cynamar nodded as she let go of Hanna. "I know, 'A tear unwept is sorrow kept.'" Cynamar smiled. "All right, old teacher. Now that you have me cured and smiling, what are we to do?"

Hanna looked about the chambers, then went to the door and opened it. The guards were outside but resting against the wall. "The queen will be taking a rest. Make sure no one disturbs her." The tone of command equaled a force leader's. The guards nodded as she shut the door.

Hanna led Cynamar to the bed where they sat. "If one were to listen to gossip on the streets, my child, there is one who you might trust. One who has earned the respect of Sykor's people."

"Go on," Cynamar said. "You and I cannot do this alone, so I must trust someone. Who is it that my people trust so?"

Hanna looked about again, nervousness showing in her eyes. "He is someone who has earned powerful enemies by helping the people."

Cynamar's impatience flared. "Who is it, Hanna? You can tell me."

"Talanvar," she said. "Lord Talanvar."

Cynamar's eyes flared with curiosity. "Talanvar ... the mysterious Lord Talanvar." She smiled. "He seems to earn respect or enmity wherever he goes. I have heard that our Force Commander would like to have him mounted on his wall next to his wolf's head."

Hanna smiled broadly. "He'll never catch this wolf."

Cynamar rubbed her bare feet on the marble floor. The cold felt good. "Hanna, I think I must talk to him. Get word to Lord Talanvar that I would like a meeting, but be careful. Give the message to someone you can trust and make sure it is someone you see on a regular schedule in case Ludar has men following you."

Hanna bowed. "He will help you, My Lady. Talanvar is a wise man, and a good one."

When Hanna left, Cynamar plopped back down on the bed, muscles relaxed. *Now, if only I could find Wisp.*

30

TALANVAR

irk stood duty at the gate to Lord Talanvar's house, four armed guards at his side. Ever since King Favian had been killed, Lord Talanvar had insisted on guards at every entrance with more at the ready inside. A well-dressed man, a gentleman it seemed, approached the gate after completing the steep climb from the merchant's district.

"I have a message for Lord Talanvar," he said, and extended his hand.

Dirk noticed the seal of Queen Cynamar and gulped. "This is from the queen?"

The man nodded. "I'm instructed to wait for a response."

Dirk struggled with what to do. His orders were to let no one in the gate, but he knew Talanvar wasn't home yet. If the queen had instructed her messenger to wait, he'd do it, and Dirk didn't think Talanvar would want him waiting outside. He looked at him again, the starched white shirt, pressed coat with a long tail, and the shiny shoes. He decided to risk it.

"Lord Talanvar is not in, but you may come in and wait." He said it in his best manners, hoping it proved to be good enough.

The messenger hid his smile as he bowed. Lord Talanvar was known for his penchant to hire the underprivileged, and this one was trying his best. "I am honored by your graciousness," he said as he straightened himself.

Dirk opened the gate to let him enter. "Watch the gate," he told the guards. "I'll be back shortly."

Before long Talanvar returned and read the letter. "Please inform the queen I will be there as requested."

The messenger bowed again, then waited for Dirk to escort him to the gate.

~

*L*ord Talanvar tapped lightly on the door of the queen's house near the merchant district. Soon a servant opened the door to grant him entry.

He bowed. "Your Majesty. I am at your service."

Cynamar dismissed her servant; then, when he was gone, she walked toward the sofa. "Please, sit, Lord Talanvar."

He took a seat, waited through silence. "What can I do for you, My Queen?"

She hesitated, then looked around to ensure they were alone. "A friend of mine, a dear friend, once told me that if ever I was in dire trouble, I should call upon you." Cynamar bowed her head low in shame. "I hesitated to act, but ... I have no one else to turn to, and he said that somehow you would help."

Talanvar stayed quiet, waiting for more of an explanation.

"Actually, it was two friends. My former nursemaid, Hannah, also suggested I speak with you."

"And here we are," Talanvar said. "What is it I can help you with?"

"I don't know why I sent for you. Please forgive me, Lord Talanvar, you must think me mad. It's just …"

"Perhaps it would help if I knew who the man was who suggested we speak."

"I cannot tell you who, but he is a man I trust completely. A man I could never betray."

Talanvar saw that she wouldn't, or at least, she thought she wouldn't tell him. "If you can't tell me who suggested my name, then how can I be expected to give you aid."

"Can you not give me aid based on my need, and the fact that I am your queen?"

"Many serve another."

"How dare you say that!" Cynamar rose up with a haughtiness mindful of earlier, happier days.

"I dare because it's true, My Queen. If you don't want to hear the truth, then we have nothing further to discuss."

"You would serve this other before me?"

Talanvar bowed. "My Lady," he said and turned to leave.

"Wait."

He turned again with a sigh. "My Lady, we have nothing further to discuss. May I have your leave, please?"

"You would let Ludar steal the land that belongs to my family?"

Talanvar stood without a response.

"Well?" she asked.

Finally, his eyes caught hers and held her fixed. His raspy, gritty voice frightened her and forced her to take a step back. "My Lady, I will only ask one more time. Do you wish the truth, or do you wish me to discontinue this discussion?"

Cynamar held her head high, her pose regal as any queen. "I wish the truth."

"The truth, My Lady, is that you have already lost these lands. But the real truth, the truth that I know, that the people know, is that these lands are not yours and not your family's. These lands belong to the people. You kings and queens and nobles ... somewhere along the line, you forgot what it was all about. You forgot that the people entrusted you to govern these lands. They're not your lands, and they are not your people."

Talanvar paused to let her speak, but he noticed her lips clenched tightly together, and her eyes were afire with rage, and perhaps hurt. When she said nothing, he continued.

"If they choose to grant you respect and pay you sovereignty and obey you, it is because they *choose* to do so. But always remember that they can rise up at any time brandishing swords and staffs and hoes and shovels. And if enough of them have the will and the mind to do it, no matter how many soldiers are in your guard—if in fact you even control the guard—they would not be enough. It is a lesson late learned by many kings and queens. And one that will be learned forthwith by our friend Ludar."

"You call him a friend!" Cynamar spat.

Talanvar thought it an un-queenly thing to do. "He is no more friend to me than the rat is to anyone."

The princess smiled.

"What makes you wear a grin? Did something I say strike you as odd?"

"Nothing. It is just ... well, a friend I once knew always thought of himself as a friend of the rat."

Talanvar's smile was broad and genuine, stretching from ear to ear, and up to his eyes. "Then we do share a common acquaintance, My Lady, in all this world, I know of only one who adores the rat like this one."

"Then you do know him? You know he is—"

"Sh. Please don't speak his name. Yes, I know him. And suffice it to say that I have done favors for him, and he has done favors for me and that either one of us would risk life for the other, though not without due cause."

"How have you known him?"

"No more questions. Let's say that our discussion regarding our acquaintance is over for now. We have established his identity satisfactorily to both of us, now, let us go into how I might help you."

"You might help me get rid of Ludar," she said, her voice firm and resolved.

"My Lady, were it so easy as that. But, don't despair, I wasn't caught unaware. I have been caught unprepared by a sudden freeze, and I once suffered losses brought on by heavy rains, but I pride myself in having never been taken unaware by a shift in the nature of man. And I have never been duped by the likes of Ludar."

"You have had dealings with him before?"

Talanvar searched her almost as if she were a suspect in a crime. "You sent a message to me by way of a messenger, who delivered it to my young gatekeeper, a lad I hold in high esteem. His name is Dirk."

She nodded her acknowledgment.

"I have heard that you are a sensitive woman, that you have kind feelings toward the animals and the servants in the palace. At least as kind as a noble can be."

Cynamar recoiled slightly at the insult, and her eyebrows raised at the way he said it, but she almost smiled. As much as the man was crude, he impressed her with his thoroughness and his forthright manner of speaking. "I like to think so."

"Then considering your kindness, your servant must have told you that Dirk was missing his thumbs."

Cynamar's heartfelt emotion showed on her face. "Yes, he did. What happened to the dear?"

Talanvar ground the words like gravel rubbed on stone. "That, My Lady, was Ludar's work. He cut off his thumbs to uncover something about me."

Cynamar gasped, and her hands flew to her mouth as she screamed. "No! He couldn't. He wouldn't."

"He did. And from that day, I have sworn vengeance upon him. His life, from that day forward, was mine. It only remains to name the day and the time."

Excitement burned in Cynamar, even though the shock of what Ludar did to Dirk saddened her. "You have plans, then? What are we to do?"

Talanvar forced a deliberate smile. "We, are to do nothing, My Lady. I, however, have many plans, some of which await the return of our mutual acquaintance."

"He's coming back!" Her cheeks flushed red with the embarrassment of her exclamation.

"He'll return unless he's dead. And like the rat, that one is difficult to kill. It would take someone clever to bring about his demise. Very clever indeed."

"Clever like you?" she asked with a hint of sarcasm.

"My Lady bestows too many compliments. Though I consider myself the better of most men, noble and peasant alike, he is far and above any I've known. He's even more clever than he knows himself to be. It's something some men are born with, and he was born with more than the best of men. Every thought he thinks, every move he makes, is instinctively right. That, My Lady, is the mark of a true hero, and a hero he is, whether he knows it or not. He'll never admit it, but one day the people will know it too."

"How can you call him a hero? Please understand, I like him. I even have feelings for him, but to call a thief a hero is going too far."

Talanvar smiled his best smile, and his cunning green eyes flickered with delight. "You think like a queen and a noble, but that won't win the hearts of your people. If you are to learn how the people think, My Lady, come with me some day to the Dongrel or to River's Edge. I'll let your eyes see 'your people' and let your ears hear their plight. If you still wish to call them your people after that, I will be surprised for one of the few times in my life about the nature of people."

Talanvar's smile had turned down, and his eyes no longer held a shine. "You might think I have digressed, but I didn't stray too far. We were speaking of our mutual friend, and I told you how he was the hero. If you accept my offer to tour the Dongrel and River's Edge, there you will see why he is thought the hero. There you will learn why your guards never caught him, at least one reason. He keeps next to nothing of what he takes. For every hungry child in the Dongrel, he feeds four, and for every lad whose bare feet grow cold when autumn brings the dampness, he has the cobblers make ten pairs of shoes. He...arranges, for a few of the local inns to give food to any woman with child, and those women also get worn bedclothes. He calls them worn, but I've seen them, and there is not a frayed edge or a stain in the lot."

Talanvar's emotions had stirred, and his voice had grown passionate. "My Lady, this is a job that your father, 'may the gods accept him' should have done. This is a responsibility of the nobles too. But I challenge you to find me one who does anything but curse those so unfortunate."

Tears welled in Cynamar's eyes. "I'll go," she said. "I want to go with you to the Dongrel and to River's Edge. She cleared her eyes and found Talanvar's stare. "Tell me when we go, and what I need to do. I'm ready to help my people."

Talanvar held her gaze for a long time. "My Lady, if you're serious about this, if you truly wish to help, then I'll be at your side the entire way. Together we will put you firmly in control of Sykor."

Cynamar smiled at the response but feared the confrontations with Ludar. "What about—"

"We will do this first, then we will plan a course of action to deal with Ludar. Though I don't know how just you and I can do this."

Talanvar was silent for a moment, then he smiled. "On second thought, there's no need to worry. I suspect we will have more help than you imagine. You let me worry about that, and I will let you worry about being the best queen you can be."

Cynamar smiled warmly and clasped Talanvar's hand in hers. "I will await your word."

"It will be soon, My Queen, soon."

(31)

VALLAH

Camissa woke in a cold sweat. She had never paid much attention to dreams, but her mother had put great stock in them. Always talked about dreams and what they could mean. Tried to interpret them at every opportunity.

She recalled a specific instance of a pregnant woman who dreamed of an eagle dropping a fish from its talons. Camissa's mother swore that meant the woman would lose the baby. Her prediction had the mother worried to death.

When the child was born healthy, everyone except Camissa's mother was relieved. Ten years later, when the child died from an accident, Camissa's mother nodded her head and said, "It was just a matter of time."

Camissa thought about her dream, the one that came again last night. It was the third time she had the same dream, and each time it had shown more details.

She was in Sethia. Lukaan was there, and they were fighting him. Rahg was there, and she thought maybe Rhaven, but there were also three women. The fighting was mostly a blur, but the one clear scene depicted one of the women yelling to Rahg that she loved him—then that woman died.

She tried to imagine a scenario where it could be anyone but her— none of them worked. It certainly wouldn't have been Mikkellana or Aentarra who said that to Rahg. Not Aenaila either. That left only her. The sad thing was that they hadn't even been together, and here she was going to die for him.

Camissa vowed to set that straight soon. Very soon, she thought, a shiver rushing from head to toe.

She sat up, feet dangling off the side of the bed, and stretched while a yawn took hold. The bed was huge—twice the size of any she had slept in before—and so comfortable. She almost slid off the satin sheet, especially while wearing the night clothes Aentarra had given her. She had been too embarrassed to try them on until Aentarra left, but when she did, she felt good. Felt alive. Felt like making love.

Another shiver raced through her with that thought. She looked at her outfit, rubbed her hands over her breasts. Experienced a tingle. Perhaps tonight.

The marble floor felt cold, though refreshing, and it woke her with a start. A deep breath brought the smell of fresh bouquets, and as she made her way to the window, a songbird greeted her with an optimistic tune—a finch, she thought and smiled.

This was so unlike the city where urine and feces assaulted a person with each inhalation, and all of the sounds were undesirable ones. Camissa leaned on the railing and stared across a landscape of gardens, waterfalls, and beautiful, clean buildings. Even the streets were clean. How nice it would be just to stay.

After relaxing for a few moments, she dressed then headed to join the rest of them for the morning meal.

"About time you got here, lass. Think I'll let you fix your own meal today if you don't mind."

Tobias was his usual cheery self, sipping khaffe and puffing on a lit pipe with his legs kicked up on a table. "Haven't been here long, but I think I could come to like this place."

"I wouldn't think of asking you to move, Tobias. I know that old people find that difficult." She almost laughed, waiting for his rejoinder.

He coughed out some smoke, sitting up as he did. "Old! I might have a year or two on my bones, but that doesn't—" He stopped when he saw her laughing, then joined in himself. "Glad to see somebody besides me is in a good mood." He leaned back in the chair and returned to his original position.

Camissa had breakfast, chatted with Mikkellana and Tobias, then announced she was leaving and asked Rahg to join her.

"Where are we going, the library?"

"There, but elsewhere too. We'll investigate Vallah. I feel like learning new things today. Doing new things."

Rahg got up from the table and followed her. "I'll go. Maybe your good mood will strike me."

Aentarra had been sitting in a casual chair on a balcony overlooking the courtyard. "Remember what I told you. No one goes in the Council room."

"I know," Camissa said. "The one at the end of the Great Path."

"Other than that, you can go anywhere."

They walked the Great Path for a while, lounged in a few of the gardens, but they spent most of their time perusing old books at the library. Before long Camissa realized it was getting late. "Rahg, it's almost time for supper. We better be going."

After dinner, Camissa and Rahg walked back toward their rooms, taking a casual stroll through the courtyard while sipping on glasses of wine. Camissa wrapped her arm around his and pulled herself closer. "I love the sound of fountains, just hearing the running water is so relaxing."

"Wish we could stay here. Forget all about Lukaan and these prophecies. Stay here and hide."

"Just the two of us," she said.

Rahg squeezed her hand, took another sip of wine, then went and sat on one of the benches next to a large fountain. "I don't know why they ever left here." He looked around at the beauty, the serenity. "If I had this, I'd stay here forever."

"Lukaan knows where this is, Rahg." Mikkellana walked out an open doorway from the Great Path. "We all shared this at one time, so it wouldn't be safe here either. Trust me, if he gets free nowhere will be safe for long."

I knew somebody would spoil the night. He stood up. "That's my cue, Mikkellana. If I'm not safe here, then I better go to bed and dream. At least I'm safe in there."

As he and Camissa left, Mikkellana stared. "Don't be too sure of that either."

They walked the long corridor to their rooms, stopping when they reached Camissa's door. She reached for the handle, then turned and stared at Rahg. "You want to come in?"

He looked at her, stunned. "Yes, I do."

Rahg walked in, finishing the last of his wine and setting the glass on a table. "She didn't have to say that to us. Spoil our night."

Camissa took a seat in one of the plush chairs. "Mikkellana says what she feels is right, regardless of the situation."

"I guess," he said, then walked around the room as if he were lost. "I'm tired, Camissa. I think—"

"Stay here, Rahg."

"What?"

"I want you to stay." She moved to him, wrapped both arms around him then kissed his lips. "I want you to spend the night."

Rahg just stared. *Does she mean ...*

"Yes, that's exactly what I mean." Camissa started taking off her top as she walked to the door. She locked it, then turned back to face Rahg. "Take your clothes off and get in bed. I'm tired of waiting for you, Rahg Fal-Thera. I won't wait any longer."

Rahg nearly fell over, but he quickly recovered and started to unbutton his shirt. "Camissa, I ..."

"Don't talk. Just get in bed."

When Rahg looked over at her, she was climbing under the sheets, naked. *By god, she's beautiful!* He finished undressing, then climbed in with her. Rahg leaned over, gently caressing her, running his fingertips up her legs, then around her bottom, then up her side.

Goosebumps chased away a shiver and Camissa laughed. "I love you, Rahg."

He kissed her on the nose, gently. Kissed her lips, short and sweet. "I love you, Camissa. I've been waiting a long time to do this."

"Then you should have done it sooner," she said, and pulled him on top of her.

The morning came early, but Rahg and Camissa greeted it with smiles. "It's going to be tough to sleep apart after this."

Camissa smiled at him. "There's no need to. Who will be offended?"

Rahg's face went blank as if a realization had just hit him. "You're right! Who cares but us?" He started to get out of bed, but Camissa grabbed him and pulled him back.

"Not so soon, lover. I'm still hungry."

He laughed, pulled the sheets up over them, and started kissing his way down her neck.

By mid-morning, Rahg and Camissa made their way to the courtyard, joining Aentarra, Rhaven, and Tobias. Aentarra greeted them with a warm voice. "I see some of us slept better than others."

Rahg's face flushed. "I had a very good sleep."

"So I see," she said. "And you, Camissa? Did you sleep as well as Rahg?"

"Even better."

Aentarra laughed. "Yes, I bet you did. Comfortable beds will do that—make you sleep soundly, I mean."

"Where's Mikkellana? Rahg asked, desperate to change the course of the conversation.

"Went somewhere to check on something. That's what my sister does best."

Camissa laughed aloud. If she weren't so afraid of Aentarra, she thought she could like her. She had a good sense of humor. Problem was, Camissa never knew when the other side of her would show, like on the ship in Entiria, when Aentarra nearly killed her.

"Don't laugh, girl. You stay with Mikkellana long enough, and you'll see what I mean."

"Did you build this city?" Rahg asked.

Aentarra shook her head. "It was here when we came. We have no idea who built it, or why."

Rahg looked up at the towering peaks of the White Mountains that surrounded the city. "How could they even get here? Those mountains—"

"Precisely. No one could get here unless they could shift, like us. But we have never found anyone else here who had powers, and as I said, it was here when we arrived."

"There must have been others here with powers," Rahg said. "Look at Wisp and Camissa. And me and Darstan. We all have powers."

Aentarra shook her head, even more bewildered. "Camissa, it's a wonder you got him to bed last night. The boy is ..."

Rahg's face reddened. "What are you saying, Aentarra? Camissa and I ... we didn't ..."

"For god's sake, boy. Everybody but the frogs knows you slept together last night. You couldn't hide that look on your face if you wore a mask."

Camissa had to cover her mouth to hide her laughter, but Rahg just stared.

Suddenly, he started laughing too. I guess Camissa was right. It's our business.

The air shimmered, and a rift opened, Mikkellana stepping through. "Sykor is in chaos. The king has been assassinated, and the guards are taking over the city."

"Who's behind it?"

"I'm sure you can guess, Aentarra. It's some pawn of Lukaan's."

"Are we going there?" Rahg asked.

"Pomanda," Aentarra said. "We need to go where he'll strike next."

Mikkellana scoffed. "You don't know that. It might be Khatara or even Genda."

"It's Pomanda. I"m sure of it. He'll want to poke that rivalry that exists between countries that share borders."

"Then that's where we set the bait," Mikkellana said. "All right. We leave in the morning. No sense going there tonight and having to find a room." She looked at Rahg. "You better get some sleep."

Rahg and Camissa left, turning down the corridor toward their rooms while Tobias and Rhaven headed in the other direction. As soon as the door closed, Mikkellana spun toward Aentarra. "I went to Council Chambers. Ghruehne and Sendra had been there."

Aentarra strolled about the room, straightening things. "I suspected as much. They wouldn't come here and not inspect everything."

"If they were there, they saw. Now they know there are only two of us."

"That is unfortunate, but it might give them the courage to face us."

Mikkellana stared at her. "That's how you are getting your strength, isn't it? You kept them alive with those Slicers, and stole their energy."

Mikkellana shook her head. "Suppose they suspect as much, suppose they—"

"What can they do? If they try to touch the Slicers, they'll regret it." Aentarra smiled. "I'm sure you already knew that though."

"How do they work? What—"

A wagging finger greeted her questions. "You should have paid more attention to father," she said, and moved toward the door. "Anyway, I believe Pomanda is the last we'll see of Ghruehne and Sendra. I intend to kill them."

"Pack some humility and caution before you go, sister. Remember, it wasn't curiosity that killed the fabled cat—it was overconfidence."

Aentarra sighed. "Yet another vice I have." She opened the door and stepped into the corridor. "Goodnight, sister. Sweet dreams."

POMANDAN POLITICS

A lot of traffic flowed in and out of Pomanda, and all freely, with no checkpoints or guard stations to stop anyone. Ghruehne, disguised as a prosperous merchant, and guarded by six mercenaries, traveled with Sendra posing as his wife.

He led a cart laden with goods onto the main street leading to the merchant district where he made arrangements for a private stable to store his goods, then left three of the men to guard it as he began a quest to find the best accommodations. Everyone they asked suggested the Dead Man's Inn as the premier establishment in Pomanda.

Ghruehne led the way as they exited the merchant district and entered the wealthier section of the city. They climbed the steep hill leading to the inn, then up the winding stone walk, decorated with flowers from all over the countryside: crocuses, moonglows, and tulips the predominant ones.

"If it is as nice inside, we will at least be comfortable," Sendra said.

A stiff, haughty man, nattily dressed hurried down the walk to greet them. He wore a fine gray coat over a shirt as white and as starched as himself. Shiny silver buttons ran from his belly to his neck and seemed to push his chin up a notch.

"I am Briston. Welcome to the Inn," he said, in a tone and with emphasis, which implied there may be only one inn in the entire city. He bowed as he greeted them in a presumptuous manner as if all patrons must claim royalty somewhere along the line. "Will you be staying with us for long?"

Sendra's smile nearly cracked her face, but she did it with the grace of an actor in a troupe performing for the king. "I'm afraid to say we will. Business will keep us here for an indeterminate period, though if the inn is as pleasant as you portray ... perhaps it will not be so tedious."

"Follow me," Briston said, and whirled as if he were a ballerina. "Before you leave, you will be begging your acquaintances to come for a visit." He led them up the walkway at the same brisk pace, with his head tilted and his back as straight as a new fencepost.

The inn smelled fresh, but with an inviting hint of garlic that wafted from the kitchens, permeating the air.

Sendra's soft leather boots met the white marble floors in near silence, but she gasped when she saw the sweeping blackthorn staircase, her left hand grabbing Ghruehne's arm as if they were tourists new to the city. "How beautiful!"

Briston stopped at a large walnut desk situated between two marble pillars. "Our finest rooms are on the first floor surrounding the lobby. And—"

"We would like privacy," Ghruehne said, and with more gruff than he intended.

Briston raised his eyebrows as he looked up at him. "Perhaps our fourth floor then. The rooms are equivalent, but they are much quieter."

Sendra answered before Ghruehne had a chance to insult someone. "That would do fine. One at the end of a corridor would suit us best."

Briston led them up the steps, then down a long corridor with plush carpeting. "This is one of our best. Away from busy servants and prying eyes."

He showed them into a spacious room, bowed his way out the door and back down the hall. Once gone, Ghruehne dropped the guise and instructed one of his guards.

"Tell him we are here."

The guard snapped to attention. "Immediately, My Lord."

Sendra let go of her guise as well, sighing. "And make sure he knows we have little patience for tardiness." As soon as the men departed, Sendra turned and glared at Ghruehne. "Why did you only get one room?"

The lecherous smile popped onto Ghruehne's face. "We are supposed to be husband and wife, remember?"

"You could have said the other was for our guards."

"No one would do that. The guards would stay in the stable or at another inn."

"Then let them think we are foolish Khatarans who squander money. Not a bad image to have anyway."

Ghruehne sat on the bed, removing his boots as he did.

Sendra opened her traveling bag, placing some of her clothes in a bureau, others in the closet. "I hope you like the chair, Ghruehne, because that will be your bed tonight, and every night until we get another room."

She smiled at the look on his face, then quickly answered a knock on the door—khaffe, served with a small dessert. "Thank you," she said to the servant, then to the guard, "Let us know when he comes."

Soon afterward another knock alerted them that the visitor had arrived. Ghruehne disguised himself then opened the door, stepping back to welcome his guest. "A fine evening to meet new friends."

Ghruehne wasted no time in greeting him with the first part of the code. He had never met the man, all he knew was a particular nobleman, high up in Pomandan society was supposed to meet him. Perhaps help.

"It is a fine evening, but one has to be careful of who their friends are these days—what with the talk of treason running rampant."

The response was perfect. "It's true. I recently heard of a mishap in Sykor."

Ghruehne smiled while he offered the man a drink. "Seems the Sykorans have blamed Pomanda." That completed the code.

The man nodded, accepted the drink, a glass of Pomanda's finest wine, then took a chair, settling comfortably into thick cushions covered with a dark floral print. He looked to Ghruehne but cast a suspicious glance at Sendra. "I presume whatever we discuss is safe among the three of us."

"As safe as if it were your own thoughts," Sendra said, and kicked off her shoes. She walked toward the nobleman, her feet treading softly across Farizi carpet, the finest in all the lands.

"I was told there would be a ... price, shall we say, for my cooperation."

Ghruehne sipped his drink, nodded, then walked over and set his glass on a fine mahogany table while he lit a candle standing tall at each end. "With every gift, there is always a reciprocal gesture."

"And what, might I ask is the gift?"

Ghruehne waved his hand toward Sendra. "The gift is from you to us," she said. "We will tell you when and how, but you will support our interests in matters dealing with Pomanda's coming war with Sykor."

The man jumped to his feet. "Support for a cause and outright treason are different matters. My associates told me nothing of this. The king is opposed to war, and I will have—"

A very fine line of Fire shot from Sendra's finger, boring into his leg just above the knee. He screamed, collapsing while he grabbed the chair for support. "What!"

Ghruehne reached and pulled him up, abandoning his Illusion at the same time. No need to waste the effort now.

The noble rose, staring at Ghruehne's face, gawking at the scar that marred him, a deep scar that ran from his ear to his eye, causing that left eye to twitch as he talked. The noble looked away then back again, and when he did, he saw fire dancing in the man's eyes. Either fear or new-found wisdom turned his head.

He shook, trembled. And his insides churned like a stew about to boil over, the chunks were inside of him now, bubbling up his throat, threatening to erupt. "What is it that you want?"

"Much better," Sendra said, and led him back to the chair. "As we said before, we will need your support. Nothing more. No blood. Not your first born."

He stared at Ghruehne, then Sendra. "And the ... reciprocal ...?"

Sendra laughed. "Even when fear has control, greed finds a way in doesn't it?" She laughed some more, straightening her hair as she did. "Fear not, dear friend. Work with us and your friends will likely be calling you Your Majesty before long."

The nobleman smiled now. "Then perhaps we should get to the details."

"Of course we should." Sendra pulled her chair closer and sat next to him.

They spoke long into the night, reviewing details of plans and alternate plans, as well as means of communicating with each other so as not to arouse suspicion. Simple letters left for each other at the Dead Man's Inn seemed to offer the most efficient, as well as the safest, way, so they opted for that. After he left, Sendra turned to Ghruehne. "How are we going to instigate this war between Sykor and Pomanda?"

"I already started. Sykoran troops will be attacking Pomandan outposts all along the border within days."

Sendra smiled, tickling the scar on her neck. "Perhaps I spoke hastily earlier today. There might be room in the bed for you after all. Then you can show me more of your strategy."

● 33

A KING'S DEMAND

The messenger woke Preman early, far too early for breakfast. Something was wrong.

"Special envoy from the king," he said. "Urgent."

Preman dressed quickly, then rushed to the foyer where the man waited. "Yes, what is it?"

The messenger stood to attention, stiff-backed and mute, his outstretched hand holding a written message.

Preman grabbed it, opened it.

"What is it, dear?"

His wife's voice echoed in the foyer, and he heard the swishing of her dress as she made her way toward him. How she could already be dressed at this time of the morning defied logic—his logic anyway. "Message from the king. He needs the Council for a meeting right away." He turned to the messenger. "Tell him I'll be there."

The man departed without another word.

When Preman arrived at the council meeting, Varga, Ciro, and four of the other five were already there, as was the king. The only one missing was Tempra, and footsteps in the hall sounded like his gait.

Preman eyed them suspiciously. They all had equal votes, but the king and the three oldest noble families—Preman's, Varga's, and Ciro's—carried the weight. The others would follow one or the other of them. As he paced the floor of the chambers, King Pendar wore a serious face. War was a serious business.

"I think we should get right to it," the king said. A servant handed him khaffe which he graciously accepted, then he nodded to each of the nobles. "Gentlemen, cast a vote to see where we stand." He smiled. "Unless that has been done already."

"War," Varga said, outspoken as always. "They have already attacked us. We have no recourse." Varga was one of those men whose face truly belied his personality. He had a round, almost cherubic face spotted with a dainty nose and soft blue eyes no larger than small buttons. His ears seemed glued to his head, and blush-red cheeks turned into a rounded chin, not one to inspire confidence.

Underneath the soft exterior though, lay Varga the man, a bitter, ruthless, vindictive man whose ambitions, driven by impressive political skills, had raised his family to the second highest in the kingdom, and anyone who knew him understood full well that he had no intentions of stopping there.

Preman was a short, stocky man, with a barrel chest and a long gait. His hair was like a shock of wheat wetted down and slicked back. He shook his head as he paced, and his long, very-strong, Pomandan nose seemed to wag as he did. "We can't be certain it was Sykor. All we know is that someone attacked our troops."

"War," Ciro said. "For once I side with Varga."

"Peace," Preman said, his fist on the table creating a resounding echo throughout the room. He hoped his vote to carry weight.

"Peace," the king said.

Three of the remaining five voted for peace, leaving the decision in their favor.

"This is nonsense!" Varga said. "Sykor is attacking our outposts, and we do nothing. If we don't declare war, at least retaliate." Fire burned inside of Varga. Perhaps it was what put the blush in his cheeks.

"I intend to send a message to Sykor. We'll demand reparations and an end to all hostilities."

A lot of arguing followed, none of it getting them anywhere. Finally, Preman asked for the floor. "Perhaps we should be more firm, My King." He broke slightly from his strict allegiance to the Crown. "A show of force, perhaps, even if we do not engage them."

Everyone except Varga agreed with Preman's proposal. He had wisely taken a middle ground, soothing the ones who wanted war—with the exception of Varga—while not offending those who sought peace. After all, who could object to a mere show of force? Varga's objections were soon overruled, and they adopted Preman's proposal as policy. Refreshments followed, then they adjourned for the day.

Ghruehne picked up the message at the Dead Man's Inn, reading it even before he went to the room.

King Pendar voted for peace, and the Council approved.

Voted peace, did he? We will see about that. He got paper and a pen from Briston, scrawled out a response, and put into the box for immediate delivery. Sendra joined him soon afterward, and they ate supper in the dining hall. He had come to enjoy the Dead Man's Inn. Despite its drawbacks, the comforts were undeniable.

After dinner, Ghruehne and Sendra went for a walk, a long walk up the Corrina Tumal, the Road of Riches, which led to the top of the hill.

An ancient cobblestone street twisted a path toward the top, lined with trees boasting hundreds of years and mansions that hid behind them slightly older. The houses seemed to get bigger as the road neared the top—Cima del Mondo—it was called, and it was the highest point in Pomanda, and it offered a breathtaking view of the city from all angles.

"Do they know to meet us here?"

"They were told."

"We are already here." A dark hooded figure stepped from behind a bush, his steps as silent as a still wind.

"Jen Pal?"

The Ligarn bowed, a simple nod of the head. His sweeping arm brought out Shatir, Triala and Suk Won. "We have been waiting."

Ghruehne gritted his teeth, restrained himself. He despised these Ligarns and their smug ways. "You did well in Sykor. Let us hope you can repeat your efforts here."

As one they all nodded. "It will be done," Jen Pal said. "When?"

"Immediately, and afterward, find the boy."

"Our hearts are eager, My Lord." He looked to Sendra, bowed a little lower. "My Lady," he said, then they all left as silently as they had come.

~

*K*ing Pendar finished his evening meal, sipped on a glass of Pomandan wine, and reflected on the day. It had been a good day overall. Sykor presented some problems, perhaps serious ones, but he felt it was possibly a misunderstanding. Why would they want a war with Pomanda?

Pendar shook his head. They wouldn't. It made no sense. He hoped the solution Preman proposed would suffice, but if not it bought them time, and at least they weren't going to war.

He set the wine down, took a short walk then a relaxing bath. He enjoyed baths, particularly at the end of a trying day. Soft towels soaked up the water then he dressed in undergarments and a heavy robe. He read for a while—a story about the early days of Pomanda—snuffed out the candles, then lay down to sleep, dreaming of peace.

~

Jen Pal led them through the shadows leading up to the king's courtyard. They scaled the wall surrounding the palace with no trouble, then made their way to a spot below the king's bedroom. Jen Pal pointed to the window, and Suk Won nodded. He handed Triala his staff then climbed the stone wall using the joints for finger holds and protruding stone faces for toeholds. At the top, he slipped into the window, silent, then crept to the king's bed.

A thin sliver of steel—a garrote—the Ligarns called it, was pulled from a hiding spot in his shirt. He grasped the padded rings at each end. Suk Won slipped the garrote over the king's head, down to his neck, then yanked it tight, crossing his hands behind the head.

Four short gasps, a spray of blood from the neck, and it was over. Pomanda would need a new king in the morning. Suk Won cleaned the garrote on the bedclothes and crept out the way he entered.

He nodded to Jen Pal when he hit the ground, then they all left as silently as they had entered. Before long they were on the road to Sykor, searching for a suitable spot to wait. Sooner or later the boy would come along this road. And Black Death would be with him.

~

"The king is dead!" Shouts rang through the poor districts first; they always seemed to, despite an attempt to keep things secret. Rumors and truths alike were often spread by maids and servants working at the palace. Soon after though, the richest districts heard the news, as it now reverberated through the lobby of the Dead Man's Inn. "The king is dead."

Briston shot up from his desk, mouth agape. "Dead? The king?" His hand covered his mouth as he rushed to give instructions to members of his staff. Patrons must be told at once, of course. Many were staunch supporters of the king or the former king. What would happen now?

Ghruehne heard the news and smiled at Sendra, whispering. "No wonder Lukaan likes the Ligarns so much. They are an efficient group."

She continued eating her melon, her smile response enough.

Briston rushed by, stopped and backed up as if an afterthought. "Have you heard the news? The king is dead!"

"We just now heard," Sendra said. "What happened?"

Briston leaned in close, his hand cupped around one side of his mouth. "Murder! And while he was in his bed." He stood, looked around. "It reeks of someone in the palace," he said, then made his apologies and hurried off.

34

A GENDAN WELCOME

The docks were always busy on good sailing days in Genda, ships coming in and going out of the harbor on a regular basis. It was a day as always when one of the men loading goods stopped, staring out to sea. "Petey, get over here. Unless my eyes have gone bad, I do believe that's the Sea Skate."

Petey stared, shielding his eyes from the sun, then he stood atop the crates they were loading to get a better view. "It is, Marco. It's her."

"Lock up the vidda!" Marco yelled. "Old Crazy's comin' home."

Word spread throughout town like a wildfire on the Nyauran Plains, and before the Sea Skate docked several hundred men stood to greet her—more than a few women too. Wild speculation about where he'd been and what he'd found raced around the dock then back again, and by the time it got to where it had started it couldn't be recognized as the same.

"Here comes Old Crazy," someone yelled, and the crowd roared its approval, granting Sennar a hero's welcome.

Water lapped at the ship's hull as Sennar walked down the plank to come ashore. Silence fell upon the people in the front row, and then spread back through the crowd as he drew nearer.

"Look at his face!" a woman yelled.

"It can't be," another said.

Sennar eyed each of them as he passed by, grasping a hand now and then to shake. Nodding his head, he breathed deep, smiled.

Genda was a fisherman's town, and the smell of fish was everywhere—in the taverns, the houses, the churches, and in every breath of air. Others might find it repulsive but not Sennar. He had grown up on fish, could string a hook when he was three years old and plot a course before he could read—and that was when he was nine.

There were days—many of them—when he had nothing but fish to eat, morning to night. Despite that, he'd take a meal of fish over most anything else. He closed his eyes, tilted his head back, and breathed as deep as he could, taking it all in: the haddock, halibut, grouper, and even the famed Gendan conk fish, which some considered good for nothing. It's good to be home.

He stopped about halfway through and turned to face the crowd, but before he opened his mouth, they peppered him with questions.

"Where have ya' been?"

"Forget that. How'd your face get fixed?"

Sennar leaned toward the man who threw that last question. He got close enough to smell the vidda on his breath. "Fixed? Lad, yer talkin' about my face as if I was a broken mast."

The man stepped back, bringing a laugh from Sennar. "If I told ya' I had to fight demons would ya' believe me?" He shook his head. "Rightly not. And you'd no more believe the tale I'd have to tell about this face."

Half a dozen people in the crowd hollered out. "What happened, Sennar? Tell us."

He looked them over before he started, knowing the truth wouldn't be good enough. "Was one of the gods—or demons—don't know which, who did this."

Fishermen leaned toward being a cynical lot, and most Gendans didn't stray from that mold.

"Why would they do that? What did you do for them?"

Sennar scratched the stubble on his chin. "Why? Good question. But they must have seen my pretty face under all that mess. Didn't want to be cruel and keep the rest of the women from enjoyin' me."

Laughter echoed off empty hulls. "Go on. Laugh. But I see a few of the men already sneakin' off, goin' home to make sure they take care of business before their wives hear about Old Crazy bein' back. And fixed too."

Three or four men had left the crowd, heading away from the dock. Sennar called to them. "Better lock the doors, lads. And keep those keys with ya'. Word will soon be out that Old Crazy's back, and he's got himself a pretty face."

The crowd exploded into laughter, many in the front row rushing up to greet him and offer their congratulations. "Well, ya' did it. Went through the Eternal Sea when no one said it could be done."

He nodded. "That I did, lad."

"Will ya' be goin' back, Sennar? I'll sail with ya' this time."

"What did you find?" more yelled.

Some scattered crates lay five paces away, and Sennar walked to them stacking six into a small pyramid, three crates high, then he climbed atop them.

Captain Jacopo Sennaro stared at the crowd, grabbing each one with his steely gaze. "I found dreams, lads. Treasures beyond your dreams. And women so beautiful they took my breath away. Long silky legs and a backside that ... well, let's just say you've never seen one like it."

Most in the crowd brushed off his tales, but a few listened intently. Someone from near the back row yelled loudly. "Tell us the truth. What's out there?"

Sennar's face no longer hurt when he smiled, didn't feel like it would crack. He let the smile linger, stayed silent long enough for them to calm down. "The truth you say. All right, lads, here it is, but the truth's not near as much fun as the tales I was gonna' tell ya." A heavy sigh firmed his resolve. 'Truth is there is no gold. No silver. No jewels."

"How about them ladies with the—"

He laughed. "Might be one or two of them, lad, but they're no different than what you've got at home. A haddock from Genda tastes about the same as one from the other side of the world."

Another pause stilled them again. "There is a land out there with good friendly people in it. And they're about as eager as we are to do some trade." He stifled them again before it got carried away. "Problem is when we were there, a Banished One got loose. Came there to kill a young lad who traveled with us."

"Banished One! There's no such thing."

Sennar shook his head. "I'd have said the same thing six months ago. Would have cursed ya' and spat in your face too." He raised his hand. "But I've seen it. I was there." He climbed down from the crates and walked into the crowd, pointing to his face. "Look at this face! Look at my hand." He grabbed hold of Pietro, an older man from the warehouse district. "You remember my face, Pietro. You were there the night the ship caught fire."

When the old man nodded, Sennar went on. "The lady who fixed my face had a sister; it was her that killed the Banished One. Mikkellana healed me. Aentarra killed the Banished One."

The smile had long since vanished, but Sennar's intensity had not. He stared through the crowd, holding up his hand as proof. "One Banished One is dead, but the time is comin' when all of them might get loose. Even Lukaan, and if that happens, we're all doomed."

"What are ya' tellin' us this for? What can we do?"

"We can raise a navy. Put sail with a force that can control the sea. Mikkellana told me there was war headin' our way. They'll want to control the sea so they can get from Jattan Kir all the way here and anywhere in between."

He made his way back toward his makeshift pulpit. "We can't let them do it. Got to stop it."

"How? We got no sea captains. Just fishermen."

Murmurs ran through the crowd, most agreeing with the man. "Can't fight Sykor. Certainly not Khatara."

Sennar was back atop his crate. A loud, shrill whistle caught their attention. "Guess I almost lied when I said I didn't find nothin' out there. Fact is, lads, I did."

A shifty grin took the place of his frown. "I found the best sea captains we could hope for, and a good start on crews to man the ships, too." Everyone was focused on Sennar now.

"Malakai," he said. "I found the Sword of the Sea."

"He's dead!" someone yelled.

"Not no more. Sea spit him back up. Guess he was too mean." Sennar laughed.

"I know he's dead," a young sailor said over the din.

"Well, if he's dead, that'll be good. What could be better than havin' a ghost command yer fleet?"

"Where is he?" one of the skeptics asked.

Sennar stared at him until he broke. "Ought to be here in two days, assuming he got my winds. And not just him but most of his men too."

35

RETURN TO THE HALL

Aentarra opened the doors leading to the Hall of Echoes and let the sounds of an eternity assault her ears. A conversation between Mikkellana and Xanthes caught her attention; she remembered it from a thousand seasons past, when the two of them had argued over Xanthes' attention to Kiris, though why he would ever cast a second glance at her puzzled Aentarra. Kiris was no more than a beanpole with hair.

Other conversations, or bits and pieces of them, floated by; some she recognized, others not. She enjoyed her visits to the Hall ... it was like eavesdropping, but when the other parties knew you would be.

There was another reason she came, a more important reason. Once before, purely by accident, she had heard the remnants of a discussion —the voices were barely whispers, indicating the event had taken place long, long ago, probably before Aentarra had even come to these lands. She had figured out the workings of the Hall of Echoes—at least some of it. The more recent a conversation took place, the stronger the resonance, even if it had been spoken in a hushed voice.

It was a particular conversation she had come to search for. The voice could barely be heard, but she had managed to make out a few words and something about it intrigued her.

Never enter ... Beware of ... She is the danger. She is ...

The whispered sounds were so faint, so light that they seemed to bounce across the room. Aentarra only caught brief parts of the conversation, though even with that she sensed it sparked with energy. Frustrated, she walked toward the doors and into the corridor.

She knew the voices didn't belong to anyone she was familiar with, and that brought to mind the Library and the entire city of Vallah. What a mystery that was. Who had built it and why? Why so far away from everything else, and how did it stay warm and pleasant when surrounded by bitter cold? And where had they gone, these people who had built Vallah?

Certainly, the puny mortals had not chased them from here. She doubted if the mortals could even find their way to Vallah, not through the Great White Mountains. The puzzles ate at her as her boots slapped noisily along the Great Path.

She intended to figure out the mystery of this hall, no matter what.

36

GOING HOME

Aenaila took Darstan and Wisp to get Adju, who was so happy to see them she thought he would burst. He ran and wrapped his arms around Wisp, hugging him, then raced to Darstan and her.

"I knew you would come back. I knew you would never leave me."

"Of course I wouldn't leave you, you little rat. You should know that by now." Wisp hugged him again. "We do need to get ready though, Adju, we're going home."

He looked up at them with huge brown eyes. "To Khatara?"

Wisp smiled. "Yes, to Khatara, but we're going to have to go to Sykor to find Takar."

"I can't wait to see the big sergeant again," Adju said. "I liked him." Adju broke away from Wisp and rushed toward his room. "I will get ready now."

Jago came over, shook hands with Wisp and Darstan then greeted Aenaila with a hug.

She held him tightly, whispering as she did. "We lost Mirana, and she was carrying Black Wolf's baby."

Jago walked over, a somber expression covering his face. "Darstan, I am sorry to hear about Mirana. She was one of my most dear friends."

Adju raced back into the room, a sack with his clothes and possessions slung over his shoulder. "I'm ready."

Aenaila laughed. "There was no need to rush, little one. I first have to have Jago send a ship for us. We can't shift to the island with nothing there."

"I'll get it done, Aenaila."

"I'm going for a walk," Darstan said.

"Where?"

"Just out. Through the city."

Aenaila eyed him suspiciously. "I didn't know you were so fond of Cartena, but if you want to walk, I will gladly accompany you." She grabbed his arm, tugging him along. "Come on."

He went with her to the door, then turned. "I want to go alone, Aenaila." He gulped, fighting emotions.

Now she understood. "Where you and Mirana went?"

He nodded.

"Go on, then. We're in no hurry. We have to wait for Jago to get a ship to the island, and that will take seven days or more."

He started to leave, and she ran after him. "Darstan!" She grabbed his arm, stared into his eyes. "No matter what, you always have that time together. She loved you, you know. Loved you more than anything."

He fought back tears. "She told you that?"

Aenaila nodded. "The night she told me she was pregnant, though I didn't need to hear the words. It had been obvious to me for a long time."

A long silence ensued, and as he lost the battle of restraint, he turned and walked toward the city. "I'll be back later."

"Come to my parent's house," she said.

A few people nodded to him, many addressed him by name, calling him BlackWolf, and some begged for him to hold their babies, heal their wounds. News had spread fast. Tobias always said news traveled on the wings of crows, but it seemed even faster here.

He finally made his way to a small plaza that had been a favorite of theirs. A pastry shop sat in the corner tucked neatly there just like the owner's goods. Darstan walked in, ordered his favorite fruit-filled tart and a khaffe.

The owner bowed to him as if he were royalty. King Marro didn't get this kind of treatment in Cartena. "It is good to see you again, BlackWolf."

Darstan smiled. He couldn't remember the man's name.

"Giacomo."

"What?" Darstan asked.

"My name is Giacomo," he said. "I wanted to save you the embarrassment in case you forgot. Not that you should remember my name, but I did it anyway."

Can he read my mind? Wouldn't be surprised. "Well, Giacomo, you happen to be right. I did forget. But I won't forget again." He pulled out some coins to pay, but Giacomo waved him off, indignant.

"You cannot pay for anything in my shop."

Darstan looked at him in surprise. "You let me pay before."

"That was before ... just before," he said.

"Giacomo, that doesn't make sense. Here, take the money." Darstan held out his hand, but Giacomo pulled away as if he had poison.

"No! Please, Black Wolf. You would dishonor me. Now take your pastry and your khaffe and sit outside where you can enjoy it."

Giacomo held out a pastry, very small and smothered in cinnamon with a thin slice of apple layered over the top. "I am sorry about Mirana. This was her favorite. Please take it. Share it with her one more time." He nodded his head toward the plaza. "Over there, by the fountain where you always sat. It will be good for you."

"All right, you convinced me." He reached over the counter and grabbed his hand, shaking it. "You're a good man, Giacomo, and a great baker. Thank you for your kindness."

Darstan walked to the fountain, a small one seldom visited; in fact, he and Mirana had often been the only ones sitting at it. There was a sculpture of a mother dolphin with a young baby at her side, both captured in mid-stream of a jump from the water.

He always liked it because it looked so real as if the sculptor had plucked them out of the sea and put them in this fountain, somehow preserving them in real life. He reached out, stroked the dolphin's head, feeling a little foolish as he did, but it felt good. Brought back memories of time spent with Mirana. All the things they had done together.

A smile popped on his face as he recalled the night she had taken off her shoes and gotten in the fountain. Threatened to take off her pants too, if he didn't get in with her. Darstan laughed aloud. She'd have done it.

Memories flooded him now, crowded his mind, confused him. Mirana swimming in the sea. Mirana laughing. Mirana and he making love. Mirana at the pass. Mirana being crushed by the boulders! Then a dramatic switch.

Rahg using his shield to topple the rocks. Rahg killing her. Killing her!

Suddenly he heard the screams and came to. Flames consumed the fountain; the dolphins were covered in flames, even the water was afire. His left hand was pouring out a column of fire, and he didn't even know it. He stopped everything. Stood. Tried to calm the people. "It's all right. I'm sorry. I didn't ..."

Giacomo emerged from the crowd that had gathered, walked over and hugged Darstan. "Come back inside now. More khaffe will do you good."

By the time he got back to Aenaila's house word had already reached them about the disaster at the fountain.

"What happened, Darstan? Are you all right?"

"I just want to go to bed, Aenaila. We'll talk tomorrow."

She nodded. I hope you sleep well, BlackWolf. There is still a lot to do.

They were three days out of the port at Cartena, sailing north. The ship was a fast one, built for speed instead of cargo, and Jago knew how to coax every bit of wind into her sails. The sea had been cooperative too, remaining calm while providing wind at their backs.

On a sunny afternoon with nothing to do, Darstan found some fishing poles and brought them on deck. "C'mon, Wisp. You too, Adju. It's time I taught you how to fish."

Jago laughed. Fishing in the sea would be quite different than Darstan's homeland.

After half the afternoon passed, and with only a few fish to show for it, Wisp grew frustrated. "This seems like the most ridiculous thing in the world. Nothing is certain."

"There's nothing better to do," Darstan said.

"Walking the deck is better than this."

Aenaila poked her head up on deck, calling out to them. "What are you men doing?"

"Just three orphans trying to fish," Darstan said, and they all laughed.

"It's about to be two orphans," Wisp said.

"One," Adju added, laughing at his joke.

As they all got back to fishing, Adju asked. "Where will we go?"

"I knew I should have left you in Cergala," Wisp said. "You ask too many questions."

"But we can't go back to Khatara. Master Bulta and the Emperor's Guards are looking for us."

"They're looking for us in Sykor too," Wisp said.

"We should go to Sykor first," Darstan said. "If Takar's alive, Ludar will surely be making him suffer."

Aenaila agreed. "We'll shift to Jago's second house in Khatara, just in case they found mine. After I rest, we'll go to Sykor."

"How will we find the big sergeant?" Adju asked.

Wisp tousled the little thief's hair. "We'll figure it out when we get there. Won't we Darstan?"

"He won't be difficult to find. Ludar will have him in the dungeons, same place he had me. He wouldn't risk the regular prison."

"And this time it will be easy to get him out," Wisp said. "Aenaila can take us in and out of there with no trouble. Only problems we'll have are the guards assigned to watch his cell."

Soon they stopped fishing, as it was time to eat dinner. They discussed their plans throughout the meal and long into the night. Finally, Aenaila announced she was going to bed.

"I'm going too," Darstan said.

Sleep usually came easy for Darstan, dreaming of childhood memories and fun times with Rahg, but tonight was different. Every time Rahg's image came up, he thought of Mirana and how she died.

He fought with himself, trying to think of anything else, but nothing stayed. At last, he drifted off, but it wasn't to restful sleep, it was another of what he termed his "real" dreams—ones that he somehow knew were real, or would become real. This one had only come to him once before, briefly, but it had made an impression because he recognized the obelisk.

It was the same obelisk that he had seen in Entiria; however, it wasn't in Entiria—it was the middle of a desert, and it was underground. He didn't know how that would be possible, but he had quit questioning his real dreams after the one that showed him what was going to happen in Entiria and the one that had predicted he'd lose his hand.

He drifted deeper into the dream, underground now, far under, and he stood in an immense cavern staring at the obelisk. There was no light, yet somehow he could see. The obelisk glowed. It pulsed—he knew that—but to a rhythm he didn't recognize, and that brought to mind the mysterious corridor at the top of the stairs in his palace—the one with the door at the end. That pulsing was dangerous. Somehow he knew.

He turned, glancing about the cavern, and this time there were people there. People with powers. He could always tell because the ones who had power glowed in his dreams.

A battle was taking place, yet he couldn't join them. Almost as if he weren't there. As if he were only an observer. The fighting continued for a while, how long he didn't know, but he couldn't tell one side from the other. Suddenly a light burst forth, blinding him. And then the dream stopped.

His eyes wide open, he tried to get out of bed but failed. He couldn't move his legs or his arms, and he felt beads of sweat sliding off his forehead. Cold sweat from his pillow seeped into his neck as he lay there, wondering why he couldn't move.

It was almost morning before he moved his legs, and the sun was up and frisky by the time he got out of bed. Wisp met him on the way to breakfast.

"Up late, Dar?" Wisp always seemed cheerful, no matter what time of day or how little sleep he had.

"Today I am."

"I'm tired too," Wisp said. "I don't like the sea. Won't be long though."

"Can't be soon enough for me."

On the eighth day, they reached the little island that Aenaila used as a Shift point for Khatara. She said goodbye to Jago and the crew, as did the others, then she, Wisp, Darstan, and Adju shifted to the safe house. Wisp stepped through the rift first, checking to ensure all was safe, then the rest came through.

"Are you all right, Aenaila?" Wisp asked.

"I don't know why but this was the easiest trip I've ever had. I'm not even tired."

"I let you use some of my power," Darstan said. "When we joined hands I let it flow into you."

"I didn't know," she said, a puzzled look on her face. "Where did you learn to do that?"

He shrugged his shoulders. "It just came to me."

Aenaila stared at him for a moment, then shook her head. "I don't understand, but if you can do it again, I won't even have to rest. We can go straight to Sykor."

"I'm ready," Darstan said.

"We should go to Cynamar's room," Wisp said. "It's the safest place."

Aenaila spun around like a viper. "No!" Fire burned in her emerald eyes. "Figure out somewhere else to go."

Jealousy burned deep behind that smooth facade. "There is another place. It could be tricky, but ..."

"Are you ready?" she asked.

He formed the image in his mind—the library, the fireplace, stone hearth. "Ready."

Aenaila took his hand, got the image then joined hands with the others, and shifted.

They appeared in a large library. A man sat in a chair by the fireplace, jumping up when he saw them. "Guards!"

Darstan tensed, drew his sword, but Wisp grabbed his arm. "It's all right." Wisp turned toward the man, now upon them, and bowed graciously. "Lord Talanvar, I am your servant."

For a moment it looked as if Talanvar would strike him, but then he laughed and embraced him. Just then guards burst through the door, weapons drawn. Talanvar held up a hand warning them off.

"It was nothing, Berto. Please have Birol bring some refreshments for our guests. These are old friends." Then he looked at Berto and winked. "Very old friends."

Berto saluted and left, taking the other guards with him.

Talanvar eyed them all, stopping at Darstan, staring at his hand. "The last time we met that wasn't gone."

Darstan said nothing.

"I've heard about you. Everyone has by now." Talanvar paced a little. "Do you know there are people who swear that you're Lukaan himself? A hundred people produce a hundred stories, few of them good."

He turned to Wisp, "Kender, I don't know your plans in Sykor, but it would be best if Darstan stayed out of sight."

Birol arrived with khaffe and te shortly afterward, questions written all over his face. "I did not hear them arrive, My Lord, or I would have been prepared." He stared at them, nodding when he saw Wisp.

"Yes, I know you would," Talanvar said. "Please have Dirk come in when he can."

Wisp's face lit up. "Dirk? The little gutter rat I used as a messenger?"

"The same."

"Fortune must have fallen on that lad if he found service with you. I'm glad. I liked him."

"Fortune was not as kind as you think," Talanvar said. "See for yourself."

The door latch twisted several times, as if someone struggled to open it, then Dirk walked in.

Wisp approached with a big smile, stopping when he saw his missing thumbs. He knelt next to Dirk, held his hands.

"Kender Darnell! How did you get in here?"

"What happened to your thumbs, boy?"

Dirk's smile vanished, replaced by a determined vengeful expression. "Ludar!"

Wisp stood up. "He did this to you? Why?"

"Wanted to know what messages I was running for you." Dirk lowered his head. "I told him everything I knew, Kender. Couldn't help it."

Wisp hugged him. "All right, lad. Don't worry about things like that. It's good to see you though. Glad you're alive."

Dirk gritted teeth. "I'll live long enough to see Ludar dead."

Wisp laid a hand on Dirk's shoulder. "Yes, you will. You will surely see that."

As they rejoined Aenaila and Darstan and the rest of them, Adju stared at his missing thumbs, unconsciously rubbing his own as if to check that they were still there.

"How did you get in here, Kender?"

"Kender Darnell is full of tricks, Dirk. Don't ever forget that."

Talanvar offered Aenaila a seat, then gestured for the rest to sit as well. "What have you come for?"

Wisp hesitated.

"Dirk knows almost everything. By the way he's staring at Darstan's arm, I'm sure he knows about him as well. And I have the same questions as Dirk, though I know your talents to be great, Kender, how did you get into my house with four people, unseen by any of my guards?"

"As talented as I am, you already know Darstan is far more gifted, but so is my dear friend, Aenaila." Wisp stared at Talanvar. "The fact is, we came to get Takar. Rescue him from Ludar."

Talanvar frowned. "Either you are too early or too late, depending on how you look at it. Either way, I am impressed with your sources."

Wisp frowned as well, accustomed to Talanvar's games of words. "Speak plainly. I'm not here to banter words about."

"Impatient men are fond of mistakes, my friend, and if you intend to get Takar out of the deep dungeons, you will need much more than patience."

"Just tell me what you know," Wisp said.

"This will require some refreshments to tell it right. Birol, get us more te and khaffe. Something else for the boy if he wants it."

Talanvar sat in one of his plush chairs, gesturing for them to accommodate themselves. "Word came just this morning that he had been recaptured."

"What do you mean recaptured?"

"Well, you have been gone long." Talanvar sat back, breathed deeply. "Ludar has had him for months, torturing him. We tried getting him out but no one could manage it, not with trickery or even bribes, and I made the purse worthy too.

"Then suddenly, he escaped. Word has it that two missing guards arranged it, and whether they are missing because Ludar caught them or because they ran away no one knows, or in any event no one is saying." Birol came with the drinks and set them on the table, pouring khaffe for Talanvar.

"Te for me, please," Aenaila said, holding out her cup.

"Khaffe," Darstan said, and Adju held his cup out to be filled as well.

"Nothing," Wisp said, then to Talanvar. "Please continue."

"We kept him hidden for a few days, then as they were trying to bring him here for safekeeping, he was caught." Talanvar grabbed a biscuit from the plate and dipped it in his khaffe despite a disapproving look from Birol.

"How did Ludar know?"

"How indeed. That is my question. It was all too convenient—the manner in which they caught him."

"How did you hear he'd been captured again?"

Talanvar finished chewing—not one to break two of the cardinal sins of etiquette at one sitting—took a gulp of khaffe, not quite cardinal, then sat upright to finish his tale. "An old friend of yours brought the news, and before the crows did. It was truly fresh."

"Who?" Wisp asked.

"The bounty-man."

Wisp's eyes grew wide. "Gregor?"

Talanvar nodded. "The one that was with you when Darstan escaped. I remember him."

"He's dead!" Darstan said.

Talanvar poured te for Aenaila, khaffe for himself. "Not as of yesterday. Said he'd be at his house or the Trader's Inn, and if I saw you to tell you."

"Let's go." Ever the impetuous one, Darstan headed for the door.

"Hold on, Darstan. We need to think this through."

"What's there to think about? Gregor's alive! Let's go." He grabbed Wisp by the shirt and tugged. "I can't wait to see him."

Talanvar's voice was like gravel scraping against gravel, and when he raised his voice, it rumbled. "No! If you want Takar alive, he needs to get out of there now."

Darstan stopped and turned around. "You're right. I wasn't thinking. Do we know where he is?"

"All I know is the dungeons."

Wisp grabbed a piece of cheese, munching on it like a rat. "Bet it's the same place he had you, Darstan. Why not?"

Darstan nodded. "Let's go."

Wisp shook his head. "Darstan, settle down. Tonight would be better. I know it's a risk, but I doubt that Ludar is there right now torturing him. He'll wait until the day is done then do it himself."

"What are you suggesting?" Aenaila asked.

"I say we go just as it turns dark. The relief guard won't be there yet, and the old guards will be tired."

"Who's going?" Darstan asked.

"Just you and me and Aenaila."

Darstan sat, satisfied with the plan. "I hope he's all right. I still remember that cell. It was ... bad."

"He'll be all right," Wisp said.

"Suppose he isn't? How can you always be so optimistic?"

"Because it's better than the alternative," he said, then grabbed another piece of cheese and headed toward the door. "Come with me, Adju. I'll teach you some bad habits."

37

WISP AND ADJU

Aenaila sat at the table to enjoy her te, but a continual thumping from behind the house proved to be too annoying. She excused herself, then got up to see what was causing the noise, though her gut told her she wouldn't like the answer.

She poked her head out the back door and gasped. "What are you doing?" Her tone was haughty with righteousness.

The knife shot from Wisp's hand and hit a target scratched into the side of a supply building. He turned to face Aenaila just as the thud struck again. "Providing Adju with an education. He needs to know how to defend himself."

"Disgusting," she said, and shook her head as she walked back into the house.

Wisp turned back to instruct Adju as he talked. "Let the blade fall back between your thumb and finger. Don't hold it too tight."

They went to retrieve their blades and, as they walked, Adju deftly lifted a pouch tied to Wisp's waist. The smile on Adju's face disappeared as Wisp's empty hand shot out. "Not like that. You need a diversion or a distraction of some kind."

Frustration clung to Adju's voice. "But you said not to bump."

"You don't need to bump, but until you're good enough, you do need a distraction. It could be anything—a noise, something to make them turn their head, a piece of conversation—anything that focuses their concentration for just a moment. That's when you strike." The wood siding squeaked as Wisp removed the blades. "Try it again."

Aenaila heard the laughter from inside and rushed out to observe Adju leaping in elation.

"I did it, Master Kender, I did it. I snatched your pouch when you got the blades."

Wisp looked at Adju and laughed. Then he grabbed him and pulled him in for a hug and laughed some more. "You're the first person that's done that to me in ten years."

Adju beamed, probably as much from the praise as the hug. Hugs were not a frequent event in the harjana.

Wisp reached behind him, undid a sheath on his shoulder, and handed it to Adju. A plain leather handle protruded from a common sheath, and when he withdrew the blade, it showed a dark, grimy face. Wisp held out his index finger, laid the blade across it and extended his hand. It didn't even teeter. He knelt and handed it to Adju. "It isn't a fancy one, but it's perfectly balanced."

Adju's eyes nearly split apart. "For me?"

"For you," Wisp said. "You earned it."

Adju felt the blade, put in in the sheath. Slid it out. Balanced it on his fingers- three of them—then he dove at Wisp and wrapped his arms around him. "You do me shame, Master Kender. I have nothing to give in return." He couldn't stop the tears from flowing down his face. "No one has ever given me a present," he managed through sobs.

Wisp hugged him. "There will be a lot more presents," he said, and lost his own battle.

Aenaila watched from the doorway, fighting an urge to laugh. Born a thief, die a thief. The adage from her village stuck in her mind, but then her mirth turned to anger. She paused for a moment studying them.

"Don't think of teaching that child any of your thieving ways. The harjana corrupted him enough as it is; your influence can only hurt him more." A short pause, then. "Besides, you've got a friend in prison, probably dying, if this Ludar is as bad as you say, you shouldn't be here having fun with Adju."

A knife lay in Wisp's hand, and for an instant, it looked as if he might throw it at Aenaila, but then the glare in his brown eyes softened, and a warm smile replaced the scowl. He walked over to her, hugged her.

"Aenaila, haven't we done everything we can until tonight?"

"Yes, but—"

He placed his finger to her lips. "Then what is the harm in letting Adju enjoy himself while we wait? There's no sense in worrying a child unnecessarily." He kissed her lips softly. "As for me, I'm planning. I know it might not look like it, but I am."

Aenaila returned the kiss passionately. Then again. "You should take a break from teaching Adju. You look tired."

His eyes lit up, and a smile covered his face. "Adju, keep practicing. I'll be back." He grabbed Aenaila's arm and led her inside.

After passionate lovemaking, they lay beside each other in bed. Aenaila wrapped her legs around him, pulled him closer. "Isn't that better use of your time?"

Wisp paused, pretending to think, then Aenaila started tickling him. The laughter continued until she jumped out of bed and began dressing. "You shouldn't be teaching him such things, you know."

"I have nothing else to give him. And besides, I give him what I think he can use. You can teach him all about manners, or what to say and not say in public, but what good will that do him in life? He's a beggar. If I can help him become a thief, he'll be ahead of where he was."

"It is better to beg than to steal."

Wisp got up from the bed, grabbed his clothes and started dressing. "A nice proverb to have handy. Well said ... for someone who has had to do neither." His voice dropped, and his tone hardened.

"I've had to do both, and I'll steal any day before I ever beg again. Nothing could be more humiliating." He shook his head. Nothing!

38

CAPTURED AGAIN

The guards hauled Takar to the dungeons, not bothering with any comforts. Ludar would have him soon anyway. When they finally tossed him into the cell, he was nearly unconscious, face bloodied, middle fingers still useless, and he had sustained numerous cuts and a few broken bones along the way.

"Why not just kill me now?"

Laughter answered him. The guard leaned in close. "Don't remember me do ya', Sergeant? I spent thirty days in prison 'cause of you, and as much as I'd love to pay that back, Ludar would have my skin for it." He straightened up but continued staring at Takar. "You must have got to him good 'cause he wants you for himself."

Takar sighed, sat in the cell, waited for death. It wouldn't be long. Ludar would torture him as long as he could, try to get information from him as to where Darstan and the thief were, but once he realized he was not going to get any answers, Ludar would have the guards kill him. Probably do it himself.

∽

"Almost time," Darstan said, pacing across Talanvar's library.

"Relax," Wisp said. "Read a book or get something to eat. We've got time yet before we leave."

Aenaila set down her cup of te, the third since she'd been sitting here. "You're sure you have a good Shift point?"

"Of course," Wisp said.

"If he doesn't, I do," Darstan said. "I spent a long time in there looking at those walls."

"But we don't want to end up in the middle of a cell," Wisp sad. "The point is to get someone out of prison."

"I'd prefer the middle of a cell rather than inside a stone wall," Aenaila said. "Anyway, if you two are ready ..."

Wisp held out his hand, and Darstan did likewise. Aenaila grabbed them, retrieved the image from Wisp's mind, then shifted.

They appeared in the chamber where Darstan had been held long ago. Two guards were posted, but when Wisp and the others appeared the guards were shocked enough to be held motionless.

Wisp and Darstan quickly got control of them, and with a tap on the head, had them knocked out. Inside the cell, on the floor in a heap, lay Takar.

"Is he alive?" Darstan asked.

Wisp grabbed the keys from the guard and opened the cell. Takar didn't move. Aenaila rushed to his side, kneeling to check him. "He's alive, but not by much. We'll take him back to Talanvar's now. Ready?"

They joined hands, and she shifted, appearing in a private room in Talanvar's upstairs, a place they had agreed would be better than the library in the event he had visitors. "Put him on the bed," Aenaila ordered. "Hurry. And get me some water."

She worked on Takar throughout the night, tending the serious wounds first: broken bones, deep cuts, and his fingers, which were nearly beyond hope.

"How is he?" Darstan asked.

"Something is still wrong with him. Must be internal."

"How do you fix it?"

"I'm not sure I can fix it."

Darstan looked at Takar then back to Aenaila, pleading in his eyes. "I can't lose someone else I care about, Aenaila. Keep trying."

A deep breath straightened her back, firmed her resolve. "I'll do it. Don't worry."

Wisp and Talanvar were on their second cup of khaffe when Darstan came downstairs.

"How's Takar?"

"Not good, but better is the last word I got. Aenaila went to sleep a little while ago. She said there are still problems, but he's safe."

Darstan sat at the table and poured khaffe for himself. "Thank whatever gods there are for that."

"We've got more problems," Talanvar said. "My people tell me Ludar has every guard in the city looking for him, and he has signed orders to conscript more guards. Soon he'll have every child over twelve in the army."

"He won't find him here."

"Don't underestimate that man's resolve. He will turn this city inside out to find him. I might hold him off for a day or two with bluffs, but if he runs out of options, he'll take this house by force."

"Let him try," Darstan said, menace tainting his voice.

Talanvar grabbed his shirt, pulled him close. "I know what you can do, some of it at least, but don't be fooled. Ludar will sacrifice a hundred men to get Takar, and if he finds out you are here, he'll sacrifice the entire army." Talanvar stood, pacing. "Not even you could stand up to that."

Before Darstan could say anything, Wisp chimed in. "He's right, Darstan. You know it. We have to do this the right way."

Aenaila trudged down the steps, sleep fresh in her eyes and heavy on her voice. A thin blue nightgown covered her, but not enough to keep feelings from stirring in the men. "He can't be moved yet. Not for days. Perhaps weeks. Even shifting might bother him."

"What are you doing up?" Wisp said. "You need sleep."

"I heard you. Couldn't sleep anyway. I was afraid you and Darstan would do something stupid."

An exaggerated expression of mock indignation greeted her, but with no words.

She bent and kissed him, smiling through the kiss. "Yes, you. Not like you haven't done it before. I've been getting you out of trouble since I've known you."

"Where's my kiss?" Darstan asked.

Aenaila blushed, but she went to him and held his face in her hands and kissed him. "I am honored to kiss BlackWolf. And I'm glad to see you with some spirit."

Darstan's smile quickly turned into a frown.

Aenaila hugged him. "I'm sorry, Darstan. I wasn't thinking, or I never would have called you that." She squeezed him tighter, his head against her breasts. "Please forgive me?"

Silence followed, then. "Nothing to forgive. I've become a lonely old man at a ripe young age. Besides, BlackWolf is my name. That's what Mirana always told me."

A question formed on Talanvar's lips, but a signal from Wisp forestalled him.

Darstan stood, stretching, though everyone must have known it to be an exercise to cover his emotions. "If we can't move him, what do we do?"

"Defend him," Talanvar said. "What else?"

Darstan smiled, a genuine smile, and went over to Talanvar, patting his back. "I see why you like him now, Wisp. I ..."

Darstan stepped back, appalled at his mistake. What did I do? He stared at Talanvar, then to Wisp. "I'm sorry. I ..."

Wisp laughed so hard he had to stand, and Talanvar joined in.

Darstan just stared, as did Aenaila. "What's going on?" Darstan asked.

Talanvar looked to Wisp. "Should you do the honors?"

Wisp bowed. "Darstan, also known as BlackWolf and Prince of Arangar, I would like you to meet Lord Talanvar, also known as Carmine, the boss of the thieves guild for Sykor."

Darstan stared, mouth agape. "He's a thief!"

Talanvar's indignation might have been real. "Not anymore."

At that, they all laughed, although it took a while for Aenaila to join them. "Seems like I can't get away from thieves."

Darstan grabbed another cup and poured the last of the khaffe. "Now that all that is in the open, what do we do about Ludar?"

"I say we sit it out and hope Ludar doesn't get here before Takar can leave." Talanvar pointed to Aenaila. "You think perhaps seven to ten days?"

She nodded.

"We might last that long, and if Ludar comes after Takar is gone, no harm done."

"And if not?" Wisp was ever the pragmatist.

"He won't come here with a full force the first time, not without knowing for sure, so we'll at least have warning."

Wisp paced, shaking his head. "I don't like it."

Talanvar walked in front of him, hands animated. "I can put all my people on the street. We'll know before Ludar, what his guards are doing."

"What if it doesn't work?" Darstan asked.

"Then we're forced to defend ourselves," Talanvar said.

Darstan and Aenaila nodded at once.

"There is another option," Wisp said.

"What?"

"Kill him."

"What?"

"Kill Ludar," Wisp said. "Get rid of him before he can come here."

Talanvar stared for a long time, then the laughter rolled up from his belly and burst out. He bent over, holding his gut he was laughing so hard. Soon, Darstan and Aenaila were laughing too. "You are the most brazen man I've ever met."

"That's what has kept me alive all these years."

Darstan stared out the window into the courtyard. "Not a bad idea, Wisp. Not bad at all."

39

WHAT GOOD ARE GUTTER RATS

Adju bounded down the steps, full of life. "Good morning, Master Kender. How is the day?"

Wisp usually tried to smile for him no matter the circumstances, but today he forgot. "Great, Adju. But I need you to hurry and get dressed. I have work for you."

"I need to eat, Master—"

"Adju, you'll get food. Just get dressed."

He ran back up the stairs, little feet pattering on the floor above.

"Harsh on him weren't you?" Aenaila asked.

"I don't have time, Aenaila." He turned to Talanvar. "I need Dirk for the day, too. Can you arrange it?"

Talanvar nodded. "Birol! Call Dirk in here. And prepare breakfast for Adju."

Darstan pushed his plate away and laid a napkin on the table. "By the way, weren't we going to see Gregor today?"

"Not good, Darstan. Not good at all. Ludar has the guards out, and you can bet they're looking for more than Takar. He might suspect we were involved." Wisp sighed, not wanting to say this. "Besides, I'm not sure I trust Gregor. I'd—"

"What! Not trust him! He almost died for us."

Wisp held up his hand, nodded. "I understand, but maybe there's something else. How come he suddenly shows up when Takar escapes? How come it's him that tells Talanvar he's captured again?" Wisp's head shook. "You know I don't like coincidences, Darstan."

"So what? We just forget him, forget he almost died?"

"No. Nothing like that. We send Dirk and Adju out to see what he's doing. Then—"

"Spy on him?"

Anger bit at Wisp, fueled by frustration. "Yes, Darstan. Spy on him. I'd rather do that than trust him, then find out we were wrong as Ludar is clamping the chains around us."

Darstan held up both arms, forgetting for a moment he only had one hand. Embarrassment set in as he realized how ridiculous it looked, and he tried hiding the fact as he lowered his other arm. "All right."

Talanvar nodded. "I have to go along with Kender. It's better to be safe." Then he looked at Wisp. "If you're sending those boys out, I have errands they can do. They'll be the least likely suspects."

Wisp nodded. "That's why I always used gutter rats."

"What are gutter rats?" Adju hit the last step and raced across the tiled floor.

Wisp grabbed him, tousling his hair as he always did. "You, my friend, are a gutter rat. As is my other friend, Dirk, who just came in the back door behind me."

"How did you know?" Dirk screamed.

"I know everything," Wisp said. "Now hurry up and eat because I have business for you."

Dirk and Adju headed down the steep hill out of High Town into the merchant's district, the ever-present wind tugging at Dirk's cap. Farley's baritone voice climbed up the hill, enticing them to his fruit stand with his sing/song chant and clever lyrics.

"Maybe we should get some fruit," Adju said.

Dirk looked at him with cold eyes. "Farlo will catch you. Ain't seen nobody that can snatch fruit from him and not get caught."

Adju's look said "I could," but he nodded and followed Dirk around the corner. "How big is Sykor?"

"Thought you been here?"

Indignant as a haughty chambermaid, Adju struck back. "I have been here. Last time we were in the princess' house."

"I bet," Dirk said, sarcasm heavy in his voice.

Adju grabbed him, spun him around, fully prepared to challenge him to a fight, but then he saw the missing thumbs. He had forgotten about them. Habit found a quick, alternate response. "You ask Master Kender. He will tell you."

Dirk stared at him. "You talk funny. And why do you call him master?"

Adju's brow wrinkled in confusion. "It is a title of respect."

Dirk digested what he said, then laughed. "Okay, Kender deserves respect." He reached out and grabbed Adju's hand with his four fingers. "Let's start fresh. We can be friends."

Adju wanted to pull his hand back, but he took Dirk's and shook it, covering up his fear. "I would like that, Dirk."

Dirk laughed. "Don't you go callin' me master," he said, then they laughed and continued down the street.

"We're going to be delivering some messages for Talanvar, but we also got to watch somebody for Kender. This guy knows me, so it's going to be up to you to do that job."

"I can follow anybody. Back in Khatara I once followed the captain of the guard for two days, and he didn't know."

Dirk's scowl said it all. "Yeah, well guards are easy and captains easier. You'll be trailing a bounty-man this time and there ain't nobody tougher except a thief."

Adju bowed to him. "I will not let you down."

"All right. Just stop that. You've got to fit into this city. Got to stop acting like a Khataran." Dirk looked him over. "First thing is we get you a cap like mine. Then you'll at least look like you belong here."

Adju frowned. "I have no money."

"Don't worry about money. Lord Talanvar gave me some. C'mon."

They went to a shop and got Adju a cap, which he treasured, then they headed to the River's Edge. The city quickly changed from clean, neat merchant shops and well-swept streets to ramshackle houses in various states of disrepair.

A fetid aroma greeted them as they turned the corner, not fifty paces into the district that so many of Sykor's citizens called home. "This reminds me of the harjana," Adju said. "That's where I came from in Khatara."

"Guess we all started out the same," Dirk said, recalling his days in the Dongrel.

They soon got to Mollie's house, where a rap on the door drew a quick response. "Well, well. Look what we have here." She grabbed both of them by the cheeks and squeezed, drawing squeals. "What brings you lads out so early?"

"Lord Talanvar says the cherry tart you sent needs more time in the oven."

Mollie's smile disappeared. "You tell him we'll do our part."

Dirk tipped his cap, then hurried off toward the Sentry's Watch. Before long, Baldomere Testa was sitting with them in the dining room.

"And what have I done to be blessed with such a visit this bright morning?"

"Lord Talanvar says the cherry tart you sent needs more time in the oven."

Testa took a long slow sip of his khaffe as he leaned back in his chair. "Ah, the cherry tart." He kicked his feet up on the seat of the chair next to him and smiled. "Would you gentlemen be so kind as to tell Lord Talanvar that I shall see to it that the tart does not burn."

Dirk smiled, finished his khaffe with a gulp and stood to leave. "C'mon, Adju."

Adju bowed to Testa, started to leave, then reached back and grabbed his mug. He downed half a cup with three swallows then hurried out the door after Dirk, Testa's laughter following him into the street.

"Where now?" Adju asked.

"The bounty-man," Dirk said. "He's probably still at home."

They stopped two blocks away from Gregor's house, waiting, watching. Finally, he made his appearance, exiting the house onto the street.

When he reached the corner, he turned left, toward the Trader's Inn.

"Up to you now, Adju. I can't be seen."

"No need to worry," Adju said and casually fell in behind Gregor, keeping a far distance from him. When Gregor turned right up a steep hill, Adju turned right a block behind him, running to the top of the hill once he was out of sight. He ducked behind a large stoop in front of a butcher's shop and watched as Gregor made his way down the street two blocks ahead. Three turns and eight blocks later, Gregor walked into the Trader's Inn.

Adju wasn't sure what to do, whether to wait for him to leave or to go inside and try to get information. Information was what Master Kender needed, so he better do that. He forced himself to walk slowly the rest of the way to the door, then walked into the inn. As soon as he entered he removed his cap, holding it in front of him in both hands.

Gregor sat at a table near the door, eating his meal and paying no attention to Adju. He passed Gregor and walked to a merchant seated at a table near the rear. "Excuse me, good sir, but could you spare enough for a small meal. Just—"

"Get away, boy. Have enough beggars bothering me during the day." The merchant went back to his meal, but when Adju didn't leave, he called the inn-keep. "Brock!"

Brock Larnigin was a giant of a man, with peeled carrots for hair and an angry red blotch that covered half his face. He stormed over and grabbed Adju by the scruff of the neck. "What are ya' doin' in here, boy?"

"Just lookin' for a meal. That's all." He stared up at Brock with pleading brown eyes.

Brock's gruff demeanor broke, and he smiled. "All right, lad. Take a seat by the kitchen. I'll have them fix you somethin' good to eat. But it's just this once, here?"

Adju smiled, nodding his head. "I am in your debt forever," he said.

"Well, I'll trade that for a good floor sweepin' sometime this week. How about that?"

Adju laughed. "I can do that. I sweep floors better than anyone."

Several guards came in, looked around, then walked over to Gregor. "Up early, Bounty-man?"

Gregor ignored them, continued eating his meal.

One of the guards pulled up a chair and put it at Gregor's table, started to sit, but Gregor grabbed his staff and pushed the chair away. "I prefer eating alone. If I wanted company, I'd have brought it."

The guards looked at each other, scowled then took a seat somewhere near the back.

Soon afterward, Adju finished his meal and left, waiting in an alcove three blocks away, though he still had a good view of the inn.

He followed Gregor all day, mostly from one inn to another, watching him eat and drink ale, then walk around and repeat it. As it neared dark, they followed him home waiting at the corner until they saw his candle light the room. "No sense in wastin' no more time here," Dirk said. "Let's go home."

As they headed up the street toward High Town, Gregor let the curtains slip back into place. Now that he had gotten rid of that little beggar he could go about his business. He snuffed out the candle, headed for the door in the darkness, knowing his way after so many years, and took the steps two at a time as he descended.

He cracked the front door, peeked out to make sure no one was watching, then exited onto the street. A slight chill had crept in since the afternoon, and he hunched his shoulders to forestall it. As he walked along, it suddenly occurred to him. There's only one person I know of who uses little boys to do his spy work. Wisp is back in town!

MAKING PLANS

Dirk and Adju returned to Lord Talanvar's house shortly after dark. Tired and hungry, they headed straight for the kitchen, only to be chased out by the cook, who told them dinner had yet to be served.

"You had better clean up before you present yourself to Lord Talanvar," Birol reminded Dirk.

Dirk raced upstairs, Adju only one step behind him the entire way. "Hurry up, Adju. I'm starved."

Dinner was being served when they came back down, and the aromas wafting up the staircase put a smile on Adju's face. "What are we having, Master Kender?"

"Does it matter? You'd eat boiled worms and swear they were good."

Adju laughed. "Master Kender, you know I don't eat worms."

Talanvar poured wine from a fine decanter, offering it to Darstan, Aenaila, and Wisp. He shot an inquisitive look to Wisp as Adju held out his glass.

"If he wants wine he can have it."

Adju shook his head. "I just want water ... please." The "please" probably more than his drink selection drew a smile from Aenaila and an approving look.

Dinner was roasted duck served with carrots, peas, and potatoes cut into little wedges and covered with a brown sauce.

Adju fidgeted while he waited for everyone to start. He knew any attempt to eat before the signal from Aenaila would draw more than just a reprimand. Finally, and not a moment too soon, Lord Talanvar invited them all to begin.

Adju started with the duck, cutting it into large pieces which he rammed into his mouth, but only when he was certain Aenaila wasn't looking. As he used his knife and fork to cut more meat, he happened to see Dirk struggling with his plate.

Without thumbs, he had a difficult time grasping things, and the knife proved elusive tonight. Twice he dropped it, and though it was quickly replaced by Birol, embarrassment showed on his face.

Dirk looked over at him, and Adju turned quickly, avoiding eye contact. Shame set in for doing this, but he couldn't help it, the sight of Dirk struggling with it made him wince.

When he had turned away, it was toward Darstan, and now he saw Darstan staring at Dirk the same way Adju had. Darstan was missing a hand, but that didn't seem as bad as Dirk; at least Darstan had one hand to hold things with.

"Tough getting used to doing things, isn't it, Dirk?" Darstan stared, awaiting the reply.

Dirk looked at his hand, then up to his face, full of sympathy. "Did it take you long?"

Laughter came out of Darstan for one of the few times since Mirana had died. "I don't know. I'm still learning."

At that, Dirk laughed too. "Me too, Darstan. Sometimes I think I'll never learn how to do the simplest things. Worst is buttoning my shirt. I still can't do it." He used the napkin to wipe his lips, though he let it slide up his face and catch the corner of his eye. "Got to get Birol to finish dressing me every day."

Darstan scooped vegetables onto his fork, then followed that with a sip of wine. "It'll get better with time, Dirk. Don't lose hope."

Dirk nodded and went back to eating. It didn't take long for either Adju or Dirk to finish, which did not go unnoticed by Wisp. Few things did.

"Tell us about your day," he said.

Adju was about to begin, but Dirk jumped in first. "We did everything you wanted, Kender. Went to Mollie's then to see Testa, then we followed Gregor the whole day." He took one final bite of meat, chewed quickly then continued. "He did nothin'. At least nothin' interesting. Wouldn't want that bounty-man's life."

"You saw nothing suspicious about Gregor?" Lord Talanvar asked.

"Nothin'."

Wisp smiled. He liked Dirk, liked him a lot, and he didn't want to hurt him, but he needed to see what could be done if he practiced. Besides, it was time to let Adju shine. "Adju, tell me exactly what you saw today. Don't leave anything out."

Adju beamed so much he almost lit up like a candle. "We saw the first patrol of guards in the merchant district; there were seventeen of them. Then we went to the River's Edge, and on the way to Mistress Mollie's house, we saw twenty-one more guards in two separate groups. Between leaving Mollie's and when we met Master Testa we did not see any guards, but six came in while we ate breakfast." Adju stopped for a moment, taking a swig of water. "Then we went to follow Gregor, who first went to the Trader's Inn."

"This is what I'm interested in, Adju. Tell me everything about what happened at the Trader's Inn."

Adju nodded. "Gregor went in first, and I followed a short while later. I took a seat by the kitchen. There was a man in the back, a merchant with green pants and a—"

"I don't care what anyone wore, just what they did and any conversations."

"Two guards came in and went straight to Gregor's table. The first guard said 'up early, Bounty-man' then pulled up a chair to sit, but Gregor pushed the chair away. He said 'I prefer eating alone. If I wanted company, I'd have brought it.'" Adju grabbed his last bite of carrots then another gulp of water.

"Seems harmless enough to me," Darstan said. "Gregor never did like the guards much."

Wisp thought, sipping wine while he did. "Could have been a code." His brow furrowed when he thought hard. "That line about 'if I wanted company I'd have brought it,' I don't like it." He looked at Adju. "You're sure that's exactly what he said?"

Adju smiled. "I knew you would question me, Master Kender, so I made sure to get everything right."

Dirk had been staring at Adju the entire time. "I can't believe you remembered this. How did you do that?"

Adju smiled. "Master Kender taught me."

"Birol, may I please have more wine?" Wisp asked. "I need to think."

"You're too suspicious," Darstan said.

"Perhaps," Wisp said. "We'll see."

After more light conversation, Adju yawned, covering his mouth. "I'm tired."

"Me too," Dirk said. "We did a lot of walking today."

"Time for you to go to bed anyway," Wisp said, and got up from his chair. "C'mon. I'll tuck you in."

They went upstairs, Dirk heading to his room and Adju to his. Wisp tucked Dirk in after helping him take off his shirt. He pulled the blanket up over him and patted his head, bending to kiss his cheek. "I'm proud of what you did today, Dirk. That was a big help."

He shook his head lightly. "I didn't do nothin'. Adju was the one who remembered all that."

Wisp thought for a moment he would cry, but he held it in.

"Can you teach me like you taught him?" Hope was in his voice.

Wisp smiled. "If I'm here long enough, I'll teach you everything."

As Wisp closed the door, Dirk called out. "Goodnight, Kender. Thanks."

"Goodnight, Dirk," he said, then went to Adju's room to repeat the process. He tucked Adju in, kissed his cheek, then started to leave.

"Master Kender, wait."

He turned about. "What?" he said, then realized Adju was shaking. "Are you cold?"

"I'm scared. I know it is a shame to admit it, but I am. In those other lands I was afraid for you, but now I'm afraid for me." Tears formed in the little beggar's eyes, real tears.

Wisp had no practice in situations like this. A joke or a snide remark would not suffice. "Adju, look at me." He waited for him to lift his head, then he held his trembling hands. "What made you afraid? You can tell me."

Adju hesitated. "Dirk's hands, Master Kender. He has no thumbs!" Adju cried freely, leaning against Wisp and holding him tight. "I do not want to be like that. Not ever."

Wisp let the tears flow until the well had almost dried. "You're not alone in your fear. And there is no shame. I've been afraid before, everyone has." Wisp held him while the sobbing stopped. "I'm still afraid. Every day I want it to be over. Every day I wish that I had chosen not to come."

Adju broke loose the bond to look at him. "You do, Master Kender? You truly do?"

Wisp nodded.

"Then why not quit? You can help Mistress Aenaila, then quit. You can quit, and we will work together."

"I thought you were afraid of losing your fingers or thumbs. Anyway, I can't quit; these are my friends."

Wisp could see Adju had not grasped the idea. "Friends are difficult to find, Adju. These are the first I've truly had."

There was sadness in Wisp's eyes, bringing tears back to Adju. "I have none either, Master Kender. I have never had a friend."

Wisp felt a pang of guilt. "You have one now, Adju. You have me. I'll be your friend, and you be mine. I'll make sure you don't ever lose those fingers. I'll teach you so well you could steal the hair from a bald man."

Adju laughed, lying back down. "Thank you, Master Kender. I feel better now."

"Goodnight, Adju. See you in the morning."

"Goodnight, Master Kender."

As Wisp walked toward the steps, he thought about Dirk and his missing thumbs. Ludar! He'll pay for this.

Kender hit the last stair with a bounce in his step, smiling as he made his way across the floor.

"All tucked in?" Aenaila asked.

"Probably asleep by now. They were both tired." He pulled a chair close to Aenaila and plopped down, resting his feet on the arm. "Did I miss anything?"

"Just your manners," Aenaila snapped and slapped his leg. "Get your feet off that chair!"

Talanvar laughed. "Not to worry. He knows he can do that here." Talanvar had moved on to water, and he took a long drink before he started. "I was just telling them that the messages worked. Between Mollie and Testa, we got word to nearly everyone, and they've already caused the guards plenty of trouble. Lost two people in the process, but six guards are hurt, and Ludar has had to double the number of patrols in the Dongrel and River's Edge."

"That's good," Wisp said. "What else do you have planned?"

"Tomorrow they're spreading it to the merchant's district. Plan on sending a dozen or more thieves to rob every shop and every patron we can. Ludar will have so many complaints he'll have to send eight or ten patrols to keep them from closing shop."

Aenaila sat in a stiff-backed chair, looking as regal as she was. Her honey hair draped over her shoulder in the front, sparkling against a dark blue dress she had worn for dinner. "How will this help?"

"With the troops he had to send to the Dongrel and the Edge, and with what he'll send tomorrow, he'll have less to use in searching for Takar." Talanvar called Birol to bring more wine, but when everyone refused, he changed it to water. "Besides, we have it planned to hit every district, then back up and hit the same ones again."

"Could be costly," Darstan said. "If he's already killed two men, what do you think he'll do when he gets frustrated?"

Talanvar swigged the last of his glass, poured more from a pitcher that Birol brought and started on that too. A glance told Birol that he would likely need more. "Then we start killing them," he said.

They discussed various plans and strategies long into the evening, until the yawning spread from Aenaila to Darstan to Talanvar.

"That does it for me," Aenaila said. "I should have gone when the boys did." She stood and set her glass on the table. "Goodnight all."

Wisp climbed the stairs, Darstan close behind. They walked down the hall and into Darstan's bedroom. Wisp closed the door and walked over, sat in a chair by the bed.

"What's on your mind, Wisp?"

"What makes you think anything is?"

"That look on your face. I can tell."

He slung his leg across the arm of the chair, leaning back as he did. "I guess it started last night. I was lying awake, thinking, and a thought popped into my head. Remember what you said the other day on the ship—when you and Adju and I were fishing?"

Darstan looked puzzled.

"You said 'I guess it's just us three orphans now' remember?"

Darstan kicked off his boots, sat on the bed. "I think so, but what has that got to do with anything?"

Wisp threw his leg around, feet planted on the floor. He sat up straight, elbows resting on his knees as he hunched forward. "Why is that, Darstan?"

The puzzled look returned. "Why is what? Have you had too much wine?"

He shook his head, standing now, and beginning to pace. "Why do you think that so many of us with powers all came together, and we all happen to be orphans?"

Darstan thought for a moment. "Camissa's not. Neither is Rahg."

"Camissa's mother was. She told me." Wisp pulled out his knife, started cleaning his nails. "And didn't you tell me Rahg's mother died giving birth?"

Darstan nodded.

"So he never actually saw her," Wisp said. "And I never heard Gregor speak of any parents."

Darstan wore a worried look on his face, but then he smiled. "Aenaila! She's no orphan."

Wisp took a long time but finally acquiesced. "Guess you're right. But still, that's only one."

"And Rahg."

"Maybe," Wisp said. "But you know how I feel about coincidences. Something's wrong."

Darstan finished undressing and climbed into bed. "Wrong or not, I'm tired. Blow out that candle when you leave."

"Am I being thrown out?"

"I believe you are. Perceptive for a thief."

Wisp closed Darstan's door then turned right and headed down the stairs. It was far too early to go to bed, and besides, there was something he needed to do.

He stepped silently through the house, then out the back door. Soon he was across the yard and into the supply building that he and Adju had used as target practice with the knives. It was dark inside, too dark to see, so he Cloaked himself, which for some reason always allowed him to see better in the dark, almost as if it were daytime.

Wisp made his way through crates of goods, tools, and miscellaneous boxes until he found the one crate that covered a secret door to the underground tunnels. He opened it, climbed down, and soon had made his way across the city to a spot below the guards' quarters.

He rested for a while, ensuring he would have enough of his power remaining to do what had to be done, then he emerged from the tunnel into a basement room rife with mildew and slime. A picked lock gained entry to the main quarters, and he made his way to where the guards were.

He was cloaked—invisible—though still able to be heard, so he had to move silently. The wait proved to be a short one, as someone came with an urgent message for Force Commander Ludar.

When the guard ran off—a recruit—Wisp followed closely behind him, careful to make no noise. A short jaunt down two corridors brought the lad to a large bronze door with a brass ring to use for knocking. Panic set in on the boy as he rapped once, then twice, though the last one was soft, reserved, as if he were afraid to disturb him.

The door popped open, and Ludar took the message, dismissing the guard without so much as a thank you. He hurried down the hall. Wisp allowed enough time for Ludar to be seated, then used the brass knocker, slamming it robustly three times. Footsteps pounded across the floor of Ludar's chambers, then the door flew open.

"What now?" he yelled, but when he saw no one, his face went blank. He poked his head out the door, then came fully into the corridor, walking half a dozen steps down to peek into an alcove on the left side, though it was barely big enough for a broom to fit in.

Once Ludar left the room, Wisp went in, still cloaked.

Ludar came back in, closed the door, then locked it, looking at the key as he made his way across the floor.

Suddenly he stopped, turning his head slowly and stared. A look of fear came over him, cold, gut-wrenching fear, and he whispered something too low for Wisp to hear. Then again. "Ghruehne?"

He walked to the table behind his reading chair, grabbed the candle and held it high. Next, he carried it toward a darkened corner.

"Ghruehne?" he called again, but a little louder this time. Ludar moved slowly toward another corner.

"Sendra?"

Wisp moved up behind him with a knife in his hand. He slowly reached around then pressed the blade to Ludar's throat, while pulling his head back by the hair.

"Don't dare move."

The candle dropped, and a loud gasp escaped, but other than that Ludar managed to keep control. "What do you want?"

"Two small things."

"What?" Ludar asked, slowly trying to straighten.

Wisp pressed the knife harder, cutting into his neck a little, enough to draw a trickle of blood.

"You don't know what you're doing. I can make you wealthy."

Wisp let go of Ludar's hair but kept the knife pressed firmly against his neck. "Listen closely, Force Commander. I'm going to remove the knife from your throat and step aside while my friend ties your hands. I will have my knife on your back the whole time. If you try anything, the blade will dig deep. I know. I've done this before."

With his free hand, he got another blade and put it into his mouth, then pressed it against Ludar's back. Then he quickly pulled his other hand back, tucked the knife in a sheath and tied Ludar's hands behind him.

"I still don't know what you want," Ludar said. "If you tell me, we can get this over with." He laughed. "I even respect a man who would dare rob the Force Commander. How did you get in?"

"Enough of your false bravado, Force Commander. Too many questions too. Besides, I already told you. I only came for two small things. Now lie on your stomach."

Ludar began to object, but Wisp pressed the knife against his throat again.

Once Ludar was on his stomach, Wisp tied his feet and gagged him. Then he tied his feet to a column behind him and on the side and put a rope from his arms to a column in front. Ludar couldn't move. He moaned and writhed a little, but he couldn't move.

A final round of testing to ensure he was secure, then Wisp knelt beside him, whispering in his ear. "Those two little things I wanted, Ludar. They're your thumbs." And with that, he started cutting.

Ludar's kicked his feet, and his arms moved from how he twisted his torso. Wisp sawed the blade back and forth. "Thumbs are difficult to remove, Force Commander. I bet you had a difficult time with Dirk's."

The thrashing continued, but Wisp sat atop him and kept cutting. "Keep still, and it might go quicker," he said.

Blood ran all over Ludar's clothes, all over the floor and all over Wisp. His hands were covered in blood, causing him to lose his grip on the knife. "Just a little more, Force Commander, then I'll be done."

By the time Wisp finished, Ludar was a mess. Twice he had passed out, only to awake in a state of shock. He lost control of his bowels too, an event that Wisp did not relish. Now Ludar lay there in tears. Weeping, sobbing.

Wisp brought a candle over then rolled him onto his back. With his face just an arm's length away, he laughed. "Get a good look, Force Commander. Know who did this to you."

Wisp took the blade and brought it close to Ludar's eye. "You might ask why I let you live? I'll tell you." He brought his face even closer, close enough for Ludar to feel his breath on him. "I want you to know what it's like to live like Dirk, even if it's just for a few days."

He saw the question come to Ludar's face. "Yes, Force Commander, a few days. After that, I'm going to kill you," he said.

Wisp put his knife away, took the candle and held it to Ludar's thumb, searing the wound. "I wouldn't want you to bleed to death," he said, but he doubted Ludar heard it over his silent screams.

REPERCUSSIONS

Ludar lay on the floor suffering. A throbbing, pounding pain started in his thumbs—or where they used to be—and ran up his arms all the way to his neck. A gag prevented him from screaming or calling for help, and the ropes on his hands and feet made it impossible to move. He only prayed the morning watch would wonder where he was and get him.

As he recalled the events from last night, he swore vengeance for the hundredth time. Oh, how he will suffer!

Before long, guards knocked on his door, calling his name. He twisted, struggled to break free, but the bindings were secure. Low moans emanated from him but the gag stifled the noise. Footsteps faded down the corridor, and Ludar prayed they returned.

By mid-day, no one had arrived, and Ludar felt as if his life was slipping away. He had lost a lot of blood before the wound was seared, and he thought he might have broken it open some time during the night in an attempt to get free.

Weak as he was, the thoughts of getting back at Darnell kept him going. He lay still, breathing slow and deep. Suddenly he heard a noise —as if a sheet flapped in a gentle breeze. And a faint aroma of ... what ... some kind of spice. He twisted his neck toward the sound.

~

A rift opened on the far side of the room, close to the fountain. Ghruehne and Sendra stepped through and scanned the area for traps. Gj walked over and stood above Ludar, who was lying on the floor.

"What mess have you gotten into, Force Commander?" He knelt, untied him, undid the gag, then helped him to his feet and onto the sofa. "Who did this?"

Ludar fought for breath, the pain taking a toll on him when he moved. "Kender Darnell, a friend of Darstan's."

"I told you he was here, Ghruehne," Sendra said. "I Sensed him."

Ghruehne nodded to her, then focused on Ludar. "This man has powers?"

Ludar shook his head. "No. He just took me by surprise. Got in behind me."

"Careless of you," Sendra said and looked closer at his thumbs. "And unfortunate that neither one of us can heal, though there isn't much we could do about that. The best we can do is sear the wound, though it seems as if your benefactor has taken care of that."

~

L udar gritted his teeth but held his tongue. The last thing he needed was to upset these two. Missing thumbs would be the least of his worries then.

"Don't let this interfere with what is important, Force Commander."

Ludar shrunk under Ghruehne's glare. "The one who did this will pay, but not at the cost of the mission."

"I should hope not," Sendra said, then, "Come, Ghruehne. We must go." With that, they shifted.

Ludar struggled with opening the door, a double latch that was simple for someone with thumbs, an unconscious act only yesterday, but now it required focus and determination. *I'll kill him slowly for this.*

He stormed down the corridor into the guards' quarters. "Who was on duty last night? I want them in my chambers."

Upon seeing all the blood, men rushed to help him, but Ludar brushed them aside.

"There's nothing to do for me now. Just find me the men who were on watch." He got something to eat, but embarrassment forced him to abandon that, and he settled for a cup of khaffe, struggling even with that, as he was forced to hold it with the palms of both hands.

"Would you like some food sent to your chambers, sir?" a sergeant asked.

At first, Ludar seemed offended, but then he nodded. "Yes, Sergeant, that would be good. Thank you."

He walked to his chambers, fumbled his way in, then went to the sofa and sat. *How could this happen to me?*

Life without his thumbs flashed before him, pictures of all the things he couldn't do, and with each thought, he vowed more pain would come to Kender Darnell.

When the guards finally found the men who were on watch the previous night, they rounded them up and brought them to the patrol leader on duty—Benton. He marched down the corridor to Ludar's chambers, a full complement of guards with him. After a rap on the door, he entered.

"These are the men?" Ludar asked.

A three-fisted salute from Benton, then he announced the watch. "Sergeant of the guard, two privates from the front gate, two privates from inside quarters, and one at each of the back gates."

They stood rigid. Fear on their faces.

"You let no one in?"

"No one, sir," the sergeant said. "There was one message for you, which we delivered, but the messenger never came through the gate."

Ludar stared at them until each one lowered their heads. "Look at me!" he said, then held his hands up. "Do you see what happened because you didn't do your duty?"

Each of them nodded.

"Benton, kill them all. Make sure everyone knows why."

"But, sir ..." the sergeant said.

"No!" one of the privates said and made a break toward the door. He made it into the corridor heading for the front.

"They will stop him, sir," Benton said, then he looked at Ludar. "Sir, I don't see—"

"If you can't do it, you can join them, Patrol Leader."

Benton's fist found his chest quickly. "Yes, sir, Force Commander. It will be done." He turned to the men under his command. "Take the prisoners. Escort them to the cells."

"As you pass the watch, tell them to send Bragh to me." He didn't need to say "immediately."

*B*ragh led the troops into the Dongrel, eight patrols in all. They were armed and ready to kill. Ludar's rage had already claimed the lives of seven guards, and no man wanted to be the eighth.

Orders had been explicit: find Kender Darnell no matter the cost; if they could find Takar that would be all the better, but Darnell was the one Ludar wanted most, and if he had to burn the city to get to him, he would.

Before noon, four citizens had fallen in the Dongrel, taking two guards with them. Bragh worried about each new street. News traveled fast, and already the streets were empty, though shades and curtains tilted slightly aside as the guards passed. He knew it wouldn't take much to turn this into a full revolt. River's Edge was next, and it might prove to be worse. "Keep sharp, men. Be ready."

Wisp, Talanvar, Darstan, and Dirk sat at the breakfast table waiting on food. Khaffe had been served, but the food was yet to come. Soon, Aenaila and Adju came down the steps and joined them.

"Just in time," Darstan said. "Food is almost ready. How is Takar this morning?"

"Each day is a little better, but he's far from healed."

"Some of Master Birol's good food will get him better," Adju said.

Birol nodded his thanks, then prepared the table. As he served the meal, a servant announced a messenger. Talanvar went to see who it was and what they wanted. He returned within moments, a scowl planted on his face.

He glared at Wisp, cold, green eyes burning a hole in him. Red brushed the tips of his ears and tinted his face. "You had to go and do it, didn't you? Had to get your revenge. Couldn't wait." It sounded as if each word scraped a rock on the way out.

"What are you talking about?" Wisp asked.

"You don't know?" Talanvar grabbed his shirt and yanked him off the chair. "Seems like someone sneaked into Ludar's chambers last night and cut off his thumbs. And for some wild reason, he believes it was you!"

Dirk dropped his fork, staring at Wisp. He jumped up and ran over to him, hugging him. "You really did?"

Wisp removed himself from Talanvar's grip, patted Dirk on the back. "It needed to be done."

Talanvar threw a spoon across the room, then picked up his khaffe cup and threw it, smashing it on the tile floor. "I would have taken care of that in due time. This was stupid! More than stupid."

"You should have just killed him," Darstan said.

"I wanted him to live like Dirk for a few days." He looked at Darstan, then Dirk. "But don't worry, he's going to die."

"I want to do it myself," Dirk said, hatred in his voice.

Wisp shook his head. "No. You don't want to get used to killing. Take satisfaction in it getting done."

Talanvar paced the room, sidestepping Birol as he cleaned up the mess from his tirade.

"Ludar is going to tear this city apart. He's already been in the Dongrel this morning." He pounded his fist into his palm. "We can't let this go on. If he doesn't find you soon, people will be hurt."

"All right," Wisp said. "Then let's make a plan."

~

With five more citizens dead and three guards seriously wounded, Bragh headed toward the merchant district. Half the city was on edge. He made a stop at the Trader's Inn, knowing he'd find nothing, but he had to look, as it was where Darnell used to work. He questioned half a dozen patrons then, pressed on Brock Larnigin. "Have you seen him since he's come back to Sykor?"

Brock stood next to a table with three customers. He moved a few steps away, then stopped and stared at Bragh. They were both big men, bigger than big.

"Either you have seen him, or you haven't," Bragh said.

"Won't tell either way."

Bragh shook his head. Frustration had been building all day. "Seize him!" he called, and the guards moved to subdue Brock.

The barkeep put up a valiant fight, injuring one guard and hurting two others, but they finally knocked him unconscious, then dragged him outside.

"Pick eight men and take him to prison. He'll talk later. And tell Ludar we're finishing our rounds and will be in afterward."

~

*D*arstan and Wisp had planned all day and come up with nothing that would satisfy everyone involved. Aenaila wanted to leave, risk it and take Takar with them. Wisp wanted to kill Ludar that night, though everyone, including himself, thought that there would be so many guards it may be impossible.

Talanvar searched for a miracle answer, and Darstan wanted to march into the guards' quarters and kill them—all of them.

As they were still discussing options, word of another messenger arrived. Talanvar once again went to the gate, returning in moments. The messenger came with him.

"Gregor!" Darstan yelled, and ran to greet him.

He was as tall and as thin as Darstan remembered, perhaps a little more gaunt, but his smile brought back memories from what seemed like long ago, happier days. Darstan hugged him, then stepped back. "I thought you were dead." He looked him over, almost lost his emotions. "In fact, Gregor, I thought I killed you."

The smile didn't disappear, but it waned. "You almost did. I was lucky to get out of there alive."

Wisp went over, hugged the bounty-man, though with less enthusiasm than Darstan. "Good to have you back, Bounty-man. you look good—well, as good as you can look."

Gregor laughed, nodded to Aenaila and Adju.

"So how did you get out of there?" Wisp asked.

Gregor looked to Aenaila and Dirk and Adju. "I can speak freely?"

"They're fine," Talanvar said.

Gregor took a seat, resting his elbow on the table as he talked. "The Wolfen took me to a ledge in a ravine, and when Darstan used his Fire, it distracted them. I threw one into the ravine, then got control of the other and killed him. I stayed quiet for a while, then when I started to come out, I saw Banished Ones. After that, it was two full days before I dared leave. When I did, it was a race to get out of the shield."

He took a long deep breath. "Before I got out, one of them caught me —Melissara." He reached for water and took a long drink. "I don't know how long they kept me, but they asked me everything I knew about Rahg and Darstan, over and over again." He shook his head as if still in disbelief. "I told them all I knew, but they repeated this every day until maybe a month ago, then they just let me loose. I guess they finally realized I knew nothing."

"You were lucky," Darstan said.

"I'd say fortune smiled on you, Bounty-man." Wisp laced his tone with more than a hint of sarcasm.

"But enough of that," Gregor said. "What I came to tell you about is Ludar." He looked at the people in the room, then continued. "I'm certain you already heard of what he did in the Dongrel and the Edge, but now he has taken Brock Larnigin captive."

"Larnigin?" Anger took over Wisp's face.

Gregor nodded. "Came into the inn this afternoon. Beat him, then hauled him off." He stared at Wisp. "Ludar wants you bad."

Wisp slammed his fist on the table. "I should have killed him last night."

Gregor put a hand on Wisp's shoulder. "Word is that he plans to speak tomorrow, try to rally the people to his cause and get their support."

"How do you know this?" Talanvar was nearly as suspicious as Kender.

"I still have friends in the guard. Ones who used to tip me off in exchange for a small reward."

"So why tell us? This would be worth a lot of money to someone?" Wisp asked. "I thought you were all about money?"

Gregor stared at Wisp. His face turned dour, grim. "If that were the case, I would have turned you in long ago." He shook his head. "I once thought I had a friend, two actually." He looked at Darstan when he said the last.

"Guess I don't have any." He turned and walked toward the door.

"Gregor, wait," Darstan said, but the bounty-man kept going.

Talanvar watched him from the window. He never looked back, just walked out the gate and down the hill. As he let the curtain fall back into place, he turned to face Wisp. "Tough on him. I think he was genuine. The man gave us information we didn't have, and I can't see how it would help him to do that."

Darstan nodded. "He was the same old Gregor as far as I'm concerned. Why did you act like that, Wisp?"

"If I'm wrong, I apologize."

Aenaila spoke for the first time since Gregor had left. "You seem to be wrong a lot these days, Kender Darnell. A bad decision last night followed by what everyone considers a bad one tonight."

"Everyone?" he looked at her with raised eyebrows.

"Everyone."

"All right. Enough of that," Talanvar said. "Now that we know what Ludar is doing, we need to make a plan. Something has to be done before he gets complete control of the city."

But do we know what he's doing? Wisp thought.

42

WORLD'S COLLIDE

T alanvar had suffered a long night with little sleep—the combination of khaffe and anxiety keeping eyelids from closing—and the day ahead promised to be even longer. All indications pointed to Ludar uprooting the city again, likely with more dead.

Birol brought te for Talanvar—an unusual request for him, but he said he had had too much khaffe the night before. Wisp, Darstan, and the others sat at the table in a state of slumber, half asleep and half awake. A servant raced in from the front gate, panting as he burst into the room.

"My Lord, gods help us; it's the queen!"

Before Talanvar spoke, Birol jumped back a step, arm covering his chest as if he would have an attack. "Here?"

"At your gate!" the servant said.

Talanvar was on his feet, wearing a mild case of panic. "Let her in. Hurry!" He stared at his manner of dress. "I can't receive the queen like this. Birol, stall until I return." He raced off toward his chambers.

Aenaila was on her way up the stairs when Talanvar left. She wore only a nightgown with a robe to cover it. Darstan and Wisp sat at the table, smiling, though Wisp's looked to be fake.

"Trouble, Wisp?"

He lost the smile. "More than you know."

"I might disappear," Darstan said.

"Don't you dare leave me. I need all the help I can get."

Darstan laughed, but he knew it wasn't funny. Put two strong-headed women like Aenaila and Cynamar in the same room—when both of them like the same man ... "Maybe I should leave."

Birol returned in a moment, ushering in Queen Cynamar. She looked regal in her soft-blue dress, and the smile she wore was the same one that had been on her face since before Wisp had known her. Blonde hair sat perfectly in a bun atop her head, and her blue eyes made her dress look even brighter.

"Kender Darnell!" She opened her arms to greet him, and Wisp went over and embraced her.

He hugged her, then pulled back, staring at her face. "You look beautiful, Cynamar. Or should I call you Queen Cynamar," he said, and bowed. It was an afterthought that reminded him she was only the queen due to the tragedy of her father's death. "I'm sorry. That was stupid of me." He leaned in and kissed her cheek, then she grabbed him and kissed his lips, passionately.

Just as the kiss began, Aenaila came down the stairs. Fire raged in her stomach. "Someone told me the queen was here." *And instead, I find a tramp.*

Wisp nearly fell over backward. He broke off the kiss, pushing away, and at the same time turning to Aenaila.

"Who is this woman?" Cynamar asked.

Wisp gulped, speechless for perhaps the first time in his life.

Darstan stepped over, bowed. "Queen Cynamar, I am Darstan. Please allow me to introduce you to—"

As Darstan spoke, Cynamar held out her hand, poised for the kiss of obeisance.

Aenaila fumed when she saw it and mimicked her every action, just as Darstan finished.

"–Queen Aenaila of Cergala."

Cynamar first saw the hand, then heard the words. She retracted her hand as if she had been stung. "What is this nonsense? I have never heard of Cergal."

"Cergala," Wisp said, almost at a whisper.

Flustered, embarrassed, and now completely flush in the cheeks, Cynamar sought an escape, finding one on the sofa. "You are a queen?" She refused to address her by name and wouldn't look at her.

"I have been for some time now, though it is only in name. My father is still the king." Aenaila walked to Cynamar's side, grabbed her hand in a consoling manner. "I am sorry about your father. It is an experience I don't ever want to have."

Cynamar fought a few tears, then looked up at her. "Where is this Cergala?"

"Across the sea, south of here."

"It is an island?"

Aenaila stifled a laugh, but before she could answer Wisp did.

"Cynamar ... excuse me, Queen Cynamar. Aenaila's land of Cergala is bigger than Sykor. Bigger even than Khatara."

She sat upright, back stiff as a board. "That is impossible. There are no islands that big, and besides, we would have known about a land that big."

"I've been there," Wisp said. "So has Darstan."

Cynamar's eyes seemed to be pried open. "Why are you here then? Why did you come back?"

"To get Takar," Darstan said. "We knew Ludar had him."

She stared at Wisp, but her eyes kept darting to Aenaila. "Is it true then? Did you do that to Ludar?"

He was silent for a while, then. "Yes. And now it looks as if I'm going to have to kill him."

Cynamar sat with her hands folded on her lap. She had dressed as "un-queenly" as she knew how, but she still looked like the "princess dolls" the merchants sold to the patrons from High Town. "After what he did yesterday, there are worse things that could happen."

Talanvar entered near the end of their conversation, waiting patiently until she had finished. "My Queen," he said, and bowed dutifully.

She looked relieved to see him, almost as if another noble amongst these cravens would equal the balance. "I had come here hoping to take you up on your offer, Lord Talanvar."

Puzzlement showed on his face. "My offer?"

"To take me to the Dongrel and the River's Edge."

Talanvar couldn't help but laugh. "My Queen, this is not the best of times for that. Perhaps if we wait—"

Her head was shaking before he finished. "No. This is precisely the time I need to go. They are in trouble. Confused. They need their queen right now."

Aenaila cleared her throat, calling attention to herself. "If the people in your Dongrel section are anything like the poor people in my lands, they are simple folks who wear their emotions on whatever garment covers them."

"What are you trying to say?"

"Simply this. They saw Ludar's men come into their homes, destroy their property, and kill their people. Ludar works for you. As far as they are concerned, that was you who caused them harm. You might as well have been leading the guards yourself."

"That is utter nonsense!"

Aenaila accepted some te from Birol. "Is it? I don't know that I'd bet my life on it." She paused, tried not to say it, but it just came out. "I don't even know that I'd bet your life on it."

A haughtiness came over Cynamar, even more than what she came in with. She unfolded her hands, stood, and announced her departure. "I should be going. Kender, you'll come with me."

Wisp didn't need to look back to know that Aenaila's eyes were on fire. He felt sure they were red now, not green. "I'll walk you to the gate if you like, but I can't go with you." His pause was noticeable. "I'm with Aenaila." Another, lesser pause. "I love her."

For Aenaila, everything softened at that moment. She could have squeezed that thief to death, ripped his clothes off, and made love to him right then and there.

For Cynamar, the exact opposite. For so long she had counted on his return. Waited for him to get back so her world could be right again. Her eyes widened. She breathed in sharply, then marched toward the door without another word. Birol had to run to get there before her so he could open it.

After she had gone, Talanvar closed the doors to the room and took a seat. "Looks as if I got dressed for nothing."

"I'm sorry, Aenaila," Wisp said. "I tried to keep it civil."

She brushed it off. "My fault as much as hers. When I came down and saw you two, I ... well, there is no other way to say it, I got jealous. I'm sure it showed. Women can tell those things."

"Regardless, we've got more important things to worry about. Remember, we still have Ludar terrorizing the city, and he's looking for us."

~

*C*ynamar stormed out of Talanvar's house, down the walk, and out the gate. She had never been so humiliated in her life. The nerve of that girl ... girl! She looked like an old woman compared to me. And she's got the audacity to call herself a queen!

"Back to the palace, My Queen?" the coach driver asked.

"Hurry up about it, too," she said and let him help her in the carriage. I'll show them. "Driver, after you drop me off, have Force Commander Ludar come see me. Tell him it's urgent."

"Yes, My Queen."

How could he do this to me? I have waited so long.

*B*efore noon, Ludar arrived at the palace, a contingent of guards with him. He met the queen in the sitting room next to the courtyard. Refreshments and food were already on the table. "You called for me, My Queen?"

"Be seated, Force Commander. Have something to eat." Cynamar grabbed a piece of fruit and bit into it. "I heard about your ... accident. I am sorry."

"Thank you."

"I also heard about the disasters that took place in the Dongrel and the River's Edge." She stared across at him. "Don't misunderstand me, Force Commander. I want no more displays like we had yesterday. This is not your city to trample as you see fit."

"But—"

"No! I am the ruler here. And I will determine what course of action we take. I will not see my father's work go to waste." She put down the fruit, picked up her te. "I am not unsympathetic to your plight, but there are always other options."

Ludar sighed. "We need to catch Takar, and I need to catch the man who did this to me."

"The guard is not your personal command. Besides, I know where this Kender Darnell is hiding."

Ludar slowly set his biscuit on the table. He stared at Cynamar, his eyes pleading, yet afire. "Where?"

"If I tell you where he is, I want it done cleanly. Neat, with no mess to clean up. If the people get stirred up by this ..."

"I already have a plan to get the people back on our side, but I need to know where he is. He is a dangerous man as you can see, and to leave him running loose ..."

Cynamar smiled. "He is traveling with a young woman. Not really so young, but pretty in her own sort of way."

Ludar nodded, likely wondering where she was going with this.

Cynamar leaned close to him, looked each way down the hall, then gritted her teeth. "When you capture him—and I want him captured, not killed—I want her killed. And I want her to suffer."

His face was blank for a moment, then a smile cracked, then unabridged laughter. "Of course, My Queen." He bowed low. "Your will is my command."

Cynamar plucked a cookie from a silver tray, nibbled on it. "He is at Lord Talanvar's home. I saw him there myself."

Rage boiled inside of Ludar. "Better and better, My Queen. Have comfort. This girl will die, and she will suffer."

She feigned indignation. "I don't know what you mean, Force Commander."

"Of course, My Queen," he said, then he bowed and took his leave.

43

DAY OF RECKONING

Ludar called his men to an early meeting. "Everything is set for today?"

"We're ready, Force Commander. We've got men stationed at every corner, and the streets will be closed off after the speech starts. If they try something, they'll be trapped."

"Either way is fine. If they don't show up, it will be just as much enjoyment going to get them at Talanvar's." *Perhaps more.*

~

Wisp paced across the tile floor of the library. "Are they ready yet?"

"You asked that on your last pass by this chair. Why don't you sit, they'll be here soon." Darstan, for once, was the calm one.

The door cracked and Aenaila entered followed by Talanvar and Adju.

"Adju's not coming," Wisp said.

Adju began to object but Aenaila's quick reprimand stopped that. "No!

You're staying with Birol. He knows what to do if we don't come back."

Birol burst into the room. "Gregor is here. He says it is urgent that he speak with you."

"Show him in," Talanvar said.

"Good. This will give us one more person," Darstan said.

"Don't trust him, Darstan. I'm telling you."

Gregor didn't bother with the greetings. "Ludar's got a trap. He assumes you're coming to the plaza, and he's planning to catch you."

"We figured as much," Talanvar said.

"There's more. He also knows you're here, Kender."

"What! How do you know?"

"My friend told me. Doesn't know who told him, but he knows. If he doesn't get you at the plaza, he'll be coming here."

Talanvar slammed his fist on the table. "That's all we need!"

Wisp smiled. "He won't be alive after the plaza."

"What do you plan to do?" the bounty-man asked.

Darstan started to respond, but Wisp cut him off. "I'll let you know when we get there. Let's get going."

*P*eople crowded the plaza long before Ludar arrived, pushing and shoving their way toward the front of the line in order to secure a good view, and to be in range to hear well.

It was the largest plaza in Sykor, with a grand stage in the center—used for plays and musical performances on nights when the weather cooperated—and a fountain graced each corner of the square. Merchants' shops guarded the perimeter with three cafes offering khaffe and te as well as pastries.

The sound of ten patrols marching down the cobblestone streets could be heard over the din of the crowd. They came from the guard's quarters, entering the plaza from the north, Ludar leading them at the forefront. Two patrols went up onto the stage with him and spread out on each side of him and behind him. The remaining eight patrols formed an inside perimeter, setting up a line between the people and Ludar.

The guards looked sharp in their calf-high black boots and their gray uniforms, swords peeking out of sheaths strapped to their shoulders. A lot of nervous citizens stood in the square, thousands of them, and the sheer number combined with the tension in the air made the guards anxious. They had strict orders to remain calm, controlled, yet despite that, many of their hands twitched—probably in anticipation of bloodshed.

At Ludar's signal, the guards snapped to attention. It had the effect the Force Commander desired, as the crowd became still. Upon seeing his opening, he began to speak.

"Good people of Sykor. I know that many of you are concerned with what has happened in our city, not just yesterday, but for some time now."

He studied the reactions on the faces he could see. Heads were nodding. people talking to each other. "First someone killed King Favian." He waited while they absorbed that. "Then someone did this to me." He slowly removed his hands from his pockets, holding them up for all to see.

Murmurs spread from the front rows. Some people even shouted it out. "They cut his thumbs off!"

Ludar let the news spread for a moment, then started up again. "That's right. They cut my thumbs off. That's why the guards got out of control yesterday. I didn't know that was happening. I was still recovering, but the guards were upset and wanted to find the men responsible."

Ludar shook his head slowly. "I don't agree with what they did. It's a shame that people had to die, but it has stopped. All I ask is that if anyone knows where Sergeant Takar or Kender Darnell are, they tell us. These men must be caught."

The crowd seemed to be favoring him, going along with all he said. One of Ludar's planted spies shouted loudly. "We'll find them, Force Commander."

The rest of the crowd soon took up the call, bringing a smile to Ludar's face. People were so easy to turn.

Leaning against a building close to the square, an older merchant and his wife observed the crowd with interest. "He is doing a remarkable job of it, don't you think?" the wife asked.

Ghruehne turned to stare at her. Despite the Illusion, her eyes always gave her away. He imagined his did the same. "I told him they wouldn't show up. Would have been fools to do so."

Sendra continued her inspection of the crowd, ever the cautious one. "They could be here the same as we are."

"They don't have the gift of Illusion. Not at that age."

"I wasn't referring to the boys," Sendra said. "Aentarra and Mikkellana could be with them."

Ghruehne nodded. "We'll keep watch for a while. Suppose we split up and mingle with the crowd."

Sendra agreed and walked to the left.

~

*W*isp and Darstan had Aenaila provide cover for them with her Illusion, and stood in the line of guards directly behind Ludar, each of them disguised as Sykoran Guards; Darstan even appeared to have two hands.

Aenaila stood to the side with Talanvar and Dirk, Illusion disguising them as well: her as an ordinary housewife so as not to draw attention, and Talanvar and Dirk as her ordinary husband and son. Gregor stood aside from them, another ordinary citizen watching the Force Commander's speech.

At Wisp's signal they moved. Darstan stepped to a spot behind Ludar and to the right. Wisp moved lightning fast, got behind Ludar to the left and put a blade to his throat, cutting him just a bit. Ludar gasped, more surprised than hurt.

Dozens of swords unsheathed as the guards raced toward the Force Commander.

Aenaila dropped the Illusion, and as she did, Darstan stepped forward, shooting a small column of fire at the guards charging from the front. One of the guard's uniform caught fire, enough to cause the rest of them to stop, then Darstan turned quickly and fired more at each group that advanced. Simultaneously, he yelled, unconsciously using Voice. "Stop! That's enough."

They all stopped, not even knowing why, and stared at him. Ludar gritted teeth. "I'll kill you for this, Darnell. I'll kill all of you."

~

Sendra made her way back to Ghruehne, weaving amongst the panicked crowd of people, trying not to look too calm, lest she draw suspicion. She let herself be nudged aside by a father rushing to get away with a small child in his arms, then hurried across an alleyway, tugging on Ghruehne's sleeve when she got near. "Did you hear? He has Voice."

"Impossible!"

"Impossible or not, he does."

Ghruehne lowered the hood on his cloak, moving toward the stage. "I'm going to kill him now."

"No," Sendra said, laying a hand on his arm. "We'll watch. See what happens."

~

The guards had stopped, but they were nervous, hands holding swords or spears, and more than a few shaking from fear.

Talanvar walked to the stage, eyes darting about warily. Aenaila and Dirk trailed behind him, and Gregor moved in from the left. Nerves were pulled taut on everyone, especially after Darstan used the Fire. Talanvar planted himself firmly, used his booming, gravelly voice to reach the people.

"You all heard Ludar talk about his love for Sykor, and how he meant no harm to the people. And you heard him whine about the loss of his thumbs, but he never told you why he lost them."

Talanvar reached his right hand back, bringing Dirk up to stand beside him. He held up Dirk's hands then continued. "You'll notice this innocent lad is also missing his thumbs." He paused. "Your Force Commander did this. Did it because he wanted information from the boy. Cut them off while the lad screamed and begged him not to."

Ludar yelled. "He's lying!"

Wisp pressed the blade to his neck drawing more blood.

"Tell them, Dirk." Talanvar said.

Dirk struggled, fear seizing his throat, but vengeance found the words. "He did it to me. I wouldn't tell him about a message I delivered for Kender Darnell, and he cut them off." Tears ran down his face. "He just cut them off," he said, then walked back to Aenaila, crying.

The crowd bought into Dirk's story. Wisp smiled. "This is for Dirk," he said, and took a firm grip on Ludar's hair then quickly removed the knife from his neck and stabbed him in the groin.

Ludar screamed, doubling over. Lightning quick, Wisp pulled the knife up to the Force Commander's throat again. "And this is for me." He slid the steel across Ludar's neck, spewing blood in a torrent. Ludar slumped to the stage, dead within a few heartbeats.

The guards rushed to attack, swords drawn.

"Stop!" Darstan shouted, but the Voice didn't work. "I don't want to do this," he shouted, but let the fire go. A column of fire struck the first group then he turned to attack the ones advancing from the side; meanwhile, Talanvar rushed Aenaila and Dirk into the crowd, forcing his way through to get them to the safety of a side street.

A patrol of guards from the right side advanced, then, when they were within range, threw their spears at Darstan.

"Look out!" Wisp yelled.

Darstan spun, saw the spears but he had no time to avoid them. Somehow, without him even calling it, BlackFire roared from his arm.

A crack like thunder in a summer storm sounded, then the spears caught fire, burning to nothing in an instant. But the BlackFire didn't stop there, it continued, engulfing the guards, then the front rows of the people, killing them all. The other guards rushed him from both sides. Darstan shook his head, thoughts of all the good things Magmar had taught him racing through his mind. *Father forgive me.*

He called BlackFire, sending large columns of flames against them. He tried to keep it restricted to the guards.

Their bodies turned to ash before they hit the ground. At that, panic set in, people and guards alike scrambling to escape, trampling each other, screaming, heads turned to ensure he wasn't coming for them. The stench of burnt flesh filled the air, seeped down the side streets and alleys. Death had come to Sykor.

Wisp stood with two knives drawn, Gregor beside him. "Just like old times, thief."

"Seems to get more dangerous as we move along," Wisp said.

"We need to get him now!" Ghruehne said.

"Don't be a fool. Our time will come."

"He's just a boy. We should kill him. Make one less to deal with."

Sendra patted his arm. "He's a very strong boy. Remember how strong Antar was at this age?"

"He isn't Antar."

"No, he's not Antar, but we have no idea who he is. Besides, did you see the way he used that BlackFire? Impressive." Sendra stared at Darstan as he stood on the stage surveying the scene. "By the Blood, Ghruehne, look at him. Look at that face!"

Ghruehne stepped forward a pace or two, stared at Darstan, then back to face Sendra. "Turn slowly. Let's leave."

44

NEW PLANS

Sykor was in a state of turmoil: the people panicked and afraid, and the guards angry and afraid. All of it was vented toward Darstan. It no longer mattered what Ludar had done to Dirk or the people of the Dongrel; all that mattered was that Darstan had used fire to kill Sykorans.

Guards roamed the streets in groups of three and four patrols, some of them incorporating citizens of Sykor on their own accord. Twice they came up to Talanvar's house, demanding he turn Darstan over to them, though they never pressed the issue beyond that.

They kept a half a strike force outside of Talanvar's mansion, guarding all means of escape. And to a man, they were armed with arrows and spears in addition to swords. Darstan might be able to stop some of them, but he wouldn't be able to stop them all.

"I'm going out there," Darstan said.

Aenaila grabbed his arm, pulling him toward her. "They'll kill you. There are too many for you to fight; besides, you don't want to have to kill those men." She embraced Darstan, laying her head on his shoulder. "Why don't we just leave?"

"And Takar?"

"By tomorrow he should be healed enough that I can leave him in Lord Talanvar's care. I can even come back to check on him once we get settled."

Wisp sat on the floor, cleaning his nails with a knife, his routine when he was bored or nervous.

"It's a good idea, Darstan. Bragh is in charge of the guards now, and he's almost as bad as Ludar. Even worse, Cynamar seems to be supporting him. We could go to Genda or even back to Khatara."

"I never did get to Khatara," Gregor said. "But we have a bigger problem than deciding on where to go." He opened the curtains and looked outside, staring at the guards. "I don't think they are just going to let us out."

Wisp laughed. Darstan too. Aenaila walked over to Gregor, smiling at him. "We travel by a different means."

Confusion showed on Gregor's face.

"Never mind, Bounty-man. You wouldn't understand anyway. Let's just say if we decide to go, we can be in Pomanda or Genda or Khatara before the guards are having their afternoon meal." Wisp stood, walking around as if he were lost. "But there is a lot we'd be leaving here." He turned to Talanvar. "Lot of risk for you."

"I can take care of things here," Talanvar said. "I'll use my contacts to try and appease the people. If we can do that, perhaps the guards will come to their senses."

Darstan paced, grabbing a piece of cheese from the table. "Pomanda."

"Why Pomanda?" Aenaila asked.

"He'll be there."

"Who?" She asked it, but she knew the answer.

"You know who—Rahg."

Wisp stopped, stared up at him. "What makes you think he'll be there? Nothing for him in Pomanda."

"I just know. I ... feel it."

Aenaila shook her head. "I'll check on Takar. You two get ready."

"What about me?" Adju asked.

"You're staying with Talanvar and Dirk," Wisp said. "It could be dangerous where we're going."

"But, Master—"

"You've got to stay here, Adju. But I'll be back."

Wisp and Darstan packed what clothes and things they needed. Aenaila finished with Takar, then packed her things. Soon, they were ready to leave. "Are you coming, Bounty-man?" Wisp asked.

Gregor nodded. "I'm coming, but I feel like I have been lost for years. What is going on and why is Darstan after Rahg? And how are we going to get to Pomanda without the guards—?"

Wisp put a finger to his mouth. "Don't worry. And besides, I think that's the most you've talked since I met you. I liked you better when you were quiet."

"At least have a meal before you go," Talanvar said.

Darstan shook his head. "We'll eat in Pomanda," he said, then turned to Aenaila. "Ready?"

She held out her hand, taking hold of Darstan, Gregor, and Wisp, then shifted.

A rift opened in their house in Pomanda, a few small rooms near the central plaza. Darstan, Gregor, Wisp, and Aenaila stepped through. She quickly looked about, knowing full well the dangers of shifting anyplace unknown, then relaxed and settled into one of the chairs by the door. "I know you two will want to eat right away, but I'd like to rest first."

Darstan plopped in the other chair, his leg finding the arm for a rest. "That's all right; we need to plan out what we're doing anyway."

"Ah, plans," Wisp said. "Glad to see we are still making them. I thought we were now relying solely on your infallible instincts."

Gregor stood in the room staring at the wall, a look on his face as if he had just seen the Evil One himself. "What just happened? And where are we?"

Aenaila laughed. "We are in Pomanda, Gregor, and that was called Shifting." She saw the questions on his face. "I can always return to a place I've been just by thinking of it, forming an image in my mind."

As Gregor stood shaking his head, Darstan paced. "We'll go to all the inns," he said, "especially the ones we stayed in before.

And I'll talk to Nirida." Darstan turned to Wisp. "You can ask Sengua."

"Let's see Sengua first," Wisp said. "The most likely chance of finding them is through him."

Darstan stood. "I'm ready."

"I'm staying here," Aenaila said. "I have no desire to spend an evening in a tavern with thieves."

"We might be late," Wisp said, then they left.

They had to search three taverns and several other known haunts before finding Sengua, tucked into a corner table at a small establishment near the Bentarina Cormal. He had a mug of ale and a half-eaten plate of beef-and-vegetables before him.

Wisp looked around, saw nothing suspicious, so he pulled up a chair, nodding to Darstan and Gregor to do the same. "Been a long time, Sengua."

Sengua stared at them, scooping up some broccoli and a few carrots while he did. He chewed in silence, still staring, then set his fork down. "A lot has happened in Pomanda since then."

Wisp looked to Darstan, then to Sengua. "We just came back today. Don't know anything."

"You must have walked the streets with your eyes and ears closed, friend. Guards are everywhere, and you can't walk two blocks without someone asking your opinion on who killed the king."

"Somebody killed the king?" Darstan asked.

Sengua took his knife and cut into the beef, slicing up a few large pieces. "Just a few days past. Think it might have been someone from inside the castle." He stared at them some more. "You really didn't know this?"

"Who's king now?" Wisp asked.

"Haven't decided on it yet. The council is meeting in the next few days to decide. It'll be Varga, Preman, or Ciro. Probably Varga." He chewed on the beef some, then, "What are you here for?"

Wisp seemed lost in thought, then he came alert, realizing Sengua was talking to him. "What?"

"I asked what you were here for?"

"Looking for old friends. Remember the ones we traveled with, Rahg and—"

"I remember the one who killed the Black Rose."

"That was Rhaven," Darstan said. "Have you seen him?"

"Not since he left with you. I'd remember if I saw him again." Sengua shook his head. "Never saw a fight like that before and probably never will again."

"Don't mean to rush, Kender, but ..."

Wisp patted Sengua on the arm. "We have to go too, but don't forget to let us know if you see any of them. We'll be checking the Inn of the Turtle often so you can leave a message."

As they left, Kender whispered to Darstan. "Lot of kings being killed lately."

"One too many for coincidence. Lukaan has to be behind this. But why?" They stepped onto a crowded walk, and it was then that Darstan noticed how many guards were roaming about; he spotted three patrols within two blocks. "Sengua wasn't kidding about the guards. Look at them."

Gregor grabbed him by the arm. "Don't stare, Darstan. As nervous as they probably are it will give them a reason to question us, and the last thing we want is to draw attention."

"I know. I was just thinking all the guards will make it more difficult," Darstan said. "I don't need guards around to interfere."

"Make what more difficult?" Gregor asked.

"Killing Rahg. I don't want a bunch of guards interfering when I find him."

Wisp stopped, pulling Darstan to the side, away from the traffic of the people. "Darstan, you still don't know what happened back there. How—"

Darstan's eyes narrowed, and his jaw clenched. "I know he killed her. That's all I need to know. Besides, if Lukaan is behind this, it's probably because he knows he's getting out soon. That's the only thing that makes sense. And if he's getting out, it's Rahg who's going to do it."

Darstan stepped back. "Remember what they said about him?" Darstan slowly nodded his head, as if agreeing with himself. "One more reason to kill him," he said, then made his way back to the street.

Wisp rushed to catch up. "Before you do anything, you should let me talk to him," he said, but he could tell his words fell on deaf ears.

BAIT

Rahg paced, shaking his head all the while. He had enjoyed his stay in Vallah, especially since he and Camissa had gotten together, but Mikkellana brought reality home.

She announced they were leaving, going to Pomanda, fishing for Banished Ones—and he was going to be the worm they used on the hook. "I'm not going. They could kill me before you even recognize them." He stared at Mikkellana with a plea in his eyes.

Aentarra chuckled. "Don't think she'll save you. What do you think you've been all along?" She rose from the chair, walked toward Rahg. "Bait, boy. Nothing but bait. Mikkellana knew they were after you. That's why she trailed you as that dog. Didn't want them to know she was around." A frown formed on her face. "Besides, we haven't come this far to turn back or hide." Anger bubbled to the surface. "They are the ones who should be hiding. Not us."

Rhaven sat on the floor against the wall. "How will they come for him? Openly?"

Mikkellana seemed to give it thought. "It depends. If they think we're setting a trap, they will be disguised. They'll wait until they are certain he's alone, or at least without us, then they'll attack. It will vary greatly depending on who escaped. We can be certain it wasn't Lukaan or Melissara, so it has to be Ghruehne and Sendra, or possibly Tirzinitzia.

Ghruehne would probably announce himself, make it a challenge. He would think himself too superior to care if Rahg was taken unaware. Sendra, however, would simply attack. Go for the kill. Tirzinitzia would study the situation and devise a clever plan. She is the most devious of them all. A careful strategist."

"I told you it was Ghruehne and Sendra," Aentarra said.

"I'm not relying on your Sense alone, sister."

Rhaven nodded, thinking it through.

"I'm not going to do it," Rahg said.

Camissa agreed. "Too much risk. We'll have to think of another way."

"Despite what I've said about my sister, this is the best way," Aentarra said.

Camissa spun around to face her, defiant. "It's not your life, Aentarra. It was different when the Banished Ones were still trapped behind the shield, when we were dealing with assassins and Victas and Wolfen, but now they're out. They could strike at any time, and Rahg will have no protection."

"Can you wrap yourself in a shield, Rahg? Maintain it all day?" Aentarra asked.

"What good will that do? I can't make a shield to hold them off."

"No, you can't, but it would stop it from being a killing attack with one blow. In fact, whatever it was those gods did to you might help enough to keep you alive. At least from any of those three."

Aentarra smiled. "It would be painful, perhaps even damaging, but it wouldn't kill you. And that would be all we'd need. Once they strike, we'll see where they are, and we can retaliate."

"You're crazy! I'm not going to let them attack me."

Aentarra glared. "You'll do what I say, or I'll strike you myself, and that little shield of yours won't help you then."

Rahg looked to Mikkellana for support but found none.

"Aentarra is right about this. It probably won't kill you, and it's our best chance to get them."

Tobias interrupted. "Not right. I don't care what you say. We ought to wait it out or hunt them down. Don't like the idea of using the lad as bait."

Mikkellana nodded. "I know you are all worried about Rahg, and rightfully so, but if we don't get them quickly, or if the others get out, then we're doomed. We are probably doomed anyway once Lukaan gets out, but no sense in making it easier for him."

The thought of Lukaan getting out gave Rahg pause; he grimaced. "I'll do it. I don't like it, but I'll do it."

They spent time formulating a plan, then set out for Pomanda.

Mikkellana disguised herself as an old lady one day, a merchant woman the next, a young girl another. Aentarra swallowed pride and assumed the guise of a plain-looking servant working at a shop in the square.

As Rahg and the others moved through the town, Mikkellana changed faces, sometimes walking ahead of them, at other times trailing them, but all the while keeping a keen eye on everything.

⁓

Ghruehne waited in the square, Illusion disguising him as a young lad. Rhaven and Rahg came out of a merchant's shop and headed in his direction. Patience was difficult to control. He wanted to strike now, but he would wait, as Sendra suggested.

Rahg and Rhaven moved toward the center of the square, Camissa and Tobias close behind them. Ghruehne kept a close watch. He saw no one following. He walked past them a dozen or so paces, looked at some goods on a peddler's cart, then turned to trail behind them. He could keep a better watch from there.

Rahg went down a side street, and the others went with him. He walked halfway down the street, and no one had followed. Now convinced that they were alone, Ghruehne waited, he felt certain they would be back.

~

A patrol of Pomandan Guards turned on the street ahead of Rahg, heading in his direction. He watched them for a moment but paid them little heed. He was more interested in trying to spot a Banished One. "Another quiet day," Rahg said.

Rhaven nodded but focused a wary eye on a beggar ahead of them. "Be alert for this beggar. Do you have your shield up?"

"It's there. Been there all day and I'm getting tired. This is the fourth day in a row we've tried this. It's beginning to wear on my nerves."

"Frayed nerves don't hurt as much as lightning," Tobias said, chuckling as he did.

The guards stopped the beggar in the street, questioning him. Rhaven's hand tensed, prepared to draw Mikkellana's sword, but the guards let the beggar go and moved on, heading straight toward Rahg and Rhaven. They stopped when they got within a few paces.

"We're looking for an escaped prisoner. Dressed in ragged clothes, about your size," the patrol leader said, and pointed to Rahg. "Dark hair and eyes, carrying a guard's sword and sheath."

"Can't say we've seen anyone like that," Tobias said, "but then again we haven't been lookin'."

The patrol leader nodded. "He's dangerous, so if you see him, tell the first guard you see. Or capture him yourself, if you feel brave. Nice reward on this one."

Rhaven studied them but saw nothing wrong. "We'll keep an eye open."

"Be plenty of patrols around today, tell any one of them," he said, then moved toward the square.

Rhaven walked halfway up the block, then turned back and led them toward the square again.

"I can't wait to get back to the inn," Rahg said. "I'm tired."

"Won't be long, lad. Kind of hungry myself."

They soon entered the square and headed across the center area toward the inn. The patrol of guards they had just met was standing in the center. A young lad approached from the side, and before anyone could react, his image changed and Ghruehne stood before them. The air exploded and lightning struck Rahg, knocking him to the ground.

Camissa screamed.

Tobias drew his sword and moved toward Ghruehne while Rhaven drew his sword and charged.

Ghruehne hurled another bolt of lightning at Rahg, then moved away from Rhaven's attack and focused attention on him, calling BlackFire.

~

Mikkellana had been in a shop, watching from the window. When she saw Ghruehne transform, she raced into the square, weaving a shield to protect Rahg just in time to stop Ghruehne's second attack. The boy might be dead already. Got to strengthen the shield, she thought. Then I'll take care of Ghruehne.

Two of the guards drew swords and attacked Tobias while one of the others went after Camissa. The patrol leader moved to the side, transformed into Sendra and called up BlackLightning, striking Mikkellana in the back. Before Mikkellana hit the ground a bolt of lightning struck her. Mikkellana's head smashed against the cobblestones, and her shield protecting Rahg fell.

Rhaven swung the sword, barely missing Ghruehne, but he pressed the attack, moving quick as a mountain cat. Ghruehne's BlackFire came at him. Rhaven fended it off with the sword, but he knew there was only so many times the sword could do that.

"See if she's alive!" Aentarra yelled. "If she dies, the shield goes down." Fire shot from her hands in pinpoint precision, striking the guards in their heads and hearts. Three bolts of lightning struck at Sendra, and simultaneously, a Slicer emerged from her pouch and flew to Ghruehne, striking him before he even knew what was happening. His body went still.

Rahg struggled to get to his feet, shaking his head, pain wracking his body. "Help me up, Camissa."

"Tend to Mikkellana, girl!" Aentarra yelled. "Rahg, attack Sendra. Rhaven, protect my body. Tobias, kill Ghruehne." With that said, Aentarra's body went still, standing in the street as if she were a statue.

More guards came and engaged Tobias, keeping him away from Ghruehne. Sendra issued BlackFire, a wall wide enough to engulf them. Rahg had just gotten to his feet, still weak. He formed the best shield he could, but it buckled as soon as the BlackFire hit it. *Next one will get us.*

Sendra sent another stream, this time it was blocked by Rhaven's sword. On the third attack, Rahg's shield failed. The Sword of Mikkellana held, but it became too hot to hold. It had nothing left in it.

"This might be it," Rhaven called out, and then he charged toward Sendra, hoping to catch her off guard.

Rahg fought to weave a shield, but he was empty. *Couldn't get anything.*

~

*D*arstan walked ahead of Wisp, Gregor, and Aenaila, always rushing, eager to question the next person. He felt a presence he recognized and knew Rahg was in Pomanda. Just then, he stopped. "Did you feel it, Aenaila? The square!" He ran toward the square, but Wisp grabbed his sleeve at the last moment.

"It will be faster if we shift."

He stopped, but anxiety had hold of him. "Hurry, Aenaila."

She joined hands with them then shifted.

Darstan stepped through the rift first, with Wisp and Aenaila right on his heels, Gregor bringing up the rear. Aenaila saw Ghruehne's strike, then Sendra's, and she noted the futile resistance Rahg and Rhaven were putting up. "Banished Ones!"

Instinct took over. BlackFire roared from Darstan's arm, racing toward Sendra.

~

*S*endra sensed it more than felt or heard, and she countered with a column of her own BlackFire, colliding with Darstan's head on. The impact jarred both of them. She recovered in time to send fire against Rhaven, who was coming at her with his sai drawn. The fire struck him, but not full force. His clothes caught aflame, and he went down, face and arms burning. Tobias broke away from the guards and rushed over. He threw his shirt over him and put the flames out; meanwhile, Gregor engaged the guards Tobias had been fighting.

Sendra surveyed the scene. Rahg and the others were about done. Mikkellana was dead, and Aentarra was in the Planes of the Mind. She focused on Darstan; he was by far the more dangerous one.

She halted the attack on Rahg, focusing everything on Darstan. She knew that Rahg would be getting some of his powers back soon, so she hurled strong bolts of lightning all over the square, knowing that he would try to protect the innocents, expend his energy and give her a chance to channel a good strike on him. Soon they would all be dead. Darstan was another matter. She had seen him kill before, and he looked as if he might enjoy it. She couldn't relax with him.

BlackLightning roared from a clear sky, striking all around Darstan. He jumped, barely avoiding the last one, then he renewed his attack in time to fend off another strike. She was fast.

Sendra caught sight of Aenaila and Wisp from the periphery, knew them to be friends of his. She funneled a ferocious attack all about Darstan, then directed several strikes at Aenaila and Wisp. Aenaila grabbed Wisp just before it struck, and shifted.

Rage fueled Darstan's fire. "Want to play that way, do you?" Darstan funneled his own onslaught at her, then, with no hesitation, directed a column of fire at Ghruehne's listless body.

Sendra didn't much care for Ghruehne, but he would be needed in this struggle with only the two of them out of Sethia. She sent a wall of fire to deflect Darstan's attack, then raced to where Ghruehne's body was, grabbed him, and shifted.

Everything in the plaza seemed to be aflame: carts, merchants' stands, even most of the stores. Darstan scanned the destruction, alert for another attack. She could have gone anywhere and could return at any time. "Keep your eyes open," he said to Wisp.

Suddenly Darstan stopped as if he remembered something. Turning his head, he stared at Rahg, kneeling on the ground next to Mikkellana. "Get up, Rahg! Get up and fight me."

Wisp grabbed his arm, but Darstan shook him off. "Stay out of it, Wisp. He's mine." Darstan stared at Rahg. "Why did you do it?"

Rahg stood, trembling. "Darstan, what are you doing? Why—"

"Shut up! Do you hear me? Shut up, or I'll kill you now."

Rhaven stepped in front of Rahg, sai drawn. "We should talk, Darstan."

Camissa, her hair a mess, got up from tending to Mikkellana and ran toward Darstan. "What's the matter with you? This is your brother!" She reached him and pounded on his chest.

Darstan stood his ground, wrapped his arm around Camissa. "He betrayed me. When we were in Cergala, he attacked when he promised to stay out of it." Tears formed in Darstan's eyes. He trembled. "He killed her, Camissa. He killed my wife. Killed my son."

Camissa stood back. "You were married?"

"Not married yet, but she was pregnant. And Rahg killed her." Darstan wiped the tears away. "Now I'm going to kill him."

Aenaila grabbed Wisp. "We need to get him out of here."

"Take him. I'm staying."

"They'll kill you!" she screamed.

"They won't hurt me. Take him away. When he calms down enough, come back for me."

"Kender, I—"

"Go!"

Aenaila grabbed Darstan, formed an image of her home in Khatara, then shifted.

"No!" Darstan screamed as he realized what was happening.

46

AENTARA'S PLOY

Ghruehne stood in the middle of nothing. Nothing! How can this be? Aentarra was nowhere in sight. There was not even a hint that she was there or had been there, yet it had been long enough, she had to be there. He wondered why, then more importantly—how. How could she be here and I can't see her?

After some thought it occurred to him that perhaps Stealth worked in the Planes, that she could see him even though he couldn't see her.

He expended enough energy to wrap a small shield about himself, not enough to stop a major attack, but something.

He built a small forest about himself. If she couldn't see him before, she definitely would now. The forest would draw attention to him, but it would also shield him from her eyes.

He wrapped the perimeter of the woods with sensor probes, enough to warn him if she approached. There was no telling what that crazy witch would do, so he needed at least this much warning. It seemed like ages that he waited. He was not a patient man. Where is she? When will she strike?

Ghruehne tried some relaxing mantras, but the anticipation ran like fire through his veins. *Where is she?*

~

*A*entara's mind twisted, swirled, rushed toward that inexplicable place called the Planes of the Mind. There is where battles were fought. There is where the fate of worlds was decided. And there were few better at fighting in the Planes than she was. Ghruehne would be there already, waiting, watching. Nervous for her to enter. Perhaps overconfident. All of this played to her advantage. She would use it all.

She hovered in the void, cloaked in Stealth. Even though anything was possible in the Planes of the Mind, a person must understand how something works in order to effect it, and since she was the only one who possessed the powers of Stealth, she was the only one who could be invisible.

She sat outside the forest Ghruehne created, watching, waiting. He couldn't see her, hear her, smell her, or sense her. On the other hand, she had to figure out a way to get to him with those sensors in place. Aentarra thought for a long time, then she smiled and got rid of the forest Ghruehne had created.

Ghruehne panicked, turning in all directions, eyes straining to find her. His sensors were still in place, but she was close, and she was toying with him.

The only thing he could do was wait for her to act. A ping hit the sensor behind him, barely a touch, but enough to trigger an alert. He jumped, spun around, then suddenly remembered who he faced— Aentarra! She would likely alert him from the rear, assuming he'd anticipate a frontal attack. He quickly spun around again to the rear, backing up instinctively as he did.

Aentarra knew she couldn't make the same mistake she'd done with Iazzo. She had almost died fighting him, and now there would be no one to save her. Ghruehne was more powerful, she knew, far more powerful than Iazzo, but still ... *How much is enough?*

If she used too much power against Ghruehne, and he was overwhelmed, it would come back to strike her when she was weakest. And she couldn't use her power to counter her own energy. The Planes of the Mind didn't work that way. She'd have to do some testing. See what he was made of. But she needed to do it quickly. If Sendra finished with Rahg and the others and came to help Ghruehne, Aentarra would be at a great disadvantage. Too much of one.

He'd have sensors set up everywhere, but the one problem with sensors was they could only tell you the power of the foremost attack. If another attack followed, the sensors could not determine its strength until the first attack was gone. So if one attack followed the other closely, Ghruehne wouldn't have time to gauge it and mount a counterattack.

Aentarra laughed. *Now the strategy comes into play. Now the games begin.*

~

Ghruehne strolled in his new makeshift forest, wary to the dangers lurking everywhere. The Planes of the Mind had always been a dangerous place, but when fighting with Aentarra, it was far more than dangerous. She was crazy enough to kill herself along with her opponent.

She had almost done it several times before, and that was when she was practicing. With that said, he knew she was also a brilliant strategist, a trait inherited from her father.

Curse her and those Slicers. I would rather have faced her outside.

He checked once again to ensure his probes were in place and active. They would be key to his survival. He tested each probe, made certain they were positioned properly, then put up a second line of probes for further defense. Nothing to do now but wait.

~

*A*entarra let him wait. And wait. Then wait some more. The longer he worried, the more reckless he would become. Patience was not a virtue of Ghruehne's. Finally, when she felt the time to be right, she sent the first wave of energy. It was designed in the shape of Fire, but she only dispatched a small Force, one measuring only twelve on the power scale developed by her father so long ago. It was nothing he could not defend with ease.

The strongest Force she had ever created was against Iazzo, and that was only a fifty-six. She could have done more, perhaps a sixty-five, but that would have trebled the Force she used on Iazzo. As far as they knew, no one could create a Force above one hundred. That was a legendary figure, and it was felt that no one could even create it, let alone survive it. So, if she used a fifty-six against Iazzo and it was far too much, what was the right amount against Ghruehne?

If he recognized a Force he could not defend, would he simply give up, not create a defense and let Aentarra die as well? Would he do that just to get even? Aentarra paused to think. Ghruehne was liable to do anything when his pride got injured.

No, she decided, she would have to ensure he defended against the attack, and with all, or most of his power. But how to do that?

Her mind kept returning to the sensors. They were the key. She had to trick the sensors, which was impossible, or, trick Ghruehne into reacting before he knew the strength of the attack.

She had to time her attacks so one came immediately after the other, almost on top of it. The first should be mild—perhaps a Force fifteen attack, followed closely, but not too close, by a Force twenty-five or thirty, and immediately behind that, riding on its back a forty-five or so.

That would tax her, to do three so close together. It was a dangerous ploy, especially if Sendra entered, or if Ghruehne countered these and then retaliated. If he did that, she would be too weak to defend herself.

Aentarra doubted that he could sustain the defense against three attacks of that magnitude, at least not without serious damage. Once he countered the twenty-five and realized there was a Force behind it, he would assume it was a strong Force and defend it vigorously. If it didn't crush him, perhaps his retaliation would leave him vulnerable.

~

Ghruehne felt the first probe go off, an alert to a breach. He leapt to his feet, formed a defense, but smiled when he realized the strength of the attack. He countered with a widespread Force of fifteen, enough to dispel the attack and send Aentarra a small message, too. It collided with Aentarra's second attack, a Force of twenty-five. This Force slowed a bit, slightly weakened, but it was still a danger approaching Ghruehne at tremendous speed.

Aentarra sent a strong force against Ghruehne from the rear, just where he expected. Ghruehne sensed it in time and turned to defend himself, but simultaneously, Aentarra issued a second attack from the front. It was weaker, but still a strong force. While Ghruehne defended against the main attack, the secondary force struck him, knocking him out. Once he was out, Aentarra called on every bit of strength she had left. She shaped her energy, worked it, then formed it into a javelin. Once it was completed, she pierced his heart.

The strain was unbearable. She stumbled, then fell. Exhaustion had taken hold of her, probably from having used too much power. She only prayed that the reverberations didn't kill her.

47

REUNION

Aenaila and Darstan reappeared in the safe house the Khataran safe house. Darstan shook his arm away from Aenaila. "You shouldn't have done that. That was my business back."

Aenaila never flinched. "I don't care one way or another about Rahg, but I do for you. If you kill him, you'll never forgive yourself. You haven't even given him a chance to explain."

"There's nothing to explain, Aenaila. He killed Mirana, and he's going to die."

"Fine, do it from here, then," she said, and shifted.

"No!" Darstan screamed as she left, fire already dancing on his fingers.

~

Wisp walked over to where Rahg stood with the rest of them. The square was empty with the exception of the stragglers peeking out from behind the fountain and from one of a few windows where the shutters had been open to slits.

Several shops smoldered from the fighting, and more than a few bodies lay in the square, marked with lightning or charred by fire. Camissa knelt next to Mikkellana, still on the ground, unconscious. And Rhaven stood guard over her while Tobias kept alert from the butcher's shop at the edge of the square.

Wisp tapped Camissa on the arm. "Camissa, good to see you again. I've missed your company." He nodded to Tobias and Rhaven, and to Rahg who stood between them. "Rahg, we need to talk."

A smile darted across Camissa's face, a brief one. "Good to see you, Kender, but right now I'm tending to Mikkellana. She's hurt badly."

"What's the matter with Darstan?" Rahg asked. "He tried to kill me!"

"Because of what you did in Arangar. We thought we had an agreement with you to stay out of it, then you used your shields, and his wife died."

"What agreement are you talking about? I didn't even know he was there. We thought you were in Khatara with Aenaila."

Wisp studied them as he talked. "You never got a message from Darstan when you were in Arangar that day at the pass?"

"I told you, Wisp, I didn't even know you were there."

Wisp nodded, and as he was thinking, Aenaila appeared. Rhaven reached for his sai but kept it sheathed when he saw who it was.

"Kender, are you all right?" Aenaila stared at the others as she moved to Wisp. "I left Darstan in Khatara."

"Is he all right?" Rahg asked.

"Not in his head. He blames you for Mirana's death, and right now so do I. What happened?"

"I just told Wisp, I didn't even know you were there. I never got a message from anyone. We thought we were helping the people of Arangar against an enemy."

Aenaila remained silent for a moment, then nodded her head as she turned to Wisp.

"Mattu," she said. "It could only have been him. He faked the message, knowing that they would attack and that Darstan would see it as a breach of trust."

"The thing he didn't count on was getting Mirana killed," Wisp said. "Even Mattu didn't want all of that killing."

"We've been to Arangar," Rhaven said. "Did Darstan do that?"

Wisp nodded. "All of that and more."

A disturbance in the air, almost as if a rift had opened, brought their attention to the side of the building next to where Tobias stood. Aentarra moved, but on legs so wobbly that she couldn't stand. Tobias grabbed hold of her and gently set her down.

"Where's Mikkellana?" she asked.

"Over there," Tobias said, pointing to where Camissa tended her. "She's hurt, but alive."

Aentarra tried to get up, but couldn't lift her head. "Need to heal her. Quickly!"

"Are you all right?" Tobias asked. "Seem mighty hurt yourself."

"I'll be fine, but she needs to be healed right away. No time to waste," she said, then fell back down.

Camissa got up and went to Aenaila. "Can you help her?"

"I'll try," Aenaila said and followed Camissa to where Mikkellana lay. She knelt by her side, running her hands over Mikkellana's back where the lightning had struck her. The dress was mostly gone, and her skin was charred, bone exposed.

Tobias stayed by Aentarra, but Rhaven, Rahg, and Wisp moved to stand over Aenaila while she worked on Mikkellana.

"There's not much blood," Rahg said.

"Wound's been seared," Rhaven said.

"She's barely breathing," Aenaila said. "I don't know if there's much I can do."

Aentarra stirred again. "Need to get out of here, fast!"

"Keep still, Lady Aentarra," Tobias said. "We'll take care of you."

Aentarra sneered. "If you don't do as I say immediately, we'll all die. I killed Ghruehne, and now that Sendra knows that, she'll be coming back to get you." Aentarra gulped, lifting her head higher. "She knows Mikkellana is dead or hurt and she'll know I'm weak. That leaves only you to defend yourselves against a Banished One. It won't take her long, so hurry."

"Get her over here," Aenaila said. "Everyone join hands and we'll shift to a safe house."

As Tobias and Rhaven helped Aentarra, a disturbance shook the square. Through the rift stepped Sendra.

SENDRA'S REVENGE

Sendra placed Ghruehne's body in a safe place, then shifted back to Pomanda. A quick, all-encompassing glance told her all she needed to know. Mikkellana was either dead, or near death, and Aentarra was too weak to do anything, needing help even to walk. The rest would be no problem. She focused, forming the images to strike. Lightning shot straight for them, two strikes at once.

Rhaven jumped to intercept the strike with his sword, catching the first one, though he could feel something wrong—it sent a shock throughout his body. He missed the second bolt, but fortunately, it missed them as well, splintering the paving stones next to where Camissa stood. "Spread out," Rhaven called and moved toward Sendra.

Wisp immediately cloaked and began sneaking around to the side of her.

Sendra struck a second time, issuing BlackFire in a low, rolling wall toward them and striking again with a massive force of BlackLightning from above.

Rhaven again intercepted the lightning, but this attack broke his sword, shattering it, and crippling his arm at the same time. He went down, his right side paralyzed.

Rahg wove a shield to stop the fire, but even with the first strike, he felt the pressure mounting. She was strong. His shield would never take another hit like that.

～

Darstan threw the vase against the wall, smashing it, then turned over the table. Fire shot from his arm, igniting the sofa but he quickly smothered the flames. He tried thinking of other things, but all that came to his mind was the fight in Pomanda. The square. Rahg! And the Statue of the Ancients. He could see it so clearly, that odd fountain where he experienced the eerie sensation. He sat on the chair, but the image of the fountain wouldn't leave his mind, nor would the feelings of vengeance.

Suddenly, he felt light-headed, dizzy, and he smelled a faint aroma of ... what, cedar? Then his ears perked up, an odd sound—like sheets rustling—silk sheets, he thought, just as he disappeared.

～

Sendra felt the rift open and turned to face Darstan, just stepping through. "Fool, that's the problem with Shifting. Come in the middle of a battle, and you're dead." She struck at once, issuing BlackFire in a massive attack. He countered, but a shade too late, absorbing the brunt of her assault.

Sendra smiled. One down, she thought and focused on her final strike.

Wisp dodged out of the way when Sendra struck Darstan, and when he did, he lost his concealment, bringing him to Sendra's attention. She hurled a quick shot of fire at him, but Rahg wove a shield just in time to save him.

Rahg had no shield left, but Darstan was on fire, and he had to do something. He drew his sword and raced toward Sendra, yelling at the top of his lungs.

She turned, struck at him with Lightning, then focused once again on Darstan.

The Lightning hit Rahg and dropped him, his head bouncing off of the cobblestones, spewing blood. If he had not been infused with Shield either the Lightning or the head wound would have killed him. As it was, he lay there fading in and out of consciousness.

Camissa knelt next to Rhaven, trying to pull him out of harm's way. She was now close enough to Aenaila, as was Tobias and Gregor with Aentarra.

"Aenaila, we should get them out of here. Can you shift with all of us?"

"As long as I don't go too far. Join hands."

"I'm stayin' here," Tobias said. "The boy needs my help."

"You can't fight a Banished One," Aenaila said and grabbed hold of Tobias's sleeve. "Camissa, grab my other arm while I hold Mikkellana."

As soon as Camissa had her arm, Aenaila shifted to their safe place in Pomanda, bringing Mikkellana, Aentarra, Rhaven, Tobias, Gregor, and Camissa with her. Once inside, she helped lay Mikkellana on the bed.

"We are still in Pomanda very near the square and the merchant's district. You can find anything you need there. I'm going back for Wisp."

Aentarra nearly jumped out of her skin. "No!" Her head shook vigorously. "If you don't heal Mikkellana, Lukaan will get out."

"But Wisp can't stay there fighting her. She—"

Aentarra forced herself to stand. "If Lukaan gets out, nothing will matter. We'll all be dead."

Aenaila struggled with the decision, but finally, she shook her head. "I don't care who gets out, or who dies. I'm going after Wisp."

She turned to Camissa. "While I'm gone, find some clean bandages. And we'll need water, a lot of it. I have to clean this before I can heal her."

"No! I'm going with you," Camissa said, determination in her eyes, and something else, perhaps love. "I won't leave Rahg there."

"I'll get the water and the bandages, lass. You see what you can do for Rahg." Tobias rushed out the door as Aenaila shifted back to the square with Camissa.

~

The BlackFire struck Darstan, bursting through his hastily made defense and consuming his body. His clothes aflame, the skin came next. He felt it burning, searing, felt the heat go through him to his bones. All he could think of was smothering it, dousing it with water or ice ... Yes, ice, he thought.

The sensation initiated in his stomach, churning. It wrapped around his bones, infused them with cold. The ice inside him spread throughout, mixing with the BlackFire from Sendra, roiling inside of him. It ran the course through his legs, his chest, and then it split, BlackFire racing down his left arm while the ColdFire sped down his right.

~

The BlackFire struck Senda first, bulling it's way through her defenses, singeing her with immense heat. She fought that off, preparing for another strike when the ColdFire struck. Sendra countered it with all of her defenses, but it pushed its way through, numbing her hands, then her arms.

Got to Shift, she thought and brought forth the image of her room in Vallah, the one where she had enjoyed her reading. Nothing! The Shift wasn't working, and as she realized that, the numbness spread into her chest, throughout her body.

Soon, numbness turned to pain, then once again to nothing, as if her body no longer existed, as if she weren't there. There was no feeling as her body shattered, pieces of flesh, bone and brain mass exploding from the spot where Sendra had stood.

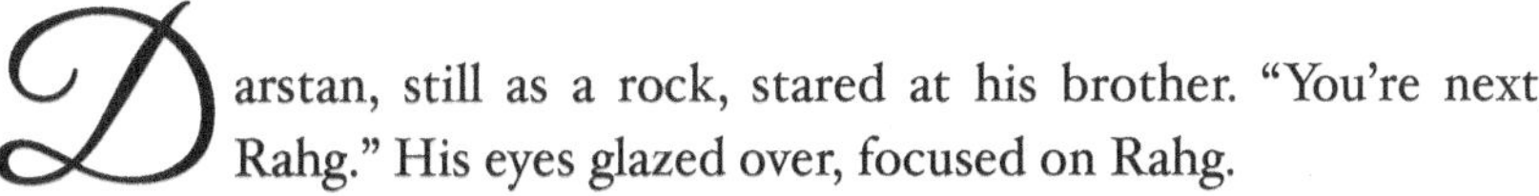

Darstan, still as a rock, stared at his brother. "You're next, Rahg." His eyes glazed over, focused on Rahg.

Wisp moved in front of Rahg. "No, Darstan. It's enough. Talk to Rahg. Listen to him."

"There's nothing to say."

Rahg moved Wisp aside. "I never got a message, Darstan. I didn't even know you were there until you attacked. I never ... I'm sorry, Dar." Tears welled in his eyes, and he moved toward Darstan. "I'm so sorry."

Heat rose in Darstan's body, flames danced inside him. He fought the emotions, restrained himself, then he collapsed.

"It must have been Mattu," Wisp said, just as Rahg reached his brother, but Darstan was already down. Aenaila appeared at the same time.

Mikkellana nearly jumped from the bed. "What was that?"

Aentarra stared at her from the chair. "You felt it too?"

"Yes, it was ... I don't know ... powerful."

"Very powerful," Aentarra said. "I can't shift yet, but we need to find out what happened. Gregor, go to the square. If Sendra is there, just leave. No matter who is hurt."

"But—"

"Run. We don't have time."

Gregor ran to the square—only a short distance away, and surveyed the scene with a glance. Wisp and Aenaila stood over Darstan, lying on the ground, and Camissa was helping Rahg to his feet. "What happened? Where's Sendra?"

Wisp turned. "Darstan killed her, but he's unconscious. Can't get him awake."

Gregor went to help Rahg and Camissa.

"Camissa felt Rahg's head, letting her hands probe.

Aenaila continued tending Darstan. "I think he's all right, but I can't get him awake. We'll take him to the house."

"Not here," Wisp said. "He wants to kill Rahg."

Aenaila looked to Rahg, then back to Darstan. "I can't take him all the way back to Khatara, then return. Besides, I have to help Mikkellana." Suddenly Aenaila's face went ashen. "Wisp, how did he get here? I left him in Khatara."

"He shifted here."

"By himself?"

Wisp nodded. "Then he did something; I don't even know what, but when he killed Sendra, she just ... exploded."

Aenaila made a sign of a holy blessing. "Maybe Rahg shouldn't go there."

Wisp glanced around. "Whatever we do, we need to get out of here. Guards will be coming once their fear wears off."

Aenaila walked to Rahg. "I'm taking Darstan to the house, but I don't think you should go. Are you all right on your own for a while?"

"Come with me, Rahg," Wisp said. "I'll keep you out of trouble."

Aenaila turned to Camissa. "I could use your help with healing after we shift back to the house." As they prepared to leave, Aenaila yelled to Wisp. "Don't take any chances. And let me know where you are."

Wisp waved his hand as he and Rahg walked off.

~

They arrived at the house just as Tobias was returning with more water. He set the pails down and ran to them. "What happened to Darstan?"

"He'll be all right. Just needs rest." Aenaila and Camissa lay Darstan on the floor, spreading a blanket out first. Rhaven limped to a chair close by and sat, his right side barely working, his arm not at all.

Aentarra walked to him, staring.

"Sword broke," he managed to say.

"Lucky it held so long," she said. "Don't worry, if we ever get Mikkellana healed, she'll fix that arm. If we don't ... well, you won't need it for long."

Aenaila sat on the bed next to Mikkellana and began working again. "Camissa, see if you can do anything for Rhaven."

"No," Aentarra said. "Leave that to Mikkellana. It's tricky when dealing with a person who is paralyzed."

"All right, see if you can help Darstan then."

Aentarra stared at Aenaila. "What happened. I thought you took him to Khatara."

"I did. He shifted."

"Did you teach him?"

"Must have taught himself."

Shouldn't be possible. "What happened to Sendra?"

"Darstan killed her."

"BlackFire?" she asked, but she knew the answer already.

Aenaila stopped, thinking, then looked at Aentarra. "I don't know. Her body was … gone. Wisp said she just … shattered."

"It's true," Camissa said. "She hit him with BlackFire, and I thought he was dead, then all of a sudden, things came out of him, both his arms, but one was fire and one … something else."

"ColdFire!" Aentarra said, then stood. She stared for a long time, remembering the nightmares from the Forbidden Lands when the dorgans had attacked them, and Lukaan used his ColdFire against them. Their bodies had also shattered, just as Wisp described. He has ColdFire, and, he taught himself to shift. This boy is dangerous!

A TIME TO HEAL

While Aenaila worked on Mikkellana, Camissa and Tobias tended to Rhaven's needs. Aentarra stared at Darstan. There was something wrong about the boy, and she intended to find out what.

The pouch at her side opened, a hint of a glow emanating from it, then a Slicer emerged and raced toward Darstan. Just as it was about to enter his head, it stopped. Just stopped!

Aentarra gasped.

"Are you all right, Lady Aentarra?"

"Fine, Camissa. Just watch Rhaven."

She dispatched another Slicer, with the exact results. It hovered a hair's breadth from Darstan's head, along with the first one she had sent. She called them both back to her, then relaxed in the chair, pondering.

How is it possible? This has never happened. It's never happened to anyone that I know of. A Slicer has never refused an order.

She sat in the chair most of the afternoon, wondering, analyzing what she knew, but nothing made sense. Soon, Darstan stirred but fell back when he tried to get up.

"You're going to be spent for quite a while after what you did." Aentarra sat straight up, staring at him, a smile on her face. "Killed Sendra, though. I'd say it was worth it."

"Where's Rahg?" he asked, jaw clenched.

Aentarra had been staring at his face when he woke. It was then the recognition hit her. She gasped again before catching herself. Gods blood! I never saw it before.

"Rahg is where you can't find him," Aenaila said. "And now that you're awake I'm taking you back to Sykor. You can stay with Talanvar until I get there." She looked at Wisp, who had just returned. "Don't let him leave."

"Let's go, Darstan. You know I'm helpless to resist a beautiful woman."

Darstan nodded, too tired to fight. He took hold of Aenaila's hand, and they shifted, coming through the rift into Talanvar's library. Immediately, Aenaila shifted back to Pomanda.

*A*nother day passed and still no sign of recovery for Mikkellana. Aentarra went to her sister's side, genuine concern registering on her face. "Any progress?"

Aenaila kept working, not bothering to look up. "Breathing is better, but nothing significant."

"She must be healed. Do you understand?"

Aenaila turned to her, eyes full of ice. "I'm doing what I can. Let me do it without interruption."

"Start trying things you don't know, girl. I can't be more specific—if she isn't healed Lukaan gets out."

Aentarra stared straight into Aenaila's green eyes. "And if he gets hold of you, pretty one, the things he'll do to you will never leave your mind—if you survive. So if you can't heal her, you'd better go hide in a dark corner and hope you grow old and ugly before he finds you."

Aenaila bit her lower lip, worried now. "Are there any suggestions you can give me?"

"I'm not a healer. I can sear a cut, heal a broken bone with Shield, but that's about all. Keep trying." She continued her pacing, and the nervousness showed.

She pointed a finger at Camissa. "See what you can do for Rhaven. Just don't butcher him. We'll probably need every sword we can get, even those without powers."

"What can I do?" Rahg asked, now back from hiding in another safe house.

A chuckle escaped Aentarra's lips. "Nothing, boy. That's the problem. You can't do enough to keep yourself out of trouble, and it's biting at your heels every time you turn."

"The lad's done good enough for himself. Fought off a Banished One. Held out against—"

Aentarra snapped her head around, staring Tobias down. "Old man, he would have been dead ten times if not for me. He can barely hold his own against a handful of guards let alone one of the Banished Ones."

She laughed aloud. "Sendra would have eaten him alive if his brother hadn't shown up, then she'd have killed us all. Lukaan would be razing cities right now if not for Darstan."

Rahg shrunk back from the berating.

Aentarra continued to pace, now wringing her hands as well.

From the other side of the room, Aenaila called out. "I think she's coming to. Either way, I've done all I can."

Aentarra raced to Mikkellana's side, kneeling as she got there. "Wake up, sister. We need you." She lay her head against Mikkellana's chest, listening to her breathing, then nodded.

Soon, Mikkellana tried lifting her head, but Aentarra caught her, supporting her with both arms. "Easy, sister. You've been hurt badly."

"The shield!" She bolted upright but fell back down, wincing at the pain. Her face wrenched in anguish, she stared at Aentarra. "I can't move my legs. Can't even get up."

Aentarra cursed. "Girl, what did you do to her? I should ..."

Mikkellana grabbed her hand. "Don't blame her. Sendra must have gotten me good, and you know how difficult it is to heal a strike to the back." She rubbed the back of her sister's hand. "I appreciate your concern, but I'll be all right. At least I've got my mind, so the shield won't go down. Have you checked it?"

"I think it's all right. We won't know until I go there, but now that you're awake we can keep the worst from happening."

"If it hasn't already." An image of Lukaan roaming free popped into her mind, but she quickly chased it away. No sense in worrying over what you didn't know.

Aentarra nodded. "Yes, if it hasn't already."

Mikkellana looked to the side, where Rhaven lay on the floor. "Rhaven! Is he—"

"I've done what I can for him," Camissa said. "But now that you are well, you can finish..." She paused. "Can you heal him? From the bed, I mean."

"I'm sure I can. Let me rest first, get some energy."

Camissa brought water for her to drink and after she sated her thirst there were many questions. "Where are we? What happened to Ghruehne and Sendra?"

"We're in a safe house I have in Pomanda," Aenaila said.

Aentarra walked over beside her. "I killed Ghruehne. Darstan killed Sendra." Mikkellana's eyes rose, but not in shock. "He killed her with ColdFire."

A sideways glance from Mikkellana told Aentarra all she needed to know. "You knew, didn't you?" Her voice was a panicked whisper. "All this time, and you knew." She nearly spat. "I suppose you know who he belongs to also."

Curiosity painted Mikkellana's face a different shade of red. "Who?"

"Did you ever look at that iron jaw."

Mikkellana tried to picture him in her mind, then she gasped. It was louder than she intended and not easy to hide.

"What's the matter?" Aenaila asked, her eyes darting between Mikkellana and Aentarra.

Mikkellana smiled. "I owe you dearly. The whole world does, but that doesn't mean I have to answer your questions."

Aenaila stood, her spine infused with steel. "I don't know what is going on, but since we are all in this together, perhaps you should tell us everything."

Mikkellana shook her head, but Aentarra stood. "It's very simple. The only way the shield in Sethia can stay up is if Mikkellana and I are alive and conscious. If either one of us goes, so does the shield."

"And that's all of it?" Aenaila stared at both of them.

"It isn't complicated," Aentarra said.

"What does Rahg have to do with this? And Darstan?"

"We don't yet know," Mikkellana said, trying to sit, but falling back again.

"That's a lie!" Aentarra said, and then helped to prop Mikkellana up against some pillows. "Might as well tell them, sister." Aentarra stared at each person in the room. "One of them is destined to free Lukaan."

All eyes darted to Rahg. And everyone wondered which one it would be.

Maybe I should have killed him, Mikkellana thought.

50

POMANDA—REST IN A SAFE HOUSE

A rift opened in the room in Pomanda, Aentarra stepping through. "The shield is still up," she said. "And it looks as if no one else got out. I could sense three of them."

"Thank the gods for something," Mikkellana said. She saw Rhaven struggling with his arm. "Bring him over here, Tobias. I feel strong enough to heal him."

She spent some time examining his arm, then the entire right side of his body. Soon, she was moving her hands up and down his arm from shoulder to wrist.

"Will he be all right?" Aentarra asked.

Mikkellana nodded. "In a day or so. He was fortunate."

"Your sword didn't fare as well."

Rahg drank several mugs filled with water, then sat on a sofa near the door. "What plans do you have, Aentarra?"

"None, but we need to make a plan before we leave here. Lukaan won't sit idly by."

"He's trapped in Sethia," Rahg said.

"Just because he's in Sethia doesn't mean he can't affect the world. Now that things have gone this far, he'll push them."

"What can he do?"

"There's a lot he can do. He'll have followers in all the cities, just like the Black Rose were, and some of those followers will be people with influence."

Aentarra sipped some khaffe Tobias had made for her. "I know in Sykor that Ludar is one of them. He—"

"He's dead," Aenaila said. "Wisp killed him."

Aentarra raised her eyebrows. "How did that come about?"

"Someone killed the king, and Ludar—"

"Lukaan killed the king. That's what he does best. He'll disrupt all the cities, then have his people try to take over. What he wants is turmoil, so his armies can destroy them."

Mikkellana sat up in the bed and stared at Aenaila. "Who rules in Sykor now?"

A scowl formed on Aenaila's face. "Cynamar, though it is tenuous. Many of the guards had been firm supporters of Ludar. We tried to weed them out, but there are likely to be quite a few left."

Mikkellana scoffed. "That girl can't rule alone."

"Talanvar is trying to counsel her," Aenaila said. "And he has support from the people. But I agree with you. She couldn't rule her household."

"Jealousy?" Mikkellana asked, then chewed on a fingernail.

"Just an observation."

"Of course, Your Majesty." Mikkellana smiled. "We'll need to prepare the other cities. Tobias, go see your friend, Preman, and tell him what happened in Sykor."

Tobias looked at Mikkellana as if she were a spirit. "How did you know I even knew Preman?"

"I was with you the last time we were here."

"I know my memory is falling short sometimes, but I'd have known if you were with us."

Mikkellana laughed. "Don't you remember Kella or the old healer woman?"

Tobias laughed, red flushing his face. "Guess I'm gettin' older than I thought. Forgettin' something like that. Forgettin' about a woman that can also be a dog."

Everyone was laughing, but he brushed it off. "All right. All right. I'm goin'. Don't know how I'm supposed to warn Preman of things he might not believe in, but I'll do it. I'll sure do that." As Tobias closed the door, they all laughed again. It was the first time in a long while they had laughed together.

Aenaila grabbed the few things she had brought with her. "Since Mikkellana is somewhat better, I'm going to join Darstan and Wisp."

"Where will you be?" Mikkellana asked.

"Either Sykor or Khatara. Though I might go home."

"Without Wisp?" Mikkellana's tone was taunting.

"Might teach him to be humble."

Rahg came to her. "What about Darstan? Will you tell him it wasn't me?" He paused. "No, I'll go with you, tell him myself."

"I don't think so. Not with him like that. Let me try, Rahg. I believe I know what happened now, and perhaps I can convince your brother."

"Please try," Rahg asked, then Aenaila shifted.

~

*T*obias stared down the servant who had answered the door. "Just tell him what I said, and be quick about it."

The servant stared right back at him as if he had lost his mind, but after a brief pause, he went off in search of Lord Preman, returning a short while later.

~

*P*reman hurried his last few steps, embracing Tobias with a warm greeting. "It's been a long time. How have you been?"

"Still above the ground, Preman, which puts me better than some I know."

Preman turned, walking toward a courtyard. "Come, join me for a meal," he said, then addressed his servant. "Wine and food for our guest. Tell Emiliana to join us as well."

Tobias's face lit up. "Emiliana! How is she? I haven't seen her since ... I believe it was since we fought in the Swamp Wars."

"Your memory's as sharp as my knife. We dined together the night you, and I left Pomanda."

Tobias nodded, recalling old times. Better times. Soon a scowl formed on his face. "What I came to tell, you won't want to hear. You probably won't even believe me, but I've got to tell it anyway."

The servant brought wine, olives, and cheese. Tobias sipped on the wine while he nibbled at the cheese. "Trust me when I tell you I've seen all this myself. We left Sethia a short while ago, and two of the Banished Ones got out."

Preman's face wrinkled, and he sipped heavily on his own glass.

"We ... I say we, but it's really the people I'm with ... they killed them just yesterday—here in Pomanda."

Preman stared at him, then nodded. "The square, by the Fountain of the Ancients."

"That's it. Craziest thing you ever seen, Preman. People with Fire and Lightning, and things I can't describe." Tobias popped three or four more olives in his mouth, chewed and swallowed. "You saw what they did. All that in the time it would take you to drink a cup of khaffe."

"What can I do to help?"

Tobias thought, then shook his head. "Don't rightly know. I came here to warn you, tell you about what plans we think Lukaan might have, but when it comes down to it, I have no idea what you can do to help."

Tobias put the wine down and lit his pipe. "All I can do is tell you what we know—that Lukaan tried taking over Sykor. He had the king killed and is blaming Pomanda for it, but you already know that. Rumor is he's causing trouble in Khatara too. No reason to think he won't try here. It would be my first guess that it was someone following his orders who killed your king."

Preman nodded. "Uses followers like he did with the Black Rose?"

"In Sykor it was the Force Commander."

"Ludar!"

"None other," Tobias said. "He got his though. Remember that skinny thief we had with us when we came for the Black Rose. Well, he gave Ludar his just rewards."

Preman seemed shocked. "I wouldn't have thought—"

"Fastest man I've ever seen with a knife. Saw him kill three people once before they even knew what they were going to do." Tobias nodded, almost to himself. "I do believe he might be faster than Rhaven with a knife if that's even possible."

"If Lukaan turned Sykor's Force Commander that means he can get to anyone. I'll have to be careful." Preman's worried look abruptly

changed to a smile. "Here comes Emiliana, let's not discuss unpleas-
antries."

"Of course not," Tobias said and rose to greet her.

Emiliana stood nearly as tall as Tobias, with long legs and a lithe form.
Her body moved gracefully, like a swan, and her dark hair bounced on
the tips of her shoulders. A warm smile revealed gleaming white teeth,
and a melodious voice followed. "Tobias, it has been a long time."

"By all the gods, I do believe you've gotten prettier since the last time
I saw you. Younger too."

"Still the same old Tobias, full of flattery."

They embraced, then he held her chair while she sat.

"I hope Preman served a good wine," Emiliana said.

"I hope not. Any wine's good enough for an old man like me. Been so
long since I've had a good one I'm afraid it would go to waste."

"Nonsense. You're royalty as far as we're concerned." Emiliana grabbed
his hand, holding it between hers. "I do miss those times with you and
Shia. How much fun we had."

Tobias tried smiling, but at the mention of her name, sadness overwhelmed him. Slowly, he pulled his hand away. "Forgive me, Emiliana,
but I still can't talk about her. Just ... well, never mind now. Got to be
going anyway." He stood, made his apologies, then walked with Preman
to the door.

Preman gripped his friend by the shoulders. "Sorry, Tobias. She
shouldn't have brought that up."

"I shouldn't be so sensitive about it after this long, but the fact is I am.
It's my fault." Tobias stared at Preman. "Don't forget what I told you.
You can't trust anyone."

"I won't." As Tobias started to leave, Preman grabbed him. "Where are
you staying? You know you're welcome to stay here."

"Thanks, but there's too many of us."

"Too many? Who?"

Tobias shook his head. "There's me and Camissa, and Rhaven, though he's hurt. Then there's the boy and those two ... I don't know, witches I guess. But they're both hurt too. Makes a motley bunch, I'll tell you that." He looked at the floor, shuffling his feet on the tiles. "No, Preman, too many of us to stay here."

"Nonsense. Your friends are all welcome. I could have the servants—"

Tobias shook his head. "No. We'll be just fine where we are."

"What, at some tavern? I won't have it."

"We've got a house, close to the square. You know where the jeweler's shop is, close to the fountain?"

"I know just the place. Those houses are nice." He patted Tobias on the back. "All right then, since there seems to be no convincing you, go with the gods."

"I got them with me. I just hope they stay with you."

51

THE OTHERS

Tobias and the rest of them relaxed in the room. Dinner was finished, and Tobias had just brewed more khaffe. Mikkel-lana sat in the bed, reading, while Rahg and Camissa played a game of cards on the floor. Aentarra finished with her khaffe, draining the last sip with a gulp then a sigh.

"Tobias, you make excellent khaffe. It reminds me of what Benna used to make for me as a child."

"Why thank you, Lass." he paused, laughed. "Here I am gettin' ready to call you lass, and you're older than me, and everybody I know put together. Can't even count that high."

～

"Tobias, if I didn't know you so well, I'd swear you were flirting." Aentarra laughed with him, then got up to cross the room. It was then that the Others struck.

The pain came in a violent wave, crushing her head. She collapsed, knees slamming onto the floor, and the mug crashed, breaking into shards and splinters. A large piece of glass dug into the palm of her hand, blood pouring out. Rhaven raced to get to her, but her fall continued, head banging the floor with a thud.

"The Others!"

She screamed, reaching for her head with one hand while attempting to push herself off the floor with the other. The glass stuck in her palm cut deep into her head as she tried to stop the pain.

Rhaven grabbed her hand, yanking it away from her head, but a Force Shield hurled him across the room. He crashed into the wall, head first, and fell unconscious to the floor.

"Aentarra! What's wrong?" Mikkellana tried getting up, but couldn't move from the bed. "Stay away from her, Tobias. You, too, Camissa. She could kill you."

Rahg wrapped himself in a shield and ran to her side, lifting her up by her arm. She thrashed wildly, muttering incoherently.

"Try to protect her with a shield, Rahg."

He wove a shield around her body, and most of her head, leaving her enough room to breathe.

The orders kept coming from Mikkellana. "Cushion her head! She could start up again at any time."

Aentarra felt them inside of her, thrashing about, sieging her mind. She fought with everything she had, but this battle seemed lost. They had taken a strong hold this time, and they weren't ceding any ground. She focused on home, on her father, on love. None of it worked. Then she recalled her heritage, the core of her strength. Revenge!

She dug deep into memory, bringing up images certain to stir revenge, bring it to a boil: her mother's murder; the Lights dishonoring her father; the exile to the Forbidden Lands; Lukaan!

From the depths of her soul, a force churned, swirling into a powerful attack. As it grew in strength it spread through her body, then regrouped and raced to her mind. She felt the rage go through her, like a shiver that goes from toe to head in an instant, but this was no shiver, and an instant seemed a lifetime in comparison.

The force struck the Others, a massive strike that knocked them out of control, dislodged them, freed her mind.

She started falling again as she moved toward the chair. Rahg caught her, carried her the rest of the way. "Are you all right, Lady Aentarra?"

"Water."

"I'll get it," Camissa said.

Mikkellana stared at her from across the room. Blood covered her face and hand. She still bled from the gash in the side of her head, and more trickled out of her nose. Even her forehead, where there was no wound. "Bring her over here, Rahg. I need to heal her."

Rahg carried her over and lay her on the bed next to Mikkellana. As she stared at her sister, she cried. "What have you done to yourself, Aentarra? By all that's holy, what have you done?"

52

PERSUASION

The patrol leader struck a three-fisted salute, then snapped to attention.

"How many men do you have with you?"

"Five patrols, sir. Enough to—"

"Enough to get you killed. Take twelve patrols." A thick wagging finger danced in front of the guard's face. "Don't underestimate this. You will likely lose a lot of men."

"I don't understand, sir."

"Remember what happened in the square? There is at least one of them there. Hurt, but still dangerous."

The patrol leader saluted and prepared to leave, but was called back. "If I were you, I would let the others go in first."

"Yes, sir," he said and made his departure. As he reached the street, he issued orders. "Sergeant, gather more patrols. Seven or eight more, and tell them all to be prepared for resistance."

"Yes, sir." He pounded out the three-fisted salute before he ran off.

~

*A*entarra sat up, struggling with the recovery from the attack. "How are you feeling, sister?"

Mikkellana lay on the bed, frustration setting in from not being able to move. From what she could tell, she may never be able to move. "I'll be fortunate to ever get off this bed. If only you could heal ... how you inherited so many talents and still can't heal I'll never know."

"We'll find a way," Aentarra said.

Mikkellana shot her a glare. "How? The only ones who could heal, you killed."

"They may not all be dead."

"For my purposes they are. If they can't heal me, they're as good as dead. And here I am stuck in bed because of it."

"I'll get that—" Aentarra sat up straighter, head cocked toward the door, listening.

"What?" Rhaven asked.

"Quiet! Someone is coming, and they're trying not to be noticed."

"Fine mess we're in," Tobias said, whispering. "Camissa and me the only ones not hurt."

A light rap at the door brought everyone to a state of alertness. "Mikkellana, can you use some Illusion?"

"Enough for what we need."

"Good, make it look like it's only you and Camissa here and only one room. Tobias, sit next to Rhaven and Rahg, and be quiet." Aentarra sat straight up. "Camissa, get the door. Everyone else stay where they are."

Camissa opened the door slowly, but as soon as it cracked the guards pushed their way in, swords drawn. They looked around, staring at Mikkellana, then Camissa, surprise evident on their faces. It was just one large room with two beds and a sofa and chairs. An older lady lay in one of the beds, and the rest of the room was empty, save the girl who had opened the door. A sofa sat against the middle of the farthest wall.

"What's behind the sofa?" he asked and pushed Camissa aside.

She grabbed his sleeve, tugged him. Her gut churned, burning inside. If he went over there, Aentarra would likely kill him, and the corridor outside was filled with guards. That meant she'd kill them all. A rumbling came from her stomach, then it seemed to pass, though she did feel light-headed. "That's nothing but a closet. No need to look in there." Her hand had taken a firm grasp on the man's uniform.

He looked to her, pulled his arm back, stepped away. "Nothing in there?"

She stared into his eyes, unflinching. "Nothing."

He took one more look around the room, nodded, then left, closing the door behind him.

Shock painted Camissa's face as she turned back around. What had just happened?

Mikkellana dropped the Illusion, and Tobias moved quickly to the door, listening. "Sh. Can't hear."

Aentarra wove a cone-shaped shield and pressed it against the wall. "Use this, Tobias."

He held his head against the shield, now able to hear what the guards were saying as they departed.

"*H*e said they'd be here, right by the jeweler's shop." There was a pause as if he was thinking, then, "We'll check the other houses. If they're not in them, I guess they left."

Tobias turned around, facing Rhaven. "They knew we were here. Knew."

"Who knew besides us? Did you tell anyone?"

Tobias started to shake his head, then stopped.

"Who?" Rhaven asked.

"Preman," Tobias said. "But I can't believe it would be him." He went and sat in the chair.

Rhaven paced. "I don't think Preman would do it. Why would he? He's the one who helped us before."

"Has to be. He's the only one I told, and they said it exactly like I told him. By the jeweler's shop. That's what I told Preman." Tobias leaned back in the chair, slumped, as if too tired to sit. "Don't understand how a man can do something like that. I've known that man all my life."

~

Aentarra watched from her spot on the sofa, lying down now, but alert, replaying the scene that had just taken place in her mind. There had been a noticeable shift in the guard's eyes as if his mind "decided" not to pursue the course of action he had set upon. And he had definitely set upon a course.

Aentarra had seen the look. She even thought that she would likely have to kill him, assuming she could muster enough energy, but once Camissa spoke to him everything changed. An unexplained change.

Camissa seemed to be in a daze as she headed back toward Mikkellana.

Aentarra's gaze followed her across the room. "Come here, girl. Just for a moment."

Camissa walked to her, knelt on the floor. "What is it, Aentarra?"

She looked deep into her eyes. "Did you do that?"

"What?"

Aentarra sat upright, leaned her head in until her nose almost touched

Camissa's. "Just what is stirring inside that head of yours?" She supported herself on Camissa's shoulder then stood, walking toward the door. "I want to go for a walk, perhaps just down the hall. Would you mind helping me?" The gaze into her eyes told her she should go along.

"Of course."

They walked a short way down the corridor to a bend that included a large alcove with a table and two chairs. Aentarra spun toward her, eyes boring into her soul. "Now, tell me how you did that?"

Camissa broke, stepping back, head bowed. "I don't know what you mean."

Aentarra's finger wagged as she walked up to Camissa again, pressing her. "You can't play those games with me. I saw what you did. Noticed some things before this too. I wouldn't be half surprised if that isn't how you got Rahg into your bed."

Anger burnt Camissa's face red. She gritted her teeth, then pushed Aentarra. "I don't need that for Rahg. Maybe you need it to get men to your bed. It's no wonder if they've ever met you. But—"

A shield wrapped around Camissa, squeezing her, holding her tight. She would have enough room to breathe, but only in small measures. Aentarra let her stand there for a while. "Take time to calm yourself. Your first reaction will be to panic because you can't breathe, but you have enough air to survive. Tell me when you are calm."

Camissa struggled to break free but immediately realized the futility. She could never get out of one of Aentarra's shields. She fought the panic, tried to calm herself. Thought of times with her mother early in life, of fun times with Kender Darnell, and of making love to Rahg. Soon her body responded, and she relaxed. "I'm ready."

Aentarra smiled. "I don't try to be cruel. And I don't care what you do with your gift." Aentarra's face hardened, and her eyes narrowed. "But I do expect to hear the truth from you when I ask a question. I need to know who can do what. It could mean a big difference, depending on our situation." She released the shield, drawing a sigh from Camissa.

Camissa's shoulders slumped, and she moved her arms about, stretching. "I can make people do things. Things I suggest in my mind."

Aentarra nodded, began to pace. "It's called Persuasion, and it is a rare gift, girl. Very rare."

"Persuasion?" Camissa smiled. "I called it Suggestion."

"Not inappropriate, but persuasion describes it better. And there are different degrees of the power. At the utmost level, well, let's just say at the highest level you could command anyone to do anything."

"Anyone?"

"Don't get any ideas. I've already blocked my mind to you, but yes, anyone, so long as they don't know your imprint and establish a block."

Camissa shook her head, confused. "Aentarra, I don't know what you are talking about."

She picked a small vase up from the table, turned it in her hand, staring, evaluating. "Yes, well, I like it like that."

Camissa laughed.

"What? Some humor I missed?"

Camissa shook her head. "It seems odd having you around so much."

She set the vase back on the table, her head bobbing up and down in a constant nod as she headed toward the room. "Things have escalated far too much. I'm going to have to protect that boy until he's capable of doing it himself." She opened the door and walked in, followed closely by Camissa.

"We're going to have to leave here sooner than I thought," Aentarra said. "Everyone better get ready."

"For where?" Rahg asked. "

"For right now, to Vallah. Give everyone a chance to heal."

"There's someplace I need to go," Rahg said, and he stared at Aentarra as he did.

"Spit it out, boy. Don't just stand there staring at me."

"Back to the mountain. I—"

"In the Paaren!" Aentarra shook her head. "Everyone I know wants to avoid that place, and you keep wanting to go back as if you were visiting your grandmother." She walked over and looked him up and down, but he didn't break under her scrutiny. "Why? Give me a good reason, and I'll take you."

"There's one left, one more of the gods to see. If I'm going to have any part in this whole thing, I better be as strong as I can, and they can help." Rahg's jaw locked. "Besides, there are things they aren't telling me. Important things. This time I intend to find out what."

Tobias laid his hand on Rahg's shoulder. "If you expect me to go with you, lad, you'll have to wait. I've got to do something first. Got to go see a man."

"Preman?" Rhaven asked, and before Tobias could respond, he continued. "Let me take care of this. At your age—"

Tobias shook his head. "I need to see it in his eyes. Hear it from him."

"All right, but I'm going with you."

Tobias started to object, but Rhaven cut him off. "There will be guards. I'll take care of them. You handle Preman."

"I'd be grateful for that," Tobias said, and he picked up his sword. "Ready to go? No sense wastin' time. As I see it, the sooner we get it done, the better off we'll be."

"We may have a problem leaving here afterward," Rhaven said. "Fact is, Tobias, we may not get out of this one. He'll be protected, and once it's done, the alarm will be raised."

He rubbed white whiskers on his chin as he thought, then went over and hugged Rahg. "Lad, if I don't get out of this … well, you know how I feel about you. And tell that brother of yours the same."

Rahg squeezed him tighter. "You'll be okay, Tobias. Nothing will happen to you."

"Where will you go afterward?" Mikkellana asked.

"Head to Sykor, I guess. Join up with Darstan and that thief."

"We'll meet you there," Aentarra said. "First I have to take Mikkellana and Camissa to Vallah, then I'll take Rahg."

Tobias and Rhaven said their farewells to everyone, then departed.

Mikkellana fluffed up a blanket that she had spread over her legs. "You can't go to the Paaren alone. That is the most absurd idea I have heard from you yet."

Aentarra shook her head. "It will be much safer, sister. If we run into any trouble, I can use Stealth for long periods of time. And besides—"

"How will you get out?"

Aentarra paused.

"Didn't think of that, did you? With no Mordi, the road back might take you a hundred years."

"We'll find our way."

Mikkellana tried sitting, latched onto the bedpost and pulled herself up. "That's no answer, Aentarra and you know it. We were trapped for hundreds of years. We—" She stopped, staring at her sister, horror and pity mixed with other emotions. "Aentarra, stop!"

Aentarra's hands tore at her hair, scratched her face. "We'll do it!" she screamed. "Just leave me alone!"

Rahg went to her, tentative, but determined to help her. He wrapped his arms around her and pulled her to him, fear bristling every hair on his body. "It will be all right. We don't have to go if you don't want."

She yanked away from him, embarrassed. A smile popped on her face as if someone had painted it there. "We're going. And don't listen to that old hag, boy. We'll find our way back. Just tell those gods that if they want you to do something they better show you the way out of there." She grabbed the amulet hanging from his neck. "If they can make this work to bring you to them, they can do something to get you out."

Aentarra straightened her hair, then her blouse.

"Come over here, sister. Let me heal that face. At least go to your death looking pretty."

Aentarra laughed. "I'd have it no other way," she said and made her way to Mikkellana's bed. After Mikkellana healed her, they prepared to shift to Vallah. From there, Aentarra took Rahg to the Paaren.

53

ANOTHER ASSASSINATION

Tobias and Rhaven walked the streets toward Preman's house, keeping to the main thoroughfares so they could mix with the crowds. "Move with the flow of the people," Rhaven said. "Not any faster or slower. Nothing to draw attention to us."

Guards roamed the streets of Pomanda, with several posted at almost every corner and a minimum of a full patrol in each of the plazas.

The king had been killed, and there had been a battle between people with powers in their main plaza; the nobles intended to keep order now, even if it meant killing some of their own.

Rhaven and Tobias kept pace with a family, two women with four children in tow, and to any casual observer, it might have appeared that they were all together. Rhaven stopped at a linen shop when they did, looking through a window at the goods, and he went inside the bakery, holding the door for all of them. When the women entered the butcher's shop, Rhaven and Tobias kept walking, a smile planted on their faces.

"Not far now," Tobias said.

"I suspect his manor will be surrounded with guards. We'll have to plan how to get in."

"Figure we'll do it the easy way. Just knock on the door and ask to see him. Last thing he'll expect is to see us."

Rhaven thought for a moment then laughed. "Might be a good plan after all, Tobias. If we assume he sent the guards, then he'll either be curious as to how we escaped, or he'll kill us straight out. Either way, we get in to see him."

"Still can't believe he did it," Tobias said, and increased his pace. Before long they entered the nobles' district, an area boasting homes similar to the ones on the Corina Tumal, but these sat on flat ground by comparison and were situated close to the king's palace by design. Two patrols kept watch at the front gate to Preman's manor, a formidable obstacle. "Your idea will get us in, Tobias, but afterward how do we get out?"

"If they don't know he's dead, they won't stop us from leaving. We'll just have to be quick and careful."

They approached the gate with smiles. "Here to see Preman," Tobias said.

The gate man stared at him as if he were a pauper. "Lord Preman."

Tobias got in close to him, leaned forward till his head nearly bumped the guard's. "Lad, I've known Preman since he was a little pup. Just had a meal with him and Emiliana a day or so ago. Send someone to fetch him and tell him Tobias is here."

The guard twitched, his eyes blinking and his legs looked a little shaky. "Benino, get Lord Preman. Tell him that ..."

"Tobias."

"tell him that Tobias is here to see him."

A grim demeanor planted itself on the guard's face. "I hope you're right about this, sir. Lord Preman doesn't like to be disturbed."

A short cackle greeted the man's statement. "He'll be surprised to see me, boy, but don't you worry, he won't blame you."

Within moments the guard came running back with orders to escort Tobias and his "guest" to Lord Preman's sitting room.

Tobias and Rhaven followed him into the house, down a long corridor, then left into a short hallway leading to a single door at the end. The guard stopped halfway down the hall, looking at Tobias. "You're supposed to go in. And you," he said, looking to Rhaven, "are supposed to wait here with me."

Tobias nodded, patting Rhaven's arm. "That's fine. I only need to give him the message, then we'll be on our way."

Rhaven leaned against the wall, trying to appear at ease while Tobias went down the hall and through the door. As he stepped into the sitting room, Preman rushed to greet him.

"Tobias, so good to see you again." He hugged him. It was a quick embrace, and Tobias could tell it wasn't genuine. "What brings you back so soon? I hope you changed your mind about staying here. I have plenty of room."

Tobias glanced about the room, searching for guards or anyone in hiding. He checked the alcoves by the back wall and the curtains to see if anyone hid behind them. A smile crossed his face. "Truth is I came back for some of that fine wine you and Emiliana served me."

Preman laughed. "Wine it shall be then," he said, and went to pour some, returning with a glass in each hand.

Tobias watched his every move while continuing to inspect the room. Tobias took a sip of the wine and smiled. "By the gods, if that's not good."

"What's the real reason you came back, Tobias? It wasn't for the wine."

Tobias laughed. "True enough, Preman. The real truth is I want to know why you sent those guards to our house to get us?"

Preman stepped back. He looked shocked.

Tobias drew a knife from behind him, one he had borrowed from Rhaven, and held it firmly against Preman's throat. "No need to set that glass down. Just keep a hold on it and don't move. And if you call out to your guards, I'll kill you."

Preman's glanced around the room, first to his left side, then to the door. He looked as if he were going to yell for help, but Tobias pressed the knife harder into his flesh, silencing him. "Let me set this glass down, Tobias, then we can—"

"No need. Just talk, and make it a whisper." Tobias stared at him. "And start thinkin' on how you're gonna' get me as much gold as I need to get out of here and to a safe place. Me and all that are with me."

A look of relief came over Preman. "I can get gold, Tobias. That's no problem."

"So you're not denying it then, you did send the guards."

Some wine spilled from the glass, but Tobias never lost contact with Preman, not with his eyes or his blade. "I'm old, Preman, but not slow. I'll kill you before you know it if you try something. Now, tell me about the guards, and why you sent them."

Preman lowered his head, staring at the floor. "There are a lot of things changing. And besides, you wouldn't have been hurt. They were only—"

Tobias leaned forward, digging deep with his blade, and at the same time, he reached behind Preman's head and pulled him forward. The knife cut the main vein in the neck, blood pouring out, mixing with the wine as it hit the floor. Tobias had stepped to his left as he slit Preman's throat, an attempt to avoid the blood. It wouldn't do to be covered in blood as they made their way out of the house. As Preman fell, Tobias pushed him to the side and jabbed the blade deep into his back as well, an extra measure of caution.

～

*R*haven heard the glass break, setting off a sequence of planned events. The guard turned, heading toward the room. Rhaven drew his sai and plunged it into the right side of the guard's neck. At the same time, he covered the man's mouth with his other hand, stifling a scream.

One more thrust with the sai—this one to the kidney—left the man with mortal wounds and no ability to sound the alarm. Rhaven laid him down gently in the hall, moved to a more suitable position, then dragged him to Preman's sitting room, placing him on the floor next to the nobleman.

"Time to go, Tobias. Hurry!"

"Just gettin' us a little money, that's all," Tobias said and finished taking the coin from Lord Preman.

As they exited, Tobias locked the door, and they walked down the hall at a normal pace. Both were laughing as they exited the manor, casual, controlled steps taking them slowly down the front walk.

It seemed as if it were twice as long leaving as it was coming in. With each step Tobias expected to hear the alarm and have a mass of guards rush them, swords drawn. His hands swung easily at his sides, but in fact, they were tensed and prepared to draw steel at any signal.

"Keep calm," Rhaven whispered. "Almost there."

About thirty more paces brought them to the front gate. "Have a fine evening, gentlemen," Tobias said as they departed, and within two blocks they had increased their walk to a still-controlled, but much faster pace.

"Stables," Rhaven said. "Let's get the horses and go."

54

WHAT DO THE GODS KNOW?

Aentarra completed the shift to Vallah, did a Sensing to ensure no trouble awaited, then helped Mikkellana to her room. "Stay with her, girl, and don't try any fancy healing. You're a novice, and though at times I'd like to kill her myself, we do need Mikkellana alive."

"Such genuine concern," Mikkellana said. "I am touched."

"I'll be back," Aentarra said, "and it won't take a hundred years either." She grabbed Rahg's hand and shifted, appearing near the entrance to the Paaren in Arangar.

"Ready, boy?"

"As ready as I'll ever be," Rahg said, and they both entered through the portal.

Another lush valley greeted them, similar to some Rahg had seen in the south of Pomanda when they were on their way to Genda. "Enjoy it while it lasts, Rahg. We have no idea what might be here tomorrow."

Rahg placed his hand on the amulet, sensing it. "This way," he said and headed west.

They marched for most of the day in silence, and at a fast pace. "Can we stop for a while?" Rahg asked. "I'd like to get some food in me."

Aentarra looked around, noting the setting sun. "Wait for darkness. I want to get there as soon as we can. We might as well use the light when it's accorded to us."

Dark followed dusk too soon, and Rahg and Aentarra found themselves tucked into a small enclave of rocks at the base of a mountain. "Cold meals only, Rahg. I'm not risking the dorgans being drawn to a fire."

Rahg unwrapped some cheese, a hunk of bread and a handful of raisins. He had already replenished their drinking supply at a nearby creek bubbling with ice-cold water. "What do you think will happen?"

Aentarra finished chewing before she answered. "If you mean with Lukaan, it's simple—we kill him, or he kills us."

Rahg gulped a large swallow of water, trying his best not to choke. "Not a bright prospect when you put it like that."

"War is never bright. And with Lukaan involved there are few prospects aside from annihilation."

Rahg sat silent for a long time. After he finished eating, he asked, "Why does he do it?"

A sigh met his question, then Aentarra propped herself against a large rock. "Long ago there was a great war on our worlds. It was called the Darkness Wars. Lukaan and my father led us to victory. They became heroes beyond imagination. The people adored them, worshiped them almost like gods." She paused for thought. "I believe it was then that it started."

Rahg waited, wondering if she had finished or had simply paused again. Just as he was about to ask, she continued.

"I don't know what happened, but ... something caused a rift between them, a rift so horrible it was the catalyst for a new war—the Wars of Light. And that lasted more than one hundred years."

She rose, walking about in a circle. "I was born during that struggle. Named Aentarra because my father had prayed for a son that would have carried on his name. This was after Ronell died."

She sighed. "If I had been a son, I would have been named Antar, after my father; instead, he got me, hence the name Aentarra." She shook her head as if waking from a daydream. "Enough of that. My ancient discomforts are of no concern to you."

Rahg jumped up. "No, Lady Aentarra, I'm interested in hearing about it. Please, go on."

Her head kept shaking. "I'm done with it, boy. The past won't help us. And we do need help, so these gods of yours better give you something more than a fancy shield to wear."

Confusion set in, coupled with fear. "Why can't we just leave him in Sethia? If the shield stays up, we'll be safe."

Aentarra continued her pacing. "He's already started it, Rahg. Lukaan is doing what he does best—put the whole world at war. You've only seen a small part of it. Killing the kings in Sykor and Pomanda were nothing. Next, he'll have the countries at each others' throats." A cynical laugh ensued. "And believe me, once he gets control of a country those people will be nothing but fodder in his bid to get to us; besides, he'll get out no matter what we do. The shield is weakening. It won't be long."

Rahg's gut ached, nerves on edge. "So what do we do?"

"I'm working on it, boy." She went over to the rock where she had been sitting and spread a blanket on the ground. "Better get some sleep. The sun might rise earlier here."

Rahg closed his eyes, but he couldn't control his mind or his fear. What were they going to do about Lukaan? And lurking in a corner of his mind was the ever-present question—what if I'm the one destined to set Lukaan free?

He wrapped the blanket tighter, rolled to the side. The Slicer tucked inside his cloak pressed against him, beckoned him. Flickers of light poked out with a rhythmic pulsing that proved enticing. Rahg's hand moved toward it, slowly, with dark determination. The clasp of his cloak undid, his hand slipping inside.

"Let it go, boy."

The voice startled him, his hand jumping back to his side. He sat up, staring at Aentarra. "What?"

"I saw what you were doing. You're not ready for that. May never be ready." She sat up, shaking her head. "Knew you had it. I should have taken it from you long ago." She held her hand out. "Give it to me."

"What?" There was innocence in his eyes, but not enough to fool Aentarra.

"I'm too tired for games. Reach in, grab hold of it and hand it to me."

Rahg shook. "Why don't you just take it? I don't want to touch it."

"You did a moment ago." She laughed but then shook her head. "Besides, I can't touch it; it belongs to you now. The only way I can touch it is if you give it to me."

Silence greeted her. "Trust me," Aentarra said. "You are losing nothing but trouble."

Rahg reached in, tentative. As he was about to touch it, he pulled back. "I don't—"

"Do it!" Her eyes burned into him.

The night air chilled Rahg, sending a shiver up his arms. Once again he reached in, this time with a grim determination. He grabbed the Slicer, yanked it out and dropped it into Aentarra's hand, retracting his arm as he did, as if he feared repercussions. "That's all?"

She smiled. "That's all, Rahg. Now you can go to sleep."

As they both lay down, she opened the pouch that was ever at her side, and the Slicer rushed into it. A warm glow emanated from the pouch as she closed it. "Someday I'll teach you about them," she said, then turned her head and closed her eyes.

~

A bright, fiery sun greeted Rahg as he woke, a good way to start any day. He rose with a smile. "Good morning, Aentarra. Looks like a fine day."

"Every day is a fine day somewhere," she said, stretching her arms as she reached for the sky. Nex,t she bent to stretch her legs and back.

Rahg watched from a few paces away.

"When you get to be a thousand years old or so, boy, you'll need to do this too."

He laughed, a hearty laugh that had been a while coming. "I guess so," he said, then laughed more.

"I'll make khaffe," Aentarra said. "Get everything ready to go."

T hey traveled quickly, making good time as both the terrain and the weather were good. At nights, Rahg slept well, knowing that the least sound alerted Aentarra. A better watchdog would be difficult to find.

He chuckled to himself, wondering what she would do to him if she read his thoughts about that. A tinge of sadness overcame him as he thought of mind-reading, Camissa popping into his head. He missed having her near, especially at night since they ... since Vallah. He wondered how far she could read minds. They had never tried to do it from any distance.

I love you, Camissa.

*A*fter nine days they were nearing the mountain and best of all, there had been no signs of the dorgans. Within two more days Rahg was making camp at the bottom of their goal, the home of the gods. Anxiety ate at him as he worked.

Daurien had not been so pleasant the last time he had been here; in fact, Rahg had feared for his life. A pocket of smoke drifted close to him, and he turned, surprised to see Aentarra building a fire. "I thought you said no fires."

"You deserve a hot meal before you go." She laughed. "Might be your last one."

Rahg ate a big meal, followed it with khaffe, then settled down to sleep, worrying about what he would face in the morning. I'm sure they won't kill me, he thought, but the pains and aches in his memory taunted him.

*T*he climb was rote by now, and it seemed to go easier than the other two. It wasn't as cold, and the rocks didn't present the same problems they had in the past. When he pulled himself over the top, the maw of the cave was waiting for him. He could almost feel the dragon beckoning.

Rahg stood, trudged over to the cave, pausing before entering.

Yours is becoming a familiar face, Young One.

"You won't see me after this."

Remember, you do not have to speak. I will know your thoughts.

"Just move aside," Rahg said, and headed toward the dragon.

So stubborn, it said, then moved enough to allow Rahg passage. Choose well, Young One.

Rahg hurried by, not intimated any more by the dragon. He stopped, staring at the two dark tunnels. There were three last time, and four prior to that. He wondered what significance it held but had no patience for further consideration.

He chose the one on the right and moved forward. Within a few paces, he unsheathed his sword to feel his way in the dark. A turbulent feeling rose in his gut, churned, twisted him. Rahg stopped, wanting to turn back. What if Daurien sends me away? Why am I even here? Fear-driven thoughts prodded him, tried to turn him around.

A throbbing feeling struck him, not a sound, but a feeling coming from the mountain itself. From up ahead. He breathed, found courage somewhere within himself and moved forward, one slow step at a time. From further down the path, a bright light shone. Daurien would be waiting for him.

As he stepped through the opening, his eyes darted about, searching, but the god was nowhere to be seen. Rahg stopped again, felt, more than heard a door closing behind him, and when he turned he discovered himself sealed in.

"Hello?" His voice was weak, not even a whisper, and it cracked when he tried again. "Hel...lo?" With no response, he crept forward.

You can stop there.

The voice boomed from all sides of him, seemed to emanate from the walls of rock. Rahg froze in place. "What do you want?"

He waited through an interminable silence, his heart racing.

You must kill the Messenger, the Prince of Arangar.

Rahg feared it would be that. "I won't do it. He's my brother."

Then all of you will die.

"I'll take that chance," Rahg said. "Besides, I don't think Darstan would ever let Lukaan go. He wouldn't do that."

More rumbling ensued as if the mountain were talking to itself. The ground moved, and Rahg teetered on shaky legs. At last, things settled down.

There is one alternative. Only one.

Hope raced through Rahg's body, lightening his mood. "What is it? I'll do anything."

"If you keep him away from Sethia, there will be no Awakening. Then—"

"I'll keep him away. Don't worry. No matter what I have to do, I'll make sure he doesn't go to Sethia."

If he tries to go to Sethia, you must kill him. Is that understood?

"Are you going to give me more power? Make me stronger? And can you help us get out of here? Mulka is not with us now."

"I am the God of Protection. When you leave here, your shielding will be as strong as anyone's." A pause followed. "Your amulet will take you out of here, but just this once."

"Will the shield stop ColdFire?"

"You will have no need to stop ColdFire. Only Lukaan has that."

"Darstan has it."

Laughter erupted from the stone walls.

No one but Lukaan has ColdFire. Now prepare yourself.

"I told you, Darstan has it. I saw him use it in Pomanda. Saw him kill Sendra with it."

Impossible!

Rahg took a firm stand. "I saw it. She attacked him with BlackFire and Darstan just absorbed it, then he attacked with BlackFire, and after that, with a light bluish-white power. When it struck her she exploded."

Rahg stared at each of the walls, not knowing where he should address his comments. "Aentarra told me it was ColdFire. She said only her father and Lukaan had it."

The silence proved to be so long that Rahg thought he had been abandoned, then he felt the contact.

I can make you stronger, but nothing can protect you against ColdFire.

"Why not? Why can't you give me a shield strong enough? Doesn't the Sethian Shield stop ColdFire?"

There are things about that shield that are unique. A person by themselves cannot weave it, nor maintain it.

More silence, then:

ColdFire is an ancient power brewed from fear and death. Every time it is used it takes a piece of the wielder's heart and soul. A massive strike will drain someone entirely. If he truly has ColdFire, your only option is to stay away from him, strike when he is not prepared. Kill when he least expects it.

"I can't just kill Darstan. He—"

Stand still.

The light came down from the ceiling again, bathing Rahg in a glorious splendor of colors, as if all the rainbows in the world had been forced into one cylindrical shape and let loose from a spot above him. An involuntary reaction closed his eyes though he could still see the colors and the light through them. No thin piece of skin was going to keep this from shining through.

His bones shook, seemed to be moving, and he felt the insides of him coalesce then solidify, then coalesce again. Muscles twitched in his legs. He struggled to keep them still, but the twitches soon evolved into spasms, knocking him to his knees. The spasms spread, first to his gut then his back, twisting him as if he were a hungry vine wrapped around an old oak.

"S ...s..top, p ...pl ...ease?" His teeth chattered, and the words sputtered out. He tried again, but nothing emerged, so he used his thoughts. *Please stop? You are killing me.*

There was no laughter, no sympathy, no response of any kind, and the unrelenting torture spread to his arms and chest. When he thought he could take no more, his head started spinning, and he fell forward, crashing against the stone floor. Blood pooled around his head, spread to his neck and shoulders.

Rahg opened his eyes. Someone was holding him, talking softly. She was beautiful, with dark hair and deep, wonderful eyes. "Camissa?"

He tried lifting his head, but a searing pain sent him straight back down.

"Don't try to sit yet," Aentarra said. "I've told you before, I'm no healer, and this is a nasty wound." She dabbed his head with a warm wet cloth. "Yet another reason to keep my sister alive."

"What happened?" Rahg asked. "How did I get here?"

"I heard a noise during the night. When I woke you were here, bleeding badly." She turned his head, inspecting the wound. "I seared the wound, and though it looks better, there is still danger of it breaking open. But enough of that, what happened up there?"

"He tried killing me."

"Don't be stupid, boy. If he wanted to kill you, you'd be dead. Tell me what happened."

Rahg sat up, brow wrinkled in thought. "He said he could increase my shield. Make me as strong as anyone with it. And he—"

"Try it."

"What?"

"Try the shield. Weave something strong." She looked around. "Over there, by that rock. Put a shield in front of it."

Rahg wove a shield, a simple one, but with strong weaves. "Go ahead."

She struck with a shot of BlackFire, then with Lightning, but neither one broke through or even damaged the shield. "Impressive," she said and walked over to it. "Did it strain you when I hit it?"

Rahg stood, smiling. "I barely felt it." His smile broadened and lit his face. "Did you really try?"

She maintained a slight smile, though it was tempered with a hint of jealousy. "More than try, boy. They have given you a gift indeed. And practice will enhance those abilities." A smirk replaced the innocent smile. "If you and Mikkellana join together you might even be able to stop me."

Rahg beamed. "I can't believe it. This is great!"

Aentarra shoved him. "Don't get a big head about it. You have a lot to learn before you can do anything useful with that power. Besides, we need to focus on getting out of here for now."

"He said the amulet would work to get us out. Just this once, he said."

"Good. We didn't need it, but it's just as well, so let's be on our way."

They packed and headed out, Rahg charged with enthusiasm and hope. As they traveled, Rahg told her about his experience with Daurien, and it seemed as if every time he told her something she had four questions to go along with it.

She continued the probing for days, often repeating the same questions to see if he answered the same way. And despite the continual questioning, she insisted on a fast pace, much faster than normal. As a result, it only took ten days to get back to the portal into Arangar. When they emerged onto the pass, Aentarra wasted no time.

"Grab hold," she said, and then they shifted, stepping through a rift into Mikkellana's room in Vallah.

"Glad to see you didn't leave me here to waste away," Mikkellana said.

"Have you been taking care of my dear sister, Camissa? I see she's still alive, at least."

Camissa laughed as she unfolded herself from Rahg's embrace. "She is an easy patient. Never complained."

"Why don't you and Rahg go for a walk. I need to discuss something with her."

Rahg stepped away from Camissa and stared at Aentarra with suspicion painted all over his face. "Talk about what?"

"If I had wanted you to be a part of it, I would have extended an invitation. As it is, perhaps you and Camissa should reacquaint yourselves with her bed."

Camissa blushed, holding Rahg's hand. "Let's go," she whispered.

Rahg pulled away. "No. I want to hear this."

"Fine. Stay then, but you might not like what you hear."

"I'm staying."

Aentarra shrugged her shoulders and turned to Mikkellana. "When he went to the mountain, they made a point of telling him not to let Darstan near Sethia." Aentarra waited in silence. "Did you hear me? They made it a strong point."

Mikkellana thought. "That means he knows."

A nod of Aentarra's head answered her.

"You better go to Sykor and keep a rein on him."

"I'm going with you," Rahg said.

"What, and let Darstan kill you?" Aentarra laughed. "Don't be too proud of that new shield of yours, boy. I've seen your brother at work." Aentarra turned back to Mikkellana. "I forgot to mention; they did grant him some very impressive shielding abilities. Perhaps even fifth degree, so I'll leave it to you to teach him."

"I'm going anyway."

"Fine. Do as you will." She held her hand out. Rahg hesitated, but she grabbed him and shifted. They stepped through a rift onto a road next to a large boulder.

Rahg recognized the site; they had passed it on their first trip to Sykor and Tobias had told them the story about some king in the past putting the marker on it. "This isn't Sykor!"

"No. It's not, but I'm sure you can find your way," she said.

"You can't just leave me here!"

"Actually I can." Aentarra smiled as she stepped through the rift.

55

OLD MEMORIES

Aentarra returned to the spot outside of the Sethian Shield, the place where she had met the Wolfen long before.

He should be back with my answer by now if he's not already baked in the sun.

The Wolfen was waiting, perhaps not patiently. He bowed when Aentarra appeared.

"I pray I wasn't too long."

The Wolfen jumped to attention. "No, My Lady. I just arrived myself."

She smiled, noting the matted fur from where he had been leaning against the rock. He had been there a while. "You may go now," she said.

The Wolfen took the dismissal with a sigh of relief and hurried off. Aentarra wove a shield on the ground that she used for a seat and sat with her back against the same rock the Wolfen had used. It wouldn't be long before Melissara arrived, and there was ample shade to keep her cool. No sense in leaving and coming back. She closed her eyes, rested her head, and drifted off into a soft sleep. It was the kind of day that made for perfect dreams.

The dreams came, but they weren't perfect, resembling nightmares more than fantasies. The dreaded time they spent in the Forbidden Lands raced through her mind, the images flashing by as if they were aligned on a gallery wall that sped by at an incomprehensible speed, slow enough to catch a blur, a sensation of what it was, but that was all. After that, the trial, and the dishonor to her father; then the Wars of Light, replete with the treachery that made it infamous.

Back further to the Wars of Darkness. But how can this be? I wasn't born yet. Despite being contrary to logic, there it was, in her mind, images of the Darkness. Staring at her as if she had been there. This is impossible!

The images seemed to slow down, focus more. Lukaan and her father were there, fighting side by side, allied with one another. And there She was, destroying everything that came near Her, unleashing powers that Aentarra had never seen before. Antar and Lukaan both used ColdFire, to no avail, then something else happened. Something she couldn't see—a rhythmic pulsing, and a blinding light. Then She was gone.

Aentarra awoke with a jump, her head darting about, breath coming in heavy gasps. She stood, issued a Sensing, but nothing registered. She was alone, as alone as anyone could get. Still, she looked about again before she sat. Things were becoming clearer.

She knew something important about the Darkness Wars that she had not known before. And that revelation told her what she needed to do next. Another trip to the Hall of Echoes was in order. And the library.

"Lonely, sister?"

Aentarra started again. The suddenness of the voice frightened her. "You startled me, Melissara. I didn't hear you coming."

Melissara smiled. "I've noticed that before. This shield does it. Even if

I'm close to it, a shift is difficult to detect. With someone on the other side, it is impossible. Voices and other sounds don't seem to be bothered, but a Shift, it seems, is muted."

Odd. "Well, enough time to investigate that later. I came to talk. Shall we?" Aentarra walked as close as she dared to the shield, then spread a shield on the ground and sat, legs folded, hands on knees.

"I have to say I was surprised, though not unhappy, to receive your letter. It has been too long since we spoke." Melissara dusted off a rock and took a seat herself, not more than a few paces from Aentarra. "You should rethink your loyalties, sister. Join us."

"And be trapped in Sethia?"

"You know the Awakening has been prophesied—"

Aentarra scoffed. "Prophecies are for blithering idiots and priests, but forgive me for being redundant."

It was now Melissara's turn to scoff. "The prophecy has been here since before we came. You cannot dispute it."

Aentarra stared. "Damn fool! Doesn't that make you wonder? Whoever made up that nonsense wasn't referring to Lukaan; he wasn't here yet."

Melissara considered it, but then brushed it aside. "Enough of that, let's move on to more important subjects. You must know that I spoke with Mikkellana not long ago."

"As you can guess, Mikkellana and I are not on the best of terms. I'm sure Ghruehne or Sendra have reported in by now."

A raised eyebrow, narrowed eyes, a smirk—all that greeted Aentarra and more. "As you can guess, I already know they're dead, dear sister. Was that you?"

Aentarra let loose unbridled laughter, then: "You ever were the one to get to the point. If curiosity is killing you, I killed Ghruehne. Iazzo, too."

"And Sendra? Was that Mikkellana?"

"Far from it. Sendra almost killed our dear sister."

Aentarra got up and walked in a circle. "Darstan killed her."

"What!"

The shock was genuine, Aentarra could tell that. "Didn't sneak up on her either. Took the full brunt of her BlackFire, then with one strike he took her out."

"That's impossible! Either you or Mikkellana helped him." Melissara stood and paced.

"Did it with ColdFire." Aentarra stopped, waiting to judge the reaction.

"ColdFire!" She bit on the end of one of her fingers. "So he's the one."

"You knew!" She nearly went through the shield after Melissara. "You knew he had ColdFire?"

"Tirzinitzia told me. She can sense these things. I don't know how, but she can."

"Zee? How is the little darling? Tell her I hate her still, that I'll kill her when I see her next."

Melissara brushed the words away, stared at her sister. "Just how strong is he?"

Aentarra raised her head in thought, sat again. "He has ColdFire. He taught himself to Shift halfway across the world on the first try. He uses BlackFire as if he has an endless supply, and ..."

She waited. "And what?"

Aentarra leaned toward the shield, looked around as if to ensure no one else was there, then whispered. "I am positive he has FearMist!"

Melissara sat on the rock, eyes staring at nothing. "Not even Lukaan has that. Not even—"

"Not even father had that," Aentarra said.

Melissara took on a different face, like the teacher she once was. "We thought it was only a legend, or at best a lost power. One that the gods determined we no longer needed." She stared some more into nothingness. "How do—"

"I saw the aftermath. He killed forty thousand men in one night. He and five thousand men, though it was mostly him. Their faces had fear written all over it. Some had gone crazy, others died when their hearts seized up, and others ... it was obvious what had happened."

"It could be an interesting battle—you, Mikkellana, and Darstan on one side. Lukaan, Tirzinitzia, and myself on the other."

"We also have Darstan's brother, Rahg, and a few others."

"I saw Rahg fight in Sethia, remember. He's not much of a factor."

"The fight could be more interesting if the sides were slightly different." Aentarra smiled. "Suppose it were Darstan, Rahg, and three sisters against Lukaan and Tirzinitzia."

"While we are supposing, why not forget your vendetta against Tirzinitzia and make it us against Lukaan?" Melissara asked.

"Why not suppose that then. I can always kill Zee later."

Melissara bit on her finger some more, then played with a strand of golden hair, twirling it around and around. "I see you still carry that pouch with you. Make much use of it?"

Laughter bounced off the rocks at Aentarra's back. "On occasion I do."

Melissara shook her head, muttering. "You and father."

Aentarra's lip curled in anger, and her eyes burned. "Don't talk about father. You have no right."

"I was only—"

"No, I've had enough of you and Mikkellana both. But I'll tell you now, sister. You had better figure out whose side you're on, because I'm coming for him soon. And when I do, there will be no survivors. Search your soul, Melissara. Test your blood. Is it Runellan red or Savarran blue?"

Aentarra leaned as close to the shield as she could. "You better decide before I return." A rift opened and Aentarra shifted.

56

A CITY IN TURMOIL

Bragh led the reinforcements up the hill to High Town. More than three hundred guards were permanently stationed around Talanvar's house, positioned far enough away to thwart any surprise attack from Darstan, yet close enough to keep an eye on who came and went through the gates, and close enough to fire a volley of arrows into Talanvar's front door if need be.

The new Force Commander brought five hundred more men. He intended to end the stalemate.

Bragh handed a message to one of his runners. "Take this to the gate keeper. Wait for the response."

As he awaited Talanvar's answer, he dispatched his strike leaders, surrounding the house. His message called for the immediate surrender of Sergeant Takar and Kender Darnell. He knew they wouldn't give them up, but that suited him fine. It provided a reason for his actions. The runner returned momentarily, handing him a sealed letter. Bragh opened it and read.

orce Commander Bragh:

Unless you are the new king of Sykor, I see no reason why I should obey your commands. Do your worst.

Lord Talanvar

Bragh ripped the letter into small pieces, letting them fall from his hand as he did. "Shoot anyone who comes out."

"Anyone?" a patrol leader asked.

The Force Commander stared at him, condescension in his eyes.

"Strike Leader! Repeat your orders for this soldier. If he still doesn't understand, dismiss him." Bragh glared at the man. He had learned that from Ludar, and he had learned it well. "Strike Leader, on my orders, shoot a volley of arrows at the house. All sides."

"Yes, sir," the strike leader said, and passed the order along to the others.

"Fire!" Bragh said, and two hundred archers released their bows.

~

nside Talanvar's manor, Darstan and Wisp paced and worried. Takar was up and about and had joined them for breakfast, only his second meal downstairs since they had brought him here. "Feels good to be alive again," Takar said. "I didn't think I'd make it for a while."

"You can thank Aenaila for that." Wisp slapped the sergeant on the back.

"Now you owe her twice, Big Sergeant," Adju chimed in. "Remember in Khatara when Mistress Aenaila healed you?"

Takar laughed. "How could I forget, little Adju? And it's good to see you again too."

The arrows hit the front of the house first, nearly a dozen of them coming in through the windows, and there were so many thuds into the sides of the house it sounded as if someone were hammering.

Aenaila jumped back when an arrow landed close to her. "We should just shift out of here," she said. "There is no sense in anyone else getting killed."

Darstan headed for the door. "I'll kill all of them."

"Don't go out there, Darstan. Even you can't stop that many arrows." Wisp moved to the side of the big front window, peering out at the guards. "Besides, they are so far away, you'd have a tough time getting to them to do much damage. Not before they fired numerous times."

Gregor paced, an old staff in his hand. "I wish I had my blackthorn staff."

"All we have to do is kill Bragh, take over the guards, and get back to my quarters. Then I'll get it for you, Bounty-man." Takar seemed to be back to his old humor.

~

*A*entarra appeared in the back of the stable behind the Trader's Inn. She had to get to Talanvar's house, and this was the closest Shift point she had. She brushed off her clothes as she exited, ignoring the stares from the stable boy, likely wondering how she had gotten in there.

A brisk pace carried her through the merchants' district, then up into High Town. Guards lined the streets. Many guards. She suspected it had something to do with Darstan, and hoped he had not dug too deep a hole. They would need Sykor in their battle against Lukaan.

"Halt!" a guard called from the side. "No one is allowed into Lord Talanvar's manor."

She felt the guard's eyes on her whenever she diverted her gaze. "I need to deliver a message to Lord Talanvar."

He held out his hand. "I'll see that he gets it."

"I'm afraid that won't do. This is something I must do myself."

He stepped in front of her, blocking her path. "I must insist, the Force Commander—"

Aentarra wove a shield and shoved him out of the way, knocking him to his knees in the street, then she continued her casual walk toward Talanvar's house. Three more guards raced to intercept her, reaching to grab for her as they drew near, but the shield prevented them from touching her.

"I can't touch her!" one screamed.

"Something blocking me," another said.

Bragh arrived with a strike leader at his side. He stared at Aentarra for a long moment. "Kill her," he said, then walked away.

Aentarra expanded her shield with a forceful shove, knocking the three guards back, bumping one of them into the Force Commander. When he turned back to her, he found her glare fixed on him. "I will remember you, Force Commander." With that, she quickened her pace to the front gate, bursting it open as she approached.

"Fire!" Bragh ordered and a volley of arrows shot straight for her, but they fell harmlessly to the ground. Gasps rang out from the guards, hinting at fear settling in.

~

From inside the manor, Wisp continued peering out the window. "Aentarra's coming up the walk," he said. "And they're firing at her."

"Aentarra!" Darstan raced to the window beside Wisp. "What's she doing here?"

A rap on the door brought an immediate response, with Talanvar opening it and rushing her inside. "Welcome to my home, My Lady."

Her smile could light up the night when she wanted it to. "No need for formalities. We are all old friends." She cast a quick glance around the room, took it all in, stopping at Gregor. "I thought you were dead until I saw you in Pomanda."

"What are you doing here?" Darstan asked.

She didn't answer at first, continuing her inspection of the library, stopping long enough to get a Shift point by the fireplace. "Saving your hide, though that's not what I came for originally."

"I can take care of this," Darstan said.

Her finger wagged at him as she walked. She picked up a book on ancient Sethian temples, flipped a few pages, then set it back down. "I've seen how you took care of things in Arangar—killed everyone." Aentarra laughed. "It's not like me to preach, but there are other options."

Darstan walked to her, stood right in front of her, staring. "Did you have anything to do with Mirana getting killed?"

Aentarra was far shorter than Darstan, yet when she stared back at him with her vindictive eyes, she seemed to be looking down from a high tower.

"Don't think you can question me, boy. Not about anything." She turned toward the kitchen, and it was then she sensed the fire building inside him. She flipped back around, wrapped him in a tight, complex weave and squeezed it tight.

He gasped, searching for breath that wouldn't come. With his arms pinned to his sides, he tried to call on his Fire, on Lightning, on anything, but nothing worked. He was trapped and soon would be out of air. Just as suddenly as he had been bound, she released him, the unexpectedness causing him to fall to the ground.

Aentarra reached her hand down and pulled him up. "I have been doing this for more than a thousand years, boy. Until your thoughts become your actions, you'll never be able to defeat me." She laughed. "You won't even come close."

Darstan seemed to have lost the fire in his belly, the anger in his eyes, though something remained.

"And another thing," Aentarra said. "Your brother knew nothing about a truce back at that pass in Arangar. There was no letter, no agreement. He didn't even know you were there until you attacked him."

Darstan looked at her as if she were lying.

She sensed the mistrust. "I have no reason to lie to you. If I wanted to, I'd just kill you."

Darstan bit his lip, seething, but then he softened. She was right. Why would she lie? Aentarra didn't care one hoot if he hated her or not, and she didn't care if he and Rahg hated each other. A laugh emerged. "Yes, I guess you would, wouldn't you."

Aentarra ruffled his hair. "Perhaps not. I almost even like you." She grabbed his arm and led him to a sofa, far away from the threat of arrows through the window. "Everyone should come here," she said. "I have a plan to discuss."

*M*oments later, Aentarra, Darstan, and Takar walked out the front door protected by one of Aentarra's shields on all sides. The arrows came immediately, striking at them from every angle, though they all fell to the ground with broken or dulled tips. They made their way to the end of the walk then into the street, heading straight for Force Commander Bragh. He had surrounded himself with several patrols of guards, all with swords drawn, and another three patrols kneeling on the street with arrows nocked in bows.

"Force Commander Bragh," Aentarra called out. "I told you I'd remember you."

"Fire!" he called, and the archers shot, again to no avail.

"Attack!" he called and the guards charged, hacking at them with swords that never reached their intended targets.

"It is futile, Force Commander. Please don't waste your men's energy. Or worse, if I grow angry, I'll be forced to kill them."

"Surround them. Keep attacking. She can't hold the shield forever."

Aentarra lost her smile, stood rigid as stone. "Now, Darstan," she said and let down a portion of her shield.

Darstan issued fire from his left arm, a huge column of fire that raged into the mass of guards, catching uniforms afire and scorching flesh. The men panicked, running back, even trampling one another; meanwhile, Aentarra wove a shield around Bragh and closed it tightly, so that his arms were pinned to his sides. He had no room to move.

Bragh struggled, tried moving his arms, his legs, but nothing worked. The more he struggled the heavier he breathed.

"You don't have long left, Force Commander. I would conserve all the air you can."

Bragh continued to struggle.

Aentarra laughed. "By now, your chest is tight, filled with pain, you're finding it difficult to breathe, and you are afraid. Very afraid."

Bragh nodded, then screamed. "Help me! Let me go! I'll do anything you want."

Aentarra paraded around him, letting her finger trace a pattern on the shield enveloping him. "Anything?"

"Anything you want."

"Would you kill your men if I asked?"

"Which ones?"

"All of them."

He paused for a moment, not knowing how to answer, but the air grew shorter. He now had few breaths left. "Yes. All of them."

Aentarra turned to the guards who remained, the ones who had not run away. "Did you hear that? Your Force Commander would kill you to save his own life. How pitiful!" She let her gaze catch them. "Fortunately for you, I am not so merciless. I think we should just let the Force Commander die instead."

Bragh had only a few breaths left, not enough to form words, but he managed to bang his head against the shield in protest. After several attempts at that, he stopped and slumped to the ground as he ran out of air.

When Aentarra was certain he was gone, she let the shield around the Force Commander go. "Your Force Commander is dead. There is no need for any more of you to die; however, if you want to, I will be glad to accommodate. Just tell me, and I'll kill every one of you where you stand."

A strike leader walked up to her, drew his sword and offered it to her, hilt first. "My sword is yours, My Lady. Do with it what you will." He knelt on the cobblestone street, head bowed in obeisance. Soon, the others followed suit.

Once they had all sworn allegiance, she had them stand. "All of you know Sergeant Takar. He is the new Force Commander. You will follow his orders as if they were mine. Send messengers to the cowards who left here. If they have any courage left, they may join the new guard, providing they can follow orders from Takar and swear their allegiance. There is a great war coming, and Sykor is critical to victory." She let her words sink in. "Furthermore, Lord Talanvar will rule Sykor in my absence. Queen Cynamar will no longer be available."

There were shocked looks among the guards, but none of them said a word. Aentarra signaled for Takar to take over and he stepped forward.

"Most of you know me. For those that don't, you soon will. We don't have time to waste, so listen well. I want full patrols to scour the city rounding up the guards. Every man must be accounted for, and either their oath of allegiance will be in place by tomorrow, or they will have a sentence of death." He noted a few dissidents. "We have no room for anything else."

"Your will, Force Commander," someone shouted from the middle of the crowd, and they all soon followed along with a three-fisted salute.

Aentarra smiled. "You have your army now. Use it well." She turned to Darstan. "Come with me."

As they walked back into the house, Aentarra remembered something she wanted to say. "Darstan, be wary of Gregor."

"Why?"

"He could be a traitor. We can't be sure. After all, he was in Sethia for a long time."

Darstan shook his head. "He already gave us information about what the guards were planning. Several times, in fact."

She stopped just as they were about to enter the door, turning to stare at him. "I know my sister, Melissara, and I find it difficult to believe she would let him go without a reason." She paused, briefly. "If we get him with Camissa again, have her probe his mind. She's good at that."

Darstan nodded. He trusted Gregor, but this was now two people who raised the question—Wisp and Aentarra. It was at least something to consider.

Back inside, Aentarra proposed the rest of her plan. "Lukaan is staging a complete war. He killed the king of Pomanda, and I suspect he will be going after the other countries. Darstan, I want you to go to Khatara and see what you can do to prevent it from falling into Lukaan's hands. Take that thief with you."

"What are you doing?" Darstan asked.

"I'm off to find Rhaven and get my sister, then I'll return to make sure things go smoothly with Takar."

"Where's Rahg?"

"I left him on the road to Sykor. He'll be here in a few days." She wagged another finger at Darstan. "But I already told you. Don't worry yourself over him. He had nothing to do with it. Besides, you'll have more than enough to do in Khatara."

She next faced Talanvar. "When Takar gets the rest of the guards in line, take a full strike force and arrest the queen. Put her in prison." Aentarra stepped aside from them and shifted.

Darstan stared at the spot where she was for a moment, locked in a trance. He didn't know whether she had anything to do with killing Mirana or not, suspected she probably didn't, but he knew Rahg did. Accident or not, he killed her. And killed his son. "Ready to go, Aenaila, Gregor, Wisp?"

"What about me?" Adju asked.

"Grab someone's hand," Aenaila said, then she formed the image of her brother's room in Khatara and Sahifted.

57

PREPARING FOR WAR

Pack Lord Dregl traipsed through the foothills of the Kamnoran Mountains, an ages-old border between Nyauran and Kamnor, and one of the few that had never been breached. The combination of rugged terrain and the peaceful nature of the Nyaurans only a few of the factors contributing to the long lasting peace. Training recruits proved to be difficult business, and Dregl needed these fresh pups to be as wily as veterans in short order.

As inevitable as the war was, so too was the death of these young ones. It sickened him. The Pack Lord raised his snout, sniffed the air, then shook his head as he moved toward a pass. He had made more noise than the frail ones, and still the pups had not found him.

What will they do when they face real war, he wondered, but his own answer was too close to the truth. An arrow in the back or a sword to the gut would be the cure.

Sharp, pointed ears pricked to full attention as he listened for sounds. Up ahead, the trail narrowed as it curved through the pass into Kamnor, a perfect spot for an ambush. They would be there waiting for him. He sighed. So little they know. And with no time to learn.

If his assumption was correct, and they were waiting for him, they would lose sight of him just as he made the turn. Dregl counted it down, then, when the time was right, he ducked behind a boulder, climbed the back, side and crept up the rocks, staying flat against them.

Four young ones lay in wait, long-knives drawn and ready. They were so focused on the trail below them, that they had no one watching their backs, and they had closed their ears to other sounds.

At five paces, Dregl raised himself to a stoop, crept closer, then charged, taking only two leaps to reach the two who guarded the rear. The first one fell to a mock stabbing in the back, the second to his throat being slit.

A gasp drew the attention of the others, but they succumbed to the superior skills of a trained Wolfen with little resistance. Shame weighed heavily on them as they stood to face the Pack Lord. Heads bowed low, they awaited the punishment.

A fierce snarl greeted them. "You have all just died. Your parents are weeping, and your siblings or loved ones shed tears of sorrow and shame. Even a frail one could have killed you.

No guards to watch. No surprises." Dregl's long, pointed claw raised the chin of one of the youngest. "Silence is the Wolfen's companion."

He moved to the next one, raising his chin with his claw as well. "Night is the Wolfen's friend."

The third recruit trembled, and though he found a measure of calm when Dregl lifted his chin, it was not enough to look him in the eyes. "Death is the Wolfen's brother."

The last recruit, the one who had functioned as the pack leader, raised his chin before Dregl arrived. The Pack Lord smiled, pressed his claw firmly into the young one's neck, drawing a trickle of blood. Amber eyes bore into him until he looked away, shamed yet again today. "Attack when they least expect."

The Pack Lord stepped away, turned and faced them. "These are the rules we live by. It is the ways of the Wolfen."

Dregl paced, waiting for a response but none came. "Fear lingered in the pass today. I caught the scent as I climbed the trail." He made his way to the first in line, and then, in succession, poked a sharp claw into the chest of each of them. "Stay in the mountains until you have rid yourselves of fear. If any of you fail ..." Dregl frowned. "You know what must be done."

The young Wolfen bowed to him, then kept their heads low until long after he was gone.

As Dregl descended the trail, the call came to him. He was to report to the master at once. *The time has come,* he thought, *and they are nowhere near ready.*

~

*B*rood Commander Vorkk used his whip on the five Victas before him. *No more than hatchlings, How will I ever have them ready for war in time to suit the master?*

Orders had come by way of Tirzinitzia to prepare all brood members for the final battle. The Viktas would, at last, take their rightful place in this realm controlled by frail ones. Vorkk licked his lips, imagining the blood of his victims. *How sweet it will taste.*

The Northern Sethian desert presented a varied terrain: large rocks and boulders sitting upon flat ground dotted with small scrub brush and cacti. A short distance away, the flat ground rose into foothills, barren, brown lands that rolled like great swells in the sea. Soon after that, the vast expanse of the Sethian Mountains—giant spires of rock that towered above the landscape and pierced the clouds, though the sky was seldom cloudy.

Vorkk's heavy boots kicked up sandy dirt as he paced in front of his recruits. These were the last five of the day, a day filled with disappointment and frustration. It sometimes seemed as if the young ones did not learn as quickly as they had in Vorkk's day. He glared at each of them, a Victa battle axe strapped to their green backs in the traditional fashion. Sharp, heavy claws protruded from three thick, scaly fingers and a short thumb-like appendage.

The Brood Commander's beady eyes found each of them. He could almost feel their slow, rhythmic heartbeats. "A poor example of how a Victa fights," he said, a hint of sibilance in A voice that dripped with disgust. It was an admonition far worse than any beating, forcing the Victas to lower their heads in shame.

Vorkk's claws clicked against his scales as he tapped with impatience. "What shall I tell the master? Reports must be detailed. Am I to say you are not ready? That the children of frail ones could defeat you with rakes and hoes?" Warmth from the afternoon sun beat on his back, one bright spot in a disastrous day.

"We will be ready," the youngest one said. There was some degree of confidence in his voice.

Humbled by the young one's courage, the others joined the chorus. "We will be ready," they said as a unit.

At least they are doing something together, Vorkk thought.

He wondered what he should do. More punishment seemed futile. They did not take to it. He thought of his own son, a younger hatchling, though almost as big as them. Encouragement is what drove him. Perhaps it would work here too. "Keep practicing. I sometimes am harsh, but it is only to make you better. Practice and you will become true soldiers."

They snapped to attention, claws scratching the scales on their chests. "Yes, Commander Vorkk. We will be ready."

He smiled, his tongue darting in and out. "That would please me," he said. "But for now I must go. I will review your progress in a few days."

The Brood Commander marched toward Sethia, a long way to go, but the walk would do him good, provide time to ponder the situation. His wife's nephew was among the trainees today, and he had been one of the worst. Could I assign him a safe post? Is that right to do?

He wondered if he would do it for his son. That would be the true test, though fortunately one he wouldn't have to face for a few more years, and, depending on the outcome of this battle, one he may never have to face.

Vorkk felt a crushing pain in his head, stopped and cupped his hands against it.

"Brood Commander. Report at once. Go to a Shift point where Tirzinitzia will meet you."

"Which one?" He spoke, before realizing all he needed to do was think.

"The oasis near the mountains."

He nodded, though no one was there to see, then he changed directions, heading toward a small oasis near the northeastern border. His pace increased, boots pounding the desert floor. Tirzinitzia did not like to wait. None of the Banished Ones did.

❧

Gnaka Night Commander Chernol loved to lead. He lived for driving men to things they thought they could not do, especially if it meant he had to beat it out of them. Gnakas were notorious for being lazy, but when properly motivated, they fought and worked better than most anyone.

All it takes is a few whips laced with thorns, he thought, and cracked the back of one of his recruits.

The master had instructed him to prepare the young ones for war, though he had yet to determine what their exact role would be.

"Shovels, pick axes, and swords" he had been told. "Perfect them in all areas and have them ready."

This could mean the master had a tunneling project for them, or he wanted them prepared for battlefield construction. Perhaps the siege of a city? No one could dig like a Gnaka, that was a well-known fact.

Gnaka bodies were made for digging: strong arms, and wiry, but tremendously strong, backs. In addition, they possessed a stamina unlike others, able to dig all day and still be fresh. Perhaps it will be both. A siege, followed by the attack of the city.

The call came to him before he had the opportunity to exercise his unique discipline.

"Report at once, Night Commander."

~

*L*ukaan sat on his throne, immersed in thought. He remembered a time when he had ruled, when he was worshiped—

"They are here, Great Lord." The Sethian Commander knelt on the floor, head bowed so that his hair scraped the marble. He shivered as the mist curled around him, wrapping itself around his body as if it were a giant snake. Tendrils of the white and gray fog sought purchase on his clothes, in his hair, caressed his eyes.

He closed his eyelids, an attempt to disguise his fear, and prayed to a long-forgotten god to let him survive this meeting. The mist swirled about, rising and falling on its own accord, sometimes in a violent rush, at other times drifting along at a lazy pace, floating by with no care.

"You may rise, Commander Shill."

Shill stood on wobbly knees, but he kept his head bowed.

Melissara arrived with Dregl, followed by Tirzinitzia with Brood Commander Vorkk and Night Commander Chernol.

"How goes the training?"

~

*D*regl responded first, knowing that to hide the truth would be death. "Not good, Great Lord." His head touched the floor as he spoke. "They are not ready."

~

*N*ight Commander Chernol lay prostrate, fear tainting his words. "I have whipped them until I break the barbs, Great Lord, but it is no use. They do not respond."

~

"*M*y men will be prepared, Great One." Pride swelled in Commander Shill, happy that he could issue such a report.

~

*V*orkk hissed, angry that he should go last and have to follow a good report. "Only a few are ready. Most are not."

"Chernl, Dregl, Vorkk. Take the worst three and kill them. All except you, Commander Shill."

Vorkk cringed, an image of his wife's nephew forming in his mind. What would he tell her? What would he tell her sister?

Darkness shone through the mist, a dark forbidding form surrounded by a coruscating light. "The time we have waited for has finally arrived. We must be prepared."

"What actions shall we take, Great Lord? The news from Sykor is not good. It remains to be seen if we will even hold it. And as you know, that city is a key factor."

Tirzinitzia had proven herself a great strategist during the Wars of Light, so much so that even Lukaan sought her advice.

Lukaan spoke his thoughts. "Pomanda is ours, or will be soon. And before long, the Victas and Wolfen will control Kamnor and the Northern lands. Once Commander Shill and Night Commander Chernol take Khatara, nothing will stop us. That will leave only Sykor and Genda."

"With Mikkellana and Aentarra on their side, and those boys, won't the fighting be unbalanced?" Shill felt he had to ask, though he risked Lukaan's wrath to do so.

"No one can stand against so many," Melissara said. "If our forces are strong enough and attack together, Aentarra and Mikkellana will be forced to abandon the cause. Their only option would be to come to Sethia, and they wouldn't dare do that."

"Besides," Lukaan said, "the Awakening will soon be here. I have seen the vision." His laughter seemed to shake the walls, and it stirred the mist into action. "Now go, all of you. Begin your march into destiny and live to reap your rewards."

~

Tirzinitzia stood tall for a woman, Lenordan bones defining a staunch frame draped with pale skin. An assortment of oils, including special soaps from the olive trees at home, kept her skin soft without Rejuvenation, and that Talent had never been hers to use.

Since ancient times she had been a pacer, and she practiced the habit while waiting for Lukaan to show, her unusually long stride carrying her past the Sethian Commander, a pacer himself—tall, too. Slender fingers clenched into tight fists slowly uncurled, stretching as far back as she could go, barely past vertical now. It seemed as if age truly was the curse of yore.

A tingle ran up her neck when she sensed the rift, and she stepped aside quickly, not wanting to be near him when he entered. It was difficult to tell what might irritate the Dark Lord, as the symbol of the suns burnt into her face reminded her daily.

Several of the Banished Ones and others stepped through the rift. The light shone bright, like the first glimpse of morning sun, then the dark aura around him seemed to absorb it. "Begin."

Tirzinitzia moved to a string of tables in the center of the room, maps of all the countries spread atop them in a continuous design. She grabbed a pointer, no more than a sharpened stick that she had carved to resemble the ones favored by her instructors at the University on Lenorda. They too had taught battle strategy. A low bow to Lukaan, followed by a nod to the others, then she began.

The Sethian Commander, Shill, stood to her left with Brood Commander Vorkk, and Pack Lord Dregl beside him. The Gnaka Leader leaned over the end of the table, hands resting on the border of wood about the perimeter of the maps.

Melissara and Lukaan graced her right side. The maps were made as if they stretched from left to right, being viewed from a spot in the Endless Sea. Tirzinitzia moved to her right, pointing to Jattan Kir, the vast desert country. She tapped the middle of it twice, calling attention to the mountains, then twice again focusing on Khatara, the large port city.

"It would be easy to say Jattan Kir is the key to it all, and it would not be far from the truth; however, as much as Jattan Kir, and especially Khatara, are strategic goals—capturing Sykor is what I believe to be the true key to success."

Her pointer moved to the walled city of Sykor as she spoke. "If we have Sykor we control the east-west roads. We also have a port to the sea, and along with Khatara, that would give us near dominance, leaving only Genda to oppose us on the water."

"I thought we were positioned to get control of Sykor," Shill said.

Tirzinitzia hesitated, but Melissara had no such reservations. "Ghruehne and Sendra failed us. As they are now dead, punishment is moot, but it should not prevent us from regaining control." Melissara tapped on the map of Pomanda. "We got Pomanda as a second prize, and it was one we didn't expect."

"How will we take Sykor?" Pack Lord Dregl asked.

Tirzinitzia smiled. She loved the strategic parts of battle. her scouts had spent years gathering details from all over the lands, details she incorporated into her maps, and now that would pay off. "First we take the Khataran Highlands," she said.

All of the commanders moved closer, eager to hear of their part in the plan.

58

KHATARAN HIGHLANDS

Commander Shill stood shorter than most Sethians, but when next to the Gnakas he appeared to be tall. Sethia bustled with activity, armies massing, recruits being trained, supply stations being set up and stocked. All for the glory to come. The pride of his race rested on him, and he could almost hear his father's words as he prepared the men.

Be loyal. Die bravely. Live forever.

It was a Sethian saying that fathers repeated to their sons from a young age, burned it into their memory, breathed it into their soul.

He looked out over the mass of men—all forty thousand of them, and felt the pride rush through his veins. It was the most important event in Sethian history, and he was commanding the attack on Jattan Kir, one of the primary concerns. His hands trembled. He had interviewed reconnaissance scouts for a year and studied battle maps for months. Now it came down to execution of the plan, and Tirzinitzia had come up with a good one.

Shill stepped to the side of his tent, admired the hint of fresh daylight just over the mountains in the eastern sky, then headed toward the center of camp. A good meal with strong khaffe should start any new journey.

Strike Leader Jirg saluted as he approached. "Good morning, Commander. The weather bodes well for our mission."

Shill nodded, surveying the scene—men scurrying about, dismantling tents, eating meals, tending to animals. It was a moving city he ruled and not a small one. "Did the Gnakas leave on time?"

Another salute, which Shill quickly brushed away. "No need to salute when there are just the two of us, Jirg. Now tell me about the Gnakas."

"They left as instructed. An advance party of five hundred."

"I hope it is enough."

"Commander, they are our best archers." Jirg cleared his throat, lowered his head. "They seem to have a special ability to dig and to be archers." Jirg straightened. "None can compare, sir. Not even Sethian archers."

Shill nodded. "That's why they were chosen. I hope they live up to it." He stared southeast toward the highest peaks of the Khataran range. "Those mountains will be riddled with Pasha's men. If we don't get them out, it will cost us dearly—in lives and time both."

"I don't think they will be expecting us, sir. They—"

"That's why you're not a commander, Jirg. You should always plan for the worst." Shill's glare proved to be as much a reprimand as his rebuke.

"Yes, sir," Jirg said and snapped out a salute.

Commander Shill accepted the salute with a tiny sneer on his face. "When I finish breakfast we leave. Make certain everyone knows."

As Jirg hurried off, Shill sat to eat his meal He stared at a mesmerizing fire and thought of his son, probably sitting down to his meal somewhere on the western border.

His son had been assigned to the army that would invade Nyauran, the horse people. They were good warriors, brave to a man, but their numbers were small even if the territory wasn't. They would be defeated with little effort. Still, he worried. As good a soldier as his son was, anyone could fall in battle.

Shill set down his plate and lowered his head, offering a silent prayer to keep his son safe. It was his last boy, the other falling in battle with Jag Tem when Iazzo took them to Entiria.

Tightness gripped his chest, throat swelling. Losing him had almost killed his wife, and though she recovered some, she had never been the same.

He sighed, finished drinking his khaffe but left the plate where it lay. This time would be different. The Master had committed his resources. This time they would be victorious.

Shill stood. It was time to go. He walked to the front of the line, never stopping to talk or issue further orders. They knew what to do.

As he moved out ahead of the camp, men fell in line behind him— forty thousand of them. All, save the five hundred Gnakas he had sent to flank the Khataran lines. If the Gnakas performed as expected, Pasha would be taken by surprise, and for the first time in a thousand years, the Khataran Pass would fall.

As the warm rays of the rising sun hit his face, Shill smiled. Perhaps his wife would even get better. She deserved to.

59

GENDA'S STAND

It didn't take long to man the ships with volunteers, not once the news arrived about Sykor and Pomanda's kings being killed, and now them at war—or near it.

Fishermen might be a stubborn lot, but their backbones were as stiff as a shark's fin, and no one was going to tell them what to do.

They didn't take kindly to government, their style of rule surviving two hundred years without a king or queen. No royalty of any kind. Fishermen lived in Genda, and they ruled Genda.

For four nights, the council met, deciding on what to do about manning the ships and the borders, debating on how many men to allocate to each area.

Seth Miska reached her hand out, accepting Maria's offer to help him stand. Ninety-one years ago Maria's great-grandmother had helped him take his first steps; now here she was helping him with some of his last.

"I wish you would let me call Niko. He's going to the meeting too."

Seth downed the last gulp of vidda, then grabbed her upper arm with one hand, his other planted on the back of his chair. He struggled, but pulled himself up, then shuffled across the wide-planked flooring of the Tern's Wing, his favorite tavern.

The owners of the Tern's Wing were the only ones that still made vidda the way it was in the old days. The way it was meant to be. "Niko will be late. He always is." Seth paused to take a deep breath. Maria waited, accustomed to his ways. "I've never been late to a meeting, Maria. You know that. Your mother and grandmother know it too."

"I know, grandpa. Being late is like not being there at all."

His teeth seemed to chatter as he walked. "Worse, girl. It shows disrespect."

"We won't be late. No need to worry."

It took a long time to climb the steep hill known as Olive Street, the street where Genda was founded. The street was as twisted and gnarled as it's namesake tree.

The council had been meeting in an ancient building near the top of the hill for more than one hundred years, transferred to that spot after their original building had been destroyed in a storm.

As they neared the entrance, Niko ran up from behind them. "Seth, you should have waited. I came to get you."

"Hah! Might have waited all night. Can't let my reputation rest on you."

Niko smiled at Maria but didn't let Seth see it. "Sorry, Seth," he said, then grabbed his arm. "Let me help him, Maria. You go on. I'll see he gets home."

Maria hesitated, but Niko insisted. "It could be very late before we get out. Don't worry."

She nodded, kissed Seth on the cheek, then turned and walked down the street, wrapping her shawl around her shoulders.

Niko opened the door at the top of the steps, helping Seth into a large room with an oval table at the center. Old wooden chairs surrounded it, chairs nearly as old as Seth and almost as wobbly.

The rest of the council arrived before the first round of vidda had been served, and once everyone was there a fresh glass was filled for the traditional toast. "Let the winds run smooth, and the fish run strong."

They all gulped it down, some calling for more afterward, others asking for khaffe.

"Pomanda and Sykor are headed for war. We've got people who know." Niko's brother, Marco, had spoken, and he was a respected member of the council.

"Krovs worry me more," Ciccio said, chewing on a pipe that looked as old as himself. Smoke hovered around his head like little clouds.

"Pomanda's the only concern. Krovs aren't gonna' get involved in no war." Seth Miska spoke as the senior member of the council. At one time there had been a title of First of Genda, but ever since Tobias Marek had shamed them, they abandoned that. Now the council members were all equal, though the elders did garner some respect even if their votes carried no more weight.

"Not if they have to fight along with someone, they won't. Krovs would just as soon fight the whole world by themselves."

Seth stood up on legs so spindly they looked as if they should squeak when he moved. "I know you had an urge to talk, Tenny, but next time say something worthwhile." He rested his hands on the table, leaning a little to the right, his weak side. "It's a narrow border we share with Pomanda, leastwise, the parts they can come through are, so I'm sayin' we send ... I don't know ... one thousand men up there?"

Tenny jumped up and slammed his fist down.

"You spilled my khaffe, Tenny!"

"Sorry," he said, "but a thousand men ain't hardly enough to stop four-fingered Milt when he goes on a binge. How you gonna' stop an army from Pomanda?"

Seth brushed the smoke from Ciccio's pipe away. "You're dumb as an oyster, Tenny. This won't stop 'em. Not meant to. We're just puttin' them there to let Pomanda know we're serious, that they can't just march in here without shedding blood." Seth's knees started shaking so he sat down.

"Pomanda's not concerned about us, and I don't think they'll risk coming in here with Sykor hovering near their border like seagulls behind a fishin' boat." Seth shook his head. "No. They won't' come here, and that'll let us send more men to sea."

"How many men we got?"

"How many men we got, and how many we can count on are two different things, Ciccio." Niko downed another vidda, stood and looked at the table. "From what I can tell we can't count on more than fifteen or sixteen thousand men. Probably get more in the long run, but better not to figure on it."

Tenny had recovered from Seth's abuse. Like most fishermen, he had thick skin. "If we agree Niko's right, then let's plan on sixteen thousand. All we need to do now is split them up."

Soon they all agreed. One thousand men would go to the Pomandan border; five thousand would stay in Genda as reserves and to guard the city; the rest of the countryside would be on alert, with men ready to go if needed; and ten thousand men would man the seventy-two ships under Malakai's command. Even if the other countries mustered an equal number of men and ships, with Malakai leading Genda the sea would belong to them.

~

*W*ord got out within a few days of what the council's decision was, and soon men were volunteering for assignments. Several thousand more men showed up than anticipated, swelling the number of men they would take to sea.

A lot of the married men, the younger ones anyway, wanted to be stationed at home, reserves for defending the city. The lazier ones volunteered for the Pomandan border, most agreeing with Seth that nothing was likely to happen there. The more adventurous begged to go to sea, where all Gendans belonged. They were born to rule the sea, and an assignment on land would be like punishment.

Sennar smiled, his new face making that a possibility. Genda had been nothing but a fishing town for a long time; perhaps now they would shine a little. Bask in the sun for a while.

He looked over the newest crop of volunteers, young and old alike, hungry for a mission. "Don't think ya' came here to rest, mates. Or to sleep."

He cackled, that grating laugh of Old Crazy had stayed with him even though his face had been fixed. "Won't be much sleepin' on this voyage. If you're not catchin' fish, you'll be fightin' minions of the Evil One or battling demons."

He laughed some more. "And the only thing that's gonna' keep ya' from a grave at the bottom of the sea is Malakai and me." He let it sink in. "So you had better listen to everything we say. First one that disobeys an order swims home—even if it's from Khatara."

A huge silence followed, then a loud roar. "We're with you, Captain Sennar."

"Follow you into the demon's mouth, we will."

Captain Jacopo Sennaro's smile was genuine this time. He finally had himself a crew. Crew! He had a lot more than a crew; this was an army.

60

THE LUCKY TALON

Rhaven and Tobias made a hasty exit from Pomanda, eager to leave the confines of the city for the expanse of the Free Lands only a day's ride from the gates. With Preman dead, it was likely that city guards, or, at the least, Preman's guards, would be scouring the countryside for suspects.

Tobias fretted over killing his friend, but constant reminders from Rhaven about Preman's betrayal allayed his concerns. "He isn't worth the worry," Rhaven said. "Anyone who betrays a trust deserves to die."

"Guess you're right," Tobias said. "Just feel bad for Emiliana. Don't know that she had anything to do with it, and I hate to think she'll hold me accountable."

"She couldn't have been that innocent, Tobias. You can't live with a man for so long and not know what he is."

Tobias said nothing, then he mumbled his agreement. "Guess you're right again," he said. "Can't eat honey and not know it came from the bees."

Rhaven nodded, then increased the pace, tapping on Argus's reins. For the rest of the day they kept to the main road, passing a few merchants and travelers, but no guards.

As night drew close, Rhaven scouted the woods for a clearing to camp. On his third trip, he found something suitable and whistled for Tobias to join him.

The clearing was of a decent size, almost ten spans across and almost as long, and surrounded by trees with thick foliage and heavy brush. They gathered firewood, cleared a spot for the bedrolls, then sat down for supper.

Rhaven favored small fires, just enough to cook with. If it was winter, enough to keep warm. After eating, they talked for a while, then went to bed.

Sometime during the night, Rhaven awakened, suspecting they were being watched. He walked the campsite, hugging the perimeter, then entered the woods, carefully searching the brush on all sides.

Memory could play tricks, and after finding nothing, he was forced to wonder if he actually heard something or just sensed it.

Something got me up, he thought. Despite the fact that he found nothing, he knew something, or someone had been there. He checked again for tracks, signs of disturbance in the forest, anything, but he found nothing. Before making an assumption, he walked the woods again, searching everywhere. He had not lived this long by assuming things.

Hand planted on his sai, he turned slowly, checking all sides before he returned to the camp. He had not seen anything, but that didn't rid him of the feeling. Someone was watching.

～

*H*ours later, as dawn threatened to break, Shatir stirred from her hiding place in the low brush. It had been a close call last night. Black Death had almost caught her. No one, not even Jen Pal, had ever sensed me before, so how did a frail one do it?

As she crawled back to her campsite, she pondered the legends. Perhaps they were correct. Perhaps Black Death was a worthy opponent.

Jen Pal greeted her as she entered the camp. "Long night, Shatir?"

"You were right, Jen Pal. Black Death is good. He sensed me even though I made no noise. Forced me to lay still all night."

Jen Pal smiled. Finally, a real mission.

"He'll be watching tonight," Shatir said.

"Then we will do the unexpected. There is an inn a few leagues up the road. We can bypass them and get there before they do."

The Lucky Talon stood alone beside the road, a beacon in the night to anyone traveling from Pomanda to Sykor, even from the Free Lands or Kamnor. It was the last good stop before reaching the city, and if a traveler left early enough, they could make Sykor the next day. The inn itself could accommodate thirty to forty, but if crowded, the stables were used to hold more.

Just after dark, four hooded figures, like priests, entered the tavern, surveying the room as if searching for someone. Jen Pal nodded to a table in the corner; it would suit their purpose well—shadows to hide them from curious eyes, but voices would still carry back to them. No sooner had they taken seats than a serving girl arrived.

"What'll you drink?"

"Ale," Jen Pal said, knowing most of the frail ones drank ale. He didn't want to arouse suspicion.

"We will all have soup to eat," Shatir said. "Bring bread and water," she added. I'll not drink this piss.

They ate the soup, a stew of potatoes and carrots with an occasional chunk of fatty meat, but that was fine; they only ate to look busy.

~

*S*uk Won pushed his bowl away and drank some water. He tilted his head back and sniffed the air. Smoke curled around candles and settled in pockets where the air was stale. His hands were folded in front of him, fingertips pressing against each other so he could feel his heartbeat. It was fast. Too fast. He breathed, reciting a calming mantra to lower his pulse and prepare him for what was to come.

~

*S*hatir felt a cold blast of air and glanced to the entrance, her eyes growing larger as Rhaven stepped through the doorway. She cursed herself for the infraction. Even something so small as a glance could be a tell-tale sign. She dare not afford to announce her presence– a dangerous precedent to set.

Her hand slipped toward her blade with anticipation, yet she did not make contact. If she could have trembled she would, but instincts prevented that—a Ligarn could no more tremble than a lion could weep.

The passing fly could not have heard her whisper, but her companions did: Jen Pal's imperceptible nod, Triala's one-eyed blink, and Suk Won's chitter all confirmed their acknowledgment—Black Death had entered the inn.

~

*J*en Pal risked a glance, at the same time wondering if his nod had been too vigorous. Black Death was said to be too good to be a frail one. He would notice anything out of the ordinary.

Jen Pal restrained his urges, too close now to their mission. He had dreamt of an assignment like this for a long time. Black Death's prowess was talked about even in Sethia. Not within earshot of a

Ligarn, none but the small gods would dare do that, but Jen Pal had heard the whispers enough when no one knew he lurked nearby.

The stories were bold, almost unimaginable, but Jen Pal knew Sethians didn't lie, a liar in Sethia risked losing a tongue, and an exaggeration was as much as a lie, so the stories were true—Black Death would not die easily.

Either way, Jen Pal couldn't lose. Death held no fear for him. Ligarns were taught of death from birth. I it was only a passing into a world where the hunts were ever-ready, and the challenges were never-ending. A world where each karn had enough assignments to keep them until they died, again, and then they would start life anew, with a different karn.

Jen Pal thought about death often, and if he would be allowed to choose new bedmates. He would like to try the staff. He always admired the way Suk Won killed with the staff.

Jen Pal sighed. If he were fortunate enough to kill Black Death, his name would be recorded in all the karn's books for all the seasons to come, and if he died while fighting Black Death, then it would be said that it took the greatest legend of all to slay Jen Pal, the legend of Black Death.

~

*R*haven scanned the room as he entered: a crowded tavern, boisterous, rancid with smoke and the stench of ale. Most men sat at their tables, talking, laughing, moving about, but a table in the corner caught his eye. Four men, or what appeared to be men, sat alone at the table.

They appeared suspicious. He couldn't say why, but they did. It struck him as odd that he would think that way, but that's how he saw it. Even though there were four of them, each one appeared to be alone. They sat rigidly, not relaxed, as if they were waiting for something to happen. Or waiting for someone.

Rhaven tapped Tobias with his left hand. "Get us a table on the left. I want to face this way."

Tobias nodded. "I see a nice spot right over there."

Rhaven walked to the bar and ordered an ale, all the while risking a glance at the corner table to his right. He checked out the rest of the inn as well, making sure no one else looked out of place. When he got the mug, he walked to the table and sat next to Tobias. The serving girl took their order, then went to get the drinks. When one of the men from the table got up, Rhaven rose also.

Deftly placed footsteps caught Rhaven's eye even before he realized those footsteps made no sound as they touched the floor. And the man's features proved to be as veiled as his walk, clothed in a hooded, dusty-brown robe that either belonged on a priest or was meant to conceal. This was no priest.

The other three remained seated at the table. They wore their robes in an identical fashion and, though he couldn't see, Rhaven knew that their eyes had fastened on him before he had even noticed them, and he had noticed them the instant he came in. There was something about their presence, perhaps the fact that they appeared so nondescript.

Instinct steered his hand toward the hilt of his sai, yet he knew, by instinct also, that he probably would not have time to draw the blade.

Rhaven pictured long, capable hands hidden under the robe of the one approaching, and he could only guess that each gripped the hilt of a weapon. He guessed this one for a knife, and perhaps a sai. The thought popped into his head like a revelation. Not many carried a sai, but those who did knew how to use them. And well.

Yes, now I'm sure of it. He carries a sai, Rhaven thought, and let his hand slip closer. The trident-shaped steel had tasted less blood since he acquired the Sword of Mikkellana. Tonight may be the time to change that.

Rhaven moved from the table at a careful pace, certain to keep one eye on the three left seated and one eye on the other. He ran strategies through his mind on how they might be handled. It was the first time since he fought Damon Pirrhar that he found himself worrying over combat. The idea was almost foreign to him—almost, but then, there was something about the ones he faced tonight that demanded this kind of attention.

He wondered how long it might take to rid himself of the one before the others joined the fray. He knew they'd be fast, could reach him within a few heartbeats, yet, given the right circumstances, he might have time to deliver a few blackthorn darts from the tube on his back.

He presumed, perhaps dangerously, that the only weapons they possessed capable of reaching him before they did themselves were knives, and though the thought of knives in the hands of someone like Wisp would kill him as surely as he could them with his darts. He prayed they weren't as quick as Wisp.

The man came to an abrupt stop with Rhaven's first movement. He had been watching,

Rhaven's left hand rested on the hilt of the sai, the leather-wrapped grip fitting his hand like the skin of a thin man. He had loosened the cinch on the knife strapped to the upper part of his arm so that it now lay resting in the palm of his hand waiting to have its taste of blood. Rhaven let his eyes flicker to the table, but only a flicker, he dare not take his focus off of this one for any longer amount of time.

Every muscle tensed as the man's hands started from the underneath fold of his robe, but they did it too slowly to be threatening. What is his plan, Rhaven thought and risked a glance to the table, a check to ensure it was no diversion.

The man's palms slid out as slow as a serpent fresh from hibernation, and they were raised in the sign of peace. Rhaven caught a glimpse of his face, but only an outline—a gaunt, ridged face that had seen and tasted battle many times. The hands continued toward the hood and when Rhaven showed no signs of hostility the man pulled the hood down to rest on his shoulders.

As it lowered, Rhaven almost gasped. The face was harder than he had first imagined, more battle-tested, and it was much darker than he thought. It proved to be no wonder he could not see the man's eyes, not with the dark face and the cherry-black eyes.

Rhaven managed to stifle the gasp, but it lingered in his throat. He knew beyond any doubt what he faced now. A Ligarn.

The Ligarn's smile was colder than a goodbye kiss and thinner than a winter rabbit. He bowed his head in respect, but not his eyes, the cherry-black eyes never left Rhaven's steel-blue glare.

Rhaven didn't bother to worry so much now that he knew what they were. He never fought a Ligarn, but he knew what they were and what to expect. He no longer chided himself for feeling a hint of fear, it was only right. But if the gods had any humor at all, they would be laughing tonight. Perhaps this is what he had been born for, what they had allowed him to live for. No matter, the course of the battle was now set. He would fight this one and this one alone.

Rhaven knew that pride and honor would keep the others at bay while either one of them lived. Besides, if they had wanted him dead, he would have died the moment he entered the inn. He would not have completed his second step.

The thin smile disappeared, but the cherry-black glare held true. His voice proved to be surprisingly warm and friendly, and his command of Sykoran was equally fresh news. "I would remove my robe, with your permission. I practice no deception."

Rhaven's nod answered him, and the Ligarn lifted the robe over his head, revealing a lean muscular body, hardened like the desert they lived in. Under the lower portions of the robe, he wore loose-fitting pants of the same design and color. Boots of supple leather clung to his feet and rose nearly to his calves.

Rhaven smiled when he saw the weapon. A sai hung from both sides of the Ligarn, with two knives between them. No doubt he had several more knives behind him, and perhaps one or two attached to the legs, but they would be well-concealed, blend with his britches. Perhaps even have the blade coated to resemble the color of them so no hint of moonlight could announce his position.

The bow was again a gesture, though this one dipped lower. Still, the eyes never moved. When the Ligarn rose, he spoke. "I am Jen Pal."

Rhaven waited, but there was no more to come. No fancy titles. No extended names. Jen Pal, that's all. Jen Pal, a Ligarn. Rhaven effected a bow identical to the Ligarn's, and when he rose, his voice flowed like the heron at dawn. "I am called Rhaven."

Tobias moved up beside them, nervous. "What's the matter?"

"Go back and eat. I'll handle this."

Several patrons passed by, sidestepping them with glares, but no one said anything.

"Does this have anything to do with Rahg?" Tobias asked.

"It seems everything has something to do with Rahg, but at least for now this is my fight." Rhaven smiled. "We are going to fight aren't we, Jen Pal?"

Jen Pal nodded. "While the gods smile from above."

"Why? About what?" Tobias asked.

"Since you are always so curious, let me introduce you. This is Jen Pal, and he is a Ligarn. If I'm not mistaken, he is likely a karn leader." Rhaven turned to Tobias. "That means he's an assassin."

The shock showed on Tobias's face, but he held his ground. "Anything happens to Rhaven, I'll kill you first. Then I'll kill everyone who came with you."

Jen Pal stared at Tobias for a long time, his cherry-black eyes burning a hole in his soul. "The small gods have given me an assignment. I have no need to kill you, though I bow to your courage."

Rhaven's hand moved toward his sai, but Jen Pal gripped his before

Rhaven. He shook his head. "Not here. There is no need for others to die."

Rhaven looked at him. "Tonight or tomorrow?"

Jen Pal bowed. "It is your honor."

"Tonight," Rhaven said. "There is a clearing off the road about half a league from here. Toward Sykor."

"We will be there," Jen Pal said, and went back to his table. Shortly afterward they left.

Tobias grabbed hold of Rhaven. "You can't do this. Suppose he—"

"Suppose he kills me?" A glaze covered his eyes. "I've waited a long time for that. Perhaps he will. He's a Ligarn."

"Let me help. I can—"

"It's my fight. But remember, if he does kill me, your job will be to warn Rahg. He will be after him next."

"Put this off till tomorrow night, Rhaven. There are only four of them, and two are women. I'll ride to Sykor tonight. Hard. Bring back some help."

Rhaven stared at him. "Already you've made a grave error. You can't think of them as two men and two women. There are four Ligarns, and that is as different as four house-cats and four lions."

Tobias shook his head. "Just put this off till tomorrow."

"I'm going tonight, Tobias. You can wait here, or you can come. You'll be safe either way."

Tobias stood and walked toward the door. "Let's go, then."

61

DESTINY

When Rhaven and Tobias got to the clearing, the Ligarns were already there, resting on the far side. Jen Pal rose, then the others did, walking toward the center.

"Since it was I who sought you, the choice of weapons is yours."

Rhaven studied him. He wore sai, so he knew he would be an expert with them, but he also carried knives, and he was likely as efficient with them.

"Sai," Rhaven said, and began stripping his other weapons: knives, darts, sword, kunai.

Jen Pal removed his knives, then stretched his legs and arms, torso too.

From three paces away, they drew their sai. With shoulders relaxed, knees bent, balanced on the balls of their feet, they stalked each other, scanning for the slightest mistake, the least advantage.

From a pace apart they tested each other with false jabs, feints, and slow, probing stabs. Half a step closer brought more urgency to the contest: the jabs became real, feints only to disguise serious attempts, and the probing stabs became attempts to draw blood.

They were now within a lethal striking distance from any angle. Focus, concentration, and agility were all important. One false step meant death. Rhaven moved quickly with his right, a straight jab toward Jen Pal's heart, and at the same time, a strike from the left side, toward his kidney.

Jen Pal fended off the jab and stepped left while diverting the strike from the other side. He twisted Rhaven's sai with his left-hand sai and moved his right with lightning speed to strike at Rhaven's gut—a double attack that would be difficult to defend.

Rhaven risked himself, defending only with his right sai, catching both of Jen Pal's weapons with his one, then he followed through with a strike toward Jen Pal's chest with his left.

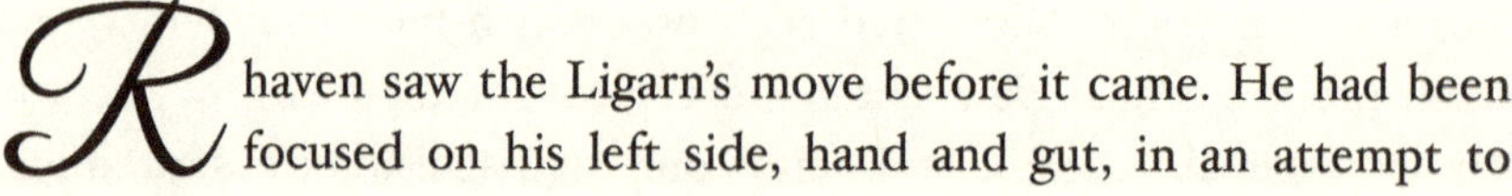

The Ligarn felt the puncture just as he leapt to the side. The sai hit him, and it did damage. Blood stained his tunic. He winced. Two quick steps backward gave him enough time to recover; his dance began anew, eyes intense, focused. Black Death had seized the advantage. He could now stall, drop into defense, let Jen Pal's wound do the work for him. *I must press the attack.*

Jen Pal stared at Rhaven's stomach while he moved, his stomach and his left hand. It seemed as if his left hand struck quicker than his right. He kept focusing on those areas, almost to the neglect of others, knowing it would not go unnoticed.

Two quick strikes with both hands brought two impressive defensive moves from Rhaven, who moved back, then advanced again. Once more, Jen pal focused on the same spot with the same hand.

Rhaven saw the Ligarn's move before it came. He had been focused on his left side, hand and gut, in an attempt to convince Rhaven he would strike elsewhere, but Rhaven knew he was going to strike there. A ploy.

Now, here he was doing it again. And wanting Rhaven to believe he would strike there again, though knowing him to be an expert, he would assume the reverse; which meant he probably would do the same. Jen Pal's left hand always moved first. That would be the tell-tale sign.

A few more feints, then the Ligarn led with his left, straight toward Rhaven's gut.

Rhaven countered with his left, immediately moving his right in a defensive strike position, thrusting down and forward, while not committing to the attack. As he pressed, Jen Pal did the same maneuver, and Rhaven countered with his right hand.

As they stepped back, the blood ran down Jen Pal's side. Rhaven breathed a slight bit easier. This fight was far from over, but he now had a definite advantage, and, he thought he had seen worry in those cherry-black eyes.

They engaged again, both trying several new attacks, then Jen Pal fell back into his old routine. Rhaven had guessed right the first two times. Which would he try now?

Rhaven felt certain that he'd try the same attack again, but this Ligarn was too clever and too quick to trust. The safe bet would be to fall back a step when he saw him start the attack, then defend whichever move he opted for. This time, though, Rhaven intended a ferocious follow through, aimed at the Ligarn's right side.

The dance continued, Jen Pal, focusing on Rhaven's left, and Rhaven observing him intently. Then, when Jen Pal led with his left sai, Rhaven stepped back, sai ready.

Jen Pal anticipated the move, and dove forward, rolling as he hit the ground, Rhaven's back-step leaving him enough room. When Jen Pal came up, his head no more than knee level, he stabbed into Rhaven's left leg with his right sai, and he jabbed upward with his left sai, into Rhaven's gut.

Tobias screamed louder than Rhaven, rushing over to help.

Rhaven's left leg collapsed, though he tried to stand and defend himself on the one leg. Blood gushed out of his stomach, and it was all he could do not to hold it.

Jen Pal moved back after the strike in an attempt to avoid a counterstrike. He stood only two paces away, sai in hands.

Rhaven was on his knees, helpless to defend himself. "Tell me your full name before you finish."

The Ligarn bowed his head. "Jen Pal, first son of Shinesa, who was wife to Bhokka."

Rhaven nodded. "So you must know that I am also Shinesa's son."

It was Jen Pal's turn to nod. "Before I kill you, tell me why she shamed herself. I will be merciful if you do."

The pain left Rhaven's face, fury dancing in his eyes as he tried to stand. "She never shamed herself. It was Lukaan."

Jen Pal never lost his composure. "Tell me."

"Lukaan raped her, left her for dead by the Caravan Trail." Rhaven paused, holding his gut while he stood, his leg barely supporting him.

"She told me that he liked to do it to all beautiful women, then he would hurt them and leave them to die. A Khataran merchant found her and took her to Sykor, where she eventually recovered, but she was with child—my older brother, Damon Pirrhar."

Jen Pal's jaw tightened as he ground his teeth.

"She knew she couldn't go back, so she stayed, marrying the man who took care of her while she was sick. He was my father and father to a younger sister as well."

"What happened?"

"People of Sykor didn't take to a Ligarn marrying one of their kind, so we left, settled in a small village in the Khataran hills. My mother told us the story, and Damon decided to tell Lukaan, announce himself as his son." Rhaven started to fall, but Jen Pal caught him, helped him to a spot where he could rest against a tree.

"Lukaan sent Victas and Sethians. They killed her and my father. Killed my sister. Left me for dead." Rhaven's icy stare went straight through Jen Pal. "I've been killing them back ever since."

Jen Pal nodded, staring off into the distance. Shatir came to his side, her arm finding his shoulder. "The shame is gone. It was not Shinesa who did wrong."

The Ligarn turned and looked at Shatir, a tear streaking his face for the first time in many many years.

"I will never tell," Shatir said. "One tear doesn't ruin a lifetime of work."

Jen Pal sheathed his sai and reached to Rhaven, pulling him up. He slid himself under Rhaven's arm to support him, then headed toward the town. "No need for you to die, brother. There are many that need killing."

"And your mission, to kill Rahg?"

"The boy will not die by a Ligarn's hand, that, I can swear to. Besides, if I am going to kill the small gods, I will need all the help I can get."

62

A WALK INTO SYKOR

Rahg cursed Aentarra for all he was worth, vowing to someday, somehow, get even. But for now, there was nothing he could do but start the long walk to Sykor.

Daurien had granted him new power, and Rahg felt as if he were bursting with energy. He couldn't wait to tell Camissa.

By mid-afternoon he was growing tired, though impatience nudged him along when he wanted to stop. Two riders approached from behind, though they seemed in no hurry to get anywhere.

"I'll pay a good price for one of those horses," Rahg said as they drew near. He eyed them with envy, a pure black mare and a big brown stallion with white feet.

They brought the horses to a stop. "What's a good price?" the one with the mare asked.

Rahg looked them over. "Ten silver crowns for the stallion. Eight for the mare."

The man astride the mare slid off, smiling. "Must be in a big hurry, but it's of no mind to me. Pay the price, and I will apologize to my feet tonight."

Rahg handed the man ten silver crowns. "Two for the saddle?"

He bowed his head, doffing his cap as he did. "I should meet so generous a patron every day," he said. "But then again, if the world surprised me every day it would not be such a joy."

*R*ahg rode at a steady pace, careful not to push the horse too hard. With luck, he'd sell her for half what he paid, perhaps more, but the time saved would be worth it. Besides, he wanted to know what was so important to Aentarra, and he wondered if Rhaven and Tobias were already there, drinking ales at the Trader's Inn.

By early evening Sykor was in sight, the once ominous wall and moat that surrounded it now a welcome sight. A gentle spur to the horse's flanks increased his pace. He could almost taste Brock Larnigin's stew as he neared the gates. The only thing better would be Mollie's pies. Rahg dismounted as he got to the line waiting to get in.

Just as before, two guards were stationed outside to document everyone who entered the city, though why they bothered Rahg didn't know. The line moved slowly, and when it came to him, he answered perfunctorily, "Rahg Fal-Thera from Kamnor."

The rest of the questions proved to be just as boring, and Rahg answered in the same nonchalant manner until he was waved on by the guard. He took hold of his mount's reins and led her into Sykor. "We're back in the city, girl. Almost feels like home."

He made his way along familiar streets, stopping to buy some fruit from Farley, then hurrying to the Trader's Inn, where he stabled the horse, throwing an extra copper to the boy to keep her brushed. "Take good care of her, and there will be more than that when I return."

"Yes, sir." The boy snapped a salute and moved her to his best stall.

Rahg smiled as he walked inside, casting sidelong glances to the rooftops, almost expecting to see a Black Rose waiting with an arrow. It seemed like a lifetime since that happened, but it wasn't that long ago. The door opened, several guards stepping out, then Rahg entered behind them.

The inn was how he remembered it. Not as large as he thought, but everything was in its place. The one thing missing was Brock Larnigin. Rahg walked up to the bar, ordered an ale, and stood while he sipped it. "Where's Brock?" he asked the serving girl.

A cautious finger touched her lips, and she flashed a warning with her eyes.

Rahg stared at her, curiosity painting an odd expression on his face. "Brock still run the bar?"

A tap on his shoulder brought his head around, bringing him face to face with a burly guard. "What business do you have with Brock Larnigin?" the guard asked.

Two more had come to stand beside him, their hands dangerously close to the swords at their sides. Must be new, Rahg thought, the old Sykoran Guards always wore their swords over their shoulders.

He stared at the man, holding his glare in check. "Brock's a friend. Haven't seen him in a while."

A smirk appeared on the face of the one guard, and he nudged the others. "Say's he's a friend of Brock."

They laughed in response, but stood a little straighter, seemed more alert. The one at the bar grabbed hold of Rahg's shirt as he leaned in closer. "Your friend Brock is in prison. Maybe you should join him. Or is there another reason why a healthy young man like you isn't in the guard?"

Rahg tensed, stared down at his crumpled shirt. He let the mug of ale stay on the bar, brushed his hands off on his pants, then slowly removed the man's grip. "You can give my regards to Brock when you see him."

Rahg lifted his head and stared straight into the man's eyes. "As to your other question, I wouldn't join the Sykoran Guard if it was full of naked women." A false smile lit Rahg's face as he wrapped himself in a shield.

The two guards at the side drew steel while the first one threw a punch to Rahg's face. He grimaced when it struck the shield, a wall as solid as the red brick on the outside of the inn. He spat a curse, drew his dagger and struck again, though he made no more progress with the knife than he did his fist.

Rahg laughed, a taunting laugh that incited the guards. The guard's two companions struck with their swords, one to the arm, the other a jab to Rahg's gut. Neither one touched flesh.

By now, most of the patrons were looking on, awe-struck by the spectacle. Rahg wove a simple blanket-weave and wrapped all three of them in it, binding them together so they couldn't move. Then, he shoved them outside, leaving them bound together on the street next to the alley.

Curses rang in his ear as he made his way up the street toward High Town. He remembered Wisp had told him that Lord Talanvar had helped them when they rescued Darstan. Perhaps he would know where they were.

~

Jen Pal led Rhaven through the woods until they stood in sight of Sykor's north wall. "I dare not risk any closer."

Rhaven gripped his hand, squeezed it. "I can make it from here. Tobias will help me." He looked into Jen Pal's cherry-black eyes. "She would have been proud of you."

The Ligarn bowed in response. "And of you," he said, then quickly turned and disappeared into the woods.

Rhaven watched him go, waiting until he was completely out of sight before turning to Tobias. "Let's go to Sykor, old friend."

"You think you can ride yet?" Tobias asked.

"Maybe in a while. Let's walk for now. If you can help me ..."

Tobias puffed on his pipe as he slipped his shoulder under Rhaven's arm to lend support. "Between the two of us we just might make it there." Tobias laughed a little, limping along with Rhaven. "I'm just glad to be alive. Never thought I'd see Sykor again when you were fighting that Ligarn." He shook his head vigorously. "Thought that fight with you and Damon Pirrhar was a good one, but this ... well, it was a dandy."

They soon reached the city, and the guards let them pass without question, Tobias quickly making his way to the Trader's Inn, expecting to find Brock or the thief, but neither one of them were there. "Lookin' for Brock Larnigin," he said, after helping Rhaven to a table. "Or Kender Darnell."

"Brock's not here. As for Kender Darnell, that's a name I haven't heard in a year." The serving girl stared at him with a suspicious glare. "You're the second one that's been here askin' for Brock today."

Tobias squinted his eyes. "Who else asked about him?"

"Young man, good lookin'. Had a little scuffle with the guards, but weren't much. I didn't see it all, but some of the people in here said the guards couldn't touch him."

Tobias noticed a man walking toward him, trying to be inconspicuous. He ordered an ale and leaned against the bar, waiting.

The man stepped to the bar next to him, ordered an ale and took a few swigs, then whispered. "Kender Darnell has had me waiting for you. I'll leave when I'm finished with this ale. Follow me soon after and head toward High Town."

Tobias nodded, ordered another ale and headed back to the table where Rhaven sat. "We found 'em," he said as he sat down. "Or rather, they found us."

Three blocks on their way to High Town, Perl stepped out of an alley. "Kender figured you'd go there, so he had me waiting." He stepped alongside Rhaven and propped up his other side. "Might as well get help while you can. This next hill's a steep one."

"Where is he?" Rhaven asked. "Who is with him?"

"He's at Talanvar's. Don't know who's with him, but there better be a lot of help. This city is in a war."

Tobias nodded. "Seems like all of 'em are."

Talanvar's gatekeeper recognized Perl and admitted them at once. Rhaven's side was bleeding by the time he got to the front door, and he was leaning heavily on Perl and Tobias.

Talanvar opened the door on the third knock and ushered them in.

Aentarra and Rahg ran to greet them. "Rhaven! What happened?" Rahg asked.

"Ligarns," Tobias said. "Nearly killed him."

They helped him to a sofa, Talanvar calling for hot water and towels. "Find a healer!" he yelled to Birol. "He needs one badly."

Aentarra knelt beside him. "He'll need more than some witch with a bag of herbs." She thought for a moment. "Stay with him, boy. I'm going to get Mikkellana."

~

*T*he rift opened in Mikkellana's bedroom in Vallah, Aentarra stepping through.

"Aentarra, it—"

"No time to waste. Rhaven is hurt, and it looks to be bad. A gut wound."

Mikkellana tried standing yet again, but couldn't. Aentarra moved quickly to her side, grabbed her hand, then looked to Camissa. "Ready, girl?"

She nodded as she touched Aentarra, and within a few heartbeats, they were stepping into Talanvar's library.

"He's up in the bedroom," Talanvar said and headed for the stairs.

Aentarra looked about. "Rahg, get someone to help you and carry Mikkellana up those steps."

He raced over. "I can do it myself," he said and picked her up in his arms.

~

*R*haven lay on the bed, blood pouring from the wound in his belly. His head was sideways on the pillow, breaths coming in short, heavy gasps.

Rahg set Mikkellana down in a chair next to the bed. She leaned over, her hand running across his stomach. "It's bad," she said. "Deep wound."

A faint blue light danced on her fingertips, sparking as it touched his wound, then the light grew brighter and disappeared into him sinking through the skin and making its way inside of him.

Rhaven moaned, shifted to the side.

"Hold him still," Mikkellana said. "Don't let him move."

Rahg grabbed Rhaven's legs while Talanvar held his arms, pinning him to the bed. Mikkellana repeated her actions, this time with more focus and more energy.

Rhaven thrashed, trying to break free but Rahg and Talanvar held him. After a while, he settled down, his head soaked in sweat.

"He'll be all right," Mikkellana said. "But it was close."

Rahg wiped sweat from his own brow. "Thank the gods for that."

"You can thank me for that," Mikkellana said. "Now get me back downstairs so I can find out what's going on."

"Aentarra has been taking care of things."

Mikkellana shook her head. "That is precisely what worries me. If I let her take care of things for long, Sykor will be in ashes."

Rahg smiled as he picked her up and headed for the stairs. Soon he and Talanvar were placing her on the sofa in the library, where Aentarra, Takar, and Tobias were discussing how to unite the city.

"Where is Darstan?" Mikkellana asked.

"I sent him to Khatara," Aentarra said, then noticed the shock on her sister's face. "I couldn't just leave him here with Rahg; besides, we need someone in Khatara. You know Lukaan isn't going to let it go, not with their seaport."

"Precisely my point. We cannot leave Darstan there by himself, especially—"

"I know," Aentarra said, "but he's not quite by himself. He's got Aenaila, Wisp, and the bounty-man with him. They should be able to keep him out of trouble. That thief is clever, too clever by half. I doubt he would let Darstan slip away."

Mikkellana smiled. "You seem fond of that thief, Aentarra."

Aentarra glared at her. "I'd keep my mouth shut if I were you. Cripples need a lot of help."

"Aentarra! What a terrible thing to say." Camissa moved to sit beside Mikkellana as if she needed protecting.

Mikkellana laughed despite the insult. "No need to worry about me, my dear. If that's the worst Aentarra does to me while I'm bedridden I shall be a happy woman. Besides, she's like that. It's in her nature."

Mikkellana used Camissa to brace herself and sat up straighter. "Seriously, Aentarra. We must keep an eye on Darstan. If Lukaan attacks Khatara, he could get killed."

"We can all get killed," she said. "But he has that girl with him, and she can shift, and he can even shift himself. Came back to Pomanda on his own, remember?"

Aentarra grabbed a glass of wine from the table, sipped it. "I hope no one minds me sharing their wine," she said, then laughed. "I don't know if we need to worry so much about Darstan. He might burn that city to the ground before they get to him."

Talanvar walked back in from the kitchen with a tray of food. "Time we decided on what to do in Sykor. We still have a guard with split allegiance."

Takar paced, favoring his right leg. "I plan on going out tomorrow. Confront them all." His face hardened. "Might not be right, but they will either join me, or they'll die." He looked to Aentarra. "I could use your help with this."

Aentarra smiled, offering him her wine glass. "Have a sip. I feel generous today. Besides, I like your way of resolving disputes—kill anyone who doesn't agree with you."

Takar accepted the glass as if it were poison, afraid to drink it but afraid not to. Finally, he took a sip and smiled. "We should get an early start."

"Indeed we will, Force Commander. Rahg and I will join you." She noted the look on Rahg's face and walked over to him. "Time you learned how to do things the right way."

"I'll go with you, Aentarra, but I'm not going to kill anyone."

"I need to get some more wine," she said, and walked away, her laughter echoing in the room.

63

GENTLE PERSUASION

Morning came too early for Rahg. He feared what would happen going out with Aentarra and wished he could just go with Takar and leave her at Talanvar's home. Perhaps I can talk her into it, he thought, but the sound of her voice from the kitchen proved to be an abrupt reminder of how strong-willed she was.

For the past six days, thieves had taken their toll on the new Force Commander's plans, reporting movements to Takar, and clubbing and beating any rogue guards found alone or even in pairs or threes.

It had gotten so bad that Force Commander Nelson forbade any of them to go to the Edge or the Dongrel with less than a full patrol. Rahg agreed with Takar—it was a good time for him to make his move. "Where are we going first, Takar?"

The big sergeant limped along, his fingers playing with the hilt of a knife tucked into his pants. "Guard barracks. Might as well start where most of them are."

Aentarra waited at the door. "Yes, I like that. If Rahg is ready, we should go. Get an early start as you said."

"I'm ready."

It was a familiar walk from Talanvar's house to the street by now, but descending from there to the merchant district was always an adventure. The street was as steep as some of the hills he and Darstan used to climb in the mountains.

Thinking of it made him wonder how Darstan was, and if he was safe in Khatara. From what he had heard about Khatara, it could be a dangerous place.

Two patrols joined them at the bottom of the hill, then three more before they reached the barracks. Rahg remembered the first time he had come here, when he and Darstan went to visit his cousin, Ludar. It was an eventful day, Rahg getting his first real sword, and Tobias nearly getting into a fight with several of the guards, including Ludar. He vowed to try and make it a peaceful day.

At the gate, a patrol leader called for them to halt. "You're not welcome here, Sergeant Takar." He bowed his head as he spoke, seemed unconvincing.

"That would be Force Commander Takar," one of the men next to Rahg said, a nasty bite to his tone.

Takar walked up to the young guard, slowly so as not to agitate. "What are you doing here, Vinson? You were one of my best recruits."

Vinson shuffled from one foot to another, refusing to give Takar his eyes. "Sorry, sir. It's just ..."

"Just what?"

"My brother, sir." He finally lifted his head to face him. "My brother was with Bragh. Stayed with the new Force Commander."

"The new Force Commander is right in front of you," the one next to Rahg yelled.

Takar placed his hand on Vinson's shoulder. "We need to go in, lad. I need to talk to the men, talk to the Force Commander too." Takar lifted the boy's chin and stared at him. "Don't try stopping us."

Vinson nodded. "Let them pass," he ordered. As Takar started to move, Vinson spoke again. "I'm coming with you, sir." He looked to the rest of his men, and they nodded. "We all are."

Takar smiled. A small victory, but a good one.

Six patrols of guards marched into the barracks, Aentarra and Rahg along with them. "Keep sharp, boy," Aentarra said. "Be prepared for anything."

As they neared the Force Commander's barracks, men streamed out from everywhere. Soon they faced a force of three to four hundred men. "You shouldn't have come, Takar." Force Commander Nelson stood as rigid as an old oak.

Takar advanced with his hands upturned. "I want no trouble, Nelson. Just want to talk."

"State your business, then."

"The city is in trouble. Lukaan is preparing for war against us."

Nelson laughed. Some of his men did, too, but only some. Others had the look of fear in their eyes. "If anyone still believes in him, they'll know he's trapped somewhere in Sethia. If he gets out, tell him to come see me." Less of them laughed this time, only the ones closest to him.

Aentarra started to move, but Takar risked putting a hand on her, and with a pleading look begged her to let him handle it. "Believe it or not, but you all saw what happened when they killed Ludar. And you saw what happened when Aentarra killed Bragh."

He waited until he was sure they had let it sink in. "I don't want any more of that." He paused. "Don't want it, but if I have to, I'll do it. I'll kill every one of you before I let you stand against this city."

Nelson stepped toward him. Only ten paces separated them now. "Brave talk for a man with so few swords."

Takar knew Aentarra would be bristling to get at him, so he whispered to her. "Please wait."

She kept still, but from the side, Rahg stepped forward. "Doesn't need many swords. Doesn't need any at all." Rahg let some fire dance on his fingers while he glared at Nelson. "Listen to Takar, or I'll start cutting those numbers down to even, Force Commander. And I'll start with you."

Several of Nelson's men slowly moved away from him. Hands that had been poised to draw steel now hung limply at their sides, and they searched for an exit rather than a course of attack.

Nelson held Rahg's glare. "I'm not afraid of you, boy. I've taken more than a few of you who could play with fire and put them in prison. Watched them rot there."

A strange sensation built inside of Rahg. Many times he had been angry in his life but never had he felt this rage. Imagine this man taunting me! Despite his fury, Rahg smiled, then, while still smiling, he called forth his power and wove a shield into a spinning disc. It raced toward Nelson so fast the Force Commander had no time to react, not that it would have mattered; he could have done nothing.

When it reached him it cut through his torso in one clean sweep. With a word still on his lips, Nelson's upper half tumbled to the ground, his legs and hips falling in the other direction.

"Rahg, no!" Takar screamed, but far too late.

Rahg wrapped himself in a shield in case they had any ideas, but he doubted any would have the courage. He approached the two strike leaders who had been standing closest to the Force Commander. "I want a show of hands as to who is with Takar and who isn't. Those with him move aside. The others will get what Nelson got."

To a man, they all raised their hands and moved aside. "We're with you, Force Commander Takar." The call was joined by everyone.

Takar patted Rahg on the back, pride in his voice as he offered his thanks. "I need to stay and discuss things with them, plan how to let the other guards know, but I think we will be all right now. Thank you."

Rahg beamed. It felt good taking control. Very good.

A wicked smile lit Aentarra's face. About time he grew up. "Come, Rahg. We have things to do." She grabbed his hand and shifted back to Talanvar's house.

64

KHATARAN BLOOD

The rift opened in Jago's old house in Khatara, Darstan stepping through first, followed by Gregor, Wisp, Aenaila, and Adju. A quick search of the other rooms confirmed that they were alone.

"Safe," Darstan said as he emerged from the bedroom.

"For now, but the house could have been compromised. They could even be watching it." Aenaila pulled a curtain aside just enough to peek out, then walked to the other side of the room and did the same at that window. "I don't see anyone, but that doesn't mean a thing. They could have neighbors watching or even have guards in a neighbor's house."

"You're getting as suspicious as Wisp," Darstan said. "Been around him too long."

"I'll have a look around tonight," Wisp said, and before he could finish, Adju announced he would join him. "Get some rest, little one, and I just might take you along."

Adju's face lit up as if it were Wish Day. "I will rest now, Master Kender. Do not forget me."

Wisp decided to stay at the house that night, but the next day he went out, being careful not to attract attention. After only a few blocks, they were spotted by Mufed, who seemed glad to see them.

Wisp watched him carefully. Mufed cast suspicious glances about, and he paid particular attention to Aenaila and Darstan Wisp wondered if he'd go straight to the Khatara guards when he left. From the look in his eyes, Wisp thought he may be counting the reward that was being offered for Darstan. "We need a place to stay," Wisp said. "Can you help us?"

"It would be my honor. I have rooms available."

"No, we couldn't do that. We need someplace safe. Quiet."

Mufed smiled. "Ah, yes, I had forgotten." He paused, as if he were thinking, but Wisp suspected differently. "Yes, I have just the place. My cousin has empty stables not far from here." Mufed bowed to Aenaila. "My apologies for suggesting stables, but it is all I could think of."

Aenaila took his hand. "That is all right. I have slept on my share of straw."

Mufed led them to the stables, then promised to return shortly with food and khaffe.

Adju tugged on Wisp's sleeve. "I'm glad we saw Mufed. Now we will have a place to stay and some food." He beamed. "You see, Master Kender, Adju takes care of everything in Khatara."

Wisp sighed. He hated to have to tell him, but it had to be done. "Adju, Mufed is not your friend. Right now, he is probably going to get the guards. He wants the reward offered for Darstan."

Adju glared at Wisp. "That is shameful to say about Mufed. He is an honorable man. He is my friend!"

Wisp knelt, hugging Adju. "I know you like him. And I know this might hurt, but Mufed is only worried about himself." He squeezed Adju lovingly. "I hope I'm wrong, but we'll soon see."

"What are we going to do?" Aenaila asked.

"Move someplace else." Wisp looked up and down the street. It was crowded with merchants' carts and men and women carrying baskets of goods to and from storage houses and stables. "See that building at the end of the street, where it intersects the other two streets? We'll go there. When they come—"

"They won't come. You'll see. It will only be Master Mufed. Then you will be ashamed."

Wisp started again. "If they come, we'll have an easy escape through the other streets."

They didn't have to wait long. Soon, Adju spotted Mufed turning the corner at the end of the street. He started to run, to yell to him, but Wisp grabbed him, covering his mouth.

Not twenty paces behind Mufed, just turning the corner, was a full patrol of Khataran Guards, all with swords drawn.

"I'm sorry, Adju. Really sorry." Wisp let go of Adju's mouth, then turned to Aenaila and Darstan. "Let's go. Now!"

They moved down the side street at a quick pace, never looking back. "Where to?" Darstan asked.

"We'll risk Jago's second house. It should be okay."

They stayed at Jago's house all day, never risking even a trip to the fruit stand after dark. Wisp cracked a window at the back of the house, lifted it, then slipped out. "Be back before morning."

"You want me to come?" Darstan asked.

He shook his head as he closed the window. "Not tonight," he said, then disappeared.

He passed by several blocks of row houses, crept down the back alleys, and climbed over walls until he got to a well-traveled street, busy with people even at this time of night.

One or two merchants still had their carts out, a bold attempt to sell the last of their goods, and two of the corners had young girls offering more than they should know about to anyone with a few silver coins.

Three guards stood opposite the girls, paying little attention to anything other than their own conversation.

Wisp ducked into a small tavern in the middle of the block. It looked as if twenty people would crowd it, and when he got inside, he saw he was right. There were four men at the table on one side and three sets of two people each on the other, with one man standing at the bar. Surprisingly, though, the establishment was clean, with an enticing aroma of fresh fruit.

Wisp opted for the bar, walked up and ordered an ale. As he sipped on his mug, the man next to him stared.

"You're the one asked me about Bulta a few months back."

Wisp looked at him, leaning heavy against the bar, mug in one hand and the other flat on the bar. The man was no threat. Wisp searched his memory for the previous conversation. "I believe I did. And you were kind enough to suggest I take the caravan trail."

The man gulped a bit of his ale, set it down with a plop, then laughed. "Guess you didn't take my advice. You got Bulta turning over every rock in the desert looking for you."

Suspicion dug a pit in Wisp's gut. "I imagine a reward is part of it, too."

"Might be, but that wouldn't tempt me no matter how big it was. Bulta broke me. Ruined my business. If I can live long enough to see him die, I'll be happy."

He took another swig of ale and moved close to Wisp. "If I were you, though, I'd find someplace good to hide until you can get out of Khatara because there aren't many like me that would pass up Bulta's money and his favors both."

A smile lit Wisp's face. "This is the second kind act you've shown me, good sir. At least let me pay for your drink."

The man started to object, but Wisp forestalled him. He grabbed his hand, holding it, then pressed the coin in his palm. "As a final kindness to me, then. Please accept my gift." With that, he dropped a silver coin onto the counter and left.

The merchant reached for his mug, and when he opened his palm, found a gold Sykoran crown in it. Not enough to put him back where he was, but enough to get him started again.

Wisp kept his head bowed as he exited the tavern but not so low as to be suspicious, just enough to look like any other man trying to mind his own business.

He walked at a normal pace, and he looked at the women on the corner—as any man would. Did all the right things to ensure the guards took no notice of him. Despite that, he could almost feel their eyes follow him as he moved down the street. At about ten paces he heard the order.

"Halt!"

A quick glance confirmed they were after him, but he was stuck in the middle of a block with guards behind him, and for all he knew, three more guards at the next intersection. Running could be more dangerous than talking. Wisp stopped, turned and faced them. "Good evening. How can I help you?" He used his most polite voice when he spoke.

They stared at him for a moment, then the one who appeared to be in charge spoke. "What is your name?"

"Perl Nostor, a merchant from Sykor. Here to purchase goods."

"Where are you staying?"

Wisp's eyebrows shot up. "Good sir, I was about to ask you for a recommendation as I have just arrived and find that sleep is calling me."

The guard leader looked him up and down. "Just arrived? Where's your horse? Your bags?" His hand slid toward the hilt of a Khataran curved sword as he spoke.

Wisp knew the game was up. "My bags are with my horse and cart, which I left at a stable not far from here. "I have a receipt as proof." He smiled as he reached to the back of his pants. Two of the guards stood right before him and the third off to the left side.

He brought a blade out with his right hand and threw it at the guard on his left, catching him square in the throat. While the blade was still in the air, he grabbed another blade with his left hand and rammed it straight into the gut of the other guard.

The last guard seized hold of Wisp, his big hands wrapping around Wisp's neck. A gasp for air brought a few chokes, but Wisp managed to reach the knife he kept in the front part of his pants, under his belt. He slid it out, and moved it up until he was close enough, then jammed it under the guard's chin.

The guard released him at once, falling to the ground. The first one was dead but the second one was only wounded, and though he had to hold his gut, he managed to draw his sword and came at Wisp. The other guards would be alerted soon if they weren't already, so Wisp risked it all, feigning a move toward the man's side, then spinning and throwing the blade instead. It worked, as the blade stuck in the man's chest, cutting deep. He went down with a loud moan.

Wisp quickly gathered his knives, checked behind him to see that no one had taken notice, other than the women on the corner, and then raced down the alley toward home.

The window opened with no noise, but as he stepped into the room, Darstan's voice greeted him. "Early night for you, isn't it?"

"Too early. Trouble with guards," he said as he closed the window and shut the blinds.

Darstan jumped up. "What happened? Are you all right?"

"Fortune was with me, Darstan. There were three of them, and they knew who I was. Seemed to be out there looking for us." Wisp shook his head.

"Something's wrong. They shouldn't be after us like this. Guards normally forget who they're looking for after a few days, let alone as long as it's been since we've been here."

"Maybe Mufed got them stirred up when he told them about us."

Wisp slumped into a chair. "Maybe," he said, and grabbed an apple from a bowl on the table beside him. He looked around the room, then sat up and looked more. "Where is the bounty-man?"

"He went out."

"Went out?" He put the apple back in the bowl and stood up. "When? Where did he go?"

"I don't know where he went. He left just after you did. Said he was going to get some ale and something to eat." Darstan stared at him. "What's the matter? Nobody knows Gregor here."

"I've told you before. I don't like coincidences, Darstan. Don't like them at all."

~

Gregor opened the door quietly, careful to make no noise. He took off his boots, then moved silently toward the back bedroom. Another surreptitious entry brought him to his cot, where he lay down for what remained of a night's sleep. Sleep, however, proved elusive. Nightmares haunted him.

He remembered that night in Sethia when the Wolfen had taken him away, and he remembered the fire that had scorched the earth, killing all the Gnakas. Then there was Melissara and Tirzinitzia, and the tortures they had put him through. And then ... something else, but what?

He struggled to recapture the memory, but it wouldn't come. No matter, though, all the other horrors could be thrown away. All the others forgotten, and he could still be a man. Be proud. But not after tonight. Never again after tonight.

65

A SPY IN OUR MIDST?

Wisp arose early, but even so, he barely caught a glimpse of Gregor as he exited the front door. "Where is he going?"

Darstan was up too, an unusual event, but he said he couldn't sleep ever since he returned to Khatara. "Said he was going to get some food for breakfast. We have nothing here."

Wisp looked out the window, quickly, then gave Adju a nudge with his foot. "Hurry up. Follow Gregor, but don't let him know it."

Adju wiped sleep from his eyes as he threw his clothes on.

"Don't worry about the boots today, just go."

"Yes, Master Kender. No one will see me."

"Remember to be careful. He's a bounty-man, not some fat greedy merchant."

"I know," he said and opened the door.

"And stay away from Mufed." Wisp threw that last bit of caution at him, though he hoped Adju had learned his lesson.

"What is all the commotion?" Aenaila asked as she entered the room.

"Just be ready to leave, that's all," Wisp said.

"Why?"

"It's just Wisp. He doesn't trust Gregor again," Darstan said.

"Why not?"

"I'm not sure. But let's be safe."

Aenaila sighed. "I'm making khaffe before I do anything. Do you want some?"

Wisp nodded as he peered out the window for the tenth time.

Darstan laughed. "He nodded, Aenaila. I guess that means yes. I'll take some, too."

They were on their second cup of khaffe when Adju returned, bursting through the door. "He'll be here right away. I ran to get ahead of him."

"Where did he go?"

"To the market, Master Kender. He got food." Adju smiled. "I could not be happier too, because I am hungry."

Darstan laughed, as did Aenaila, but Wisp wouldn't let the scowl leave his face. "That's all? He only went to the market? Did he talk to anyone?"

Adju's smile disappeared, replaced by a curious look. "Just the merchant. I was close enough to hear him. He said he needed breakfast enough for five people. That's all he said."

Wisp looked at Adju. "Exactly what did they say? Can you remember as I taught you?"

Adju focused. He closed his eyes and replayed the scene in his mind. "Gregor walked up and said good morning. The merchant said it is a fine day. Gregor said I hope you have enough food to feed five hungry people. All new in town. The merchant said—"

Wisp peeked out the window. "He's coming now, so we don't have much time. But we'll need to get out of here before tonight."

"Why?" Darstan asked.

"Because Gregor is a traitor."

"Wisp, I've heard enough of that. He's—"

Wisp spun toward him, a ferocious look on his face. "Trust me, Darstan," he said, then opened the door. "Bounty-man, glad you finally got here. I'm starving." Wisp ushered him in, glanced down the street, then closed the door. "Aenaila, do we have any khaffe left? I'm sure Gregor would like some."

Gregor sipped his khaffe while the others ate the biscuits and pastries he brought back. "Where are we going today?"

Wisp smiled. "To kill a traitor," he said, and when he did, he stared straight into Gregor's eyes.

"A traitor?"

"The worst kind. One who pretended to be a friend." Wisp caught Adju's shocked look from the corner of his eye and turned to him. "I'm sorry, Adju, but Mufed brought this on himself. We can't have him out there knowing what we look like, waiting to collect a reward on us." Wisp shook his head as he finished the last of the pastries. "He must go, and it must be today."

"Perhaps there is a reason," Gregor said.

Wisp's glare could have frozen a man. "There is never a reason for betraying a friend." He slammed his empty mug on the table. "Let's go."

A tear formed in Adju's eyes. "Are we really doing that, Master Kender?"

Wisp never looked back as he headed toward the door. "Traitors must die."

~

A patrol of Khataran Guards sat in a house at the end of the street, the leader pulling aside a curtain now and then to check their target. Orders had come to watch that house, and to apprehend the people inside when it was safe.

The patrol leader frowned and glanced down the street one more time as he mumbled. "What did they mean by 'Wait till it's safe'? There are only three men, a woman, and a boy." He had a full patrol with him and two more patrols at the other end of the street.

Several people had come and gone since they arrived, but never had all of them left at the same time. His orders were to wait, so wait he did. He pulled the curtain aside, anticipation rising as he saw someone exit, a tall, thin man with a crooked nose. Next came a man with one hand, then the other three. "Prepare yourselves!"

The guards jumped to alert and moved toward the door. The patrol leader saw them heading in their direction, ignored the orders about getting reinforcements, and commanded his men to follow him. They stepped into the street, spreading wide to block the way. "Stop and be searched," he called, hand gripping the hilt of his sword.

~

*F*ear and excitement ran concurrently through Darstan, each battling for dominance of his emotions. Fear because at any moment any of them could be killed. The patrol in front of them had four archers and nine others with swords. No doubt there were likely reinforcements coming from either the front or the rear. The excitement felt like a surge of energy, the euphoria that rushed through Darstan when he used the power. The feeling of being a god!

Darstan stepped to the front of the line, staring at the Khataran patrol, his eyes fixed on their leader. "Move aside."

"I have orders. No one will be hurt if you come with me."

Darstan never flinched. "I have orders too. Move aside."

The patrol leader lifted his arm. "Archers!"

The four archers nocked arrows and drew back their bowstrings, poised to fire. The others unsheathed their swords and adopted a strike position.

"You don't know what you're doing," Wisp said to the Khataran as he stepped in front of Darstan. "Stop now, and no one will be hurt."

The patrol leader's hand, still raised, began its descent as his voice called out, "Fire!"

Darstan shoved Wisp aside and unleashed a wall of Fire that filled the street. Blue flames spread from side to side and rolled toward the guards, an unrelenting wall of death.

Wisp rolled to the side then popped up. "You shouldn't have, Darstan!"

"Run!" the patrol leader called, but it was far too late for that, the fire had already caught the first of them, and within heartbeats screams echoed through the street.

"More coming from behind," Gregor yelled.

Darstan turned, saw the guards running toward them. He issued another wall of fire, enough to hold them at bay, then headed in the other direction.

"This way," Wisp called, and found an opening in the wall of blue flame to breach.

Adju hesitated, afraid, but Darstan snatched him up and ran with him tucked into his chest. "You'll be safe with me."

One of the guards was still alive as he passed. Wisp noticed it was the patrol leader. He looked back, saw he had time, so he knelt next to the man, flames torturing him. "Answer my questions, and I'll put an end to your misery."

"Kill me?" he pleaded.

"Only if you tell me the truth."

"Wh ... What?"

"Who sent you here?"

He coughed, gasped.

Wisp grabbed his shirt by the collar, one of the only parts not aflame or smoldering, and shook him. "Who?"

"Bulta!"

Wisp drew a blade and slit the man's throat, then got up and ran down the block. Bulta! And I would have sworn it was Gregor. He turned left at the end of the street, then a right and another left. Soon they were in the bustling traffic of Khatara's morning trade district, blending in with everyone else.

"We need somewhere to stay," Aenaila said.

"How about Sykor?"

"It's not funny, Kender Darnell."

Wisp tapped Adju on the shoulder. "I always know I'm in trouble when she uses both of my names."

"Where will we go?" Adju asked.

"Not to Sykor." Wisp sighed. "I've got to take care of Harun Bulta, and Darstan seems intent on burning Khatara to the ground, so it looks as if we'll be staying here for a while."

Darstan stopped, staring at Wisp. "There was nothing else to do."

"I could have shifted us," Aenaila said. "We had time." She laid a hand on Darstan's shoulder. "You have got to stop thinking that death is the only solution."

"With what we have to do, it is the only solution. Maybe now the guards will think twice about coming after us."

"We can discuss this later," Gregor said. "For now, I suggest we get someplace safe."

"I know a woman who will help." Aenaila looked straight at Wisp. "I know you are suspicious of everyone, but this is a lady I healed before. She will help me."

Wisp nodded. "Go on, then. But stay to main streets. We would draw too much attention otherwise."

They made it the eight or ten blocks to the woman's house, where she embraced Aenaila with open arms. "I am so happy to see you, My Lady. Come into my home, but please forgive me not being prepared."

Aenaila smiled, her warm, soothing smile that seemed to put everyone at ease. "How could you have been prepared, Bethia, when you had no warning we would come?" She hugged her again, then stepped back to introduce the others. "These are my friends: Darstan, Kender, Adju, and Gregor."

Aenaila looked at her to see if there was any recognition on her face. "You might have heard of the guards looking for some of them. They might have even said we did horrible things, but trust me, Bethia, whatever we did was necessary."

Bethia's smile was as warm as Aenaila's. "My Lady, far be it from me to doubt anything you say. Please sit while I make some te." She started toward the kitchen then turned, hand to her mouth. "Forgive my manners. Perhaps you want khaffe instead of te."

"I would prefer khaffe, Bethia, if you don't mind." Aenaila looked to the others then back to her host. "It seems as if we will all have khaffe, even the little one."

While Bethia prepared the khaffe, Wisp moved next to Aenaila. "You shouldn't have told her about us. She probably didn't know."

Bethia called out from the kitchen. "I suppose I should have told you that ever since Aenaila healed me, my hearing has been better than ever. And yes, Kender, I already knew, as does most of Khatara."

"It must be old people," Wisp said. "Bethia hears like an owl, and

Tobias sees like a hawk. Perhaps I have something to look forward to after all."

When she returned with the drinks, Wisp questioned her. "How is it that so many people know about us? Normally these things are forgotten with the first rains."

"You can thank Master Bulta for that." She placed two khaffes on a small tray then went back for more, Aenaila joining her. She was already speaking when she returned. "Bulta controls the guards. Not all of them, but enough of the leaders to get what he wants. So if he wants you dead, you should make plans to leave Khatara. Master Bulta does not give up."

"How many guards in Khatara?" Gregor asked. "Do you know?"

"Thirty thousand," Adju said. "I know it as fact. My friend—"

"We believe you, Adju." Darstan finished his khaffe with a gulp. "And that is a lot of guards."

"It might have been a bad idea coming here alone," Aenaila said. "We should have waited for Aentarra."

"What we need is an army," Darstan said. "Refugio and his men."

Wisp got up to let Bethia take his seat, then sat on the floor, back against the wall. He pulled out his favorite knife and started the ritual of cleaning his nails. "A lot of our problems will be solved once I kill Bulta."

"Killing Bulta is not going to be such an easy task." Gregor fondled his staff as he spoke. "He will be protected. And he will surely have traps."

"Anyone can be killed, Bounty-man." A smile lit Wisp's face as he put his knife away and stood. "Anyone."

66

A HEALTHY BREAKFAST

For once, Wisp didn't wake first. Bethia and Adju were having te and khaffe when he made his way to the kitchen.

"Are we going after Bulta today, Master Kender?"

"Maybe after breakfast, little one."

Adju got up from his chair. "What do you want? I can make you anything."

"I was thinking of going out for breakfast. Perhaps to Mufed's."

Adju sank. The light in his eyes turned dull, and he lost his smile. "Master Kender, do we have to? We could just avoid him. Leave him alone."

Wisp hugged the little thief, his voice warm and compassionate. "We could, Adju. We could do that, and no one but us would ever know." There was a long pause. "But that is exactly the problem. We would know. And we can't leave a man out there who would sell our souls for a few silver coins."

Adju kept hugging him. "But, Master Kender, now that we know—"

Wisp knelt next to Adju, held his hands, stared into tear-stained eyes. "Listen, Adju. I know you like Mufed, but you have to remember that what you liked about Mufed was a lie. He is not the man you thought he was. This man that you know now, this traitor, is the real Mufed."

The sobbing continued but slowed.

Wisp squeezed him. "It's like when people look at you and only see a thief. They don't see the little boy with a big smile and a bigger heart."

Adju pulled back from him, then kissed his cheek. "I love you, Master Kender. You are like a father to me. I never had a father, you know."

Wisp turned to see Bethia wiping away a tear of her own. "You've heard a lot from us, Bethia. I hope we can trust you."

She grabbed hold of Wisp, holding him like an old grandmother. "I would slit my own throat before I whispered a single word."

Wisp patted her back. "Sweet mother, I believe you," he said, then booted Adju in the backside. "Go wake Aenaila and Darstan. The bounty-man too. We need to get going."

When everyone was ready, Wisp explained his plan. As they were about to exit the door, he looked at Adju. "You don't have to come. You can stay with Bethia."

"No, I'm going."

"All right," Wisp said, and headed down the street.

It was a ten-block walk to Mufed's. They stopped at the corner to review the plan.

"I'll be out back," Darstan said. "Gregor, you come with me."

Aenaila held Adju's hand as she and Wisp walked down the street and into Mufed's.

Mufed was serving a table with six patrons when they entered. He cast a quick glance in their direction at the sound of the door, then, when recognition hit him he did a double-take, eyebrows raised.

He called a serving girl to take over for him, then rushed to greet them as if they were old friends. "I am honored to have you back, my friends." He bent down, squeezing Adju's cheek. "Especially you. And to think you once worked for me. Now you travel the world."

Adju hugged him. "It is good to see you, Master Mufed. I have missed you." He stepped back. "How is Khalina?"

Mufed laughed. "Khalina is growing older and putting fear in her father's heart. If only you were here to watch over her." Suddenly he stopped talking and began making an odd clicking sound with his tongue as he spoke, but all the while he smiled. "But listen to me, ranting on when my honored guests have empty stomachs." He pulled a chair out for Aenaila. "Please sit, My Lady."

As she sat, he raced to do the same for Wisp, then Adju. "I will serve khaffe first, then a meal."

"Maybe I want te," Wisp said.

Mufed's smile stretched ear to ear, and his wagging finger danced in front of Wisp. "Such good humor, my old friend, but Mufed never forgets. You always drink khaffe—dark, if my feeble mind recalls." His laughter faded as he left to get the drinks.

Aenaila patted Adju's hand, whispering. "You did well."

Wisp looked around, checking to see if anyone seemed to be leaving in a hurry. "You're sure there are only two ways out, Adju?"

"Just the door we entered and the one out back."

"He'll probably feed us first, then get the guards, or send someone to get them."

"Suppose they go out the front door?" Aenaila asked.

"Then I'll have to excuse myself. But knowing Mufed, I would guess he would opt for the back door. He doesn't seem to be a deep thinker."

Mufed served them khaffe, then took the breakfast order. He called Sameena, the serving girl, and introduced her, then instructed her to take care of them while he prepared their meal. "You will be in good hands with Sameena," he said, then headed toward the kitchen.

After Sameena left, Wisp said to the others. "I hope Darstan is ready."

~

*M*ufed turned the corner in the kitchen, now out of sight of the ones in the dining hall. He raced, calling out orders. "Prepare this meal, then give it to Sameena." He threw off his apron as he hurried to the back door. He swung it open, ran down the steps, and as he hit the street, gasped. "You!"

Darstan stared at him, smiling. "Yes, Mufed. Me. We knew you would betray us. I've been waiting."

Mufed ran back up the stairs, but Wisp met him at the door, Aenaila and Adju right behind him.

"The worst thing is that you had this little boy convinced you were a good man, Mufed. He respected you."

Mufed folded his hands in prayer, bowed his head. "I am an old man who begs to be forgiven." He stared at Wisp, then Adju. "Please, I have a wife. Children."

Wisp grabbed his shirt, dragging him down the steps. "You didn't seem to think much about children when you betrayed Adju." He tugged harder on him, pulling him off balance. "And you did this for what ... a few gold coins?"

Wisp looked down the side street, saw no one, and dragged Mufed along behind him. Gregor grabbed hold of him and helped Wisp, making headway toward a small alley halfway down the street.

As they moved into the alley, Wisp turned to Aenaila. "Keep Adju out of here. He doesn't need to see this."

She nodded, taking hold of Adju and walking up the street.

"Please," Mufed begged, "I will make amends. If you—"

"Just say your prayers." Wisp shook his head. "You should have chosen a different path, Mufed."

When Wisp hesitated, Darstan took hold of Mufed. "Let me do it."

"No. It's my job." Wisp took his knife out and slid it along the side of Mufed's throat, making sure to keep away from the spray of blood. Mufed slumped to the ground, neck pumping blood like a fountain.

Darstan grabbed Wisp's arm. "Let's go. We're done here."

They met Aenaila and Adju at the top of the street, then headed toward the merchant's district.

"I wish you did not have to do that, Master Kender."

"Me too, Adju."

"Gregor, since no one knows you here, why don't you scout ahead."

"We should just go back to the house. Bulta will be surrounded by guards," Gregor said, then shook his head. "What we should do is just go back to Sykor. I get a bad feeling about this place."

"Aentarra wanted us here, but I doubt it was to kill Bulta," Darstan said. "Maybe we should stay out of sight and see what develops."

"If Bulta is controlling the guards, nothing good will develop, and I'm not letting Bulta have his way." Wisp looked at each one of them. "Bounty-man, scout the area. Aenaila, stay close in case we need to shift. Master Bulta will soon learn what it's like to be hunted."

67

HUNTING MERCHANTS

Arvin Maziar, the Captain of the Khataran Guard, waited in the sitting room of Harun Bulta's house. The servants brought him khaffe and offered him a meal, but none of that assuaged the insult of having to wait so long. No one kept Arvin Maziar waiting.

Maziar's boots pounded the floor as he paced, his large bony hands clasped behind his back. Black hair covered his head, and though it was not yet noon, the stubble on his face was dark and looked a day old. After waiting a few more moments, a servant arrived and led him to Harun Bulta's receiving room. The servant bowed low then announced the guest.

"Captain Maziar to see you Master Bulta."

Bulta sat in a large chair, feet clad in slippers resting on a footstool in front of him. With a wave of his hand, the servant was dismissed, then he extended that same hand to greet Maziar, though he didn't bother to stand.

Captain Arvin Maziar had the eyes of a ferret and the lean, hungry look of a wolf. He kissed Bulta's hand, hiding his scowl as he did. "Another fine Khataran day," he said, then stared into Bulta's eyes.

After a quick glance to ensure the servant had gone, Bulta addressed him. "Any news from our friend?"

"Not for several days."

Bulta nodded, picked a date from the bowl beside him. "Patience is a virtue."

"We should hunt him down," Maziar said. "Let me do it my way."

A thick finger wagged at him. "I prefer a more subtle approach, my dear Captain. I would not want him killed right off. It would ruin the pleasure one gets from vengeance."

"Killing him is vengeance enough for me."

"Ah, my good man, but it was not you who suffered the insult was it?" Bulta's laugh rumbled through the room, echoed off the walls.

"Death is underrated, Captain Maziar. Simply killing him would be like swallowing a whole meal in one bite." His laugh continued to reverberate. "I prefer to savor each flavor," he said, then looked around as he leaned forward.

His eyes narrowed to little slits in a massive head. "I want him to suffer for what he did to me. No quick deaths for this one."

Maziar nodded. Stood erect. "As you wish, Master Bulta. I shall continue our surveillance."

"And keep our friend informed. Or better, have him keep us informed." Bulta popped another date in his mouth. "And, Captain, do not fret. Your payment will be in direct proportion to the pleasure I derive from my revenge."

Maziar saluted. "Your will." With that, he departed.

~

*W*isp convinced Aenaila that they needed to move to her original house. "They'll never guess we'd go back there."

With Darstan in agreement, they opted to go along with his plan and shifted there. Wisp popped through the rift first, knife in hand, but after checking the other rooms and peering out the curtains into the streets, he came to the conclusion that it was safe.

Bethia relaxed. She heated water for khaffe and te, while Darstan kept a wary eye on the outside.

"Stop opening the curtains, Darstan. Even if someone is watching the house, they won't' know we're here."

"We do have candles lit, Kender."

Wisp laughed. "All right, Aenaila. My mistake. I guess they know a few candles are here."

Everyone laughed at that, even Bethia, who was entering the room with khaffe. "I'm sure no one is watching. They can't watch every home in the city."

Wisp forced a smile. "In any case, I'm going out, so keep a keen watch. Post a guard tonight."

Darstan sipped the first of his khaffe. "This is good, Bethia. Thanks." Then to turned toward Wisp. "You are a suspicious one, aren't you?"

"Better to be alive and suspicious, than trusting and dead." He stared at Gregor. "Right, Bounty-man?"

Gregor scoffed. "Where are you going, thief?"

"To do something I should have done long ago."

"Not much of an answer."

"I would have to agree, Bounty-man. It isn't. But then I like to keep things close to my chest." He opened a window at the back, peeked out into the alley, and slipped outside. "Don't wait up."

he merchants' district had only a smattering of people left in, most of them merchants tallying the day's take, or preparing for the next morning. Merchandise was moved from large display tents to the more secure shops behind them, complete with iron gates and heavy locks.

Three men moved the last of Harun Bulta's goods into the building as he and two of his guards watched. He dismissed the men, told the guards to wait outside, then put his large frame into an even larger chair behind the desk.

As he counted the money for the second time, a blade touched the side of his throat. He froze, hands still grasping the money. "Whoever you are, know that I have guards posted outside."

"They're dead," a voice whispered in his ear.

Bulta strained to see outside, hoping the man was lying, but he could see no one. He let go of the money, spread his hands wide, slowly, so his move did not appear to threaten. "Take it, then. Money is not worth a life."

The blade pressed into his neck, drawing a trickle of blood. "Odd to hear you say that, fat merchant. From the stories I've been told, money is everything to you. Worth many lives."

"Different tongues tell different tales, my friend." Bulta hoped to talk his way out of this. "For a man such as yourself—able to enter my shops without being caught—that shows talent. I am a man who appreciates talent. Perhaps I could use you in my employ."

"For what? To steal from the other merchants? Don't you do enough of that already with your fake pirate scams?"

Bulta slammed his hands on the table, risking the repercussions. "Enough of this! I shall not be blind to an accuser." With that said, he turned his head. "You!"

Wisp smiled, kept the knife pressed to his neck, but this time the point of the blade held him fast. In his other hand, he held another knife—longer, thinner. "I understand you've been searching for me, Merchant Bulta."

Bulta's large pouty lips squeezed together, and he squinted his eyes. "You will never leave here alive, thief."

"Imagine that, you steal my words, then call me the thief." When Wisp saw that his words had sunk in, he pressed the blade deep into Bulta's neck, puncturing the artery. Blood erupted as if he had just bled a bull, and he leapt aside to avoid the spray.

Bulta jumped up, hands clamped around his neck to stop the bleeding. Wisp got out of his way as he stumbled around the room, bumping into furniture and overturning things, gasping for breath and gurgling blood all the while.

"Now you'll never get your necklace back, Merchant Bulta. If you had kept your end of the bargain things would have been different."

Bulta fell to his knees, still holding his neck with both hands, but life had left his eyes.

Wisp cleaned his blade, put it away, then walked to the desk and picked up the money. He exited through the back door. Before long he was back in Aenaila's house but told them nothing.

The next morning brought a new day and a lot of hungry people. "Nothing to eat here," Darstan said. "Guess we forgot about that."

"Bethia can get us some food," Aenaila said. "They're not looking for her."

Bethia dressed, then went to the market. When she hadn't returned by mid-morning, Aenaila worried. "Something has happened. I know it."

Wisp shook his head. "We don't know anything yet, Aenaila. Be patient."

"Why would she take this long?" Aenaila paced. "She wouldn't. I know something happened."

"She's coming now," Gregor said, from his perch at the window. "Baskets full of food."

No one rushed out to help her as they didn't want to be seen, but the moment she came through the door, Adju and Wisp grabbed the load from her and took it to the kitchen.

Aenaila hugged her. "I was worried, Bethia. What took you so long?"

"Whole city is a mess. Someone killed Merchant Bulta last night, and guards are everywhere searching for the killer."

Aenaila shot Wisp a glare. "It was you, wasn't it? Is that where you went last night?" Aenaila threw a spoon at him. "How could you be so stupid? Now look what you've done."

Wisp tried biting his tongue, but that wasn't his style. He walked straight to Aenaila, got close, and raised his voice, one of the few times he had ever done that with her.

"The man needed killing. He was the one causing us the trouble to begin with. Besides, it should be better with him gone. Trouble might last a few days, but they'll soon forget about who killed Harun Bulta and go back to their own business. With no one to pay them, they'll have no reason to hunt us."

Bethia stood to the side shaking her head. "Not this time. Bulta's wife offered five gold crowns as a reward, and that's got not only the guards looking but regular people as well. I was stopped twice on my way home by people asking questions about you and Adju. They know what you look like." She pointed to Darstan. "And you, they're calling you the one-handed man."

"We need information," Wisp said. "I'm going out."

"Don't be a fool!" Aenaila's face wrinkled into a scowl. "The whole city is looking for you. Before you reach the market you'll be dead."

Wisp stared at her with a determined look. "I took care of myself long before you arrived, Aenaila." He opened the back window, checked the alley, then slipped out.

Aenaila shook her head. "Damn him!"

"He'll be all right," Darstan said.

"Damn him!" She said again.

68

RAISING ARMIES

Wisp waited across the street from the guards' barracks, huddled in a doorway. When Maziar came out, he turned his head, waited for him to get half a block away, then followed at a safe distance.

After Maziar went into Bulta's shop, Wisp cloaked himself and went in as well, finding a corner to sit where he could hear the conversation.

Captain Arvin Maziar walked through Merchant Bulta's shop, careful not to step in the blood that seemed to be everywhere. Bulta's wife had found him after she woke. Her first reaction was to call guards to protect the property and the jewels he had in the shop and at his home.

Maziar smiled as he eyed her body. This was not a woman who grieved over a lost love. If anything, she had probably been waiting for this day, and that thought made him wonder if she had done this or had someone else do it. Who else would Bulta allow to get this close? As he pondered it more, she walked over to him.

"Good morning, Captain."

Maziar caught his breath. Her beauty was so stunning, and her charms so alluring, that he had to remind himself that she might have done this. She seemed remarkably unconcerned for someone who had just lost her husband.

"I understand from my officers that you have offered a reward for the capture of the killer."

"I did. I want this man caught."

Every time she spoke, his breathing suffered, heart seemed to truly skip a beat, as the poets mentioned often enough. She is a Qorami. A Qorami.

He forced himself to recite this often; otherwise, he would be trapped, like all other men. Though to be trapped by her … Maziar shook his head. Stomped on his foot with his other boot. Anything to cause pain, bring him out of this stupor.

He had not believed the tales about the Qorami, but now that he had met one, he realized the tales did not do them justice. "What can you tell me, Lady Bulta? Do you know anything about what happened?"

She smiled, and a thousand candles lit her eyes. When she reached a single finger toward his face, Maziar jumped back, afraid. He couldn't let her touch him. All resistance would fall.

Despite his defenses, he found himself smiling like a little boy with a pocketful of sweets. He stepped toward her, wanting to be touched. Praying to be touched.

A long white fingernail scratched his cheek, just barely, but it sent shivers racing through his body. He trembled, reached for her, but she had moved back. Her smile was both inviting and mocking. "Will you find him for me, Captain? It would please me if you did."

Maziar couldn't find the words to answer, so he simply nodded.

"Good. I will have a special reward for you once he is caught."

She turned and walked away, taking his heart with her. He stared for a long time, tried to burn her image into his mind, but he found it was already there. Finally, he found his voice. "I will get him," he called out, though she could not have heard. *I will.*

As Maziar walked back toward the guards' barracks, what she said resounded in his ears. *Special reward.* He could hear it over and over, and there was something about the way she emphasized "special" that captured him. His dreams began immediately.

~

Commander Shill opened the curtain leading to a back room, stepping lightly as he entered the shop. He had arrived in Khatara under cover of the night and stayed in an older house owned by the Bultas.

It would not do for a Sethian Commander to be seen roaming the streets, not with what had happened in the Highlands and now in Jattan Kir. Word might not have reached them yet, but it would soon enough. "A magnificent performance, Lady Bulta, or was it? I have heard reports of the Qorami. Is that what you do, entrance poor souls like Maziar?"

Her reaction came instinctively. A smile, eyes aglitter, a sway in her hips as she moved toward him. When she reached for his face, he grabbed her hand. Not a gentle squeeze. "My master warned me of your guiles, but he prepared me for it. Your time would be better spent on the Khataran."

"He will do as I say, Commander Shill."

"Good. My armies will be here in two days. Three at the most. With the Highlands and the capital city under our control, Khatara is the only remaining obstacle, and with Maziar on our side it should fall easily."

"There is another captain in the harbor district, and he has a sizable force under him. But with the people stirred up by the reward, the city will be a mess. Maziar should have little problem."

Commander Shill bowed low. "Your reward will be rightly earned, My Lady. Khatara will flourish under your rule."

"And the emperor?"

"His head is on its way to Sethia."

She smiled. "I love efficiency."

The commander bowed and went back through the curtains to the room behind the shop. Lady Bulta exited through the front door.

Wisp waited a long time after they left, then exited through a rear door and made his way back to Aenaila's house.

*I*t was late afternoon when Wisp returned, sneaking in the same back window he exited earlier that day.

Aenaila ran to him, threw her arms around him. "Thank the gods you are safe." She grabbed his face and kissed him.

Wisp smiled. "Had I known this was all I had to do ..."

Darstan laughed, but it stopped short. Memories of Mirana flashed before him. Then memories of Rahg.

"Learn anything, thief?"

"Quite a bit," Wisp said and grabbed an apple from a bowl on the table. "Captain Maziar is going to be hunting us down like dogs, driven by the most primal of emotions—lust."

"What?" Aenaila appeared confused.

"Lust for the unbelievably charming Lady Bulta, who, I am certain, is a Qorami."

Adju bounced up, raced to Wisp. "A Qorami? Is that true, Master Kender? What did she look like?"

"I'm afraid it is true, little one. While I was in hiding she almost had me convinced to switch sides, and—" Suddenly he realized Aenaila was there, and at the same time caught her glare. If her eyes had not been green before, they would have been today. "But of course, when I am so blessed as to spend every day in the company of Queen Aenaila, even a Qorami means little."

The quick turn brought laughter to Aenaila and an embarrassed look. "You do have a silver tongue, Kender Darnell."

Wisp leaned close to Adju and whispered. "There she goes with the two names again. That means I'm not quite back in good graces."

Darstan paced. "What else?"

"Believe it or not, Maziar is the least of our worries. There was a Sethian Commander hiding in the back room, and he said an army is marching here from Jattan Kir."

"Jattan Kir? That is good news, Kender. The emperor will put this to a quick death once his troops arrive."

Wisp shook his head. "The army is a Sethian army, and the emperor's head is on its way to Sethia."

"What?" Darstan shouted.

"Worse. The Sethians have also taken the Highlands. Khatara is all that stands in their way."

Aenaila chewed on her fingernails. "We can't let them take Khatara, then they would have control of the sea and the land from the far east all the way to Nyauran. And if Sethia is marching so brazenly, Nyauran is not long for this world."

"Aenaila is right," Darstan said. "We can't let them take Khatara. Aentarra warned me they would do this. The problem is, two or three days doesn't give us much time. We need an army, Aenaila. Can you raise one? Would they come here for you?"

"I can get one, but how to get them here is the question."

"I think I know how. We can go to Sykor and get Aentarra and Mikkellana. With the four of us, we could bring back a lot of men."

Aenaila thought for a moment, then nodded. "All right. We'll do it." She turned to Kender. "Get ready, and get Adju dressed. That boy never has all of his clothes on."

"Can't go," Wisp said. "I've got to stay here and get the Harbor Guard on our side. There's no way you'll be back in time, so it will be up to them to hold the city."

Gregor joined in. "I have to agree with him, though I am loath to. With the way their barracks are stationed for defense, they could hold out a good while."

Darstan agreed. "From what I've heard there's no love lost between Maziar and the captain of the Harbor Guard. It shouldn't be difficult to convince him. You might even consider staying there. It would be safer."

Though reluctant, Aenaila agreed as well but cautioned him to seek shelter with the captain. "And go nowhere! We won't be long."

"Of course," Wisp said. "How long can a trip halfway around the world take?"

Aenaila reached out for Darstan's hand. "Ready? We're going to Talanvar's house."

~

Before leaving, Aenaila called Darstan to the side. "When we get to Sykor, keep control of yourself. Rahg will be there, and I don't want to have to get between the two of you and end up dead."

Darstan nodded, but he seemed to be staring off into nothing.

Aenaila grabbed him by the cheeks, turned him to face her. "I don't know how else to tell you, Darstan. I don't think Rahg did it."

"He did it all right. I saw him."

"But he didn't know." Her eyes softened, almost teared. "I loved

Mirana. She was my best friend. But I don't think Rahg and the rest of them are lying when they say they never got a message. I think it was Mattu." She waited for a response but got none. "Never mind, just take hold. We're going."

Darstan and Aenaila stepped through the rift into Talanvar's library, Darstan's hand balled into a fist as he emerged. He cast a quick glance around to see if Rahg was there.

"If you're looking for Rahg, he's not here," Aentarra said. "What do you want?" She got off the sofa, walked to him. "Why did you leave Khatara?"

"We need help. The guards are taking over, and worse than that, Lukaan's men have taken over the rest of Jattan Kir. They're on their way to Khatara now."

"God's Blood! I knew it."

"Aenaila can raise an army in Cergala, but we have to be able to get them here in time. Can you shift that many people?"

Aentarra turned to Aenaila. "How many men can you get?"

"Probably six or seven columns. There are two thousand soldiers in a column."

"With all of us, we can definitely do it."Mikkellana is still hurt, but we don't need her to walk, just use her mind." As she pondered more thoughts, Tobias, Rahg, and Talanvar entered the library.

Darstan tensed. Anger rising in his gut.

Rahg nodded to him. "Darstan, good to see you. I hope we can talk."

Tobias got between them, walked right up to Darstan, stared into his eyes. "Lad, you know I've always told you the truth, so hear me out. We never got a message from anyone in Cergala. Never even knew you were there. Feel badly about your wife and child." He shook his head. "Been more than twenty years and I still remember losing my Shia ...." a long pause followed, then he stared into Darstan's eyes again. "But the truth is we didn't know. Someone down there lied to you. Don't know why, but they did."

Darstan thought about what Aenaila had said, and what Aentarra had said—how she could just kill him so why lie? Then he thought about how Rahg tried to save him in Pomanda. Mattu! It must have been Mattu.

Without further deliberations, he walked around Tobias and headed for Rahg, embracing him when he got there. He wasn't sure what to feel, but for now, at least, he was going to have to trust his gut. "Sorry, Rahg."

Rahg pushed back from the embrace, tears in his eyes as he spoke. "Sorry? Dar, I'm the one who's sorry." He pulled him close to hug him again. "I didn't know. I'm so sorry about her. I ..."

"Mirana," Darstan said. "Her name was Mirana."

"That's a pretty name."

Darstan nodded and wiped tears away. "Rahg, I don't know how to say this, but it's going to take me a while. All this time I've been thinking you did this to Mirana."

Rahg pulled him close. Patted his back. "Don't worry. I understand. I'm just glad we got this far. Now we can work on fixing it up."

Tobias put his arms around both of them. "You boys would have made your father proud. Had me worried for a while, Darstan. Thought I might have to take a paddle to you like I did when you were young."

Darstan laughed through tears, and hugged Tobias, and as he did he noticed that even Aentarra had misty eyes. She never ceased to surprise him. "Well, enough of this," Darstan said. "We have to get moving. Khatara is not going to last long if we don't."

A confused look came to Rahg's face. "Khatara? What's wrong?"

Aentarra stepped forward. "Lukaan has taken Jattan Kir and the Highlands. Khatara is next, and we can't let him have it. We're going to get an army from Cergala, but before we do, I need to go see that crazy sea captain."

"Sennar?" Rahg asked.

Aentarra smiled. "I have a plan that should surprise the Khataran Guards." She looked to Darstan. "I won't be long."

⌐

*A*s the Sea Skate plowed through roiling waves driven by a wild wind, a rift appeared next to the main mast. A faint scent of cinnamon was whisked away by the wind and the sea, and as Aentarra stepped through, salty water splashed her face. She spun a quick shield to protect herself, then looked around, finally spying Captain Jacopo Sennar on the top deck. He raced to greet her.

"Welcome aboard, My Lady. Nasty time to show up though. The sea seems to disagree with my course."

She smiled. "We should go inside where we can speak better."

Once inside of Sennar's cabin, she let go her shield and accepted the towel he handed to her. "I have new plans for you, Captain Sennar. You will go to Khatara, position your ships so that you can block any advance from Jattan Kir, should one come, but mostly so that you can reinforce a small army at the harbor in Khatara."

Sennar stared in confusion.

Aentarra sighed, as if she shouldn't have to explain everything. "Lukaan has taken control of Jattan Kir. We have a small force of Khataran Guards in the Harbor District that need help." She then explained what she had in mind for the Cergalan soldiers once they came back with them.

"And don't forget, if you find out one of the Banished Ones is loose, like Iazzo in Entiria, get your ships far out of range. If any of them so much as see you, their lightning will cut those ships down as if they were—"

"I believe we know—"

Aentarra grabbed him by the neck. "Don't ever interrupt me." She stared for a moment longer, waiting to see if he would respond, then she continued. "You might know about casting nets and catching fish, but you know nothing about Lukaan."

She waited for his nod. "Take your ships and guard the coastline at Jattan Kir. And when you get there, get in touch with the captain of the Harbor Guard immediately. Tell him we won't be long." She leaned in close to Sennar. "Don't fail me, Captain. I detest failure."

Sennar bowed to her, and then she shifted back to Talanvar's house.

*A*entarra explained her plan to Aenaila, and the rest of them, then turned to Rahg. "We have to leave you here," she said. "Someone has to watch over Sykor. It's too important to let it fall into Lukaan's hands."

Rahg reluctantly agreed, then said goodbye to Darstan and the others.

When they were ready to leave, Aenaila reached out, taking hold of Darstan with one hand and Mikkellana with her other. Aentarra supported Mikkellana from the other side. Soon, they stepped through a rift into King Marro's house in Cartena. No one was in the room when they appeared, so Aenaila went to get them.

After joyous greetings and introductions, Marro had food and drinks served, and he sat down with Queen Genea to join Mikkellana, Aentarra, and Darstan.

Aenaila watched every word, anxious about having Aentarra here in case someone offended her. Marro had wanted his advisors there as well, but Aenaila refused, partly because of time, but mostly due to Aentarra. The more people she came into contact with the more chance someone would get killed. Though right now she was sipping khaffe and holding conversation as if she were a well-bred princess.

Marro was talking, but Aenaila decided to interrupt. "Father, forgive me, but we are in desperate need to move quickly."

"I'm sorry. I was too busy enjoying the company. What can I do?"

"We need an army to take back to Khatara, and we need it now."

"How much of an army?"

"As many as you can spare," Aentarra said, then she smiled as if it were an afterthought. "Forgive my rudeness, King Marro, but there is nothing short of your country's safety at stake. I know you do not know Lukaan, but he is a very powerful and dangerous man." She paused. "Perhaps more than a man now." Another slight pause, then. "If he takes control of Khatara, he will eventually come here. Nothing will stop him."

Marro listened to everything she said, his brow wrinkled with worry. When Aentarra finished, he stood. "Stay and rest. I will speak with my generals."

"Do you have a room for my sister to rest?" Aentarra asked. "Mikkel-lana seems tired and sitting up wears on her."

"Of course, let me help," Marro said and rushed to her side. He picked her up, then carried her to a guest bedroom. Queen Genea had gotten there ahead of him and arranged the bed, then tucked her in once Marro set her down. "I will close the door, but someone will be posted outside. Just call if you need anything."

"You are both kind. Thank you. Just make sure I am called when your generals arrive. I want to be part of that."

"Try to rest," Marro said, then closed the door and left, rejoining the others.

Darstan got up and walked toward the door. "I'm going out."

"Where?" Aentarra asked, her tone demanding.

"Find some memories."

"You should rest. We have a lot ahead of us."

"You rest your way. I'll rest my way," he said, and walked out the door.

The street leading down to the plaza was familiar, bringing back memories, good and bad. He had his hand tucked into his pocket and his head hung low, hoping no one noticed him. He made it all the way to the baker's shop without being recognized. The shop was empty when Darstan entered. "Hello, Giacomo."

Giacomo looked up from his spot behind the counter. A smile covered his face. "BlackWolf! You have returned." He raced to greet Darstan, giving him a huge hug. "Sit. Relax. I will fix khaffe and a dessert."

"I didn't come for that, Giacomo. Just to remember."

Giacomo laughed, and it was a contagious laugh. "There is nothing that goes better with memories than Giacomo's khaffe. Sit. It won't take long."

Darstan smiled, despite his mood. Giacomo always made him smile. He had always made Mirana smile too.

Darstan stared at the walls, at the empty chairs. It was late afternoon, not a busy time for a bakery, but still, there should be people here. He could almost hear Mirana's laughter echoing off the walls. She, too, had a contagious laugh and it never failed to make him smile.

Giacomo set the glass on the table, filled with hot khaffe, and next to it he set a pastry smothered in cinnamon with a thin slice of apple on top. "It is a beautiful day, BlackWolf, you should go outside and enjoy this. Perhaps by the fountain."

Darstan looked to the fountain, almost afraid to go there, recalling the last time he was there, and he nearly destroyed it with his fire. He stared across the square.

"It is fixed," Giacomo said.

Darstan smiled. "Thanks, Giacomo. I think I will." He picked up his plate and his khaffe and walked to the fountain, taking a seat on the ledge. They had done a good job of fixing it. It looked just like it did when Mirana first brought him here—two beautiful dolphins in mid jump.

He ate the pastry, the same one they used to share, then sipped on the khaffe, still too hot to gulp down, and he let the breeze spray him with a light mist from the fountain. He sat for a while, and when he had taken the last sips of his khaffe, he reached out and patted the dolphins on the head, then walked back to Giacomo's shop to return his cup and plate. "Goodbye, Giacomo."

"And to you, BlackWolf. Come back soon."

"I just might do that, Giacomo."

*M*arro's house was crowded by the time he returned, with Generals Baldo, Leto, and even Mattu waiting for him. Aenaila and Aentarra were there, as was Mikkellana.

Marro and Genea had made a sofa into a makeshift bed so that she was more comfortable, and though she was lying down, she seemed as alert as ever.

Darstan moved to a chair beside Aentarra and Aenaila. "I hope I didn't miss much."

"We have been waiting," Aenaila said, and as she did, the generals rose to greet him.

Leto bowed, reaching for Darstan's hand. "BlackWolf, it is good to see you again."

Darstan frowned. "General Leto, there is no need to bow to me. I'm not your king, and I'm not your commander. I'm just here with Aenaila to get some help."

Leto saluted. "You will always be my commander, Black Wolf." And with that, he returned to his chair.

Baldo and Mattu were in line to address Darstan, but he forestalled it. "Sit. We need to get something resolved without wasting time." It was all Darstan could do to hold his ire. Seeing Mattu brought him to the edge, but he didn't know for sure if it was him who had betrayed Mirana.

Marro stood, staring at Darstan. "We have almost five columns in Cartena that you could take right now. There are several more in Solero, and in Arangar, near the pass. All told, you could easily have ten columns but you would need to transport them."

Mikkellana shook her head. "Too much shifting. It will be strain enough to take ten thousand men across the sea. We might do more, but with me weakened there is no sense risking it." She raised her head up a little. "Exactly how many men can we take now."

Baldo stood. "Nine thousand men right now. Right here. I could have them ready to go by morning."

Mikkellana nodded. "Then that is what we'll do. Get them ready to leave after breakfast."

Baldo saluted her, then asked his king for leave. As the other generals got up, Darstan did too. "Just a moment, Mattu. I have a question for you."

Mattu came to face him. "What is it, Black Wolf?"

Darstan's hand clenched, and the veins in his head bulged. "When we were in the pass, did you send that message to my brother Rahg? The one asking for peace?"

Mattu looked confused. "You know I did. He even responded."

Darstan stared. "And you know this as fact?"

"I sent the messenger myself. You heard his report back to you in Queen Aenaila's tent."

"You mean Mosca, the soldier who got killed right after that?"

Mattu bowed. "Yes, it was unfortunate."

Aentarra walked over, pushed Darstan aside, then stared at Mattu. "You never sent the messenger."

He looked at her, indignation written on his face, then stared at Darstan. "I don't know who this is, but it is an insult to accuse me."

Aentarra grabbed his cheeks and pulled him toward her. "Listen to me, General, I can tell when someone is lying to me, and you are lying."

Darstan looked to Aentarra. "You can do that?"

She nodded. "He did it. And he had Mosca killed too."

"Thank the Gods," Darstan said. "It really wasn't Rahg."

He grabbed hold of Mattu and dragged him outside. Once out the door, Mattu drew his sword, but Darstan already had fire coming from his arm. It struck Mattu in the face, then the stomach. He fell to the ground, writhing and screaming, but only for a moment. Darstan let him burn, refusing to allow anyone to put an end to his suffering. After a short while it was over.

Baldo and Leto had come out, and just stared at Mattu's charred body. "Take him away," Darstan said. "And have someone clean up the mess."

Darstan went back inside, apologized to Marro and Genea, then sat down in a chair, breathing a sigh of relief.

～

*M*ikkellana tugged on Aentarra's sleeve, pulling her close, then whispered. "I didn't know you could do that, sister? Since when—"

Aentarra smiled. "I can't. But I had to get Darstan's mind straight. Couldn't have him wondering whether it really was Rahg or not."

Aentarra looked at Mikkellana's shocked face. "And get that look off of your face. He's one man. Well worth the price even if he didn't do it."

"Then I guess it's settled," Aenaila said as she stood, stretching. "We can all get a good night's sleep and leave in the morning."

Aentarra stood and smiled at Genea and Marro. "I will be sorry to leave such wonderful hosts."

Mikkellana lay back on the sofa, seething. How could she ever trust someone like Aentarra.

69

STRATEGY

Tirzinitzia walked around the table, staring at her maps. She wore the green gown she made from the Victory Cloak she won for her battle strategy at Katsintal so long ago. What an honor that had been. Raised before her peers and the Council of Light, she stood alone on the dais, listened to the roar of the crowds as they praised her.

If only those times could come again, she thought, then returned her gaze to the maps. She placed a red marker on Jattan Kir and another on the Highlands. Commander Shill had completed his initial assignments admirably. All that was left for him was Khatara, and early reports indicated he would have control within days.

For a brief moment, she toyed with putting a marker there but thought better of it. Lukaan would not like to be misled. It was best to wait until it was official. She set a yellow marker on Pomanda. They didn't yet have military control, but fortune had smiled on them, and the greed of the nobles delivered the city without casualties.

With her left hand full of green markers, she set one in Nyauran, and the other two in Kamnor and the Free Lands. The final green one would be for Sykor, and that would be soon. As soon as the other territories fell.

She walked to another table, unrolling charts on military strategy, charts she had made very long ago. "Advanced Tactics in the Prairies," "Moving Forward in the Forest," and "Using Defense in a Mountain Setting." A rush of exhilaration swept over her, and she smiled as she pulled another chart from the case—"Siege of a City"—her favorite.

She unrolled it, glanced at a few diagrams. Sighed. Sykor would come soon enough.

A sound alerted her, and she turned to see Dregl and Vorkk coming in together. If it had only been the Wolfen, she might not have heard, but Victas were notoriously noisy. The Gnaka commander arrived within moments, leaving Melissara and Lukaan late for the session.

Tirzinitzia liked promptness. It irked her when someone was late. A flash of anger heated her face, and she paced to cool off. Afraid that it might show when Lukaan finally did arrive. A whiff of spice floated in the air just before the rift opened. She turned to face them. Long ago she had learned never to have your back face a rift in case an enemy came through.

Melissara stepped onto the marble floors, feet clad in soft leather boots. "Are we ready?"

Tirzinitzia looked to Lukaan for his acknowledgment. It came with a simple nod of the head. Not what she wanted, but it would suffice.

She turned to the charts on the wall, pointing to the one on the far right, "Using Defense in a Mountain Setting." She tapped it with her pointer. "Brood Commander Vorkk, this will be yours. The Free Lands between Kamnor and Pomanda are mountainous and riddled with caves and ravines. Cliffs and uncertain terrain will give Victas an edge there." She faced the group again. "How many men do you have, Commander?"

His chest puffed up even larger than it normally was. "Ten thousand. And we are training recruits every day."

"Good. Very good." She pointed to the chart again. I have a complete strategy mapped out for you. Take it with you to study, and as we prepare for the final strike, we will review it together. Often."

He saluted. "As you wish, Mistress Tirzinitzia."

A smile lit her face. Respect. That's what one lived for.

"Pack Lord Dregl!"

He stepped forward, bowing and offering his salute. "I am honored to serve," he said to Lukaan, then turned to Tirzinitzia, ears pricked to attention and eyes alert.

"The Kamnoran forest lies next to the Free Lands and serves as the majority of the northern border of Sykor. That will be your responsibility." She paused.

"Listen well, Pack Lord, because yours is the heaviest burden.

Vorkk will be fighting a defensive battle with occasional raids into Sykor, but mostly waiting until the time is right. And when it is, he will strike with all of his men. Something they will not expect. Your forces will take the brunt of the offense. You will have to be relentless and perform to perfection."

A tiny snarl to one side of his face bared teeth. It gave the appearance he was smiling. "I am honored, Mistress."

"You might not feel that way when I provide details." She tapped the chart on "Moving Forward in the Forest."

"You will have five thousand Victas as a primary attack, supported by two thousand of your own."

"How many will Sykor have?"

Tirzinitzia consulted notes she had next to the maps. "Altogether they could mass sixty thousand, possibly a few more. But they will leave some in the city, and they will have to put some at the Pomandan border and the Free Lands. I suspect at least ten thousand at the Nyauran border. The rest will go to the Kamnoran border."

"Why give us so few, then?"

"You are the decoy, Pack Lord. I pray you will be a good one."

"Night Commander Chernol!"

The Gnaka leader stepped forward when Tirzinitzia called. He knelt on the floor, head kissing the marble until she told him to rise. "How may I serve?"

"Since you will be least suspected of leading a massive strike, you will be our focal point. You will lead the force that will drive us to victory over Sykor."

Her pointer had traced a route from Sethia across Nyauran and into Sykor. Surprise is a powerful weapon; the Nyaurans will not expect you, and since Sykor will count on them to help hold the border it will be left all but unprotected."

The Night Commander gulped. Fear was not a companion of his, but common sense was. "The Nyauran horsemen are the best, Mistress. And we have no horses, only soldiers."

"Exactly why they will not suspect this."

"But, Mistress—"

She advanced, glaring. "Yes, Chernol?"

"It's just that horsemen against soldiers ..."

She smiled. "Are you imagining a massacre, Night Commander?" Taunting laughter rolled around the room. "Don't worry. I have a plan, little one."

Before Chernol could respond, Lukaan's message emanated to all of them. *You have your missions. Go. Study the plans Tirzinitzia has provided you and work with her to refine them. There is little time.*

Chernol, Dregl, and Vorkk all bowed low as they backed out of the room. Tirzinitzia watched them leave with mixed emotions. Pride swelled within her; after all, they would be marching under her battle plans.

But even with that, regret filled her heart that she was forced to remain in Sethia. How she loved a battlefield. A sharp intake of air raced through her as she tilted her head back, eyes closed. Images of past battles floated in her mind like petals on a pond. If she guessed right, she would be pitting her strategy up against Mikkellana.

She would likely be the one defining the battle plan for them, and that would be almost as good as going against her father. After all, he had taught her everything she knows. Tirzinitzia smiled. It would almost be like fighting Antar. How glorious a victory that would be!

Tirzinitzia and Melissara stood before Lukaan, awaiting his instructions. He smiled, something he seldom did, then walked to a door leading to a balcony and went outside. Tirzinitzia followed, standing next to Melissara as he stared into the emptiness of the desert.

"There is much yet to do," he said. "But I feel the shield weakening every day. It won't be long. Not long at all." He gripped the railing, squeezing with both hands until his veins bulged. "I cannot wait to see Aentarra again." When he said that, flames flickered from his body, from his arms and the back of his head. Tirzinitzia took a step back, head bowed.

Without warning, Lukaan shifted, leaving Tirzinitzia alone with Melissara. "If I were you, Tirzinitzia, I'd make certain that the commanders were ready. It would not do to fail in this mission." She did not wait for a response but shifted when she was done.

Tirzinitzia closed the doors to the balcony, walked to the table and rolled up her charts, then straightened her maps, taking time to review her strategy one more time. She nodded her head. Yes, this was a good strategy. One Mikkellana would not expect. One that ... A cold chill raced up her spine, triggered shivers that froze her.

Suppose it was not Mikkellana defining the strategy. Suppose it is Aentarra! She ran to the door, holding up her green gown with one hand.

Foolish of her to have worn this anyway. Only idiots acted like this. Old idiots! The doors flung open at her will, and she called outside to waiting servants. "More te! And bring me some fruit. I have work to do."

Once inside, she unrolled her charts, laid them on the table beside the corresponding maps and started anew. If Aentarra is involved in this, I have a lot of work to do.

70

A DEFENSIVE STRATEGY

Rahg and Camissa sat with Talanvar in the kitchen, waiting for Takar to show. He sent a message earlier that said to expect him by supper with important news to discuss.

"Bound to be news about the attacks," Talanvar said.

Camissa nudged closer to Rahg. "From what I've heard, Nyauran has been invaded."

"They will have a tough go of it there," Rahg said. "The Nyauran horsemen are the best."

Just then, Birol came in, followed by Takar. After exchanging pleasantries, Takar sat in one of the chairs between Camissa and Talanvar. Rahg stood.

"What news have you got, Takar?" Talanvar was not one to beat around the bush.

"Not good. As you've probably heard, the Sethians attacked Nyauran, but what you don't know is they have also attacked the Free Lands and Kamnor."

"Kamnor!" Rahg came over to stand beside Takar. "Who attacked? How many?"

"We don't have all the reports yet, but it sounds like a combination of Victas and Wolfen. A lot of them."

"What about the Free Lands?" Camissa asked.

Takar turned to her. "Victas. Thousands of them." The Force Commander shook his head. "I doubt they can hold. We tried to reinforce them, but the Victas already held the key pass. No way we were getting through with them holding that."

"We should ask Pomanda for help."

Talanvar shook his head. "Pomanda is likely going to be against us. Their king was assassinated, and the new ruler, Varga, doesn't look kindly on Sykor. Doesn't look kindly on anyone but himself."

"You think they'd take arms against us?" Takar asked.

"At best we can expect neutrality."

Takar stood. "I'm taking the rest of the army to the border. We can't let them take Kamnor and the Free Lands."

"What about Nyauran?" Talanvar asked.

"I can post a small force at the border, but we're going to have to rely on Nyauran to hold their own. The northern border is our main concern right now."

"How many men do you have?" Rahg asked.

"I'll leave twenty thousand men here. Have to wait and see where to post the ones I take, but I imagine I'll send a small strike force to the Pomandan border. Won't be enough to stop them if they decide to come over, but with the locals supporting them, they'll hold for a while."

Takar scratched the old scar on his face. "I'll have almost 40,000 men to protect the northern border—that is, once I count all the outposts. That should be enough to keep a few Victas and Wolfen out."

"A few, yes," Talanvar said, "but you know it won't be just a few."

Takar placed a hand on Rahg's shoulder. "I'm counting on you to keep things peaceful while I'm gone. Some of the guards might think they can get away with things once I leave. Some of the people too." He stared hard at Rahg. "Don't let them. Be tough. Brutal if you have to."

"Don't worry. I'll take care of it."

"When are you leaving?" Camissa asked.

"First light. Need to get up there. Kamnor can't survive without help."

～

Tobias walked down the steep hill from Hightown, whistling a merry tune. Things had been going well of late: Ludar dead, they survived an attack by Sendra and Ghruehne, and now the boys were back together. That's what made him happy.

He had looked after those boys for a long time, seen them being raised. It broke his heart when they were at odds; now it was better. Even the thief seemed to be doing well, and Tobias had grown to like that thief. He was like broccoli, didn't care for him at first, but the more he was around, the more he tolerated him, then one day he realized he even liked him.

Yep, he's like broccoli, Tobias thought.

Tobias tipped his hat to a young lady walking with her child, then smiled at a merchant with a basket of fruit. He thought about what he would do once he got those boys out of trouble, and for the first time in ages, he considered settling down. Maybe in Sykor.

Thoughts of settling down made him think of Mollie. She was as sassy as spice, but he sure did like her. Didn't make a bad pie either.

As he turned the corner toward the Edge, two guards approached him, hands dangerously close to their swords. Tobias went on alert, reached for his sword, but as he did, someone struck him on the head from behind. He went down, hitting the pavement hard. Blood pooled in the low spots of the cobblestone street while they stripped him of his sword, money, and even his pipe and tobacco. Afterward, they dragged him into the alley.

~

When Tobias didn't show for supper, Rahg worried, but when he failed to come back to Talanvar's that night, he knew something was wrong. "I'm going to look for him."

"I am too," Camissa said, and she started for the door, Rahg right behind her.

She set a fast pace, and as they went down the hill leaving Hightown, she kept five paces ahead of Rahg.

"We should check with Mollie first. He said he was going to get a pie when he went out."

"Too late for that, Rahg; besides, the Trader's Inn is on the way. We'll stop there."

"Do you know where Mollie lives?"

"No. We'll have to ask around.'"

They went to four inns and talked to dozens of people, but no one had seen him, and no one knew where Mollie lived. If they did, they weren't saying.

It was getting late, and Camissa was tired, but Rahg pushed, and Camissa went along; she was not one to give up, especially when a friend was involved. At the sixth inn, as they walked in the door, Camissa stopped, lifted her head and sniffed the air. "He's here, Rahg. I smell his pipe."

Rahg looked but didn't see Tobias, and the room was small enough that he couldn't have missed him. "Not here, Camissa."

She continued looking. "I'm telling you, that's his pipe I smell."

"A lot of people smoke pipes."

Camissa's expression grew stern, and her eyes narrowed. "Do a lot of them smoke blackthorn pipes?" she asked and nodded toward two men sitting at a table toward the center of the inn.

Anger arrived quickly in Rahg. "Nobody smokes a blackthorn pipe."

He walked over to them, stood staring at the man with the pipe in his mouth. As he was about to speak, two guards joined the men at the table, sitting down, but staring at Rahg.

"Where did you get the pipe?" Rahg asked.

"None of your business."

"Take it from an old man? Bald, with white hair on the sides?"

The man stopped, moved his chair back, giving him access to his sword. "I said none of your business."

"It happens to be my business because I know the man who owns that pipe, and he's a friend. Where is he?"

All of them stood, hands reaching for swords. Rahg smiled. He infused himself with a shield, strengthening what he already had, then he drew his sword.

"Rahg, no!" Camissa said, but he was already moving.

He lunged for the one nearest him to the right. The man stood with his left side exposed, facing Rahg, and no room to move. Rahg's first thrust took him in the left side, and the man fell. The other three moved to attack, one of them striking at Rahg's left side, which he countered, but when he did the second one struck him on the right side. The steel met Rahg's shield and did nothing.

The man stepped back, eyes wide. "I hit him!" he said, and while he questioned what happened, Rahg dealt him a blow that crippled his sword hand.

Only two remained, and they appeared to be losing interest in fighting. When Rahg thought they were seeking an escape route, he wrapped them in a shield and squeezed them tightly, forcing the air from around them. They gasped, struggling to breathe.

"Where is he?" Rahg asked.

The first one said nothing, but the other one nodded to Rahg, and he opened a gap large enough to give them air. "I'll take you to him."

Rahg nodded to the ones on the floor. "Bring them with you. I'll follow."

"They need healers."

"Bring them," Rahg said, "or you'll be on the floor with them."

A short while later, they led Rahg to the spot where they had left Tobias. One man went in the alley, then came back out, dragging Tobias.

His head was covered in blood, and he wasn't moving. "Is he alive?" Rahg asked.

Camissa knelt beside him, examining the wound, then listening for a heartbeat. "His heart is beating fast, Rahg, He's alive, but we might be too late."

One of the guards tried running, but Rahg wove a shield into a spinning disc and flung it toward him, cutting deeply into his back. His scream pierced the night as he fell. Next Rahg wove a shield into a sword and attacked the others, killing all three in less than a moment. He gathered Tobias's things: his sword, pipe, and tobacco, and then took the guards' money before racing back to Tobias.

"We need help!" Camissa said.

"Can't you heal him?"

"I've tried. The bleeding is stopped, but I don't know what else to do. I think he has lost too much blood."

Rahg panicked. "What can we do?"

She looked up at him, crying. "Nothing."

71

A DIFFERENT KIND OF HEALING

Rahg wove a shield around Tobias's head, and then he carried him out of the Edge until he found someone with a horse and cart. He offered to pay for it, but the man offered to take them.

"Just sit in the back with your friend, and tell me where to go."

When they arrived at Talanvar's house, Camissa gave the man several silver pieces, then rushed with Rahg into the house. Birol met them at the door, then ushered them to the bedroom that Tobias had been using. Camissa and Rahg sat with him all through the night, taking turns resting and watching. Rhaven, still not healed from the wounds he suffered when he fought Jen Pal, came in for a while, but he had to get rest.

During the early morning, just before dawn, Rahg woke to see Camissa sitting at the side of Tobias's bed.

"How is he?"

She shook her head. "It doesn't look good, Rahg. You better get everyone here."

The sun was almost coming up. Rahg went downstairs, had Birol make khaffe and te, and then woke Dirk, sending him on a mission to get Mollie and tell her what happened. Mollie would want to know.

Mollie came rushing in with Dirk not too long afterward, and after learning of Tobias's location, she climbed the stairs and pulled up a chair alongside the bed. She talked to him most of the morning, telling him stories and telling him how much people would miss his funny ways and his long-winded stories. Now and then she would get a hot towel from Birol and wipe his forehead, and when she had te, she would dab a taste of it to his lips.

Camissa watched when she could, but without being obvious, and making sure to leave them time alone.

At noon, Mollie came to the kitchen to eat with everyone. She looked as if she had been awake for days.

Camissa brought her te and something to eat. "It is kind of you to sit with him, Mollie."

Mollie looked at her with a discerning eye, the kind of look that analyzed a person with a glance, the kind of eye a person could only get through a lifetime of dealing with people.

"Young lady, I'm not just sitting with him. I'm here to get him better. You might think he's gone, but he ain't."

She looked around the room at all of them. "I can see in your eyes what you think. But he's not finished telling tales. A man's not gone till that something special inside of him goes."

Camissa smiled warmly, wrapped her arms around Mollie. "He's lost too much blood. All the healing in the world won't help him now."

Mollie patted Camissa's hand and laughed, that same kind of wise old laugh that Tobias did when he knew something to be true. "Every time I see a pretty young thing like you, I find myself wishing I was young again. Wishing I could just smile and get a man to fawn over me. Or forget the top button of my blouse and have them follow me all day long, asking what chores I need to be done."

She sighed. "But then, when I think that, I remember the reasons why I can't go back." She leaned close to Camissa and whispered. "Because I know too much. Would plain drive me crazy to be that young and silly and know what I know now. What it would do is spoil it. Spoil all the fun. So why do it?" She laughed. "Not like I have a choice, but for the sake of wishin', well, there you have it."

Mollie sipped the last of her te and faced Camissa again. "Fact is, girl, that all the healing in the world is right inside a person."

She pointed her finger to her head and tapped on it. "Right in here. That's what heals a man—or a woman. Got to want to be healed. That's why I'm talking to him. That's why I'm telling him all those stories." Mollie got up from the table and pushed her chair in. "Don't you worry, he'll get better. Old Mollie will see to that."

After Mollie left the room, Camissa sat in silence and thought about what she had said. Suppose Mollie was right. Suppose that a person could heal themselves? She pondered that for a moment, then paced the room. Then suppose a person had help!

She almost ran to Tobias's room, slowing down only when she got close. Mollie was there, holding his hand and talking to him again. Camissa walked up to her. "Do you mind if I join you and just rest in the chair?"

"Don't mind at all. Just make a wish or two for old Tobias, would you?"

"I will," Camissa said and sat in the chair. She closed her eyes and focused, going deep within herself. She had her mind separated into neat little cottages lining a river bank. Each cottage had a special quality about it. She remembered exactly where the one she needed was, it was all the way at the end, where the river flooded the most.

When she got there, she opened the door and let "hope" come out. Then she called it to follow her, and when it did, she sent it to Tobias. She let it swirl about his head, enveloping him, then she sent it into him, deep into him. Infused him with it. Live, Tobias. You want to live. Mollie is waiting for you.

When she felt confident it was done, she opened her eyes and stared at Mollie—so dedicated. If ever two people deserved a chance to share lives, it was them. I hope you are right about this, Mollie.

72

CAPTAIN OF THE GUARD

Wisp ate breakfast, then prepared to leave. "I'm going to see the captain of the Harbor Guard, Adju. After that, I'll be back." He pointed a finger at him. "Stay here. Don't leave the house."

Shortly after he had gone, Gregor said he was going out for food. "Wouldn't do to have the guards see Bethia out every day, and buying so much food," he said.

When he hadn't returned after a while, Bethia began to worry. "Maybe I should go look for him."

"I think you should," Adju said. "I can stay here by myself."

"No, you come with me."

"Master Kender told me I had to stay here. If he comes back and finds me gone, I will be in big trouble."

Bethia stared at him.

"Besides," Adju said. "I will be safer here than outside."

Bethia patted his head. "All right, Adju. I won't be long. Stay inside and don't go anywhere."

##

After announcing himself at the Harbor Guard and convincing them he had an urgent message for the captain, they ushered him in to see Captain Darius Vespa. The captain greeted him when he entered, then motioned for him to sit. "My man tells me you have urgent news from Jattan Kir."

Wisp took the seat, waited for Darius to take his, then he leaned forward. "Jattan Kir has been captured. The emperor is dead."

Darius jumped up. "What?"

"The Highlands are gone too. Under Sethia's control."

Darius headed toward the door. "I've heard nothing." Disbelief drenched his words. "Guard, come here." When the guard showed up, Darius instructed him. "Go see Maziar and ask if he has heard anything about Jattan Kir."

Wisp rose. "I wouldn't do that, Captain."

"Why not?" Suspicion rang in his tone.

"Maziar is in with them."

Darius thought a moment before turning to his guard. "Wait until you hear from me," he said and started to close the door. "And say nothing to anyone about this," he added. Once back inside, he stared at Wisp. "How do you know this?"

Wisp decided to risk it all. "I'm the thief that Maziar is turning this city upside down to find."

Darius reached for his sword, but Wisp forestalled him, moving so quickly that he had a knife to the captain's throat before he could even draw it. "Please, Captain, I mean no harm. Just listen."

Darius nodded, staring at the knife against his neck from the corner of his eye.

Wisp knew he had better make this good. He had only one chance. "I was planning to rob Harun Bulta, not for the normal reasons, but because he had cheated me. None of that matters now; however, what matters is that while hiding in his shop, waiting for him to close so that I could rob him, Captain Arvin Maziar came in. I overheard the two of them talking about the whole thing—"

Vespa began to interrupt, but Wisp stopped him. "Then, someone else came to the door. It was a Sethian General, and he told them that the emperor was dead, the capital city was taken, and the Highlands taken. He said his troops would be here in two to three days. When they left, I killed Bulta, took money enough to compensate myself, and left."

Wisp removed the knife from his throat, though he stood close by.

"Why should I believe you?"

After much thinking, Wisp said. "What you should ask yourself is why not? Why would a thief come in here, and tell you he killed Merchant Bulta and overheard this nonsense?"

He stared at Darius. "I could have left the city. Gone to Jattan Kir, if it really isn't in the hands of Sethia, or to Sykor, or anywhere else, so why would I come here and tell you such a fantastic tale?"

Vespa looked at Wisp with suspicion. "Taking chances by putting your blade away aren't you?"

"I never intended to use it. Just needed to get my story told."

"So what is it you want? Why come tell me?"

"First thing I want is to ask for protection for a young boy and an older woman who were seen with me. They could be in danger.

If it isn't too much to ask, for myself as well, though I can manage on my own if I have to."

"And what else? Money?"

Wisp laughed. "No, my good Captain, I am not after money. If you heard the reports, you will note that nothing of value was taken from Merchant Bulta when he died, which is why they suspect his lovely wife.

Nothing of value was taken because I only took what he had cheated me out of, nothing more."

Wisp looked straight into the captain's eyes. "What I want is for you to stand tall for Khatara. Protect the city against Maziar and his Sethian allies until help arrives."

Vespa shook his head. "What help? Who—"

"I know this is difficult to understand, but I also have many allies, powerful allies, and they are coming to help. You will have to trust me."

Vespa thought, then shook his head. "I can't. I—"

"Two days!" Wisp said. "Trust me for two days. If you still don't believe me, turn me over to Maziar."

"You'll stay here, then?"

"First I must get my friends."

Vespa looked suspicious.

"No tricks, Captain. Send a patrol of guards with me. In fact, that would be much appreciated for protection."

Vespa narrowed his eyes, then nodded his head. "All right, thief. I don't know why, but I'm going to trust you. But for two days only."

Wisp reached out his hand to the captain. "You will not be sorry, sir. I thank you."

～

*V*espa decided to send three guards with Wisp. They made good time getting back to the house where he was staying. Wisp opened the front door, calling Adju's name as he did.

Adju came bouncing out of the back room, a smile covering his face, but terror in his eyes.

"It's all right," Wisp said, realizing the guards must have frightened him. Then he looked around. "Where's Bethia and Gregor?"

The boun—I mean, Gregor left early this morning and has not come back. Bethia went to look for him later, and now she is gone. I was worried."

Wisp ran to the curtains, peeked outside, then ran to the back window. "Hurry, Adju, and forget getting dressed. We've got to get out of here, now!" He turned to the guards who had come with him. "Follow me. We're going out the back," he said and headed for the kitchen window.

By the time Adju's feet had hit the alley, guards were coming at them from both ends, swords drawn. "Back inside, Adju. Quick!" He reached to pull him up, but halfway through the window, they grabbed him from the other side. At the same time, Wisp heard the front door burst open, and guards issuing orders. "Halt, no one move."

❧

*D*arstan walked slowly as he approached the column of Cergalans. These were the men who had fought with him before, fought for him, but he didn't know how they felt about him. Didn't know if they resented him or respected him.

Refugio bowed—a low bow, then pounded out a salute. "Welcome home, BlackWolf."

At least a thousand voices behind him echoed the greeting. It rang warm in Darstan's heart. He smiled, hugged Refugio. "Good to see you, old friend." He looked at Refugio and then down the line to Tesla. "Why are you here instead of at the pass or in Arangar?"

"Came back to be with family, BlackWolf. They missed me."

Darstan smiled. "I'm glad you did that, Tesla." Darstan walked a few steps and put his hand on Refugio's shoulder. "We've got a dark need right now, Commander. Worse trouble than Arangar or anything you could imagine. I'm going to need you with me. Do you think your family can spare you a while longer?"

"They will do what is right for Cergala."

Darstan patted his back. "This is what is right, believe me." He turned and walked the line until he got to Tesla again, finding a fond embrace for him and a few of the other soldiers, nodding to many he recognized but couldn't recall their names. A few rows back he saw a face he knew and walked to see him. "Benson, isn't it? We met in Arangar."

The young man beamed, pride covering his face. "I am honored you remember, BlackWolf."

Darstan smiled. "We're not so different as you might think. Both soldiers fighting for Cergala." He started to walk away, then returned. "You still think I'm not fit to lead?"

Benson got on his knees. "Forgive me, BlackWolf. I was a foolish young boy back then. You have helped me grow."

Darstan pulled him up. Hugged him. "I have never helped anyone grow, Benson. I've killed people. Broken families apart. Ruined dreams. But that is all destruction. Helping someone grow is a different talent, and it's one I haven't learned yet."

Darstan looked at the men staring at him. "You've heard me. I'm a demon. I kill, and I do it well." He let the words sink in. "Fact of the matter is, that there is a man—a demon—a god—no matter what you call him, he's bad, and he is about to be loosed on this world. And stories say he kills better than me."

Darstan stared at each soldier as he moved down the line, using Voice so that his words carried to all of them. "He will kill everyone he can if we don't stop him. This will be a big war. The biggest ever."

As he moved back to the front of the line, passing by Refugio and Tesla, he climbed atop a rock so that the men in the back could see him. "This world will need a lot of building once the war is over. I'm not the man to help you with that."

He let his gaze catch a few of the soldiers who looked frightened. "But you know me. Know what I *am* good at. Know I can kill. And kill well." Darstan smiled. "That, is where I can help you. With you at my side, we'll stop this demon. Kill his soldiers. Kill the creatures that follow him. Then, we'll kill him."

A soldier named Yago was the first to scream. "Black Wolf! Black Wolf!"

Soon the chant was taken up by Refugio and Tesla, then rows and rows of men until all two columns had joined in.

Aenaila smiled. Darstan had become a leader as well as a general. "When do we leave, Black Wolf?"

"Now," Darstan said. "Let everyone eat first, then we'll leave. We will be killing Sethians by this time tomorrow."

Aentarra interrupted him as he walked back to the house. "Nice speech. I particularly liked the part about killing Lukaan."

"Me, too," Darstan said. "Now all we have to do is deliver."

Aentarra laughed. Then laughed more. "You and I would make a fine team, Darstan. A fine team."

~

*I*n a cell underneath the barracks of the City Guard, Wisp and Adju sat in the dark, each in a separate cell. "I am afraid, Master Kender. What will they do to us?"

Wisp ran his hand along the walls, then across the bars of the cell feeling for any indication he could break out of there. "Don't worry,

Adju. We'll get out." They had stripped him and Adju both when they came in, took away the wire and pick he normally used to escape. "Search the ground. See if you feel anything sharp and thin. Anything at all."

Footsteps sounded in the corridor outside, then the door opened, bringing light in along with two guards. Captain Maziar accompanied them.

"So, the man who stole Merchant Bulta's jewels is finally caught."

"I have no idea what you're talking about," Wisp said.

"But you do know a one-handed man?"

"Not that I can recall."

Maziar paced. "Take the boy out."

The guards set their candles on a table in the hallway, then opened the cell next to Wisp and dragged Adju out. He was barefoot and had no shirt.

Maziar picked up a hammer from the table. "Put his right hand here," he said and pointed to a spot near the center of the table.

Wisp jumped to the cell, hands gripping the bars. "No! Don't do it! I'll tell you whatever you want."

Maziar stared at him, then turned to his guards. "I gave an order."

"No!" Wisp shouted. "What do you want? I'll give you anything." When Maziar showed no reaction, Wisp pleaded. "Captain, he is but a boy. If you want punishment, take it out on me. I'm the thief, smash my hand."

Maziar held up his hand, forestalling the guards. He walked to the front of Wisp's cell. Stared at him, smiling. "In due time, good man," he said, then returned to the table. "Hold him still."

Adju fought, scratching, kicking, even trying to bite, but they subdued him and held him still. The hammer struck, followed by a crunch of bones and a deafening scream. "Master Kender! Help!"

Wisp shook the bars. "Maziar, no! Take me!"

"Left hand," Maziar said, and raised his hammer as the guards yanked Adju's left hand to the table. He fought, and he screamed, but mostly he cried. "Master Kender!"

The hammer struck again, followed by the same scream and more crunching of bones. Adju fell to the ground when the guards let go of him, and he lay there, crying.

Wisp banged on the bars, punched the wall. Started crying himself. He couldn't even promise Adju he'd help him. *What have I done? I should have left him on the streets.*

He had to do something to stop this. "Maziar, what do you want to know? I'll tell you anything."

"I know you will, but I'm not done with your little friend. We'll let him rest before we start again." The guards threw him back in the cell, grabbed their candles, then left.

Adju crawled to the bars that separated his cell from Kender's. He tried talking but couldn't stop crying.

Wisp held him through the bars, kissed his head. "I'm sorry, Adju. I'm so sorry." He kissed his head some more, crying himself. "I don't know how, but I'll get you out of this."

"They are coming back for me." Adju managed through huge sobs.

"I'll protect you, Adju. Somehow I will."

"My pants ..."

Wisp wondered if he had soiled his pants. "Don't worry about your pants."

Adju fought to control his tears. "No, reach in my pants. I took the guard's knife before they smashed my left hand."

Wisp reached through the bars into the back of Adju's pants, pulling out a thin-bladed knife. He felt the shape of it and smiled.

"Will it work, Master Kender?"

He rubbed Adju's hair. "It's not perfect, Adju, but we'll make it work. Don't worry about that." *Now Maziar will pay. Oh, gods will he pay.*

73

PRISONS ARE DARK

Guardsman Bharva stumbled down the street holding his gut, trying to stop the bleeding. He banged on the door two houses away from where the City Guard patrol had ambushed them, killed his fellow soldiers, and taken that other one prisoner, along with the little boy. An older man answered the door, reaching out to support him as soon as he saw the situation.

"Get word to the captain at the Harbor Guard. Tell him to come here."

The man helped him to a chair, called for his wife to tend him, then hurried out the door. It was only several blocks to the barracks, and the man ran most of the way. Soon, Darius Vespa had dispatched men and had Bharva back in the safety of the barracks, his wounds being tended.

Vespa paced as he heard the story again. *So the thief was telling the truth. I didn't believe him.* He turned to a patrol leader standing beside him. "Get all soldiers called to duty. And send out word to all citizens nearby. Tell them the city is in danger. Bring any who are willing to fight. If they don't have weapons, we will provide them."

Vespa caught the patrol leader's sleeve as he headed for the door. "And tell the guards at the gate that these people are to allowed entry." As the man left, Vespa called again, more thoughts coming to him. "And we need carpenters and masons. I want these walls reinforced."

After he left Vespa comforted Guardsman Bharva, then headed toward his room. There was much more to do. Food had to be brought in. Animals. Fresh water. Fletchers to make arrows. So much to do, and if the thief was right, little time to do it.

*V*espa addressed the men in his guard, most of whom had come that morning or had been on duty since the night before. "This is a grave situation, men. The City Guard and the Perimeter Guard are now in the hands of an enemy. Captain Arvin Maziar is a traitor, and he will likely be coming here after us."

Murmurs and mumbling raced through the rows of men. "Believe me or don't, but ask Bharva, who is lying in a bed, maybe not getting up, because Maziar's men attacked him. Or ask Gezza or Kavier?" He paused. "But you can't ask them because Maziar's men killed them."

"What?" a soldier asked.

"Killed them? Why?" someone else called out.

"Killed them because they were protecting a man I had taken in as a guest. The one who told me about what is happening in our city." The men seemed interested now. "And there's worse news, men. The emperor is dead. Killed by Maziar and his allies."

"How can we stop them? There are too many." a soldier in the second row said.

"They have ten times our numbers, Captain."

Vespa nodded. "It is true. We are outnumbered, and badly, but we have help coming. Help from Sykor and Genda. Other places too."

"When will they get here?" somebody asked.

"How many?" another called out.

"Valid questions, all. But I don't know the answers. I just know that help is coming and it will be here soon."

He stared out over the crowd. "It is our duty to hold out until they get here. We cannot let them take the harbor and get the fleet." There seemed to be a concurrence among the men about that. "In fact, my orders to every man here are this: if I die, or if the barracks looks as if it will fall, burn the fleet. Destroy every ship."

A rousing cheer went up from the men. There was fear there, Vespa knew, but there was a lot of pride too. Pride in the fleet, pride in Khatara, and pride in being a Harbor Guard. *I just hope that thief was right about help coming.*

~

"Full sails!" Sennar called. "I want every deckhand that death hasn't bitten to be on board. Need to be in Khatara in less than two days."

"Pushin' mighty hard, Captain." The first mate had a question on his mind, but wouldn't ask it. "Storm looks bad for full sails."

"Ever seen a sea witch?" Sennar asked.

"Few times. When I've had too much vidda."

Sennar nodded. "I've seen them too, but I'm talkin' about real sea witches. The kind that can make that storm we're facin' seem like a sweet Gendan breeze."

He shook his head. "Can't say I have."

Sennar's head bobbed up and down as he walked. "Full sails!" he ordered again, then he turned to the first mate. "Just had one tell me to get to Khatara in two days. I plan on doin' it."

As the men scrambled across decks and climbed masts, the first mate's voice could be heard calling out the orders. "Full sails, men. Full sails or I'll have your hides nailed to the mizzen."

"Where will we shift to?" Aenaila asked. "We can't just show up in the city with nine thousand men."

"I know a spot north of the city," Mikkellana said. "Do you remember where you found Kella, and then shifted to Entiria?"

Aenaila appeared confused. "I remember the occasion, but you weren't there. How would you know that spot?"

Mikkellana laughed. "I forgot you and Darstan weren't with us when everyone else found out." She stared at Aenaila. "I am Kella."

"What?" Darstan said, jumping up.

Aenaila just stared. "Kella?"

"It's called Bonding, and—"

"And she nearly let me get killed to keep it a secret," Aentarra said. "Still don't think she would have revealed herself if not for—"

"Enough of your nonsense, Aentarra. We have no time for that."

Aenaila shook her head. "Well, if you have the Shift point, that spot will certainly do. It is remote enough."

While they waited for Refugio and Tesla to come, Darstan pondered. He tried to recall just when Kella had come to their rescue in Twin Forks. Had she been there when Magmar died? Could she have saved him?

The memory was hazy, and he couldn't be sure. He did remember how Tonka, the little boy felt so much better after sleeping with Kella. She must have healed him. And he recalled how Kella had saved so many in Entiria, though if she had transitioned to Mikkellana, she could have probably saved more. Most of all though, he remembered that night in Sethia, how Kella had been in the camp when the Wolfen attacked. How Kella—if she had been Mikkellana—could have prevented him from getting his hand cut off. That, was a memory that wasn't hazy. It was as clear as if it were yesterday.

Darstan glared at her. How does it feel to be a cripple, Mikkellana? As he stared back at his hand, his missing hand, the one he could still feel now and then, the one that still ached now and then, he wondered what it would be like to have it back. To be whole again. There always seems to be someone to kill, he thought, then tried to smother that emotion. He had spent enough time hating people of late.

Aentarra paced. "Once we arrive, if we're not too tired, I'll take Mikkellana to Sykor." She looked to Aenaila. "You'll have to go with me, so you can take me to the harbor afterward."

"Good. After that, I will get Kender, Adju, and Gregor then join Darstan."

"Here comes Refugio," Marro said, then he and Genea hugged Aenaila, sending her off with tears. "Take care of her, BlackWolf."

Darstan embraced them both. "I'll keep her safe."

Refugio and Tesla carried Mikkellana down to the camp where the soldiers waited. Once there, they all joined hands, completing the connection with a link to Mikkellana, who effected the Shift.

The rift was loud, with so many coming through, and the smell, this time of berries, was strong. Darstan stepped through first, checking to ensure no trap awaited. "Good," he said, then let go of Aenaila as his feet grounded. The rest soon followed until all of them were safe in Khatara.

Mikkellana slumped, not able to even sit. "This wore me out more than I thought it would."

Aentarra supported her. "I'm tired too, but there is enough to get us to Sykor, and we might as well do that now." She reached toward Aenaila. "Ready?"

Aenaila grabbed her hand, then they shifted to Talanvar's library, where a quick search brought Birol and another servant to help Mikkellana to her room. Birol ordered food and drinks for them while they waited. Aentarra and Aenaila rested.

"I have never been this exhausted, Aentarra."

"It will wear you out, especially as many men as we just moved." Aentarra sipped on water and ate a piece of fruit. "Don't worry, though. If you can provide the Shift point, I can take us back to Khatara."

They rested a few more moments, then Aentarra took her hand, got the Shift point and took them to the Harbor Guard, stepping out into the square just outside the door. The square was filled with guards, Maziar's guards, and they opened fire with arrows as soon as Aentarra stepped through. She wove a shield, and though a weak one, it afforded them the protection they needed until they could get inside the gates.

Darius came to greet them, a thousand questions on his mind, but Aentarra had no patience for him. "Captain, all you need to know is that help is coming. I have ten thousand men coming by sea, and they should be here soon, and we have ten thousand more on the northern edge of the city."

"That's good," Darius said, "but it won't be good enough. Maziar has at least that many and now I've heard he has been reinforced by Sethian troops. Maybe twice that number."

Aentarra smiled. "We have a few more tricks, Captain. Trust me."

Aenaila was leaning on Aentarra for support. "Get her somewhere she can rest," Aentarra said. "And get her food and water."

"Not time for that. I need to get to the house."

"You're not strong enough," Aentarra said.

"I can make it. It's not far, and once I'm there, I can rest a few moments then bring them back."

Aentarra nodded. "All right then." She turned to Darius. "Show me what you have for defenses, Captain. I might be able to reinforce them."

⁓

$\mathcal{A}$enaila rested for a moment, then formed the image of her house and shifted. When she stepped through the rift into her room, several patrols of guards awaited, knocking her unconscious before she could do anything.

"Take her to Maziar," one of the guards said.

"Shame to waste such beauty. Maybe—"

"To Maziar," the other one said. "We need to wait here for the other one."

⁓

$\mathcal{W}$isp used the knife Adju had taken from the guard, and with a little difficulty managed to open the cell door. He moved over to Adju's cell and got him out also, then relocked both cells.

After checking around, he determined that he couldn't get out; the only door was bolted from the outside. He retreated to the corner to devise a strategy.

"We'll have to wait until they come back, Adju. And it's going to be dangerous, so listen to my plan. You're going to have to be braver than you've ever been."

They stayed in the corner, waiting for someone to come. The only way he could get out was if a guard came in, and Wisp was able to conceal them both and sneak around the guard to get out. After what seemed like days, but was probably only hours, he heard footsteps.

"Sh. Quiet, Adju. I'm going to conceal us so don't pull away from me. As long as I'm holding you, no one can see us. But remember, they can hear us."

"I know."

The door opened, some light from candles showing as three guards walked in. Wisp went on alert. They had someone as a prisoner. As they moved near, he could see it was Aenaila. Rats blood!

One of the guards walked to Adju's cell and held the candle close. "Captain, he's gone!" He then ran to Wisp's cell and checked it as well. "Both gone!"

Maziar quickly shut the door, then looked around, hand gripping his blade. "See if they are locked."

The guard checked. "This one is," he said, then moved back to Adju's. "This one too."

Maziar smiled. "He's in there. Remember what our friend told us? I guess he was right."

Wisp put his hand over Adju's mouth, hoping to muffle the sound of his breathing, still a little labored due to his pain. He thought of rushing them, but with three of them and only one knife, he might not get them all in time, and he couldn't risk Aenaila's life. Worse, suppose they caught him or killed him, then Adju and Aenaila would be at their mercy.

What to do? If they thought he was still in the cell, what would they do? They must think he is still in the cell. Thank the Lady he locked them. He patted Adju's head, soothing him. Praying he could keep quiet. He could feel him breathing heavy. Knew he must be in terrible pain. Oh, but he was going to make Maziar suffer.

"Tie her to the shackles," Maziar said. "Then she can't leave."

Gregor! Wisp thought. He told them about her being able to Shift and about my cloaking. That's how they know.

Once Aenaila was secure, the first guard reached for his knife. Wisp prayed it wasn't the guard Adju had taken it from. He pulled it out, used it to cut her clothes off, not being careful about bleeding her some while he did. Wisp started to go after them, but Adju stepped on his foot, a warning. He rubbed Adju's head again. Reassuring him.

"Are you here, thief? Still watching? Good. I hope you enjoy this as much as we will." Maziar nodded to the first guard, who undid his pants, dropping them to the floor. The second guard began pawing Aenaila's breasts.

Adju stepped on Wisp's foot again, then buried his head in his stomach. Wisp analyzed the situation. The guard with the knife had his pants down, and the second guard had no knife, only a sword, not easy to wield in these tight quarters.

That left Maziar. Wisp could get to him in time, though he hated to kill him. He wanted so much to torture that man. Can't risk it, he thought. Have to act now.

He gently moved Adju aside, slowly, then grasped the knife in his right hand, while holding onto Adju with his left to keep him cloaked. It would take a while to creep across the floor silently, and he didn't have the time. The one guard was about to dishonor Aenaila. He couldn't let that happen.

Just as the first guard pulled her to him, Wisp let go of Adju with his left hand and lunged for the first guard, jamming the blade into the man's right kidney. Wasting no time, he spun, switching grips on the knife and plunged it into Maziar's neck.

Maziar's hands flew to his neck, while he fell to the floor. Wisp though had time to grab the blade from Maziar's belt. Now, armed with two blades, he turned to face the second guard, who had his sword drawn and was coming for him. Blood covered his hands, and he didn't want to risk throwing it for fear it would slip.

Circumstances afforded him no room for error. Wisp cloaked, ducking to the floor as he did and crawled toward the guard, who would likely think he moved to either side. The man swung wildly to his left, then as he brought the sword around to go right, Wisp shoved the blade into his groin.

Before he finished screaming, the second blade cut his throat. Wisp popped up, moved two steps to the first guard and stabbed straight into the man's face, just below the eye. The knife slid off of bone and pushed up into his eye socket, finishing him.

Wisp spun around, went to Maziar, but he was down, no threat, though he was dying. *Thank the Lady he is still alive.* Wisp took the man's pants down, then cut off his balls as Maziar screamed.

Adju laughed until he started crying again.

Wisp ran to Aenaila, hugged her. Cried with her. "Oh, gods, I'm sorry. I'm so sorry."

Aenaila had her legs crossed, embarrassed, ashamed. "Get me out of here. Hurry, please." Then she saw Adju, his hands raised, all bloody. "Adju! What happened?"

He was crying. "They smashed my hands, Mistress Aenaila. It hurts real bad." He moved toward her but kept his head turned. "Can you help me? Can you make it stop hurting?"

Wisp undid her shackles and got her clothes to cover up with. Though they were torn, it offered some protection.

She hugged Adju, careful not to touch his hands. "Don't worry, Adju. I'll get you fixed." She looked to Wisp, a question on her face. "Kender, I am too weak to get us out of here now. Too weak to even help Adju. What are we going to do? More guards will be here soon."

"I don't know, Aenaila. Just stay together for now. And hope no one comes until you can get us out of here."

74

RELIEF COMES AT LAST

Darstan paced the line, casting glances every few moments to the spot where they came through the rift. *Where is she? Can't be taking this long?*

He ran through all of the reasons why it might take so long, and kept coming up with the same logical answer—she was exhausted from the shift and had to rest. Despite that, he couldn't shake the feeling that something was wrong.

"Refugio, take command. I'll be back soon."

Darstan formed the image in his mind of Aenaila's house, then shifted. A rift opened, and Darstan stepped through, two full patrols of guards waiting for him. The guard nearest him stabbed with his sword, but Darstan showed no effect.

He focused on his power, and a column of BlackFire shot from his arm, cutting a swath through the guards in front of him, and at the same time, his body erupted in flames. The guardsmen moved back, fear on their faces. Darstan took advantage, cutting one down with a focused strike.

He raised his left arm to defend against a sword strike, and when the sword hit, it activated the blade the metalsmith had built into the shield. With a quick reflexive action, he jabbed and gutted the man. Five of the guards were now down, and Darstan's body was aflame. He moved amongst them, fear thinning their ranks. Several of the guards stabbed him, or he thought they did, but he felt nothing. Driven by anger, he let fire rage, sweeping the room, and he followed up with clean strikes to the gut and neck with his blades.

Soon, he was the only one standing, though the house was aflame. A noise from the other room caught his attention, and he entered, caution with him. Gregor sat in the corner, choking back smoke.

"Where are they, Gregor? What happened?" Suspicion tainted Darstan's voice.

He sat there, mumbling, head down. "Gone. Maziar took them."

"Where?"

"Barracks." He lifted his head, stared at Darstan. "I'm sorry. I—"

Darstan threw him a knife. "Do it, Gregor. Don't make me do it for you."

Gregor looked at him with pleading eyes. "Darstan, I—"

"Do it, Gregor. Now!" Darstan glared at him. "I swear if I have to do it, you will regret it."

Gregor took the knife, stared at it, then pressed it to his wrist, head turned.

"Wisp says the throat is faster," Darstan said.

Gregor nodded, cast one more pleading glance at Darstan, but saw nothing. He placed the knife against his neck and cut quick and deep. Blood gushed out in spurts, not an even flow. It covered his neck and shoulders. Gregor sunk to the floor, blood pooling on the hard planks.

Darstan waited until he was sure it was done, then he raced for the front door. He didn't have a Shift point to the barracks, so he was going to have to run there. He hoped that someone would come to put out the fire, though with the city in turmoil as it was, it might burn the whole block, or worse.

The streets were crowded, mostly with guards, but they paid no attention to him as he moved through the streets. As he was going through the merchant's district, a patrol leader spotted him, recognizing his face or his missing hand.

"Halt!" a guardsman called.

Darstan paid him no mind and continued on his way, though he kept a wary eye on the man.

"Halt!" he called again, and this time he issued orders for the men to draw bows.

Darstan spun around, shot a column of fire straight at them. As soon as he did, he turned and continued his race to the barracks. If Maziar had Wisp, there was no telling what he would do.

~

"How long before you can shift?" Wisp asked.

Aenaila focused, concentrated, but nothing came. "A while still, Kender. I can't even call up a Shift point."

A moan from Adju turned their attention elsewhere. "I don't suppose there's anything you can do for him," Wisp asked.

She shook her head, though she held Adju close, patting his back. "Won't be long, Adju. I'll get us out of here."

"Do it before they come back, Mistress Aenaila. Please?"

"I will, Adju. I promise."

Wisp hugged both of them. "Nobody is coming through that door alive; I can tell you that."

~

*D*arstan approached the barracks with caution, scanning the walls for archers and the side streets for reinforced patrols. Ten guards held the front gate on the outside. No doubt there would be more inside. Plenty more.

"Halt!" a guard called as Darstan drew near.

"Came to see a friend," Darstan said, and he didn't stop.

"Halt!" the guard called again, this time drawing steel. Three others with him drew swords as well.

Darstan kept moving toward them, though he slowed his advance so he could judge the defenses better. "Here to see Captain Maziar."

The guards looked at each other. Mentioning Maziar must have thrown them off. "Stay where you are. Captain Maziar is inside and not to be disturbed."

Darstan was close enough now. Archers might be a problem if they were positioned on the walls, but no one else. "Open the gate."

Six more guards drew steel. He was within striking distance. "Halt!"

One of the guards in the rear stared at Darstan's missing hand. "It's him, the one-handed one." His alert sent the four guards in the front line into attack mode.

Darstan let the first guard's sword strike his arm, activating the blade the metalsmith had built into his shield, which he quickly used to jab into the man's throat. Then he called his fire to deal with the others. A bolt of Lightning shattered the gate; where it had come from Darstan didn't know. He had never called Lightning before.

More guards came from both sides and the front, but Darstan was now an inferno—walking death. He moved to the main barracks, killing everyone who got in his way, setting everything afire. "Find me Maziar, and I'll let you live," he told them, but no one listened. Halfway through the first floor, one of the guards talked, telling Darstan that Maziar was with prisoners on the floor below.

Darstan glared at him. "Leave here. Leave Khatara, too; otherwise, you'll be dead." He continued until he found the door leading downstairs. It was a large oak door with bronze hinges. Darstan focused, then blasted it with Lightning, his new friend, and started down the stairs.

~

The whole building seemed to shake, walls trembling. "That has to be Darstan," Aenaila said. "There's no one else it could be."

"I hope so," Wisp said. "But he might just as easily kill us if he comes through that door."

"Get us in the cells," Aenaila suggested.

Wisp opened the cell door, and they helped Adju inside, then huddled against the stone wall. Outside, the explosions grew louder. The door leading into them blew open, tearing stone from the walls and spraying it across the room. A bright light lit the dark room, and a magnificent warmth filled the room as Darstan entered.

"Darstan!" Wisp called. "Darstan, it's me."

Darstan turned, saw Wisp, and Adju, and Aenaila. He focused on calming himself, and when he finally got control, he ran to them. "I was worried," he said and reached to hug everyone.

"Careful of Adju," Wisp said. "They nearly killed him." He nodded to the hands. "Broke the bones in the backs of both of them."

Darstan fumed, balling his fist. "Don't worry, Adju, we'll get you healed." He then turned to Aenaila and Wisp. "You all right?"

Wisp nodded. Aenaila cried. "Thank the gods you are here, Darstan." She threw her arms around him, and it was then Darstan noticed her torn clothes and the bruises on her.

He pushed back, stared. "Did they do this to you?"

Wisp grabbed his arm. "It's all right. I was able to stop them."

Darstan's body shook, started smoldering, skin turning red with heat. "Let's go. I'll get you to safety, then ..."

"Then, what?" Wisp asked.

Darstan stared at a blank wall. "Then they will all pay." He held out his hand for them to grab, and once they connected, he shifted to Talanvar's library.

*D*arstan stepped through the rift first, still holding on to Wisp, who was carrying Adju. "Let's get him to Mikkellana. She should be able to heal him."

Birol met them as they made their way to the stairs. "He's hurt bad," Wisp said. "Is Mikkellana upstairs?" At Birol's nod, Wisp climbed the steps, careful not to bump Adju.

Darstan and Aenaila went with him, moving quickly to Mikkellana's room. She was sitting up in bed when they entered. Camissa sat in a chair nearby.

"It's Adju!" Wisp said. "Hurt bad."

Mikkellana struggled to get straighter, leaning forward as she did. "What happened?"

"Guards in Khatara. They smashed his hand with a hammer."

Tears were rolling down Adju's cheek, though he sobbed and sniffled, trying to hold them back. Mikkellana reached for him, gently touching his hands. Adju winced, pulling back.

"Don't hurt him!" Darstan said, and moved to stand in front of her.

Mikkellana glared. "I'm looking to see what needs fixing. When the bones get broken like that, it can be difficult."

"Just fix him good."

Mikkellana stopped, staring at Darstan. "You don't like me, do you, Darstan?"

There was no hesitation. "Not one bit."

"Because of the hand?"

He paused. "At first, maybe. But now it's because of many things. The hand. Gregor. What happened to Aenaila and Adju." He shook his head. "All of it."

"I'll take the blame for your hand, but the rest—"

"It's all your fault. You and Aentarra and Lukaan, the whole bunch of you people."

"Don't forget that you're one of us people."

"I might be cursed with some of your blood or somebody's blood, but I'll never be one of you." He turned to go. "Heal him good. That boy doesn't deserve this."

"Don't threaten me—"

Darstan spun to face her again. "I'll threaten whoever I want. And by the way, how does it feel to be a cripple?" He didn't wait for an answer, just left.

Aenaila reached to stop him, but he shook her off, then he leaned over and kissed her cheek. "I'll be back."

"Where are you going?"

"Khatara must pay for this."

~

Commander Shill saw the fires burning over Khatara long before he made the city proper. He knew instantly that there was trouble. He increased the pace of the march and sent a half a strike force ahead at an even faster pace. The Master would not accept failure at this point. At any point. By nightfall, the fire in the barracks had been controlled, and Khatara was now reinforced with thirty thousand soldiers under Shill's command.

"Where is your captain?" Shill asked the patrol leader.

"Dead, along with his two sub-commanders. The captain of the Perimeter Guard is alive, though. Name is Shamada, but he's in the north preparing his defenses."

Shill appeared confused. Defending the north? "Defending against what?"

"An army, sir. Reports put them at ten thousand men. We don't know where they came from. Never saw their uniforms before."

Shill shook his head. It seemed impossible, but he'd not question the man at this point. Would have to see for himself. "And the Harbor Guard?"

"Holding out, sir. We can't break them. They got reinforcements by sea, and last I heard they had a witch defending the barracks, too."

The Sethian commander tried to digest all that he had learned since arriving in Khatara. Things had changed drastically in a few short days, and not for the better. "How many men under Captain Shamada?"

The patrol leader paused, seemed to be lost in thought. "Mettu," he called to another guard standing nearby. "How many men does Shamada have?"

"At least twenty thousand," he said. "Half of them got no experience, though."

Shill nodded. Twenty thousand in the north. Another fifteen thousand to throw against the Harbor Guard if his numbers were correct, and now, with his reinforcements thirty thousand to divide amongst them. A formidable force even against the resistance they had somehow managed to muster. He ordered his two best scouts to inspect the city's defenses and report back to him.

The river bordered Khatara on the west, and he had just come in from the east, which was secure. All he had to worry about was the north and the harbor.

By the next day, the scouts returned with the information Shill needed. He consulted his advisors, then dispatched ten thousand men to support Shamada in the north and twelve thousand under his own Captain Jeffern in the south. He opted to keep a reserve of eight thousand as a stabilizing force in the city under his command. They would all be in position by nightfall.

Commander Shill sipped a glass of Khataran wine while he waited for his dinner. He smiled. Tomorrow he would show these people what Sethians were made of.

75

THE NORTHERN BORDER

A rift opened north of Khatara, and Darstan stepped through into the middle of a raging battle. Instinct brought his hand and arm up to cover his head, and a blow from a sword activated the plate in his arm. Another blade scraped his side, triggering him to erupt into flames.

An area cleared around him, spreading wider as the flames grew. Gripping his emotions firmly, he searched for the Cergalans, but when he saw no uniforms he recognized, he let loose his powers. BlackFire shot from his arm, and a wall of it seemed to rise from the ground all around him. Screams from Khataran soldiers could not stop it as it cut a swath through their ranks, sending them into retreat, despite the admonitions of superiors.

When Darstan saw a clear path, he headed for the Cergalan line, greeting Refugio with a weary smile. "Testing me, Commander?"

"Sorry, BlackWolf. They attacked with an overwhelming force. We could not hold them."

Darstan patted his back. "No harm," he said, but then rubbed his side, looking at the blood on his hands. "Although I could use some bandages. One of them got me."

Refugio signaled a nearby soldier. "Healer for BlackWolf. Hurry!"

"What I could use more is some water, Refugio. A lot of it."

Refugio leaned to the side. "Water!"

Darstan looked to the Khatarans, still in retreat, but showing initial signs of regrouping. "We don't have much time, Refugio. Gather your advisors. We need a plan, and quickly."

"Get Tesla and Borlo here," Refugio said to an aide, "and make sure someone alerts us if the Khatarans advance."

"Yes, sir," the aide said, then saluted and ran off.

Once Tesla and Borlo arrived, Darstan described the situation to them. He drew a fair representation of the city on a chart, delineating their position, the docks, and the river and desert borders on the east and west. "How many men are we facing, Refugio?"

"Tesla can tell you better," he said.

"My guess is close to thirty thousand. I can have Tiko scout them if you need to know better."

Darstan remembered Tiko from Cergala. He was widely known for his ability to estimate troop size down to the finest detail. His prowess had grown to near legendary status. "Your guess is good enough for me," Darstan said. "It served us well in Arangar."

Tesla nodded.

"Do you have any idea what they might send against the docks?"

Refugio accepted a large flask of water from the soldier who brought it, then handed it to Darstan. "They would have scouted it, BlackWolf. Probably sent the same proportion of men they did here—maybe three to one." His brow wrinkled as he said it, then he added a correction.

"Perhaps more to the docks, since it is fortified. That's what I would do."

"It would be nice to know," Tesla said. "We don't want to base a strategy on the numbers we have here, then find out they've got a lot more."

Darstan frowned. "I don't have a Shift point at the docks." He paced, drank more water, then shook his head. "We can wait no longer, though. I'm going to trust that Sennar got there in time, so we'll move accordingly."

"But, sir ..." Refugio seemed concerned.

"Yes, Commander?"

"It will be tough making headway in the city, especially if they control it all. With the docks, we can put pressure on their rear, but without controlling the docks, we'll be at a disadvantage."

"Don't worry. I have faith in them." Darstan smiled. "Now, here's what we'll do."

For the next hour, Darstan laid out his plans. He had almost finished when a messenger said the forward scouts had spotted movement from the Khataran side. "Guess that ends any debate about the plan," Darstan said. "Gentlemen, let's go."

The terrain was slightly rolling, with few trees. Mostly an open valley that had not seen water in a thousand years. To his right, over a small embankment, lay the Khataran River, and to the left, the paucity of the endless desert, which legends claim was protected by the laughing wolves. Khataran soldiers would not venture there, no matter how many medals they had for bravery.

That left the direct route through the valley into Khatara, and they had crammed almost thirty thousand men into the geographic funnel that guarded the city.

Darstan positioned Borlo with his archers on the hills along the river, a strong deterrent to any forces moving against his right flank. On the left flank, though, he made his boldest move, daring the gods themselves by crossing the sacred grounds. He sent almost half of his men with Tesla—four thousand of them—to attack the enemy's right flank from the region of the laughing wolves. That left him only a few thousand men to hold against nearly thirty thousand in the center, taking the brunt of the attack.

Refugio moved the men slowly up the valley, timing it to coincide with the positioning of Tesla and Borlo on the right and left flanks. Before they were all in place, however, the Khatarans charged.

~

*D*arius braced himself for defeat, but he didn't want to go like this. Dreaded the thought of Khatara falling to traitors. Nearly thirty thousand of the enemy lay outside the barracks, crowding the square, filling the streets, and perched in windows of houses and nearby buildings. They seemed to be evenly split between Khataran and Sethian soldiers, and they were fully prepared—armed with siege equipment and an abundance of archers.

They could keep him pinned down for days if they wanted. More than enough time to effect a siege. To counter that, would cost him men. A lot of men. Calculating his forces, he came up with four, maybe five thousand soldiers, and another five hundred volunteers from the citizen rank. A defense like that would last a few days at most.

Sighing, he resigned himself to the inevitable. Khatara was his city, his home, but not for long. He would, however, defend it to the death. A clamor from the wall brought him to the top, where he saw them massing for another charge.

"Archers, prepare!"

They had been busy making arrows for days and had amassed a significant supply. Enough to cause a lot of trouble for those traitors. "Ready!" he said, holding up his arm. Then, when they got within range, he dropped his arm. "Fire!"

A volley of arrows flew into the Khataran force in the streets, dropping many of them. His arm came down again, and another volley swept through their ranks. The third volley didn't take nearly as many, as they had raised shields and taken cover under nearby buildings.

Darius frowned. That was likely his first, and last, surprise attack. As he studied the situation and the horrendous odds he faced, he wondered why he had ignored his father's advice to become a jeweler. Even a farrier would do right now.

Retaliation came swiftly and unmercifully. Thousands of arrows flew over the walls, many of them aflame, and struck houses and buildings, as well as soldiers and animals that had been brought in for food. Darius ordered them to seek shelter, but the barrages proved to be both relentless and unexpected.

"Raise shields and brace the walls," Darius ordered. "They will be coming for us soon, and we need to hold these gates." Even as he issued the orders, he heard the battering rams against the front gates. Where were the reinforcements?

~

Commander Shill watched from a vantage point high above the valley. With the river on his left and the sacred desert on his right, he had only two choices: behind him lay the city of Khatara and ahead, the valley. His best scouts had reported already that the bulk of the enemy was moving to flank his right side, going through the desert where they knew the Khatarans would not venture. Another contingent, what appeared to be archers, were positioning themselves on the hills overlooking the river. They would likely have a strong guard for the front lines and archers in the rear. The rest of them were in the valley, and the scouts had estimated their numbers to be less than four thousand. Why would they be so foolish? Was their commander that green?

It was obvious that their general was trying some variation of an envelopment maneuver, but he had left himself far too few men to effect it properly. Shill shook his head. Victory was to be savored at any rate, but he preferred to earn it in a hard-fought battle, not a slaughter.

He knew that at least one of them had powers similar to the small gods in Sethia, but he also knew that they could not last long. If they pressured him, he would eventually succumb.

Leaving ten thousand men to guard the rear, Shill issued orders to drive the others forward. Upon his command, twenty thousand Khatarans and Sethians rushed into the valley. It would not take long to destroy the few men they had, then, once he took command of the front, he could turn his attention to the others, crushing them in a pincer movement. Many would die today.

~

*D*arstan let them advance, holding Refugio and his men steady until the Khatarans were almost upon them. When they got within a hundred paces of the line, Darstan let loose, spraying their lines with fire. It was a tactic he had used with great success in Arangar.

Once the enemy soldiers faced fire, discipline and order fell apart. And once order was gone, he could advance and clear the ranks. Hundreds of the enemy burned, their screams a chilling sound. Darstan watched, waiting for them to break ranks. This time, however, they stayed in rank, stayed organized. Worse, they continued their advance, the commanders from the rear driving them forward relentlessly.

Wearing a worried frown, Darstan unleashed a wall of BlackFire that rolled ahead on a course to intercept them right in the center.

He smiled. This would show them who held the upper hand. Darstan's smile soon turned, though, for the Khatarans absorbed the casualties without missing a beat and continued the advance at an even faster pace. Instead of panicking, as he had expected, they had regrouped and charged. He stared, appalled. He had killed hundreds. Maybe thousands. What would it take to stop them? "Refugio! Form the lines. Prepare for engagement."

The Khatarans charged, rushing through the wall of BlackFire amidst screams and valor and chants that promised the rewards of an afterlife.

Refugio and his men drew swords, bracing for an attack. Darstan waited until they got within fifty paces, then he focused his strength and searched deep within himself. He took a trip to the palace in his mind, where he quickly found the ColdFire. Soon, his body heated to an inferno, then, it started reversing, turning cold. With his eyes open, but in a fixed trance, he issued the ColdFire. It exploded from his arm, spreading out in a wave, almost like a storm cloud, but blue mist in the shape of flames.

When it hit, many bodies shattered as if they were fine crystal. Others froze, cracked, then fell apart. The ColdFire ran through the ranks of soldiers as if it were an ancient plague, taking many thousands in one sweep. Panic set in, row upon row of soldiers succumbing to fear.

Commander Shill advanced from the rear to restore discipline, once again forcing the remaining ones to attack.

A series of flags, used as signals, rose from all over the field and soon, the Khatarans had completely regrouped, functioning as a cohesive unit. Darstan tried to call the ColdFire again, but this time he collapsed instead. Refugio rushed to him, but couldn't wake him. "Hold the guard, men! I have to get BlackWolf to safety."

~

*S*ennar cursed and threatened until he could barely speak, and it finally had an effect. On the day he promised Aentarra he would be there, he looked across the bow at Khatara's harbor. "Thank the sea gods for something," he said and wiped his brow. He did not want to think of the consequences of being late.

"Smoke from the harbor," the first mate said.

Sennar took the looking glass and peered through it. Not only smoke but in the pre-dawn light, he could see flames tickling the sky above the fortress. "Sharpen your swords, mates. And get those harpoons ready. We'll be spearing more than whales today."

He turned to the first mate. "Send a signal to the others. We're joining a battle in mid-stream, so landing might be testy." As the mate started to go, Sennar added. "Tell 'em to keep a skeleton crew on deck and send everyone else in on the small boats." Sennar's cackle cut through the morning mist. "Tell 'em to arm to the teeth. This one is for all the fish."

By the time the sun showed its full face, Sennar and half of his men had reinforced the barracks to the delight of Darius. With five thousand fresh troops already there, and another four or five thousand coming, he would breathe much easier.

"Do your men know how to shoot?" he asked Sennar.

"Got no archers," Sennar said, "but we do know how to spear a whale." He laughed as he held up a long harpoon, its barbed point a chilling prospect for a victim. "Put us on the wall, Captain. When the rest of my men get here, we'll show them what it means to fight a seaman."

Darius had no time to answer, as rousing cheers rose from the back of the barracks. "Malakai. Malakai!" A thousand men joined the chorus, welcoming the pirate into the fray.

Darius smiled for the first time in days. He had heard that Malakai was dead. This was one rumor he was glad had been spread false. He turned as the big man stepped inside, then held out his hand to greet him. "You're a welcome sight, my friend. My name is Captain Darius."

Malakai grabbed him by the shoulders and pulled him into a big bear hug. "I imagine I'll be more welcome once I kill a few dozen of those men at your gates, mate. So get me some ale, then get me a few men to guard my flanks, and let me at them."

Sennar laughed until his sides hurt. "It's not even time for lunch yet, pirate, and you're wanting ale."

"Can't go killing men on an empty stomach, Jacopo. Just isn't right."

The men that had gathered around laughed, the first time in a while for most of them. Darius could see the confidence building in them. He smiled. The odds were still horribly against them, but confidence was what won battles. Maybe they had a chance after all.

Sennar clanked his mug against the two held by Darius and Malakai. In the middle of preparing a toast, he suddenly stopped, sniffing the air. "Smell that?" he asked. "Smells like figs."

Just then a rift opened, and he and Malakai both moved aside quickly. Aentarra stepped through, warily eyeing everyone. Darius held his ground, confused as much as curious. "Who is in charge here?" Aentarra asked.

"I am. Who are you?" Darius asked, though his voice held more fear than brusqueness.

"I am your new commander, Commander." She smiled at her cleverness, then turned to Sennar. "Hello, Jacopo. I see you and the pirate made it."

Sennar bowed. "Wouldn't have missed it, My Lady."

A volley of arrows flew by, striking some soldiers only a few paces from where Aentarra stood. "Enough of this!" she said. "Captain, open the gates at my signal." She turned to Sennar. "You and Malakai get your men to support me."

A worried look came to Darius's face. "Where are you going?"

"To kill some insolent people," she said, then turned to face Sennar and Malakai. "Let's go."

When the gates opened, the Khatarans tried flooding in, but a wall of fire met them, cutting through their ranks as if they were fields of wheat. From atop the walls, Sennar's men harpooned the Khatarans, the wide-tipped point digging huge gashes into their flesh, then, when pulled back, ripping large chunks from their bodies. Men screamed, some on fire, others bleeding profusely.

The Khataran commander ordered them to focus on Aentarra, which angered her more than anything. She wove a shield around herself, then, as she moved amongst them, she suddenly lowered it while she struck with fire or Lightning before closing it again.

Before long, the besiegers were in retreat, and Aentarra organized a force to track them down. Suddenly, though, she felt the unmistakable presence of ColdFire being used. And close by. That fool! She turned to Sennar. "Take charge. I must leave for a while." After that, she shifted.

~

The rift opened just behind the Cergalan line, not far from where Refugio was tending to Darstan. Aentarra surveyed the scene with a glimpse, then shifted to a spot on the hill left of the Khatarans. The moment she appeared, she issued a wall of BlackFire against the Khataran flank. While they were reeling from that, she attacked with bolts of Lightning all through their ranks, each strike in a different place, designed to instill fear more than damage them.

Even in their panic, though, Shill was able to drive them forward. Aentarra re-evaluated, then erected a shield between the Khatarans and the Cergalans separating them before continuing with her assault from the rear. The Khatarans were now trapped, unable to move forward and blocked by fire to the rear.

Once fear had a firm grip on them Aentarra let the shield drop, allowing the Cergalans to move in for the slaughter.

As this was going on, the archers had begun firing on the ten thousand troops that Shill had left in reserve, and the four thousand men Darstan had sent to flank them from the desert side advanced as well. It soon turned into a full-scale rout, with Sethians and Khatarans scrambling to reach safety inside the city.

Exhausted, Aentarra went to Darstan, who was just regaining consciousness. She stood above him, frowning. "I warned you about that, boy. You can't use ColdFire unless you know you are going to win, right then. Try it again, and it will kill you."

Darstan sat up, head still groggy. "Thanks, I—"

"Don't apologize. I didn't do it to save you." She glared at him. "If you're strong enough, get up and get your men ready. It's time to show the Khatarans they chose the wrong side."

"What do you mean, My Lady?" Refugio asked.

Aentarra cast another glare at Refugio, but then turned to Darstan and grabbed his cheeks. "Drive them to me, boy. Drive them like they are sheep. I will be at the docks waiting." With that, she shifted.

Refugio looked as if he had seen the goddess herself. "Orders, BlackWolf?"

Darstan smiled. "You heard her, Refugio. I'm just a pawn in this game." He stared at his commander. "You only thought you should be afraid of me," he said, then laughed. "Little did you know I was protecting you."

Refugio bowed low, then said a prayer, and wished he had stayed with his family.

～

For the rest of the day, Darstan and Refugio drove Khatarans through the city streets, funneling them toward the docks and into the waiting arms of Aentarra. The Cergalans took five or six streets at a time, with Darstan clearing a path down one, then attacking the rear of any force moving against them. Before long, the bulk of the Khataran force had been channeled into a large area before the barracks.

Each time fresh troops arrived, Aentarra wove a shield around them, then issued fire into the shield, burning them alive. Soon, the stench from the harbor district was so bad even veteran soldiers were throwing up. All afternoon this went on, and by the end of the day, the battle for Khatara was over. Aentarra ordered Darius and his men to track down any of the enemy still roaming the streets.

"Kill the Sethians, but if the Khatarans want to join with you, allow them. We will need more troops." She then turned to Sennar. "Have someone put together several forces to try and put these fires out. It looks as if more than half the city is in flames."

Darius bowed to Aentarra and Darstan. "Khatara is grateful. We are in your debt forever."

Aentarra's smirk was telling. "Don't worry, Captain. I will collect in due time. For now, just keep control of this city."

Sennar soon returned with a bottle of wine and a bottle of vidda. "Didn't know who wanted what, but thought we all needed something."

Aentarra accepted a glass of wine, and Darstan took the vidda, as did Sennar, Malakai, and Darius. After a few drinks, the two sea captains drifted off with Darius, leaving Darstan alone with Aentarra. She smiled at him. "We did a good job today. Good combination—your fire and my shields."

He nodded, then, after some thought, he said. "That brings something to mind. When I shifted into a house earlier, it was a trap, and several guards stabbed me, but nothing happened. How is that possible?"

Aentarra looked at him with questioning eyes. "Perhaps they missed you."

He shook his head. "Couldn't have. I shifted right into the middle of them, and I even saw them stab me. I was on fire though, when they did it, so maybe that did something."

As Aentarra thought, Darstan brought up another point. "I just thought of this, but today, the same thing happened, but I did get cut by the sword."

She stared, walked over to him and lifted his shirt, looking at where the bandages were. "Were you on fire then?"

He thought, then shook his head. "No. It was after I got cut that the fire came."

She paced, nodding and talking out loud. "Sometimes, when faced with emergency situations, a person's shield will activate from the subconscious."

"But I can't shield."

Aentarra stopped, her eyes rolling in her head. "Maybe you can and just don't know it yet."

"How is that possible?"

I can think of only three ways. "I don't know, Darstan, but I'm certain we will figure it out."

He nodded. "So what now?"

"Sennar will stay with Darius and help him hold Khatara. I'm going to Sykor to see what help Mikkellana and your brother need." She turned to Darstan. "You can either stay here or come with me."

"Where I need to go is wherever that second obelisk is."

She spun to him like a weasel to a rat. "What?"

"An obelisk, like the one in Entiria. I've been dreaming about it for months."

She nearly jumped on him, and her face contorted. "Don't dare go near that obelisk. Do you hear me?"

Shocked, he stepped back. "Why? What is it?"

She glared. "Do not go near it. Not if you want to live." She paused, thinking. "I must go somewhere. I'll be back soon, so stay here." Once again she held his gaze. "Stay!" she said, and then shifted.

76

LIGARNS GO HOME

Suk Won led the karn through the last remaining woods of Sykor, exiting onto the open plains that consumed the vast expanse of Nyauran. "We will need to be more careful. The horsemen keep a close watch."

Jen Pal nodded. "Stay to the tall grasses, and we should see them first."

Shatir moved to the lead, eyes scanning the distance for signs of the Nyaurans. They walked all day with less than a few dozen words among them; in fact, there had not been many more than that spoken since they abandoned the mission, but now that they were nearing home the matter would need to be addressed.

Shatir waited until after supper then broached the subject. "Jen Pal, we must discuss this."

His attention had been focused on the small fire until Shatir spoke. He lifted his head, stared at her. "I have given it much thought. Once we return, I will surrender myself to the master and admit my guilt, but then I will try to kill him."

"Impossible," Triala said. It was the first she'd spoken since the day before.

"Anyone can be killed," Jen Pal said. "Even the master."

Suk Won squatted next to the fire, his feet planted on the ground. He used a stick to stir the flames. "Not if he knows your mind. And once you surrender, he will know it."

"Your only chance is surprise," Shatir said.

"There can be no surprise. I must free you from guilt."

Triala laughed, a rare sound from any Ligarn but from Triala it sounded utterly foreign. "Jen Pal, we were all dead as soon as we failed to kill you."

The flicker of light from the fire lit Suk Won's smile. "I even thought about it."

Jen Pal shifted his eyes from Triala to Suk Won. "Why then?"

Shinesa was not my mother, but if she had been ... he looked around as if someone might be watching. "...I would try to kill him also."

Triala nodded. "We are a karn. We live or die together."

Jen Pal turned to Shatir, sitting silently on the side. "And you, quiet sister?"

She did not face him, continued staring into the distance, then, after a moment, she stood and turned to face them all. "We have no chance. All of you know that. And my house does not sit empty like yours, Jen Pal, or yours," she said to Triala and Suk Won. "I have two children and a husband. Lukaan will do more than kill us. He will make us suffer through our families."

Jen Pal felt a chill run through him. How shameful he had been to think of only his concerns. He bowed low to Shatir. "You are right. I have been selfish."

"You have been stupid!" Shatir said. The harshness of her words stopped Jen Pal. He stared at her with his eyes wide open.

Shatir paced, and when she did she resembled a mountain cat, grace and danger merged into one being. "How do you fight a sangra? Do you get in the swamps with it and wrestle?"

She looked to Suk Won and Triala. "Or a bear? Go into its cave?" She paused now, shaking her head. "We will fight Lukaan, but we will do it our way. The Ligarn way. It is time we chased the small gods out of Sethia. It is time to reclaim our lands."

Jen Pal could have cried but to shed a tear twice would be tempting the fates too much. He did allow himself to hug her, though, a tight squeeze. "Thank you, Shatir."

It seemed to be a night for Ligarn laughter, as one burst forth from Shatir. "Thank me when this is done, Jen Pal. If any of us live."

~

They made plans throughout the night, agreeing on little other than the sacredness of continuing the race, then they devised a plan to usher the children and old ones to safety in Jattan Kir.

"How do we hurt him the most?" Suk Won asked.

"First we must convince the other karns to join us." Jen Pal paced, a nervousness even he did not know existed under his calm demeanor.

"If even one of them goes to Lukaan, we will all die," Triala said. "How do we make sure?"

"Kill them if we suspect anything," Shatir said, and when she drew strange looks, she frowned. "It will be them or us. If you look at it that way, it makes the decision easier."

"One karn at a time," Triala said. "That is the only way to do it."

"No!" Jen Pal said. "It must be all at once. That way, if anyone objects, the others will pressure them to stay quiet or join us."

"Jen Pal is right," Shatir said. "Even Ligarns experience emotions, and a crowd can excite more than anything." She turned to Jen Pal. "You must be the one to speak for us. Only you can inspire them."

Jen Pal nodded. "So it will be, then. For tonight, though, let us sleep."

*I*t took six more days for them to reach Sethia and, when they did, they made sure to stay out of sight of the palace guards or anyone who had contact with the small gods. For two more days they remained hidden, planning, then late on day nine they crept into the Ligarn home, each one retiring to their own houses.

～

*T*riala opened her door, stepped inside carefully. She checked each room, caution her partner, and when she finished, she lit a fire and boiled water for te. She intended to savor this one as it might be the last time in her own home. After contemplation, she stripped to basics—a cloth to cover her genitals and soft leather shoes, then she headed into the magnificent pre-dawn of the desert.

Her strides were long and measured, her head raised. Deep breaths filled her lungs with fresh morning air. There was nothing as satisfying in life as a run across the desert sands early in the morning before the sun chased life away.

For two leagues she ran, a pace she had set years ago and one that few could match, but as the Sethian sun heated the air and the sands, she turned toward home, saying her farewells to the plants and the wildlife she had come to call friends. It was time to leave. Jen Pal was waiting.

～

*S*uk Won closed his eyes before entering his home, a silent prayer preceding entry. He left his windows open, doors ajar —allowing free access to the wildlife of the desert—everything from the voles to the birds and wild dogs. Somehow, they all got along when in his presence. People did not understand animals, failed to realize they shared a world with them. Most people thought the world was theirs, to do with whatever they wished. Pitiful fools. If only they would open their eyes.

Suk Won kept his eyes closed as he walked through the house. He knew his home as a blind man does his domain. A deep breath told him the wild dogs had visited, perhaps taking the bones he left in the kitchen before leaving with the karn.

Another intake brought the tangy scent of Chupa birds, no doubt feasting on the berries he put in baskets hanging from the ceiling. Even though his eyes were closed, he could see the red on their wings as they flew, and he could hear the sharp chirping of the babies waiting for the food their parents would bring.

A sense of urgency forced his eyes open, only to find an empty house. It would be easy to stay here all day—all year even—but he knew he must prepare to meet Jen Pal.

He set his house in order, opening all windows and all doors. Might as well let the animals have their comfort while he was gone. After he prepared everything, he went to the courtyard one final time and said his prayers. When he was done, he rose, grabbed his staff and walked out into the night. Jen Pal was waiting.

~

*S*hatir's silent footsteps brought her to the front door of her house. She listened, her keen senses detecting the low snoring of her husband and the soft breathing of her children. She opened the door, making no noise, and crept across the kitchen floor on her way to the bedroom.

The door was open, as she suspected, and she entered undetected. Bhaka had always been a sound sleeper. A few quick movements undid her snaps, releasing her clothes to the floor, then she crept into bed, curling up next to him.

He sighed, feeling her warmth, and turned.

"Shatir?"

"Who else would it be, husband?"

She felt his smile more than saw it as he answered.

"Only your body could warm me like that."

"I hope so," she said and pulled him close.

"Then the karn proved a success?"

She said nothing, but kissed him hard, her hand running up and down his back.

Bhaka pulled back. "You were successful?"

She raised herself on her left elbow, stared at him, barely visible in the pre-dawn light. "No."

Bhaka sat up. Startled. "No? And yet, you returned?"

She said nothing for a while, then, "Things are changing, husband. I need you to be brave for me. For us."

Bhaka got off the bed. "Perhaps we should talk."

"Perhaps we should," she said, and also stood, staring at him.

"You have no clothes on," Bhaka said.

"You might listen better this way."

Bhaka smiled and pulled her back into the bed, wrapping his arms around her. "We will talk later."

~

A meeting with all the Ligarns had been set for the next night. Questions flowed through the camps like the summer mating bugs, but no one dared to speak against it. Tradition held that a karn leader could call an assembly at any time, and if called, all must obey.

During supper, small talk was made, and stories were traded, mostly old Ligarn legends, but afterward, all eyes fell to Jen Pal in anticipation. Tradition only carried so far.

Jen Pal finished his sarmac juice, then stood, facing the crowd. A circle had formed, each karn leader situated on the inner ring with the other karn members behind them.

"What brings us here, Jen Pal?" the question came from Matta Tez, an ancient amongst the Ligarns, one who had led nine karns.

Jen Pal gulped. Nervous for the first time since naming day. "As you know, we have just returned from our mission." He paused, knowing they expected him to tell his tales of success. He walked straight to Matta Tez, knelt before him. "We failed," he said and bowed his head.

A collective gasp arose from the crowd gathered, accompanied by whispers and secret language.

"Why did you call us?" Matta asked. "You should never have returned."

"I called you because we need your help." Jen Pal stood and faced each of the karn leaders. "All of you know Shinesa, my mother, who I have mourned these many years."

Heads nodded throughout the camp.

"And of those who knew her well, you know what a fine woman she was. A warrior."

More nods.

"And of those of you who knew her—do you also know of a frail one called Black Death?"

Angry murmurs spread throughout them. Some even cursed.

"I went to kill Black Death. I almost did."

Another gasp at the mention of "almost"—but Jen Pal calmed them.

"I say almost because I learned that Black Death is Shinesa's son. My brother."

Several of the karn leaders stood, prepared to leave.

"No!" Jen Pal's shout stopped them. "Stay and listen to what I have to say. If you want my head afterward, it is yours."

They sat.

"Our Master, Lukaan, raped my mother. Tortured her. Sent her out into the world of the frail ones."

The karn leaders seemed shocked but listened.

"A frail one befriended her, married her, and she bore the one we know as Black Death. But her first born betrayed her and killed her, leaving Black Death for dead."

"Where is he now?" Matta asked.

"Black Death killed his brother and now dedicates his life to killing Lukaan." Jen Pal walked in front of each of them, holding their eyes. "Can I do any less?"

Quiet overtook the gathering until Sim Tol spoke. "Are we to sacrifice our lives—our families, to avenge you?"

Jen Pal shook his head. Almost violently. "No! I will not have it." He stared at them. "But ask yourselves how long it will be until he takes your mother, your wife, or your daughter." He let it sink in. "What happened to Mara Fan, the beautiful one, who disappeared four years ago? What about Sensa Tikki, so young to have left us? Where is she? Where did she go?"

Jen Pal paced. "Do Ligarns get lost? Or does someone take them?"

Matta stood on wobbly legs. "I am with you, Jen Pal. Tell us what to do."

"And I," Sim Tol said.

"My karn will follow you," a woman from the left said, then more joined, until all agreed.

Pride swelled Jen Pal's heart. He bowed. "I owe my life to you. It is yours forever."

"Just teach us how to win," Sim Tol said.

"I have a plan, but I will let Shatir tell it."

~

Tiny clouds of dust kicked up as Shatir paced, arms folded behind her. After a few minutes, Jen Pal signaled her, but she waited until she had everyone's attention, then stood before them and bowed. "Jen Pal has honored me by allowing me to present the plan. I pray it is a success."

She held out a list in her left hand. "Eighteen of our warriors have been selected by the elders. They will lead the youngest and the oldest to a new home."

Murmurs arose from those sitting. A few of the Ligarns stood, voicing objections, but Shatir remained firm. "Sit. Stay quiet until I finish."

She waited, let her gaze rake the crowd. "The young must go. They are our future. The old must go for their wisdom and advice. And the protectors—to protect and to breed."

"Who will go?" a young boy shouted.

"Anyone under fourteen years and anyone over fifty."

More murmurs, but no objections.

"The protectors are all young enough to breed."

"Where will we go?" a young girl asked.

"The protectors will decide once they leave here. We are not to know."

"Why? How will you find us?"

Shatir sighed. "For what we have to do, we will likely die. If any of us are captured by the small gods, we do not want the knowledge to fall into their hands. If we do not know—we cannot say."

"But how will you find us?" another worried girl asked.

"If we cannot find you here, we will find you at the Gates of the Sun," Shatir said, and bowed.

"When do we leave?"

"Tomorrow."

In the morning Shatir separated them into groups. The young, along with anyone over fifty, said their goodbyes, then moved to the side, awaiting orders. The breeders, the eighteen who would be the guardians, were chosen by the council, then allowed time to say their goodbyes. Shatir's husband was among them.

He came to her with wet eyes. "Shatir, you must stop this. I cannot leave you."

"Someone must protect the children. I trust no one else."

Bhaka lowered his head and folded his hands in prayer. When he finished, he stared at her. "I will not take another mate."

"You will do as the council instructs." Her voice carried stern warnings. "If you do not, you will shame the children and your name."

He reached for her, but she pushed him away. "We are no longer together."

Bhaka fought tears, it was obvious, but he won the struggle and kept his pride. "I will go then," he said and bowed to her. "Until we meet at the Gates of the Sun."

She returned the bow. "Until then."

Shatir watched him go and did all she could to stop her tears. Tears brought disgrace and death; besides, if she were fortunate, she would survive this mission and be able to find them. Once again lay with

Bhaka during the cold winter nights and play with her children in the light of the sun. If she survived.

Bhaka turned one final time to wave goodbye, then he joined his fellow protectors for their long journey. The council had chosen wisely—six men and twelve women, a good mix for breeding and protection. Soon enough some of the younger ones could breed, then the Ligarns would be strong again.

Shatir fought the tears, fought them hard, then she lifted her hand and waved to Bhaka and her children. She knew it would be the last time she ever saw them. When she had composed herself, she turned to Jen Pal, nodding. "We are ready?"

Jen Pal bowed. "The march awaits you, Shatir. I have chosen you to lead the right flank when the time comes."

"The honor is too much, Jen Pal. Others are more deserving."

"Others may be more deserving, but none are more qualified." He stepped close and hugged her. "I have learned much on our journey, including how to shed tears and still be a Ligarn—thanks to you. And I have learned what it is to trust someone."

Jen Pal let his cherry-black eyes burn into her. "If I had been blessed with a sister, I would have wanted them to be like you."

She bowed. "We should go, Jen Pal. The others await us."

~

Jen Pal approached the Ligarns gathered together under the few trees offering shade. He stood on a rock to give himself a view over the crowd. "We are off on a journey that will likely be our last," he said. "Few, if any, of us, will survive."

A few murmurs bounced around the still air, but most simply stared at him.

"We cannot fight the small gods, that would be foolish. But we can fight their minions, and right now the Wolfen and Victas are running rampant over the frail ones in Sykor. They cannot hold for long."

"Why help the frail ones?" someone from the middle shouted.

"Because we are out to defeat the Master. To do that we need allies, and the frail ones have small gods of their own." Jen Pal waited for them to digest his information. "Perhaps with our help they can prevail."

"And if we fail?" one asked.

"Then we die," Jen Pal said. "It is the Ligarn way."

"I have never liked Wolfen," a young warrior from the front row said.

"Nor I, the Victas." This from the woman standing next to him.

Ballisan, tallest of all the Ligarns, towered over the group from the rear. His voice carried to the front. "I have sharpened my weapons," he said, holding up his sai. "We should march while the sun is low."

Everyone joined in the shouts of approval, forcing a smile to Jen Pal's face. "Let us begin," he said, and led the way toward Kamnor, with Shatir, Suk Won, and Triala at his side. As soon as we reach Kamnor, we will show the world what being a Ligarn means.

77

WHERE IS AENTARRA?

A rift opened in Talanvar's library—a busy spot of late—and Aentarra stepped through. She hurried up the stairs to Mikkellana's room, bursting through the door. "Get out!" she ordered Camissa. Her tone brooked no argument.

Once Camissa left, Mikkellana spoke. "What is so urgent? You act as if—"

"Darstan can shield!"

Mikkellana sat straighter, gathered her thoughts. "How?"

Aentarra glared. "That is precisely what I want to know."

After a lengthy pause, Mikkellana shook her head. "Impossible. You must be wrong. There is no way he can shield."

Aentarra paced, cracking her knuckles as she did. "You tell me what it is when guards stab him, and he doesn't bleed." She stopped to stare at her sister again. "I call that shielding."

Mikkellana nodded to the door, and Aentarra opened it, checking the hall both ways. "No one is here," she said, then sat beside her on the bed.

"Since you are here, I presume Khatara is under our control?"

Aentarra stood, resumed her pacing. "Khatara is, but we had to destroy half the city to do it. I left Darstan with Sennar and his men." She cast a glance to Mikkellana before continuing. "Lukaan controls the rest of Jattan Kir, but I think we could take it if we need to."

Staring straight into Aentarra's eyes, Mikkellana resumed her questioning. "Getting back to Darstan—does he belong to you?"

"Of course not! Do you think—"

"I stopped thinking about what you might do long ago," she said. "And don't give me any nonsense about motherly love. I've seen snakes with more concern for their children."

Aentarra grabbed a pitcher of water from the nightstand and filled a glass. She drank it straight down, then poured another. "Was that a question to throw me off? Is he yours?" Aentarra asked.

"Don't be ridiculous," Mikkellana said.

Aentarra laughed. "You're right. That would be ridiculous." Her comment drew a raised eyebrow from Mikkellana, but nothing more. "Then who?" She finished her water, set the glass on the table. "While you ponder those possibilities, I have something to do."

"What?"

"I need to check on something."

Mikkellana struggled, trying to get situated on the bed. "What you need to do is make sure that Darstan doesn't go to Sethia."

"I already told him to wait for me in Khatara."

"That one is far from a trained pet, Aentarra. He doesn't listen to anything."

Aentarra nodded. "I know that, but I believe he'll stay put for a while; besides, I won't be long."

"Where are you going?"

"See you soon, sister," she said and shifted.

Mikkellana cursed as the rift closed, then she called for Camissa.

~

The library in Vallah was one of Aentarra's favorite spots. So many books. So much knowledge. And much of it still a mystery to her. There were entire volumes that she did not even understand.

She searched through the shelves, recalling from memory the general location of the book that came to mind when Darstan mentioned the obelisk. That mere mention had triggered something, and she needed to find it.

It was a particular passage in a book, an obscure passage at the time she had read it. Perhaps now it would have more meaning. She recalled the book had read almost like an autobiography, but of whom?

She pulled out several of the books—ancient tomes, all—and leafed through them, careful not to tear pages. After a half a dozen or so, she found the one she was looking for and took it to the table. It didn't take long to find the spot.

...the transition from simple exile to complete incarceration would not be favorable, yet, the route to freedom seemed easy enough—find two champions, then await the victor. How to draw them to the obelisk, though—that was the key. And such a short time to decide. Only days before they are finished ...

Aentarra placed a marker in the book then shut it, resting her hands on top. She stared into the silence of the library and fixed on a late-afternoon bar of light shining through the window. Find two champions ... What did they mean by that? She opened it and read it once more. ...draw them to the obelisk ... that was the key.

Aentarra pondered more, flipped more pages, then read the original passage one final time. Nothing else of significance came to her, so she reviewed what she had learned. Tried fitting it into what she already knew.

After a trip to her room to make khaffe, she returned and began searching through more books. She sustained herself on water, khaffe, and fruits as hours turned into days, and all the while, she took breaks to walk and think.

Suddenly, while walking down the Great Path, pieces began to fit. As the thoughts merged, a clear picture formed. Aentarra smiled. She didn't have the answers, yet, but one thing was certain. She could not let Darstan enter Sethia.

Mikkellana was right, but for different reasons. I better get to Khatara, she thought, but before she took two more steps, the Others struck.

Her hands flew to her head as if she could hold it together. Stop it from exploding. "No!" She screamed just as she fell to the floor.

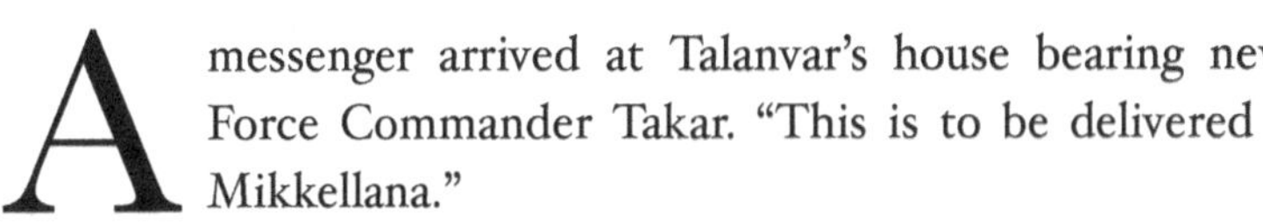

SIGNS OF TROUBLE

A messenger arrived at Talanvar's house bearing news from Force Commander Takar. "This is to be delivered to Lady Mikkellana."

Birol accepted the message and took it to Mikkellana. "Thank you, Birol. And please ask Camissa to come see me." As he left, Mikkellana opened the letter and read the reports, her frown increasing the more she read.

Victas had control of the Free Lands; Kamnor was lost in two days, and the Wolfen had infiltrated the forest north of Sykor. Even worse than that though, if initial reports were to be believed, Nyauran was all but overrun, and a massive army was on its way across the plains to Sykor.

"Where is Aentarra?" Mikkellana asked as Camissa entered the room. "Has anyone seen her?"

Camissa had been tending Mikkellana for nearly a month, but there had been no sign of improvement, and it was showing in her attitude. "No one has seen or heard from Aentarra since she came from Khatara." Camissa brought fresh te to Mikkellana. "Should I ask Aenaila—"

"That girl does nothing besides fix her hair." Mikkellana adjusted herself on the bed, propping pillows behind her back. "Get me Talanvar and Rhaven. And be quick!"

Camissa scurried out of the room and headed for the stairs. Mikkellana's temper was becoming unbearable. Halfway down the steps, Camissa heard her yelling. "And get Rahg up here, too. He needs to do something."

She passed Dirk and Adju in the kitchen, and though she managed a smile, it was difficult. She had not known Adju for long, but she had grown to like him. And no one deserved what happened to him.

Mikkellana had not been able to heal him fully, and while Camissa wanted to try, she was afraid of hurting him more than helping. Mikkellana told her before that healing can hurt as much as help if done wrong. At least he was no longer in severe pain, but he had little use of his hands. And Aenaila wasn't much better, which is what prompted Mikkellana's attitude.

Since her attack in Khatara, it seemed as if she could not get a firm ground to stand on. She was too brave to show it in front of Adju, but the hurt was there. Camissa felt it. Aenaila hurt and hurt badly.

Rahg was in the library when she passed. "Mikkellana wants you, Rahg. I'm getting Rhaven and Talanvar. Tell her they'll be up soon."

He finished his conversation with Wisp, then headed up the stairs to see her, Wisp following close behind. Within moments, Rhaven and Talanvar joined him, and shortly after, Camissa as well.

When they were all gathered in the room, Mikkellana sat as straight as she could and waved the letter at them. "Takar sends grim news. The Free Lands and Kamnor are gone, in complete control of Lukaan's forces. And if scouts are to be believed, Nyauran is in trouble as well."

Rhaven's hand twitched as if he were prepared to draw steel. "We can't let them get any closer to Sykor. If they—"

Mikkellana glared, her voice raising. "We cannot let them keep what they have, let alone come closer. Lukaan already has Pomanda and everything to our north. Assuming he takes Nyauran, that gives him the entire east, save Khatara." She sipped on the te Camissa had brought. "And with him having Jattan Kir and Sethia, we cannot expect to hold Khatara for long. Right now it is only Darstan keeping him out of there."

"I'm going to help Takar," Rahg said. He stepped up to Mikkellana. "I don't care what you say. I'm going."

"You should go, Rahg, but tell him I suggested putting you on the Pomandan border. They are not used to people with powers of any kind and will be frightened by it. The Victas and Wolfen will have experience, not with shields, but with powers, and Lukaan will have trained them to deal with it. We'll be better off fighting them with our troops."

"I'm going with him," Camissa said.

Mikkellana shook her head. "You will stay here, and do as I say."

Rahg pulled Camissa to him. "Mikkellana, I'm sorry about your back, but other people are hurt, too, and you have no reason to talk to Camissa like that." He stared. "Look at Adju, he's laughing every day, and he can't even use his hands."

"I can speak for myself, Rahg," Camissa said. "But thank you, anyway."

Mikkellana's head was bobbing up and down. "He is right, Camissa. And I do apologize. Not just to you, to all of you. I have been miserable. Worried, mostly. If you only knew the dangers ..." Now her head was shaking. "No matter. We'll do what we can."

"I can help," Wisp said.

"Won't find a better spy," Rhaven said.

"And Takar will likely need one," Mikkellana said, "but I need you for something else first." She turned to Camissa. "You, too. Afterward, you can join Rahg."

When Camissa objected, Mikkellana stopped her. "It won't be long, so just kiss Rahg goodbye and tell him you will see him soon." She laughed at the expression on Rahg's face. "There, I knew that would embarrass him."

"Rahg, you and Rhaven will be riding out together, but I'm going to have Talanvar send some more troops with you. Takar will need them." She looked to Talanvar. "I'll speak with you in a moment about that."

"What do you want with me?" Wisp asked.

"For now, to get Aenaila and bring her here. And be prepared to leave." She turned to Talanvar again. "I'm going to trust you to run this city while we are gone. Protect it and keep it under control. The people can grow restless and unruly when danger threatens, so it might take a firm hand."

He bowed. "My Lady."

Mikkellana stared at him. "I know what you are, Lord Talanvar, but that doesn't bother me. Times like this call for tough-minded men."

"How long until you return, My Lady?"

She shook her head. "That depends on our success. Soon or never are the easy answers, but there might be a few in between. Regardless, do what you have to do."

As he turned to leave, Mikkellana said. "And get with the Barracks Commander. Send as many men as you can to support Takar. Leave at least five thousand here."

The door had barely closed behind him when Rhaven spoke.

"I'd feel better staying here with you."

"You have lived your life taking care of yourself. Same way I've lived mine. No need for either of us to change now. If fate puts us together, we'll still be there." She squeezed his hand. "Takar needs you. Besides, I need to go somewhere with Aenaila."

Rhaven went on alert. "Where? You can't be traveling."

"It's my back, not my mind that is damaged."

He began to object, but she held up her hand. "If I don't find my sister, Lukaan will get out. I can already feel the shield weakening. Something is wrong. Very wrong. And I have little time to set it right."

"If there is little time, then the place I want to be is here with you."

Mikkellana sighed, looked at him with soft eyes. "I might never recover from this. I might be crippled all my life, and that could be a long one. If—"

Rhaven sat on the bed beside her, put his finger to her lips. "As long as I am alive, you will never be crippled. I will take care of you."

She shook her head. "And when you are too old to carry a fat old woman who can't walk? What happens then?"

"If you try to get fat on me, I'll stop feeding you."

Mikkellana laughed at that. Laughed hard, the way she used to when she was a little girl with no worries. With a broad smile still on her face, she grabbed Rhaven with both hands and kissed him. Then kissed him again. They stayed locked in an embrace for a moment, saying nothing.

"You have to promise me one thing," Rhaven said.

"Anything."

"Promise me that now and then you will become Kella so we can hunt together."

"It will be my greatest honor," she said. "Now, go. Rahg will be waiting."

As Rhaven left, tears streamed down Mikkellana's face, but she wiped them away before anyone came.

Moments later, Aenaila and Wisp entered. Aenaila had an almost blank stare on her face, and she walked with a listlessness that spoke of sadness. "You wanted to see me?"

"I need you to take me some places."

"Where?"

"If I were to tell you names, it wouldn't matter. Just know that if we don't hurry and do this, the troubles and woes you think you have now will be magnified by a thousand."

Aenaila wrinkled her brow and walked closer. "Tell me what's going on, Mikkellana. I have no time for your games."

"Aentarra is missing, as you know." Mikkellana stared at Wisp, then back to Aenaila. "The shield is weakening. If I can't find my sister soon, Lukaan will get out."

She grabbed Aenaila's sleeve. "If he does, we're all dead. We are not strong enough to fight him. Not even all of us combined." When Aenaila didn't respond, Mikkellana took a harsh tact. "If you think what happened to you in Khatara was bad, think again. If Lukaan doesn't kill you during the battle and he finds someone as pretty as you later ..." she laughed a cynical laugh. "there are not words to describe the agony he will put you through. If we lose this battle, or if you fall into his hands, either kill yourself or mar your face beyond the point of desire."

Aenaila's face grew red, and she gritted her teeth, but then she simply nodded. "What do I need to do?"

Mikkellana turned to Wisp. "Kender, if you can get Camissa, I'd like her to come with us. You too. We might need your skills."

"I'll be right back."

When there were just the two of them left, Mikkellana addressed her. "Aenaila, I know what happened in Khatara. You cannot blame yourself or feel bad about it."

Aenaila walked over, shut the door, then began crying. "Kender was there. He saw them touch me." She cried more, then tried wiping away the tears. "I didn't even do anything. Just froze."

Mikkellana reached for her, now sorry about the things she had said earlier. "I know that thief pretty well by now. If there is anything I'm certain of, it's that he would not give one single thought to the things you are worried over. He is an honorable man, despite being a thief."

She sobbed a few more times but eventually lifted her head. She accepted a cloth from Mikkellana to use for wiping her eyes, and then smiled for the first time in days. "Perhaps you are right. He is an honorable man, isn't he?"

"One of the best men I know," Mikkellana said. "After Rhaven."

"I've noticed the attraction."

"Yes, well ... enough of that nonsense. How about if both of us make up our minds to tend to business that will allow us to enjoy these wonderful men."

Aenaila held her hand out. "Mikkellana, you have a bargain."

They chatted for a moment more before Wisp and Camissa arrived.

"Ready?" Aenaila asked, and when Mikkellana nodded, she took her hand, got the image from Mikkellana's mind, then shifted. The rift opened into Mikkellana's room in Vallah, where Camissa stepped through first, followed by Aenaila and Wisp, supporting Mikkellana. Wisp carried her to the bed and lay her down, propping her head up on a few pillows.

"Kender, stay with me while they search."

He started to say something, but Mikkellana interrupted. "Camissa knows the palace, so it makes more sense for her to go with Aenaila." She turned to Aenaila, "If you get a Shift Point of the room—"

"I already have one. Don't worry; we'll be all right." Aenaila turned to Camissa. "Let's go."

Camissa led her through the range of bedrooms, fondly recalling the time she spent with Rahg here. After finding nothing in this section, she led Aenaila across the courtyard toward the main building, stepping onto the Great Path as they entered. Almost halfway around the perimeter, Camissa saw something ahead. She ran, gasping as she got close. "Aentarra!"

79

THE ART OF HEALING

Aenaila cracked her knuckles while Camissa knelt on the floor next to Aentarra. "Is she alive?"

"Alive, yes, but ..."

"What?"

"Look at her eyes!"

Aenaila got down with Camissa and looked. Aentarra's eyes were rolled toward the top of her head and stared at nothing. Aenaila waved her hand in front of her, then got closer and snapped her fingers. Nothing.

"No response at all," Camissa said. "But she is breathing."

"We need to get her to Mikkellana."

"No." Camissa stood. "We can't risk moving her. Get Mikkellana. I'll wait here."

"Be right back," Aenaila said, and shifted.

～

*A*enaila stepped through the rift into Mikkellana's room. "We found her, but she's hurt badly. You need to come. Quick!"

Wisp went to the bed, helped Mikkellana sit up, then he and Aenaila put their arms around her and prepared to shift. Aenaila formed the image in her mind of where she left Camissa and then shifted, appearing on the Great Path. They stepped through the rift together, bringing Mikkellana to where Aentarra lay on the floor.

"Put me down next to her," Mikkellana said, then to Camissa. "What happened?"

"We found her like this. I can't get her to respond, but I haven't tried much. I didn't want to hurt her."

Mikkellana felt her head, then leaned in to listen to her heart. "Where did the blood come from? I see no wounds."

"There was blood coming from her ears and mouth when I got here. I cleaned it up."

Mikkellana ran her hands up and down Aentarra's legs and then her arms, felt nothing out of place. "Roll her gently to the side," Mikkellana said. "I want to feel her back."

Wisp got down with Camissa and helped roll her to her side, then Mikkellana touched her at the base of the spine and all up and down it. "Nothing!" She seemed lost in thought. "I don't know what is wrong with her."

"Can we move her?" Wisp asked.

"I don't know, but I don't know why not either." She looked at Wisp. "Take her to my room with Aenaila, then come back and get me. Be careful, though."

Wisp and Camissa got their arms under her, then, when they were ready, they signaled Aenaila, and she grabbed hold of them and shifted. Once situated on Mikkellana's bed, they went back and got Mikkellana.

"We should take her to Talanvar's house," Aenaila said. "At least he has beds and food, and there are people who can take care of her."

"I think you are right, Aenaila, but we cannot do this all at once. With both of us crippled it will require two trips. Take her first."

She turned to Camissa. "Go with them and make sure she is kept warm. And try to get water in her. Don't let anyone move her or touch her." Before they left, Mikkellana added. "And don't try to heal her before I get there." She then turned to Aenaila. "If you need to rest before coming back that's fine. I'll be all right by myself."

Aenaila shifted, got Aentarra situated once again, then went back for Mikkellana. Moments later she returned with her, and they took her to the bedroom where Aentarra lay. "Get me something that I can sit in while I tend to her."

"You should rest," Aenaila said.

Mikkellana spun to her, anger flashing on her face. "Rest! If I don't do something soon, and I mean very soon, Lukaan will get out."

80

BATTLEFIELD REPORTS

Tirzinitzia smiled as soon as she saw the messenger. She knew he bore news from the attacks, and she had no doubts about what those reports would be. They were, after all, her plans being carried out.

It was a Sethian who brought the news, and his breath was short by the time he got to her. "Lady Tirzinitzia, we have reports from all of the regions."

She held out her hand to receive them, still smiling. She had already sent a message to Melissara and Lukaan, advising them that news awaited. "You may go now," she said to the messenger. "And have someone bring water for us to drink."

He bowed as he left. Tirzinitzia itched to open the reports, but she would wait for Lukaan. He would want to know the news as it is learned. As she paced, she sensed the rift opening. Melissara came through first, followed by Lukaan.

Is the news good, Tirzinitzia?

"I was waiting for you."

"Good. Then let us share it together," he said, now communicating with his voice.

She opened the scroll and read the report from the Free Lands, ecstasy planted on her face. "The Free Lands are ours. Almost no resistance." She scrambled to the next report, but a frown came quickly to her face, then fear. "Khatara has fallen to the enemy." She looked to Lukaan, afraid he would blame her. "Jattan Kir is ours, but they have taken Khatara."

"Keep reading," he said.

She fumbled through the next two scrolls, reading as fast as she could, desperate for good news. "The Wolfen have taken Kamnor." Her nerves were pressing her. "And Nyauran is in our ... no, wait."

She read more. "The eastern territory of Nyauran is in our control, and they anticipate the rest to fall soon. Their horsemen reduced by half in the first few battles."

She froze while Lukaan sat silent. "They will strike back at us in Kamnor and the Free Lands. And they will do everything to hold Nyauran." He got off his seat and walked around. "Pomanda needs to deliver on its promises. Tell them to move men to the border. And keep up the pressure in Nyauran."

Tirzinitzia bowed low. "Your will." She was almost afraid to ask but had to. "And Khatara?"

Lukaan looked to the sky as if he saw something she did not. "Do you feel the shield, Tirzinitzia? Reach out with your senses and tell me what you feel?"

Tirzinitzia concentrated, tried to sense it. She let her mind wander toward the border, probing, sensing. She saw it wavering in the hot sun as if it were collapsing. She gasped. "It's failing!"

Lukaan smiled, and when he did it was so sinister, it frightened her. "Yes, Tirzinitzia. It is failing. Soon, we will be free. Then I will show Khatara what it means to defy me."

Tirzinitzia bowed even lower this time, and as she did she almost felt sorry for Khatara, and its people.

81

LORN REINFORCEMENTS

Rahg and Rhaven were heading down the street from Hightown when Rhaven stopped him. "Rahg, you go ahead without me. I need to see Mikkellana about something."

"Doesn't matter to me," Rahg said, "we were going different routes anyway."

Rhaven went back to Talanvar's house and settled in, waiting for Mikkellana to return. He told Birol to tell him the instant she got back. His stomach still hurt from the stab wound Jen Pal had given him, and he didn't feel ready for battle, but there were times when things needed to be done regardless. He settled into a chair in the library and rested.

Before long, Birol awakened him, with news of Mikkellana's arrival, and Rhaven rushed up the stairs to see her.

When he opened the door, he found Camissa, Wisp, and Aenaila positioning Aentarra on a makeshift bed, with Mikkellana sitting against the wall on her bed.

"If that's all you need, Mikkellana, Wisp and I are going to eat," Aenaila said.

As they left, Rhaven turned to Mikkellana. "What happened to Aentarra?"

"We don't know," Mikkellana said, "but she's bad. We can't get her to regain consciousness."

Rhaven moved closer, looked at the blood staining her head and face. "This is like what happened in Pomanda."

"I'm afraid it might be," Mikkellana said. "And if that is the case, there isn't much I can do other than wait."

"There must be something!" Camissa said while she applied cold water to her head with a towel.

"This isn't some fever, girl. This is ... never mind, you wouldn't understand anyway." Mikkellana turned toward Rhaven. "What are you doing here? I told you to go with Rahg."

"I have an idea."

Mikkellana sighed. "Be quick about it. We don't have time to waste."

"The Lorns," Rhaven said. "We use the Lorns to attack the Victas in the Free Lands from Skyebridge."

"Nonsense! All it would take are a few dozen Victas to hold that bridge. It would be a massacre."

"Not if the Lorns got across undetected. Then they could hold the bridge from the other side and mount an assault from the rear. It would provide Takar the support he needs."

Mikkellana sat silent for a moment. "And you think you can get them to do this?"

Rhaven smiled. "I know I can. And I know just the places in the Free Lands where we can—"

"You're not going with them. I told you where I needed you."

"I should be with the Lorns. That's where I can be the most help."

"You'll be the most help where I tell you. Now find me Aenaila. She can take you there."

Rhaven stormed out of Mikkellana's room and headed downstairs. Things had to be done, and she was as hard-headed as Kella used to be. He needed to find Aenaila and quick. He looked in the kitchen, where Birol told him she was in the library. When he entered the library, Wisp and Aenaila were in the middle of a conversation with Talanvar.

"Don't mean to interrupt, but I need to talk to you, Aenaila."

She looked at Wisp, eyebrows raised, then excused herself and went with Rhaven. When they got outside the library, he turned. "I need to get to Skythorne right away. Wisp knows the area if you can take us."

Aenaila looked at him with a question on her face. "Do you feel good enough to go?"

"Mikkellana doesn't want me to go, but it needs to be done. Takar won't hold the border without help, and the Lorns can provide that."

"If Kender says he knows a spot well enough, I can take you."

"When?"

"Whenever you want. Now, if you're ready."

"Let me get my weapons. I'll be right back."

Aenaila got Wisp, and he told her he could do it. "When are we going?"

"I need to speak with Mikkellana, then we can leave."

When Rhaven returned they shifted to Skythorne, the capital city of the Lorns. After stepping through the rift, Rhaven thanked Aenaila. "Tell Mikkellana I hope to see her when this is over with."

"I will," Aenaila said. "But I need to rest before I shift back."

"Of course," Rhaven said. "Come with me. We'll get you food and a drink."

Wisp stared at Aenaila with a suspicious glance, but he said nothing.

As they walked with Rhaven, dozens of Lorns ran to him. Greetings seemed to last forever. Finally, Rhaven dispensed with the formalities and got Rhalan, the young leader of the Lorns, to take them to the council room where his father waited.

Introductions were made, then Rhalan sent for food and ale to be brought in. Rhalan's sister, Rhiana, asked Aenaila to walk with her.

"Te for me, please," Aenaila said, then turned to Wisp. "I am going with Rhiana. She wants to talk."

Soon after, Rhaven was talking strategy with the Lorns. "Victas have taken over the Free Lands, and reports claim there to be upward of ten thousand of them. Perhaps more. They have Kamnor too."

"What do you need from us?" Rhalan asked.

"Try not to think of it as what I need. If we fail, we all lose. The Lorns must fight if you are to live."

Rhalan looked to his father, whose nod said it all. "We have known for a long time that a day such as this would come. You can count on us to do our part."

Rhaven smiled. "We need to put troops on the Pomandan border too. Not many, but enough to threaten them. Make them think twice about attacking Sykor. But most importantly, we need to go into the Free Lands and support Takar's back."

"Not the best use of Lorn soldiers," Rhalan said.

Rhaven nodded. "I know you would rather be in the forest, but we can't choose the battlefield this time. Takar is getting slaughtered. If we attack from the rear, we should distract them and give him a chance to gain a foothold."

"How many men can you raise?" Wisp asked.

Rhalan looked to his father before answering, and somehow they seemed to communicate a number. "A thousand, perhaps more."

"Not much against their force, but something."

Rhaven laughed. "A lot more than you think, Wisp. These are the greatest archers in the world. And they will all be armed with blackthorn arrows coated with the same poison I use on my darts."

Wisp smiled, bowing low. "A formidable army indeed."

Rhalan bowed to him in return. "And you, Kender Darnell, also called Wisp, have you had occasion to use the gifts we gave you?"

Wisp thought back to the poison darts they had given him on his first visit with Rhaven. It seemed so long ago. "I am glad to say that I haven't, Rhalan, though I have come close a few times."

Another smile lit Rhalan's face. "Close is good. I am pleased they are still there to protect you."

Aenaila had just returned. "Time for us to go."

Rhalan bowed to Rhaven, offering the formal farewell of the Lorns. "May the light of the sun ever touch you. You are ever well come to home."

"I'm not leaving, Rhalan. I'm going with you to the Free Lands."

Wisp took Aenaila's hand, then just as she was about to shift, she grabbed hold of Rhaven, taking him along with them.

Rhalan smiled as they shifted. "Don't worry, Rhaven, we will take care of everything."

They appeared in Talanvar's library, Rhaven cursing as he stepped through the rift.

Aenaila stared him down. "Mikkellana gave me orders. I had no choice."

Rhaven fumed. "Did you know, Wisp?"

"Not a thing."

As Rhaven stormed up the stairs toward Mikkellana's room, Wisp laughed. "Would love to see that."

"So would I," Aenaila said.

82

DREAMS OF FREEDOM

Tirzinitzia studied the newest reports. They arrived daily now, and each one seemed to supersede the one before. Victas had complete control of the Free Lands and were poised to strike into Sykor. And the Wolfen were sweeping through the forests in northern Sykor, already claiming hundreds of guards as casualties, with only a dozen deaths in their own ranks.

News from Nyauran was even better. The famed Nyauran horsemen had fallen victim to her battle tactics and were now in full retreat. Sethians and Gnakas occupied the east and central plains and were pushing to the western border on forced marches.

A frown formed on her face. Khatara was the only disappointment. Even the new assault from Jattan Kir had been beaten back, apparently with the help of someone with powers. The messenger claimed it was a man, but it couldn't be. Not if their reports were accurate. Neither of those boys could be that strong. It must be Aentarra. They spoke of BlackFire and Lightning, and although Tirzinitzia knew that Darstan had the ability, he couldn't be so strong—had to be her.

She chased away the sadness. Would not allow bad news to dampen such a glorious day. She had grown fonder of the Sethian days of late, ever since she realized they were short-lived. That she would soon be free to choose what kind of days she would wake up to. Would it be the sunny shores of the Gendan Sea or the crisp mountain air of the White Mountains? She laughed but felt the impatience that came with longing to once again have that pleasure.

Tirzinitzia walked the perimeter of the shield, testing it every few paces.

Ever since Lukaan had mentioned it weakening, she had dreams of freedom. What would it feel like after all of these years? She closed her eyes and formed images in her mind of silly things, things that seemed so trivial, but they were so real to her she felt if she reached out she could almost touch them. The shield lay in front of her, within reach. She touched it, pressed against it, but felt nothing different.

Still, it was coming. She could feel it, too. Something had happened outside. Whatever, or whoever, controlled the shield was weakening. Soon they would all be out. Then they would pay. Especially you, Aentarra. I can't wait.

~

Mikkellana sat in her chair, staring at Aentarra. Pondering the dilemma. Something had to be done. And quickly. But what? She had tried everything she knew. Nothing worked. Never, had she seen anything like this.

Camissa came in, probably the tenth time she had, and Mikkellana was losing patience. It wasn't the girl's fault. She was trying, but there was too much at stake, and little things were wearing on her.

"Anything new, Mikkellana?"

Mikkellana tried calming herself. "Nothing, dear. Same as last time."

Camissa sat on the bed, staring into Aentarra's eyes. "It is like nothing is in there. Is she still alive?"

Mikkellana sighed. "She is alive, but ... I don't know, Camissa. I just don't know."

Camissa turned to her. "I'm sorry, Mikkellana. I know she's your sister. I'm just worried. Despite what Aentarra has done, she has helped us a lot."

Mikkellana felt like smacking her. Maybe it would knock sense in the girl. Did she think this was about one person's life? This was everything. "Yes, she has, hasn't she."

Rhaven came in just then, saving Mikkellana from further idle talk. He had said few words since the incident with the Lorns, but Mikkellana knew he would get over it. If not, he'd die with it. Either way, it would be long forgotten in her mind.

"I'm going to try reading to her," Camissa said. "It helped Tobias. Maybe—"

"It won't," Mikkellana said, then thought better of her attitude. "But you can try if you like."

Camissa sat close, held Aentarra's hand and began reading a book she brought to the bedroom. She read all morning, ate supper, then continued in the early afternoon, pausing only for water breaks and to use the facilities Talanvar had for the ladies. Afterward, she returned and tried her Persuasion.

She waited until Mikkellana was napping, then closed her eyes and focused, going deep into her mind.

She found the cottages, the ones lining the river bank, and walked past the ones she didn't need: courage, confidence, love—she almost laughed at that, but didn't. Even Aentarra needed love. Maybe she would use that in the future.

Now, where was she—oh, yes, love, revenge, another one Aentarra didn't need. Continuing, she finally found it—hope, the one that helped Tobias. She called Hope to her, led it out, directed it to

Aentarra and let it swirl about her head. Then she directed it into her mind, ordering it to infuse her body.

As Camissa relaxed, proud of herself, a jolt struck her, knocking her to the floor. She jumped up, astonished. What had happened? Something —or someone—would not let Hope inside of Aentarra. But it can't be her. She's unconscious.

Camissa shivered, her body shaking and twitching. This emotion she recognized. Fear!

●83

THE SETHIAN SHIELD

Tirzinitzia came to Lukaan's chambers, heart racing. It may have been the first time she entered his room when she wasn't frightened.

"What is it, Tirzinitzia?"

She bowed to the floor. "The shield, Great Lord. It is down!"

Silence was followed by exuberant exultation. "Call Melissara. Gather my Sethian Troops. We leave at once."

"For where, My Lord?"

"Melissara, take Tirzinitzia with you and support the west. One of you in Kamnor and one in the Free Lands." He paused. "And if you encounter either of those impetuous boys, kill them."

Melissara's brow wrinkled. "Both of them?"

Lukaan glared. "Don't get soft on me, Melissara. They both must die. I have no need for them now."

She bowed low. "And you, Lord, where do you go?"

"Khatara! It needs to be taught a lesson."

~

*L*ukaan departed Sethia with 15,000 seasoned Sethian troops, leaving the rest to guard the homeland. From long ago he had a Shift Point, but he didn't trust it after all of these years, so he moved the men by sight-shifting only. When they got within sight of Khatara, he stopped to address the men.

"Captain, no one in the city shall live. We must teach them what insolence brings."

The captain pounded his fist to his chest in salute. "Yes, Great Lord. Your will."

~

*R*efugio raced through the lines, panting as he addressed Darstan. "Fresh troops coming in from Jattan Kir. The Khatarans say they are Sethians."

A moment of silence followed. "Take the men from the Northern Border and all the soldiers who have rested. I'll be there soon."

Refugio saluted. "Don't be long, Black Wolf," he whispered. "The men need your confidence."

"I won't be long."

By the time Refugio got the men assembled, and positioned, the Sethians were within sight of the lines, fast approaching the city's border.

~

*L*ukaan watched as they formed their lines, in anticipation of a charge by him. They had no idea what they faced. He called the captain aside and issued his orders. "Captain, prepare the men to charge."

~

*R*efugio paced the line, twenty thousand soldiers standing anxiously behind him. The enemy was approaching, but he had Tico scout them, and he reported no more than fifteen thousand men. And Tico was seldom wrong.

Confidence topped Refugio's cap. He was accustomed to fighting with the worst odds; this would be a welcome advantage. The Cergalans and Khatarans lined up in column formation awaiting orders from Refugio. He mixed the units up, keeping his stalwart troops as leaders of each column. They were trained. Patient. They could wait until an enemy was almost upon them before reacting, but then it would be devastating.

"Hold," Refugio ordered as the Sethians charged. "Hold!" he repeated when they drew near.

Fifteen thousand of them, roaring toward Refugio's front line. "Ready!" he shouted.

Darstan stepped through a rift, nodded to Refugio. "You're in command, General. Tell me what to do."

"Wait until they are almost here, BlackWolf, then use your fire against them. When they retreat, we will set upon them and finish it."

Moments later the Sethians charged, racing toward the front lines. Just as they were about to engage, though, the Sethians veered left and right in a typical envelopment maneuver, but the entire army went with them, leaving the middle with no one. As Darstan wondered what kind of tactic this was, a massive wall of BlackFire roared toward him. He had never seen a wall of fire that big, nor one that moved so fast.

Using his concentration, he focused on a defensive wall, but what he erected was crushed by Lukaan's fire. The impact sent him reeling, knocked him back a hundred paces or more, but the rest of the men, it engulfed. Screams shattered his ears, and the smell of flesh burning assaulted his nose. He struggled to his feet, tried to call more fire, but it, too, was crushed as soon as it met the wall.

As he ran toward the line, he issued orders to those in retreat. "Get to the harbors. Tell them to get everyone to sea. As far as they can."

"Refugio! Refugio!" He called for his general, but he was nowhere to be found.

A Cergalan ran past Darstan, his arm still smoldering. "Refugio is gone, BlackWolf. Just gone!"

Darstan felt the weight on him. More people dead because of him. And a real friend this time. He had taken Refugio from his home. From his family.

"What can we do, BlackWolf?"

Darstan looked at a young soldier in tears. "Grab hold of me!" he said. "Tell everyone to grab hold of each other."

Several hundred, maybe more, finally joined, but then he had to shift before Lukaan's assault got them again. He took them to the docks.

Sennar came running toward him. "What happened? We heard—"

"Lukaan!" Darstan said, and he looked around. "Lukaan is out."

"What!"

"Has to be. He's the only one strong enough to do that to me." Darstan turned to Sennar. "Get the men on the ships and get them out of here. Take everyone you can and get as far to sea as you can."

"But—"

Darstan grabbed him. "Listen, Sennar. If he can see you, you're dead!"

"What about you?"

"Don't worry about me. I'll take care of myself."

Leaving Sennar and Malakai to take care of them, Darstan shifted back to the lines to try and save some more. By the time he returned though, they were gone. Burnt to ashes. He saw Lukaan staring at him from a distance, and he felt the malice in him. His blood boiled. Rage building. "You'll pay for this, Lukaan! Believe me; you'll pay."

84

BATTLE FOR KAMNOR

Takar paced in front of his tent, a limp showing from the torture Ludar had put him through. The night had a chill, but other than that it was a good night, with both moons hanging low. They needed all the light they could get. He had set up camp in an old Sykoran outpost near the Kamnoran border, yet close enough to the Free Lands to provide easy access.

Across the border in the Free Lands, ten thousand Victas waited for them, gathering strength each day. And to the northeast, in the forests of Kamnor, another five thousand. Worse, though, were the two thousand Wolfen that supported the force that had invaded Kamnor. It was nearly impossible to fight Wolfen in the forest. They were silent and all but invisible. It was like fighting the trees.

A horse galloped into camp, and the rider dismounted and raced to Takar. The three-fisted salute was done quickly, and he began speaking before he finished. "Right flank's secure, Sergeant." The soldier shook his head and cursed. "Sorry, sir. Meant Force Commander."

Takar laughed. "I don't care what you call me as long as you do your job." Takar thought a moment while the man waited. "Secure all the way? Who's holding the border with Nyauran?"

"They said Vonner's got that held tight. I know him, Force Commander. They won't get through."

"All right. Eat something, then rest. You'll be going out again tomorrow."

"Yes, sir," he said and pounded out a salute.

Takar returned to pacing, a young recruit by his side. "Tell Mennar I want him."

The lad rushed off, returning with Mennar in moments. Takar started as soon as Mennar saluted.

"I want riders posted every half league, with messengers going back and forth all day. I don't want any surprises." He glared when he said it.

As Mennar departed, Takar smiled, but then a frown pounced on his face like it had been waiting. He turned to the recruit again. "Get the Force Leaders and any Strike Leader not on duty. I want them here. And tell someone to get me khaffe. We might be up a while."

*T*akar sipped on khaffe as the men made their way to his tent. Three Force Leaders and four Strike Leaders had already shown up. He expected two more.

Salardi came in, running. "Sorry, Force Commander, caught me at the pits."

Takar laughed. "That's all right, Jenkins isn't here yet either."

Salardi's face grew somber. "Won't be, sir. Took a Victa ax today. Not too long ago."

Takar closed his eyes and gritted his teeth. "Falek!"

The recruit came running. "Yes, sir."

"Find out why I wasn't told about Jenkins."

"Yes, sir!" he said, and raced off.

"Falek?" Salardi asked. "Wasn't that the bandit in the Freeland's name?"

"Might be his son for all I know, but he works well. Listens, too."

Salardi grabbed a khaffe, handing another one to Takar when he did. "What have we got, sir?"

"What we have is a lot of trouble. We're barely holding the Nyauran border, and as you know, Kamnor is gone. The enemy has complete control. We're facing maybe seven thousand Victas and Wolfen in Kamnor and another ten thousand in the Free Lands."

"I'll take the Free Lands," Salardi said, and laughed.

The Force Commander nodded. "I'd agree with you on that. The Wolfen are tough in the woods, but ten thousand Victas hiding behind rocks in the Free Lands doesn't give me any comfort."

"What about Pomanda?" Force Leader Nardo asked. "Can we expect any help from them?"

Takar cursed. "I've got three full strike forces at the border. I don't know that we can count on them not to attack us, let alone help us." He raised his cup and drained it, tossing the last drop or two aside. "Sure could use those men here."

"What are we going to do?" Nardo asked.

"That's what I brought you here for. I want ideas, plans. We need a strategy that's going to work."

Takar paced, limp exaggerated from overuse. "And we can't sit here and wait them out. They're getting reinforced every day." Takar threw his khaffe mug on the ground. "Where in god's name are they getting these troops?"

Salardi paced, too. "We got that boy, don't we? The one with powers?"

"Darstan?" Takar shook his head. "No, he's in Khatara and from the last report I got, he's in trouble there."

"How could he be in trouble with powers like that?"

Takar stared at him. "No different than having a quiver full of arrows and the high ground. Seems like you're invincible until you run out of arrows."

"What about the other one?"

"We've got him, Nardo. Or soon will, I hope. I put him on the Pomandan border until we see what they're doing. If they attack and we've only got three strike forces, they'll run over them. But with Rahg, they could hold out quite a while."

"Couldn't we make better use of him up here?" Salardi asked.

Takar shook his head. "If the Pomandans attack and Rahg shows his powers, it might be enough to hold them back for some time."

The force commander pointed to the woods. "Up here, against them, he's only as good as his powers. The Wolfen and Victas aren't going to be afraid of Rahg, not with what they've seen in Sethia."

"Then it's just us, so we better get smart."

Twice the fire had to be stoked and twice they had to add wood. Shortly before sunrise, they broke off. "Get what rest you can, men. It's going to be a long day."

"Least we got a plan," Nardo said.

"Just hope it works," Salardi added. "Anyway, I've got to get going. Need to get over to the Free Lands before the Victas do anything."

~

*P*ack Commander Drogg sniffed the air, cool and crisp, and tainted with the scent of fear carried from the Sykoran camp.

One of three fingers rubbed the silver hilt of his Wolfen long knife, a gift from his father when he had been just a pup. He breathed in again, a long, deep breath, reveling in Kamnor's fresh air. It would be good to rid these lands of the frail ones, then he and his packs could roam freely, feel the cold mountain air and taste the snow.

~

*P*ack Leader Vanya stood half a step behind him, a snarl painted on his face whenever the commander wasn't looking. Vanya thought it should have been him leading the forces in Kamnor, but they put Drogg in charge; it irked Vanya. "How should we prepare the day?" Vanya asked.

"We'll watch them to see what they do. They know they have to attack soon."

Vanya nodded. "More Victas came in last night. Almost two hundred."

"No more packs?"

Vanya shook his head. "They sent them to Nyauran, trying to break them at the border."

Drogg growled, a fierce guttural sound called up from ancestral times. "They should have sent us the packs and put the Victa Broods on the line. Fools!"

Vanya looked about nervously. "The orders came from the Master. He—"

"He might be a god, but that doesn't mean he knows how to fight."

Vanya's eyes darted about, but he kept silent, afraid to stir more conversation.

*D*rogg watched the enemy camp without a sound. "You see how nervous they are today. And how they are eating their meal early." He smiled. "Tell Brood Commander Mazza that I want to see him. I suspect the frail ones will attack soon."

The Pack Leader darted off, not bothering to salute. As he raced through the forest, he wondered how Drogg would position them. He hoped he would lead the front, that would honor his family forever.

～

*D*rogg put Vanya on the left flank, poised to go in first and draw the fire of the Sykorans. With a force of nine hundred Victas and several hundred Wolfen, they would know it was a major attack. Once they focused on Vanya, Brood Commander Mazza, now with eight thousand troops, would press the full weight of his attack on the center line, while leaving a reserve of two thousand Victas to contain their right flank.

Simultaneously, the Victa forces in the Free Lands would launch a southerly attack through the pass. Drogg's forces would wait until he saw where the Sykoran Commander committed his men.

～

*T*akar paced an imaginary line within the camp. He had barely slept the previous night, and not at all during the day. To complicate things, his limp was growing worse as the new night wore on. Nerves ate at his gut, and the vast amount of coffee he drank roiled in his stomach. "Falek! Any word?"

Falek seemed to appear from nowhere, saluting as he did. "Nothing, sir. We've got scouts everywhere though. We'll hear as soon as they make a move against us."

Takar nodded and kept his hands folded behind his back. He faced Nardo and asked, "Any word from Salardi?"

Force Leader Nardo shook his head. "He hasn't had time to get there, let alone get a message back." He handed Takar another khaffe. "I know this doesn't go together, but drink this to relax, then try to get some sleep."

Takar laughed. "You're right, Nardo. Don't plan on being a healer in your next life."

"I'm not done with this one yet."

Takar sipped the khaffe Nardo gave him and looked at the sky. Clouds had moved in to cover the faint glow of the moons in daytime. Not a good sign for them. "I hope you're right, Nardo. I'd like to live a little while longer myself."

Nardo placed his cup near the fire. "Got to get back, sir. Don't want that flank unsupervised for long."

"See you soon," Takar said.

~

Drogg waited until the reports were in, then issued his orders. "It's time, Vanya. Kill their scouts first." After acknowledging Vanya's nod, he turned to his Pack Assassin. "Help take out their scouts, then send us the signal."

He pounded out a salute before disappearing into the darkness, five of his fellow Wolfen trailing behind him.

Drogg looked at the ever-darkening sky and smiled. The frail ones would not have a chance against them. Before the clouds changed, he gave the orders—attack!

Pack Assassins had moved in ahead of the forces and had been successful in taking out almost every scout the Sykorans had. They would have no advance warning of the attack. The pack assassins now switched roles and moved to take over the role of spy.

When Vanya's forces got close enough, he issued the orders to charge, surprising the Sykorans. As Takar's men rallied and threw their forces against them, Brood Commander Mazza launched his assault from the center, simultaneously moving his reserve troops to hold the right flank.

~

Falek ran into camp, out of breath. "Force Commander! They've attacked!"

Takar rushed out of his tent, buckling his sword onto his belt. "Where, Falek? Calm down and tell me."

"Wolfen and Victas on the left, and lots of Victas in the center."

"How many are lots?"

Falek settled himself and straightened up. "Sorry, sir. Lost myself for a moment. They said there were about two thousand on the left flank and maybe two or three times that many in the center."

Takar grabbed hold of a young soldier nearby. "Get Nardo, tell him I need him now."

He thought about what Falek told him. If the reports were accurate, that would account for almost all of the troops they had—if, their estimates had been correct.

Takar still had them outnumbered, but they had taken advantage with the surprise attack. Where the hell had his scouts been? He thought about what the Wolfen would do. They would be the ones running this strategy. "Falek, tell them to hold the left, let the center fall back a little, but hold! Don't let them break."

Falek turned to leave.

"Not yet, boy! I'm not done with you. Tell the commander we are looking for an envelopment. I'll send troops to support his right."

Falek stared at him, then lowered his head. "Sir, won't they recognize that? I mean, everybody knows that strategy."

Takar's head was bobbing up and down. "True, lad. And it's not something the Wolfen commander would fall for, but the Victas might. I think it's worth a gamble."

"Yes, sir." Falek snapped out a salute. "That all, sir?"

Takar thought for a moment, then, "Tell him if the Victas don't fall for it, to attack with everything they've got. Push straight up the center."

"Yes, sir," Falek said and sped off.

Nardo arrived moments later. "Yes, sir?"

"Nardo, take five thousand men and attack the right flank. They will likely have a small reserve there, so be prepared to take them out first, but once you do, close in on them."

"Sir, that won't leave us much in reserve. Only a few hundred."

"I know, Nardo. It's a risk we'll have to take."

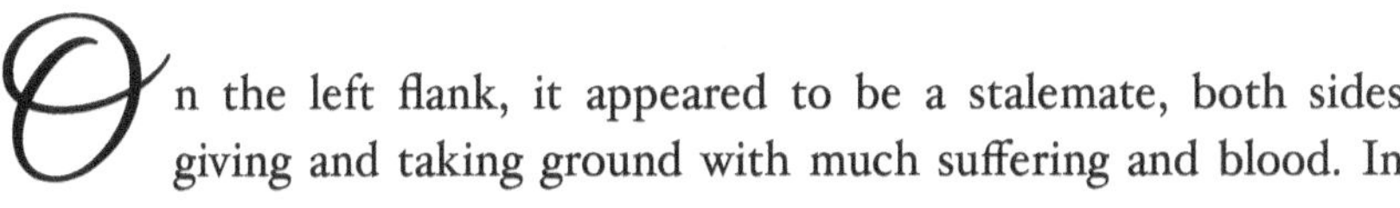

*F*alek rode his mount hard toward the front line. This was his most important duty assignment yet, and he felt the pride swell inside him. Perhaps this would make up for the wrongs his father had done as a bandit.

He repeated the orders over and over in his head, making sure he didn't forget a thing. This was for Sykor, even more, if Takar was to be believed.

As he turned a bend and slowed to cross the creek, Pack Assassin Jarrven moved from behind a tree and shoved his long knife into Falek's side, yanking him from the horse as he did.

Falek shouted, and attempted to draw his sword, but the Wolfen struck two more times with his knife before Falek could clear the sheath. The young recruit slumped to the ground, moaning.

*O*n the left flank, it appeared to be a stalemate, both sides giving and taking ground with much suffering and blood. In the center, Commander Mazza was making headway, pushing the Sykorans back with little resistance. Too little, he thought, recalling what Tirzinitzia had told him about the Sykoran strategy, that they might try something like this.

He issued orders to halt the advance. If they are trying to lure us into a trap, then the right flank is in danger.

Mazza considered it a moment longer, then moved half his troops to the right flank and sent another thousand to support the left. "We will hold the center, brood members. Do not fail the Master. He is watching."

~

Free Lands--Calgar Pass

Salardi paced behind the front line. The scouts had already reported movement in the pass. "Keep alert, men. They could come at any moment."

A veteran soldier holding watch on the line stopped him. "You think this is it, sir?"

"No way to tell, soldier." Salardi wished he hadn't said that. He wished he had known his name, a good commander would have. "Soldier, what's your name?"

"Baumgartner, sir."

"Well, Baumgartner, all I can tell you is we're going to kill a lot of Victas when they come out. If they get past us, they'll know they had one demon-cursed fight. I guarantee that."

He saluted. "You bet, sir. I'll make sure of it on my end."

Salardi patted him on the shoulder. "I know you will. We all will."

~

Through the night Victas from the rear positions moved toward the pass, crowding the border with Sykor. A messenger had come earlier in the day informing them of the attack from Kamnor, and early reports showed it going well, with the Sykorans suffering heavy casualties.

Four veteran brood leaders stood alongside Commander Noll, waiting for orders. Noll listened to the latest scouting report, then dismissed the soldier and addressed his officers. "The pack assassins have taken out their scouts between Kamnor and Nyauran. They won't know that their eastern border is being overrun before it is too late."

"But the scouts delivered messages. We saw them."

"Tirzinitzia insisted. We will let them worry for a while, perhaps until tonight, then we will attack during the dark."

Brood Commander Noll looked at each in turn. "Are your troops ready? Do they know that failure is death?"

Each one nodded. "It has been related, Commander," the most seasoned veteran said.

Noll acknowledged him. "Good. Have everyone rest. We attack tonight."

85

DEATH IN KHATARA

Lukaan watched as Darstan shifted with the few troops remaining after Lukaan's last attack. It was all right; he wouldn't get far, not taking so many with him. More than likely he was already exhausted from the battle, not to mention bewildered and confused. A smile lit Lukaan's face. Now would be the time to kill him.

He looked to his Sethian commander, anxiously awaiting orders. "Leave no survivors, Commander."

The commander bowed low, stuttering out his response. "Your will, Great Master," he said, then turned to his officers. "Put all prisoners to the sword. The Master commands it."

Lukaan marched the rest of the way into Khatara with no resistance. He set fire to every building he saw, and he had his men kill any person, male or female, child or adult. As he burnt a path toward the harbor, smoke filled the sky, and the screams of the dying filled the air.

*S*ennar and Malakai roused the men they had brought, forcing them to abandon the city and head for the ships. "Row till your head hurts, mates, because what's coming after you is worse than a sea demon. Even worse than that witch who came aboard."

Many of his men had died in the struggle, as many as two thousand by Malakai's calculations, but that was a small number compared to what the Khatarans had lost. And from what he was hearing from the city, lots more dead would need to be counted.

Sennar tried one last time to convince Darius to come with him, but the man would have nothing of it. Can't say he blamed him. It was his city. If someone had been doing this to Genda, Sennar imagined he'd stay and fight. He'd like to think so anyway.

Darius held his hand out in gratitude. "Captain Sennar, I want to thank you and your men. We might not have saved the city, but we tried."

Sennar shook his head. "Wish you'd come with us. It's gonna be bad here."

"I'll stay."

Sennar nodded and climbed into the last boat leaving the dock. He could hear the cracking of lightning and the terrifying screams of the people as he pulled away from shore. "Put your backs into it, boys. This is not over yet."

～

*L*ukaan and his men moved down the street that ran from the market to the dock. Normally lined with vendors selling food, clothes, and just about any kind of goods anyone could want, it sat empty today. As Lukaan passed, flames engulfed the buildings, leaving them nothing but ashes before he hit the next block.

As he approached the harbor district, archers fired from the walls of the fortress. A wave of BlackFire eliminated them before any had a chance to strike, then Lukaan stopped and stared at them. Calling forth Lightning, he blasted away at the wall until a huge section of it collapsed to the right of the main gate. Darius and his men rushed to guard the gap, swords drawn.

Lukaan waited until they had packed the opening, then he issued BlackFire against them. It rolled forward, disintegrating the bodies that covered the square, then eating through the resistance that Darius had prepared. Soon, his men occupied the fortress, and all prisoners were dead.

Lukaan walked to the dock, staring at the small boats, some still racing to reach the ships. He judged the distance, then fired Lightning at them, missing many, but striking many more. With each hit, the boat exploded, killing most of the men instantly.

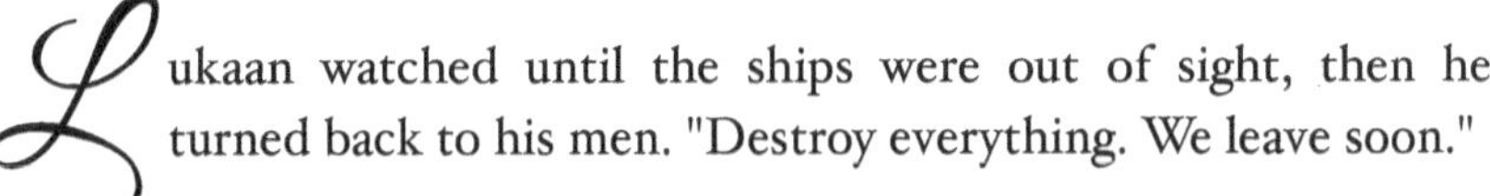

*A*s Sennar climbed the rope ladder to the Sea Skate, a bolt of lightning struck the ship next to him, blasting a huge hole in it and setting it afire. "Get us out of here," he yelled.

By the time he got out of ranged, Sennar had lost six of his ships and more than a dozen of the small boats filled with crewmen. As he looked through his glass at the harbor, he saw Lukaan staring at him. It looked as if Lukaan's eyes had locked onto him, and Sennar felt as if he couldn't let go. Never thought I'd be praying to have that witch around, but I'd sure like her here now.

*L*ukaan watched until the ships were out of sight, then he turned back to his men. "Destroy everything. We leave soon."

86

THE TIDE TURNS

Rahg walked the lines by himself, worried if he was up to the task entrusted to him. He couldn't afford a mistake. If the Pomandan border fell, it would put Takar and his men in danger of a rear attack. Early scouting reports estimated there to be ten thousand Pomandans poised to advance into Sykor. *And here I am with less than a thousand men.*

Further thoughts were interrupted by Strike Leader Dorran's arrival. He saluted Rahg, then stood at attention. "Sir, we've got reports that more Pomandans are ready to move at the crossing by Fetter's Creek."

Rahg's gut tightened. He prayed they were wrong. "And these reports are reliable?"

Dorran didn't sigh, but he seemed as if he might. "Sir, I would not have come to you unless I felt they were reliable."

Rahg nodded. "Of course. My apologies." He stared at Dorran for a moment before speaking, trying to determine what to say. He decided the truth was best.

"Strike Leader, I'm sure Takar told you I'm not experienced. The fact is, I'm not much more than a farm boy who happens to have powers to do things others can't."

He looked around him, saw the tents and supply carts. "If I wanted to I could set everything you see near us on fire. I could surround us with a shield, too, so nothing could hurt us. Not arrows, or swords, or anything. But this is only temporary. It doesn't last long." Rahg sighed. "And worst of all, I don't know the first thing about warfare, so you are going to have to help me. I'm counting on you to make the decisions."

Dorran seemed relieved. "Sir, that is the most refreshing thing a commander has ever said to me."

Rahg laughed, and when he did, Dorran laughed with him. "Good, then consider me as you would a shovel or a pick. Use me as you would one of them."

"Then, sir, this is what I suggest. We keep the same number of scouts close to the border, so we can tell if any of them come through. The last thing we want is them finding out how few men we have. We also disperse more of our men to the north and south of Fetter's Creek, keeping no more than a hundred with us at the crossing."

"So few?"

"Here's where I'm counting on you, sir. If they cross at the creek, they will also test us up and down, but with only a few men. We need to be ready to hold them back. If you hit them with your fire it will likely scare them so much it will send half of them home. I promise you, sir, take it from one who doesn't like these things. It's frightening."

Rahg thought for a moment then nodded. "I know. I'm scared of it myself."

After another round of short laughter, Rahg grew somber. "Guess it's time we go then."

By the time they got to the crossing at Fetter's Creek, Rahg could almost feel the tension in the air, a blend of anxiety and fear that had men jittery, kept them from napping.

A patrol leader rushed up to Dorran, snapping out a three-fisted salute. "Sir, they've been testing us regularly. I expect them to come across soon."

"They're testing you to keep you awake and nervous. I doubt they plan on attacking until morning." Dorran looked around, saw the panic building in his men. They had no confidence in this young boy, Rahg, and he didn't blame them. If it hadn't been for Takar, he wouldn't either. He tugged on Rahg's sleeve and walked to the side, out of earshot.

"What is it?" Rahg asked.

"I think we need to take the initiative, sir. Perhaps we should attack them."

"They haven't done anything to warrant it!"

Dorran looked at him as if he were a child. "Sir, I know you're not a veteran, but you're not a child either. And you're not a diplomat." He turned to face the border. "Look over there. It's as plain as it can be. They're planning on attacking, and soon."

Rahg took time to stare, but he didn't need to. He could feel it, just like he knew when it was going to snow on those days when the air felt wet, and the skies were gray. "What do you suggest?"

Dorran smiled. "For that, sir, you'll have to tell me a little more of what you can do."

~

*N*ardo's men charged headlong into what they thought was going to be a small reserve of Victas, only to discover thousands of them, and positioned to make the worst scenario for him. Three thousand to the front, meeting him head-on, and several thousand more to his right flank. He had to do something to counteract this, or his men would be in trouble.

Nardo dispatched messengers to both Takar and the commanders of the other strike forces in the center and on the left flank. He only hoped they got there in time.

~

A messenger reached Sykoran Strike Leader Greenwell while he pondered his situation. The Victa commander had suddenly stopped his advance even though Greenwell had conveniently given him ground.

The strike leader thought he might have acted too hastily, let the Victa have it too easily. Even an animal suspects a trap when it comes too easily. Greenwell cursed. Takar would have his hide for this.

Greenwell took the lad aside, not wanting his men to hear if the news was bad. "What news have you, lad?"

"Force Leader Nardo said he is being surrounded." The soldier panted, out of breath from his run through the woods. "He said they surprised him with a strong right flank and even more in reserve to encircle him."

So that's what they did? "And nothing on the left? No news there?"

"None that I know of, sir."

Greenwell clasped his hands behind his back as he walked slowly around the tent. "You must be thirsty, or cold, if not both. Do you want te or khaffe?"

"Te, please, sir."

The strike leader ordered his aide to bring te for both of them, then he sat. "When we're done here, I'm going to have to ask you to make one more run, lad. I need to get this message back to Force Leader Nardo."

"Not a problem, sir."

"Good. Tell Nardo that I'm going to send half of my force to support his flank so we can cut them off at the neck. Meantime, I'll push ahead with the rest as if we were falling into their trap. That way, they won't suspect anything."

"Yes, sir." The young soldier stood, making ready to depart.

"Wait for your te, lad. It won't be long."

"Sir, nothing more I'd rather do, but Commander Nardo will be waiting for this. I need to get it to him."

Greenwell stood with him, clapped him on the back. "You're a good soldier. Stay alert. We need you to live long enough to be a commander yourself."

The boy smiled and saluted. "Yes, sir."

~

Takar was taking a nap when the messenger from Salardi arrived. His new aide entered the tent to wake him, as per instructions.

"Sir, message from Commander Salardi."

Takar got up, rubbing too little sleep from his eyes. "Any news about Falek?"

"No, sir. We have people out searching for him, but no sign as yet, and he never arrived at the front."

Takar kicked a stool out of his way. "Blasted Wolfen probably got him. Can't even see them in these woods." He focused on the business at hand. "Send in the messenger and get me some khaffe. See if he wants food and drink too. It's a long way from the Free Lands."

The force commander spent the better part of two cups of khaffe with the messenger, and the news was not good. The Victas had swarmed out of the pass, attacking with full force. Salardi's men were holding, but he said it was only a matter of time.

While he was finishing his instructions to take back to Salardi, news of a messenger from Nardo arrived. "Tell Salardi to hold as long as he can, but not to sacrifice an undue number of men. And remember, if he has to retreat, get word to me quickly. We don't want to be surprised by ten thousand Victas on our backs."

"Yes, sir!" the soldier said, and pounded his chest in salute. "I could use a fresh horse, sir, then I'll be off."

"Tell my aide," Takar said, then shook his hand. "May the gods protect you, soldier."

"Thank you, sir. And you."

When he had gone, Takar signaled for Nardo's messenger to come up. "I hope you've got good news for me."

"Actually, sir. It's not the best, but not too bad."

This was a veteran soldier, not the young recruits they normally used for messengers. That thought brought Falek to mind again, and Takar cursed himself for using him. He was too green. "Go on."

"Commander Nardo said to tell you the right flank will hold. He got support from Greenwell on that, but that has put Commander Greenwell in a spot, and his line is weakening."

"And the left?"

The soldier sighed. "That's the bad part, sir. It's failing. Probably won't hold through the night."

Takar paced. And I don't have a blasted soul to send them. "Tell them to hang on. Tell them I said this is for Sykor. They are the last line."

"Yes, sir. Is that all?"

Takar thought for a minute, then nodded. "I'm afraid it is. I'd like to send you back with a few strike forces, but I can't even give you a companion rider right now."

The soldier saluted. "Don't worry, sir. We'll hold it."

After the man left, Takar sat on the edge of his cot, burying his head in his hands. He had not heard from Pomanda or the Eastern border, but he hadn't expected to; they were too far off.

News from the two Northern borders had not been as good as he'd hoped for, and that worried him. They had to hold all fronts, or they would lose all fronts. He braced his hands on his knees and with great effort, stood. "Boy! I need more khaffe."

The recruit came running, scared half out of his wits by Takar's gruff voice. He shouldn't be so hard on the lad, but it was difficult. This one was no Falek, and now Falek was probably dead.

Takar's hand played with the hilt of his sword. He intended to kill more than a few Wolfen to settle that score.

● **87**

THE LIGARNS' REVENGE

Shatir led them through the mountains north of the Nyauran border, taking seldom-traveled paths and hidden trails so their advance would remain undetected.

Once they reached the Kamnoran forests they had no worries; no one could detect them once they got there. Not even the Wolfen. They walked for several hours, then ran at double the pace for several more hours. A short rest followed before repeating the same. Meals and sleep accounted for less than seven hours a day. At this rate, they would be within striking distance by the next night.

The thick forests of Kamnor welcomed the Ligarns by mid-afternoon. Shatir dispatched scouts to see where the Wolfen and Victas were, and what forces they faced. Shortly after dusk, they returned with reports.

"Not more than a league ahead, they are fighting the frail ones. Victas have the right flank and are barely holding on, but they are advancing in the center. If they push through, they will be able to reinforce the right. The left should be theirs soon."

"The Sykorans are holding their own?" Jen Pal asked.

The Ligarn scout who led the expedition shook his head. "The Wolfen have a strong reserve just ahead. Waiting, no doubt to see where it is needed most."

He looked to Jen Pal then Shatir. "If I were him, I would throw them at the left, overrun them, then sweep around their rear flank."

"How many Wolfen?" Jen Pal asked.

"Far too many for us. Perhaps fourteen hundred."

Shatir snickered as she locked eyes with Jen Pal. "Not so bad of odds."

"Not if done properly," Jen Pal said.

He thought for a moment, then instructed Shatir to bring Suk Won and Triala. "We need a strategy."

A short while later, Suk Won showed, followed soon after by Triala. Once they were all together, Jen Pal started. "The Wolfen must be stopped before they can reinforce the left flank, and as you know, they have us outnumbered ten or twelve to one. Perhaps more."

Suk Won muttered something unintelligible, but when Shatir pressed him, he spoke up. "I am not complaining, Jen Pal, but we did not come this far to fail so early. Those odds are not reasonable."

Triala shook her head. "The odds are not bad if you know how the Wolfen operate, Suk Won. They never attack as a single group. Their pack commander will split them up into sections with four or five packs in each one. If my guess is correct, these will be spaced out to attack the frail ones at various points, striking quickly, then retreating while another group strikes in another area. Each time the frail ones respond to move toward an attack, the packs will attack their flank."

Shatir leaned in close, listening intently. "So you are saying that they will have no more than fifty or sixty in each group?"

"For the flanks, yes, but they will likely keep a large force, one of perhaps two hundred at the rear, in the center."

Jen Pal smiled. "If we isolate the packs individually and attack each of them with our full force—"

"Then we will take them before they can get word to the others," Triala said.

"Are you are sure this is what they will do?" Suk Won asked.

"As certain as anyone can be of what the enemy is thinking. In my youth, I spent time with a Wolfen pack. I know how they work."

"It will be easy enough to determine," Jen Pal said. "We will watch and see what they do. If they divide their forces as Triala said, we will take them apart one by one."

Shatir stood. "We should eat for nourishment. We have a long night ahead of us."

~

Salardi rode his horse from one side of the line to the other, trying every trick he knew to keep the men inspired. It was difficult with ten thousand Victas charging the front line.

The Sykorans had dug trenches in front of their lines and erected barricades, but the Victas didn't seem to care about the loss of men; they kept coming, letting the dead bodies fill the ditches so they could cross, and use them as steps to climb over the berms Salardi's men had built.

It was that disrespect for their own comrades' lives, as much as their appearance, which put the fear of the gods into the Sykoran soldiers. It was one thing to fight another man, a Pomandan or a Khataran, but to fight these ... lizards was something else.

Two columns of archers fired from the back rows, putting arrow after arrow into the green-scaled monsters, but unless they happened to catch them in the throat or the face, the arrows did little but slow them down. It might have even worked as a disadvantage. When enemy soldiers approached with three arrows sticking out of their sides, it frightened the men.

Salardi shouted encouragement to his men as he passed them, now and then dismounting to offer a hand in the fighting. Nothing inspired men more than that. Despite their courage, he didn't know how much longer he could last. He had told Takar he'd hold as long as possible, and it might have just reached that limit.

As the strike leader prepared to issue orders for a retreat and to call for volunteers to guard the rear, shouts rang out from the front line.

"Commander, something's happening at the rear. Archers attacking the Victas."

Puzzled, Salardi rushed to get to the man, curious as to what he meant. He had no archers that could have flanked them. As he neared his left flank, he saw volleys of arrows, hundreds of them, if not more, flying out from the pass and the crevices in the rocks above it. Each time they flew, dozens of Victas dropped, and with only one shot. Salardi stared, but couldn't make out anything.

"What do you make of it, soldier?"

The man who called it out first shook his head. "Can't make out anything but arrows and the fact that Victas are dropping like vermin."

"But who is it?" Salardi wondered.

"Don't rightly care who it is, sir. Just glad they're here."

Salardi moved back, climbing a rock to get a better view. "Someone get me a looking glass. Quickly!"

Before long a soldier rushed up to him with one in his hand. Salardi fixed the sights, then focused on the pass. He smiled as wide as the morning sun when it came into view. "Lorns, men. We've got us a whole blasted army of Lorns ahead of us, and they're cutting down Victas with every shot."

A rousing shout went up from everyone within earshot, then Salardi ordered them to pass the word down the line. "We're going to give them a short time, then put the squeeze on these lizards. Hold that line! And wait for my signal. Then we go in."

*R*ahg told Dorran what he could do, and he told him his limitations, then he sat back and listened to the strike leader's plan, taking it all in without saying a word. When Dorran finished, Rahg stared at him. "We can't just attack them. They haven't done anything yet?"

Dorran hadn't touched his food and had barely sipped his ale. "Rahg, I know you're not a soldier, but Takar told me you were a smart lad. Have you seen them over there across the creek? What do you think they're doing, if not preparing to attack us? If we wait for them to make the first move, we're going to lose a lot of men."

Ragh thought for a while, then resigned himself to accepting the inevitable. Pomanda was planning to attack, and he had to stop them. "Shouldn't we try some kind of diplomacy first?"

Dorran grabbed him by the shoulders and shook him. "Lad, this is diplomacy. It's just a different kind."

Rahg smiled. "All right, Dorran. Tell me what to do, and I'll do it."

88

BETWEEN THE PLANES OF SANITY

Camissa felt it before she saw anything, and that feeling is what put the fear into her. She stood, trying to back away, but she stumbled over the leg of a chair.

Before she got back to her feet, the pouch Aentarra always wore on at her side opened, and several Slicers emerged. Two of them took up positions on each side of Aentarra's head while one hovered above her —just like they had when she when she was hurt in Sethia.

The noise from Camissa falling caused Mikkellana to awaken. She managed to lift her head enough to gawk. "Don't move, Camissa. Not one iota."

Both of them froze in place, and while they watched, a dozen more Slicers emerged from the pouch at Aentarra's side. They took up posts by her head, over her heart, and around her stomach and legs. Two of them made slow circles knee-high above her head, almost daring anyone to approach.

Mikkellana glared and spoke through gritted teeth. "What did you do?"

Camissa was afraid to speak, but she managed to whisper while staring at Aentarra. "Nothing. I didn't do anything."

"Liar! You must have done something to trigger them. They wouldn't have just come out on their own."

Camissa remained silent for a moment, then responded with regret. "I tried to heal her. I didn't—"

"You fool! You blithering idiot! I told you to leave her alone." Mikkellana wove a shield, ready to strike her with it, but she managed to restrain herself. Their odds were bad enough already. They didn't need to lose anyone else.

Tears filled Camissa's eyes. "I'm sorry, Mikkellana. What can we do?"

"Other than wait for her to awaken, I have no idea." Silence followed, then Mikkellana's voice softened. "Let's just pray she does awaken. If not, we could both be in trouble."

~

A rift opened in Talanvar's library, Darstan stepping out. Wisp and Aenaila were sitting there, talking.

"Where's Mikkellana?" Darstan asked.

"Upstairs," Wisp said. "Why?"

"Come with me. You'll hear when I tell her."

Darstan burst into Mikkellana's room, and when he did, Mikkellana and Camissa shouted at once. "Do not move!"

Darstan froze, staring. The Slicers caught his eye, and he closed the door behind him, cautioning Wisp and Aenaila to remain outside. "God's blood! What are they?"

"I don't quite know," Mikkellana said. "They are called Slicers, and trust me; they can kill you before you take another breath if they want to."

"My legs are cramping," Camissa said. "I don't know how much longer I can stand like this."

"As long as you want to live," Mikkellana said.

"Should I try—"

Mikkellana turned to him. "Don't try anything, Darstan. I mean it."

"Well, while we're together, I might as well spread more good news. Lukaan is out."

"What!" Mikkellana forgot about the Slicers and tried sitting but couldn't raise herself. "Lukaan? Are you certain?"

"I just came from Khatara. Fought him." Darstan paused to take a few breaths. "I used everything I had, and his fire collapsed mine. Unless there is someone else out there with that kind of power, it was Lukaan."

"Had to be," Mikkellana said.

"But how?" Camissa asked.

Mikkellana shook her head. "The shield was weakening even before I got hurt. It was only a matter of time. I just hoped it would hold a little longer."

"Who else?" Darstan asked.

"Tirzinitzia and Melissara." Camissa breathed harder while Mikkellana gnawed on her nails. "Tirzinitzia is a strategist. She would prefer not to fight herself, but she will if cornered. Melissara, on the other hand, is brutal. She can kill you with a single strike, and she won't hesitate to do it."

"She's your sister?" Darstan asked.

"I don't like to admit it, but she is a sibling."

"Scary enough," Darstan said, then looked over to where Aentarra lay on the bed. "What's wrong with her?"

"We don't know. We haven't been able to do anything," Mikkellana said, "But now we have no choice. We have to try and heal her."

"With those Slicers there?" Camissa asked.

Mikkellana scoffed. "It won't matter, Camissa. If we don't heal her, we're all dead." *Probably are anyway.*

"I think if you two walk very slowly toward me, you might be all right. They are there to protect her, not me."

*L*et me see what I can do," Darstan said.

"No! Don't go near her, Darstan."

As he approached, a dozen more Slicers flew from the pouch and surrounded his head, threatening him. He stopped, frightened, but confident that he had to find a way to help Aentarra. *I am not going to hurt her. I am here to help her.*

Nothing happened. He seemed to sense some kind of relief of tension, but the Slicers didn't budge. *I will not hurt her. I want to help.*

"What are you doing, Darstan?" Mikkellana asked.

Camissa put her finger to her lips, cautioning Mikkellana to be quiet.

Darstan tried one more time, hoping they could communicate with him at this level. *Help me to heal her. We need to have her back.*

The Slicers that had surrounded Darstan's head slid aside, not much, but enough to allow him to pass. He barely moved, but then advanced slowly, keeping alert for any signs of aggression. When he reached Aentarra, he spoke aloud. "I'm going to sit next to her now. I'm not going to hurt her."

The Slicers had followed him across the room, staying close to his head, never more than a finger's width away. He sat with no trouble from them, and once he was situated, he took a few deep breaths. *What now?* he wondered.

Open your mind.

Darstan almost jumped, but he managed to control himself. "What?"

Open your mind. Do not fight.

No sooner had he heard his, then two of the Slicers darted into his head, right through his temple. He hollered, almost panicked, but he offered no resistance. Within a few minutes, he had calmed down. He reached for Aentarra with his hand, placing it on her forehead. The Slicers guarding her moved aside to let him through.

Mikkellana gasped.

Darstan moved his hand across her forehead, then around her head, slowly. Sometimes he applied pressure, other times he brought fire to his hand and let it infuse her.

For almost an hour he kept this up, and all the while, the Slicers hovered and danced, watching, waiting. Another fifteen minutes went by, and suddenly Darstan began breathing heavily. Within seconds he collapsed to the floor. When he did, the Slicers exited his head and went back to the pouch at Aentarra's side. Soon after, the other Slicers did, too. And after that, Aentarra opened her eyes and tried sitting up.

Camissa rushed to see to Darstan while Mikkellana, almost too shocked to speak, looked to her sister. "Are you all right?"

Aentarra rubbed her head, pain showing on her face. "I think so." She looked down at the floor. "What happened to Darstan? What is he doing here?" Panic set in. "Who is taking care of Khatara?"

Mikkellana's exhilaration turned quickly to realism. "As to what happened to him, I don't know. He healed you. I know that much."

"Healed me? Impossible!"

"Yes, it is, isn't it. And yet, he did."

Aentarra knelt beside him and Camissa. "Any indication of what is wrong?"

"Nothing," Camissa said.

"In case you are still interested in your other questions, Aentarra. Lukaan now holds Khatara."

She spun around, eyes registering shock. "Lukaan is out!"

"And in full bloom. Darstan said he was destroying everything. By now the entire city is probably gone."

"That means he'll be coming here," Aentarra said. She turned to Camissa. "Heal him, girl. Find some way to heal him."

"Mikkellana can—"

Aentarra waved her hand in the air, as if to dismiss the statement. "My sister is good at some things, but when it comes to healing things of the mind she fails miserably. It's up to you. And you better be good."

89

SPECIAL REINFORCEMENTS

Melissara and Tirzinitzia rode with the massive army that the Sethians and Gnakas had put together. Tirzinitzia's strategy called for them to march through the Great Plains of Nyauran and break the border at Sykor.

The Sykorans were counting on the horsemen to keep them at bay, but Tirzinitzia's plans had nullified the benefits of their cavalry. And when they reached the border, no matter how many men the Sykorans had, it wouldn't matter. Melissara would see to that. She had to hurry, too. Lukaan was expecting her back in Sethia by the time he arrived.

His plan called for them to break the Sykoran border, then let Tirzinitzia move forward with the army while Melissara got a Shift point and returned to get Lukaan. It had been five days since they left Sethia, and she assumed he would be about through with Khatara by now. If not, it wouldn't be much longer.

"Commander Ovenni, how much longer until we reach the border?"

"Tomorrow, My Lady. And the scouts have reported that the horsemen have joined forces with the Sykorans."

"Does that present a problem?"

He shook his head. "None; in fact, it may help us. They won't know how to work together as well as our soldiers do, especially with—"

"With us?" Melissara asked, a hint of danger in her tone.

He bowed low. "Forgive me, My Lady. I meant no disrespect. It is simply that they will not be accustomed to fighting people with your talents."

Melissara smiled. "You are a diplomat as well as a commander. I like that."

Ovenni bowed again. "Yes, My Lady, thank you. Should we make camp here tonight? It will leave us plenty of time to reach them tomorrow."

"Good, make camp then. I could use some nourishment."

~

Jen Pal listened to the scouting report, then issued the orders. The Wolfen had split into groups, just as Triala suggested they would, and the group dispatched to the southwest sector had almost sixty pack members, split into four patrols. The plan was to surround them and attack as a single unit.

With the Ligarns outnumbering them almost two to one, it should not take long. The Ligarns who had chosen the bow as a bedmate were spaced out evenly, then, when Jen Pal gave the orders, they started the attack, firing rapidly into the rear of the Wolfen ranks. Within minutes, almost half of the Wolfen were gone, then the archers joined their brethren in completing the mission, using knives, sai, staff, and swords to kill the Wolfen before a signal could be sent.

When they had finished, Jen Pal ordered them to fall back, then move to attack the next group. They continued in this manner until they had eliminated the packs from the western side. Now facing the center force, the Ligarns changed strategy, relying on the archers to cut the Wolfen ranks down until their numbers were almost even.

~

*S*hatir took out the pack commander first; then the other archers focused on the Wolfen who were nearest to them. Within two hours they had whittled the Wolfen down to several dozen pack members, and Jen Pal had put Triala in charge of tracking them through the forest. They had sent runners to their relief forces on the eastern side, so they would arrive soon, but that meant that their front lines would be getting no support. The mission had already been successful, and they were far from through with it. Many more would die before Jen Pal pulled back.

*R*ahg waited for Dorran's signal, then just before dawn, he wove a shield inside the Pomandan ranks, cutting off one or two hundred of their soldiers from retreat. He left it open on the creek side, sealing them in on the rear and flanks. When Dorran issued the orders, Rahg released small columns of fire across the creek and into their ranks. They had camped in a heavily wooded area, filled with pines and an assortment of hardwoods, and since it had been dry of late, they caught aflame easily.

He cringed when he heard the screams of the men. At first, they tried retreating, but when they hit the shield and realized there was no escape they turned and charged ahead into Dorran's men, getting butchered by steel instead of flames.

"Keep it up," Dorran yelled. "Pretty soon they'll grow tired of this."

Rahg hated what he was doing, but he knew something had to be done. If he could convince the Pomandans to turn back, he could then help Takar at the Kamnoran border.

He waited until Dorran had finished with his butchering, then he wove another shield around more Pomandans. As soon as they realized they were caught, they moved across the creek, preferring to die fighting than by fire. But as they tried to climb the banks of the creek on the Sykoran side, Rahg unleashed his flames on them, not sparing a one.

Within a few hours they had slaughtered hundreds of Pomandans, and the rest of them moved back from the border, out of range of Rahg's shields or his fire.

"What do we do now?" Rahg asked.

"Wait them out," Dorran said. "They'll think twice before coming across now."

~

Melissara paced the camp late into the night. She spent half her time chewing on fingernails—a habit she shared with her sister—and the other half of the time, she worried about the outcome of the next few days. After the countless years she had spent in Sethia, swearing to get even with Mikkellana for locking them inside, she now discovered that vengeance was not as sweet as she thought it would be. Apparently, she had not inherited that from her father. Aentarra seemed to have gotten that trait.

She woke early despite being up most of the night. "Commander, are we ready to move?"

Commander Ovenni bowed to her. "My Lady, we are ready. How would you have us proceed?"

Melissara pointed to Tirzinitzia. "She's the strategist. Ask her?"

Tirzinitzia explained her plan to Ovenni, who listened intently, asking questions as she explained the details.

"What about the archers, My Lady? They will certainly have archers and likely many of them."

Tirzinitzia nodded. "Tell me just before we hit their range. We'll stay outside of it while I prepare them for our arrival."

"Yes, My Lady," Ovenni said, and issued orders to move the men out.

For two hours they marched, then as the plains gave way to lightly forested hills, they could see the Sykorans massed at the border, just beyond the crest of a small hill.

Ovenni called a halt and approached Tirzinitzia. "We are within one, perhaps two hundred paces of their archers."

Tirzinitzia studied the terrain ahead of them. "Where would their archers be?"

He pointed to the left, "There, behind the rise and in the woods." Then he pointed to the right. "And there, where the rocks are at the top of that hill."

"Fine. You can rest for now. Please ask Melissara to join me, and have your men be ready to go at my command."

"Yes, My Lady."

Tirzinitzia waited for Melissara, then told her what they would do. As soon as she was ready, they both unleashed Lightning on the areas where Ovenni indicated the archers would be.

Panic ran through the ranks of the Sykoran soldiers as they tried to retreat and hide from the strikes. Tirzinitzia continued to assault the archers, and Melissara struck wherever she saw huge congregations of soldiers. Soon, the massive army had turned into a disorganized mess of soldiers retreating for cover deeper into the woods of Sykor.

"Now!" Tirzinitzia ordered, and Ovenni had his men move ahead at a fast pace. Every time the Sykorans tried to regroup and form a stand, Melissara and Tirzinitzia sent a barrage of Lightning against them. It wasn't long before the Sethians and Gnakas had overrun the border and were putting hundreds of soldiers to the sword.

When they had the situation in control, Melissara announced she was leaving. "Ovenni, Tirzinitzia will be in charge while I am gone."

He bowed to her quickly, not much more than a nod. "Your will, My Lady."

"Practice your bowing, Ovenni. I am going to get the Master, and when he comes, your head better be much closer to the ground than it is now. If not, he may place it on the ground."

This time the bow was very low. "Apologies, My Lady."

"That's better, Commander. Now get busy. I shouldn't be long." Melissara turned to Tirzinitzia. "I'm going to get him now. I assume you are heading to Kamnor?"

"Kamnor, then the Free Lands. I'm hoping there isn't much to do, but we'll see."

"You're taking them with you to Kamnor?"

Tirzinitzia smiled. "I'm not taking many at all to Kamnor, enough to protect me when I tire—the rest are heading to Sykor, cut off their retreat, assuming any survive."

Melissara stared at her. "I will stall as long as I can to give you time. The more you have conquered before he gets here, the better it will be."

"Thank you, Melissara. I can use the help." Tirzinitzia started to go, but then turned back. "Melissara, what should I do if I run into those boys?"

Melissara's brow creased, and her eyes narrowed. "What do you mean? I'm certain you heard Lukaan's orders, and it's not like you to forget."

"I did hear his orders, but I also saw your hesitation. And you did help me one time."

Melissara thought long before answering. She still didn't know if she could trust Tirzinitzia or not. She wanted to think she could, but she wasn't sure. "Kill them, Tirzinitzia," she said and turned to depart. If you can.

90

PREPARATIONS

Camissa struggled with her attempts at healing Darstan. She had tried using her powers of Persuasion, calling on all the emotions she could think of that might benefit him, but nothing worked. He lay there, unconscious, and seemingly dead, though nothing seemed to be wrong; there was no blood, no marks, no signs of anything.

"I give up," she said, and stood to stretch her legs. "I have tried everything I know, but it's hopeless."

Aentarra poked her finger at Camissa. "Keep trying. Something will work sooner or later. It's only a matter of time."

"How do you know? It's—"

Anger flashed in her eyes. "I know because I know what did this to him." She seemed to settle down after pacing for a minute, then, "Keep trying."

Mikkellana called Aentarra to her. "Get Talanvar and the others up here. We need a plan."

Aentarra stared at her sister. "If you know anything, tell me now."

Mikkellana hesitated, but only for a minute. "I know that Melissara and Tirzinitzia weren't with Lukaan in Khatara. Which means—"

Aentarra banged her fist against the wall. "They're here, in Sykor. Not here, but out there fighting Takar and Rahg." Aentarra looked at Mikkellana. "She's going to kill him. You know that, don't you?"

"Not if we get a message to them first."

"I have no Shift points to call on. The fact is, Mikkellana, I don't even know where they are."

"I know you don't, but that thief might have some idea. He could get Aenaila to take him, deliver the message, then return."

"How can he remember a Shift point when he doesn't have the ability?" Aentarra asked.

"I think he has the ability and doesn't know it," Mikkellana said. "Even more so, somehow that talent of memorizing Shift points, which usually only comes with the ability, has infused his whole mind. He can remember everything! Even when he's not trying."

Aentarra stood and headed for the door. "Enough of this, I'm going to get them."

*S*he returned in a few moments, Talanvar coming through the door first, followed by Rhaven, Aenaila, and Wisp. Lord Talanvar nodded to Mikkellana. "You said you needed to see me?"

"I do, but first I need to talk to Aenaila and Kender."

Mikkellana told them what she wanted, then cautioned them. "You won't be able to bring everyone back. I know that. So bring back Takar, and whoever else he feels is needed to defend the city. Tell him the rest will have to make it on their own."

Wisp spoke first. "No way Takar will do that. He'll stay with the men."

"Tell him it's an order," Mikkellana said, and the look in her eyes was enough to frighten Wisp.

"I'll try, but I don't think it will work. Anyway, I know several spots I could take Aenaila. I don't know how close it is to where Takar is, but it shouldn't be too far."

"You don't have to worry about guessing," Rhaven said. "He'll be in the old outpost by the Kamnoran border with the Free Lands. Do you know it?"

Wisp nodded. "I've been there before." He turned to Aenaila. "I can get us right inside it."

"All right, hurry," Mikkellana said.

After they left, she turned to Talanvar. "We've got a bad situation coming. Lukaan is out, and that means once he is through with Takar's men, he'll be coming here."

"Then we've got to get out."

Mikkellana shook her head. "No time for that, and besides, we've got nowhere to go. He'll have the north covered, Pomanda is already against us, and Lukaan owns the east."

"And we don't have ships, so we can't go down the river," Talanvar said. "So how do we protect ourselves?"

"Gather every bow we have in the city and all the arrows. Assign them to anyone who can wield it, and man the walls. Have people get all the animals inside. Stock food and move everyone in from the surrounding countryside. Once that is done, brace the gates with stone. We need to prepare for a siege like you have never seen."

"I'll get Tobias to help," Rhaven said. "We'll start manning the north wall first."

"It's useless to try to stay here," Aentarra said.

Mikkellana shook her head. "I've seen cities hold out for thirty days against him in Nelstar."

"And I've seen them fall in a matter of hours," Aentarra said. "How do you plan on defending it? You can't even walk."

Mikkellana began to respond, but then saw Darstan raising his head. He got halfway up, struggling, then Camissa helped him sit. "Are you all right, Darstan?"

"Hurting, but yes, I'm all right."

"What happened?" Mikkellana asked. "You were helping Aentarra, then you passed out."

He blinked his eyes a few times, then rubbed his head. "I don't know. All I remember is falling."

Rhaven helped him to his feet. "Glad to see you, Darstan. We're going to need you for this."

"For what?"

"They have attacked in Kamnor, the Free Lands, and at the Nyauran border. Probably Pomanda too. And from what you told Mikkellana about what happened in Khatara, I feel certain they'll be coming here next."

"Meaning Lukaan and your sister?"

"And Tirzinitzia, yes. So we've got to prepare for them," Mikkellana said.

Rhaven clapped Darstan on the back. "I've got to go."

"Where's Rahg?"

"At the Pomandan border," Aentarra said. "Until they find him, then he'll be dead."

"I'm going to get him."

"Sit down, Darstan." Mikkellana seemed disgusted. "You have no idea where he is or how to get there. Unless you tell me you have a Shift point, you'd be wasting your energy."

"I hate to agree with my sister, but she's right. If I knew where he was, I would have gotten him already."

"I guess all we can do is wait."

"While you're waiting, why don't you try healing me the way you did her?"

"You just reminded me of that, sister." Aentarra spun around to face Darstan. "What did you do? And how did you know what to do?"

"I didn't do anything," he said and sat in the chair. "I can't heal you."

Mikkellana scoffed. "He won't tell you. He's as stubborn as an ass. He doesn't like me, so he won't heal me; it's that simple."

Darstan started to say something, but then he saw the despair on her face, the disappointment and frustration. He got up and walked over then sat on the bed beside her.

"I don't like you; you're right about that. And I do blame you for the loss of my hand and other things. But none of that has anything to do with my refusal to heal you."

She stared at him, and Darstan felt the pleading in her eyes. "If you want me to try, I will, but I can't promise anything."

Her look softened. "Aentarra, help Darstan turn me over. He'll need to see my back."

After they turned her over, carefully, Darstan lifted her top and placed his hand on her back, just above her buttocks, rubbing gently. If this were any other woman, he might have gotten excited. Even Aentarra. Perhaps especially Aentarra, but not Mikkellana. He still loathed her, and he couldn't change those feelings. He explored for a moment, then felt something that seemed out of place. When he went back to it, there was nothing.

"What is it?" Aentarra asked.

"Nothing. No, that's not right. I thought I felt something, but when I went back to it, it wasn't there."

"How did you do it with me?"

He didn't know if he should tell or not, but the way things looked, with Lukaan out, it hardly mattered. "When you were unconscious, the Slicers surrounded you. I came up to you, and two of them went into my head. After that, I could see into your head. I could see what was wrong with you."

Aentarra stared at him. "The Slicers went into your head?"

"Yes."

"You're certain of that?"

"I saw them," Camissa said, from her seat across the room.

Aentarra shook her head but continued staring at him. "Let's see what happens then." She opened up her pouch, and two Slicers emerged, glowing as if they were aflame. They rose slowly, then circled Darstan's head. On the second pass, they entered.

Darstan reeled back, surprised by the feeling, but he soon sat up. He had a blank look in his eyes as he placed his hand on Mikkellana's back, rubbing gently. "I see what is wrong now," he said.

A Slicer flew from his head and entered Mikkellana's back. She panicked. "What is going on, Darstan? What are you doing?"

Her back emitted a glow, a faint blue light; then it faded to nothing. Soon, Darstan stopped what he was doing and stood. The second Slicer emerged from his head and returned to Aentarra's pouch. "Stand up," Darstan said.

"What? I can't stand."

"Now you can."

Mikkellana looked at him as if he were crazy, but she attempted to sit. Suddenly a smile lit her face as she moved herself to a sitting position. "By the gods! By the sweet and mighty gods!"

Aentarra reached her hand out and helped her sister to her feet. With some struggling, Mikkellana stood. Tears filled her eyes.

"Darstan, I never thought I would walk again. How did you do it?"

"I don't know, Mikkellana, so quit asking me."

"But how?"

Darstan stared at her. "Listen, I'm not hiding anything. I truly don't know. When those Slicers entered me, it was like I could see inside your body. I could see what was wrong, and then I fixed it."

"Okay, I won't ask again how you did it, I'm just thankful that it worked." She walked, with Aentarra's help, to Darstan's side and hugged him. "I know you don't like me, Darstan, but I am eternally grateful for what you've done."

He nodded. "We need you for this battle, Mikkellana. Can't have a cripple fighting Lukaan can we?"

She laughed. "No, I guess we can't."

91

ALL THE NEWS IS BAD

Melissara waited in the Sethian Palace, sometimes pacing, at other times lounging in a chair in the reception hall. Lukaan would be here soon enough, and in the interim, she could reminisce about the good times in life, when things were happy.

It caused her to think about her life, and the hundreds of years she had spent in Sethia. All that time she had waited for revenge, wishing nothing more than to see the last breaths of her two sisters—now though, she found herself longing for the family she had sworn to kill.

Peals of Aentarra's laughter rang in Melissara's head as she recalled the tricks her little sister had played on their father. And the warm smile of her mother, always the patient one, always the sacrificial one, occupied a permanent spot in the corner of her mind, safe from vengeance or evil thoughts. Her mother had always let her father have all the fun and all the love. And she never asked for anything in return.

Try as she might to hate Mikkellana, fond remembrances of her as a child trying to organize events, even playtime, brought a smile to Melissara's face. Her older sister always had rules, even for the games they played as children. She must have been born with a rule book in her brain.

And those boys ...

She felt the disturbance in the air, smelled a hint of nutmeg, then prepared for Lukaan's entrance.

~

Shatir led her force of Ligarns to the left flank of the Wolfen, waiting only for the signal from Triala and Suk Won that they were ready. As soon as all were in place, they would attack from three sides while Jen Pal held his position in the north to preclude any escape. She had never liked the Wolfen.

As she lay behind some brush, tucked into shadows, a bolt of Lightning lit the air around her. Then another and more after that. She looked around, then at the sky. This was no storm!

Signaling to those closest to her, she ordered them to fall back and report to Jen Pal; meanwhile, she advanced further south to see what she could find out. The sounds of battle had grown more prominent during the past few moments.

Jen Pal listened patiently while the Ligarn gave her report. Though he had not needed to hear this, he listened in case new information arose. He had seen the Lightning also, as did all of them. And they all knew exactly what it was—the small gods had arrived. They were out!

He looked around, worry tearing at him. "Where is Shatir?"

"She went to scout them."

Triala arrived and heard the conversation. "I will find her."

"No!" Jen Pal said. "It is my duty." He looked about, then spoke to Triala. "Take everyone and find the young ones."

"We have no idea where they went."

"The world is not so large, Triala. I have three guesses, knowing the ones who guard them. The mountains north of Jattan Kir would be my first choice."

"And where else?"

"The swamps where the Krovs live, though that would make them travel through the frail ones' lands, so it is my last choice. The other would be the White Mountains. No one goes there."

"There is a reason for that. No one can live there."

"A Ligarn can. They might lose some of the old ones, but the rest will survive." Jen Pal thought for a minute. "As I think on it, Triala, I would choose there before the others. Besides, it is closest."

She embraced him and let the hug linger, an emotion long lost on Ligarns. "I will see you at the Gates of the Sun, Jen Pal."

He laughed. "The Gates may be crowded my good friend, but I will find you. And give my thanks to Suk Won for experience we shared."

Jen Pal started off at a fast pace, heading south to find Shatir. Many things crossed his mind as he made his way through the forest. He kept an eye open for Wolfen, but the drive to get Shatir fueled his body.

Several times he passed bodies of Wolfen with their throats slit, a sure sign he was on her trail. He only hoped she had not tried something stupid with the small god.

As he made his way further south, the Lightning increased, striking in many places through the forest, but he also saw a huge section of the woods aflame. The small gods had taken to their destruction once again, not caring for anything but their objective. He passed another dead Wolfen and smiled. That made six she had taken out. There was no one like Shatir.

Those thoughts brought regrets as well as smiles. He should have taken her as his wife long ago. They had been lovers once, before she wed, but Jen Pal had been too obsessed with his selfish mission of vengeance. Now he would pay the price for the rest of his life.

A noise alerted him, and he stopped, backing toward a tree. Six Wolfen surrounded him, and four more were moving in from the outskirts. The rest of his life seemed short now. He should have been paying closer attention to what he was doing, not what he should have done years ago.

Jen Pal drew his two sai, very slowly, and he smiled at them. "It is time to die, my furry brethren. Who would like to join me?"

A gasping moan came from behind him, and as he turned to look, a short howl followed. Two Wolfen had fallen, their throats slit by the steel in Shatir's hands.

She moved quickly, standing beside Jen Pal. "I thought those two should go before you," she said.

Jen Pal handed her a sai, and she gave him one of her knives in return. They turned slightly, backs facing each other, and keeping a large oak on their right side. The odds were still too much. "I will see you at the Gates of the Sun, Shatir."

"And you, Jen Pal, brother I never had."

She didn't say, "husband I should have had," but Jen Pal could feel she meant it. "May the karn reunite in the next life."

"And the hunts last forever," Shatir said, and moved swiftly to strike at a Wolfen who had advanced to within range. The sai struck his side, possibly puncturing a lung, then she stepped back to where she had been.

One of the Wolfen, probably the leader, ordered the attack charge and they rushed at once. Six of them eventually went down, but so, too, did Shatir and Jen Pal, their bodies riddled with marks from the Wolfen long-knife.

akar saw the messenger racing toward the camp as if a demon followed him, and for all he knew one did. He wouldn't put anything out of the question.

"Sir, I—"

Takar placed his hand on the soldier's shoulder. "Easy. Wait and catch your breath, then tell me."

The man waited only a short while, then started off, still out of breath. "It's a massacre, sir. Everybody's trying to run, but they got somebody there with fire and lightning. Our men don't stand a chance."

The force commander nodded. He had seen the smoke and the light from the flames and wondered what had happened. Did this mean the Banished Ones were out? Didn't matter what it meant. His men were being slaughtered. That was all that mattered.

He looked to the messenger, now more composed. "Do you know anything else? What of the left flank?"

"Gone, sir." A tear came to the man's eyes. "I mean all gone. My brother was with them too."

Takar patted his back. "I'm sorry, soldier."

"Yes, sir. Sorry to break down like that. Anyway, left flank is gone, center has broken and in full retreat, and the right is trying to hold, but the fire hasn't reached them. They'll go too, once it does."

The camp was littered with young recruits, aides, cooks, and wounded soldiers. Not much of anything else. Takar considered what to do. "Soldier, I hate to ask this, but I need you to get a message back to the lines. I can give you a horse to take."

"I can do it, sir."

"Good. I want you to get to the right flank commander; Nardo is his name. Tell him that I said to retreat now. Now! Tell him to retreat like we did when we fought at Landers Bend."

Takar's aide had brought up a horse, already saddled. "Take this mount and get there as fast as you can."

"Yes, sir," he snapped and started to mount the horse.

"Soldier!"

"Yes, sir."

"I really am sorry about your brother, but know that what you are doing is saving a lot of lives."

He didn't salute this time, just turned and headed off on the horse.

Takar's aide stood by his side. "What now, sir?"

"Get me four of our best horses and men who can ride them. I want two to go to Salardi and warn him of what's coming. Tell him to take whatever action he thinks is best, but if he retreats to Sykor, they might be able to cut him off. And the other two I want to go to the Pomandan border. Tell Dorran to get everyone back to the city."

"Yes, sir."

"And tell Dorran I said to hurry." Almost an afterthought, he said, "and tell him to use the south gate."

Takar yelled for one of the young recruits. "Get everyone gathered and all the horses we've got. We're leaving now."

"I'll start packing things—"

"No packing. Leave everything as it is. The only things we're taking are people and horses. Spread the word."

"Yes, sir."

Takar moved toward the wounded. He helped the few that could ride onto horses, and others he moved onto stretchers, which they put onto the few wagons they had used to bring supplies. "If we run out of room on the wagons, they're going to have to stack up or turn on their sides."

"But, sir—"

Takar snapped. "No sense arguing. If we don't move fast, we're going to die." He saw the look on the lad's face. "There, I said it. Don't mean to frighten you, boy, but that's the way it is. Now move!"

As the force commander loaded a man with a leg wound onto a cart, he wondered if it was all going to be in vain. If the Sethians were already in Kamnor that meant they had busted through the Nyauran border, and, if they did that, they probably sent forces to cut off the path to Sykor. That's what he would have done.

92

SIEGE OF SYKOR

Wisp looked to Aenaila. "If you're ready, I'm going to conceal us. Just in case."

"Where are we going?"

"It's a Sykoran outpost. We'll be shifting into the stables. It's all I can remember."

She grabbed Wisp's hand. "Let's go," she said and shifted.

The rift opened, but just as Wisp was about to step through, Aenaila yelled. "Don't. It's on fire!"

He stepped back, and they both emerged into Talanvar's library. "Doesn't look good for Takar if they've burnt the outpost."

"Not good, but not necessarily his doom," Wisp said. He thought a moment. "Perhaps we can shift to another spot and try tracking him."

"We better do it quickly."

"I know where to go," Wisp said. "Take hold."

Aenaila grabbed him and retrieved the image from his mind. Within a few heartbeats, they had emerged onto a roadside where two large stones sat on either side, one with a marker on it indicating the distance to Sykor. Wisp looked around quickly but saw nothing to worry over. "Looks safe here."

"So how do we find Takar now that we're here?"

"You can shift by sight like you did in Entiria."

"That takes a long time."

"Then we keep doing it until we find him."

Aenaila stared. "I'm not going to wear myself out and get trapped out here with an army of Sethians."

"And I'm not leaving Takar. He stuck his neck out for me. There's no way I'm leaving without finding him."

Aenaila sighed. "Which way?"

"North. We'll take this road until we get to the outpost. If we don't find them, we'll head west and south."

Aenaila grabbed hold of his arm and began shifting. Using this method she could shift as far as she could see, so in open stretches, it carried them a long way. As they hit the crest of a small hill, Wisp pulled her down. "Something ahead," he said. "Keep low. I'll cloak us so we can get closer and see if they're Takar's men or the Sethians."

One more shift had them close enough. "Sethians!" Aenaila said. "Now what?"

Wisp pointed toward the southwest. "That way. Even if we can't find Takar, this will take us toward where Rahg is, in case Takar didn't get to warn him."

"I can't do this forever, Kender."

"I know, but we've got to try."

After half a dozen leagues, Aenaila had to stop and rest. "This is what I was talking about. If any Sethians come now, we're dead. I can't shift at all."

"Don't worry, if anyone comes, I can hide us until you recover."

"I hadn't thought about that." She hugged him. "Now I feel better." She sat silent for a long time, then she turned to Wisp and held him. "You know I'm not worried about myself. It's you."

He smiled. "I know. And you might be the first person who has ever cared about me. That makes it all the more important."

She kissed him. "You know if I weren't so tired ..."

Wisp laughed. "That's all we need, a bunch of Victas coming up on us while we're naked." He kissed her for a long time. "I can wait until we get back. The bed will be far more comfortable."

They stayed for a short while until Aenaila felt strong enough to continue. "Okay, Kender, let's go. The sooner we get this over with the sooner we can get into that bed you mentioned."

"I'm all for that," he said and took hold of her hand. "Keep going southwest. We're bound to run into someone soon."

Within two more leagues, they saw a large force of Sethians and Gnakas moving west, coming from the direction of the north gate. "That answers our questions about that route. If Takar isn't on his way to the south gate, he's likely dead. Hurry up," Wisp said.

"I can't go any faster than this." Aenaila shifted almost ten more times until they caught sight of another force of men.

"Looks like they're Sykorans," Wisp said.

Two more shifts brought them within range. She shifted one more time to get even with the lead. Takar was in front, leading a mass of wounded men and a small force of able-bodied soldiers. He seemed surprised to see them, grabbing his chest.

"Not that I'm not happy to see you, Kender, but you could have put me in the grave. I thought you might be one of them."

"Meaning Lukaan's people?"

"I guess. They came in with fire and lightning, cutting us to pieces."

"Just as well," Wisp said. "There is a sizable army right behind you, heading this way."

Takar's face scrunched into a mass of wrinkles. "I knew they would come this way! They're trying to cut off all paths to the city."

"And doing a good job of it," Aenaila said. "You won't make the south gate ahead of them."

Takar thought for a moment. "I need to try and join with Rahg and his men. If Salardi made it there, too, perhaps with all of our forces we can—"

Wisp shook his head. "Don't even think about it. If they had one of Lukaan's people with them, Rahg wouldn't stand a chance against them. And neither will you, no matter how many men you have." Wisp stared at him. "And while you're thinking about it, you will never outrun them. Not carrying these wounded men."

"They'll just have to take me then."

Wisp shook his head. "My orders are to bring you back."

Takar's face solidified as if it turned to stone. "I'm not going back without these men."

Wisp thought for a long while. He could have Aenaila grab hold of him and shift, and that would be the end of it. But he couldn't do that to Takar. He surely wouldn't want someone to do it to him. "If that's the way it is going to be, then we better get moving, Force Commander, and I mean fast."

～

The messenger rode into camp on a horse that looked as if it would drop from exhaustion at any moment. He dismounted, though it was more like falling off than a formal dismount. "Here to see Commander Dorran." His breaths came in short gasps, but he managed a strong salute.

"This way," the soldier who met him said, and hurried through the camp. When they reached Dorran, the man saluted again.

"Sir, message from the force commander. He said to tell you that the Sethians are coming. That all is lost in Kamnor and that you should retreat to the city. And he said to use the south gate."

Dorran waited to see if that was all the man had to say. "Where is Takar now?"

"He's going to try to get back to the city, sir."

"And Salardi?"

"Don't know. We sent a messenger to him, too."

"And Kamnor is lost?"

"Not just Kamnor, sir. Nyauran also."

"Soldier, join my men. Get some food and drink first, but then be ready to leave."

"Yes, sir," he said, and went off.

Dorran addressed the soldier who had brought him in. "You heard him, Mika. Spread the word to the strike leaders. We'll be leaving but without breaking camp. I don't want the Pomandans to know we're going until it is too late."

~

Salardi and his men were in full retreat when the messenger reached them. He listened in earnest to the news, worry creasing his face. The soldier told him of Takar's plight and the likely events that had taken place on the Nyaruan border, and what he could expect if he headed south. All the while the sounds of battle resounded from the rear, as Victas moved in to take advantage of Salardi's withdrawal. Most retreats turned into slaughters; at least he had kept that from happening.

"Do you have anywhere else to go, soldier?" Salardi asked the messenger.

"No, sir."

The force leader pointed to a wagon parked near the rear of the camp. "Get some food; then you're free to either go on your way, or join us and die fighting."

"Which way are you going, sir?"

"Don't know yet, but it sounds like the outcome won't be much different."

Salardi sent his aides to bring the men, except those guarding the front line, to a meeting. When the majority of them had arrived, he stood up on a boulder and addressed them. "Men, we've just gotten word from the force commander. No reinforcements are coming. Not for us. Fact is, the Victas are likely going to get help before we do, and it will be a crushing blow." He paused for a minute. "Looks like we're facing the Evil One himself on our rear, so we can go fight him and die trying, or we can turn ourselves around and kill some Victas." He waited for the murmurs to slow down, then shouted. "Well! Which is it?"

"Lizards!" someone yelled, and the call was picked up by nearly everyone.

"Let's kill us some Victas."

Salardi smiled. Just what he had hoped. He unsheathed his sword and waved it in the air. "Let's go get some green blood on these blades, men. Lots of it."

A rousing cheer answered him, and they turned to rush the line.

∼

*C*enaila pestered Wisp as they rode. "Mikkellana said to bring him in, not to ride with him and get us killed."

"We're not dead yet."

"It's the yet part that keeps ringing in my ears," she said.

Wisp was about to respond when a scout came racing up from the southwest. Wisp rode alongside Takar so he could hear the report.

"Sir, up ahead, not a half a league. It's Dorran's men, the whole bunch."

"How many?" Takar asked.

"Nearly two full strike forces, sir."

A smile popped onto Takar's face. This wasn't enough to hold off the Sethians who were heading to cut them off, but it was getting them closer. "Lead us there, soldier."

He steered them almost due south, but by the time they got within sight of the others, they were already under attack from Sethian forces.

Takar sought out Dorran at once. "Strike Leader, report!"

"Small force attacked us a short while ago, sir. We're taking care of them."

"This is only an expeditionary force, Dorran. They have several thousand men they're moving between us and the city."

"Blasted nasty Sethians!" Dorran looked over the men Takar had with him. "This all you got, sir?"

"And most of mine are wounded."

"Not enough to handle a force like that. Not even with the lad."

Takar sat up straight and searched for Rahg. "How did he do?"

Dorran smiled. "He didn't like the killing part, but he did it, sir. And if I must say so, he did a blasted nice job of it." Dorran rubbed his chin. "Can't say that I wouldn't mind having a few of those talents myself."

"We could use more than a few right now."

"Maybe we can have more than a few," Wisp said.

Takar and Dorran turned to him and stared. "What do you mean?"

Wisp leaned in close. "Get everyone close together. Form as tight a circle as you can make, but leaving plenty of breathing room, of course. Have Rahg make a shield that covers the whole bunch of you."

"All well and good," Dorran said, "but he can't hold it for long. He already told me that."

Wisp looked at Takar. "Force Commander, I would have thought you taught your men better. This man has no patience."

Dorran acknowledged with a bow of his head, then Wisp continued.

"Rahg can hold it long enough for Aenaila to go back to Sykor, and then she can bring some real help."

Dorran looked puzzled, but Takar smiled. "Who's in Sykor?"

"Darstan, Aentarra, and Mikkellana."

Takar beamed. "Dorran, do what the lad suggested and do it fast." As Dorran rode away, Takar mumbled. "Blasted thief, I might have to make him a commander."

Wisp explained his plan to Aenaila, and she prepared to leave. She pointed to a wagon next to Takar. "Keep that exactly where it is, and don't let anyone move it. I'll be coming back right here."

Takar issued orders to surround the wagon and stabilize it, then he placed himself near the front. "Don't worry, My Lady, it won't move."

～

Aenaila focused on the Shift point in Talanvar's house, then opened up the rift. An instant later, she was heading up the long sweeping staircase to Mikkellana's room. When she entered, all of them were there, and Mikkellana was even up and walking, albeit with a limp.

"Mikkellana! You're healed!"

"Thanks to Darstan, yes."

She turned her head. "Darstan?"

Aentarra stepped forward. "It's a long story. Now tell me what you are doing here."

Aenaila told them what happened and before she finished, Darstan and Aentarra were latching onto her.

"Take us there," Aentarra said. "I'll teach those Sethians to come out of the desert."

"I'm coming, too," Mikkellana said. "I might not be complete yet, but I can weave a shield, and it sounds as if you might need that."

Aenaila waited for them to grab hold, then she shifted, stepping through the rift onto the field next to the wagon. They were under siege by thousands of Sethians, arrows and swords alike hacking away at the barrier Rahg had created.

Mikkellana sought out Rahg and noted the weary look on his face. He was faltering. "Open a small channel in the rear for me, Rahg."

When he did, she wove a shield outside of his that formed a wider circle, while leaving a perimeter space wide enough to hold ten men deep. Taken all around, there were at least several hundred of them, perhaps more. Once the shield was complete, she called to Aentarra. "Do what you do best, sister."

She smiled, then tugged on Darstan's sleeve. "Let's have some fun."

arstan positioned himself on one side of the circle. Aentarra took the other. At her signal, Rahg opened up two gaps where they stood. They unleashed barrages of fire into the perimeter space, filling it with deadly flames.

The screams of the Sethians echoed throughout, piercing the shield that Rahg had constructed. The stench followed, permeating the smallest of pores in the shield, gagging the men inside.

Rahg called out to Mikkellana. "I can't hold it any longer."

"I've got it, Rahg. You can lower yours."

Rahg let go the shield, but Mikkellana's held true. There were still Sethians clamoring to get inside, but with not so much vigor as before. "Aentarra, Darstan," Mikkellana called to them.

When they came up, she pointed to a spot near the north wall. "Position yourselves there, and be ready. When I lower the shield, attack."

Mikkellana lowered her shield, and Aentarra and Darstan fired into the mass of soldiers, using fire and lightning. The soldiers fell as wheat to the onslaught, and those that didn't fall, fled, screaming in terror. Soon, they stopped the attack.

"Time to go home," Mikkellana said.

Takar came up to her. "That won't keep them away for long, and we still need to get to Sykor."

Aentarra looked to Mikkellana. "Are you strong enough, sister?"

She nodded. "If you are, and Darstan."

He smiled. "Plenty left in me."

Mikkellana turned to Takar. "Have everyone join hands together. When it is done, I will take us back to the city."

"What? How? Where?"

"The *where* is the biggest obstacle with so many." She turned to Aenaila. "Go ahead of us and make sure that the main square is cleared of everyone and everything. We will arrive there shortly."

ikkellana allowed Aenaila plenty of time to accomplish her task, then she ordered them to join together, and they shifted.

After they appeared in the square, Takar fell to his knees thanking the gods for delivering his men to safety.

"Don't thank them, Force Commander," Aentarra said. "Thank me."

"Don't thank anyone yet," Mikkellana said. "As soon as Lukaan gets here, we will all likely die."

93

NEW PLANS

Before nightfall, ten thousand archers had surrounded the city from the north gate to the south gate, and by morning ten thousand more joined their ranks. Constant barrages of arrows flew over the walls, killing or wounding many. The guards Mikkellana had posted on the parapets were forced to seek cover, hiding inside the towers, and citizens took their lives in their hands by daring to go to the tavern or across the street.

The gates had been reinforced with stone, so they withstood the ongoing assaults of battering rams, and the moat proved to be a formidable barrier. Back in Talanvar's house, everyone argued about what to do.

Mikkellana sat in a chair in the kitchen area. It seemed as if it had been a year since she was out of that bedroom. "I have already infused the walls with shield. Even when Lukaan shows, he won't break them, at least not easily."

"How is that, sister? I've seen him take down walls far stronger than these."

"Not the way I do it."

"Can you do anything about the arrows?" Takar asked.

She nodded. "I can put a dome up, but it's going to take a while. And it is difficult to do while they are firing at us."

"I can stop the arrows," Darstan said and moved toward the library.

"Wait. Where do you think you're going?" Mikkellana asked. "There are twenty thousand of them, if not more. No matter how powerful you think you are, you can do nothing about such numbers."

"I'm going to stop them," he said and turned to Aentarra. "I'll need your help to do it."

She got a puzzled look on her face, shrugging to Mikkellana. "If it involves killing more Sethians, I'm ready to go."

Mikkellana moved to block his way. "Did you hear what I said? There are twenty thousand of them."

Darstan gently nudged her aside. "I heard, Mikkellana, and I have a plan."

Aentarra grabbed hold of him. "Let's go." They walked out of the kitchen and into the library. She wanted to get him alone before leaving. "What are you planning?"

"I need you to get me behind them, to a place where they can't see us. And we'll need to be able to stay cloaked for a while."

Questions formed in her mind and were reflected on her face. "What do you have in mind?"

"I don't even know how to explain it, just trust me."

She hesitated, but then accepted it. "Good enough. I'll get us outside the gates, close enough to their ranks to avoid the arrows, then we can sight-shift behind them."

"Whatever works," Darstan said.

~

*C*amissa paced from one side of the library to the other, nerves eating at her. "What are we doing here? If we know Lukaan is coming why don't we leave?"

Mikkellana took on an indignant look. "Of all people, how can you say that? We've got an entire city to save." She limped to where Camissa stood. "What do you think Lukaan will do with these people if we abandon them?"

"Why would he hurt them? It's not them he's after."

"He would torture every one of them until someone told him where we were. And if no one knew, he would kill them all, down to the smallest child. Depending on his mood, he might even kill the animals."

Camissa stood silent for a moment, then said. "I understand you have a feud with him, but no one is that bad."

Mikkellana looked as if she might burst. "He killed my mother, who never did anything wrong to him." She took a long deep breath. "She was Lukaan's sister, and he killed her."

Aenaila gasped. "Then how do we help Sykor? You said yourself that you couldn't keep him out forever."

Mikkellana sat on the sofa. "That's true. I can't hold him off forever, but I can for a while, and I hope long enough to let you do your work."

Aenaila seemed shocked. "Me?"

"Yes. While I keep him at bay, you can start shifting people from the city to another location. Perhaps Genda." She thought for a moment. "Yes, Genda would be good. Sennar should be there by now, or soon. And then he can take people to Entiria. Lukaan has no way of getting to Entiria."

"Why not stay and make a stand here?" Rahg asked.

Camissa leaned to him and kissed his cheek. "I'm proud, Rahg. I sense your fear, but even so, you want to do the right thing.

Mikkellana laughed. "It's difficult to explain how strong Lukaan is. We would be like a few rats fighting a pack of wolves, Rahg. He would destroy us."

"Then how do you plan to hold him?"

"I have a few tricks left. I won't be able to hold him forever, but it will give us enough time to get people to safety. Perhaps."

~

*A*entarra appeared a hundred paces or so in front of the Sethian line, cloaked so no one could see them. "What now, Darstan?"

"Get behind them."

She picked out a spot to the left, then shifted, and continued shifting until she had appeared behind them in a small wooded section. "Good enough?" she asked.

"Good enough," he said.

He looked around, saw no one, then peered into the masses of Sethian soldiers before him. Conflicting emotions ran through him as he recalled the horrors of what had happened in Arangar. He had sworn he would never do that again, and yet here he was prepared to kill thousands more.

"What are you doing, Darstan?"

More hesitation. "Getting ready," he said, but he wondered if he had lost his nerve.

"Getting ready for what?"

Yet another pause. "I don't know. Something that should stop them."

Aentarra searched her memory. "Is this about FearMist?"

Darstan turned to her. "You know it?"

"I know of it. I saw the effects of what you did in Arangar. But I've never seen it work."

He lowered his head. "You don't want to. Not even you."

She looked at the Sethian soldiers surrounding them. "Regardless, let's get on with it. We need to do something to help Mikkellana."

He nodded. "Keep watch for me."

Darstan sat on the ground, arms folded. He let his fingertips touch the spot on his left arm, where his hand used to be, then he closed his eyes and focused.

Soon he felt the beat of his heart, slow, pulsing. He listened to it for a while, felt its rhythm, let his breathing fall in step. It felt as if he still had both of his hands, but before long the pulsing stopped, replaced by a vibration that traveled up his arms and into his chest. It circled in his stomach, then moved down his legs and back to his head.

He entered a world where he ruled, where everything was pure and simple. When he first came here, he didn't know what it was he wanted. Now he did though, and it was a dangerous path to take.

He entered the palace and immediately sought the room he needed. No sense in wasting time with Fire or Lightning or any of the others. He had to get to one specific room, that special one that endowed him with the gift no one else had.

He passed by the room that he had seen before, the one in a constant state of flux. He now knew that to be the shifting room, but since he had mastered that, it was no longer locked.

He climbed to the next level, then several more beyond that until he found what he wanted—ColdFire. The door was a whitish blue, like blue ice. He shivered when he saw it. A cold, eerie feeling called to him when he neared the room, but he proceeded anyway, walking toward the door surrounded with fog.

As he approached, a strange, ominous sound from that strangest of all doors called to him from up the stairs. He had investigated it once before, but only to the point of looking at it. It had frightened him enough to drive him back down the stairs. Today he had neither the time nor the desire, to look into it.

When he got back to his destination, he opened the door and walked in. The room was cold, very cold, and a mist filled the room from floor to ceiling, a thick fog that swirled and moved as if it had a life of its own. Memory cleared his head. *This is it. This is what I need.*

He opened his mind—opened his soul—and let the fog in. It seeped in through the pores of his skin, chasing goosebumps away with fear. Somehow it got into his veins, raced through him as if it were his blood. Filled him. Flooded him.

The palace disappeared, and Darstan opened his eyes. Aentarra stared at him with a strange look in her eyes.

"I presume you are ready," she said.

He rose, walked to the outer rim of the bushes. "I don't know what you know about this, but if you're not certain, don't go near the fog you'll see."

Aentarra nodded. "I'll keep my distance."

He focused, reaching inside himself to call on the FearMist. Of all the powers he had, he dreaded this the most. This was the one that made him less of a person, more of a monster.

The fog oozed from his stump in a cylindrical column that moved across the plains, hugging the ground. Soon, his fingertips glowed, and more mist emerged, tendrils of thick smoke that twisted and turned as it made its way toward the Sethians.

Somehow Darstan had more command of it this time. He instructed it to follow a path throughout the encampment, mixing with the men until it had engulfed them all.

The first screams began moments later, followed by the sound of swords clashing and the crying of crazed ones.

Aentarra grabbed hold of Darstan's arm. The experience a new one for her. She wasn't entirely sure what the FearMist could do, as she had only heard tales of it from ages past, but she had seen the effects when she was in Arangar, and she could hear what was going on in the Sethian camp right now. Both the memory and the present experience were more than she cared for.

"Are you ready, Darstan?" There was a newfound reverence in her voice when she spoke to him.

He seemed somber, almost lost, but he nodded his head and held out his hand.

She took hold and focused on the image in Talanvar's house, then shifted.

When they stepped through the rift into the library, Darstan collapsed. She was able to catch him and helped him to a sofa. "Someone call Mikkellana. Darstan needs help."

~

*M*ikkellana came at as fast a pace as she could manage, considering her condition. "What happened? Is he all right?"

"That depends on how you look at it," Aentarra said.

"Speak plainly, Aentarra. None of your stupid riddles."

She looked around, made certain no one else could hear. "He used FearMist again."

Mikkellana's eyes nearly bulged from her head. "You witnessed this?"

"Not only did I see him do it, but it started working immediately. I don't think we'll have any more problems from the Sethian archers."

"We'll have to continue this discussion later. For now, let me look at him."

Mikkellana examined Darstan for more than an hour but nothing she tried even stirred him. "I'm at my wit's end. I've tried everything I know, and nothing works."

"Let him rest. That might be all he needs," Aentarra said. "In the meantime, what do you propose to do now that we've stopped the archers, or should I say now that Darstan has stopped the archers."

"Now I can erect a good shield, one that will hold for a while against Lukaan."

"You better hope so. He'll kill whoever is in the city if he gets in."

Mikkellana moved to a chair and sat, propping her feet up. "And while I am defending Sykor, what do you propose to be doing, sister?"

"I'll take Rahg and Darstan with me. We've got to find a way to stop him."

Mikkellana smiled, but it was a taunting smile. "You three against Lukaan, Melissara, and Tirzinitzia." Mikkellana scoffed. "You couldn't take Lukaan by himself, let alone with those two at his side."

It was Aentarra's turn to smile. "I've got a few tricks."

Mikkellana threw a glass at her. "You stupid little witch. Your Slicers won't help you against Lukaan. You get him in a Mind Battle, and you won't be coming back."

Darstan roused as they were talking, and at the same time, Camissa and Rahg came in. Darstan rubbed his head as he sat. "Guess we did all right, huh, Aentarra?"

She laughed. "We make a good team, Darstan."

As they laughed, Birol entered the library, fear outlining his face. "My Lady," he said to Mikkellana, "reports have come in that claim that the one you call Lukaan is here!"

"What!" Mikkellana jumped from her chair.

"Time to go," Aentarra said. "We need to prepare."

"Go where? What are you going to do?"

"Find somewhere to put up a stand," Aentarra said. "It surely isn't here."

Darstan stood up and walked between them. "The obelisk."

"What?" Mikkellana said.

"The obelisk," Darstan said. "I dreamt about it. That's where we need to be. I don't know how I know, or where it is, but that's where I saw us fighting Lukaan."

"The obelisk is in Entiria," Mikkellana said.

Aentarra stared at Darstan, a curious look in her eyes. "Is it like the one in Entiria?"

"Exactly like that, but under the ground."

"This is nonsense," Mikkellana said. "Right now, we need everyone here to defend the city."

"We've got to find the obelisk," Darstan said. "I saw it in the dream."

"It's in Sethia," Camissa said, but her voice was almost a whisper.

"What?" Aentarra asked. "What did you say?"

She looked up at her. "I said it's in Sethia. I dreamt it too."

Aentarra nodded her head. "We're going to Sethia."

"That's suicide!" Mikkellana said.

"Only if we die," Aentarra said, "besides, it's what he would least expect."

Mikkellana let her frustration show. "There is no obelisk in Sethia."

Aentarra looked as if she was afraid for the first time in her life. "Yes, sister, I'm afraid there is."

94

STRANGE RESEMBLANCE

Mikkellana watched as Darstan walked across the room. She couldn't let them go without exploring this avenue of thought. "Darstan, come here a moment."

A curious look came to his face, but he went and stood beside her. "If you're going to apologize, it's not necessary."

She reached up, her finger tracing his cheek. "You are a handsome one aren't you. Just like your father was."

Aentarra rushed to intercept the conversation. "Time enough for family discussions later. We need to go."

Darstan looked to Aentarra, then back to Mikkellana. "What are you talking about? You didn't know my father."

"I knew him all right, and when the shadows hit your face like they are now, you are the spitting image of him. When you're angry too."

"You don't know my father."

"Oh, I do, boy. I've known him for thousands of years. I suspected long ago, that first night in Sethia when you found your powers. No one except my father and Lukaan have ever been able to wield ColdFire, but you did it that night. That's why I told Wisp to never let you near Sethia. I didn't want him to have you if he was your father."

She looked him over some more. "I didn't know for a while. Thought I saw some of Antar in you, but now that you are stronger I can see the changes in your face. Runellan blood runs in those veins. You are Lukaan's son."

"That can't be!"

"Anyone on this world who has powers got them ultimately from one of us. We are, after all, driven by the same desires. So you, Rahg, Camissa, Aenaila, and even you, Wisp, are descendants, one way or another, of one of us. There were twenty-one of us who made it through the first few years on this world, so it could be anybody."

Wisp looked as if he were panicking. "What about Aenaila? Who—"

"I'm not sure about her," Mikkellana said, then stared at Camissa. "You neither, child. I haven't figured out yet who you belong to, though the list could be long."

Wisp gulped. "It would be nice if we knew."

"Yes, it would be nice to know, wouldn't it. Don't want to be sleeping with your sister, or any relation for that matter."

Aentarra grabbed hold of Darstan's arm and led him away, but not before shredding Mikkellana with a look that could kill. "And you say I'm the evil sister. I would never do such a thing to a child."

"You still are a child. Besides, I needed to give him more reason to hate his father. Now that he knows what he did to him, he'll be less likely to join sides against you."

Darstan spun back to face her. "Aentarra is right. You're the evil one. I should never have healed you."

Aentarra and Darstan walked out of the room, and as they did, Rahg got up to follow.

"Where do you think you're going, Rahg? I need to speak with you as well."

He wore a scowl on his face that equaled the one Darstan had when he left. "Why, to tell me something bad about my father?"

"No, something else entirely."

When Rahg got next to her, she reached her hand out and got him to help her up. "Walk with me so that we may speak privately."

They walked through the house and out the back door onto a patio. As the door closed behind them, Mikkellana spoke. "Do you remember when you swore that oath to me back in Pomanda?"

Shock covered Rahg's face, but he said nothing.

"Thought I'd forgotten about it didn't you? Well, I didn't. Oaths are not something to be taken lightly. Remember, I told you that at the time."

He nodded. "What do you want?"

Her voice lowered, and the tone seemed sincere. "You must keep an eye on Darstan when you get to Sethia. If he tries to support Lukaan, in any way, kill him."

"I can't kill Darstan. I won't."

"If he helps Lukaan, you will. Or you will die from the oath."

"What do you mean? I can't—"

"This wasn't some silly game you played. If you break this oath, you'll die."

Rahg headed for the door, but he turned to face her before he went in. "I'm with Darstan. Aentarra is the better one of you two."

"Don't forget what I said about Darstan."

"I'll die first," Rahg said, and slammed the door. He stormed into the kitchen, where Aentarra sat with Darstan. His brother looked as sad as Rahg had ever seen him. "Are we almost ready to go?"

Aentarra laughed. "This isn't a festival. We'll likely all die, with the odds being what they are."

Darstan tapped his fingers on the table. "Three of us against three of them—what could be more fair."

"I'm going, too," Camissa said as she entered the kitchen.

Rahg pointed his finger at her. "You stay right here."

Before the scowl even formed on Camissa's face, Aentarra spoke up. "I think she should come with us. We might have use of her special talents."

Rahg shook his head. "There is no use in you—"

"Rahg, I admit, I'm scared, and I would rather stay, but I saw it in the dream. I saw you in a dark place, underground with the obelisk, and I was there too."

"Then I'm sure you saw us as well," Wisp said, "because we're going with you."

Camissa lowered her head. "You were both there."

Aentarra slapped her hand on the table. "I knew it! This is where it ends. This is where Lukaan dies."

"Do we even know where the obelisk is?" Darstan asked.

Aentarra searched her memory. "I sensed something the last time we were in Sethia. I think I might know where it is."

Darstan stood and reached out to Rahg. "Ready?"

"I'm ready," he said and held Camissa's hand, squeezing it gently.

She grabbed hold of Wisp, and then he and Aenaila joined with Aentarra. An instant later they were stepping through a rift by an enclave of rocks.

Rhaven walked over to Mikkellana after they left. "Pretty hard on Darstan weren't you?"

"I needed him to hate Lukaan as much as he hates me."

95

TIME TO DIE

Aentarra let her sensing roam the area, feeling for that prickly sensation of power. She let the probes expand slowly, encompassing a larger area with each sweep. Within moments, she recognized the feeling. "There," she said, pointing to the east. "Not far either."

Rahg led them up a hill and through a wide pass riddled with scrub brush and an assortment of large rocks that appeared to have fallen from the mountains on either side. As they stepped through the pass, a vast plain opened before them, filling a gap between two ranges of mountains.

"Are you sure it was close?" Rahg asked.

Aentarra shaded her eyes and looked over the valley. "It has to be out there somewhere."

"It is an obelisk, isn't it?" Wisp asked.

"Just like the one in Entiria," Aentarra said. "The difference is this one is underground."

"You get me close, and I'll find it," Darstan said.

Aentarra looked at him, puzzled. "How?"

"I'm not sure, but somehow I know I can."

As they descended from the pass, Aentarra pointed to a spot in the desert that appeared darker than the areas surrounding it. "Over there, Darstan. See if that's where it is."

Darstan stopped, closed his eyes and focused. "That's it. Let's go."

They made their way to the other side of the mountain and onto the plains. Many hours later they arrived at the area and found the entrance to an underground cavern. "This has to be it," Aentarra said.

Darstan stepped in front of her, leading the way. The steps took many turns, twisting a path ever downward. "How deep is this thing? Darstan asked.

"If there is an obelisk like the one in Entiria, it must be very deep," Aentarra said. "Keep going."

Torches lined the walls in a few places and long before they hit the bottom, Darstan had to call fire to his hand to light a path so they could see. "Grab a torch if you see one," he called to the others. "We'll need all the light we can get."

They emerged into a wide passage that eventually led them to a huge cavern. "Rats blood," Darstan said. "Look at that."

Aentarra pushed past him, then stopped dead, staring at the sight before her. An obelisk, likely five-span high rose from the floor. "Can you feel the power," she asked.

"I don't feel anything," Rahg said.

"I do," Darstan said. "It's strong."

"And possibly dangerous," Aentarra said, then looked to the others. "Don't touch it. No matter what."

*M*ikkellana finished her breakfast, then called for Talanvar. "How are we coming on the evacuation of the countryside?"

"Most of the people are in the city now, but the animals have proven to be far more difficult."

"As long as we have enough for several weeks of food, it will suffice." She turned to Rhaven. "And the people in the city, they know what to expect?"

"Your instructions were given out," Rhaven said.

"I don't want panic when Lukaan strikes. It will be difficult enough to hold him off for a while. I don't need a city full of wild-eyed lunatics."

"Takar and Tobias will see to that. They have their orders."

"Good," Mikkellana said. "Now come with me. We need to strengthen these walls and build a dome."

Rhaven looked at her as if she were nuts, but he took hold of her hand, and they shifted. An instant later they appeared at the north gate to the city, being reinforced with stone after getting the last of the citizens from the north side in. The south gate was still open, awaiting a few stragglers.

Mikkellana went to the side walls, the old ones, and lay her hands upon them, focusing on their core. She reached down into the earth, below the surface, all the way to where the stone foundations started. Once she found the bottom, she began weaving Shield into the stone, through the mortar joints and into the stone itself, infusing it with Shield. Her shield both strengthened it and gave it elasticity, a key component for withstanding an assault from the kind of attacks Lukaan would offer.

When she finished, she moved to another spot, this one on the eastern wall, where she knew it to be weakest—close to where the river ate at the banks. This time she stretched the shield all the way to the edge of the water, then far below the bottom of the river's bed.

Like an anchor on a ship, this shield would ground the wall and stabilize it. After securing the south and west walls, she returned to the gate and strengthened both the heavy wooden gates and the new stone wall behind it. A crowd had gathered while the wall was being built, people already worrying about how they would get out of the city if something were to happen.

"What if a fire strikes?" someone asked.

Mikkellana restrained her laughter. "This is meant to stop something far worse than fire from coming in."

Before the morning had gotten old, the walls were done, and Mikkellana climbed to the parapets on the north wall. She stared at what was left of the armies and wondered when Lukaan would arrive. Not if, but when.

It still puzzled her what Darstan had done, but whatever it was, Fear-Mist or something else, it had worked; the Sethian archers were gone. She turned to Rhaven. "I need privacy for what I'm doing now. Make sure that no one bothers me."

"I will," Rhaven said, and from the look in his eye, Mikkellana would not have wanted to be the one to ignore a command he gave. Powers or not, Rhaven had a commanding presence.

She closed her eyes and sank deep inside herself, calling upon every iota of her power. Once it formed, she reached down through the walls into the earth, going deeper than the foundation, far deeper.

As she dug further, the shield spread out, searching for cracks, no matter how minuscule, and once found, the shield insinuated itself into those cracks and spread, anchoring to the earth itself.

Mikkellana did this for hours, finding cracks that even water would find hard to breach until she had secured points at numerous places on each of the walls.

Once she had accomplished that, she raised her shield, bringing it up through the stone, and forming it into a dome that rose above the city. By the time the shield met and closed off at the top, she collapsed.

Rhaven caught her, setting her down while he stood guard. He called for water to be brought and wiped her forehead with a damp cloth. After a few minutes, she awakened, alert, but tired. "We have a shield," she said. "A good one."

"Strong enough to keep him out?" Rhaven asked.

"It's not like the Sethian Shield was, but being a smaller area, I could do wonders with it. This is strong, probably strong enough to hold him for a good while."

"Long enough to get everyone out?"

Mikkellana's face covered with worry. "That, I don't know." She used Rhaven to help her stand. "But I do know I'm hungry and tired. Let's go back to Talanvar's and get some rest." She grabbed hold of Rhaven and shifted, entering the library.

"I'll get something for you to eat," Rhaven said.

Talanvar came in, and the three of them shared food, along with te and khaffe. "How long before we start getting people out of here?" Talanvar asked.

"I need to rest a while, but by tonight we should be able to begin. After that, it will be up to Captain Sennar to get them to Entiria."

Talanvar sipped his khaffe. "Tell me again why Lukaan won't be able to find them on Entiria."

"What we do is called Shifting. It only works if you have been to the place before. Since Lukaan, nor any of his people have been there, they won't be able to go."

"Unless he goes by boat," Rhaven said.

Mikkellana shook her head. "He is far too concerned about his life to go by boat."

"I thought—"

"No, he's not immortal. None of us are. We will die just like anyone else. It is simply that we won't die from old age or disease. But a knife to the heart, or having our head cut off, or drowning, will certainly do it."

"Couldn't he just shift himself back to land if something happened?"

"Yes, he could, but he doesn't know how far it is to land, and there are limits to how far we can go. For some reason, it is easier to shift from one world to another than it is to go across the seas. We found this true on our worlds and never understood why."

Rhaven got up and paced, a somber look on his face.

"What's wrong?" Mikkellana asked.

"I should be with Rahg and Darstan, not here drinking khaffee."

"You're helping me."

"That's a lie. You kept me here to keep me safe." He turned to face her. "I need to go, Mikkellana. I can't stay here and let them face Lukaan alone."

"But you can let me face him?" A tone crept into her voice.

"If you tell me that we're going out there, swords drawn, to wage war; I'll gladly stay with you. But to stand by your side and do nothing is not right. Not for me."

"Fine, do what you want, but I can't take you there, so if you're going, you'll have to find your own way."

Rhaven let the cup fall too heavily on the table. "I have been finding my own way all of my life," he said and stormed out of the room.

Before he got halfway down the hill leading from Hightown, the first crack of lightning hit, striking the dome by the north walls. The sound reverberated throughout the city, exaggerated by the hollow sound from the dome.

Rhaven stopped and looked up, as did anyone who was out at the time. As he stared, three more strikes came, hitting almost simultaneously and not five-span apart from one another. He placed his hands over his ears and held them, the sound almost deafening, like heavy thunder in a closed room.

A baby cried not far off, and the mother stood crying, holding her ears while the child sat on the ground. Rhaven scooped the little boy up in his arms. "Where do you live?"

At first, she didn't answer, but then he shouted to her, and she pointed down the street toward the Trader's Inn. "Come, show me."

With her leading the way, he took the baby home and told her to stay inside. "It will be all right. Just stay inside." Afterward, he ran for the north wall. If things were going to falter, it would be there, where the attacks seemed to be centered. He climbed the wall and looked out onto the fields. There were three of them firing lightning at the city, and surrounding them was an enormous army.

"You wanted to fight him," a voice said from behind. "There he is."

Rhaven turned to see Mikkellana. "That's Lukaan?"

"That's him."

"I couldn't tell from this far off. We were closer in Sethia."

"Don't worry; he'll get closer. He's only toying with us now. Wait until he gets angry."

"And the shield?"

"Holding. But I expected no problem with this. It's what comes after that I dread."

"What can he do that is worse than this?"

Mikkellana laughed. "It's difficult to explain. He can do so much more." She paused for a minute. "You heard my sister talk about Darstan using something called ColdFire?"

Rhaven nodded.

"That's what he used on Arton in Sethia, when Arton's body shattered. If he uses that, I don't think the shield will hold. Not for long, anyway."

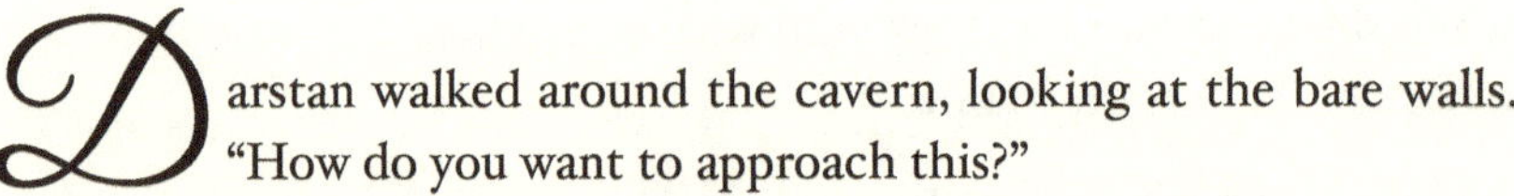

*D*arstan walked around the cavern, looking at the bare walls. "How do you want to approach this?"

Aentarra stared at the walls, and then the obelisk. "Not much here to use, but that might play to our advantage."

Rahg started to question her, but she forestalled him. "Let me think this through."

As she pondered their situation, she assessed the cavern for strategic purposes. If they were to defend themselves against Lukaan, she would need every advantage she could get. She walked the perimeter, inspecting the walls. They were a mix of rock and dirt in most places, and someone had used BlackFire to fuse the two together.

Near the back of the cavern, though, the walls were almost pure rock, top to bottom. "This is where we'll make a stand," she said. "We can make use of the stone to brace our shields."

She called the rest of them to join her, then addressed Rahg. "I want you to practice on making convex shields that you can brace against these walls."

She pointed to a few large boulders that protruded from the sides. "Lock your shield here, in the corner of this one," she said, then walked across to the other side, pointing out its counterpart, "and here, where this meets the side wall. Doing that will take advantage of the earth itself, and the shape of your shield will push the force in that direction."

Rahg took a close look at the areas she pointed out. "I can make the shield, but I don't know how long I can hold off Lukaan. Remember when we were in Sethia—"

"You are a lot stronger than you were in Sethia," Aentarra said. "I tested your shield when we were in the Paaren. Don't worry, it will hold long enough."

"Long enough for what?" Darstan asked.

"For us to do what we need. If not, we'll all be dead."

"You better have a lot more planned than Rahg using a shield, because that isn't going to work by itself." Darstan stood rigid, awaiting an answer.

Aentarra sighed. "The whole plan relies on impeccable timing. If I have miscalculated, by even an iota, we will likely see each other next in whatever comes after this life."

"Then I think you better tell us what you have in mind," Darstan said.

"Yes, it is time," Aentarra said and signaled them to come closer. She detailed her strategy; then they went over it several times, then several more, until she was comfortable that they knew exactly what to do and when.

Aentarra looked at each one of them. "Is everyone ready?"

Upon receiving an affirmative response, she nodded to Rahg. "Give us a shield. I don't know what this will do."

After Rahg put up a shield to protect them, he opened a slot for her, and she fired a bolt of lightning at the obelisk before he quickly closed the shield again.

When the bolt struck, the obelisk shook, but then a huge forcebolt lashed out at the spot where Aentarra had been standing, almost buckling Rahg's shield.

"What in god's name was that?" Rahg asked.

"Indeed," Aentarra said. "Exactly what I want to know. It was strong, wasn't it." She looked at the obelisk, then at Rahg. Very strong.

As she turned to face Darstan, she issued more instructions. "You and Aenaila take hold of Wisp and get to your position. Remember, stay cloaked."

"Won't he be able to sense us?" Aenaila asked.

"He will sense something," Aentarra said, "but he will think it is the obelisk, especially since he can't see you."

As the others rushed to stand beside the obelisk, Aentarra turned to Camissa. "Stay behind that boulder I showed you, and be strong. This entire plan might rest on your shoulders."

Camissa nodded, and though her voice quavered a little, it had conviction. "I'll do my part, Aentarra. Count on it."

"We all are, dear. And it won't be long." Aentarra paced. "He will have felt that. Anyone would. And that means he'll be here soon."

❧

*L*ukaan stood several hundred paces outside the gates of Sykor, hurling bolt after bolt of lightning, interspersed with walls of BlackFire, all to no avail. "It's like the one she used in Sethia," he said. "I can't get through."

Melissara and Tirzinitzia joined him, adding their power to his assault, but there didn't seem to be any dent in the defenses. "This is something she learned from my father," Melissara said. "He had a similar structure surrounding our manor."

"It's not the same," Lukaan said. "Antar's never had this strength for such a wide area. He could protect the manor, but not far beyond, and if he tried, the manor suffered. Somehow Mikkellana has managed to improve upon that."

"She can't withstand this for long," Melissara said, "it's not the ..." She looked around her, then to the city, then at Lukaan. "What was that? Did you feel it?"

"I sense something, but it felt as if it was in Sethia," Lukaan said.

"Mikkellana is here. How could—"

"Mikkellana might be here, but Aentarra is in Sethia. I should have known." He reached out to Melissara and Tirzinitzia. "Get some of the guards. We're going back."

"What about Sykor?" Tirzinitzia asked.

Lukaan felt the scar on his head where Aentarra stabbed him. "Sykor will wait. I want her now."

96

FINAL BATTLE

Lukaan stepped through the rift first, followed by Melissara, Tirzinitzia, and more than fifty of his special Sethian Guard, the elite of his troops.

As soon as she felt the rift, Aenaila put her Illusion in place, making it appear as if there was nothing but a stone wall behind Rahg and his shield.

Rahg also put his part of the plan in place, erecting the strongest shield he could weave and bracing it into the rocks on either side.

～

Camissa remained hidden behind the projection of a huge boulder, not far behind Rahg. As soon as she saw them, she focused on her Persuasion, drawing images from a Slicer that Aentarra had dispatched to her just before Lukaan arrived.

Melissara was easy to identify, she looked exactly as Aentarra had described her, but even without that she would have recognized her from the familial resemblance.

When she felt as if she were ready, Camissa released the Persuasion, sending it to Melissara. She was able to see it now, whereas when she first discovered it, she could only feel where it was going. This was more like a cloud that she could steer to where she wanted it to go, and she sent this straight into Melissara's head. *Don't let him do this. Not to Aentarra. Not to your favorite little sister.*

Camissa let it pause. She noticed the blank look on Melissara's face, and the shake of her head as she turned from side to side, searching for whatever did this to her. She would let that sit with her for a while, a short while to be sure, but it might be best to let that percolate.

～

*A*entarra, cloaked in stealth, waited on the opposite side of the cavern, behind the Sethian Guard, facing Lukaan's back. He was searching the cavern, confused. Right now he would be using his Sensing to try and find them, knowing she had Stealth, and wondering where she might be. She would wait for the right moment before striking.

～

*L*ukaan saw nothing but obelisk, but he Sensed something, and even that puzzled him. He knew Aentarra had Stealth, but if she were cloaked like that, he wouldn't be able to sense her, so what … His eyes were drawn to the obelisk, a dull coruscating, pulsing, rhythmic beat from the shadows on the far wall. It lurked there, almost a shadow itself.

Lukaan's first instinct was to strike it, but something inside him steered him away from that, so he continued his scan. He turned to Melissara and Tirzinitzia. "Remember, she has Stealth. Keep alert."

"Do you know anything about this place?" he asked Melissara, all the while continuing to search for Aentarra.

Melissara shot Tirzinitzia a scathing glance before responding. "We can discuss that later. Right now, let's look for my sisters."

"Mikkellana is in Sykor," Lukaan said. It's only Aentarra—" he stopped in midstream, staring at where Rahg was, flattened against the wall. "I correct myself. Aentarra and the boy are both here." Lukaan's laughter rang through the cavern. "I'll get to you shortly, boy. Don't leave."

Aentarra focused until she built the strongest force she could and then unleashed it all in a single strike of BlackLightning at Lukaan's back. As soon as she let it go, she shifted to a spot behind Rahg's shield for protection. As soon as she got there, she put Illusion into effect so Aenaila could leave, then reinforced Rahg's shield with her own in anticipation of Lukaan's retaliation. She prayed that Aenaila had initiated her second phase of the plan and had gone to get Mikkellana. Hurry, girl. Whatever you do, hurry.

A primal scream shook the walls as the bolt struck him. Lukaan went to his knees, hands holding his back where the Lightning had hit him. After a few seconds, though, he stood and focused his attention on Aentarra and Rahg. "A good game, Aentarra, but now you will die."

Lukaan, still in a rage after suffering the attack from Aentarra, took a moment to regain his strength, then he issued a wall of BlackFire that spread as wide as the shield that Rahg and Aentarra hid behind. It raced across the cavern and crashed into the shield, searing the floor and everything else along the course. Upon meeting the resistance, the BlackFire reached all the way to the ceiling, searching for a way in, but then settled back to an assault along the base, applying continuous pressure.

"Now, Melissara," Lukaan said, and at that command, all three of them blasted the shield with a combination of Lightning and Fire, testing it at various spots along the center and the seams. "Keep it up," Lukaan said. "They can't hold for long."

Aentarra had woven her shield to complement Rahg's, and as Lukaan assaulted their defenses, she felt the strength of the pounding, and she knew Rahg must be suffering. He was strong, his shield the equal of anyone's except Mikkellana, but his mental capacity for endurance had not been tested. Not like this. "Keep strong, Rahg. Not much longer."

"I'm all right."

Aentarra didn't bother turning her head, but she called back to Camissa. "Are you still at it, girl? We could use a break from Melissara."

"I'm trying, Aentarra," Camissa said, then closed her eyes to focus once again. It was time to try some more after giving Melissara a rest. She formed the cloud again—and realized as she did that no one but her could see it—then directed it toward Melissara. It passed through Rahg's shield and straight toward Melissara's head, through the Black-Fire and the Lightning and with not a quaver to show for it.

Camissa paused to gather her thoughts while it hovered there, then she directed it into Melissara's mind with all the force she could.

Melissara, it's me, Aentarra. Remember me? I'm the one you played hide and seek with. The one who brushed your hair with for hours on end when we were both little.

Melissara stopped her attack, shaking her head as if something was attached to it. "Get out!" she screamed.

Camissa smiled. It was working. By all that's holy it was working. She let no time elapse but went right to work again, this time incorporating images with the messages.

She sent images of Aentarra as a little girl, sitting on the floor in the manor with a brush and comb, doing Melissara's hair, and she showed pictures of the puppy they both loved and the games they played with it among the rows of hedges. We could do this again, Melissara. We could be friends again if you only stop him. Stop him, Melissara. Please?

Aentarra called back to Camissa. "It's working, girl. I can see it working. Don't let up." Things were looking better than Aentarra hoped for. They might not die after all—if the rest of the plan went well—and if that blasted sister of hers would hurry and get here

~

$\mathcal{A}$enaila stepped through the rift into Talanvar's library. "Mikkellana! Where are you?"

Mikkellana almost ran in from the kitchen. "What is it? Is he there?"

Aenaila seemed out of breath, but it was anxiety, not exertion that strained her voice. "Yes, and he is mad. Truly."

"Let's go," Mikkellana said.

Rhaven grabbed hold of Aenaila, but Mikkellana tried to tear his hand away. "Oh no, you don't."

"You're not stopping me this time, Mikkellana. I don't care what you say."

She curled her lower lip as if she were preparing for an argument, then shrugged her shoulders. "I don't have time. Come on."

Aenaila looked to Mikkellana. "We're going to be in an underground cavern, and we will be coming out by an obelisk. Wisp will keep us cloaked, but remember, that is just for sight. They can still hear us and sense us."

"Enough of this, let's go. If it's just Rahg and Aentarra, they'll be hard-pressed to hold him for long."

"One more thing," Aenaila said. "Aentarra warned us not to touch the obelisk, no matter what."

"Let's go!" Mikkellana hollered.

They stepped through the rift onto the floor next to the obelisk—Rhaven, Aenaila, and Mikkellana now joining Aentarra, Darstan, Rahg, Wisp, and Camissa.

As soon as they arrived, Mikkellana shifted to a spot behind the shield with Rahg and Aentarra, leaving Wisp, Rhaven, Aenaila, and Darstan where they were. She erected a new shield in front of theirs, and when it was woven, she turned to Aentarra. "Take a rest, sister. I know you both must be exhausted."

At the appearance of Mikkellana, Lukaan's rage took on new meaning. He unleashed a series of BlackLightning strikes that should have collapsed any shield, but Mikkellana's held. Even so, she felt the pain and once more was awed by his strength. "I hope you don't need long, Aentarra. At this rate, he'll kill us all before your plan works."

~

Melissara had stopped attacking, and Lukaan must have noticed. "What's wrong with you, Melissara? You're not letting family get in the way of this are you?"

She stuttered. "I seem to be weak for some reason. I can't muster the energy."

He looked to Tirzinitzia, still with use of her powers and scowled. "Your strength better return soon."

Mikkellana buckled from the shock of a dozen strikes in a row but held her shield. She wished she had been able to infuse it to the walls and floor of this place, but there was no time for anything like that. "I'm going to need help soon," she said.

"I'm ready," Rahg said, and wove a shield to interweave with hers.

"I'm going to try something to distract him," Aentarra said, and shifted behind Lukaan, fully cloaked. Lukaan had his body surrounded by BlackFire now, a strong force that would deflect most attacks or absorb them, but still, a strong bolt of BlackLightning or a force five shield assault would do some damage.

Aentarra focused and struck, once again using BlackLightning, but this time he absorbed it without much effect. His knees buckled, and he stumbled, but all it seemed to do was enrage him. He spun to fire at the place where Aentarra had been standing, but fortunately, she had shifted back to safety by then.

A dozen or so of the Sethian Guard were not so fortunate, and Lukaan's attack disintegrated them. She wondered why he had even brought them to a battle like this, although they could prove to be a nuisance if it came to a closely fought contest. That gave her an idea, though. Twice more she shifted to a spot behind Lukaan, and each time she picked a spot using the Sethian Guard as a barrier. With the first attack she hit Lukaan pretty good, this time using a shield, but by the time she attacked the second time she was weakening and her strike did almost nothing. The combined effect eliminated almost twenty more of the guards though, so it had been worth something. And it had distracted him long enough to give Mikkellana and Rahg a short break.

"I'm wasted," Aentarra said to Mikkellana. "Let me rest for a few minutes then I'll help with the shield. It is time for the last piece." She walked back to where Camissa was hiding. "Get ready for the final play. It will be all or nothing for us, so don't hold back."

$\sim$

Camissa nodded, but fear had taken hold of her. "I'll do it even if it is with my last breath," she said, and when she did, she remembered her dream showing a woman telling Rahg she loved him, and then that woman dying. The only person that could be was her. Regardless, she prepared herself for the end, calling all images that Aentarra had provided her, and all of the other information. Once together, she started the assault on Melissara's mind. If she resisted this, they were goners.

$\sim$

Infuriated by their resistance, Lukaan mounted an endless barrage against them, using the strongest of the forces at his command. He struck mostly with Lightning and BlackFire, though Aentarra worried that he might at any time resort to ColdFire. If he did, they would all die, but she had gambled that he wouldn't unless he felt his life was in jeopardy. People who used ColdFire risked a short period of unconsciousness from using it, and she bet that he wouldn't use it unless he had to; in fact, her plan called on that very thing—pushing him to that point, but at just the right time.

The shield was being pounded by all three of them, Melissara included, and it was beginning to show signs of weakening. "Aentarra, we could use your help."

"I'm ready, Mikkellana." Aentarra turned to Camissa. "Keep working on my sister. We need her out of this battle."

"Whenever you're ready, Aentarra, we could use you." The repeated request carried a sense of urgency.

Aentarra stood beside Rahg and Mikkellana and wove her shield to support theirs. "Good to be here with you, sister."

"Just hold your shield. I don't need your comments."

"We need to wear him down for our plan to work. If that means I have to hold a shield until I'm near dead, I'll do it," Aentarra said.

~

Camissa dug deep inside herself, forming the strongest mass of Persuasion she could, using every bit of strength she had to form the images and make them real. *Look what he is doing to your sister, and you are helping him. Shame on you. Look! This is the man who killed your mother.*

With that message, she sent an image of Molina as Melissara would have remembered her, but with a knife in her gut and blood all over her hands and stomach, her face wrenched in pain. *Do you want to help the man who killed your mother?*

Melissara stopped firing and turned to face Tirzinitzia. She stared for a long time, then, with nothing said, opened fire on Tirzinitzia. The first strike sent her reeling, knocking her to the floor on her back. Before Melissara could strike again, Tirzinitzia managed to mount a defense, issuing a column of BlackFire to counter Melissara's attack.

Aentarra was staggering from weakness. She dropped her shield. "Mikkellana, it is time."

"It's too risky," Mikkellana said. "We can—"

"We have no choice," Aentarra said. "Keep the shield up until you get my signal."

Aentarra shifted to stand before the obelisk. She knew Aenaila was close by. "When I signal, shift to behind the shield, and remember, if all goes wrong take everyone and get out of here."

"Good luck," Darstan said.

Part of Aentarra wanted to let Darstan attack now, risk it all and see if they could defeat Lukaan. But if that failed they would all die. This way was better, if not almost as risky. Part of it hinged on Camissa getting Melissara's help; that was already done. But the rest relied on a hunch that Aentarra had about the obelisk.

If she could get Lukaan to the brink of madness with rage, then draw his fire at her while she stood in front of the obelisk, it would work. As soon as she knew Darstan and the others were safe behind the shield, she released the cloaking and became visible, firing all she had at Lukaan at the same time. A bolt of her strongest lightning hit him but did little besides make him stagger. She felt faint from the exertion and wobbled with dizziness. "I'm through with hiding, Lukaan. It's just the two of us now." After saying this, she hurled a ball of BlackFire at him.

Lukaan righted himself after the insolent attack from Aentarra. He turned, focused and called ColdFire. "It is time to end this game, Aentarra."

Aentarra sensed the power building within him and positioned herself for the shift. She would have to time this just right. If she shifted too early, all of them would die, too late and she would die alone. It had to be just right. Nobody could stop ColdFire, and she knew he was building up to that. Mikkellana and Rahg were supposed to have a shield in place to slow it down, but that was all it could do. She focused, keeping every part of her body alert.

Lukaan fired, a huge blast of ColdFire emitting from his hands and racing across the cavern too fast to see. Aentarra saw it coming. "Now!" she screamed, and then called her shift, but not soon enough. The ColdFire hit the shield Mikkellana and Rahg wove and shattered it without even slowing, then, what was left of it hit Aentarra head on. It hurled her backward, her body striking against the obelisk as if she were a twig blown around in a storm. Her head cracked the stone, and she crumbled to the ground.

The ground shook, and the obelisk seemed to sway. Suddenly a force-bolt shot from the obelisk and struck Lukaan, throwing him across the cavern and into the wall on the other side.

Darstan had been mustering his power all of this time, and when Aentarra's signal came, he focused everything he had on a massive strike of ColdFire, aiming it at Lukaan. It struck him just as he seemed to be recovering from the forcebolt attack. His head reared back into the wall, blood splattering as it cracked against stone. Lukaan tried straightening, raising his hands as if he would fire, but Darstan had been advancing and all the time firing a relentless barrage of ColdFire. The second shot took Lukaan to the ground.

Tirzinitzia must have realized all was lost when Lukaan collapsed. She shifted out of the cavern, freeing Melissara to join Darstan.

Melissara turned and fired at Lukaan while he was on the ground, her BlackFire mixed with Darstan's ColdFire hammering him until he lay still.

Darstan wobbled, hand going to his head as he reeled from the use of the ColdFire. He started to fall, but Melissara caught him and helped him to the ground. "Mikkellana, come help him."

Mikkellana ran to Darstan, while Rahg rushed to see Aentarra, along with Camissa and Rhaven. Wisp and Aenaila went to see to Darstan with Mikkellana.

Aentarra lay on the floor, barely breathing. "Do something," Rahg said.

She shook her head. "Can't do anything for me now, Rahg. It's over."

He turned to Camissa. "Help her, Camissa. Or get Mikkellana."

"It won't do any good," Aentarra said. "He got me good with ColdFire. Too much of it." She struggled, trying to lift her head, but nothing seemed to work. "Is he ..."

"He's dead," Rahg said. "Darstan and Melissara killed him."

"Make sure," Aentarra said. "Cut off his head."

"Let me take care of that," Rhaven said, and unsheathed his sword as he headed to where Lukaan lay. He stared at the body of the once-godlike being and thanked the real gods for giving him this chance.

"This is for Shinesa," Rhaven said, and swung the sword, cutting a huge gash into Lukaan's neck. "And for Jen Pal." The second swing almost severed the head, but not quite. The third one did. He walked away feeling better, though unimpressed. It almost seemed as if there should have been something happen when he killed him, ground shaking or a thunderous roar. Instead, it was nothing. Not even a last whimper.

Rhaven stopped where Darstan was just managing to raise his head. "Are you all right, Darstan?"

"Is he dead?"

"He is now," Rhaven said.

"Help me," Rahg called.

Mikkellana got to her feet and ran to see to her sister. "Move aside, Rahg."

She knelt beside her and ran her hands over her head and heart. "She's almost gone."

"Can't you do something?"

Mikkellana shook her head.

"Rahg," Aentarra called to him.

He and Camissa knelt next to her, holding her hand.

"Before anyone says anything, know that I love you."

"What?" Rahg asked.

"I wanted you …" Her head dropped to the side, and she was gone.

Rahg wiped a tear away with his sleeve but continued holding her hand. "I never thought I'd see her die."

"Neither did I," Camissa said.

"I wonder what she was trying to say."

Mikkellana held her hand on his shoulder. "She was trying to tell you she was your mother."

He bolted up. "What! That's impossible. My mother—"

"Your mother what—died when you were born?" Mikkellana stared at him, then pointed to Darstan. "And he was an orphan, parents died of a disease when he was young." Then she pointed to Wisp, and he is a thief abandoned in the alleys of Pomanda or Genda or some such city."

Rahg paced, rubbing his head. "It can't be. It's impossible. My father—"

"Was not your father either."

"How do you know? Did she tell you?"

"I didn't know at first, but eventually I figured it out. Figured out most of you anyway." She turned to Wisp. "He's your real brother. The only one he could have gotten Stealth from is Aentarra, so he belonged to her too."

While Mikkellana spoke, the pouch at Aentarra's side opened, and a Slicer emerged. It crept around the cavern as if it were on a hunt, then after it hovered above Lukaan's body, it returned at blinding speed and entered Rahg's head. As soon as it positioned itself, it began disseminating information that Aentarra had instructed, informing him of his heritage, showing him images of his ancestors. He learned about the Wars of Light and the Darkness Wars. And he learned what the Lights had done to Antar. Lastly, he learned of his duties.

Rahg's eyes glazed over and he turned from Mikkellana while she was still talking, and knelt beside Aentarra once again. He removed the family knife from a belt at her side and a ring from her finger. He held both in his hand as he repeated the words that came to him.

An oath of life I swear by Blood, to be an oath of death.

Mikkellana screamed. "No!" She tried yanking him from the floor, but he wouldn't budge. Even Melissara joined in, slapping his face as he droned on.

And each page of the Sacred Book I whisper with each breath.

"Don't do it, Rahg!" Melissara said. "Don't dare do it."

To the Seven Lights of Nelstar—this day I swear your death.

When he had finished, he stood, placing the ring in his pocket and the knife in a sheath at his belt.

"You blithering idiot," Mikkellana said, and slapped him. "You bloody, blithering idiot." She reached back to slap him again.

The pouch at Aentarra's side opened wide, and hundreds, if not thousands of Slicers came out, surrounding Rahg and Mikkellana both. They moved to within a hair's breadth of Mikkellana's eyes and her head and heart, and they positioned themselves around Rahg, moving slowly in a circular fashion.

Mikkellana breathed slowly, not daring to move.

"Call them off, Rahg," Melissara said. She hadn't moved either.

"What do you mean?"

"Tell them to cease."

"How?"

"Think it," Melissara said. "Just think it."

In an instant, the Slicers disappeared into the pouch. Rahg stooped to retrieve it and placed it on his belt.

"Let's get out of here," Mikkellana said. "I need to bury my sister."

Darstan reached down to help with Aentarra, and as he did, he brushed against the obelisk. The obelisk shook briefly, then glowed where he had touched it. He reached to examine the stone, and when he did his arm went straight through the stone, pulling him in with it.

Rahg moved quickly to the obelisk and examined it, but there was nothing there. No opening, just a small crack where Lukaan's ColdFire had struck. "Where's Darstan?"

Mikkellana stared, saying nothing, but Melissara had a curious look on her face. "I think we should all leave here," Melissara said.

"We can't leave without Darstan," Rahg said.

"Unless I'm wrong, Darstan is lost to us. And if we don't leave, we'll all be lost."

The ground shook, bringing silence to the room. Then the obelisk shook and the same glow that appeared where Darstan had touched it spread from side to side and bottom to top. A deep rumbling filled the room, and the earth shuddered, moved under their feet.

A crack developed near the top of the obelisk, and from each of its four eyes, cracks descended toward the base, rending the impenetrable stone as if it were a sheet of decayed parchment. When the obelisk split apart, Darstan stumbled from the base of it in what appeared to be a delirious state.

"I don't like this," Mikkellana said, and as she did, a vapor, an ominous miasma, like a storm stretching across the lands, oozed from the cracks and spread through the air, reminiscent of blood spilled in a clear pond.

Out of the mist, a shape took form, dark and forbidding. So dark the light collapsed into it, and even the brown of the desert earth seemed to glow in comparison.

Mikkellana didn't utter a word, yet she knew who this was—the goddess herself, Anciara, come back from ancient legends shared by so many lost worlds.

The sky in the cavern continued to blacken, a black darker than the worst of storms, and the air tingled with a sensation of power. Eyes, like twin suns burnt beyond use, stared at them and a voice like the clashing of worlds paused in the air. "You have done well, my champion. Now kneel to your goddess."

Mikkellana shivered, the kind of shiver she got when a wet winter wind wouldn't let go of her, and she had to tuck herself under the covers to stay warm.

Her teeth chattered as fear rose within her for the first time in many many years. She recalled the stories her father had told her of Anciara, and the horrible things she had done, and could do. She didn't know what she was going to do, but she knew they had to get out of here. "Take my hand, everyone. And someone make sure to grab hold of Aentarra."

Once she saw they had taken hold, she Shifted to Sykor, into Talanvar's library.

"What was that?" Aenaila asked.

"That," Melissara said, "is the Goddess of Death."

97

NO PLACE TO HIDE

Once in Talanvar's library, they lay Aentarra's body on the sofa. "We've got to bury her," Rahg said.

"What we've got to do is get out of here," Mikkellana said. "She'll find us here in no time."

"Where can we go?" Aenaila asked.

"Entiria," Mikkellana said. "I have a feeling we might be safe there."

"What about the people in Sykor?" Camissa asked. "We can't just leave everyone here."

"We can, and we will," Mikkellana said. "She won't kill them for the sake of killing. They might not like living under her rule, but they'll survive. Besides, we can't take them all with us."

She looked around, found Talanvar. "Get those two boys, Birol, anyone else you feel should go with us and gather them here. Quickly."

She turned to Rhaven. "Find Tobias and Mollie. I know he won't go without her, and get Takar. Tell him to bring a handful of men at best. The rest will have to stay."

Rhaven started to head off, and she called him back, kissing him on the cheek. "I'm sorry about the trouble earlier. I had thought it best at the time."

"I never thought any more about it," he said.

"Why Entiria?" Darstan asked.

"The obelisk," she said. "Something about it seemed different. I think we'll be safe there."

"Let's hope so," Melissara said. "If we stay here, she'll kill us."

"Of that, I have no doubt," Mikkellana said.

~

*A*nciara searched the area, a feeling of euphoria at being free after all of these aeons. Stragglers from the Sethian Guard huddled in a corner, crouched in shadows. For so long she had waited, and now she would wait no longer.

Anciara reached out, extracting the life from their bodies. She felt the surge in power as their energy flowed into her. She could now draw power from both life and death, and best of all there were no more gods to test her. No one to stop her from what she wanted to do.

ACKNOWLEDGMENTS

It is with great honor that I give eternal gratitude to my wife and all four of my grandkids. They give me the inspiration to keep going.

ABOUT THE AUTHOR

Giacomo Giammatteo is the author of gritty crime dramas about murder, mystery, and family. He also writes non-fiction books including the No Mistakes Careers series, No Mistakes Publishing, No Mistakes Grammar, and No Mistakes Writing.

When Giacomo isn't writing, he's helping his wife take care of the animals on their sanctuary. At last count they had forty-five animals—eleven dogs, a horse, six cats, and twenty-six pigs.

Oh, and one crazy—and very large—wild boar, who takes walks with Giacomo every day and happens to also be his best buddy.

nomistakespublishing.com
gg@giacomog.com

ALSO BY GIACOMO GIAMMATTEO

You can see all of my books here.

And you can buy them on the platform of your choice.

This brings up a thought: with more than fifty books out now, it is becoming difficult to try to update the list in the back of all of them. If you want to know what books I have out, use the link above, which takes you to my website, or download the latest copy of my GG recommended reading list, which is free.

Nonfiction :

Careers:

No Mistakes Resumes, Book I of No Mistakes Careers

No Mistakes Interviews, Book II of No Mistakes Careers

Grammar:

Misused Words, No Mistakes Grammar, Volume I

Misused Words for Business, No Mistakes Grammar, Volume II

More Misused Words, No Mistakes Grammar, Volume III

Visual Grammar (this is a compilation of volumes I–III with a bit of new information added. It also includes pictures. The world's first visual grammar book)

Misused Words and Then Some, No Mistakes Grammar, Volume V

More Grammar:

No Mistakes Grammar Bites, Volume I, Lie, Lay, Laid, and It's and Its

No Mistakes Grammar Bites, Volume II, Good and Well, and Then and Than

No Mistakes Grammar Bites, Volume III, That, Which, and Who, and There Is and There Are

No Mistakes Grammar Bites, Volume IV, Affect and Effect, and Accept and Except

No Mistakes Grammar Bites, Volume V, You're and Your, and They're, There, and Their

No Mistakes Grammar Bites, Volume VI, Passed and Past, and Into, In To and In

No Mistakes Grammar Bites, Volume VII, Farther and Further, and Onto, On, and On To

No Mistakes Grammar Bites, Volume VIII, Anxious and Eager, and Different From and Different Than

No Mistakes Grammar Bites, Volume IX, A While and Awhile, and Envy and Jealousy

No Mistakes Grammar Bites, Volume X, Could've and Should've, and Irony and Coincidence

Writing:

No Mistakes Writing, Volume I—Writing Shortcuts

No Mistakes Writing, Volume II—How to Write a Bestseller

No Mistakes Writing, Volume III—Editing Made Easy

Publishing:

How to Publish an eBook, No Mistakes Publishing, Volume I

How to Format an eBook, No Mistakes Publishing, Volume II

eBook Distribution, No Mistakes Publishing, Volume III

Print on Demand—Who to Use to Print Your Books, No Mistakes Publishing, Volume IV

Other nonfiction

Uneducated

Whiskers and Bear—Volume I, Sanctuary Tales *A Collection of Animal Stories, Volume II,* Sanctuary Tales

More Animal Stories, Volume III, Sanctuary Tales *Surviving a Stroke—or Two*

Life and Then Some

Fiction:

Friendship & Honor Series:

Murder Takes Time

Murder Has Consequences

Murder Takes Patience

Murder Is Invisible

Murder Is a Promise

Blood Flows South Series:

A Bullet For Carlos: A Connie Gianelli Mystery

Finding Family, a Novella

A Bullet From Dominic

The Good Book

Redemption Series:

Necessary Decisions: A Gino Cataldi Mystery

Old Wounds

Promises Kept, the Story of Number Two

Premeditated

Rules of Vengeance Series: (Fantasy)

Light of Lights (the beginning, a novella)

A Promise of Vengeance

Undeniable Vengeance

Consummate Vengeance

Note. The Light of Lights is a novella. It's about 100 pages long and sets the stage for the series. The other books in the series are about 800 pages long.

OTHER BOOKS

You can always see the current and coming-soon books on my website.

Fiction:

***Memories for Sale* (mystery/sf)**

***The Joshua Citadel* (SF novella)**

Children's Books:

No Mistakes Grammar for Kids, Volume I—Much and Many

No Mistakes Grammar for Kids, Volume II—Lie and Lay

No Mistakes Grammar for Kids, Volume III—Bring and Take

No Mistakes Grammar for Kids, Volume IV, "Would've, Should've" and "Your and You're"

No Mistakes Grammar for Kids, Volume V, "There, They're, and Their" and "To, Too, and Two"

Shinobi Goes to School—Life on the Farm for Kids, Volume I

Fiona Gets Caught, Life on the Farm for Kids, Volume II

Coco Gets a Donut, Life on the Farm for Kids, Volume III

Squeak Gets a Home, Life on the Farm for Kids, Volume IV

Biscotti Saves Punch, Life on the Farm for Kids, Volume V

Coming Soon:

The Adventures of Adalina, Volume I, Adalina and the Five Tiny Bears

The Adventures of Adalina, Volume II, Adalina and the Underwater Bears

Get on the mailing list and you'll be sure to be notified of release dates and sales.

<u>Mailing list</u>

And don't forget to leave a review!